MASTERPIECES IN MINIATURE

MASTER

STORIES BY

AGATHA
CHRISTIE

PIECES

IN MINIATURE

THE DETECTIVES

Copyright acknowledgments appear on page vii

ISBN0-7394-6017-X

COPYRIGHT ACKNOWLEDGMENTS

CONTENTS

PART I

PARKER PYNE

MEETING PARKER PYNE

One day, having lunch at a Corner House, I was enraptured by a conversation on statistics going on at a table behind me. I turned my head and caught a vague glimpse of a bald head, glasses, and a beaming smile—I caught sight, that is, of Mr. Parker Pyne. I had never thought about statistics before (and indeed seldom think of them now!) but the enthusiasm with which they were being discussed awakened my interest. I was just considering a new series of short stories. Then and there I decided on the general treatment and scope, and in due course enjoyed writing them. My own favorites are "The Case of the Discontented Husband" and "The Case of the Rich Woman," the theme for the latter being suggested to me by having been addressed by a strange woman ten years before when I was looking into a shop window. She said with the utmost venom: "I'd like to know what I can do with all the money I've got. I'm too seasick for a yacht—and I've got a couple of cars and three fur coats—and too much rich food fair turns my stomach." Startled, I murmured, "Hospitals?" She snorted, "Hospitals? I don't mean charity. I want to get my money's worth," and departed wrathfully. That, of course, was now twenty-five years ago. Today all such problems would be solved for her by the income tax inspector, and she would probably be more wrathful still!

—From the introduction to the
1953 Penguin U.K. edition
of *Parker Pyne Investigates*

1. THE CASE OF THE MIDDLE-AGED WIFE

Four grunts, an indignant voice asking why nobody could leave a hat alone, a slammed door, and Mr. Packington had departed to catch the eight-forty-five to the City. Mrs. Packington sat on at the breakfast table. Her face was flushed, her lips were pursed, and the only reason she was not crying was that at the last minute anger had taken the place of grief.

"I won't stand it," said Mrs. Packington. "I won't stand it!" She remained for some moments brooding, and then murmured: "The minx. Nasty sly little cat! How George can be such a fool!"

Anger faded; grief came back. Tears came into Mrs. Packington's eyes and rolled slowly down her middle-aged cheeks.

"It's all very well to say I won't stand it, but what can I do?"

Suddenly she felt alone, helpless, utterly forlorn. Slowly she took up the morning paper and read, not for the first time, an advertisement on the front page.

"Absurd!" said Mrs. Packington, "Utterly absurd." Then: "After all, I might just see . . ."

Which explains why at eleven o'clock Mrs. Packington, a little nervous, was being shown into Mr. Parker Pyne's private office.

As has been said, Mrs. Packington was nervous, but somehow or other, the mere sight of Mr. Parker Pyne brought a feeling of reassurance. He was large, not to say fat; he had a bald head of noble proportions, strong glasses and little twinkling eyes.

"Pray sit down," said Mr. Parker Pyne. "You have come in answer to my advertisement?" he added helpfully.

"Yes," said Mrs. Packington, and stopped there.

"And you are not happy," said Mr. Parker Pyne in a cheerful, matter-of-fact voice. "Very few people are. You would really be surprised if you knew how few people are happy."

"Indeed?" said Mrs. Packington, not feeling, however, that it mattered whether other people were unhappy or not.

"Not interesting to you, I know," said Mr. Parker Pyne, "but very interesting to *me*. You see, for thirty-five years of my life I have been engaged in the compiling of statistics in a government office. Now I have retired, and it has occurred to me to use the experience I have gained in a novel fashion. It is all so simple. Unhappiness can be classified under five main heads—no more, I assure you. Once you know the cause of a malady, the remedy should not be impossible.

"I stand in the place of the doctor. The doctor first diagnoses the patient's disorder, then he proceeds to recommend a course of treatment. There are cases where no treatment can be of any avail. If that is so, I say frankly that I can do nothing. But I assure you, Mrs. Packington, that if I undertake a case, the cure is practically guaranteed."

Could it be so? Was this nonsense, or could it, perhaps, be true? Mrs. Packington gazed at him hopefully.

"Shall we diagnose your case?" said Mr. Parker Pyne, smiling. He leaned back in his chair and brought the tips of his fingers together. "The trouble concerns your husband. You have had, on the whole, a happy married life. Your husband has, I think, prospered. I think there is a young lady concerned in the case—perhaps a young lady in your husband's office."

"A typist," said Mrs. Packington. "A nasty made-up little minx, all lipstick and silk stockings and curls." The words rushed from her.

Mr. Parker Pyne nodded in a soothing manner. "There is no real harm in it—that is your husband's phrase, I have no doubt."

"His very words."

"Why, therefore, should he not enjoy a pure friendship with this young lady, and be able to bring a little brightness, a little pleasure, into her dull existence? Poor child, she has so little fun. Those, I imagine, are his sentiments."

Mrs. Packington nodded with vigor, "Humbug—all humbug! He takes her on the river—I'm fond of going on the river myself, but five or six years ago he said it interfered with his golf. But he can give up golf for *her*. I like the theater—George has always said he's too tired to go out at night. Now he takes her out to dance—*dance!* And comes back at three in the morning. I—I—"

"And doubtless he deplores the fact that women are so jealous, so unreasonably jealous when there is absolutely no cause for jealousy?"

Again Mrs. Packington nodded. "That's it." She asked sharply: "How do you know all this?"

"Statistics," Mr. Parker Pyne said simply.

"I'm so miserable," said Mrs. Packington. "I've always been a good wife to George. I worked my fingers to the bone in our early days. I helped him to get on. I've never looked at any other man. His things are always mended, he gets good meals, and the house is well and economically run. And now that we've got on in the world and could enjoy ourselves and go about a bit and do all the things I've looked forward to doing some day—well, this!" She swallowed hard.

Mr. Parker Pyne nodded gravely. "I assure you I understand your case perfectly."

"And—can you do anything?" She asked it almost in whisper.

"Certainly, my dear lady. There is a cure. Oh, yes, there is a cure."

"What is it?" She waited, round-eyed, and expectant.

Mr. Parker Pyne spoke quietly and firmly. "You will place yourself in my hands, and the fee will be two hundred guineas."

"Two hundred guineas!"

"Exactly. You can afford to pay such a fee, Mrs. Packington. You would pay that sum for an operation. Happiness is just as important as bodily health."

"I pay you afterward, I suppose?"

"On the contrary," said Mr. Parker Pyne. "You pay me in advance."

Mrs. Packington rose. "I'm afraid I don't see my way—"

"To buying a pig in a poke?" said Mr. Parker Pyne cheerfully. "Well, perhaps you're right. It's a lot of money to risk. You've got to trust me, you see. You've got to pay the money and take a chance. Those are my terms."

"Two hundred guineas!"

"Exactly. Two hundred guineas. It's a lot of money. Good morning, Mrs. Packington. Let me know if you change your mind." He shook hands with her, smiling in an unperturbed fashion.

When she had gone he pressed a buzzer on his desk. A forbidding-looking young woman with spectacles answered it.

"A file, please, Miss Lemon. And you might tell Claude that I am likely to want him shortly."

"A new client?"

"A new client. At the moment she has jibbed, but she will come back. Probably this afternoon about four. Enter her."

"Schedule A?"

"Schedule A, of course. Interesting how everyone thinks his own case unique. Well, well, warn Claude. Not too exotic, tell him. No scent and he'd better get his hair cut short."

It was a quarter past four when Mrs. Packington once more entered Mr. Parker Pyne's office. She drew out a check book, made out a check and passed it to him. A receipt was given.

"And now?" Mrs. Packington looked at him hopefully.

"And now," said Mr. Parker Pyne, smiling, "you will return home. By the first post tomorrow you will receive certain instructions which I shall be glad if you will carry out."

Mrs. Packington went home in a state of pleasant anticipation. Mr. Packington came home in a defensive mood, ready to argue his position if the scene at the breakfast table was reopened. He was relieved, however, to find that his wife did not seem to be in a combative mood. She was unusually thoughtful.

George listened to the radio and wondered whether that dear child Nancy would allow him to give her a fur coat. She was very proud, he knew. He didn't want to offend her. Still, she had complained of the cold. That tweed coat of hers was a cheap affair; it didn't keep the cold out. He could put it so that she wouldn't mind, perhaps . . .

They must have another evening out soon. It was a pleasure to take a girl like that to a smart restaurant. He could see several young fellows were envying him. She was uncommonly pretty. And she liked him. To her, as she had told him, he didn't seem a bit old.

He looked up and caught his wife's eye. He felt suddenly guilty, which annoyed him. What a narrow-minded, suspicious woman Maria was! She grudged him any little bit of happiness.

He switched off the radio and went to bed.

Mrs. Packington received two unexpected letters the following morning. One was a printed form confirming an appointment at a noted beauty specialist's. The second was an appointment with a dressmaker. The third was from Mr. Parker Pyne, requesting the pleasure of her company at lunch at the Ritz that day.

Mr. Packington mentioned that he might not be home to dinner that evening as he had to see a man on business. Mrs. Packington merely nodded absently, and Mr. Packington left the house congratulating himself on having escaped the storm.

The beauty specialist was impressive. Such neglect! Madam, but *why?* This should have been taken in hand years ago. However, it was not too late.

Things were done to her face; it was pressed and kneaded and steamed. It had mud applied to it. It had creams applied to it. It was dusted with powder. There were various finishing touches.

At last she was given a mirror. "I believe I *do* look younger," she thought to herself.

The dressmaking seance was equally exciting. She emerged feeling smart, modish, up-to-date.

At half-past-one, Mrs. Packington kept her appointment at the Ritz. Mr. Parker Pyne, faultlessly dressed and carrying with him his atmosphere of soothing reassurance, was waiting for her.

"Charming," he said, an experienced eye sweeping her from head to foot. "I have ventured to order you a White Lady."

Mrs. Packington, who had not contracted the cocktail habit, made no demur. As she sipped the exciting fluid gingerly, she listened to her benevolent instructor.

"Your husband, Mrs. Packington," said Mr. Parker Pyne, "must be made to Sit Up. You understand—to Sit Up. To assist in that, I am going to introduce to you a young friend of mine. You will lunch with him today."

At that moment a young man came along, looking from side to side. He espied Mr. Parker Pyne and came gracefully toward them.

"Mr. Claude Luttrell, Mrs. Packington."

Mr. Claude Luttrell was perhaps just short of thirty. He was graceful, debonair, perfectly dressed, extremely handsome.

"Delighted to meet you," he murmured.

Three minutes later Mrs. Packington was facing her new mentor at a small table for two.

She was shy at first, but Mr. Luttrell soon put her at her ease. He knew Paris well and had spent a good deal of time on the Riviera. He asked Mrs. Packington if she were fond of dancing. Mrs. Packington said she was, but that she seldom got any dancing nowadays as Mr. Packington didn't care to go out in the evenings.

"But he couldn't be so unkind as to keep *you* at home," said Claude Luttrell, smiling and displaying a dazzling row of teeth. "Women will not tolerate male jealousy in these days."

Mrs. Packington nearly said that jealousy didn't enter into the question. But the words remained unspoken. After all, it was an agreeable idea.

Claude Luttrell spoke airily of night clubs. It was settled that on the following evening Mrs. Packington and Mr. Luttrell should patronize the popular Lesser Archangel.

Mrs. Packington was a little nervous about announcing this fact to her husband. George, she felt, would think it extraordinary and possibly ridiculous. But she was saved all trouble on this score. She had been too nervous to make her announcement at breakfast, and at two o'clock a telephone message came to the effect that Mr. Packington would be dining in town.

The evening was a great success. Mrs. Packington had been a

good dancer as a girl and under Claude Luttrell's skilled guidance she soon picked up modern steps. He congratulated her on her gown and also on the arrangement of her hair. (An appointment had been made for her that morning with a fashionable hairdresser.) On bidding her farewell, he kissed her hand in a most thrilling manner. Mrs. Packington had not enjoyed an evening so much for years.

A bewildering ten days ensued. Mrs. Packington lunched, teaed, tangoed, dined, danced and supped. She heard all about Claude Luttrell's sad childhood. She heard the sad circumstances in which his father lost all his money. She heard of his tragic romance and his embittered feelings toward women generally.

On the eleventh day they were dancing at the Red Admiral. Mrs. Packington saw her spouse before he saw her. George was with the young lady from his office. Both couples were dancing.

"Hello, George," said Mrs. Packington lightly, as their orbits brought them together.

It was with considerable amusement that she saw her husband's face grow first red, then purple with astonishment. With the astonishment was blended an expression of guilt detected.

Mrs. Packington felt amusedly mistress of the situation. Poor old George! Seated once more at her table, she watched them. How stout he was, how bald, how terribly he bounced on his feet! He danced in the style of twenty years ago. Poor George, how terribly he wanted to be young! And that poor girl he was dancing with had to pretend to like it. She looked bored enough now, her face over his shoulder where he couldn't see it.

How much more enviable, thought Mrs. Packington contentedly, was her own situation. She glanced at the perfect Claude, now tactfully silent. How well he understood her. He never jarred—as husbands so inevitably did jar after a lapse of years.

She looked at him again. Their eyes met. He smiled; his beautiful dark eyes, so melancholy, so romantic, looked tenderly into hers.

"Shall we dance again?" he murmured.

They danced again. It was heaven!

She was conscious of George's apoplectic gaze following them. It had been the idea, she remembered, to make George jealous.

What a long time ago that was! She really didn't want George to be jealous now. It might upset him. Why should he be upset, poor thing? Everyone was so happy. . . .

Mr. Packington had been home an hour when Mrs. Packington got in. He looked bewildered and unsure of himself.

"Humph," he remarked. "So you're back."

Mrs. Packington cast off an evening wrap which had cost her forty guineas that very morning. "Yes," she said, smiling. "I'm back."

George coughed. "Er—rather odd meeting you."

"Wasn't it?" said Mrs. Packington.

"I—well, I thought it would be a kindness to take that girl somewhere. She's been having a lot of trouble at home. I thought—well, kindness you know."

Mrs. Packington nodded. Poor old George—bouncing on his feet and getting so hot and being so pleased with himself.

"Who's that chap you were with? I don't know him, do I?"

"Luttrell, his name is. Claude Luttrell."

"How did you come across him?"

"Oh, someone introduced me," said Mrs. Packington vaguely.

"Rather a queer thing for you to go out dancing—at your time of life. Mustn't make a fool of yourself, my dear."

Mrs. Packington smiled. She was feeling much too kindly to the universe in general to make the obvious reply. "A change is always nice," she said amiably.

"You've got to be careful, you know. A lot of these lounge-lizard fellows going about. Middle-aged women sometimes make awful fools of themselves. I'm just warning you, my dear. I don't like to see you doing anything unsuitable."

"I find the exercise very beneficial," said Mrs. Packington.

"Um—yes."

"I expect you do, too," said Mrs. Packington kindly. "The great thing is to be happy, isn't it? I remember your saying so one morning at breakfast, about ten days ago."

Her husband looked at her sharply, but her expression was devoid of sarcasm. She yawned.

"I must go to bed. By the way, George, I've been dreadfully extravagant lately. Some terrible bills will be coming in. You don't mind, do you?"

"Bills?" said Mr. Packington.

"Yes. For clothes. And massage. And hair treatment. Wickedly extravagant I've been—but I know you won't mind."

She passed up the stairs. Mr. Packington remained with his mouth open. Maria had been amazingly nice about this evening's business; she hadn't seemed to care at all. But it was a pity she had suddenly taken to spending money. Maria—that model of economy!

Women! George Packington shook his head. The scrapes that girl's brothers had been getting into lately. Well, he'd been glad to help. All the same—and dash it all, things weren't going too well in the City.

Sighing, Mr. Packington in his turn slowly climbed the stairs.

Sometimes words that fail to make their effect at the time are remembered later. Not till the following morning did certain words uttered by Mr. Packington really penetrate his wife's consciousness.

Lounge lizards; middle-aged women; awful fools of themselves.

Mrs. Packington was courageous at heart. She sat down and faced facts. A gigolo. She had read all about gigolos in the papers. Had read, too, of the follies of middle-aged women.

Was Claude a gigolo? She supposed he was. But then, gigolos were paid for and Claude always paid for her. Yes, but it was Mr. Parker Pyne who paid, not Claude—or, rather, it was really her own two hundred guineas.

Was she a middle-aged fool? Did Claude Luttrell laugh at her behind her back? Her face flushed at the thought.

Well, what of it? Claude was a gigolo. She was a middle-aged fool. She supposed she should have given him something. A gold cigaret case. That sort of thing.

A queer impulse drove her out there and then to Asprey's. The cigaret case was chosen and paid for. She was to meet Claude at Claridge's for lunch.

As they were sipping coffee she produced it from her bag. "A little present," she murmured.

He looked up, frowned. "For me?"

"Yes. I—I hope you like it."

His hand closed over it and he slid it violently across the table. "Why do you give me that? I won't take it. Take it back. Take it back, I say." He was angry. His dark eyes flashed.

She murmured, "I'm sorry," and put it away in her bag again.

There was constraint between them that day.

The following morning he rang her up. "I must see you. Can I come to your house this afternoon?"

She told him to come at three o'clock.

He arrived very white, very tense. They greeted each other. The constraint was more evident.

Suddenly he sprang up and stood facing her. "What do you think I am? That is what I've come to ask you. We've been friends, haven't we? Yes, friends. But all the same, you think I'm—well, a gigolo. A creature who lives on women. A lounge lizard. You do, don't you?"

"No, no."

He swept aside her protest. His face had gone very white. "You *do* think that! Well, it's true. That's what I've come to say. It's true! I had my orders to take you about, to amuse you, to make love to you, to make you forget your husband. That was my job. A despicable one, eh?"

"Why are you telling me this?" she asked.

"Because I'm through with it. I can't carry on with it. Not with *you*. You're different. You're the kind of woman I could believe in, trust, adore. You think I'm just saying this; that it's part of the game." He came closer to her. "I'm going to prove to you it isn't. I'm going away—because of you. I'm going to make myself into a man instead of the loathsome creature I am because of you."

He took her suddenly in his arms. His lips closed on hers. Then he released her and stood away.

"Good-by. I've been a rotter—always. But I swear it will be different now. Do you remember once saying you liked to read the advertisements in the Agony column? On this day every year you'll find there a message from me saying that I remember and am making good. You'll know, then, all you've meant to me. One thing more. I've taken nothing from you. I want you to take something from me." He drew a plain gold seal ring from his finger. "This was my mother's. I'd like you to have it. Now Good-by."

He left her standing there amazed, the gold ring in her hand.

George Packington came home early. He found his wife gazing into the fire with a far-away look. She spoke kindly but absently to him.

"Look here, Maria," he jerked out suddenly. "About that girl?"

"Yes, dear?"

"I—I never meant to upset you, you know. About her. Nothing in it."

"I know. I was foolish. See as much as you like of her if it makes you happy."

These words, surely, should have cheered George Packington. Strangely enough, they annoyed him. How could you enjoy taking a girl about when your wife fairly urged you on? Dash it all, it wasn't decent! All that feeling of being a gay dog, of being a strong man playing with fire, fizzled out and died an ignominious death. George Packington felt suddenly tired and a great deal poorer in pocket. The girl was a shrewd little piece.

"We might go away together somewhere for a bit if you like, Maria?" he suggested timidly.

"Oh, never mind about me. I'm quite happy."

"But I'd like to take you away. We might go to the Riviera."

Mrs. Packington smiled at him from a distance.

Poor old George. She was fond of him. He was such a pathetic old dear. There was no secret splendor in his life as there was in hers. She smiled more tenderly still.

"That would be lovely, my dear," she said.

Mr. Parker Pyne was speaking to Miss Lemon. "Entertainment account?"

"One hundred and two pounds, fourteen and sixpence," said Miss Lemon.

The door was pushed open and Claude Luttrell entered. He looked moody.

"Morning, Claude," said Mr. Parker Pyne. "Everything go off satisfactorily?"

"I suppose so."

"The ring? What name did you put in it, by the way?"

"Matilda," said Claude gloomily. "1899."

"Excellent. What wording for the advertisement?"

"'Making good. Still remember. Claude.'"

"Make a note of that, please. Miss Lemon. The Agony column. November third for—let me see, expenses a hundred and two pounds, fourteen and six. Yes, for ten years, I think. That leaves us a profit of ninety-two pounds, two and fourpence. Adequate. Quite adequate."

Miss Lemon departed.

"Look here," Claude burst out. "I don't like this. It's a rotten game."

"My dear boy!"

"A rotten game. That was a decent woman—a good sort. Telling her all those lies, filling her up with this sob stuff, dash it all, it makes me sick!"

Mr. Parker Pyne adjusted his glasses and looked at Claude with a kind of scientific interest. "Dear me!" he said dryly. "I do not seem to remember that your conscience ever troubled you during your somewhat—ahem!—notorious career. Your affairs on the Riviera were particularly brazen, and your exploitation of Mrs. Hattie West, the Californian Cucumber King's wife, was especially notable for the callous mercenary instinct you displayed."

"Well, I'm beginning to feel different," grumbled Claude. "It isn't—nice, this game."

Mr. Parker Pyne spoke in the voice of a head master admonishing a favorite pupil. "You have, my dear Claude, performed a meritorious action. You have given an unhappy woman what every woman needs—a romance. A woman tears a passion to pieces and gets no good from it, but a romance can be laid up in lavender and looked at all through the long years to come. I know human nature, my boy, and I tell you that a woman can feed on such an incident for years." He coughed. "We have discharged our commission to Mrs. Packington very satisfactorily."

"Well," muttered Claude, "I don't like it." He left the room.

Mr. Parker Pyne took a new file from a drawer. He wrote: "Interesting vestiges of a conscience noticeable in hardened Lounge Lizard. Note: Study developments."

2. THE CASE OF THE DISCONTENTED SOLDIER

Major Wilbraham hesitated outside the door of Mr. Parker Pyne's office to read, not for the first time, the advertisement from the morning paper which had brought him there. It was simple enough:

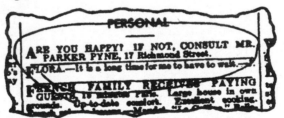

PERSONAL

ARE YOU HAPPY? IF NOT, CONSULT MR. PARKER PYNE, 17 Richmond Street.

FLORA.—It is a long time for me to have to wait.—

FRENCH FAMILY RECEIVE PAYING GUESTS. 10 minutes Park. Large house in own grounds. Up-to-date comfort. Excellent cooking.

The major took a deep breath and abruptly plunged through the swing door leading to the outer office. A plain young woman looked up from her typewriter and glanced at him inquiringly.

"Mr. Parker Pyne?" said Major Wilbraham, blushing.

"Come this way, please."

He followed her into an inner office—into the presence of the bland Mr. Parker Pyne.

"Good morning," said Mr. Pyne. "Sit down, won't you? And now tell me what I can do for you."

"My name is Wilbraham—" began the other.

"Major? Colonel?" said Mr. Pyne.

"Major."

"Ah! And recently returned from abroad? India? East Africa?"

"East Africa."

"A fine country, I believe. Well, so you are home again—and you don't like it. Is that the trouble?"

"You're absolutely right. Though how you knew—"

Mr. Parker Pyne waved an impressive hand. "It is my business to know. You see, for thirty—five years of my life I have been engaged in the compiling of statistics in a government office. Now I have retired and it has occurred to me to use the experience I have gained in a novel fashion. It is all so simple. Unhappiness can be classified under five main heads—no more, I assure you. Once you know the cause of a malady, the remedy should not be impossible.

"I stand in the place of the doctor. The doctor first diagnoses the patient's disorder, then he recommends a course of treatment. There are cases where no treatment can be of any avail. If that is so, I say quite frankly that I can do nothing about it. But if I undertake a case, the cure is practically guaranteed.

"I can assure you, Major Wilbraham, that ninety-six percent of retired empire builders—as I call them—are unhappy. They exchange an active life, a life full of responsibility, a life of possible danger, for—what? Straitened means, a dismal climate and a general feeling of being a fish out of water."

"All you've said is true," said the major. "It's the boredom I object to. The boredom and the endless tittle—tattle about petty village matters. But what can I do about it? I've got a little money besides my pension. I've a nice cottage near Cobham. I can't afford to hunt or shoot or fish. I'm not married. My neighbors are all pleasant folk, but they've no ideas beyond this island."

"The long and short of the matter is that you find life tame," said Mr. Parker Pyne.

"Damned tame."

"You would like excitement, possibly danger?" asked Mr. Pyne.

The soldier shrugged. "There's no such thing in this tinpot country."

"I beg your pardon," said Mr. Pyne seriously. "There you are wrong. There is plenty of danger, plenty of excitement, here in London if you know where to go for it. You have seen only the surface of our English life, calm, pleasant. But there is another side. If you wish it, I can show you that other side."

Major Wilbraham regarded him thoughtfully. There was something reassuring about Mr. Pyne. He was large, not to say fat; he had a bald head of noble proportions, strong glasses and little twinkling eyes. And he had an aura—an aura of dependability.

"I should warn you, however," continued Mr. Pyne, "that there is an element of risk."

The soldier's eye brightened. "That's all right," he said. Then, abruptly: "And—your fees?"

"My fee," said Mr. Pyne, "is fifty pounds, payable in advance. If in a month's time you are still in the same state of boredom, I will refund your money."

Wilbraham considered. "Fair enough," he said at last. "I agree. I'll give you a check now."

The transaction was completed. Mr. Parker Pyne pressed a buzzer on his desk.

"It is now one o'clock," he said, "I am going to ask you to take a young lady out to lunch." The door opened. "Ah, Madeleine, my dear, let me introduce Major Wilbraham, who is going to take you out to lunch."

Wilbraham blinked slightly, which was hardly to be wondered at. The girl who entered the room was dark, languorous, with wonderful eyes and long black lashes, a perfect complexion and a voluptuous scarlet mouth. Her exquisite clothes set off the swaying grace of her figure. From head to foot she was perfect.

"Er—delighted," said Major Wilbraham.

"Miss de Sara," said Mr. Parker Pyne.

"How very kind of you," murmured Madeleine de Sara.

"I have your address here," announced Mr. Parker Pyne. "Tomorrow morning you will receive my further instructions."

Major Wilbraham and the lovely Madeleine departed.

. . .

IT WAS THREE O'CLOCK when Madeleine returned.

Mr. Parker Pyne looked up. "Well?" he demanded.

Madeleine shook her head. "Scared of me," she said. "Thinks I'm a vamp."

"I thought as much," said Mr. Parker Pyne. "You carried out my instructions?"

"Yes. We discussed the occupants of the other tables freely. The type he likes is fair—haired, blue-eyed, slightly anemic, not too tall."

"That should be easy," said Mr. Pyne. "Get me Schedule B and let me see what we have in stock at present." He ran his finger down a list, finally stopping at a name. "Freda Clegg. Yes, I think Freda Clegg will do excellently. I had better see Mrs. Oliver about it."

THE NEXT DAY Major Wilbraham received a note, which read:

> On Monday morning next at eleven o'clock go to Eaglemont, Friars Lane, Hampstead, and ask for Mr. Jones. You will represent yourself as coming from the Guava Shipping Company.

Obediently on the following Monday (which happened to be Bank Holiday), Major Wilbraham set out for Eaglemont, Friars Lane. He set out, I say, but he never got there. For before he got there, something happened.

All the world and his wife seemed to be on their way to Hampstead. Major Wilbraham got, entangled in crowds, suffocated in the tube and found it hard to discover the whereabouts of Friars Lane.

Friars Lane was a cul-de-sac, a neglected road full of ruts, with houses on either side standing back from the road. They were largish houses which had seen better days and had been allowed to fall into disrepair.

Wilbraham walked along peering at the half-erased names on the gateposts, when suddenly he heard something that made him stiffen to attention. It was a kind of gurgling, half-choked cry.

It came again and this time it was faintly recognizable as the word "Help!" It came from inside the wall of the house he was passing.

Without a moment's hesitation, Major Wilbraham pushed open the rickety gate and sprinted noiselessly up the weed-covered drive. There in the shrubbery was a girl struggling in the grasp of two enormous Negroes. She was putting up a brave fight, twisting and turning and kicking. One Negro held his hand over her mouth in spite of her furious efforts to get her head free.

Intent on their struggle with the girl, neither of the blacks had noticed Wilbraham's approach. The first they knew of it was when a violent punch on the jaw sent the man who was covering the girl's mouth reeling backward. Taken by surprise, the other man relinquished his hold of the girl and turned. Wilbraham was ready for him. Once again his fist shot out, and the Negro reeled backward and fell. Wilbraham turned on the other man, who was closing in behind him.

But the two men had had enough. The second one rolled over, sat up; then, rising, he made a dash for the gate. His companion followed suit. Wilbraham started after them, but changed his mind and turned toward the girl, who was leaning against a tree, panting.

"Oh, thank you!" she gasped. "It was terrible."

Major Wilbraham saw for the first time who it was he had rescued so opportunely. She was a girl of about twenty-one or -two, fair-haired and blue-eyed, pretty in a rather colorless way.

"If you hadn't come!" she gasped.

"There, there," said Wilbraham soothingly. "It's all right now. I think, though, that we'd better get away from here. It's possible those fellows might come back."

A faint smile came to the girl's lips. "I don't think they will—not after the way you hit them. Oh, it was splendid of you!"

Major Wilbraham blushed under the warmth of her glance of admiration. "Nothin' at all," he said indistinctly. "All in day's work.

Lady being annoyed. Look here, if you take my arm, can you walk? It's been a nasty shock, I know."

"I'm all right now," said the girl. However, she took the proffered arm. She was still rather shaky. She glanced behind her at the house as they emerged through the gate. "I can't understand it," she murmured. "That's clearly an empty house."

"It's empty, right enough," agreed the major, looking up at the shuttered windows and general air of decay.

"And yet it *is* Whitefriars." She pointed to a half-obliterated name on the gate. "And Whitefriars was the place I was to go."

"Don't worry about anything now," said Wilbraham. "In a minute or two we'll be able to get a taxi. Then we'll drive somewhere and have a cup of coffee."

At the end of the lane they came out into a more frequented street, and by good fortune a taxi had just set down a fare at one of the houses. Wilbraham hailed it, gave an address to the driver and they got in.

"Don't try to talk," he admonished his companion. "Just lie back. You've had a nasty experience."

She smiled at him gratefully.

"By the way—er—my name is Wilbraham."

"Mine is Clegg—Freda Clegg."

Ten minutes later, Freda was sipping hot coffee and looking gratefully across a small table at her rescuer.

"It seems like a dream," she said. "A bad dream." She shuddered. "And only a short while ago I was wishing for something to happen—anything! Oh, I don't like adventures."

"Tell me how it happened."

"Well, to tell you properly I shall have to talk a lot about myself, I'm afraid."

"An excellent subject," said Wilbraham, with a bow.

"I am an orphan. My father—he was a sea captain—died when I was eight. My mother died three years ago. I work in the City. I am with the Vacuum Gas Company—a clerk. One evening last week I found a gentleman waiting to see me when I returned to my lodgings. He was a lawyer, a Mr. Reid from Melbourne.

"He was very polite and asked me several questions about my family. He explained that he had known my father many years ago. In fact, he had transacted some legal business for him. Then he told me the object of his visit. 'Miss Clegg,' he said, 'I have reason to suppose that you might benefit as the result of a financial transaction entered into by your father several years before he died.' I was very much surprised, of course.

"'It is unlikely that you would ever have heard anything of the matter,' he explained. 'John Clegg never took the affair seriously, I fancy. However, it has materialized unexpectedly, but I am afraid any claim you might put in would depend on your ownership of certain papers. These papers would be part of your father's estate, and of course it is possible that they have been destroyed as worthless. Have you kept any of your father's papers?'

"I explained that my mother had kept various things of my father's in an old sea chest. I had looked through it cursorily but had discovered nothing of interest.

"'You would hardly be likely to recognize the importance of these documents, perhaps,' he said, smiling.

"Well, I went to the chest, took out the few papers it contained and brought them to him. He looked at them, but said it was impossible to say offhand what might or might not be connected with the matter in question. He would take them away with him and would communicate with me if anything turned up.

"By the last post on Saturday I received a letter from him in which he suggested that I come to his house to discuss the matter. He gave me the address: Whitefriars, Friars Lane, Hampstead. I was to be there at a quarter to eleven this morning.

"I was a little late finding the place. I hurried through the gate and up toward the house, when suddenly those two dreadful men sprang at me from the bushes. I hadn't time to cry out. One man put his hand over my mouth. I wrenched my head free and screamed for help. Luckily you heard me. If it hadn't been for you—" She stopped. Her looks were more eloquent than further words.

"Very glad I happened to be on the spot. By Gad, I'd like to get hold of those two brutes. You'd never seen them before, I suppose?"

She shook her head. "What do you think it means?"

"Difficult to say. But one thing seems pretty sure. There's something someone wants among your father's papers. This man Reid told you a cock-and-bull story so as to get the opportunity of looking through them. Evidently what he wanted wasn't there."

"Oh!" said Freda. "I wonder. When I got home on Saturday I thought my things had been tampered with. To tell you the truth, I suspected my landlady of having pried about in my room out of curiosity. But now—"

"Depend upon it, that's it. Someone gained admission to your room and searched it, without finding what he was after. He suspected that you knew the value of this paper, whatever it was, and that you carried it about on your person. So he planned this ambush. If you had had it with you, it would have been taken from you. If not, you would have been held prisoner while he tried to make you tell where it was hidden."

"But what can it possibly *be*?" cried Freda.

"I don't know. But it must be something pretty good for him to go to this length."

"It doesn't seem possible."

"Oh, I don't know. Your father was a sailor. He went to out-of-the-way places. He might have come across something the value of which he never knew."

"Do you really think so?" A pink flush of excitement showed in the girl's pale cheeks.

"I do indeed. The question is, what shall we do next? You don't want to go to the police, I suppose?"

"Oh, no, please."

"I'm glad you say that. I don't see what good the police could do, and it would only mean unpleasantness for you. Now I suggest that you allow me to give you lunch somewhere and that I then accompany you back to your lodgings, so as to be sure you reach them safely. And then, we might have a look for the paper. Because, you know, it must be somewhere."

"Father may have destroyed it himself."

"He may, of course, but the other side evidently doesn't think so, and that looks hopeful for us."

"What do you think it can be? Hidden treasure?"

"By Jove, it might be!" exclaimed Major Wilbraham, all the boy in him rising joyfully to the suggestion. "But now, Miss Clegg, lunch!"

They had a pleasant meal together. Wilbraham told Freda all about his life in East Africa. He described elephant hunts, and the girl was thrilled. When they had finished, he insisted on taking her home in a taxi.

Her lodgings were near Notting Hill Gate. On arriving there, Freda had a brief conversation with her land-lady. She returned to Wilbraham and took him up to the second floor, where she had a tiny bedroom and sitting room.

"It's exactly as we thought," she said. "A man came on Saturday morning to see about laying a new electric cable; he told her there was a fault in the wiring in my room. He was there some time."

"Show me this chest of your father's," said Wilbraham.

Freda showed him a brass-bound box. "You see," she said, raising the lid, "It's empty."

The soldier nodded thoughtfully. "And there are no papers anywhere else?"

"I'm sure there aren't. Mother kept everything in here."

Wilbraham examined the inside of the chest. Suddenly he uttered an exclamation. "Here's a slit in the lining." Carefully he inserted his hand, feeling about. A slight crackle rewarded him. "Something's slipped down behind."

In another minute he had drawn out his find. A piece of dirty paper folded several times. He smoothed it out on the table; Freda was looking over his shoulder. She uttered an exclamation of disappointment.

"It's just a lot of queer marks."

"Why, the thing's in Swahili. *Swahili*, of all things!" cried Major Wilbraham. "East African native dialect, you know."

"How extraordinary!" said Freda. "Can you read it, then?"

"Rather. But what an amazing thing." He took the paper to the window.

"Is it anything?" asked Freda tremulously. Wilbraham read the thing through twice, and then came back to the girl. "Well," he said with a chuckle, "here's your hidden treasure, all right."

"Hidden treasure? Not *really*? You mean Spanish gold—a sunken galleon—that sort of thing?"

"Not quite so romantic as that, perhaps. But it comes to the same thing. This paper gives the hiding place of a cache of ivory."

"Ivory?" said the girl, astonished.

"Yes. Elephants, you know. There's a law about the number you're allowed to shoot. Some hunter got away with breaking that law on a grand scale. They were on his trail and he cached the stuff. There's a thundering lot of it—and this gives fairly clear directions how to find it. Look here, we'll have to go after this, you and I."

"You mean there's really a lot of money in it?"

"Quite a nice little fortune for you."

"But how did that paper come to be among my father's things?"

Wilbraham shrugged. "Maybe the Johnny was dying or something. He may have written the thing down in Swahili for protection and given it to your father, who possibly had befriended him in some way. Your father, not being able to read it, attached no importance to it. That's only a guess on my part, but I dare say it's not far wrong."

Freda gave a sigh. "How frightfully exciting!"

"The thing is—what to do with the precious document," said Wilbraham. "I don't like leaving it here. They might come and have another look. I suppose you wouldn't entrust it to me?"

"Of course I would. But—mightn't it be dangerous for you?" she faltered.

"I'm a tough nut," said Wilbraham grimly. "You needn't worry about me." He folded up the paper and put it in his pocketbook.

"May I come to see you tomorrow evening?" he asked. "I'll have worked out a plan by then, and I'll look up the places on my map. What time do you get back from the City?"

"I get back about half-past-six."

"Capital. We'll have a powwow, and then perhaps you'll let me take you out to dinner. We ought to celebrate. So long, then. Tomorrow at half-past-six."

Major Wilbraham arrived punctually on the following day. He rang the bell and inquired for Miss Clegg. A maid-servant had answered the door.

"Miss Clegg? She's out."

"Oh!" Wilbraham did not like to suggest that he come in and wait. "I'll call back presently," he said.

He hung about in the street outside, expecting every minute to see Freda tripping toward him. The minutes passed. Quarter to seven. Seven. Quarter past seven. Still no Freda. A feeling of uneasiness swept over him. He went back to the house and rang the bell again.

"Look here," he said, "I had an appointment with Miss Clegg at half-past-six. Are you sure she isn't in or hasn't—er—left any message?"

"Are you Major Wilbraham?" asked the servant.

"Yes."

"Then there's a note for you. It come by hand."

Wilbraham took it from her and tore it open. It ran as follows:

Dear Major Wilbraham:

Something rather strange has happened. I won't write more now, but will you meet me at Whitefriars? Go there as soon as you get this.

Yours sincerely,
Freda Clegg

Wilbraham drew his brows together as he thought rapidly. His hand drew a letter absentmindedly from his pocket. It was to his tailor. "I wonder," he said to the maidservant, "if you could let me have a stamp."

"I expect Mrs. Parkins could oblige you."

She returned in a moment with the stamp. It was paid for with a shilling. In another minute Wilbraham was walking toward the tube station, dropping the envelope in a box as he passed.

Freda's letter had made him mot uneasy. What could have taken the girl, alone, to the scene of yesterday's sinister encounter?

He shook his head. Of all the foolish things to do! Had Reid reappeared? Had he somehow or other prevailed upon the girl to trust him? What had taken her to Hampstead?

He looked at his watch. Nearly half-past-seven. She would have counted on his starting at half-past-six. An hour late. Too much. If only she had had the sense to give him some hint.

The letter puzzled him. Somehow, its independent tone was not characteristic of Freda Clegg.

It was ten minutes to eight when he reached Friars Lane. It was getting dark. He looked sharply about him; there was no one in sight. Gently he pushed the rickety gate so that is swung noiselessly on its hinges. The drive was deserted. The house was dark. He went up the path cautiously, keeping a lookout from side to side. He did not intend to be caught by surprise.

Suddenly he stopped. Just for a minute a chink of light had shone through one of the shutters. The house was not empty. There was someone inside.

Softly Wilbraham slipped into the bushes and worked his way round to the back of the house. At last he found what he was looking for. One of the windows on the ground floor was unfastened. It was the window of a kind of scullery. He raised the sash, flashed a torch (he had bought it at a shop on the way over) around the deserted interior and climbed in.

Carefully he opened the scullery door. There was no sound. He flashed the torch once more. A kitchen—empty. Outside the kitchen were half a dozen steps and a door evidently leading to the front part of the house.

He pushed open the door and listened. Nothing. He slipped

through. He was now in the front hall. Still there was no sound. There was a door to the right and a door to the left. He chose the right-hand door, listened for a time, then turned the handle. It gave. Inch by inch he opened the door and stepped inside.

Again he flashed the torch. The room was unfurnished and bare.

Just at that moment he heard a sound behind him, whirled round—too late. Something came down on his head and he pitched forward into unconsciousness . . .

How much time elapsed before he regained consciousness Wilbraham had no idea. He returned painfully to life, his head aching. He tried to move and found it impossible. He was bound with ropes.

His wits came back to him suddenly. He remembered now. He had been hit on the head.

A faint light from a gas jet high up on the wall showed him that he was in a small cellar. He looked around and his heart gave a leap. A few feet away lay Freda, bound like himself. Her eyes were closed, but even as he watched her anxiously, she sighed and they opened. Her bewildered gaze fell on him and joyous recognition leaped into them.

"You, too!" she said. "What has happened?"

"I've let you down badly," said Wilbraham. "Tumbled headlong into the trap. Tell me, did you send me a note asking me to meet you here?"

The girl's eyes opened in astonishment. "*I?* But you sent *me* one."

"Oh, I sent you one, did I?"

"Yes. I got it at the office. It asked me to meet you here instead of at home."

"Same method for both of us," he groaned, and he explained the situation.

"I see," said Freda. "Then the idea was—"

"To get the paper. We must have been followed yesterday. That's how they got on to me."

"And—have they got it?" asked Freda.

"Unfortunately, I can't feel and see," said the soldier, regarding his bound hands ruefully.

And then they both started. For a voice spoke, a voice that seemed to come from the empty air.

"Yes, thank you," it said. "I've got it, all right. No mistake about that."

The unseen voice made them both shiver.

"Mr. Reid," murmured Freda.

"Mr. Reid is one of my names, my dear young lady," said the voice. "But only one of them. I have a great many. Now, I am sorry to say that you two have interfered with my plans—a thing I never allow. Your discovery of this house is a serious matter. You have not told the police about it yet, but you might do so in the future.

"I very much fear that I cannot trust you in the matter. You might promise—but promises are seldom kept. And you see, this house is very useful to me. It is, you might say, my clearing house. The house from which there is no return. From here you pass on—elsewhere. You, I am sorry to say, are so passing on. Regrettable—but necessary."

The voice paused for a brief second, then resumed: "No bloodshed. I abhor bloodshed. My method is much simpler. And really not too painful, so I understand. Well, I must be getting along. Good evening to you both."

"Look here!" It was Wilbraham who spoke. "Do what you like to me, but this young lady has done nothing—nothing. It can't hurt you to let her go."

But there was no answer.

At that moment there came a cry from Freda. "The water—the water!"

Wilbraham twisted himself painfully and followed the direction of her eyes. From a hole up near the ceiling a steady trickle of water was pouring in.

Freda gave a hysterical cry. "They're going to drown us!"

The perspiration broke out on Wilbraham's brow. "We're not done yet," he said. "We'll shout for help. Surely somebody will hear. Now, both together."

They yelled and shouted at the top of their voices. Not till they were hoarse did they stop.

"No use, I'm afraid," said Wilbraham sadly. "We're too far underground and I expect the doors are muffled. After all, if we could be heard, I've no doubt that brute would have gagged us."

"Oh!" cried Freda. "And it's all my fault. I got you into this."

"Don't worry about that, little girl. It's you I'm thinking about. I've been in tight corners before now and got out of them. Don't you lose heart. I'll get you out of this. We've plenty of time. At the rate that water's flowing in, it will be hours before the worst happens."

"How wonderful you are!" said Freda. "I've never met anybody like you—except in books."

"Nonsense—just common sense. Now, I've got to loosen these infernal ropes."

At the end of a quarter of an hour, by dint of straining and twisting, Wilbraham had the satisfaction of feeling that his bonds were appreciably loosened. He managed to bend his head down and his wrists up till he was able to attack the knots with his teeth.

Once his hands were free, the rest was only a matter of time. Cramped, stiff, but free, he bent over the girl. A minute later she also was free.

So far the water was only up to their ankles.

"And now," said the soldier, "to get out of here."

The door of the cellar was up a few stairs. Major Wilbraham examined it.

"No difficulty here," he said. "Flimsy stuff. It will soon give at the hinges." He set his shoulders to it and heaved.

There was the cracking of wood—a crash, and the door burst from its hinges.

Outside was a flight of stairs. At the top was another door—a very different affair—of solid wood, barred with iron.

"A bit more difficult, this," said Wilbraham. "Hello, here's a piece of luck. It's unlocked."

He pushed it open, peered round it, then beckoned the girl to come on. They emerged into a passage behind the kitchen. In another moment they were standing under the stars in Friars Lane.

"Oh!" Freda gave a little sob. "Oh, how dreadful it's been!"

"My poor darling." He caught her in his arms. "You've been so wonderfully brave. Freda—darling angel—could you ever—I mean, would you—I love you, Freda. Will you marry me?"

After a suitable interval, highly satisfactory to both parties, Major Wilbraham said with a chuckle:

"And what's more, we've still got the secret of the ivory cache."

"But they took it from you!"

The major chuckled again. "That's just what they didn't do! You see, I wrote out a spoof copy, and before joining you here tonight, I put the real thing in a letter I was sending to my tailor and posted it. They've got the spoof copy—and I wish them joy of it! Do you know what we'll do, sweetheart? We'll go to East Africa for our honeymoon and hunt out the cache."

MR. PARKER PYNE LEFT his office and climbed two flights of stairs. Here in a room at the top of the house sat Mrs. Oliver, the sensational novelist, now a member of Mr. Pyne's staff.

Mr. Parker Pyne tapped at the door and entered. Mrs. Oliver sat at a table on which were a typewriter, several notebooks, a general confusion of loose manuscripts and a large bag of apples.

"A very good story, Mrs. Oliver," said Mr. Parker Pyne genially.

"It went off well?" said Mrs. Oliver. "I'm glad."

"That water-in-the-cellar business," said Mr. Parker Pyne. "You don't think, on a future occasion, that something more original—perhaps?" He made the suggestion with proper diffidence.

Mrs. Oliver shook her head and took an apple from the bag. "I think not Mr. Pyne. You see, people are used to reading about such things. Water rising in a cellar, poison gas, et cetera. Knowing about it beforehand gives it an extra thrill when it happens to oneself. The public is conservative, Mr. Pyne; it likes the old well-worn gadgets."

"Well, you should know," admitted Mr. Parker Pyne, mindful of the authoress' forty-six successful works of fiction, all best sellers in England and America, and freely translated into French, German,

Italian, Hungarian, Finnish, Japanese and Abyssinian. "How about expenses?"

Mrs. Oliver drew a paper toward her. "Very moderate, on the whole. The two Negroes, Percy and Jerry, wanted very little. Young Lorrimer, the actor, was willing to enact the part of Mr. Reid for five guineas. The cellar speech was a phonograph record, of course."

"Whitefriars has been extremely useful to me," said Mr. Pyne. "I bought it for a song and it has already been the scene of eleven exciting dramas."

"Oh, I forgot," said Mrs. Oliver. "Johnny's wages. Five shillings."

"Johnny?"

"Yes. The boy who poured the water from the watering cans through the hole in the wall."

"Ah, yes. By the way, Mrs. Oliver how did you happen to know Swahili?"

"I didn't."

"I see. The British Museum, perhaps?"

"No. Delfridge's Information Bureau."

"How marvelous are the resources of modern commerce!" he murmured.

"The only thing that worries me," said Mrs. Oliver, "is that those two young people won't find any cache when they get there."

"One cannot have everything in this world," said Mr. Parker Pyne. "They will have had a honeymoon."

MRS. WILBRAHAM WAS sitting in a deck chair. Her husband was writing a letter. "What's the date, Freda?"

"The sixteenth."

"The sixteenth. By Jove!"

"What is it, dear?"

"Nothing. I just remembered a chap named Jones."

However happily married, there are some things one never tells.

"Dash it all," thought Major Wilbraham, "I ought to have called at that place and got my money back." And then, being a fair-minded man, he looked at the other side of the question. "After all, it was I who broke the bargain. I suppose if I'd gone to see Jones something would have happened. And anyway, as it turns out, if I hadn't been going to see Jones, I should never have heard Freda cry for help, and we might never have met. So, indirectly, perhaps they have a right to that fifty pounds!"

Mrs. Wilbraham was also following out a train of thought. "What a silly little fool I was to believe in that advertisement and pay those people three guineas. Of course, they never did anything for it and nothing ever happened. If I'd only known what was coming—first Mr. Reid, and then the queer, romantic way that Charlie came into my life. And to think that *but for pure chance* I might never have met him!"

She turned and smiled adoringly at her husband.

3. THE CASE OF THE DISTRESSED LADY

The buzzer on Mr. Parker Pyne's desk purred discreetly.

"Yes?" said the great man.

"A young lady wishes to see you," announced his secretary. "She has no appointment."

"You may send her in, Miss Lemon." A moment later he was shaking hands with his visitor. "Good morning," he said. "Do sit down."

The girl sat down and looked at Mr. Parker Pyne. She was a pretty girl and quite young. Her hair was dark and wavy with a row of curls at the nape of the neck. She was beautifully turned out from the white knitted cap on her head to the cobweb stockings and dainty shoes. Clearly she was nervous.

"You are Mr. Parker Pyne?" she asked.

"I am."

"The one who—who—advertises?"

"The one who advertises."

"You say that if people aren't—aren't happy—to—to come to you."

"Yes."

She took the plunge. "Well, I'm frightfully unhappy. So I thought I'd come along and just—and just see."

Mr. Parker Pyne waited. He felt there was more to come.

"I—I'm in frightful trouble." She clenched her hands nervously.

"So I see," said Mr. Parker Pyne. "Do you think you could tell me about it?"

That, it seemed, was what the girl was by no means sure of. She stared at Mr. Parker Pyne with a desperate intentness. Suddenly she spoke with a rush.

"Yes, I will tell you.—I've made up my mind now. I've been nearly crazy with worry. I didn't know what to do or whom to go to. And then I saw your advertisement. I thought it was probably just a ramp, but it stayed in my mind. It sounded so comforting, somehow. And then I thought—well, it would do no harm to come and *see*. I could always make an excuse and get away again if I didn't—well, if I didn't—"

"Quite so; quite so," said Mr. Pyne.

"You see," said the girl, "it means—well, *trusting* somebody."

"And you feel you can trust me?" he said, smiling.

"It's odd," said the girl with unconscious rudeness, "but I do. Without knowing anything about you! I'm *sure* I can trust you."

"I can assure you," said Mr. Pyne, "that your trust will not be misplaced."

"Then," said the girl, "I'll tell you about it. My name is Daphne St. John."

"Yes, Miss St. John."

"Mrs. I'm—I'm married."

"Pshaw!" muttered Mr. Pyne, annoyed with himself as he noted the platinum circlet on the third finger of her left hand. "Stupid of me."

"If I weren't married," said the girl, "I shouldn't mind so much. I mean, it wouldn't matter so much. It's the thought of Gerald—Well, here—here's what all the trouble's about!"

She dived in her bag, took something out and flung it down on the desk where, gleaming and flashing, it rolled over to Mr. Parker Pyne.

It was a platinum ring with a large solitaire diamond.

Mr. Pyne picked it up, took it to the window, tested it on the pane, applied a jeweler's lens to his eye and examined it closely.

"An exceedingly fine diamond," he remarked, coming back to the table; "worth, I should say, about two thousand pounds at least."

"Yes. And it's stolen! I stole it! And I don't know what to do."

"Dear me!" said Mr. Parker Pyne. "This is very interesting."

His client broke down and sobbed into an inadequate handkerchief.

"Now, now," said Mr. Pyne. "Everything's going to be all right."

The girl dried her eyes and sniffed. "Is it?" she said. "Oh, *is* it?"

"Of course it is. Now, just tell me the whole story."

"Well, it began by my being hard up. You see, I'm frightfully extravagant. And Gerald gets so annoyed about it. Gerald's my husband. He's a lot older than I am, and he's got very—well, very austere ideas. He thinks running into debt is dreadful. So I didn't tell him. And I went over to Le Touquet with some friends and I thought perhaps I might be lucky at chemmy and get straight again. I did win at first. And then I lost, and then I thought I must go on. And I went on. And—and—"

"Yes, yes," said Mr. Parker Pyne. "You need not go into details. You were in a worse plight than ever. That is right, is it not?"

Daphne St. John nodded. "And by then, you see, I simply couldn't tell Gerald. Because he hates gambling. Oh, I was in an awful mess. Well, we went down to stay with the Dortheimers near Cobham. He's frightfully rich, of course. His wife, Naomi, was at school with me. She's pretty and a dear. While we were there, the setting of this ring got loose. On the morning we were leaving, she asked me to take it up to town and drop it at her jeweler's in Bond Street." She paused.

"And now we come to the difficult part," said Mr. Pyne helpfully. "Go on, Mrs. St. John."

"You won't ever tell, will you?" demanded the girl pleadingly.

"My clients' confidences are sacred. And anyway, Mrs. St. John, you have told me so much already that I could probably finish the story for myself."

"That's true. All right. But I hate saying it—it sounds so awful. I went to Bond Street. There's another shop there—Viro's. They—copy jewelry. Suddenly I lost my head. I took the ring in and said I wanted an exact copy; I said I was going abroad and didn't want to take real jewelry with me. They seemed to think it quite natural.

"Well, I got the paste replica—it was so good you couldn't have told it from the original—and I sent it off by registered post to Lady Dortheimer. I had a box with the jeweler's name on it, so that was all right, and I made a professional-looking parcel. And then I—I—pawned the real one." She hid her face in her hands. "How could I? How *could* I? I was just a low, mean, common thief."

Mr. Parker Pyne coughed. "I do not think you have quite finished," he said.

"No, I haven't. This, you understand, was about six weeks ago. I paid off all my debts and got square again, but of course I was miserable all the time. And then an old cousin of mine died and I came into some money. The first thing I did was to redeem the wretched ring. Well, that's all right; here it is. But something terribly difficult has happened."

"Yes?"

"We've had a quarrel with the Dortheimers. It's over some shares that Sir Reuben persuaded Gerald to buy. He was terribly let in over them and he told Sir Reuben what he thought of him—and oh, it's all dreadful! And now, you see, I can't get the ring back."

"Couldn't you send it to Lady Dortheimer anonymously?"

"That gives the whole thing away. She'll examine her own ring, find it's a fake and guess at once what I've done."

"You say she is a friend of yours. What about telling her the whole truth—throwing yourself on her mercy?"

Mrs. St. John shook her head. "We're not such friends as that. Where money or jewelry is concerned, Naomi's as hard as nails. Perhaps she couldn't prosecute me if I gave the ring back, but she could tell everyone what I've done and I'd be ruined. Gerald would know and he would never forgive me. Oh, how awful everything is!" She began to cry again. "I've thought and I've thought, and I can't see *what* to do! Oh, Mr. Pyne, can't you do anything?"

"Several things," said Mr. Parker Pyne.

"You can? Really?"

"Certainly. I suggested the simplest way because in my long experience I have always found it the best. It avoids unlooked-for complications. Still, I see the force of your objections. At present no one knows of this unfortunate occurrence but yourself?"

"And you," said Mrs. St. John.

"Oh, I do not count. Well, then, your secret is safe at present. All that is needed is to exchange the rings in some unsuspicious manner."

"That's it," the girl said eagerly.

"That should not be difficult. We must take a little time to consider the best method—"

She interrupted him. "But there is no time! That's what's driving me nearly crazy. She's going to have the ring reset."

"How do you know?"

"Just by chance. I was lunching with a woman the other day and I admired a ring she had on—a big emerald. She said it was the newest thing—and that Naomi Dortheimer was going to have her diamond reset that way."

"Which means that we shall have to act quickly," said Mr. Pyne thoughtfully.

"Yes, yes."

"It means gaining admission to the house—and if possible not in a menial capacity. Servants have little chance of handling valuable rings. Have you any ideas yourself, Mrs. St. John?"

"Well, Naomi is giving a big party on Wednesday. And this friend of mine mentioned that she had been looking for some exhibition dancers. I don't know if anything has been settled—"

"I think that can be managed," said Mr. Parker Pyne. "If the matter is already settled it will be more expensive, that is all. One thing more, do you happen to know where the main light switch is situated?"

"As it happens I *do* know that, because a fuse blew out late one night when the servants had all gone to bed. It's a box at the back of the hall—inside a little cupboard."

At Mr. Parker Pyne's request she drew him a sketch.

"And now," said Mr. Parker Pyne, "everything is going to be all right, so don't worry, Mrs. St. John. What about the ring? Shall I take it now, or would you rather keep it till Wednesday?"

"Well, perhaps I'd better keep it."

"Now, no more worry, mind you," Mr. Parker Pyne admonished her.

"And your—fee?" she asked timidly.

"That can stand over for the moment. I will let you know on Wednesday what expenses have been necessary. The fee will be nominal, I assure you."

He conducted her to the door, then rang the buzzer on his desk.

"Send Claude and Madeleine here."

Claude Luttrell was one of the handsomest specimens of lounge lizard to be found in England. Madeleine de Sara was the most seductive of vamps.

Mr. Parker Pyne surveyed them with approval. "My children," he said, "I have a job for you. You are going to be internationally famous exhibition dancers. Now, attend to this carefully, Claude, and mind you get it right . . ."

LADY DORTHEIMER WAS fully satisfied with the arrangements for her ball. She surveyed the floral decorations and approved, gave a few last orders to the butler, and remarked to her husband that so far nothing had gone wrong!

It was a slight disappointment that Michael and Juanita, the dancers from the Red Admiral, had been unable to fulfill their contract at the last moment, owing to Juanita's spraining her ankle, but instead, two new dancers were being sent (so ran the story over the telephone) who had created a furor in Paris.

The dancers duly arrived and Lady Dortheimer approved. The evening went splendidly. Jules and Sanchia did their turn, and most sensational it was. A wild Spanish Revolution dance. Then a dance called the Degenerate's Dream. Then an exquisite exhibition of modern dancing.

The "cabaret" over, normal dancing was resumed. The handsome Jules requested a dance with Lady Dortheimer. They floated away. Never had Lady Dortheimer had such a perfect partner.

Sir Reuben was searching for the seductive Sanchia—in vain. She was not in the ballroom.

She was, as a matter of fact, out in the deserted hall near a small box, with her eyes fixed on the jeweled watch which she wore round her wrist.

"You are not English—you cannot be English—to dance as you do," murmured Jules into Lady Dortheimer's ear. "You are the sprite, the spirit of the wind. *Droushcka petrovka navarouchi.*"

"What is that language?"

"Russian," said Jules mendaciously. "I say something to you in Russian that I dare not say in English."

Lady Dortheimer closed her eyes. Jules pressed her closer to him.

Suddenly the lights went out. In the darkness Jules bent and kissed the hand that lay on his shoulder. As she made to draw it away, he caught it, raised it to his lips again. Somehow, a ring slipped from her finger into his hand.

To Lady Dortheimer it seemed only a second before the lights went on again. Jules was smiling at her.

"Your ring," he said. "It slipped off. You permit?" He replaced it on her finger. His eyes said a number of things while he was doing it.

Sir Reuben was talking about the main switch. "Some idiot. Practical joke, I suppose."

Lady Dortheimer was not interested. Those few minutes of darkness had been very pleasant.

MR. PARKER PYNE ARRIVED at his office on Thursday morning to find Mrs. St. John already awaiting him.

"Show her in," said Mr. Pyne.

"Well?" She was all eagerness.

"You look pale," he said accusingly.

She shook her head. "I couldn't sleep last night. I was wondering—"

"Now, here is the little bill for expenses. Train fares, costumes, and fifty pounds to Michael and Juanita. Sixty-five pounds, seventeen shillings."

"Yes, yes! But about last night—was it all right? Did it happen?"

Mr. Parker Pyne looked at her in surprise. "My dear young lady, naturally it is all right. I took it for granted that you understood that."

"What a relief! I was afraid—"

Mr. Parker Pyne shook his head reproachfully. "Failure is a word not tolerated in this establishment. If I do not think I can succeed I refuse to undertake a case. If I do take a case, its success is practically a foregone conclusion."

"She's really got her ring back and suspects nothing?"

"Nothing whatever. The operation was most delicately conducted."

Daphne St. John sighed. "You don't know the load off my mind. What were you saying about expenses?"

"Sixty-five pounds, seventeen shillings."

Mrs. St. John opened her bag and counted out the money. Mr. Parker Pyne thanked her and wrote out a receipt.

"But your fee?" murmured Daphne. "This is only for expenses."

"In this case there is no fee."

"Oh, Mr. Pyne! I couldn't, *really!*"

"My dear young lady, I insist. I will not touch a penny. It would be against my principles. Here is your receipt. And now—"

With the smile of a happy conjurer bringing off a successful trick, he drew a small box from his pocket and pushed it across the table. Daphne opened it. Inside, to all appearances, lay the identical diamond ring.

"Brute!" said Mrs. St. John, making a face at it. "How I hate you! I've a good mind to throw you out of the window."

"I shouldn't do that," said Mr. Pyne. "It might surprise people."

"You're quite sure it isn't the real one?" said Daphne.

"No, no! The one you showed me the other day is safely on Lady Dortheimer's finger."

"Then that's all right." Daphne rose with a happy laugh.

"Curious your asking me that," said Mr. Parker Pyne. "Of course Claude, poor fellow, hasn't many brains. He might easily have got muddled. So, to make sure, I had an expert look at this thing this morning."

Mrs. St. John sat down again rather suddenly. "Oh! And he said?"

"That it was an extraordinarily good imitation," said Mr. Parker Pyne, beaming. "First-class work. So that sets your mind at rest, doesn't it?"

Mrs. St. John started to say something, then stopped. She was staring at Mr. Parker Pyne.

The latter resumed his seat behind the desk and looked at her benevolently. "The cat who pulled the chestnuts out of the fire," he said dreamily. "Not a pleasant rôle. Not a rôle I should care to have any of my staff undertake. Excuse me. Did you say anything?"

"I—no, nothing."

"Good. I want to tell you a little story, Mrs. St. John. It concerns a young lady. A fair-haired young lady, I think. She is not married. Her name is not St. John. Her Christian name is not Daphne. On the contrary, her name is Ernestine Richards, and until recently she was secretary to Lady Dortheimer.

"Well, one day the setting of Lady Dortheimer's diamond ring became loose and Miss Richards brought it up to town to have it fixed. Quite like your story here, is it not? The same idea occurred to Miss Richards that occurred to you. She had the ring copied. But she was a farsighted young lady. She saw a day coming when Lady Dortheimer would discover the substitution. When that happened, she would remember who had taken the ring to town and Miss Richards would be instantly suspected.

"So what happened? First, I fancy, Miss Richards invested in a La Merveilleuse transformation—Number Seven side parting, I think"—his eyes rested innocently on his client's wavy locks—"shade dark brown. Then she called on me. She showed me the ring, allowed me to satisfy myself that it was genuine, thereby disarming suspicion on my part. That done and a plan of substitution arranged, the young lady took the ring to the jeweler who in due course returned it to Lady Dortheimer.

"Yesterday evening the other ring, the false ring, was hurriedly handed over at the last minute at Waterloo Station. Quite rightly, Miss Richards did not consider that Mr. Luttrell was likely to be an authority on diamonds. But just to satisfy myself that everything was aboveboard I arranged for a friend of mine, a diamond merchant, to be on the train. He looked at the ring and pronounced at once, 'This is not a real diamond; it is an excellent paste replica.'

"You see the point, of course, Mrs. St. John? When Lady Dortheimer discovered her loss, what would she remember? The charming young dancer who slipped the ring off her finger when the lights went out! She would make inquiries and find that the dancers originally engaged were bribed not to come. If matters were traced back to my office, my story of a Mrs. St. John would seem feeble in the extreme. Lady Dortheimer never knew a Mrs. St. John. The story would sound a flimsy fabrication.

"Now you see, don't you, that I could not allow that? And so my friend Claude replaced on Lady Dortheimer's finger *the same ring that he took off*." Mr. Parker Pyne's smile was less benevolent now.

"You see why I could not take a fee? I guarantee to give happiness. Clearly I have not made *you* happy. I will say just one thing more. You are young; possibly this is your first attempt at anything of the kind. Now I, on the contrary, am comparatively advanced in years, and I have had a long experience in the compilation of statistics. From that experience I can assure you that in eighty-seven percent of cases dishonesty does not pay. Eighty-seven percent. Think of it!"

With a brusque movement the pseudo Mrs. St. John rose. "You oily old brute!" she said. "Leading me on! Making me pay expenses! And all the time—" She choked, and rushed toward the door.

"Your ring," said Mr. Parker Pyne, holding it out to her.

She snatched it from him, looked at it and flung it out of the open window.

A door banged and she was gone.

Mr. Parker Pyne was looking out of the window with some interest. "As I thought," he said. "Considerable surprise has been created. The gentleman selling Dismal Desmonds does not know what to make of it."

4. THE CASE OF THE DISCONTENTED HUSBAND

Undoubtedly one of Mr. Parker Pyne's greatest assets was his sympathetic manner. It was a manner that invited confidence. He was well acquainted with the kind of paralysis that descended on clients as soon as they got inside his office. It was Mr. Pyne's task to pave the way for the necessary disclosures.

On this particular morning he sat facing a new client, a Mr. Reginald Wade. Mr. Wade, he deduced at once, was the inarticulate type. The type that finds it hard to put into words anything connected with the emotions.

He was a tall, broadly built man with mild, pleasant blue eyes and a well-tanned complexion. He sat pulling absent-mindedly at a little mustache while he looked at Mr. Parker Pyne with all the pathos of a dumb animal.

"Saw your advertisement, you know," he jerked. "Thought I might as well come along. Rum sort of show, but you never know, what?"

Mr. Parker Pyne interpreted these cryptic remarks correctly. "When things go badly, one is willing to take a chance," he suggested.

"That's it. That's it, exactly. I'm willing to take a chance—any chance. Things are in a bad way with me, Mr. Pyne. I don't know what to do about it. Difficult, you know; damned difficult."

"That," said Mr. Pyne, "is where I come in. I *do,* know what to do! I am a specialist in every kind of human trouble."

"Oh, I say—bit of a tall order, that!"

"Not really. Human troubles are easily classified into a few main heads. There is ill health. There is boredom. There are wives who are in trouble over their husbands. There are husbands"—he paused—"who are in trouble over their wives."

"Matter of fact, you've hit it. You've hit it absolutely."

"Tell me about it," said Mr. Pyne.

"There's nothing much to tell. My wife wants me to give her a divorce so that she can marry another chap."

"Very common indeed in these days. Now you, I gather, don't see eye to eye with her in this business?"

"I'm fond of her," said Mr. Wade simply. "You see—well, I'm fond of her."

A simple and somewhat tame statement, but if Mr. Wade had said, "I adore her. I worship the ground she walks on. I would cut myself into little pieces for her," he could not have been more explicit to Mr. Parker Pyne.

"All the same, you know," went on Mr. Wade, "what can I do? I mean, a fellow's so helpless. If she prefers this other fellow—well, one's got to play the game; stand aside and all that."

"The proposal is that she should divorce you?"

"Of course. I couldn't let her be dragged through the divorce court."

Mr. Pyne looked at him thoughtfully. "But you come to me? Why?"

The other laughed in a shamefaced manner. "I don't know. You see, I'm not a clever chap. I can't think of things. I thought you might—well, suggest something. I've got six months, you see. She agreed to that. If at the end of six months she is still of the same mind—well, then, I get out. I thought you might give me a hint or two. At present everything I do annoys her.

"You see, Mr. Pyne, what it comes to is this: I'm not a clever chap! I like knocking balls about. I like a round of golf and a good set of tennis. I'm no good at music and art and such things. My wife's clever. She likes pictures and the opera and concerts, and naturally she gets bored with me. This other fellow—nasty long-haired chap—he knows all about these things. He can talk about them. I can't. In a way, I can understand a clever, beautiful woman getting fed up with an ass like me."

Mr. Parker Pyne groaned. "You have been married—how long? . . . Nine years? And I suppose you have adopted that attitude from the start. Wrong, my dear sir; disastrously wrong! Never adopt an apologetic attitude with a woman. She will take you at your own valuation—and you deserve it. You should have gloried in your athletic prowess. You should have spoken of art and music as 'all that nonsense my wife likes.' You should have condoled with her on not being able to play games better. The humble spirit, my dear sir, is a washout in matrimony! No woman can be expected to stand up against it. No wonder your wife has been unable to last the course."

Mr. Wade was looking at him in bewilderment. "Well," he said, "what do you think I ought to do?"

"That certainly is the question. Whatever you should have done nine years ago, it is too late now. New tactics must be adopted. Have you ever had any affairs with other women?"

"Certainly not."

"I should have said, perhaps, any light flirtations?"

"I never bothered about women much."

"A mistake. You must start now."

Mr. Wade looked alarmed. "Oh, look here, I couldn't really. I mean—"

"You will be put to no trouble in the matter. One of my staff will be supplied for the purpose. She will tell you what is required of you, and any attentions you pay her she will, of course, understand to be merely a matter of business."

Mr. Wade looked relieved. "That's better. But do you really think—I mean, it seems to me that Iris will be keener to get rid of me than ever."

"You do not understand human nature, Mr. Wade. Still less do you understand feminine human nature. At the present moment you are, from the feminine point of view, merely a waste product. Nobody wants you. What use has a woman for something that no one wants? None whatever. But take another angle. Suppose your wife discovers that you are looking forward to regaining your freedom as much as she is?"

"Then she ought to be pleased."

"She ought to be, perhaps, but she will not be! Moreover, she will see that you have attracted a fascinating young woman—a young woman who could pick and choose. Immediately your stock goes up. Your wife knows that all her friends will say it was you who tired of her and wished to marry a more attractive woman. That will annoy her."

"You think so?"

"I am sure of it. You will no longer be 'poor dear old Reggie.' You will be 'that sly dog Reggie.' All the difference in the world! Without relinquishing the other man, she will doubtless try to win you back. You will not be won. You will be sensible and repeat to her all her arguments. 'Much better to part.' 'Temperamentally unsuited.' You realize that while what she said was true—that you had never understood her—it is also true that *she* had never understood *you*. But we need not go into this now; you will be given full instructions when the time comes."

Mr. Wade seemed doubtful still. "You really think that this plan of yours will do the trick?" he asked dubiously.

"I will not say I am absolutely sure of it," said Mr. Parker Pyne cautiously. "There is a bare possibility that your wife may be so overwhelmingly in love with this other man that nothing you could say or do will affect her, but I consider that unlikely. She has probably been driven into this affair through boredom—boredom with the atmosphere of uncritical devotion and absolute fidelity with which you have most unwisely surrounded her. If you follow my instructions, the chances are, I should say, ninety-seven percent in your favor."

"Good enough," said Mr. Wade. "I'll do it. By the way—er—how much?"

"My fee is two hundred guineas, payable in advance."

Mr. Wade drew out a check book.

THE GROUNDS OF Lorrimer Court were lovely in the afternoon sunshine. Iris Wade, lying on a long chair, made a delicious spot of color. She was dressed in delicate shades of mauve and by skillful make-up managed to look much younger than her thirty-five years.

She was talking to her friend Mrs. Massington, whom she always found sympathetic. Both ladies were afflicted with athletic husbands who talked stocks and shares and golf alternately.

"—and so one learns to live and let live," finished Iris.

"You're wonderful, darling," said Mrs. Massington and added too quickly: "Tell me, who *is* this girl?"

Iris raised a weary shoulder. "Don't ask me! Reggie found her. She's Reggie's little friend! So amusing. You know he never looks at girls as a rule. He came to me and hemmed and hawed, and finally said he wanted to ask this Miss de Sara down for the week-end. Of course I laughed—I couldn't help it. *Reggie*, you know! Well, here she is."

"Where did he meet her?"

"I don't know. He was very vague about it all."

"Perhaps he's known her some time."

"Oh, I don't think so," said Mrs. Wade. "Of course," she went on, "I'm delighted—simply delighted. I mean, it makes it so much easier for me, as things are. Because I *have* been unhappy about Reggie; he's such a dear old thing. That's what I kept saying to Sinclair—that it would hurt Reggie so. But he insisted that Reggie would soon get over it; it looks as if he were right. Two days ago Reggie seemed heartbroken—and now he wants this girl down! As I say, I'm *amused*. I like to see Reggie enjoying himself. I fancy the poor fellow actually thought I might be jealous. Such an absurd idea! 'Of course,' I said, 'have your friend down.' Poor Reggie—as though a girl like that could ever care about him. She's just amusing herself."

"She's extremely attractive," said Mrs. Massington. "Almost dangerously so, if you know what I mean. The sort of girl who cares only for men. I don't feel, somehow, she can be a really nice girl."

"Probably not," said Mrs. Wade.

"She has marvelous clothes," said Mrs. Massington.

"Almost too exotic, don't you think?"

"But very expensive."

"Opulent. She's too opulent-looking."

"Here they come," said Mrs. Massington.

Madeleine de Sara and Reggie Wade were walking across the lawn. They were laughing and talking together and seemed very happy. Madeleine flung herself into a chair, tore off the béret she was wearing and ran her hands through her exquisitely dark curls. She was undeniably beautiful.

"We've had such a marvelous afternoon!" she cried. "I'm terribly hot. I must be looking too dreadful."

REGGIE WADE STARTED nervously at the sound of his cue. "You look—you look—" He gave a little laugh. "I won't say it," he finished.

Madeleine's eyes met his. It was a glance of complete understanding on her part. Mrs. Massington noted it alertly.

"You should play golf," said Madeleine to her hostess. "You miss such a lot. Why don't you take it up? I have a friend who did and became quite good, and she was a lot older than you."

"I don't care for that sort of thing," said Iris coldly.

"Are you bad at games? How rotten for you! It makes one feel so out of things. But really, Mrs. Wade, coaching nowadays is so good that almost anyone can play fairly well. I improved my tennis no end last summer. Of course I'm hopeless at golf."

"Nonsense!" said Reggie. "You only need coaching. Look how you were getting those brassie shots this afternoon."

"Because you showed me how. You're a wonderful teacher. Lots of people simply can't teach. But you've got the gift. It must be wonderful to be you—you can do everything."

"Nonsense. I'm no good—no use whatever." Reggie was confused.

"You must be very proud of him," said Madeleine, turning to Mrs. Wade. "How have you managed to keep him all these years? You must have been very clever. Or have you hidden him away?"

Her hostess made no reply. She picked up her book with a hand that trembled.

Reggie murmured something about changing, and went off.

"I do think it's so sweet of you to have me here," said Madeleine to her hostess. "Some women are so suspicious of their husbands' friends. I do think jealousy is absurd, don't you?"

"I do indeed. I should never dream of being jealous of Reggie."

"THAT'S WONDERFUL OF you! Because anyone can see that he's a man who's frightfully attractive to women. It was a shock to me when I heard he was married. Why do all the attractive men get snapped up young?"

"I'm glad you find Reggie so attractive," said Mrs. Wade.

"Well, he is, isn't he? So good-looking, and so frightfully good at games. And that pretended indifference of his on women. That spurs us on, of course."

"I suppose you have a lot of men friends," said Mrs. Wade.

"Oh, yes. I like men better than women. Women are never really nice to me. I can't think why."

"Perhaps you are too nice to their husbands," said Mrs. Massington with a tinkly laugh.

"Well, one's sorry for people sometimes. So many nice men are tied to such dull wives. You know, 'arty' women and highbrow women. Naturally, the men want someone young and bright to talk to. I think the modern ideas of marriage and divorce are so sensible. Start again while one is still young with someone who shares one's tastes and ideas. It's better for everybody in the end. I mean, the highbrow wives probably pick up some longhaired creature of their own type who satisfies them. I think cutting your losses and starting again is a wise plan, don't you, Mrs. Wade?"

"Certainly."

A certain frostiness in the atmosphere seemed to penetrate Madeleine's consciousness. She murmured something about changing for tea and left them.

"Detestable creatures these modern girls are," said Mrs. Wade. "Not an idea in their heads."

"She's got one idea in hers, Iris," said Mrs. Massington. "That girl's in love with Reggie."

"Nonsense!"

"She is. I saw the way she looked at him just now. She doesn't care a pin whether he's married or not. She means to have him. Disgusting, I call it."

Mrs. Wade was silent a moment, then she laughed uncertainly. "After all," she said, "what does it matter?"

Presently Mrs. Wade, too, went upstairs. Her husband was in his dressing room changing. He was singing.

"Enjoyed yourself, dear?" said Mrs. Wade.

"Oh, er—rather, yes."

"I'm glad. I want you to be happy."

"Yes, rather."

Acting a part was not Reggie Wade's strong point, but as it happened, the acute embarrassment occasioned by his fancying he was doing so did just as well. He avoided his wife's eye and jumped when she spoke to him. He felt ashamed; hated the farce of it all. Nothing could have produced a better effect. He was the picture of conscious guilt.

"How long have you known her?" asked Mrs. Wade suddenly.

"Er—who?"

"Miss de Sara, of course."

"Well, I don't quite know. I mean—oh, some time."

"Really? You never mentioned her."

"Didn't I? I suppose I forgot."

"Forgot indeed!" said Mrs. Wade. She departed with a whisk of mauve draperies.

After tea Mr. Wade showed Miss de Sara the rose garden. They walked across the lawn conscious of two pairs of eyes raking their backs.

"Look here." Safe out of sight in the rose garden, Mr. Wade unburdened himself. "Look here, I think we'll have to give this up. My wife looked at me just now as though she hated me."

"Don't worry," said Madeleine. "It's quite all right."

"Do you think so? I mean, I don't want to put her against me. She said several nasty things at tea."

"It's all right," said Madeleine again. "You're doing splendidly."

"Do you really think so?"

"Yes." In a lower voice she went on: "Your wife is walking round the corner of the terrace. She wants to see what we're doing. You'd better kiss me."

"Oh!" said Mr. Wade nervously. "Must I? I mean—"

"Kiss me!" said Madeleine fiercely.

Mr. Wade kissed her. Any lack of élan in the performance was remedied by Madeleine. She flung her arms round him. Mr. Wade staggered.

"Oh!" he said.

"Did you hate it very much?" said Madeleine.

"No, of course not," said Mr. Wade gallantly. "It—it just took me by surprise." He added wistfully: "Have we been in the rose garden long enough, do you think?"

"I think so," said Madeleine. "We've put in a bit of good work here."

They returned to the lawn. Mrs. Massington informed them that Mrs. Wade had gone to lie down.

Later, Mr. Wade joined Madeleine with a perturbed face.

"She's in an awful state—hysterics."

"Good."

"She saw me kissing you."

"Well, we meant her to."

"I know, but I couldn't say that, could I? I didn't know what to say. I said it had just—just—well, happened."

"Excellent."

"She said you were scheming to marry me and that you were no better than you should be. That upset me—it seemed such awfully rough luck on you. I mean, when you're just doing a job. I said that I had the utmost respect for you and that what she said wasn't true at all, and I'm afraid I got angry when she went on about it."

"Magnificent!"

"And then she told me to go away. She doesn't want ever to speak to me again. She talked of packing up and leaving." His face was dismayed.

Madeleine smiled. "I'll tell you the answer to that one. Tell her that you'll be the one to go; that you'll pack up and clear out to town."

"But I don't want to!"

"That's all right. You won't have to. Your wife would hate to think of you amusing yourself in London."

The following morning Reggie Wade had a fresh bulletin to impart.

"She says she's been thinking, and that it isn't fair for her to go away when she agreed to stay six months. But she says that as I have my friends down here she doesn't see why she shouldn't have hers. She is asking Sinclair Jordan."

"Is he *the* one?"

"Yes, and I'm damned if I'll have him in my house!"

"You must," said Madeleine. "Don't worry. I'll attend to him. Say that on thinking things over you have no objection, and that you know she won't mind your asking me to stay on, too."

"Oh, dear!" sighed Mr. Wade.

"Now don't lose heart," said Madeleine. "Everything is going splendidly. Another fortnight—and all your troubles will be over."

"A fortnight? Do you really think so?" demanded Mr. Wade.

"Think so? I'm sure of it," said Madeleine.

A WEEK LATER Madeleine de Sara entered Mr. Parker Pyne's office and sank wearily into a chair.

"Enter the Queen of Vamps," said Mr. Parker Pyne, smiling.

"Vamps!" said Madeleine. She gave a hollow laugh. "I've never had such uphill work being a vamp. That man is obsessed by his wife! It's a disease."

Mr. Parker Pyne smiled. "Yes, indeed. Well, in one way it made our task easier. It is not every man, my dear Madeleine, whom I would expose to your fascination so light-heartedly."

The girl laughed. "If you knew the difficulty I had to make him even kiss me as though he liked it!"

"A novel experience for you, my dear. Well, is your task accomplished?"

"Yes. I think all is well. We had a tremendous scene last night. Let me see, my last report was three days ago?"

"Yes."

"Well, as I told you, I only had to look at that miserable worm, Sinclair Jordan, once. He was all over me—especially as he thought from my clothes that I had money. Mrs. Wade was furious, of course. Here were both her men dancing attendance on me. I soon showed where my preference lay. I made fun of Sinclair Jordan, to his face and to her. I laughed at his clothes, and at the length of his hair. I pointed out that he had knock-knees."

"Excellent technique," said Mr. Parker Pyne appreciatively.

"Everything boiled up last night. Mrs. Wade came out in the open. She accused me of breaking up her home. Reggie Wade mentioned the little matter of Sinclair Jordan. She said that that was only the result of her unhappiness and loneliness. She had noticed her husband's abstraction for some time but had had no idea as to the cause of it. She said they had always been ideally happy, that she adored him and he knew it, and that she wanted him and only him.

"I said it was too late for that. Mr. Wade followed his instructions splendidly. He said he didn't give a damn! He was going to marry me! Mrs. Wade could have her Sinclair as soon as she pleased. There was no reason why the divorce proceedings shouldn't be started at once; waiting six months was absurd.

"Within a few days, he said, she should have the necessary evidence and could instruct her solicitors. He said he couldn't live without me. Then Mrs. Wade clutched her chest and talked about her weak heart and had to be given brandy. He didn't weaken. He went up to town this morning, and I've no doubt she's gone after him by this time."

"So that's all right," said Mr. Pyne cheerfully. "A very satisfactory case."

The door flew open. In the doorway stood Reggie Wade.

"Is she here?" he demanded, advancing into the room. "Where is she?" He caught sight of Madeleine. "Darling!" he cried. He seized both her hands. "Darling, darling. You knew, didn't you, that it was real last night—that I meant every word I said to Iris? I don't know why I was blind so long. But I've known for the last three days."

"Known what?" said Madeleine faintly.

"That I adored you. That there was no woman in the world for me but you. Iris can bring her divorce and when it's gone through you'll marry me, won't you? Say you will. Madeleine, I adore you."

He caught the paralyzed Madeleine in his arms just as the door flew open again, this time to admit a thin woman dressed in untidy green.

"I thought so!" said the newcomer. "I followed you! I knew you'd go to her!"

"I can assure you—" began Mr. Parker Pyne, recovering from the stupefaction that had descended upon him.

The intruder took no notice of him. She swept on: "Oh, Reggie, you can't want to break my heart! Only come back! I'll not say a word about all this. I'll learn golf. I won't have any friends you don't care about. After all these years, when we've been so happy together—"

"I've never been happy till now," said Mr. Wade, still gazing at Madeleine. "Dash it all, Iris, you wanted to marry that ass Jordan. Why don't you go and do it?"

Mrs. Wade gave a wail. "I hate him! I hate the very sight of him." She turned to Madeleine. "You wicked woman! You horrible vampire—stealing my husband from me."

"I don't want your husband," said Madeleine distractedly.

"Madeleine!" Mr. Wade was gazing at her in agony.

"Please go away," said Madeleine.

"But look here, I'm not pretending. I mean it."

"Oh, go away!" cried Madeleine hysterically. "Go *away!*"

Reggie moved reluctantly toward the door. "I shall come back," he warned her. "You've not seen the last of me." He went out, banging the door.

"Girls like you ought to be flogged and branded!" cried Mrs. Wade. "Reggie was an angel to me always till you came along. Now he's so changed I don't know him." With a sob, she hurried out after her husband.

Madeleine and Mr. Parker Pyne looked at each other.

"I can't help it," said Madeleine helplessly. "He's a very nice man—a dear—but I don't want to marry him. I'd no idea of all this. If you knew the difficulty I had making him kiss me!"

"Ahem!" said Mr. Parker Pyne. "I regret to admit it, but it was an error of judgment on my part." He shook his head sadly, and drawing Mr. Wade's file toward him, wrote across it:

FAILURE—owing to natural causes.

N.B. They should have been foreseen.

5. THE CASE OF THE CITY CLERK

Mr. Parker Pyne leaned back thoughtfully in his swivel chair and surveyed his visitor. He saw a small sturdily built man of forty-five with wistful, puzzled, timid eyes that looked at him with a kind of anxious hopefulness.

"I saw your advertisement in the paper," said the little man nervously.

"You are in trouble, Mr. Roberts?"

"No—not in trouble exactly."

"You are unhappy?"

"I shouldn't like to say that either. I've a great deal to be thankful for."

"We all have," said Mr. Parker Pyne. "But when we have to remind ourselves of the fact it is a bad sign."

"I know," said the little man eagerly. "That's just it! You've hit the nail on the head, sir."

"Supposing you tell me about yourself," suggested Mr. Parker Pyne.

"There's not much to tell, sir. As I say, I've a great deal to be thankful for. I have a job; I've managed to save a little money; the children are strong and healthy."

"So you want—what?"

"I—I don't know." He flushed. "I expect that sounds foolish to you, sir."

"Not at all," said Mr. Parker Pyne.

By skilled questioning he elicited further confidences. He heard of Mr. Roberts' employment in a well-known firm and of his slow but steady rise. He heard of his marriage; of the struggle to present a decent appearance, to educate the children and have them "looking nice"; of the plotting and planning and skimping and saving to put aside a few pounds each year. He heard, in fact, the saga of a life of ceaseless effort to survive.

"And—well, you see how it is," confessed Mr. Roberts. "The wife's away. Staying with her mother with the two children. Little change for them and a rest for her. No room for me and we can't afford to go elsewhere. And being alone, and reading the paper, I saw your advertisement and it set me thinking. I'm forty-eight. I just wondered . . . Things going on everywhere," he ended, all his wistful suburban soul in his eyes.

"You want," said Mr. Pyne, "to live gloriously for ten minutes?"

"Well, I shouldn't put it like that. But perhaps you're right. Just to get out of the rut. I'd go back to it thankful afterward—if only I had something to think about." He looked at the other man anxiously. "I suppose there's nothing possible, sir? I'm afraid—I'm afraid I couldn't afford to pay much."

"How much could you afford?"

"I could manage five pounds, sir." He waited, breathless.

"Five pounds," said Mr. Parker Pyne. "I fancy—I just fancy we might be able to manage something for five pounds. Do you object to danger?" he added sharply.

A tinge of color came into Mr. Roberts' sallow face. "Danger, did you say, sir? Oh, no, not at all. I—I've never done anything dangerous."

Mr. Parker Pyne smiled. "Come to see me again tomorrow and I'll tell you what I can do for you."

. . .

THE BON VOYAGEUR is a little-known hostelry. It is a restaurant frequented by a few habitués. They dislike newcomers.

To the Bon Voyageur came Mr. Pyne and was greeted with respectful recognition. "Mr. Bonnington here?" he asked.

"Yes, sir. He's at his usual table."

"Good. I'll join him."

Mr. Bonnington was a gentleman of military appearance with a somewhat bovine face. He greeted his friend with pleasure.

"Hello, Parker. Hardly ever see you nowadays. Didn't know you came here."

"I do now and then. Especially when I want to lay my hand on an old friend."

"Meaning me?"

"Meaning you. As a matter of fact, Lucas, I've been thinking over what we were talking about the other day."

"The Peterfield business? Seen the latest in the papers? No, you can't have. It won't be in till this evening."

"What is the latest?"

"They murdered Peterfield last night," said Mr. Bonnington, placidly eating salad.

"Good heavens!" cried Mr. Pyne.

"Oh, I'm not surprised," said Mr. Bonnington. "Pig-headed old man, Peterfield. Wouldn't listen to us. Insisted on keeping the plans in his own hands."

"Did they get them?"

"No; it seems some woman came round and gave the professor a recipe for boiling a ham. The old ass, absent-minded as usual, put the recipe for the ham in his safe and the plans in the kitchen."

"Fortunate."

"Almost providential. But I still don't know who's going to take 'em to Geneva. Maitland's in the hospital. Carslake's in Berlin. I can't leave. It means young Hooper." He looked at his friend.

"You're still of the same opinion?" asked Mr. Parker Pyne.

"Absolutely. He's been got at! I know it. I haven't a shadow of proof, but I tell you, Parker, I know when a chap's crooked! And I want those plans to get to Geneva. The League needs 'em. For the first time an invention isn't going to be sold to a nation. It's going to be handed over voluntarily to the League.

"It's the finest peace gesture that's ever been attempted, and it's got to be put through. And Hooper's crooked. You'll see, he'll be drugged on the train! If he goes in a plane it'll come down at some convenient spot! But confound it all, I can't pass him over. Discipline! You've got to have discipline! That's why I spoke to you the other day."

"You asked me whether I knew of anyone."

"Yes. Thought you might in your line of business. Some fire eater spoiling for a row. Whoever I send stands a good chance of being done in. Your man would probably not be suspected at all. But he's got to have nerve."

"I think I know of someone who would do," said Mr. Pyne.

"Thank God there are still chaps who will take a risk. Well, it's agreed, then?"

"It's agreed," said Mr. Parker Pyne.

MR. PARKER PYNE WAS summing up instructions. "Now, that's quite clear? You will travel in a first-class sleeper to Geneva. You leave London at ten-forty-five, via Folkestone and Boulogne, and you get into your first-class sleeper at Boulogne. You arrive at Geneva at eight the following morning. Here is the address at which you will report. Please memorize it and I will destroy it. Afterward go to this hotel and await further instructions. Here is sufficient money in French and Swiss notes and currency. You understand?"

"Yes, sir." Roberts' eyes were shining with excitement. "Excuse me, sir, but am I allowed to—er—know anything of what it is I am carrying?"

Mr. Parker Pyne smiled beneficently. "You are carrying a cryptogram which reveals the secret hidding place of the crown jewels of Russia," he said solemnly. "You can understand, naturally, that Bolshevist agents will be alert to intercept you. If it is necessary for you to talk about yourself, I should recommend that you say you have come into money and are enjoying a little holiday abroad."

MR. ROBERTS SIPPED A cup of coffee and looked out over the Lake of Geneva. He was happy but at the same time he was disappointed.

He was happy because, for the first time in his life, he was in a foreign country. Moreover, he was staying in the kind of hotel he would never stay in again, and not for one moment had he had to worry about money! He had a room with private bathroom, delicious meals and attentive service. All these things Mr. Roberts had enjoyed very much indeed.

He was disappointed because so far nothing that could be described as adventure had come his way. No disguised Bolshevists or mysterious Russians had crossed his path. A pleasant chat on the train with a French commercial traveler who spoke excellent English was the only human intercourse that had come his way. He had secreted the papers in his sponge bag as he had been told to do and had delivered them according to instructions. There had been no dangers to overcome, no hair-breadth escapes. Mr. Roberts was disappointed.

It was at that moment that a tall, bearded man murmured, *"Pardon,"* and sat down on the other side of the little table. "You will excuse me," he said, "but I think you know a friend of mine. 'P. P.' are the initials."

Mr. Roberts was pleasantly thrilled. Here, at last, was a mysterious Russian. "Qu-quite right."

"Then I think we understand each other," said the stranger.

Mr. Roberts looked at him searchingly. This was far more like the real thing. The stranger was a man of about fifty, of distinguished though foreign appearance. He wore an eyeglass, and a small colored ribbon in his buttonhole.

"You have accomplished your mission in the most satisfactory manner," said the stranger. "Are you prepared to undertake a further one?"

"Certainly. Oh, yes."

"Good. You will book a sleeper on the Geneva-Paris train for to-morrow night. You will ask for Berth Number Nine."

"Supposing it is not free?"

"It will be free. That will have been seen to."

"Berth Number Nine," repeated Roberts. "Yes, I've got that."

"During the course of your journey someone will say to you, 'Pardon Monsieur, but I think you were recently at Grasse?' To that you will reply, 'Yes, last month.' The person will then say, 'You are interested in scent?' and you will reply, 'Yes, I am a manufacturer of synthetic Oil of Jasmine.' After that you will place yourself entirely at the disposal of the person who has spoken to you. By the way, are you armed?"

"No," said little Mr. Roberts in a flutter. "No; I never thought. That is—"

"That can soon be remedied," said the bearded man. He glanced around. No one was near them. Something hard and shining was pressed into Mr. Roberts' hand. "A small weapon but efficacious," said the stranger, smiling.

Mr. Roberts, who had never fired a revolver in his life, slipped it gingerly into a pocket. He had an uneasy feeling that it might go off at any minute.

They went over the passwords again. Then Roberts' new friend rose.

"I wish you good luck," he said. "May you come through safely. You are a brave man, Mr. Roberts."

"Am I?" thought Roberts, when the other had departed. "I'm sure I don't want to get killed. That would never do."

A pleasant thrill shot down his spine, slightly adulterated by a thrill that was not quite so pleasant.

He went to his room and examined the weapon. He was still uncertain about its mechanism and hoped he would not be called upon to use it.

He went out to book his seat.

The train left Geneva at nine-thirty. Roberts got to the station in good time. The sleeping-car conductor took his ticket and his passport, and stood aside while an underling swung Roberts' suitcase onto the rack. There was other luggage there: pigskin case and a Gladstone bag.

"Number Nine is the lower berth," said the conductor.

As Roberts turned to leave the carriage he ran into a big man who was entering. They drew apart with apologies—Roberts' in English and the stranger's in French. He was a big burly man, with a closely shaven head and thick eyeglasses through which his eyes seemed to peer suspiciously.

"An ugly customer," said the little man to himself.

He sensed something vaguely sinister about his traveling companion. Was it to keep a watch on this man that he had been told to ask for Berth Number Nine? He fancied it might be.

He went out again into the corridor. There was still ten minutes before the train was due to start and he thought he would walk up and down the platform. Halfway along the passage he stood back to allow a lady to pass him. She was just entering the train and the conductor preceded her, ticket in hand. As she passed Roberts she dropped her hand bag. The Englishman picked it up and handed it to her.

"Thank you, Monsieur." She spoke in English but her voice was foreign, a rich low voice very seductive in quality. As she was about to pass on, she hesitated and murmured: "Pardon, Monsieur, but I think you were recently at Grasse?"

Roberts' heart leaped with excitement. He was to place himself at the disposal of this lovely creature—for she *was* lovely, of that there was no doubt. Not only lovely, but aristocratic and wealthy. She wore a traveling coat of fur, a chic hat. There were pearls round her neck. She was dark and her lips were scarlet.

Roberts made the required answer: "Yes, last month."

"You are interested in scent?"

"Yes, I am a manufacturer of synthetic Oil of Jasmine."

She bent her head and passed on, leaving a mere whisper behind her: "In the corridor as soon as the train starts."

The next ten minutes seemed an age to Roberts. At last the train started. He walked slowly along the corridor. The lady in the fur coat was struggling with a window. He hurried to her assistance.

"Thank you, Monsieur. Just a little air before they insist on closing everything." And then in a soft, low, rapid voice: "After the frontier, when our fellow traveler is asleep—not before—go into the washing place and through into the compartment on the other side. You understand?"

"Yes." He let down the window and said in a louder voice: "Is that better, Madame?"

"Thank you very much."

He retired to his compartment. His traveling companion was already stretched out in the upper berth. His preparations for the night had evidently been simple. The removal of boots and a coat, in fact.

Roberts debated his own costume. Clearly, if he were going into a lady's compartment he could not undress.

He found a pair of slippers, substituted them for his boots, and then lay down, switching out the light. A few minutes later, the man above began to snore.

Just after ten o'clock they reached the frontier. The door was thrown open; a perfunctory question was asked. Had Messieurs anything to declare? The door was closed again. Presently the train drew out of Bellegarde.

The man in the upper berth was snoring again. Roberts allowed twenty minutes to elapse, then he slipped to his feet and opened the door of the lavatory compartment. Once inside, he bolted the door behind him and eyed the door on the farther side. It was not bolted. He hesitated. Should he knock?

Perhaps it would be absurd to knock. But he didn't quite like entering without knocking. He compromised, opened the door gently about an inch and waited. He even ventured on a small cough.

The response was prompt. The door was pulled open, he was seized by the arm, pulled through into the farther compartment, and the girl closed and bolted the door behind him.

Roberts caught his breath. Never had he imagined anything so lovely. She was wearing a long foamy garment of cream chiffon and lace. She leaned against the door into the corridor, panting. Roberts had often read of beautiful hunted creatures at bay. Now, for the first time, he saw one—a thrilling sight.

"Thank God!" murmured the girl.

She was quite young, Roberts noted, and her loveliness was such that she seemed to him like a being from another world. Here was romance at last—and he was in it!

She spoke in a low, hurried voice. Her English was good but the inflection was wholly foreign. "I am so glad you have come," she said. "I have been horribly frightened. Vassilievitch is on the train. You understand what that means?"

Roberts did not understand in the least what it meant, but he nodded.

"I thought I had given them the slip. I might have known better. What are we to do? Vassilievitch is in the next carriage to me. Whatever happens, he must not get the jewels. Even if he murders me, he must not get the jewels."

"He's not going to murder you and he's not going to get the jewels," said Roberts with determination.

"Then what am I to do with them?"

Roberts looked past her at the door. "The door's bolted," he said.

The girl laughed. "What are locked doors to Vassilievitch?"

Roberts felt more and more as though he were in the middle of one of his favorite novels. "There's only one thing to be done. Give them to me."

She looked at him doubtfully. "They are worth a quarter of a million."

Roberts flushed. "You can trust me."

The girl hesitated a moment longer, then: "Yes, I will trust you," she said. She made a swift movement. The next minute she was holding out to him a rolled-up pair of stockings—stockings of cobweb silk. "Take them, my friend," she said to the astonished Roberts.

He took them and at once he understood. Instead of being light as air, the stockings were unexpectedly heavy.

"Take them into your compartment," she said. "You can give them to me in the morning—if—if I am still here."

Roberts coughed. "Look here," he said. "About you." He paused. "I—I must keep guard over you." Then he flushed in an agony of propriety. "Not in here, I mean. I'll stay in there." He nodded toward the lavatory compartment.

"If you like to stay here—" She glanced at the upper unoccupied berth.

Roberts flushed to the roots of his hair. "No, no," he protested. "I shall be all right in there. If you need me, call out."

"Thank you, my friend," said the girl softly.

She slipped into the lower berth, drew up the covers and smiled at him gratefully. He retreated into the wash-room.

Suddenly—it must have been a couple of hours later—he thought he heard something. He listened—nothing. Perhaps he had been mistaken. And yet it certainly seemed to him that he had heard a faint sound from the next carriage. Supposing—just supposing . . .

He opened the door softly. The compartment was as he had left it, with the tiny blue light in the ceiling. He stood there with his eyes straining through the dimness till they got accustomed to it. He made out the outline of the berth.

He saw that it was empty. The girl was not there!

He switched the light full on. The compartment was empty. Suddenly he sniffed. Just a whiff but he recognized it—the sweet, sickly odor of chloroform!

He stepped from the compartment (unlocked now, he noted) out into the corridor and looked up and down it. Empty! His eyes fastened on the door next to the girl's. She had said that Vassilievitch was in the next compartment. Gingerly Roberts tried the handle. The door was bolted on the inside.

What should he do? Demand admittance? But the man would refuse—and after all, the girl might not be there! And if she were, would she thank him for making a public business of the matter? He had gathered that secrecy was essential in the game they were playing.

A perturbed little man wandered slowly along the corridor. He paused at the end compartment. The door was open, and the conductor lay there sleeping. And above him, on a hook, *hung his brown uniform coat and peaked cap.*

. . .

IN A FLASH Roberts had decided on his course of action. In another minute he had donned the coat and cap and was hurrying back along the corridor. He stopped at the door next to that of the girl, summoned all his resolution and knocked peremptorily.

When the summons was not answered, he knocked again.

"Monsieur," he said, in his best accent.

The door opened a little way and a head peered out—the head of a foreigner, clean-shaven except for a black mustache. It was an angry, malevolent face.

"*Qu'est-ce-qu'il y a?*" he snapped.

"*Votre passeport, monsieur.*" Roberts stepped back and beckoned.

The other hesitated, then stepped out into the corridor. Roberts had counted on his doing that. If he had the girl inside, he naturally would not want the conductor to come in. Like a flash, Roberts acted. With all his force he shoved the foreigner aside—the man was unprepared and the swaying of the train helped—bolted into the carriage himself, shut the door and locked it.

Lying across the end of the berth was the girl, a gag across her mouth and her wrists tied together. He freed her quickly, and she fell against him with a sigh.

"I feel so weak and ill," she murmured. "It was chloroform, I think. Did he—did he get them?"

"No." Roberts tapped his pocket. "What are we to do now?" he asked.

The girl sat up. Her wits were returning. She took in his costume.

"How clever of you. Fancy thinking of that! He said he would kill me if I did not tell him where the jewels were. I have been so afraid—and then you came." Suddenly she laughed. "But we have outwitted him! He will not dare do anything. He cannot even try to get back into his own compartment.

"We must stay here till morning. Probably he will leave the train at Dijon; we are due to stop there in about half an hour. He will telegraph to Paris and they will pick up our trail there. In the meantime, you had better throw that coat and cap out of the window. They might get you into trouble."

Roberts obeyed.

"We must not sleep," the girl decided. "We must stay on guard till morning."

It was a strange, exciting vigil. At six o'clock in the morning, Roberts opened the door carefully and looked out. No one was about. The girl slipped quickly into her own compartment. Roberts followed her in. The place had clearly been ransacked. He regained his own carriage through the washroom. His fellow traveler was still snoring.

They reached Paris at seven o'clock. The conductor was declaiming at the loss of his coat and cap. He had not yet discovered the loss of a passenger.

Then began a most entertaining chase. The girl and Roberts took taxi after taxi across Paris. They entered hotels and restaurants by one door and left them by another. At last the girl gave a sigh.

"I feel sure we are not followed now," she said. "We have shaken them off."

They breakfasted and drove to Le Bourget. Three hours later they were at Croydon. Roberts had never flown before.

At Croydon a tall old gentleman with a far-off resemblance to Mr. Roberts' mentor at Geneva was waiting for them. He greeted the girl with especial respect.

"The car is here, madam," he said.

"This gentleman will accompany us, Paul," said the girl. And to Roberts: "Count Paul Stepanyi."

The car was a vast limousine. They drove for about an hour, then they entered the grounds of a country house and pulled up at the door of an imposing mansion. Mr. Roberts was taken to a room furnished as a study. There he handed over the precious pair of stockings. He was left alone for a while. Presently Count Stepanyi returned.

"Mr. Roberts," he said, "our thanks and gratitude are due to you. You have proved yourself a brave and resourceful man." He held out a red morocco case. "Permit me to confer upon you the Order of St. Stanislaus—tenth class with laurels."

As in a dream Roberts opened the case and looked at the jeweled order. The old gentleman was still speaking.

"The Grand Duchess Olga would like to thank you herself before you depart."

He was led to a big drawing-room. There, very beautiful in a flowing robe, stood his traveling companion.

She made an imperious gesture of the hand, and the other man left them.

"I owe you my life, Mr. Roberts," said the grand duchess.

She held out her hand. Roberts kissed it. She leaned suddenly toward him.

"You are a brave man," she said.

His lips met hers; a waft of rich Oriental perfume surrounded him. For a moment he held that slender, beautiful form in his arms. . . .

He was still in a dream when somebody said to him: "The car will take you anywhere you wish."

An hour later, the car came back for the Grand Duchess Olga. She got into it and so did the white-haired man. He had removed his beard for coolness. The car set down the Grand Duchess Olga at a house in Streatham. She entered it and an elderly woman looked up from a tea table.

"Ah, Maggie dear, so there you are."

In the Geneva-Paris express this girl was the Grand Duchess Olga; in Mr. Parker Pyne's office she was Madeleine de Sara, and in the house at Streatham she was Maggie Sayers, fourth daughter of an honest, hardworking family.

How are the mighty fallen!

MR. PARKER PYNE WAS lunching with his friend. "Congratulations," said the latter, "your man carried the thing through without a hitch. The Tormali gang must be wild to think the plans of that gun have gone to the League. Did you tell your man what it was he was carrying?"

"No. I thought it better to—er—embroider."

"Very discreet of you."

"It wasn't exactly discretion. I wanted him to enjoy himself. I fancied he might find a gun a little tame. I wanted him to have some adventures."

"Tame?" said Mr. Bonnington, staring at him. "Why, that lot would murder him as soon as look at him."

"Yes," said Mr. Parker Pyne mildly. "But I didn't want him to be murdered."

"Do you make a lot of money in your business, Parker?" asked Mr. Bonnington.

"Sometimes I lose it," said Mr. Parker Pyne. "That is, if it is a deserving case."

THREE ANGRY GENTLEMEN were abusing one another in Paris.

"That confounded Hooper!" said one. "He let us down."

"The plans were not taken by anyone from the office," said the second. "But they went Wednesday, I am assured of that. And so I say *you* bungled it."

"I didn't," said the third sulkily; "there was no Englishman on the train except a little clerk. He'd never heard of Peterfield or of the gun. I know. I tested him. Peterfield and the gun meant nothing to him." He laughed. "He had a Bolshevist complex of some kind."

MR. ROBERTS WAS SITTING in front of a gas fire. On his knee was a letter from Mr. Parker Pyne. It enclosed a check for fifty pounds "from certain people who are delighted with the way a certain commission was executed."

On the arm of his chair was a library book. Mr. Roberts opened it at random. "She crouched against the door like a beautiful hunted creature at bay."

Well, he knew all about that.

He read another sentence: "He sniffed the air. The faint, sickly odor of chloroform came to his nostrils."

That he knew about, too.

"He caught her in his arms and felt the responsive quiver of her scarlet lips."

Mr. Roberts gave a sigh. It wasn't a dream. It had all happened. The journey out had been dull enough, but the journey home! He had enjoyed it. But he was glad to be home again. He felt vaguely that life could not be lived indefinitely at such a pace. Even the Grand Duchess Olga—even that last kiss—partook already of the unreal quality of a dream.

Mary and the children would be home tomorrow. Mr. Roberts smiled happily.

She would say: "We've had such a nice holiday. I hated thinking of you all alone here, poor old boy." And he'd say: "That's all right, old girl. I had to go to Geneva for the firm on business—delicate bit of negotiation—and look what they've sent me." And he'd show her the check for fifty pounds.

He thought of the Order of St. Stanislaus, tenth class with laurels. He'd hidden it, but supposing Mary found it! It would take a bit of explaining. . . .

Ah, that was it—he'd tell her he'd picked it up abroad. A curio.

He opened his book again and read happily. No longer was there a wistful expression on his face.

He too, was of that glorious company to whom Things Happened.

6. THE CASE OF THE RICH WOMAN

The name of Mrs. Abner Rymer was brought to Mr. Parker Pyne. He knew the name and he raised his eyebrows.

Presently his client was shown into the room.

Mrs. Rymer was a tall woman, big-boned. Her figure was ungainly and the velvet dress and the heavy fur coat she wore did not disguise the fact. The knuckles of her large hands were pronounced. Her face was big and broad and highly colored. Her black hair was fashionably dressed, and there were many tips of curled ostrich in her hat.

She plumped herself down on a chair with a nod. "Good morning," she said. Her voice had a rough accent. "If you're any good at all you'll tell me how to spend my money!"

"Most original," murmured Mr. Parker Pyne. "Few ask that in these days. So you really find it difficult, Mrs. Rymer?"

"Yes, I do," said the lady bluntly. "I've got three fur coats, a lot of Paris dresses and such like. I've got a car and a house in Park Lane. I've had a yacht but I don't like the sea. I've got a lot of those high-class servants that look down their nose at you. I've traveled a bit and seen foreign parts. And I'm blessed if I can think of anything more to buy or do." She looked hopefully at Mr. Pyne.

"There are hospitals," he said.

"What? Give it away, you mean? No, that I won't do! That money was worked for, let me tell you, worked for hard. If you think I'm going to hand it out like so much dirt—well, you're mistaken. I want to spend it; spend it and get some good out of it. Now, if you've got any ideas that are worthwhile in that line, you can depend on a good fee."

"Your proposition interests me," said Mr. Pyne. "You do not mention a country house."

"I forgot it, but I've got one. Bores me to death."

"You must tell me more about yourself. Your problem is not easy to solve."

"I'll tell you and willing. I'm not ashamed of what I've come from. Worked in a farmhouse, I did, when I was a girl. Hard work it was, too. Then I took up with Abner—he was a workman in the mills near by. He courted me for eight years, and then we got married."

"And you were happy?" asked Mr. Pyne.

"I was. He was a good man to me, Abner. We had a hard struggle of it, though; he was out of a job twice, and children coming along. Four we had, three boys and a girl. And none of them lived to grow up. I dare say it would have been different if they had." Her face softened; looked suddenly younger.

"His chest was weak—Abner's was. They wouldn't take him for the war. He did well at home. He was made foreman. He was a clever fellow, Abner. He worked out a process. They treated him fair, I will say; gave him a good sum for it. He used that money for another idea of his. That brought in money hand over fist. He was a master now, employing his own workmen. He bought two concerns that were bankrupt and made them pay. The rest was easy. Money came in hand over fist. It's still coming in.

"Mind you, it was rare fun at first. Having a house and a tiptop bathroom and servants of one's own. No more cooking and scrubbing and washing to do. Just sit back on your silk cushions in the drawing-room and ring the bell for tea—like any countess might! Grand fun it was, and we enjoyed it. And then we came up to London. I went to swell dressmakers for my clothes. We went to Paris and the Riviera. Rare fun it was."

"And then?" said Mr. Parker Pyne.

"We got used to it, I suppose," said Mrs. Rymer. "After a bit it didn't seem so much fun. Why, there were days when we didn't even fancy our meals properly—us, with any dish we fancied to choose from! As for baths—well, in the end, one bath a day's enough for anyone. And Abner's health began to worry him. Paid good money to doctors, we did, but they couldn't do anything. They tried this and they tried that. But it was no use. He died." She paused. "He was a young man, only forty-three."

Mr. Pyne nodded sympathetically.

"That was five years ago. Money's still rolling in. It seems wasteful not to be able to do anything with it. But as I tell you, I can't think of anything else to buy that I haven't got already."

"In other words," said Mr. Pyne, "your life is dull. You are not enjoying it."

"I'm sick of it," said Mrs. Rymer gloomily. "I've no friends. The new lot only want subscriptions, and they laugh at me behind my back. The old lot won't have anything to do with me. My rolling up in a car makes them shy. Can you do anything, or suggest anything?"

"It is possible that I can," said Mr. Pyne slowly. "It will be difficult, but I believe there is a chance of success. I think it's possible I can give you back what you have lost—your interest in life."

"How?" demanded Mrs. Rymer curtly.

"That," said Mr. Parker Pyne, "is my professional secret. I never disclose my methods beforehand. The question is, will you take a chance? I do not guarantee success, but I do think there is a reasonable possibility of it."

"And how much will it cost?"

"I SHALL HAVE to adopt unusual methods, and therefore it will be expensive. My charges will be one thousand pounds, payable in advance."

"You can open your mouth all right, can't you?" said Mrs. Rymer appreciatively. "Well, I'll risk it. I'm used to paying top price. Only when I pay for a thing, I take good care that I get it."

"You shall get it," said Mr. Parker Pyne. "Never fear."

"I'll send you the check this evening," said Mrs. Rymer, rising. "I'm sure I don't know why I should trust you. Fools and their money are soon parted, they say. I dare say I'm a fool. You've got nerve, to advertise in all the papers that you can make people happy!"

"Those advertisements cost me money," said Mr. Pyne. "If I could not make my words good, that money would be wasted. I *know* what causes unhappiness, and consequently I have a clear idea of how to produce an opposite condition."

Mrs. Rymer shook her head doubtfully and departed, leaving a cloud of expensive mixed essences behind her.

The handsome Claude Luttrell strolled into the office. "Something in my line?"

Mr. Pyne shook his head. "Nothing so simple," he said. "No, this is a difficult case. We must, I fear, take a few risks. We must attempt the unusual."

"Mrs. Oliver?"

Mr. Pyne smiled at the mention of the world-famous novelist. "Mrs. Oliver," he said, "is really the most conventional of all of us. I have in mind a bold and audacious coup. By the way, you might ring up Doctor Antrobus."

"Antrobus?"

"Yes. His services will be needed."

A WEEK LATER Mrs. Rymer once more entered Mr. Parker Pyne's office. He rose to receive her.

"This delay, I assure you, has been necessary," he said. "Many things had to be arranged, and I had to secure the services of an unusual man who had to come half across Europe."

"Oh!" She said it suspiciously. It was constantly present in her mind that she had paid out a check for a thousand pounds and the check had been cashed.

Mr. Parker Pyne touched a buzzer. A young girl, dark, Oriental-looking, but dressed in white nurse's kit, answered it.

"Is everything ready, Nurse de Sara?"

"Yes. Doctor Constantine is waiting."

"What are you going to do?" asked Mrs. Rymer, with a touch of uneasiness.

"Introduce you to some Eastern magic, dear lady," said Mr. Parker Pyne.

Mrs. Rymer followed the nurse up to the next floor. Here she was ushered into a room that bore no relation to the rest of the house. Oriental embroideries covered the walls. There were divans with soft cushions and beautiful rugs on the floor. A man was bending over a coffeepot. He straightened as they entered.

"Doctor Constantine," said the nurse.

The doctor was dressed in European clothes, but his face was swarthy and his eyes were dark and oblique with a peculiarly piercing power in their glance.

"So this is my patient?" he said in a low, vibrant voice.

"I'm not a patient," said Mrs. Rymer.

"Your body is not sick," said the doctor, "but your soul is weary. We of the East know how to cure that disease. Sit down and drink a cup of coffee."

Mrs. Rymer sat down and accepted a tiny cup of the fragrant brew. As she sipped it the doctor talked.

"Here in the West, they treat only the body. A mistake. The body is only the instrument. A tune is played upon it. It may be a sad, weary tune. It may be a gay tune full of delight. That last is what we shall give you. You have money. You shall spend it and enjoy. Life shall be worth living again. It is easy—easy—so easy . . ."

A feeling of languor crept over Mrs. Rymer. The figures of the doctor and the nurse grew hazy. She felt blissfully happy and very sleepy. The doctor's figure grew bigger. The whole world was growing bigger.

The doctor was looking into her eyes. "Sleep," he was saying. "Sleep. Your eyelids are closing. Soon you will sleep. You will sleep. You will sleep . . ."

Mrs. Rymer's eyelids closed. She floated with a wonderful great big world. . . .

. . .

WHEN HER EYES opened it seemed to her that a long time had passed. She remembered several things vaguely—strange, impossible dreams; then a feeling of waking; then further dreams. She remembered something about a car and the dark, beautiful girl in nurse's uniform bending over her.

Anyway, she was properly awake now, and in her own bed.

At least, was it her own bed? It felt different. It lacked the delicious softness of her own bed. It was vaguely reminiscent of days almost forgotten. She moved, and it creaked. Mrs. Rymer's bed in Park Lane never creaked.

SHE LOOKED ROUND. Decidedly, this was not Park Lane. Was it a hospital? No, she decided, not a hospital. Nor was it a hotel. It was a bare room, the walls an uncertain shade of lilac. There was a deal washstand with a jug and basin upon it. There was a deal chest of drawers and a tin trunk. There were unfamiliar clothes hanging on pegs. There was the bed covered with a much-mended quilt and there was herself in it.

"Where *am* I?" said Mrs. Rymer.

The door opened and a plump little woman bustled in. She had red cheeks and a good-humored air. Her sleeves were rolled up and she wore an apron.

"There!" she exclaimed. "She's awake. Come in, doctor."

Mrs. Rymer opened her mouth to say several things—but they remained unsaid, for the man who followed the plump woman into the room was not in the least like the elegant, swarthy Doctor Constantine. He was a bent old man who peered through thick glasses.

"That's better," he said, advancing to the bed and taking up Mrs. Rymer's wrist. "You'll soon be better now, my dear."

"What's been the matter with me?" demanded Mrs. Rymer.

"You had a kind of seizure," said the doctor. "You've been unconscious for a day or two. Nothing to worry about."

"Gave us a fright, you did, Hannah," said the plump woman. "You've been raving, too, saying the oddest things."

"Yes, yes, Mrs. Gardner," said the doctor repressively. "But we mustn't excite the patient. You'll soon be up and about again, my dear."

"But don't you worry about the work, Hannah," said Mrs. Gardner. "Mrs. Roberts has been in to give me a hand and we've got on fine. Just lie still and get well, my dear."

"Why do you call me Hannah?" said Mrs. Rymer.

"Well, it's your name," said Mrs. Gardner, bewildered.

"No, it isn't. My name is Amelia. Amelia Rymer. Mrs. Abner Rymer."

The doctor and Mrs. Gardner exchanged glances.

"Well, just you lie still," said Mrs. Gardner.

"Yes, yes; no worry," said the doctor.

They withdrew. Mrs. Rymer lay puzzling. Why did they call her Hannah, and why had they exchanged that glance of amused incredulity when she had given them her name? Where was she, and what had happened?

She slipped out of bed. She felt a little uncertain on her legs, but she walked slowly to the small dormer window and looked out— on a farmyard! Completely mystified, she went back to bed. What was she doing in a farmhouse that she had never seen before?

Mrs. Gardner re-entered the room with a bowl of soup on a tray.

Mrs. Rymer began her questions. "What am I doing in this house?" she demanded. "Who brought me here?"

"Nobody brought you, my dear. It's your home. Leastways, you've lived here for the last five years—and me not suspecting once that you were liable to fits."

"*Lived* here? *Five* years?"

"That's right. Why, Hannah, you don't mean that you still don't remember?"

"I've never lived here! I've never seen you before."

"You see, you've had this illness and you've forgotten."

"I've never lived here."

"But you have, my dear." Suddenly Mrs. Gardner darted across to the chest of drawers and brought to Mrs. Rymer a faded photograph in a frame.

It represented a group of four persons: a bearded man, a plump woman (Mrs. Gardner), a tall, lank man with a pleasantly sheepish grin, and somebody in a print dress and apron—herself!

Stupefied, Mrs. Rymer gazed at the photograph. Mrs. Gardner put the soup down beside her and quietly left the room.

Mrs. Rymer sipped the soup mechanically. It was good soup, strong and hot. All the time her brain was in a whirl. Who was mad? Mrs. Gardner or herself? One of them must be! But there was the doctor, too.

"I'm Amelia Rymer," she said firmly to herself. "I know I'm Amelia Rymer and nobody's going to tell me different."

She had finished the soup. She put the bowl back on the tray. A folded newspaper caught her eye and she picked it up and looked at the date on it, October 19. What day had she gone to Mr. Parker Pyne's office? Either the fifteenth or the sixteenth. Then she must have been ill for three days.

"That rascally doctor!" said Mrs. Rymer wrathfully.

All the same, she was a shade relieved. She had heard of cases where people had forgotten who they were for years at a time. She had been afraid some such thing had happened to her.

She began turning the pages of the paper, scanning the columns idly, when suddenly a paragraph caught her eye.

Mrs. Abner Rymer, widow of Abner Rymer, the "button shank" king, was removed yesterday to a private home for mental cases. For the past two days she has persisted in declaring she was not herself, but a servant girl named Hannah Moorhouse.

"Hannah Moorhouse! So that's it," said Mrs. Rymer. "She's me, and I'm her. Kind of double, I suppose. Well, we can soon put *that* right! If that oily hypocrite of a Parker Pyne is up to some game or other—"

But at this minute her eye was caught by the name Constantine staring at her from the printed page. This time it was a headline.

DR. CONSTANTINE'S CLAIM

At a farewell lecture given last night on the eve of his departure for Japan, Dr. Claudius Constantine advanced some startling theories. He declared that it was possible to prove the existence of the soul by transferring a soul from one body to another. In the course of his experiments in the East he had, he claimed, successfully effected a double transfer—the soul of a hypnotized body A being transferred to a hypnotized body B and the soul of B to the body of A. On recovering from the hypnotic sleep, A declared herself to be B, and B thought herself to be A. For the experiment to succeed, it was necessary to find two people with a great bodily resemblance. It was an undoubted fact that two people resembling each other were *en rapport*. This was very noticeable in the case of twins, but two strangers, varying widely in social position but with a marked similarity of feature, were found to exhibit the same harmony of structure.

MRS. RYMER CAST the paper from her. "The scoundrel! The black scoundrel!"

She saw the whole thing now! It was a dastardly plot to get hold of her money. This Hannah Moorhouse was Mr. Pyne's tool—possibly an innocent one. He and that devil Constantine had brought off this fantastic coup.

But she'd expose him! She'd show him up! She'd have the law on him! She'd tell everyone—

Abruptly Mrs. Rymer came to a stop in the tide of her indignation. She remembered that first paragraph. Hannah Moorhouse had not been a docile tool. She had protested; had declared her individuality. And what had happened?

"Clapped into a lunatic asylum, poor girl," said Mrs. Rymer.

A chill ran down her spine.

A lunatic asylum. They got you in there and they never let you get out. The more you said you were sane, the less they'd believe you. There you were and there you stayed. No, Mrs. Rymer wasn't going to run the risk of that.

The door opened and Mrs. Gardner came in.

"Ah, you've drunk your soup, my dear. That's good. You'll soon be better now."

"When was I taken ill?" demanded Mrs. Rymer.

"Let me see. It was three days ago—on Wednesday. That was the fifteenth. You were took bad about four o'clock."

"Ah!" The ejaculation was fraught with meaning. It had been just about four o'clock when Mrs. Rymer had entered the presence of Doctor Constantine.

"You slipped down in your chair," said Mrs. Gardner. "'Oh!' you says. 'Oh!' just like that. And then: 'I'm falling asleep,' you says in a dreamy voice. 'I'm falling asleep.' And fall asleep you did, and we put you to bed and sent for the doctor, and here you've been ever since."

"I suppose," Mrs. Rymer ventured, "there isn't any way you could know who I am—apart from my face, I mean."

"Well, that's a queer thing to say," said Mrs. Gardner. "What is there to go by better than a person's face, I'd like to know? There's your birthmark, though, if that satisfies you better."

"A birthmark?" said Mrs. Rymer, brightening. She had no such thing.

"Strawberry mark just under the right elbow," said Mrs. Gardner. "Look for yourself, my dear."

"This will prove it," said Mrs. Rymer to herself. She knew that she had no strawberry mark under the right elbow. She turned back the sleeve of her nightdress. The strawberry mark was there.

Mrs. Rymer burst into tears.

FOUR DAYS LATER, Mrs. Rymer rose from her bed. She had thought out several plans of action and rejected them.

She might show the paragraph in the paper to Mrs. Gardner and the doctor and explain. Would they believe her? Mrs. Rymer was sure they would not.

She might go to the police. Would they believe her? Again she thought not.

She might go to Mr. Pyne's office. That idea undoubtedly pleased her best. For one thing, she would like to tell that oily scoundrel what she thought of him. She was debarred from putting this plan into operation by a vital obstacle. She was at present in Cornwall (so she had learned), and she had no money for the journey to London. Two and four-pence in a worn purse seemed to represent her financial position.

And so, after four days, Mrs. Rymer made a sporting decision. For the present she would accept things! She was Hannah Moorhouse. Very well, she would be Hannah Moorhouse. For the present she would accept that rôle, and later, when she had saved sufficient money, she would go to London and beard the swindler in his den.

And having thus decided, Mrs. Rymer accepted her rôle with perfect good temper, even with a kind of sardonic amusement. History was repeating itself indeed. This life here reminded her of her girlhood. How long ago that seemed!

THE WORK WAS a bit hard after her years of soft living, but after the first week she found herself slipping into the ways of the farm.

Mrs. Gardner was a good-tempered, kindly woman. Her husband, a big, taciturn man, was kindly also. The lank, shambling man of the photograph had gone; another farmhand came in his stead, a good-humored giant of forty-five, slow of speech and thought, but with a shy twinkle in his blue eyes.

The weeks went by. At last the day came when Mrs. Rymer had enough money to pay her fare to London. But she did not go. She put it off. Time enough, she thought. She wasn't easy in her mind about asylums yet. That scoundrel, Parker Pyne, was clever. He'd get a doctor to say she was mad and she'd be clapped away out of sight with no one knowing anything about it.

"Besides," said Mrs. Rymer to herself, "a bit of a change does one good."

She rose early and worked hard. Joe Welsh, the new farmhand, was ill that winter, and she and Mrs. Gardner nursed him. The big man was pathetically dependent on them.

Spring came—lambing time; there were wild flowers in the hedges, a treacherous softness in the air. Joe Welsh gave Hannah a hand with her work. Hannah did Joe's mending.

Sometimes, on Sundays, they went for a walk together. Joe was a widower. His wife had died four years before. Since her death he had, he frankly confessed it, taken a drop too much.

He didn't go much to the Crown nowadays. He bought himself some new clothes. Mr. and Mrs. Gardner laughed.

Hannah made fun of Joe. She teased him about his clumsiness. Joe didn't mind. He looked bashful but happy.

After spring came summer—a good summer that year. Everyone worked hard.

Harvest was over. The leaves were red and golden on the trees.

It was October eighth when Hannah looked up one day from a cabbage she was cutting and saw Mr. Parker Pyne leaning over the fence.

"You!" said Hannah, alias Mrs. Rymer. "You . . ."

It was some time before she got it all out, and when she had said her say, she was out of breath.

Mr. Parker Pyne smiled blandly. "I quite agree with you," he said.

"A cheat and a liar, that's what you are!" said Mrs. Rymer, repeating herself. "You with your Constantines and your hypnotizing and that poor girl Hannah Moorhouse shut up with—loonies."

"No," said Mr. Parker Pyne, "there you misjudge me. Hannah Moorhouse is not in a lunatic asylum, because Hannah Moorhouse never existed."

"Indeed?" said Mrs. Rymer. "And what about the photograph of her that I saw with my own eyes?"

"Faked," said Mr. Pyne. "Quite a simple thing to manage."

"And the piece in the paper about her?"

"The whole paper was faked so as to include two items in a natural manner which would carry conviction. As it did."

"That rogue, Doctor Constantine!"

"An assumed name—assumed by a friend of mine with a talent for acting."

Mrs. Rymer snorted. "Ho! And I wasn't hypnotized either, I suppose?"

"As a matter of fact, you were not. You drank in your coffee a preparation of Indian hemp. After that, other drugs were administered and you were brought down here by car and allowed to recover consciousness."

"Then Mrs. Gardner has been in it all the time?" said Mrs. Rymer. Mr. Parker Pyne nodded.

"Bribed by you, I suppose! Or filled up with a lot of lies!"

"Mrs. Gardner trusts me," said Mr. Pyne. "I once saved her only son from penal servitude."

Something in his manner silenced Mrs. Rymer on that tack. "What about the birthmark?" she demanded.

Mr. Pyne smiled. "It is already fading. In another six months it will have disappeared altogether."

"And what's the meaning of all this tomfoolery? Making a fool of me, sticking me down here as a servant—me with all that good money in the bank. But I suppose I needn't ask. You've been helping yourself to it, my fine fellow. That's the meaning of all this."

"It is true," said Mr. Parker Pyne, "that I did obtain from you, while you were under the influence of drugs, a power of attorney and that during your—er—absence, I have assumed control of your financial affairs, but I can assure you, my dear madam, that apart from that original thousand pounds, no money of yours has found its way into my pocket. As a matter of fact, by judicious investments your financial position is actually improved." He beamed at her.

"Then why—" began Mrs. Rymer.

"I am going to ask you a question, Mrs. Rymer," said Mr. Pyne. "You are an honest woman. You will answer me honestly, I know. I am going to ask you if you are happy."

"Happy! That's a pretty question! Steal a woman's money and ask her if she's happy. I like your impudence!"

"You are still angry," he said. "Most natural. But leave my misdeeds out of it for the moment. Mrs. Rymer, when you came to my office a year ago today, you were an unhappy woman. Will you tell me that you are unhappy now? If so, I apologize, and you are at liberty to take what steps you please against me. Moreover, I will refund you the thousand pounds you paid me. Come, Mrs. Rymer, are you an unhappy woman now?"

MRS. RYMER LOOKED AT Mr. Parker Pyne, but she dropped her eyes when she spoke at last.

"No," she said. "I'm not unhappy." A tone of wonder crept into her voice. "You've got me there. I admit it. I've not been as happy as I am now since Abner died. I—I'm going to marry a man who works here—Joe Welsh. Our banns are going up next Sunday; that is, they *were* going up next Sunday."

"But now, of course," said Mr. Pyne, "everything is different."

Mrs. Rymer's face flamed. She took a step forward. "What do you mean—different? Do you think if I had all the money in the world it would make me a lady? I don't want to be a lady, thank you; a helpless, good-for-nothing lot they are. Joe's good enough for me and I'm good enough for him. We suit each other and we're going to be happy. As for you, Mr. Nosey Parker, you take yourself off and don't interfere with what doesn't concern you!"

Mr. Parker Pyne took a paper from his pocket and handed it to her. "The power of attorney," he said. "Shall I tear it up? You will assume control of your own fortune now, I take it."

A strange expression came over Mrs. Rymer's face. She thrust back the paper.

"Take it. I've said hard things to you—and some of them you deserved. You're a downy fellow, but all the same I trust you. Seven hundred pounds I'll have in the bank here—that'll buy us a farm we've got our eye on. The rest of it—well, let the hospitals have it."

"You cannot mean to hand over your entire fortune to hospitals?"

"That's just what I do mean. Joe's a dear, good fellow, but he's weak. Give him money and you'd ruin him. I've got him off the drink now, and I'll keep him off it. Thank God, I know my own mind. I'm not going to let money come between me and happiness."

"You are a remarkable woman," said Mr. Pyne slowly. "Only one woman in a thousand would act as you are doing."

"Then only one woman in a thousand's got sense," said Mrs. Rymer.

"I take off my hat to you," said Mr. Parker Pyne, and there was an unusual note in his voice. He raised his hat with solemnity and moved away.

"And Joe's never to know, mind!" Mrs. Rymer called after him.

She stood there with the dying sun behind her, a great blue-green cabbage in her hands, her head thrown back and her shoulders squared. A grand figure of a peasant woman, outlined against the setting sun. . . .

7. HAVE YOU GOT EVERYTHING YOU WANT?

PAR ici, Madame."

A tall woman in a mink coat followed her heavily encumbered porter along the platform of the Gare de Lyon.

She wore a dark brown knitted hat pulled down over one eye and ear. The other side revealed a charming tiptilted profile and little golden curls clustering over a shell-like ear. Typically an American, she was altogether a very charming-looking creature and more than one man turned to look at her as she walked past the high carriages of the waiting train.

Large plates were stuck in holders on the sides of the carriages.

PARIS—ATHÉNES. PARIS—BUCHAREST. PARIS—STAMBOUL.

At the last named the porter came to an abrupt halt. He undid the strap which held the suitcases together and they slipped heavily to the ground. *"Voici, Madame."*

The *wagon-lit* conductor was standing beside the steps. He came forward, remarking, *"Bonsoir, Madame,"* with an empressement perhaps due to the richness and perfection of the mink coat.

The woman handed him her sleeping-car ticket of flimsy paper. "Number Six," he said; "this way."

He sprang nimbly into the train, the woman following him. As she hurried down the corridor after him, she nearly collided with a portly gentleman who was emerging from the compartment next to hers. She had a momentary glimpse of a large bland face with benevolent eyes.

"*Voici, Madame.*"

The conductor displayed the compartment. He threw up the window and signaled to the porter. A lesser employee took in the baggage and put it up in the racks. The woman sat down.

Beside her on the seat she had placed a small scarlet case and her hand bag. The carriage was hot, but it did not seem to occur to her to take off her coat. She stared out of the window with unseeing eyes. People were hurrying up and down the platform. There were sellers of newspapers, of pillows, of chocolate, of fruit, of mineral waters. They held up their wares to her, but her eyes looked blankly through them. The Gare de Lyon had faded from her sight. On her face were sadness and anxiety.

"If Madame will give me her passport?"

The words made no impression on her. The conductor, standing in the doorway, repeated them. Elsie Jeffries roused herself with a start.

"I beg your pardon?"

"Your passport, Madame."

She opened her bag, took out the passport and gave it to him.

"That will be all right, Madame, I will attend to everything." A slight significant pause. "I shall be going with Madame as far as Stamboul."

Elsie drew out a fifty-franc note and handed it to him. He accepted it in a businesslike manner, and inquired when she would like her bed made up and whether she was taking dinner.

These matters settled, he withdrew and almost immediately the restaurant man came rushing down the corridor ringing his little bell frantically, and bawling out, "*Premier service. Premier service.*"

Elsie rose, divested herself of the heavy fur coat, took a brief glance at herself in the little mirror, and picking up her hand bag and jewel case, stepped out into the corridor. She had gone only a few steps when the restaurant man came rushing along on his return journey. To avoid him, Elsie stepped back for a moment into the doorway of the adjoining compartment, which was now empty. As the man passed and she prepared to continue her journey to the dining car, her glance fell idly on the label of a suitcase which was lying on the seat.

It was a stout pigskin case, somewhat worn. On the label were the words, "J. Parker Pyne, passenger to Stamboul." The suitcase itself bore the initials "P. P."

A startled expression came over the girl's face. She hesitated a moment in the corridor, then going back to her own compartment she picked up a copy of the *Times* which she had laid down on the table with some magazines and books.

She ran her eye down the advertisement columns on the front page, but what she was looking for was not there. A slight frown on her face, she made her way to the restaurant car.

The attendant allotted her a seat at a small table already tenanted by one person—the man with whom she had nearly collided in the corridor. In fact, the owner of the pigskin suitcase.

Elsie looked at him without appearing to do so. He seemed very bland, very benevolent, and in some way impossible to explain, delightfully reassuring. He behaved in reserved British fashion, and it was not till the fruit was on the table that he spoke.

"They keep these places terribly hot," he said.

"I know," said Elsie. "I wish one could have the window open."

He gave a rueful smile. "Impossible! Every person present except ourselves would protest."

She gave an answering smile. Neither said any more.

Coffee was brought and the usual indecipherable bill. Having laid some notes upon it, Elsie suddenly took her courage in both hands.

"Excuse me," she murmured. "I saw your name upon your suitcase—Parker Pyne. Are you—are you, by any chance—?"

She hesitated and he came quickly to her rescue.

"I believe I am. That is"—he quoted from the advertisement which Elsie had noticed more than once in the *Times*, and for which she had searched vainly just now—"'Are you happy? If not, consult Mr. Parker Pyne.' Yes, I'm that one, all right."

"I see," said Elsie. "How—how extraordinary!"

He shook his head. "Not really. Extraordinary from your point of view, but not from mine." He smiled reassuringly, then leaned forward. Most of the other diners had left the car. "So you are unhappy?" he said.

"I—" began Elsie, and stopped.

"You would not have said 'How extraordinary' otherwise," he pointed out.

Elsie was silent a minute. She felt strangely soothed by the mere presence of Mr. Parker Pyne. "Ye-es," she admitted at last. "I am—unhappy. At least, I am worried."

He nodded sympathetically.

"You see," she continued, "a very curious thing has happened—and I don't know in the least what to make of it."

"Suppose you tell me about it," suggested Mr. Pyne.

Elsie thought of the advertisement. She and Edward had often commented on it and laughed. She had never thought that she . . . Perhaps she had better not . . . If Mr. Parker Pyne were a charlatan . . . But he looked—nice!

Elsie made her decision. Anything to get this worry off her mind.

"I'll tell you. I'm going to Constantinople to join my husband. He does a lot of Oriental business, and this year he found it necessary to go there. He went a fortnight ago. He was to get things ready for me to join him. I've been very excited at the thought of it. You see, I've never been abroad before. We've been in England six months."

"You and your husband are both American?"

"Yes."

"And you have not, perhaps, been married very long?"

"We've been married a year and a half."

"Happily?"

"Oh, yes! Edward's a perfect angel." She hesitated. "Not, perhaps, very much go to him. Just a little—well, I'd call it strait-laced.

Lot of Puritan ancestry and all that. But he's a *dear*," she added hastily.

Mr. Parker Pyne looked at her thoughtfully for a moment or two, then he said, "Go on."

"It was about a week after Edward had started. I was writing a letter in his study, and I noticed that the blotting paper was all new and clean, except for a few lines of writing across it. I'd just been reading a detective story with a clue in a blotter and so, just for fun, I held it up to a mirror. It really *was* just fun, Mr. Pyne—I mean, I wasn't spying on Edward or anything like that. I mean, he's such a mild lamb one wouldn't dream of anything of that kind."

"Yes, yes; I quite understand."

"The thing was quite easy to read. First there was the word 'wife,' then 'Simplon Express,' and lower down, 'just before Venice would be the best time.'" She stopped.

"Curious," said Mr. Pyne. "Distinctly curious. It was your husband's handwriting?"

"Oh, yes. But I've cudgeled my brains and I cannot see under what circumstances he would write a letter with just those words in it."

"'Just before Venice would be the best time,'" repeated Mr. Parker Pyne. "Distinctly curious."

Mrs. Jeffries was leaning forward looking at him with a flattering hopefulness. "What shall I do?" she asked simply.

"I am afraid," said Mr. Parker Pyne, "that we shall have to wait until just before Venice." He took up a folder from the table. "Here is the schedule time of our train. It arrives at Venice at two-twenty-seven tomorrow afternoon."

They looked at each other.

"Leave it to me," said Mr. Parker Pyne.

IT WAS FIVE minutes past two. The Simplon Express was eleven minutes late. It had passed Mestre about a quarter of an hour before.

Mr. Parker Pyne was sitting with Mrs. Jeffries in her compartment. So far the journey had been pleasant and uneventful. But now the moment had arrived when, if anything was going to happen, it presumably would happen. Mr. Parker Pyne and Elsie faced each other. Her heart was beating fast, and her eyes sought his in a kind of anguished appeal for reassurance.

"Keep perfectly calm," he said. "You are quite safe. I am here."

Suddenly a scream broke out from the corridor.

"Oh, look—look! The train is on fire!"

With a bound Elsie and Mr. Parker Pyne were in the corridor. An agitated woman with a Slav countenance was pointing a dramatic finger. Out of one of the front compartments smoke was pouring in a cloud. Mr. Parker Pyne and Elsie ran along the corridor. Others joined them. The compartment in question was full of smoke. The first comers drew back, coughing. The conductor appeared.

"The compartment is empty!" he cried. "Do not alarm yourselves, *messieurs et dames. Le feu,* it will be controlled."

A dozen excited questions and answers broke out. The train was running over the bridge that joins Venice to the mainland.

Suddenly Mr. Parker Pyne turned, forced his way through the little pack of people behind him and hurried down the corridor to Elsie's compartment. The lady with the Slav face was seated in it, drawing deep breaths from the open window.

"Excuse me, Madame," said Parker Pyne. "But this is not your compartment."

"I know. I know," said the Slav lady. "*Pardon.* It is the shock, the emotion—my heart." She sank back on the seat and indicated the open window. She drew her breath in great gasps.

Mr. Parker Pyne stood in the doorway. His voice was fatherly and reassuring. "You must not be afraid," he said. "I do not think for a moment that the fire is serious."

"Not? Ah, what a mercy! I feel restored." She half rose. "I will return to my own compartment."

"Not just yet." Mr. Parker Pyne's hand pressed her gently back. "I will ask of you to wait a moment, Madame."

"Monsieur, this is an outrage!"

"Madame, you will remain."

His voice rang out coldly. The woman sat still looking at him. Elsie joined them.

"It seems it was a smoke bomb," she said breathlessly. "Some ridiculous practical joke. The conductor is furious. He is asking everybody—" She broke off, staring at the second occupant of the carriage.

"Mrs. Jeffries," said Mr. Parker Pyne, "what do you carry in your little scarlet case?"

"My jewelry."

"Perhaps you would be so kind as to look and see that everything is there."

There was immediately a torrent of words from the Slav lady. She broke into French, the better to do justice to her feelings.

In the meantime Elsie had picked up the jewel case. "Oh!" she cried. "It's unlocked."

". . . et je porterai plainte à la Compagnie des Wagons-Lits," finished the Slav lady.

"They're gone!" cried Elsie. "Everything! My diamond bracelet. And the necklace Pop gave me. And the emerald and ruby rings. And some lovely diamond brooches. Thank goodness I was wearing my pearls. Oh, Mr. Pyne, what shall we do?"

"If you will fetch the conductor," said Mr. Parker Pyne, "I will see that this woman does not leave this compartment till he comes."

"Scélérat! Monstre!" shrieked the Slav lady. She went on to further insults. The train drew in to Venice.

The events of the next half hour may be briefly summarized. Mr. Parker Pyne dealt with several different officials in several different languages—and suffered defeat. The suspected lady consented to be searched—and emerged without a stain on her character. The jewels were not on her.

Between Venice and Trieste Mr. Parker Pyne and Elsie discussed the case.

"When was the last time you actually saw your jewels?"

"This morning. I put away some sapphire earrings I was wearing yesterday and took out a pair of plain pearl ones."

"And all the jewelry was there intact?"

"Well, I didn't go through it all, naturally. But it looked the same as usual. A ring or something like that might have been missing, but not more."

Mr. Parker Pyne nodded. "Now, when the conductor made up the compartment this morning?"

"I had the case with me—in the restaurant car. I always take it with me. I've never left it except when I ran out just now."

"Therefore," said Mr. Parker Pyne, "that injured innocent, Madame Subayska, or whatever she calls herself, *must* have been the thief. But what the devil did she do with the things? She was only in here a minute and a half—just time to open the case with a duplicate key and take out the stuff—yes, but what next?"

"Could she have handed them to anyone else?"

"Hardly. I had turned back and was forcing my way along the corridor. If anyone had come out of this compartment I should have seen them."

"Perhaps she threw them out of the window to someone."

"An excellent suggestion; only, as it happens, we were passing over the sea at that moment. We were on the bridge."

"Then she must have hidden them actually in the carriage."

"Let's hunt for them."

With true transatlantic energy Elsie began to look about. Mr. Parker Pyne participated in the search in a somewhat absent fashion. Reproached for not trying, he excused himself.

"I'm thinking that I must send a rather important telegram at Trieste," he explained.

Elsie received the explanation coldly. Mr. Parker Pyne had fallen heavily in her estimation.

"I'm afraid you're annoyed with me, Mrs. Jeffries," he said meekly.

"Well, you've not been very successful," she retorted.

"But my dear lady, you must remember I am not a detective. Theft and crime are not in my line at all. The human heart is my province."

"Well, I was a bit unhappy when I got on this train," said Elsie, "but nothing to what I am now! I could just cry buckets. My lovely,

lovely bracelet—and the emerald ring Edward gave me when we were engaged."

"But surely you are insured against theft?" Mr. Parker Pyne interpolated.

"Am I? I don't know. Yes, I suppose I am. But it's the *sentiment* of the thing, Mr. Pyne."

The train slackened speed. Mr. Parker Pyne peered out of the window. "Trieste," he said. "I must send my telegram."

"EDWARD!" ELSIE'S FACE lighted up as she saw her husband hurrying to meet her on the platform at Stamboul. For the moment even the loss of her jewelry faded from her mind. She forgot the curious words she had found on the blotter. She forgot everything except that it was a fortnight since she had seen her husband last, and that in spite of being sober and strait-laced he was really a most attractive person.

They were just leaving the station when Elsie felt a friendly tap on the shoulder and turned to see Mr. Parker Pyne. His bland face was beaming good-naturedly.

"Mrs. Jeffries," he said, "will you come to see me at the Hotel Tokatlian in half an hour? I think I may have good news for you."

Elsie looked uncertainly at Edward. Then she made the introduction. "This—er—is my husband—Mr. Parker Pyne."

"As I believe your wife wired you, her jewels have been stolen," said Mr. Parker Pyne. "I have been doing what I can to help her recover them. I think I may have news for her in about half an hour."

Elsie looked inquiringly at Edward. He replied promptly:

"You'd better go, dear. The Tokatlian, you said, Mr. Pyne? Right; I'll see she makes it."

It was just half an hour later that Elsie was shown into Mr. Parker Pyne's private sitting room. He rose to receive her.

"You've been disappointed in me, Mrs. Jeffries," he said. "Now, don't deny it. Well, I don't pretend to be a magician, but I do what I can. Take a look inside here."

He passed along the table a small stout cardboard box. Elsie opened it. Rings, brooches, bracelet, necklace—they were all there.

"Mr. Pyne, how marvelous! How—how too wonderful!"

Mr. Parker Pyne smiled modestly. "I am glad not to have failed you, my dear young lady."

"Oh, Mr. Pyne, you make me feel just mean! Ever since Trieste I've been horrid to you. And now—this. But how did you get hold of them? When? Where?"

Mr. Parker Pyne shook his head thoughtfully. "It's a long story," he said. "You may hear it one day. In fact, you may hear it quite soon."

"Why can't I hear it now?"

"There are reasons," said Mr. Parker Pyne.

And Elsie had to depart with her curiosity unsatisfied.

When she had gone, Mr. Parker Pyne took up his hat and stick and went out into the streets of Pera. He walked along smiling to himself, coming at last to a little café, deserted at the moment, which overlooked the Golden Horn. On the other side, the mosques of Stamboul showed slender minarets against the afternoon sky. It was very beautiful. Mr. Pyne sat down and ordered two coffees. They came thick and sweet. He had just begun to sip his when a man slipped into the seat opposite. It was Edward Jeffries.

"I have ordered some coffee for you," said Mr. Parker Pyne, indicating the little cup.

Edward pushed the coffee aside. He leaned forward across the table. "How did you know?" he asked.

Mr. Parker Pyne sipped his coffee dreamily. "Your wife will have told you about her discovery on the blotter? No? Oh, but she will tell you; it has slipped her mind for the moment."

He mentioned Elsie's discovery.

"Very well; that linked up perfectly with the curious incident that happened just before Venice. For some reason or other you were engineering the theft of your wife's jewels. But why the phrase 'just before Venice would be the best time'? There seemed no sense in that. Why did you not leave it to your—agent—to choose her own time and place?

"And then, suddenly, I saw the point. *Your wife's jewels were stolen before you yourself left London and were replaced by paste duplicates.* But that solution did not satisfy you. You were a high-minded, conscientious young man. You have a horror of some servant or other innocent person being suspected. A theft must actually occur—at a place and in a manner which will leave no suspicion attached to anybody of your acquaintance or household.

"Your accomplice is provided with a key to the jewel box and a smoke bomb. At the correct moment she gives the alarm, darts into your wife's compartment, unlocks the jewel case and flings the paste duplicates into the sea. She may be suspected and searched, but nothing can be proved against her, since the jewels are not in her possession.

"And now the significance of the place chosen becomes apparent. If the jewels had merely been thrown out by the side of the line, they might have been found. Hence the importance of the one moment when the train is passing over the sea.

"In the meantime, you make your arrangements for selling the jewelry here. You have only to hand over the stones when the robbery has actually taken place. My wire, however, reached you in time. You obeyed my instructions and deposited the box of jewelry at the Tokatlian to await my arrival, knowing that otherwise I should keep my threat of placing the matter in the hands of the police. You also obeyed my instructions in joining me here."

Edward Jeffries looked at Mr. Parker Pyne appealingly. He was a good-looking young man, tall and fair, with a round chin and very round eyes. "How can I make you understand?" he said hopelessly. "To you I must seem just a common thief."

"Not at all," said Mr. Parker Pyne. "On the contrary, I should say you are almost painfully honest. I am accustomed to the classification of types. You, my dear sir, fall naturally into the category of victims. Now, tell me the whole story."

"I can tell you that in one word—blackmail."

"Yes?"

"You've seen my wife; you realize what a pure, innocent creature she is—without thought or knowledge of evil."

"Yes, yes."

"She has the most marvelously pure ideals. If she were to find out about—about anything I had done, she would leave me."

"I wonder. But that is not the point. What *have* you done, my young friend? I presume this is some affair with a woman?"

Edward Jeffries nodded.

"Since your marriage—or before?"

"Before—oh, before."

"Well, well, what happened?"

"Nothing; nothing at all. This is just the cruel part of it. It was at a hotel in the West Indies. There was a very attractive woman—a Mrs. Rossiter—staying there. Her husband was a violent man; he had the most savage fits of temper. One night he threatened her with a revolver. She escaped from him and came to my room. She was half crazy with terror. She—she asked me to let her stay there till morning. I—what else could I do?"

Mr. Parker Pyne gazed at the young man, and the young man gazed back with conscious rectitude. Mr. Parker Pyne sighed. "In other words, to put it plainly, you were had for a mug, Mr. Jeffries."

"Really—"

"Yes, yes. A very old trick—but it often comes off successfully with quixotic young men. I suppose, when your approaching marriage was announced, the screw was turned?"

"Yes. I received a letter. If I did not send a certain sum of money, everything would be disclosed to my prospective father-in-law. How I had—had alienated this young woman's affection from her husband; how she had been seen coming to my room. The husband would bring a suit for divorce. Really, Mr. Pyne, the whole thing made me out the most utter blackguard." He wiped his brow in a harassed manner.

"Yes, yes, I know. And so you paid. And from time to time the screw has been put on again."

"Yes. This was the last straw. Our business has been badly hit by the slump. I simply could not lay my hands on any ready money. I hit upon this plan." He picked up his cup of cold coffee, looked at it absently, and drank it. "What am I to do now?" he demanded pathetically. "What *am* I to do, Mr. Pyne?"

"You will be guided by me," said Parker Pyne firmly. "I will deal with your tormentors. As to your wife, you will go straight back to her and tell her the truth—or at least a portion of it. The only point where you will deviate from the truth is concerning the actual facts in the West Indies. You must conceal from her the fact that you were—well, had for a mug, as I said before."

"But—"

"My dear Mr. Jeffries, you do not understand women. If a woman has to choose between a mug and a Don Juan, she will choose Don Juan every time. Your wife, Mr. Jeffries, is a charming, innocent, high-minded girl, and the only way she is going to get any kick out of her life with you is to believe that she has reformed a rake."

Edward Jeffries was staring at him open-mouthed.

"I mean what I say," said Mr. Parker Pyne. "At the present moment your wife is in love with you, but I see signs that she may not remain so if you continue to present to her a picture of such goodness and rectitude that it is almost synonymous with dullness."

Edward winced.

"Go to her, my boy," said Mr. Parker Pyne kindly. "Confess everything—that is, as many things as you can think of. Then explain that from the moment you met her you gave up all this life. You even stole so that it might not come to her ears. She will forgive you enthusiastically."

"But when there's nothing really to forgive—"

"What is truth?" said Mr. Parker Pyne. "In my experience it is usually the thing that upsets the apple cart! It is a fundamental axiom of married life that you *must* lie to a woman. She likes it! Go and be forgiven, my boy. And live happily ever afterward. I dare say your wife will keep a wary eye on you in future whenever a pretty woman comes along—some men would mind that, but I don't think you will."

"I never want to look at any woman but Elsie," said Mr. Jeffries simply.

"Splendid, my boy," said Mr. Parker Pyne. "But I shouldn't let her know that if I were you. No woman likes to feel she's taken on too soft a job."

Edward Jeffries rose. "You really think—?"

"I *know*," said Mr. Parker Pyne, with force.

8. THE GATE OF BAGHDAD

"Four great gates has the city of Damascus. . . ."

Mr. Parker Pyne repeated Flecker's lines softly to himself.

*"Postern of Fate, the Desert Gate, Disaster's
    Cavern, Fort of Fear,
The Portal of Bagdad am I, the Doorway of
    Diarbekir."*

He was standing in the streets of Damascus and drawn up outside the Oriental Hotel he saw one of the huge six-wheeled Pullmans that was to transport him and eleven other people across the desert to Baghdad on the morrow.

*"Pass not beneath, O Caravan, or pass not
    singing. Have you heard
That silence where the birds are dead yet
    something pipeth like a bird?
"Pass out beneath, O Caravan, Doom's
    Caravan, Death's Caravan!"*

Something of a contrast now. Formerly the Gate of Baghdad *had* been the gate of Death. Four hundred miles of desert to traverse by caravan. Long weary months of travel. Now the ubiquitous petrol-fed monsters did the journey in thirty-six hours.

"What were you saying, Mr. Parker Pyne?"

It was the eager voice of Miss Netta Pryce, youngest and most charming of the tourist race. Though encumbered by a stern aunt with the suspicion of a beard and a thirst for Biblical knowledge, Netta managed to enjoy herself in many frivolous ways of which the elder Miss Pryce might possibly have not approved.

Mr. Parker Pyne repeated Flecker's lines to her.

"How thrilling," said Netta.

Three men in Air Force uniform were standing near and one of them, an admirer of Netta's, struck in.

"There are still thrills to be got out of the journey," he said. "Even nowadays the convoy is occasionally shot up by bandits. Then there's losing yourself—that happens sometimes. And we are sent out to find you. One fellow was lost for five days in the desert. Luckily he had plenty of water with him. Then there are the bumps. Some bumps! One man was killed. It's the truth I'm telling you! He was asleep and his head struck the top of the car and it killed him."

"In the six-wheeler, Mr. O'Rourke?" demanded the elder Miss Pryce.

"No—not in the six-wheeler," admitted the young man.

"But we must do some sight seeing," cried Netta.

Her aunt drew out a guide book.

Netta edged away.

"I know she'll want to go to some place where St. Paul was lowered out of a window," she whispered. "And I do so want to see the Bazaars."

O'Rourke responded promptly.

"Come with me. We'll start down the Street called Straight—"

They drifted off.

Mr. Parker Pyne turned to a quiet man standing beside him, Hensley by name. He belonged to the public works department of Baghdad.

"Damascus is a little disappointing when one sees it for the first time," he said apologetically. "A little civilized. Trams and modern houses and shops."

Hensley nodded. He was a man of few words.

"Not got—back of beyond—when you think you have," he jerked out.

Another man drifted up, a fair young man wearing an old Etonian tie. He had an amiable but slightly vacant face which at the moment looked worried. He and Hensley were in the same department.

"Hullo, Smethurst," said his friend. "Lost anything?"

Captain Smethurst shook his head. He was a young man of somewhat slow intellect.

"Just looking round," he said vaguely. Then he seemed to rouse himself. "Ought to have a beano tonight. What?"

The two friends went off together. Mr. Parker Pyne bought a local paper printed in French.

He did not find it very interesting. The local news meant nothing to him and nothing of importance seemed to be going on elsewhere. He found a few paragraphs headed *Londres*.

The first referred to financial matters. The second dealt with the supposed destination of Mr. Samuel Long, the defaulting financier. His defalcations now amounted to the sum of three million and it was rumored that he had reached South America.

"Not too bad for a man just turned thirty," said Mr. Parker Pyne to himself.

"I beg your pardon?"

Parker Pyne turned to confront an Italian General who had been on the same boat with him from Brindisi to Beirut.

Mr. Parker Pyne explained his remark. The Italian General nodded his head several times.

"He is a great criminal, that man. Even in Italy we have suffered. He inspired confidence all over the world. He is a man of breeding, too, they say."

"Well, he went to Eton and Oxford," said Mr. Parker Pyne cautiously.

"Will he be caught, do you think?"

"Depends on how much of a start he got. He may be still in England. He may be—anywhere."

"Here with us?" the General laughed.

"Possibly." Mr. Parker Pyne remained serious. "For all you know, General, *I* may be he."

The General gave him a startled glance. Then his olive brown face relaxed into a smile of comprehension.

"Oh! that is very good—very good indeed. But you—"

His eyes strayed downward from Mr. Parker Pyne's face.

Mr. Parker Pyne interpreted the glance correctly.

"You mustn't judge by appearances," he said.

"A little additional—er—*embonpoint*—is easily managed and has a remarkably aging effect."

He added dreamily,

"Then there is hair dye, of course, and face stain, and even a change of nationality."

General Poli withdrew doubtfully. He never knew how far the English were serious.

Mr. Parker Pyne amused himself that evening by going to a Cinema. Afterward he was directed to a "Nightly Palace of Gaieties." It appeared to him to be neither a palace nor gay. Various ladies danced with a distinct lack of *verve*. The applause was languid.

Suddenly Mr. Parker Pyne caught sight of Smethurst. The young man was sitting at a table alone. His face was flushed and it occurred to Mr. Parker Pyne that he had already drunk more than was good for him. He went across and joined the young man.

"Disgraceful, the way these girls treat you," said Captain Smethurst gloomily. "Bought her two drinks—three drinks—lots of drinks. Then she goes off laughing with some dago. Call it a disgrace."

Mr. Parker Pyne sympathized. He suggested coffee.

"Got some araq coming," said Smethurst. "Jolly good stuff. You try it."

Mr. Parker Pyne knew something of the properties of araq. He employed tact. Smethurst, however, shook his head.

"I'm in a bit of a mess," he said. "Got to cheer myself up. Don't know what you'd do in my place. Don't like to go back on a pal, what? I mean to say—and yet—what's a fellow to do?"

He studied Mr. Parker Pyne as though noticing him for the first time.

"Who are you?" he demanded with the curtness born of his potations. "What do you do?"

"The confidence trick," said Mr. Parker Pyne gently.

Smethurst gazed at him in lively concern.

"What—you too?"

Mr. Parker Pyne drew from his wallet a cutting. He laid it on the table in front of Smethurst.

"Are you unhappy? (So it ran) *If so, consult Mr. Parker Pyne."*

Smethurst focused it after some difficulty.

"Well, I'm damned," he ejaculated. "You meantersay—people come and tell you things?"

"They confide in me—yes."

"Pack of idiotic women, I suppose."

"A good many women," admitted Mr. Parker Pyne. "But men also. What about you, my young friend? You wanted advice just now?"

"Shut your damned head," said Captain Smethurst "No business of anybody's—anybody's 'cept mine. Where's that goddamned araq?"

Mr. Parker Pyne shook his head sadly.

He gave up Captain Smethurst as a bad job.

THE CONVOY FOR Baghdad started at seven o'clock in the morning. There was a party of twelve. Mr. Parker Pyne and General Poli, Miss Pryce and her niece, three Air Force officers, Smethurst and Hensley and an Armenian mother and son by name Pentemian.

The journey started uneventfully. The fruit trees of Damascus were soon left behind. The sky was cloudy and the young driver looked at it doubtfully once or twice. He exchanged remarks with Hensley.

"Been raining a good bit the other side of Rutbah. Hope we shan't stick."

They made a halt at mid-day and square cardboard boxes of lunch were handed round. The two drivers brewed tea which was served in cardboard cups. They drove on again across the flat interminable plain.

Mr. Parker Pyne thought of the slow caravans and the weeks of journeying. . . .

Just at sunset they came to the desert fort of Rutbah.

The great gates were unbarred and the six-wheeler drove in through them into the inner courtyard of the fort.

"This feels exciting," said Netta.

After a wash she was eager for a short walk. Flight Lieutenant O'Rourke and Mr. Parker Pyne offered themselves as escorts. As they started the manager came up to them and begged them not to go far away as it might be difficult to find their way back after dark.

"We'll only go a short way," O'Rourke promised.

Walking was not, indeed, very interesting owing to the sameness of the surroundings.

Once Mr. Parker Pyne bent and picked something up.

"What is it?" asked Netta curiously.

He held it out to her.

"A prehistoric flint, Miss Pryce—a borer."

"Did they—kill each other with them?"

"No—it had a more peaceful use. But I expect they could have killed with it if they'd wanted to. It's the *wish* to kill that counts—the mere instrument doesn't matter. *Something* can always be found."

It was getting dark, and they ran back to the fort.

After a dinner of many courses of the tinned variety they sat and smoked. At twelve o'clock the six-wheeler was to proceed.

The driver looked anxious.

"Some bad patches near here," he said. "We may stick."

They all climbed into the big car and settled themselves. Miss Pryce was annoyed not to be able to get at one of her suitcases.

"I should like my bedroom slippers," she said.

"More likely to need your gum boots," said Smethurst "If I know the look of things we'll be stuck in a sea of mud."

"I haven't even got a change of stockings," said Netta.

"That's all right. You'll stay put. Only the stronger sex has to get out and heave."

"Always carry spare socks," said Hensley, patting his overcoat pocket. "Never know."

The lights were turned out. The big car started out into the night.

The going was not too good. They were not jolted as they would have been in a touring car, but nevertheless they got a bad bump now and then.

Mr. Parker Pyne had one of the front seats. Across the aisle was the Armenian lady shrouded in wraps and shawls. Her son was behind her. Behind Mr. Parker Pyne were the two Miss Pryces. The General, Smethurst, Hensley and the R.A.F. men were at the back.

The car rushed on through the night. Mr. Parker Pyne found it hard to sleep. His position was cramped. The Armenian lady's feet stuck out and encroached on his preserve. She, at any rate, was comfortable.

Everyone else seemed to be asleep. Mr. Parker Pyne felt drowsiness stealing over him, when a sudden jolt threw him up toward the roof of the car. He heard a drowsy protest from the back of the six-wheeler. "Steady. Want to break our necks?"

Then the drowsiness returned. A few minutes later, his neck sagging uncomfortably, Mr. Parker Pyne slept. . . .

He was awakened suddenly. The six-wheeler had stopped. Some of the men were getting out. Hensley spoke briefly.

"We're stuck."

Anxious to see all there was to see, Mr. Parker Pyne stepped gingerly out in the mud. It was not raining now. Indeed there was a moon and by its light the drivers could be seen frantically at work with jacks and stones, striving to raise the wheels. Most of the men were helping. From the windows of the six-wheeler the three women looked out, Miss Pryce and Netta with interest, the Armenian lady with ill-concealed disgust.

At a command from the driver, the male passengers obediently heaved.

"Where's that Armenian fellow?" demanded O'Rourke. "Keeping his toes warmed and comfortable like a cat? Let's have him out too."

"Captain Smethurst, too," observed General Poli. "He is not with us."

"The blighter's asleep still. Look at him."

True enough, Smethurst still sat in his armchair, his head sagging forward and his whole body slumped down.

"I'll rouse him," said O'Rourke.

He sprang in through the door. A minute later he reappeared. His voice had changed.

"I say. I think he's ill—or something. Where's the doctor?"

Squadron Leader Loftus, the Air Force doctor, a quiet-looking man with graying hair detached himself from the group by the wheel.

"What's the matter with him?" he asked.

"I—don't know."

The doctor entered the car. O'Rourke and Parker Pyne followed him. He bent over the sagging figure. One look and touch was enough.

"He's dead," he said quietly.

"Dead? But how?" Questions shot out. "Oh! how dreadful!" from Netta.

Loftus looked round in an irritated manner.

"Must have hit his head against the top," he said. "We went over one bad bump."

"Surely that wouldn't kill him? Isn't there anything else?"

"I can't tell unless I examine him properly," snapped Loftus. He looked round him with a harassed air. The women were pressing closer. The men outside were beginning to crowd in.

Mr. Parker Pyne spoke to the driver. He was a strong, athletic young man. He lifted each female passenger in turn, carrying her across the mud and setting her down on dry land. Madame Pentemian and Netta he managed easily, but he staggered under the weight of the hefty Miss Pryce.

The interior of the six-wheeler was left clear for the doctor to make his examination.

The men went back to their efforts to jack up the car. Presently the sun rose over the horizon. It was a glorious day. The mud was drying rapidly, but the car was still stuck. Three jacks had been broken and so far no efforts had been of any avail. The drivers started preparing breakfast—opening tins of sausages and boiling water for tea.

A little way apart Squadron Leader Loftus was giving his verdict.

"There's no mark or wound on him. As I said he must have hit his head against the top."

"You're satisfied he died naturally?" asked Mr. Parker Pyne.

There was something in his voice that made the doctor look at him quickly.

"There's only one other possibility."

"Yes?"

"Well, that someone hit him on the back of the head with something in the nature of a sandbag." His voice sounded apologetic.

"That's not very likely," said Williamson, the other Air Force officer. He was a cherubic-looking youth. "I mean, nobody could do that without our seeing."

"If we were asleep?" suggested the doctor.

"Fellow couldn't be sure of that," pointed out the other. "Getting up and all that would have roused someone or other."

"The only way," said General Poli, "would be for anyone sitting behind him. He could choose his moment and need not even rise from his seat."

"Who was sitting behind Captain Smethurst?" asked the doctor.

O'Rourke replied readily.

"Hensley, sir—so that's no good. Hensley was Smethurst's best pal."

There was a silence. Then Mr. Parker Pyne's voice rose with quiet certainty.

"I think," he said, "that Flight Lieutenant Williamson has something to tell us."

"I, sir? I—well—"

"Out with it, Williamson," said O'Rourke.

"It's nothing, really—nothing at all."

"Out with it."

"It's only a scrap of conversation I overheard—at Rutbah—in the courtyard. I'd got back into the six-wheeler to look for my cigaret case. I was hunting about. Two fellows were just outside talking. One of them was Smethurst. He was saying—"

He paused.

"Come on, man, out with it."

"Something about not wanting to let a pal down. He sounded very distressed. Then he said: 'I'll hold my tongue till Baghdad—but not a minute afterward. You'll have to get out quickly.'"

"And the other man?"

"I don't know, sir. I swear I don't. It was dark and he only said a word or two and that I couldn't catch."

"Who among you knows Smethurst well?"

"I don't think the words—a pal—could refer to anyone but Hensley," said O'Rourke slowly. "I knew Smethurst, but very slightly. Williamson is new out—so is Squadron Leader Loftus. I don't think either of them have ever met him before."

Both men agreed.

"You, General?"

"I never saw the young man until we crossed the Lebanon in the same car from Beirut."

"And that Armenian rat?"

"He couldn't be a pal," said O'Rourke with decision. "And no Armenian would have the nerve to kill anyone."

"I have, perhaps, a small additional piece of evidence," said Mr. Parker Pyne.

He repeated the conversation he had had with Smethurst in the café at Damascus.

"He made use of the phrase—"don't like to go back on a pal,'" said O'Rourke thoughtfully. "And he was worried."

"Has no one else anything to add?" asked Mr. Parker Pyne.

The doctor coughed.

"It may have nothing to do with it—" he began.

He was encouraged.

"It was just that I heard Smethurst say to Hensley, 'You can't deny that there is a leakage in your department.'"

"When was this?"

"Just before starting from Damascus yesterday morning. I thought they were just talking shop. I didn't imagine—" He stopped.

"My friends, this is interesting," said the General. "Piece by piece you assemble the evidence."

"You said a sandbag, doctor," said Mr. Parker Pyne. "Could a man manufacture such a weapon?"

"Plenty of sand," said the doctor dryly. He took some up in his hand as he spoke.

"If you put some in a sock," began O'Rourke and hesitated.

Everyone remembered two short sentences spoken by Hensley the night before.

"Always carry spare socks. Never know."

There was silence. Then Mr. Parker Pyne said quietly, "Squadron Leader Loftus, I believe Mr. Hensley's spare socks are in the pocket of his overcoat which is now in the car."

Their eyes went for one minute to where a moody figure was pacing to and fro on the horizon. Hensley had held aloof since the discovery of the dead man. His wish for solitude had been respected since it was known that he and the dead man had been friends.

Mr. Parker Pyne went on.

"Will you get them and bring them here?"

The doctor hesitated.

"I don't like—" he muttered. He looked again at that pacing figure. "Seems a bit low down—"

"You must get them please," said Mr. Parker Pyne. "The circumstances are unusual. We are marooned here. And we have got to know the truth. If you will fetch those socks I fancy we shall be a step nearer."

Loftus turned away obediently.

Mr. Parker Pyne drew General Poli a little aside.

"General, I think it was you who sat across the aisle from Captain Smethurst."

"That is so."

"Did anyone get up and pass down the car?"

"Only the English lady, Miss Pryce. She went to the wash place at the back."

"Did she stumble at all?"

"She lurched a little with the movement of the car, naturally."

"She was the only person you saw moving about?"

"Yes."

The General looked at him curiously and said, "Who are you, I wonder? You take command, yet you are not a soldier."

"I have seen a good deal of life," said Mr. Parker Pyne.

"You have traveled, eh?"

"No," said Mr. Parker Pyne. "I have sat in an office."

Loftus returned carrying the socks. Mr. Parker Pyne took them from him and examined them. *To the inside of one of them wet sand still adhered.*

Mr. Parker Pyne drew a deep breath.

"Now I know," he said.

All their eyes went to the pacing figure on the horizon.

"I should like to look at the body if I may," said Mr. Parker Pyne.

He went with the doctor to where Smethurst's body had been laid down covered with a tarpaulin.

The doctor removed the cover.

"There's nothing to see," he said.

But Mr. Parker Pyne's eyes were fixed on the dead man's tie.

"So Smethurst was an old Etonian," he said.

Loftus looked surprised.

Then Mr. Parker Pyne surprised him still further.

"What do you know of young Williamson?" he asked.

"Nothing at all. I only met him at Beirut. I'd come from Egypt. But why? Surely—"

"Well, it's on his evidence we're going to hang a man, isn't it?" said Mr. Parker Pyne cheerfully. "One's got to be careful."

He still seemed to be interested in the dead man's tie and collar. He unfastened the studs and removed the collar. Then he uttered an exclamation.

"See that?"

On the back of the collar was a small round bloodstain.

He peered closer down at the uncovered neck.

"This man wasn't killed by a blow on the head, doctor," he said briskly. "He was stabbed—at the base of the skull. You can just see the tiny puncture."

"And I missed it!"

"You'd got your preconceived notion," said Mr. Parker Pyne apologetically. "A blow on the head. It's easy enough to miss this. You can hardly see the wound. A quick stab with a small sharp instrument and death would be instantaneous. The victim wouldn't even cry out."

"Do you mean a stiletto? You think the General—"

"Italians and stilettos go together in the popular fancy—Hullo, here comes a car!"

A touring car had appeared over the horizon.

"Good," said O'Rourke as he came up to join them. "The ladies can go on in that."

"What about our murderer?" asked Mr. Parker Pyne.

"You mean Hensley—"

"No, I don't mean Hensley," said Mr. Parker Pyne. "I happen to know that Hensley's innocent."

"You—but why?"

"Well, you see, he had sand in his sock."

O'Rourke stared.

"I know, my boy," said Mr. Parker Pyne gently, "it doesn't sound like sense, but it is. Smethurst wasn't hit on the head, you see, he was stabbed."

He paused a minute and then went on.

"Just cast your mind back to the conversation I told you about—the conversation we had in the café. You picked out what was, to you, the significant phrase. But it was another phrase that struck me. When I said to him that I did the Confidence Trick he said 'What, you too?' Doesn't that strike you as rather curious? I don't know that you'd describe a series of peculations from a Department as a 'Confidence Trick.' Confidence Trick is more descriptive of someone like the absconding Mr. Samuel Long, for instance."

The doctor started. O'Rourke said. "Yes—perhaps . . ."

"I said in jest that perhaps the absconding Mr. Long was one of our party. Suppose that that is the truth."

"What—but it's impossible!"

"Not at all. What do you know of people besides their passports and the accounts they give of themselves? Am I really Mr. Parker Pyne? Is General Poli really an Italian General? And what of the masculine Miss Pryce senior who needs a shave most distinctly."

"But he—but Smethurst—didn't know Long?"

"Smethurst is an old Etonian. Long, also, was at Eton. Smethurst may have known him although he didn't tell you so. He may have recognized him among us. And if so, what is he to do? He has a simple mind, and he worries over the matter. He decides at last to say nothing till Baghdad is reached. But after that he will hold his tongue no longer."

"You think one of *us* is Long," said O'Rourke, still dazed.

He drew a deep breath.

"It must be the Italian fellow—it *must*. . . . Or what about the Armenian?"

"To make up as a foreigner and get a foreign passport is really much more difficult than to remain English," said Mr. Parker Pyne.

"Miss Pryce?" cried O'Rourke incredulously.

"No," said Mr. Parker Pyne. "*This* is our man!"

He laid what seemed an almost friendly hand on the shoulder of the man beside him. But there was nothing friendly in his voice, and the fingers were vice-like in their grip.

"Squadron Leader Loftus or Mr. Samuel Long, it doesn't matter which you call him!"

"But that's impossible—impossible," spluttered O'Rourke. "Loftus has been in the service for years."

"But you've never met him before, have you? He was a stranger to all of you. It isn't the *real* Loftus, naturally."

The quiet man found his voice.

"Clever of you to guess. How did you, by the way?"

"Your ridiculous statement that Smethurst had been killed by bumping his head. O'Rourke put that idea into your head when we were standing talking in Damascus yesterday. You thought—how simple! You were the only doctor with us—whatever you said would be accepted. You'd got Loftus's kit. You'd got his instruments. It was easy to select a neat little tool for your purpose. You lean over to speak to him and as you are speaking you drive the little weapon home. You talk a minute or two longer. It is dark in the car. Who will suspect?

"Then comes the discovery of the body. You give your verdict. But it does not go as easily as you thought. Doubts are raised. You fall back on a second line of defense. Williamson repeats the conversation he has overheard Smethurst having with you. It is taken to refer to Hensley and you add a damaging little invention of your own about a leakage in Hensley's department. And then I make a final test. I mention the sand and the socks. You are holding a handful of sand. I send you to find the socks so *that we may know the truth.* But by that I did not mean what you thought I meant. *I had already examined Hensley's socks.* There was no sand in either of them. You put it there."

Mr. Samuel Long lit a cigarette.

"I give it up," he said. "My luck's turned. Well, I had a good run while it lasted. They were getting hot on my trail when I reached Egypt. I came across Loftus. He was just going to join up in Baghdad—and he knew none of them there. It was too good a chance to be missed. I bought him. It cost me twenty thousand pounds. What was that to me? Then, by cursed ill luck, I run into Smethurst—an ass if there ever was one! He was my fag at Eton. He had a bit of hero worship for me in those days. He didn't like the idea of giving me away. I did my best and at last he promised to say nothing till we reached Baghdad. What chance should I have then? None at all. There was only one way—to eliminate him. But I can assure you I am not a murderer by nature. My talents lie in quite another direction."

His face changed—contracted. He swayed and pitched forward. O'Rourke bent over him.

"Probably prussic acid—in the cigaret," said Mr. Parker Pyne. "The gambler has lost his last throw."

He looked round him—at the wide desert. The sun beat down on him. Only yesterday they had left Damascus—by the gate of Baghdad.

> "Pass not beneath, O Caravan, or pass not
>   singing. Have you heard
> That silence where the birds are dead yet
>   some thing pipeth like a bird?"

9. THE HOUSE AT SHIRAZ

It was six in the morning when Mr. Parker Pyne left for Persia after a stop in Baghdad.

The passenger space in the little monoplane was limited, and the small width of the seats was not such as to accommodate the bulk of Mr. Parker Pyne with anything like comfort. There were two fellow travelers—a large, florid man whom Mr. Parker Pyne judged to be of a talkative habit, and a thin woman with pursed-up lips and a determined air.

"At any rate," thought Mr. Parker Pyne, "they don't look as though they would want to consult me professionally."

Nor did they. The little woman was an American missionary, full of hard work and happiness, and the florid man was employed by an oil company. They had given their fellow traveler a résumé of their lives before the plane started.

"I am merely a tourist, I am afraid," Mr. Parker Pyne had said deprecatingly. "I am going to Teheran and Ispahan and Shiraz."

And the sheer music of the names enchanted him so much as he said them that he repeated them. Teheran. Ispahan. Shiraz.

Mr. Parker Pyne looked out at the country below him. It was flat desert. He felt the mystery of these vast, unpopulated regions.

At Kermanshah the machine came down for passport examinations and customs. A bag of Mr. Parker Pyne's was opened. A certain small cardboard box was scrutinized with some excitement. Questions were asked. Since Mr. Parker Pyne did not speak or understand Persian, the matter was difficult.

The pilot of the machine strolled up. He was a fair-haired young German, a fine-looking man, with deep blue eyes and a weather-beaten face. "Please?" he inquired pleasantly.

Mr. Parker Pyne, who had been indulging in some excellent realistic pantomine without, it seemed, much success, turned to him with relief. "It's bug powder," he said. "Do you think you could explain to them?"

The pilot looked puzzled. "Please?"

Mr. Parker Pyne repeated his plea in German. The pilot grinned and translated the sentence into Persian. The grave and sad officials were pleased; their sorrowful faces relaxed; they smiled. One even laughed. They found the idea humorous.

The three passengers took their places in the machine again and the flight continued. They swooped down at Hamadan to drop the mails, but the plane did not stop. Mr. Parker Pyne peered down, trying to see if he could distinguish the rock of Behistun, that romantic spot where Darius describes the extent of his empire and conquests in three different languages—Babylonian, Median and Persian.

It was one o'clock when they arrived at Teheran. There were more police formalities. The German pilot had come up and was standing by smiling as Mr. Parker Pyne finished answering a long interrogation which he had not understood.

"What have I said?" he asked of the German.

"That your father's Christian name is Tourist, that your profession is Charles, that the maiden name of your mother is Baghdad, and that you have come from Harriet."

"Does it matter?"

"Not the least in the world. Just answer something; that is all they need."

Mr. Parker Pyne was disappointed in Teheran. He found it distressingly modern. He said as much the following evening when he happened to run into Herr Schlagal, the pilot, just as he was entering his hotel. On an impulse he asked the other man to dine, and the German accepted.

The Georgian waiter hovered over them and issued his orders. The food arrived. When they had reached the stage of *la tourte,* a somewhat sticky confection of chocolate, the German said:

"So you go to Shiraz?"

"Yes, I shall fly there. Then I shall come back from Shiraz to Ispahan and Teheran by road. Is it you who will fly me to Shiraz tomorrow?"

"*Ach,* no. I return to Baghdad."

"You have been long here?"

"Three years. It has only been established three years, our service. So far, we have never had an accident—*unberufen!*" He touched the table.

Thick cups of sweet coffee were brought. The two men smoked.

"My first passengers were two ladies," said the German reminiscently. "Two English ladies."

"Yes?" said Mr. Parker Pyne.

"The one she was a young lady very well born, the daughter of one of your ministers, the—how does one say it?—the Lady Esther Carr. She was handsome, very handsome, but mad."

"Mad?"

"Completely mad. She lives there at Shiraz in a big native house. She wears Eastern dress. She will see no Europeans. Is that a life for a well-born lady to live?"

"There have been others," said Mr. Parker Pyne. "There was Lady Hester Stanhope—"

"This one is mad," said the other abruptly. "You could see it in her eyes. Just so have I seen the eyes of my submarine commander in the war. He is now in an asylum."

Mr. Parker Pyne was thoughtful. He remembered Lord Micheldever, Lady Esther Carr's father, well. He had worked under him when the latter was Home Secretary—a big blond man with laughing blue eyes. He had seen Lady Micheldever once—a noted Irish beauty with her black hair and violet-blue eyes. They were both handsome, normal people, but for all that there *was* insanity in the Carr family. It cropped out every now and then, after missing a generation. It was odd, he thought, that Herr Schlagal should stress the point.

"And the other lady?" he asked idly.

"The other lady—is dead."

Something in his voice made Mr. Parker Pyne look up sharply.

"I have a heart," said Herr Schlagal. "I feel. She was, to me, most beautiful, that lady. You know how it is, these things come over you all of a sudden. She was a flower—a flower." He sighed deeply. "I went to see them once—at the house at Shiraz. The Lady Esther, she asked me to come. My little one, my flower, she was afraid of something, I could see it. When next I came back from Baghdad, I hear that she is dead. Dead!"

He paused and then said thoughtfully: "It might be that the other one killed her. She was mad, I tell you."

He sighed, and Mr. Parker Pyne ordered two Benedictines.

"The curaçao, it is good," said the Georgian waiter, and brought them two curaçaos.

JUST AFTER NOON the following day, Mr. Parker Pyne had his first view of Shiraz. They had flown over mountain ranges with narrow, desolate valleys between, and all arid, parched, dry wilderness. Then suddenly Shiraz came into view—an emerald-green jewel in the heart of the wilderness.

Mr. Parker Pyne enjoyed Shiraz as he had not enjoyed Teheran. The primitive character of the hotel did not appall him, nor the equally primitive character of the streets.

He found himself in the midst of a Persian holiday. The Nan Ruz festival had begun on the previous evening—the fifteen-day period in which the Persians celebrate their New Year. He wandered through the empty bazaars and passed out into the great open stretch of common on the north side of the city. All Shiraz was celebrating.

One day he walked just outside the town. He had been to the tomb of Hanfiz the poet, and it was on returning that he saw and was fascinated by a house. A house all tiled in blue and rose and yellow, set in a green garden with water and orange trees and roses. It was, he felt, the house of a dream.

That night he was dining with the English consul and he asked about the house.

"Fascinating place, isn't it? It was built by a former wealthy governor of Luristan, who had made a good thing out of his official position. An Englishwoman's got it now. You must have heard of her. Lady Esther Carr. Mad as a hatter. Gone completely native. Won't have anything to do with anything or anyone British."

"Is she young?"

"Too young to play the fool in this way. She's about thirty."

"There was another Englishwoman with her, wasn't there? A woman who died?"

"Yes; that was about three years ago. Happened the day after I took up my post here, as a matter of fact. Barham, my predecessor, died suddenly, you know."

"How did she die?" asked Mr. Parker Pyne bluntly.

"Fell from that courtyard or balcony place on the first floor. She was Lady Esther's maid or companion, I forget which. Anyway, she was carrying the breakfast tray and stepped back over the edge. Very sad; nothing to be done; cracked her skull on the stone below."

"What was her name?"

"King, I think; or was it Wills? No, that's the missionary woman. Rather a nice-looking girl."

"Was Lady Esther upset?"

"Yes—no, I don't know. She was very queer; I couldn't make her out. She's a very—well, imperious creature. You can see she is somebody, if you know what I mean; she rather scared me with her commanding ways and her dark, flashing eyes."

He laughed half apologetically, then looked curiously at his companion. Mr. Parker Pyne was apparently staring into space. The match he had just struck to light his cigaret was burning away unheeded in his hand. It burned down to his fingers and he dropped it with an ejaculation of pain. Then he saw the consul's astonished expression and smiled.

"I beg your pardon," he said.

"Woolgathering, weren't you?"

"Three bags full," said Mr. Parker Pyne enigmatically.

They talked of other matters.

That evening, by the light of a small oil lamp, Mr. Parker Pyne wrote a letter. He hesitated a good deal over its composition. Yet in the end it was very simple:

Mr. Parker Pyne presents his compliments to Lady Esther Carr and begs to state that he is staying at the Hotel Fars for the next three days should she wish to consult him.

He enclosed a cutting—the famous advertisement:

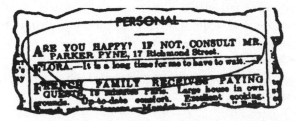

"That ought to do the trick," said Mr. Parker Pyne, as he got gingerly into his rather uncomfortable bed. "Let me see, nearly three years; yes, it ought to do it."

On the following day about four o'clock the answer came. It was brought by a Persian servant who knew no English.

Lady Esther Carr will be glad if Mr. Parker Pyne will call upon her at nine o'clock this evening.

Mr. Parker Pyne smiled.

It was the same servant who received him that evening. He was taken through the dark garden and up an outside staircase that led round to the back of the house. From there a door was opened and he passed through into the central court or balcony, which was open to the night. A big divan was placed against the wall and on it reclined a striking figure.

Lady Esther was attired in Eastern robes, and it might have been suspected that one reason for her preference lay in the fact that they suited her rich, Oriental style of beauty. Imperious, the consul had called her, and indeed imperious she looked. Her chin was held high and her brows were arrogant.

"You are Mr. Parker Pyne? Sit down there."

Her hand pointed to a heap of cushions. On the third finger there flashed a big emerald carved with the arms of her family. It was an heirloom and must be worth a small fortune, Mr. Parker Pyne reflected.

He lowered himself obediently, though with a little difficulty. For a man of his figure it is not easy to sit on the ground gracefully.

A servant appeared with coffee. Mr. Parker Pyne took his cup and sipped appreciatively.

His hostess had acquired the Oriental habit of infinite leisure. She did not rush into conversation. She, too, sipped her coffee with half-closed eyes. At last she spoke.

"So you help unhappy people," she said. "At least, that is what your advertisement claims."

"Yes."

"Why did you send it to me? Is it your way of—doing business on your travels?"

There was something decidedly offensive in her voice, but Mr. Parker Pyne ignored it. He answered simply, "No. My idea in traveling is to have a complete holiday from business."

"Then why send it to me?"

"Because I had reason to believe that you—are unhappy."

There was a moment's silence. He was very curious. How would she take that? She gave herself a minute to decide that point. Then she laughed.

"I suppose you thought that anyone who leaves the world, who lives as I do, cut off from my race, from my country, must do so because she is unhappy! Sorrow, disappointment—you think something like that drove me into exile? Oh, well, how should you understand? There—in England—I was a fish out of water. Here I am myself. I am an Oriental at heart. I love this seclusion. I dare say you can't understand that. To you, I must seem"—she hesitated a moment—"mad."

"You're not mad," said Mr. Parker Pyne.

There was a good deal of quiet assurance in his voice. She looked at him curiously.

"But they've been saying I am, I suppose. Fools! It takes all kinds to make a world. I'm perfectly happy."

"And yet you told me to come here," said Mr. Parker Pyne.

"I will admit I was curious to see you." She hesitated. "Besides, I never want to go back there—to England—but all the same, sometimes I like to hear what is going on in—"

"In the world you have left?"

She acknowledged the sentence with a nod.

Mr. Parker Pyne began to talk. His voice, mellow and reassuring, began quietly, then rose ever so little as he emphasized this point and that.

He talked of London, of society gossip, of famous men and women, of new restaurants and new night clubs, of race meetings and shooting parties and country-house scandals. He talked of clothes, of fashions from Paris, of little shops in unfashionable streets where marvelous bargains could be had. He described theaters and cinemas, he gave film news, he described the building of new garden suburbs, he talked of bulbs and gardening, and he came last to a homely description of London in the evening, with the trams and the busses and the hurrying crowds going homeward after the day's work and of the little homes awaiting them, and of the whole strange intimate pattern of English family life.

It was a very remarkable performance, displaying as it did wide and unusual knowledge and a clever marshaling of the facts. Lady Esther's head had drooped; the arrogance of her poise had been abandoned. For some time her tears had been quietly falling, and now that he had finished, she abandoned all pretense and wept openly.

Mr. Parker Pyne said nothing. He sat there watching her. His face had the quiet, satisfied expression of one who has conducted an experiment and obtained the desired result.

She raised her head at last. "Well," she said bitterly, "are you satisfied?"

"I think so—now."

"How shall I bear it; how shall I bear it? Never to leave here; never to see—anyone again!" The cry came as though wrung out of her. She caught herself up, flushing. "Well?" she demanded fiercely. "Aren't you going to make the obvious remark? Aren't you going to say, 'If you want to go home so much, why not do so?'"

"No." Mr. Parker Pyne shook his head. "It's not nearly so easy as that for you."

For the first time a little look of fear crept into her eyes. "Do you know why I can't go?"

"I think so."

"Wrong." She shook her head. "The reason I can't go is a reason you'd never guess."

"I don't guess," said Mr. Parker Pyne. "I observe—and I classify."

She shook her head. "You don't know anything at all."

"I shall have to convince you, I see," said Mr. Parker Pyne pleasantly. "When you came out here, Lady Esther, you flew, I believe, by the new German Air Service from Baghdad."

"Yes?"

"You were flown by a young pilot, Herr Schlagal, who afterward came here to see you."

"Yes."

A different "yes" in some indescribable way—a softer "yes."

"And you had a friend, or companion, who—died." A voice like steel now—cold, offensive.

"My companion."

"Her name was———?"

"Muriel King."

"Were you fond of her?"

"What do you mean, fond?" She paused, checked herself. "She was useful to me."

She said it haughtily and Mr. Parker Pyne was reminded of the consul's saying: "You can see she is somebody, if you know what I mean."

"Were you sorry when she died?"

"I—naturally! Really, Mr. Pyne, is it necessary to go into all this?" She spoke angrily, and went on without waiting for an answer: "It has been very good of you to come. But I am a little tired. If you will tell me what I owe you—?"

But Mr. Parker Pyne did not move. He showed no signs of taking offense. He went quietly on with his questions. "Since she died, Herr Schlagal has not been to see you. Suppose he were to come, would you receive him?"

"Certainly not."

"You refuse absolutely?"

"Absolutely. Herr Schlagal will not be admitted."

"Yes," said Mr. Parker Pyne thoughtfully. "You could not say anything else."

The defensive armor of her arrogance broke down a little. She said uncertainly: "I—I don't know what you mean."

"Did you know, Lady Esther, that young Schlagal fell in love with Muriel King? He is a sentimental young man. He still treasures her memory."

"Does he?" Her voice was almost a whisper.

"What was she like?"

"What do you mean, what was she like? How do I know?"

"You must have looked at her sometimes," said Mr. Parker Pyne mildly.

"Oh, that! She was quite a nice-looking young woman."

"About your own age?"

"Just about." There was a pause, and then she said: "Why do you think that—that Schlagal cared for her?"

"Because he told me so. Yes, yes, in the most unmistakable terms. As I say, he is a sentimental young man. He was glad to confide in me. He was very upset at her dying the way she did."

Lady Esther sprang to her feet. "Do you believe I murdered her?"

Mr. Parker Pyne did not spring to his feet. He was not a springing kind of man. "No, my dear child," he said. "I do *not* believe that you murdered her, and that being so, I think the sooner you stop this play-acting and go home, the better."

"What do you mean, play-acting?"

"The truth is, you lost your nerve. Yes, you did. You lost your nerve badly. You thought you'd be accused of murdering your employer."

The girl made a sudden movement.

Mr. Parker Pyne went on. "You are not Lady Esther Carr. I knew that before I came here, but I've tested you to make sure." His smile broke out, bland and benevolent. "When I said my little piece just now, I was watching you, and every time you reacted *as Muriel King*, not as Esther Carr. The cheap shops, the cinemas, the new garden suburbs, going home by bus and tram—you reacted to all those. Country-house gossip, new night clubs, the chatter of Mayfair, race meetings—none of those meant anything at all to you."

His voice became even more persuasive and fatherly. "Sit down and tell me about it. You didn't murder Lady Esther, but you thought you might be accused of doing so. Just tell me how it all came about."

She took a long breath; then she sank down once more on the divan and began to speak. Her words came hurriedly, in little bursts.

"I must begin—at the beginning. I—I was afraid of her. She was mad—not quite mad—just a little. She brought me out here with her. Like a fool I was delighted; I thought it was so romantic. Little fool. That's what I was, a little fool. There was some business about a chauffeur. She was man-mad—absolutely man-mad. He wouldn't have anything to do with her, and it got out; her friends got to know about it and laughed. And she broke loose from her family and came out here.

"It was all a pose to save her face—solitude in the desert—all that sort of thing. She would have kept it up for a bit, and then gone back. But she got queerer and queerer. And there was the pilot. She—she took a fancy to him. He came here to see me, and she thought—Oh, well, you can understand. But he must have made it clear to her. . . .

"And then she suddenly turned on me. She was awful, frightening. She said I should never go home again. She said I was in her power. She said I was a slave. Just that—a slave. She had the power of life and death over me."

Mr. Parker Pyne nodded. He saw the situation unfolding. Lady Esther slowly going over the edge of sanity, as others of her family had gone before her, and the frightened girl, ignorant and untraveled, believing everything that was said to her.

"But one day something in me seemed to snap. I stood up to her. I told her that if it came to it I was stronger than she was. I told her I'd throw her down onto the stones below. She was frightened, really frightened. I suppose she'd just thought me a worm. I took a step toward her—I don't know what she thought I meant to do. She moved backward; she—she stepped back off the edge!" Muriel King buried her face in her hands.

"And then?" Mr. Parker Pyne prompted gently.

"I lost my head. I thought they'd say I'd pushed her over. I thought nobody would listen to me. I thought I should be thrown into some awful prison out here." Her lips worked. Mr. Parker Pyne saw clearly enough the unreasoning fear that had possessed her. "And then it came to me—if it were I! I knew that there would be a new British consul who'd never seen either of us. The other one had died.

"I thought I could manage the servants. To them we were two mad Englishwomen. When one was dead, the other carried on. I gave them good presents of money and told them to send for the British consul. He came and I received him as Lady Esther. I had her ring on my finger. He was very nice and arranged everything. Nobody seemed to have the least suspicion."

Mr. Parker Pyne nodded thoughtfully. The prestige of a famous name. Lady Esther Carr might be mad as a hatter, but she was still Lady Esther Carr.

"And then afterward," continued Muriel, "I wished I hadn't. I saw that I'd been quite mad myself. I was condemned to stay on here playing a part. I didn't see how I could ever get away. If I confessed the truth now, it would look more than ever as though I'd murdered her. Oh, Mr. Pyne, what shall I do? What shall I do?"

"Do?" Mr. Parker Pyne rose to his feet as briskly as his figure allowed. "My dear child, you will come with me now to the British consul, who is a very amiable and kindly man. There will be certain unpleasant formalities to go through. I don't promise you that it will be all plain sailing, but you won't be hanged for murder. By the way, why was the breakfast tray found with the body?"

"I threw it over. I—I thought it would look more like me to have a tray there. Was it silly of me?"

"It was rather a clever touch," said Mr. Parker Pyne. "In fact, it was the one point which made me wonder if you might, perhaps, have done away with Lady Esther—that is, until I saw you. When I saw you, I knew that whatever else you might do in your life, you would never kill anyone."

"Because I haven't the nerve, you mean?"

"Your reflexes wouldn't work that way," said Mr. Parker Pyne, smiling. "Now, shall we go? There's an unpleasant job to be faced, but I'll see you through it, and then—home to Streatham Hill—it is Streatham Hill, isn't it? Yes, I thought so. I saw your face contract when I mentioned one particular bus number. Are you coming, my dear?"

Muriel King hung back. "They'll never believe me," she said nervously. "Her family and all. They wouldn't believe she could act the way she did."

"Leave it to me," said Mr. Parker Pyne. "I know something of the family history, you see. Come, child, don't go on playing the coward. Remember, there's a young man in Teheran sighing his heart out. We had better arrange that it is in his plane you fly to Baghdad."

The girl smiled and blushed. "I'm ready," she said simply. Then as she moved toward the door, she turned back. "You said you knew I was not Lady Esther Carr before you saw me. How could you possibly tell that?"

"Statistics," said Mr. Parker Pyne.

"Statistics?"

"Yes, Both Lord and Lady Micheldever had blue eyes. When the consul mentioned that their daughter had flashing *dark* eyes I knew there was something wrong. Brown-eyed people may produce a blue-eyed child, but not the other way about. A scientific fact, I assure you."

"I think you're wonderful!" said Muriel King.

10. THE PEARL OF PRICE

The party had had a long and tiring day. They had starte from Amman early in the morning with a temperature of ninety-eight in the shade, and had come at last just as it was growing dark into the camp situated in the heart of that city of fantastic and preposterous red rock which is Petra.

There were seven of them. Mr. Caleb P. Blundell, that stout and prosperous American magnate. His dark and good-looking, if somewhat taciturn, secretary, Jim Hurst. Sir Donald Marvel, M.P., a tired-looking English politician. Doctor Carver, a world-renowned elderly archaeologist. A gallant Frenchman, Colonel Dubosc, on leave from Syria. A Mr. Parker Pyne, not perhaps so plainly labeled with his profession, but breathing an atmosphere of British solidity. And lastly, there was Miss Carol Blundell—pretty, spoiled, and extremely sure of herself as the only woman among half a dozen men.

They dined in the big tent, having selected their tents or caves for sleeping in. They talked of politics in the Near East—the Englishman cautiously, the Frenchman discreetly, the American somewhat fatuously, and the archaeologist and Mr. Parker Pyne not at all. Both of them, it seemed, preferred the role of listeners. So also did Jim Hurst.

Then they talked of the city they had come to visit.

"It's just too romantic for words," said Carol. "To think of those—what do you call 'em?—Nabataeans living here all that while ago, almost be fore time began!"

"Hardly that," said Mr. Parker Pyne mildly. "Eh, Doctor Carver?"

"Oh, that's an affair of a mere two thousand years back, and if racketeers are romantic, then I suppose the Nabataeans are, too. They were a pack of wealthy blackguards I should say, who compelled travelers to use their own caravan routes, and saw to it that all other routes were unsafe. Petra was the storehouse of their racketeering profits."

"You think they were just robbers?" asked Carol. "Just common thieves?"

"Thieves is a less romantic word, Miss Blundell. A thief suggests a petty pilferer. A robber suggests a larger canvas."

"What about a modern financier?" suggested Mr. Parker Pyne with a twinkle.

"That's one for you, Pop!" said Carol.

"A man who makes money benefits mankind," said Mr. Blundell sententiously.

"Mankind," murmured Mr. Parker Pyne, "is so ungrateful."

"What is honesty?" demanded the Frenchman. "It is a *nuance,* a convention. In different countries it means different things. An Arab is not ashamed of stealing. He is not ashamed of lying. With him it is from *whom* he steals or to *whom* he lies that matters."

"That is the point of view—yes," agreed Carver.

"Which shows the superiority of the West over the East," said Blundell. "When these poor creatures get education—"

Sir Donald entered languidly into the conversation. "Education is rather rot, you know. Teaches fellows a lot of useless things. And what I mean is, nothing alters what you are."

"You mean?"

"Well, what I mean to say is, for instance, once a thief always a thief."

There was a dead silence for a moment. Then Carol began talking feverishly about mosquitoes, and her father backed her up.

Sir Donald, a little puzzled, murmured to his neighbor, Mr. Parker Pyne: "Seems I dropped a brick—what?"

"Curious," said Mr. Parker Pyne.

Whatever momentary embarrassment had been caused, one person had quite failed to notice it. The archaeologist had sat silent, his eyes dreamy and abstracted. When a pause came, he spoke suddenly and abruptly.

"You know," he said, "I agree with that—at any rate, from the opposite point of view. A man's fundamentally honest, or he isn't. You can't get away from it."

"You don't believe that sudden temptation, for instance, will turn an honest man into a criminal?" asked Mr. Parker Pyne.

"Impossible!" said Carver.

Mr. Parker Pyne shook his head gently. "I wouldn't say impossible. You see, there are so many factors to take into account. There's the breaking point, for instance."

"What do you call the breaking point?" asked young Hurst, speaking for the first time. He had a deep, rather attractive voice.

"The brain is adjusted to carry so much weight. The thing that precipitates the crisis—that turns an honest man into a dishonest one—may be a mere trifle. That is why most crimes are absurd. The cause, nine times out of ten, is that trifle of overweight—the straw that breaks the camel's back."

"It is the psychology you talk there, my friend," said the Frenchman.

"If a criminal were a psychologist, what a criminal he could be!" said Mr. Parker Pyne. His voice dwelt lovingly on the idea. "When you think that of ten people you meet, at least nine of them can be induced to act in any way you please by applying the right stimulus."

"Oh, explain that!" cried Carol.

"There's the bullyable man. Shout loud enough at him—and he obeys. There's the contradictory man. Bully him the opposite way from that in which you want him to go. Then there's the suggestible person, the commonest type of all. Those are the people who have *seen* a motor, because they have heard a motor horn; who *see* a postman because they hear the rattle of the letter box; who *see* a knife in a wound because they are *told* a man has been stabbed; or who will have *heard* the pistol if they are told a man has been shot."

"I guess no one could put that sort of stuff over on me," said Carol incredulously.

"You're too smart for that, honey," said her father.

"It is very true what you say," said the Frenchman reflectively. "The preconceived idea, it deceives the senses."

Carol yawned. "I'm going to my cave. I'm tired to death. Abbas Effendi said we had to start early tomorrow. He's going to take us up to the place of sacrifice—whatever that is."

"It's where they sacrifice young and beautiful girls," said Sir Donald.

"Mercy, I hope not! Well, good night, all. Oh, I've dropped my earring."

Colonel Dubosc picked it up from where it had rolled across the table and returned it to her.

"Are they real?" asked Sir Donald abruptly. Discourteous for the moment, he was staring at the two large solitaire pearls at her ears.

"They're real, all right," said Carol.

"Cost me eighty thousand dollars," said her father with relish. "And she screws them in so loosely that they fall off and roll about the table. Want to ruin me, girl?"

"I'd say it wouldn't ruin you even if you had to buy me a new pair," said Carol fondly.

"I guess it wouldn't," her father acquiesced. "I could buy you three pairs of earrings without noticing it in my bank balance." He looked proudly around.

"How nice for you!" said Sir Donald.

"Well, gentlemen, I think I'll turn in now," said Blundell. "Good night." Young Hurst went with him.

The other four smiled at one another, as though in sympathy over some thought.

"Well," drawled Sir Donald, "it's nice to know he wouldn't miss the money. Purse-proud hog!" he added viciously.

"They have too much money, these Americans," said Dubosc.

"It is difficult," said Mr. Parker Pyne gently, "for a rich man to be appreciated by the poor."

Dubosc laughed. "Envy and malice?" he suggested. "You are

right, Monsieur. We all wish to be rich; to buy the pearl earrings several times over. Except, perhaps, Monsieur here."

He bowed to Doctor Carver who, as seemed usual with him, was once more far away. He was fiddling with a little object in his hand.

"Eh?" He roused himself. "No, I must admit I don't covet large pearls. Money is always useful, of course." His tone put it where it belonged. "But look at this," he said. "Here is something a hundred times more interesting than pearls."

"What is it?"

"It's a cylinder seal of black hematite and it's got a presentation scene engraved on it—a god introducing a suppliant to a more important enthroned god. The suppliant is carrying a kid by way of an offering, and the august god on the throne has the flies kept off him by a flunky who wields a palm-branch fly whisk. That neat inscription mentions the man as a servant of Hammurabi, so that it must have been made just four thousand years ago."

He took a lump of plasticine from his pocket and smeared some on the table, then he oiled it with a little vaseline and pressed the seal upon it, rolling it out. Then, with a penknife, he detached a square of the plasticine and levered it gently up from the table.

"You see?" he said.

The scene he had described was unrolled before them in the plasticine, clear and sharply defined.

For a moment the spell of the past was laid upon them all. Then, from outside, the voice of Mr. Blundell was raised unmusically.

"Say, you fellows! Change my baggage out of this darned cave and into a tent! The no-see-ums are biting good and hard. I shan't get a wink of sleep."

"No-see-ums?" Sir Donald queried.

"Probably sand flies," said Doctor Carver.

"I like no-see-ums," said Mr. Parker Pyne. "It's a much more suggestive name."

.   .   .

THE PARTY STARTED early the following morning, getting under way after various exclamations at the color and marking of the rocks. The "rose-red" city was indeed a freak invented by Nature in her most extravagant and colorful mood. The party proceeded slowly, since Doctor Carver walked with his eyes bent on the ground, occasionally pausing to pick up small objects.

"You can always tell the archaeologist—so," said Colonel Dubosc, smiling. "He regards never the sky, nor the hills, nor the beauties of nature. He walks with head bent, searching."

"Yes, but what for?" said Carol. "What are the things you are picking up, Doctor Carver?"

With a slight smile the archaeologist held out a couple of muddy fragments of pottery.

"That rubbish!" cried Carol scornfully.

"Pottery is more interesting than gold," said Doctor Carver. Carol looked disbelieving.

They came to a sharp bend and passed two or three rock-cut tombs. The ascent was somewhat trying. The Bedouin guards went ahead, swinging up the precipitous slopes unconcernedly, without a downward glance at the sheer drop on one side of them.

Carol looked rather pale. One guard leaned down from above and extended a hand. Hurst sprang up in front of her and held out his stick like a rail on the precipitous side. She thanked him with a glance, and a minute later stood safely on a broad path of rock. The others followed slowly. The sun was now high and the heat was beginning to be felt.

At last they reached a broad plateau almost at the top. An easy climb led to the summit of a big square block of rock. Blundell signified to the guide that the party would go up alone. The Bedouins disposed themselves comfortably against the rocks and began to smoke. A few short minutes and the others had reached the summit.

It was a curious, bare place. The view was marvelous, embracing the valley on every side. They stood on a plain rectangular floor, with rock basins cut in the side and a kind of sacrificial altar.

"A heavenly place for sacrifices," said Carol with enthusiasm. "But my, they must have had a time getting the victims up here!"

"There was originally a kind of zigzag rock road," explained Doctor Carver. "We shall see traces of it as we go down the other way."

They were some time longer commenting and talking. Then there was a tiny chink, and Doctor Carver said:

"I believe you've dropped your earring again, Miss Blundell."

Carol clapped a hand to her ear. "Why, so I have."

Dubosc and Hurst began searching about.

"It must be just here," said the Frenchman. "It can't have rolled away, because there is nowhere for it to roll to. The place is like a square box."

"It can't have rolled into a crack?" queried Carol.

"There's not a crack anywhere," said Mr. Parker Pyne. "You can see for yourself. The place is perfectly smooth. Ah, you have found something, Colonel?"

"Only a little pebble," said Dubosc, smiling and throwing it away.

Gradually a different spirit—a spirit of tension—came over the search. They were not said aloud, but the words "eighty thousand dollars" were present in everybody's mind.

"You are sure you had it, Carol?" snapped her father. "I mean, perhaps you dropped it on the way up."

"I had it just as we stepped onto the plateau here," said Carol. "I know, because Doctor Carver pointed out to me that it was loose and he screwed it up for me. That's so, isn't it, doctor?"

Doctor Carver assented. It was Sir Donald who voiced the thoughts in everybody's mind.

"This is rather an unpleasant business, Mr. Blundell," he said. "You were telling us last night what the value of these earrings is. One of them alone is worth a small fortune. If this earring is not found, and it does not look as though it will be found, every one of us will be under a certain suspicion."

"And for one, I ask to be searched," broke in Colonel Dubosc. "I do not ask, I demand it as a right!"

"You can search me, too," said Hurst. His voice sounded harsh.

"What does everyone else feel?" asked Sir Donald, looking around.

"Certainly," said Mr. Parker Pyne.

"An excellent idea," said Doctor Carver.

"I'll be in on this too, gentlemen," said Mr. Blundell. "I've got my reasons, though I don't want to stress them."

"Just as you like, of course, Mr. Blundell," said Sir Donald courteously.

"Carol, my dear, will you go down and wait with the guides?"

Without a word the girl left them. Her face was set and grim. There was a despairing look upon it that caught the attention of one member of the party, at least. He wondered just what it meant.

The search proceeded. It was drastic and thorough—and completely unsatisfactory. One thing was certain. No one was carrying the earring on his person. It was a subdued little troop that negotiated the descent and listened halfheartedly to the guide's descriptions and information.

Mr. Parker Pyne had just finished dressing for lunch when a figure appeared at the door of his tent.

"Mr. Pyne, may I come in?"

"Certainly, my dear young lady, certainly."

Carol came in and sat down on the bed. Her face had the same grim look upon it that he had noticed earlier in the day.

"You pretend to straighten out things for people when they are unhappy, don't you?" she demanded.

"I am on holiday, Miss Blundell. I am not taking any cases."

"Well, you're going to take this one," said the girl calmly. "Look here, Mr. Pyne, I'm just as wretched as anyone could well be."

"What is troubling you?" he asked. "Is it this business of the earring?"

"That's just it. You've said it. Jim Hurst didn't take it, Mr. Pyne. I know he didn't."

"I don't quite follow you, Miss Blundell. Why should anyone assume he had?"

"Because of his record. Jim Hurst was once a thief, Mr. Pyne. He was caught in our house. I—I was sorry for him. He looked so young and desperate—"

"And so good-looking," thought Mr. Parker Pyne.

"I persuaded Pop to give him a chance to make good. My father will do anything for me. Well, he gave Jim his chance and Jim has made good. Father's come to rely on him and to trust him with all his business secrets. And in the end he'll come around altogether, or would have if this hadn't happened."

"When you say 'come around'—?"

"I mean that I want to marry Jim and he wants to marry me."

"And Sir Donald?"

"Sir Donald is Father's idea. He's not mine. Do you think I want to marry a stuffed fish like Sir Donald?"

Without expressing any views as to this description of the young Englishman, Mr. Parker Pyne asked: "And Sir Donald himself?"

"I dare say he thinks I'd be good for his impoverished acres," said Carol scornfully.

Mr. Parker Pyne considered the situation. "I should like to ask you about two things," he said. "Last night the remark was made, 'once a thief, always a thief.'"

The girl nodded.

"I see now the reason for the embarrassment that remark seemed to cause."

"Yes, it was awkward for Jim—and for me and Pop, too. I was so afraid Jim's face would show something that I just trotted out the first remarks I could think of."

Mr. Parker Pyne nodded thoughtfully. Then he asked: "Just why did your father insist on being searched today?"

"You didn't get that? I did. Pop had it in his mind that I might think the whole business was a frame-up against Jim. You see, he's crazy for me to marry the Englishman. Well, he wanted to show me that he hadn't done the dirty on Jim."

"Dear me," said Mr. Parker Pyne, "this is all very illuminating. In a general sense, I mean. It hardly helps us in our particular inquiry."

"You're not going to hand in your checks?"

"No, no." He was silent a moment, then he said: "What is it exactly you want me to do, Miss Carol?"

"Prove it wasn't Jim who took that pearl."

"And suppose—excuse me—that it was?"

"If you think so, you're wrong—dead wrong."

"Yes, but have you really considered the case carefully? Don't you think that the pearl might prove a sudden temptation to Mr. Hurst? The sale of it would bring in a large sum of money—a foundation on which to speculate, shall we say?—which will make him independent, so that he can marry you with or without your father's consent."

"Jim didn't do it," said the girl simply.

This time Mr. Parker Pyne accepted her statement. "Well, I'll do my best."

She nodded abruptly and left the tent. Mr. Parker Pyne in his turn sat down on the bed. He gave himself up to thought. Suddenly he chuckled.

"I'm growing slow-witted," he said, aloud. At lunch he was very cheerful.

The afternoon passed peacefully. Most people slept. When Mr. Parker Pyne came into the big tent at a quarter past four only Doctor Carver was there. He was examining some fragments of pottery.

"Ah!" said Mr. Parker Pyne, drawing up a chair to the table. "Just the man I want to see. Can you let me have that bit of plasticine you carry about?"

The doctor felt in his pockets and produced a stick of plasticine, which he offered to Mr. Parker Pyne.

"No," said Mr. Parker Pyne, waving it away, "that's not the one I want. I want that lump you had last night. To be frank, it's not the plasticine I want. It's the contents of it."

There was a pause, and then Doctor Carver said quietly. "I don't think I quite understand you."

"I think you do," said Mr. Parker Pyne. "I want Miss Blundell's pearl earring."

There was a minute's dead silence. Then Carver slipped his hand into his pocket and took out a shapeless lump of plasticine.

"Clever of you," he said. His face was expressionless.

"I wish you'd tell me about it," said Mr. Parker Pyne. His fingers were busy. With a grunt, he extracted a somewhat smeared pearl earring. "Just curiosity, I know," he added apologetically. "But I should like to hear about it."

"I'll tell you," said Carver, "if you'll tell me just how you happened to pitch upon me. You didn't see anything, did you?"

Mr. Parker Pyne shook his head. "I just thought about it," he said.

"It was really sheer accident, to start with," said Carver. "I was behind you all this morning and I came across it lying in front of me—it must have fallen from the girl's ear a moment before. She hadn't noticed it. Nobody had. I picked it up and put it into my pocket, meaning to return it to her as soon as I caught her up. But I forgot.

"And then, halfway up that climb, I began to think. The jewel meant nothing to that fool of a girl—her father would buy her another without noticing the cost. And it would mean a lot to me. The sale of that pearl would equip an expedition." His impassive face suddenly twitched and came to life. "Do you know the difficulty there is nowadays in raising subscriptions for digging? No, you don't. The sale of that pearl would make everything easy. There's a site I want to dig—up in Baluchistan. There's a whole chapter of the past there waiting to be discovered . . .

"What you said last night came into my mind—about a suggestible witness. I thought the girl was that type. As we reached the summit I told her her earring was loose. I pretended to tighten it. What I really did was to press the point of a small pencil into her ear. A few minutes later I dropped a little pebble. She was quite ready to swear then that the earring had been in her ear and had just dropped off. In the meantime I pressed the pearl into a lump of plasticine in my pocket. That's my story. Not a very edifying one. Now for your turn."

"There isn't much of my story," said Mr. Parker Pyne. "You were the only man who'd picked up things from the ground—that's what made me think of you. And finding that little pebble was significant. It suggested the trick you'd played. And then—"

"Go on," said Carver.

"Well, you see, you'd talked about honesty a little too vehemently last night. Protesting overmuch—well, you know what Shakespeare says. It looked, somehow, as though you were trying to convice *yourself*. And you were a little too scornful about money."

The face of the man in front of him looked lined and weary. "Well, that's that," he said. "It's all up with me now. You'll give the girl back her gewgaw, I suppose? Odd thing, the barbaric instinct for ornamentation. You find it going back as far as paleolithic times. One of the first instincts of the female sex."

"I think you misjudge Miss Carol," said Mr. Parker Pyne. "She has brains—and what is more, a heart. I think she will keep this business to herself."

"Father won't, though," said the archaeologist.

"I think he will. You see, 'Pop' has his own reasons for keeping quiet. There's no forty-thousand-dollar touch about this earring. A mere fiver would cover its value."

"You mean—?"

"Yes. The girl doesn't know. She thinks they are genuine, all right. I had my suspicions last night. Mr. Blundell talked a little too much about all the money he had. When things go wrong and you're caught in the slump—well, the best thing to do is to put a good face on it and bluff. Mr. Blundell was bluffing."

Suddenly Doctor Carver grinned. It was an engaging small-boy grin, strange to see on the face of an elderly man. "Then we're all poor devils together," he said.

"Exactly," said Mr. Parker Pyne and quoted, "'A fellow feeling makes us wondrous kind.'"

11. DEATH ON THE NILE

Lady Grayle was nervous. From the moment of coming on board the S. S. Fayoum she complained of everything. She did not like her cabin. She could bear the morning sun, but not the afternoon sun. Pamela Grayle, her niece, obligingly gave up her cabin on the other side. Lady Grayle accepted it grudgingly.

She snapped at Miss MacNaughton, her nurse, for having given her the wrong scarf and for having packed her little pillow instead of leaving it out. She snapped at her husband, Sir George, for having just bought her the wrong string of beads. It was lapis she wanted, not carnelian. George was a fool!

Sir George said anxiously, "Sorry, me dear, sorry. I'll go back and change 'em. Plenty of time."

She did not snap at Basil West, her husband's private secretary, because nobody ever snapped at Basil. His smile disarmed you before you began.

But the worst of it fell assuredly to the dragoman—an imposing and richly dressed personage whom nothing could disturb. When Lady Grayle caught sight of a stranger in a basket chair and realized that he was a fellow passenger, the vials of her wrath were poured out like water.

"They told me distinctly at the office that we were the only passengers! It was the end of the season and there was no one else going!"

"That right, lady," said Mohammed calmly. "Just you and party and one gentleman, that's all."

"But I was told that there would be only ourselves."

"That quite right, lady."

"It's not all right! It was a lie! What is that man doing there?"

"He come later, lady. After you take tickets. He only decide come this morning."

"It's an absolute swindle!"

"That all right, lady; him very quiet gentleman, very nice, very quiet."

"You're a fool! You know nothing about it. Miss MacNaughton, where are you? Oh, there you are. I've repeatedly asked you to stay near me. I might feel faint. Help me to my cabin and give me an aspirin, and don't let Mohammed come near me. He keeps on saying 'That right, lady,' till I feel I could scream."

Miss MacNaughton proffered an arm without a word. She was a tall woman of about thirty-five, handsome in a quiet, dark way. She settled Lady Grayle in the cabin, propped her up with cushions, administered an aspirin and listened to the thin flow of complaint.

Lady Grayle was forty-eight. She had suffered since she was sixteen from the complaint of having too much money. She had married that impoverished baronet, Sir George Grayle, ten years before.

She was a big woman, not bad-looking as regarded features, but her face was fretful and lined, and the lavish make-up she applied only accentuated the blemishes of time and temper. Her hair had been in turn platinum-blond and henna-red, and was looking tired in consequence. She was overdressed and wore too much jewelry.

"Tell Sir George," she finished, while the silent Miss MacNaughton waited with an expressionless face—"tell Sir George that he *must* get that man off the boat! I *must* have privacy. All I've gone through lately—" She shut her eyes.

"Yes, Lady Grayle," said Miss MacNaughton, and left the cabin.

The offending last-minute passenger was still sitting in the deck chair. He had his back to Luxor and was staring out across the Nile to where the distant hills showed golden above a line of dark green. Miss MacNaughton gave him a swift, appraising glance as she passed.

She found Sir George in the lounge. He was holding a string of beads in his hand and looking at it doubtfully

"Tell me, Miss MacNaughton, do you think these will be all right?"

Miss MacNaughton gave a swift glance at the lapis. "Very nice indeed," she said.

"You think Lady Grayle will be pleased—eh?"

"Oh, no, I shouldn't say that, Sir George. You see, nothing *would* please her. That's the real truth of it. By the way, she sent me with a message to you. She wants you to get rid of this extra passenger."

Sir George's jaw dropped. "How can I? What could I say to the fellow?"

"Of course you can't." Elsie MacNaughton's voice was brisk and kindly. "Just say there was nothing to be done." She added encouragingly, "It will be all right."

"You think it will, eh?" His face was ludicrously pathetic.

Elsie MacNaughton's voice was still kinder as she said: "You really must not take these things to heart, Sir George. It's just health, you know. Don't take it seriously."

"You think she's really bad, nurse?"

A shade crossed the nurse's face. There was something odd in her voice as she answered: "Yes, I—I don't quite like her condition. But please don't worry, Sir George. You mustn't. You really mustn't." She gave him a friendly smile and went out.

Pamela came in, very languid and cool in her white. "Hullo, Nunks."

"Hullo, Pam, me dear."

"What have you got there? Oh, nice!"

"Well, I'm glad you think so. Do you think your aunt will think so, too?"

"She's incapable of liking anything. I can't think why you married the woman, Nunks."

Sir George was silent. A confused panorama of unsuccessful racing, pressing creditors and a handsome, if domineering woman rose before his mental vision.

"Poor old dear," said Pamela. "I suppose you had to do it. But she does give us both rather hell, doesn't she?"

"Since she's been ill—" began Sir George.

Pamela interrupted him. "She's not ill! Not really. She can always do anything she wants to. Why, while you were up at Assouan she was as merry as a—a cricket. I bet you Miss MacNaughton knows she's a fraud."

"I don't know what we'd do without Miss MacNaughton," said Sir George, with a sigh.

"She's an efficient creature," admitted Pamela. "I don't exactly dote on her as you do, though, Nunks. Oh, you do! Don't contradict. You think she's wonderful. So she is, in a way. But she's a dark horse. I never know what she's thinking. Still, she manages the old cat quite well."

"Look here, Pam, you mustn't speak of your aunt like that. Dash it all, she's very good to you."

"Yes, she pays all our bills, doesn't she? It's the hell of a life, though."

Sir George passed on to a less painful subject. "What are we to do about this fellow who's coming on the trip? Your aunt wants the boat to herself."

"Well, she can't have it," said Pamela coolly. "The man's quite presentable. His name's Parker Pyne. I should think he was a civil servant out of the Records Department—if there is such a thing. Funny thing is, I seem to have heard the name somewhere. Basil!" The secretary had just entered. "Where have I seen the name Parker Pyne?"

"Front page of the *Times*. Agony Column," replied the young man promptly. "'Are you happy? If not, consult Mr. Parker Pyne.'"

"Never! How frightfully amusing! Let's tell him all our troubles all the way to Cairo."

"I haven't any," said Basil West simply. "We're going to glide down the golden Nile, and see temples"—he looked quickly at Sir George, who had picked up a paper—"together."

The last word was only just breathed, but Pamela caught it. Her eyes met his.

"You're right, Basil," she said lightly. "It's good to be alive."

Sir George got up and went out. Pamela's face clouded over.

"What's the matter, my sweet?"

"My detested aunt-by-marriage—"

"Don't worry," said Basil quickly. "What does it matter what she gets in her head? Don't contradict her. You see," he laughed, "it's good camouflage."

The benevolent figure of Mr. Parker Pyne entered the lounge. Behind him came the picturesque figure of Mohammed, prepared to say his piece.

"Lady, gentlemans, we start now. In a few minutes we pass temples of Karnak right-hand side. I tell you story now about little boy who went to buy a roasted lamb for his father . . ."

MR. PARKER PYNE MOPPED his forehead. He had just returned from a visit to the Temple of Dendera. Riding on a donkey was, he felt, an exercise ill suited to his figure. He was proceeding to remove his collar when a note propped up on the dressing table caught his attention. He opened it. It ran as follows:

Dear Sir,

I should be obliged if you would not visit the Temple of Abydos but would remain on the boat, as I wish to consult you.

Yours truly,
Ariadne Grayle

A smile creased Mr. Parker Pyne's large, bland face. He reached for a sheet of paper and unscrewed his fountain pen.

Dear Lady Grayle (he wrote),

I am sorry to disappoint you, but I am at present on holiday and am not doing any professional business.

He signed his name and dispatched the letter by a steward. As he completed his change of toilet, another note was brought to him.

Dear Mr. Parker Pyne,

I appreciate the fact that you are on holiday, but I am prepared to pay a fee of a hundred pounds for a consultation.

Yours truly,
Ariadne Grayle

Mr. Parker Pyne's eyebrows rose. He tapped his teeth thoughtfully with his fountain pen. He wanted to see Abydos, but a hundred pounds was a hundred pounds. And Egypt had been even more wickedly expensive than he had imagined.

Dear Lady Grayle (he wrote),

I shall not visit the Temple of Abydos.

Yours faithfully,
J. Parker Pyne

Mr. Parker Pyne's refusal to leave the boat was a source of great grief to Mohammed.

"Very nice temple. All my gentlemans like see that temple. I get you carriage. I get you chair, and sailors carry you."

Mr. Parker Pyne refused all these tempting offers.

The others set off.

Mr. Parker Pyne waited on deck. Presently the door of Lady Grayle's cabin opened and the lady herself trailed out on deck.

"Such a hot afternoon," she observed graciously. "I see you have stayed behind, Mr. Pyne. Very wise of you. Shall we have some tea together in the lounge?"

Mr. Parker Pyne rose promptly and followed her. It cannot be denied that he was curious.

It seemed as though Lady Grayle felt some difficulty in coming to the point. She fluttered from this subject to that. But finally she spoke in an altered voice.

"Mr. Pyne, what I am about to tell you is in the strictest confidence! You do understand that, don't you?"

"Naturally."

She paused, took a deep breath. Mr. Parker Pyne waited.

"I want to know whether or not my husband is poisoning me."

Whatever Mr. Parker Pyne had expected, it was not this. He showed his astonishment plainly. "That is a very serious accusation to make, Lady Grayle."

"Well, I'm not a fool and I wasn't born yesterday. I've had my suspicions for some time. Whenever George goes away I get better. My food doesn't disagree with me and I feel a different woman. There must be some reason for that."

"What you say is very serious, Lady Grayle. You must remember I am not a detective. I am, if you like to put it that way, a heart specialist—"

She interrupted him. "Eh—and don't you think it worries me, all this? It's not a policeman I want—I can look after myself, thank you—it's certainty I want. I've got to *know*. I'm not a wicked woman, Mr. Pyne. I act fairly by those who act fairly by me. A bargain's a bargain. I've kept my side of it. I've paid my husband's debts and I've not stinted him in money."

Mr. Parker Pyne had a fleeting pang of pity for Sir George.

"And as for the girl, she's had clothes and parties and this, that and the other. Common gratitude is all I ask."

"Gratitude is not a thing that can be produced to order, Lady Grayle."

"Nonsense!" said Lady Grayle. She went on: "Well, there it is! Find out the truth for me! Once I *know*—"

He looked at her curiously. "Once you know, what then, Lady Grayle?"

"That's my business." Her lips closed sharply.

Mr. Parker Pyne hesitated a minute, then he said: "You will excuse me, Lady Grayle, but I have the impression that you are not being entirely frank with me."

"That's absurd. I've told you exactly what I want you to find out."

"Yes, but not the reason *why?*"

Their eyes met. Hers fell first.

"I should think the reason was self-evident," she said.

"No, because I am in doubt upon one point."

"What is that?"

"Do you want your suspicions proved right or wrong?"

"Really, Mr. Pyne!" The lady rose to her feet, quivering with indignation.

Mr. Parker Pyne nodded his head gently. "Yes, yes," he said. "But that doesn't answer my question, you know."

"Oh!" Words seemed to fail her. She swept out of the room.

Left alone, Mr. Parker Pyne became very thoughtful. He was so deep in his own thoughts that he started perceptibly when someone came in and sat down opposite him. It was Miss MacNaughton.

"Surely you're all back very soon," said Mr. Parker Pyne.

"The others aren't back. I said I had a headache and came back alone." She hesitated. "Where is Lady Grayle?"

"I should imagine lying down in her cabin."

"Oh, then that's all right. I don't want her to know I've come back."

"You didn't come back on her account, then?"

Miss MacNaughton shook her head. "No, I came back to see you."

Mr. Parker Pyne was surprised. He would have said offhand that Miss MacNaughton was eminently capable of looking after her troubles herself without seeking outside advice. It seemed that he was wrong.

"I've watched you since we all came on board. I think you're a person of wide experience and good judgment. And I want advice very badly."

"And yet—excuse me, Miss MacNaughton—but you're not the type that usually seeks advice. I should say that you were a person who was quite content to rely on her own judgment."

"Normally, yes. But I am in a very peculiar position." She hesitated a moment. "I do not usually talk about my cases. But in this instance I think it is necessary. Mr. Pyne, when I left England with Lady Grayle, she was a straightforward case. In plain language, there was nothing the matter with her. That's not quite true, perhaps. Too much leisure and too much money do produce a definite pathological condition. Having a few floors to scrub every day and five or six children to look after would have made Lady Grayle a perfectly healthy and a much happier woman."

Mr. Parker Pyne nodded.

"As a hospital nurse, one sees a lot of these nervous cases. Lady Grayle *enjoyed* her bad health. It was my part not to minimize her sufferings, to be as tactful as I could—and to enjoy the trip myself as much as possible."

"Very sensible," said Mr. Parker Pyne.

"But Mr. Pyne, things are not as they were. The suffering that Lady Grayle complains of now is real and not imagined."

"You mean?"

"I have come to suspect that Lady Grayle is being poisoned."

"Since when have you suspected this?"

"For the past three weeks."

"Do you suspect—any particular person?"

Her eyes dropped. For the first time her voice lacked sincerity. "No."

"I PUT IT to you, Miss MacNaughton, that you do suspect one particular person, and that that person is Sir George Grayle."

"Oh, no, no, I can't believe it of him! He is so pathetic, so child-like. He couldn't be a cold-blooded poisoner." Her voice had an anguished note in it.

"And yet you have noticed that whenever Sir George is absent his wife is better, and that her periods of illness correspond with his return."

She did not answer.

"What poison do you suspect? Arsenic?"

"Something of that kind. Arsenic or antimony."

"And what steps have you taken?"

"I have done my utmost to supervise what Lady Grayle eats and drinks."

Mr. Parker Pyne nodded. "Do you think Lady Grayle has any suspicion herself?" he asked casually.

"Oh, no, I'm sure she hasn't."

"There you are wrong," said Mr. Parker Pyne. "Lady Grayle *does* suspect."

Miss MacNaughton showed her astonishment.

"Lady Grayle is more capable of keeping a secret than you imagine," said Mr. Parker Pyne. "She is a woman who knows how to keep her own counsel very well."

"That surprises me very much," said Miss MacNaughton slowly.

"I should like to ask you one more question, Miss Mac-Naughton. Do you think Lady Grayle likes you?"

"I've never thought about it."

They were interrupted. Mohammed came in, his face beaming, his robes flowing behind him.

"Lady, she hear you come back; she ask for you. She say why you not come to her?"

Elsie MacNaughton rose hurriedly. Mr. Parker Pyne rose also.

"Would a consultation early tomorrow morning suit you?" he asked.

"Yes, that would be the best time. Lady Grayle sleeps late. In the meantime, I shall be very careful."

"I think Lady Grayle will be careful, too."

Miss MacNaughton disappeared.

Mr. Parker Pyne did not see Lady Grayle till just before dinner. She was sitting smoking a cigaret and burning what seemed to be a letter. She took no notice at all of him, by which he gathered that she was still offended.

After dinner he played bridge with Sir George, Pamela and Basil. Everyone seemed a little distrait and the bridge game broke up early.

It was some hours later when Mr. Parker Pyne was roused. It was Mohammed who came to him.

"Old lady, she very ill. Nurse, she very frightened. I try get doctor."

Mr. Parker Pyne hurried on some clothes. He arrived in the doorway of Lady Grayle's cabin at the same time as Basil West. Sir George and Pamela were inside. Elsie MacNaughton was working desperately over her patient. As Mr. Parker Pyne arrived, a final convulsion seized the poor lady. Her arched body writhed and stiffened. Then she fell back on her pillows.

Mr. Parker Pyne drew Pamela gently outside.

"How awful!" the girl was half sobbing. "How awful! Is she, is she—?"

"Dead? Yes, I am afraid it is all over."

He put her into Basil's keeping. Sir George came out of the cabin, looking dazed.

"I never thought she was really ill," he was muttering. "Never thought it for a moment."

Mr. Parker Pyne pushed past him and entered the cabin.

Elsie MacNaughton's face was white and drawn. "They have sent for a doctor?" she asked.

"Yes." Then he said: "Strychnine?"

"Yes. Those convulsions are unmistakable. Oh, I can't believe it!" She sank into a chair, weeping. He patted her shoulder.

Then an idea seemed to strike him. He left the cabin hurriedly and went to the lounge. There was a little scrap of paper left unburned in an ash tray. Just a few words were distinguishable:

"Now, that's interesting," said Mr. Parker Pyne.

MR. PARKER PYNE SAT in the room of a prominent Cairo official. "So that's the evidence," he said thoughtfully.

"Yes, pretty complete. Man must have been a damned fool."

"I shouldn't call Sir George a brainy man."

"All the same!" The other recapitulated: "Lady Grayle wants a cup of Bovril. The nurse makes it for her. Then she must have sherry in it. Sir George produces the sherry. Two hours later, Lady Grayle dies with unmistakable signs of strychnine poisoning. A packet of strychnine is found in Sir George's cabin and another packet actually in the pocket of his dinner jacket."

"Very thorough," said Mr. Parker Pyne. "Where did the strychnine come from, by the way?"

"There's a little doubt over that. The nurse had some—in case Lady Grayle's heart troubled her—but she's contradicted herself once or twice. First she said her supply was intact, and now she says it isn't."

"Very unlike her not to be sure," was Mr. Parker Pyne's comment.

"They were in it together, in my opinion. They've got a weakness for each other, those two."

"Possibly; but if Miss MacNaughton had been planning murder, she'd have done it a good deal better. She's an efficient young woman."

"Well, there it is. In my opinion, Sir George is in for it. He hasn't a dog's chance."

"Well, well," said Mr. Parker Pyne, "I must see what I can do."

He sought out the pretty niece.

Pamela was white and indignant. "Nunks never did such a thing—never—never—never!"

"Then who did?" said Mr. Parker Pyne placidly.

Pamela came nearer. "Do you know what I think? *She did it herself.* She's been frightfully queer lately. She used to imagine things."

"What things?"

"Queer things. Basil, for instance. She was always hinting that Basil was in love with her. And Basil and I are—we are—"

"I realize that," said Mr. Parker Pyne, smiling.

"All that about Basil was pure imagination. I think she had a down on poor little Nunks, and I think she made up that story and told it to you, and then put the strychnine in his cabin and in his pocket and poisoned herself. People have done things like that, haven't they?"

"They have," admitted Mr. Parker Pyne. "But I don't think that Lady Grayle did. She wasn't, if you'll allow me to say so, the type."

"But the delusions?"

"Yes, I'd like to ask Mr. West about that."

He found the young man in his room. Basil answered his questions readily enough.

"I don't want to sound fatuous, but she took a fancy to me. That's why I daren't let her know about me and Pamela. She'd have had Sir George fire me."

"You think Miss Grayle's theory a likely one?"

"Well, it's possible, I suppose." The young man was doubtful.

"But not good enough," said Mr. Parker Pyne quietly. "No, we must find something better." He became lost in meditation for a minute or two. "A confession would be best," he said briskly. He unscrewed his fountain pen and produced a sheet of paper. "Just write it out, will you?"

Basil West stared at him in amazement. "Me? What on earth do you mean?"

"My dear young man"—Mr. Parker Pyne sounded almost paternal—"I know all about it. How you made love to the good lady. How she had scruples. How you fell in love with the pretty, penniless niece. How you arranged your plot. Slow poisoning. It might pass for natural death from gastroenteritis—if not, it would be laid to Sir George's doing, since you were careful to let the attacks coincide with his presence.

"Then your discovery that the lady was suspicious and had talked to me about the matter. Quick action! You abstracted some strychnine from Miss MacNaughton's store. Planted some of it in Sir George's cabin, and some in his pocket and put sufficient into a cachet which you enclosed with a note to the lady, telling her it was a 'cachet of dreams.'

"A romantic idea. She'd take it as soon as the nurse had left her, and no one would know anything about it. But you made one mistake, my young man. It is useless asking a lady to burn letters. They never do. I've got all that pretty correspondence, including the one about the cachet."

Basil West had turned green. All his good looks had vanished. He looked like a trapped rat.

"Damn you!" he snarled. "So you know all about it. You damned interfering Nosey Parker."

Mr. Parker Pyne was saved from physical violence by the appearance of the witnesses he had thoughtfully arranged to have listening outside the half-closed door.

MR. PARKER PYNE WAS again discussing the case with his friend the high official.

"And I hadn't a shred of evidence! Only an almost indecipherable fragment, with *'Burn this!'* on it. I deduced the whole story and tried it on him. It worked. I'd stumbled on the truth. The letters did it. Lady Grayle had burned every scrap he wrote, but *he didn't know that.*

"She was really a very unusual woman. I was puzzled when she came to me. What she wanted was for me to tell her that her husband was poisoning her. In that case, she meant to go off with young West. But she wanted to act fairly. Curious character."

"That poor little girl is going to suffer," said the other.

"She'll get over it," said Mr. Parker Pyne callously. "She's young. I'm anxious that Sir George should get a little enjoyment before it's too late. He's been treated like a worm for ten years. Now, Elsie MacNaughton will be very kind to him."

He beamed. Then he sighed. "I am thinking of going incognito to Greece. I really *must* have a holiday!"

12. THE ORACLE AT DELPHI

Mrs. Willard J. Peters did not really care for Greece. And of Delphi she had, in her secret heart, no opinion at all.

Mrs. Peters' spiritual homes were Paris, London and the Riviera. She was a woman who enjoyed hotel life, but her idea of a hotel bedroom was a soft-pile carpet, a luxurious bed, a profusion of different arrangements of electric light, including a shaded bedside lamp, plenty of hot and cold water and a telephone beside the bed, by means of which you could order tea, meals, mineral waters, cocktails and speak to your friends.

In the hotel at Delphi there were none of these things. There was a marvelous view from the windows, the bed was clean and so was the whitewashed room. There was a chair, a washstand and a chest of drawers. Baths took place by arrangement and were occasionally disappointing as regarded hot water.

It would, she supposed, be nice to say that you had been to Delphi, and Mrs. Peters had tried hard to take an interest in Ancient Greece, but she found it difficult. Their statuary seemed so unfinished; so lacking in heads and arms and legs. Secretly, she much preferred the handsome marble angel complete with wings which was erected on the late Mr. Willard Peters' tomb.

But all these secret opinions she kept carefully to herself, for fear her son Willard should despise her. It was for Willard's sake that she was here, in this chilly and uncomfortable room, with a sulky maid and a disgusted chauffeur in the offing.

For Willard (until recently called Junior—a title which he hated) was Mrs. Peters' eighteen-year-old son, and she worshiped him to distraction. It was Willard who had this strange passion for bygone art. It was Willard, thin, pale, spectacled and dyspeptic, who had dragged his adoring mother on this tour through Greece.

They had been to Olympia, which Mrs. Peters thought a sad mess. She had enjoyed the Parthenon, but she considered Athens a hopeless city. And a visit to Corinth and Mycenae had been agony to both her and the chauffeur.

Delphi, Mrs. Peters thought unhappily, was the last straw. Absolutely nothing to do but walk along the road and look at the ruins. Willard spent long hours on his knees deciphering Greek inscriptions, saying, "Mother, just listen to this! Isn't it splendid?" And he would then read out something that seemed to Mrs. Peters the quintessence of dullness.

This morning Willard had started early to see some Byzantine mosaics. Mrs. Peters, feeling instinctively that Byzantine mosaics would leave her cold (in the literal as well as the spiritual sense), had excused herself.

"I understand, Mother," Willard had said. "You want to be alone just to sit in the theater or up in the Stadium and look down over it all and let it sink in."

"That's right, pet," said Mrs. Peters.

"I knew this place would get you," said Willard exultantly, and departed.

Now, with a sigh, Mrs. Peters prepared to rise and breakfast.

She came into the dining room to find it empty save for four people. A mother and daughter, dressed in what seemed to Mrs. Peters a most peculiar style (not recognizing the peplum as such), who were discoursing on the art of self-expression in dancing; a plump, middle-aged gentleman who had rescued a suitcase for her when she got off the train and whose name was Thompson; and a newcomer, a middle-aged gentleman with a bald head who had arrived on the preceding evening.

This personage was the last left in the breakfast room, and Mrs. Peters soon fell into conversation with him. She was a friendly woman and liked someone to talk to. Mr. Thompson had been distinctly discouraging in manner (British reserve, Mrs. Peters called it), and the mother and daughter had been very superior and highbrow, though the girl had got on rather well with Willard.

Mrs. Peters found the newcomer a very pleasant person. He was informative without being highbrow. He told her several interesting, friendly little details about the Greeks, which made her feel much more as though they were real people and not just tiresome history out of a book.

Mrs. Peters told her new friend all about Willard and what a clever boy he was, and how Culture might be said to be his middle name. There was something about this benevolent and bland personage which made him easy to talk to.

What he himself did and what his name was, Mrs. Peters did not learn. Beyond the fact that he had been traveling and that he was having a complete rest from business (what business?) he was not communicative about himself.

Altogether, the day passed more quickly than might have been anticipated. The mother and daughter and Mr. Thompson continued to be unsociable. They encountered the latter coming out of the museum, and he immediately turned in the opposite direction.

Mrs. Peters' new friend looked after him with a little frown.

"Now, I wonder who that fellow is!" he said.

Mrs. Peters supplied him with the other's name, but could do no more.

"Thompson—Thompson. No, I don't think I've met him before, and yet somehow or other his face seems familiar. But I can't place him."

In the afternoon Mrs. Peters enjoyed a quiet nap in a shady spot. The book she took with her to read was not the excellent one on Grecian Art recommended to her by her son, but was, on the contrary, entitled "The River Launch Mystery." It had four murders in it, three abductions, and a large and varied gang of dangerous criminals. Mrs. Peters found herself both invigorated and soothed by the perusal of it.

It was four o'clock when she returned to the hotel. Willard, she felt sure, would be back by this time. So far was she from any presentiment of evil that she almost forgot to open a note which the proprietor said had been left for her by a strange man during the afternoon.

It was an extremely dirty note. Idly she ripped it open. As she read the first few lines, her face blanched and she put out a hand to steady herself. The handwriting was foreign but the language employed was English.

Lady (it began):

This to hand to inform you that your son is being held captive by us in place of great security. No harm shall happen to honored young gentleman if you obey orders of yours truly. We demand for him ransom of ten thousand English pounds sterling. If you speak of this to hotel proprietor or police or any such person your son will be killed. This is given you to reflect. Tomorrow directions in way of paying money will be given. If not obeyed the honored young gentleman's ears will be cut off and sent you. And following day if still not obeyed he will be killed. Again this is not idle threat. Let the Kyria reflect and—above all—be silent.

Demetrius the Black Browed

It were idle to describe the poor lady's state of mind. Preposterous and childishly worded as the demand was, it yet brought home to her a grim atmosphere of peril. Willard, her boy, her pet, her delicate, serious Willard.

She would go at once to the police; she would rouse the neighborhood. But perhaps, if she did . . . She shivered.

Then, rousing herself, she went out of her room in search of the hotel proprietor—the sole person in the hotel who could speak English.

"It is getting late," she said. "My son has not returned yet."

The pleasant little man beamed at her. "True. Monsieur dismissed the mules. He wished to return on foot. He should have been here by now, but doubtless he has lingered on the way." He smiled happily.

"Tell me," said Mrs. Peters abruptly, "have you any bad characters in the neighborhood?"

Bad characters was a term not embraced by the little man's knowledge of English. Mrs. Peters made her meaning plainer. She received in reply an assurance that all around Delphi were very good, very quiet people—all well disposed toward foreigners.

Words trembled on her lips, but she forced them back. That sinister threat tied her tongue. It might be the merest bluff. But suppose it wasn't? A friend of hers in America had had a child kidnaped, and on her informing the police, the child had been killed. Such things did happen.

She was nearly frantic. What was she to do? Ten thousand pounds—what was that?—between forty or fifty thousand dollars! What was that to her in comparison with Willard's safety? But how could she obtain such a sum? There were endless difficulties just now as regarded money and the drawing of cash. A letter of credit for a few hundred pounds was all she had with her.

Would the bandits understand this? Would they be reasonable? Would they *wait*?

When her maid came to her, she dismissed the girl fiercely. A bell sounded for dinner, and the poor lady was driven to the dining room. She ate mechanically. She saw no one. The room might have been empty as far as she was concerned.

With the arrival of fruit, a note was placed before her. She winced, but the handwriting was entirely different from that which she had feared to see—a neat, clerkly English hand. She opened it without much interest, but she found its contents intriguing:

At Delphi you can no longer consult the Oracle (so it ran), but you *can* consult Mr. Parker Pyne.

Below that was a cutting of an advertisement pinned to the paper, and at the bottom of the sheet a passport photograph was attached. It was the photograph of her bald-headed friend of the morning.

Mrs. Peters read the printed cutting twice.

Are you happy? If not, consult Mr. Parker Pyne.

Happy? Happy? Had anyone ever been so *un*-happy? It was like an answer to prayer.

Hastily she scribbled on a loose sheet of paper she happened to have in her bag:

Please help me. Will you meet me outside the hotel in ten minutes?

She enclosed it in an envelope and directed the waiter to take it to the gentleman at the table by the window. Ten minutes later, enveloped in a fur coat, for the night was chilly, Mrs. Peters went out of the hotel and strolled slowly along the road to the ruins. Mr. Parker Pyne was waiting for her.

"It's just the mercy of heaven you're here," said Mrs. Peters breathlessly. "But how did you guess the terrible trouble I'm in? That's what I want to know."

"The human countenance, my dear madam," said Mr. Parker Pyne gently. "I knew at once that *something* had happened, but what it is I am waiting for you to tell me."

Out it came in a flood. She handed him the letter, which he read by the light of his pocket torch.

"H'm," he said. "A remarkable document. A most remarkable document. It has certain points—"

But Mrs. Peters was in no mood to listen to a discussion of the finer points of the letter. What was she to do about Willard? Her own dear, delicate Willard.

Mr. Parker Pyne was soothing. He painted an attractive picture of Greek bandit life. They would be especially careful of their captive, since he represented a potential gold mine. Gradually he calmed her down.

"But what am I to *do?*" wailed Mrs. Peters.

"Wait till tomorrow," said Mr. Parker Pyne. "That is, unless you prefer to go straight to the police."

Mrs. Peters interrupted him with a shriek of terror. Her darling Willard would be murdered out of hand!

"You think I'll get Willard back safe and sound?"

"There is no doubt of that," said Mr. Parker Pyne soothingly. "The only question is whether you can get him back without paying ten thousand pounds."

"All I want is my boy."

"Yes, yes," said Mr. Parker Pyne soothingly. "Who brought the letter, by the way?"

"A man the landlord didn't know. A stranger."

"Ah! There are possibilities there. The man who brings the letter tomorrow might be followed. What are you telling the people at the hotel about your son's absence?"

"I haven't thought."

"I wonder, now." Mr. Parker Pyne reflected. "I think you might quite naturally express alarm and concern at his absence. A search party could be sent out."

"You don't think these fiends—?" She choked.

"No, no. So long as there is no word of the kidnaping or the ransom, they cannot turn nasty. After all, you can't be expected to take your son's disappearance with no fuss at all."

"Can I leave it all to you?"

"That is my business," said Mr. Parker Pyne.

They started back toward the hotel again but almost ran into a burly figure.

"Who was that?" asked Mr. Parker Pyne sharply.

"I think it was Mr. Thompson."

"Oh!" said Mr. Parker Pyne thoughtfully. "Thompson, was it? Thompson—h'm."

MRS. PETERS FELT AS she went to bed that Mr. Parker Pyne's idea about the letter was a good one. Whoever brought it *must* be in touch with the bandits. She felt consoled, and fell asleep much sooner than she could ever have believed possible.

When she was dressing on the following morning she suddenly noticed something lying on the floor by the window. She picked it up—and her heart missed a beat. The same dirty, cheap envelope; the same hated characters. She tore it open.

> Good morning, lady. Have you made reflections? Your son is well and unharmed—so far. But we must have the money. It may not be easy for you to get this sum, but it has been told us that you have with you a necklace of diamonds. Very fine stones. We will be satisfied with that, instead. Listen, this is what you must do. You, or anyone you choose to send must take this necklace and bring it to the Stadium. From there go up to where there is a tree by a big rock. Eyes will watch and see that only one person comes. Then your son will be exchanged for necklace. The time must be to-morrow six o'clock in morning just after sunrise. If you put police on us afterward we shoot your son as your car drives to station.
>
> This is our last word, lady. If no necklace tomorrow morning your son's ears sent you. Next day he die.
>
> With salutations, lady,
> Demetrius

Mrs. Peters hurried to find Mr. Parker Pyne. He read the letter attentively.

"Is this true," he asked, "about a diamond necklace?"

"Absolutely. A hundred thousand dollars, my husband paid for it."

"Our well-informed thieves," murmured Mr. Parker Pyne.

"What's that you say?"

"I was just considering certain aspects of the affair."

"My word, Mr. Pyne, we haven't got time for aspects. I've got to get my boy back."

"But you are a woman of spirit, Mrs. Peters. Do you enjoy being bullied and cheated out of ten thousand pounds? Do you enjoy giving up your diamonds meekly to a set of ruffians?"

"Well, of course, if you put it like that!" The woman of spirit in Mrs. Peters wrestled with the mother. "How I'd like to get even with them—the cowardly brutes! The very minute I get my boy back, Mr. Pyne, I shall set the whole police of the neighborhood on them. And if necessary I shall hire an armored car to take Willard and myself to the railway station!" Mrs. Peters was flushed and vindictive.

"Ye-es," said Mr. Parker Pyne. "You see, my dear madam, I'm afraid they will be prepared for that move on your part. They know that once Willard is restored to you nothing will keep you from setting the whole neighborhood on the alert. Which leads one to suppose that they have prepared for that move."

"Well, what do you want to do?"

Mr. Parker Pyne smiled. "I want to try a little plan of my own." He looked round the dining room. It was empty and the doors at both ends were closed. "Mrs. Peters, there is a man I know in Athens—a jeweler. He specializes in good artificial diamonds—first-class stuff." His voice dropped to a whisper. "I'll get him by telephone. He can get here this afternoon, bringing a good selection of stones with him."

"You mean?"

"He'll extract the real diamonds and replace them with paste replicas."

"WHY, IF THAT isn't the cutest thing I've ever heard of!" Mrs. Peters gazed at him with admiration.

"Sh! Not so loud. Will you do something for me?"

"Surely."

"See that nobody comes within earshot of the telephone."

Mrs. Peters nodded.

The telephone was in the manager's office. He vacated it obligingly, after having helped Mr. Parker Pyne to obtain the number. When he emerged, he found Mrs. Peters outside.

"I'm just waiting for Mr. Parker Pyne," she said. "We're going for a walk."

"Oh, yes, Madam."

Mr. Thompson was also in the hall. He came toward them and engaged the manager in conversation. Were there any villas to be let in Delphi? No? But surely there was one above the hotel.

"That belongs to a Greek gentleman, Monsieur. He does not let it."

"And there are no other villas?"

"There is one belonging to an American lady. That is the other side of the village. It is shut up now. And there is one belonging to an English gentleman, an artist—that is on the cliff edge looking down to Itéa."

Mrs. Peters broke in. Nature had given her a loud voice and she purposely made it louder. "Why," she said, "I'd just adore to have a villa here! So unspoiled and natural. I'm simply crazy about the place, aren't you, Mr. Thompson? But of course you must be if you want a villa. Is it your first visit here? You don't say so."

She ran on determinedly till Mr. Parker Pyne emerged from the office. He gave her just the faintest smile of approval.

Mr. Thompson walked slowly down the steps and out into the road, where he joined the highbrow mother and daughter, who seemed to be feeling the wind cold on their exposed arms.

All went well. The jeweler arrived just before dinner with a car full of other tourists. Mrs. Peters took her necklace to his room. He grunted approval. Then he spoke in French.

"*Madame peut être tranquille. Je reussirai.*" He extracted some tools from his little bag and began work.

At eleven o'clock, Mr. Parker Pyne tapped on Mrs. Peters' door. "Here you are!"

He handed her a little chamois bag. She glanced inside.

"My diamonds!"

"Hush. Here is the necklace with the paste replacing the diamonds. Pretty good, don't you think?"

"Simply wonderful."

"Aristopoulos is a clever fellow."

"You don't think they'll suspect?"

"How should they? They know you have the necklace with you. You hand it over. How can they suspect the trick?"

"Well, I think it's wonderful," Mrs. Peters reiterated, handing the necklace back to him. "Will you take it to them? Or is that asking too much of you?"

"Certainly I will take it. Just give me the letter, so that I have the directions clear. Thank you. Now, good night and *bon courage*. Your boy will be with you tomorrow for breakfast."

"Oh, if only that's true!"

"Now, don't worry. Leave everything in my hands."

Mrs. Peters did not spend a good night. When she slept, she had terrible dreams. Dreams where armed bandits in armored cars fired off a fusillade at Willard, who was running down the mountain in his pajamas. She was thankful to wake. At last came the first glimmer of dawn. Mrs. Peters got up and dressed. She sat— waiting.

At seven o'clock there came a tap on her door. Her throat was so dry she could hardly speak.

"Come in," she said.

The door opened and Mr. Thompson entered. She stared at him. Words failed her. She had a sinister presentiment of disaster. And yet his voice when he spoke was completely natural and matter-of-fact. It was a rich, bland voice.

"Good morning, Mrs. Peters," he said.

"How dare you, sir! How dare you—"

"You must excuse my unconventional visit at so early an hour," said Mr. Thompson. "But you see, I have a matter of business to transact."

Mrs. Peters leaned forward with accusing eyes. "So it was you who kidnaped my boy! It wasn't bandits at all!"

"It certainly wasn't bandits. Most unconvincingly done, that part of it, I thought. Inartistic, to say the least of it."

Mrs. Peters was a woman of a single idea. "Where's my boy?" she demanded, with the eyes of an angry tigress.

"As a matter of fact," said Mr. Thompson, "he's just outside the door."

"Willard!"

The door was flung open. Willard, sallow and spectacled and distinctly unshaven, was clasped to his mother's heart. Mr. Thompson stood looking benignly on.

"All the same," said Mrs. Peters, suddenly recovering herself and turning on him, "I'll have the law on you for this. Yes, I will."

"You've got it all wrong, Mother," said Willard. "This gentleman rescued me."

"Where were you?"

"In a house on the cliff point. Just a mile from here."

"And allow me, Mrs. Peters," said Mr. Thompson, "to restore your property."

He handed her a small packet loosely wrapped in tissue paper. The paper fell away and revealed the diamond necklace.

"You need not treasure that other little bag of stones, Mrs. Peters," said Mr. Thompson, smiling. "The real stones are still in the necklace. The chamois bag contains some excellent imitation stones. As your friend said, Aristopoulos is quite a genius."

"I just don't understand a word of all this," said Mrs. Peters faintly.

"You must look at the case from my point of view," said Mr. Thompson. "My attention was caught by the use of a certain name. I took the liberty of following you and your fat friend out of doors and I listened—I admit it frankly—to your exceedingly interesting conversation. I found it remarkably suggestive, so much so that I took the manager into my confidence. He took a note of the number to which your plausible friend telephoned, and he also arranged that a waiter should listen to your conversation in the dining room this morning.

"The whole scheme worked out very clearly. You were being made the victim of a couple of clever jewel thieves. They know all about your diamond necklace; they follow you here; they kidnap your son, and write the rather comic 'bandit' letter, and they arrange that you shall confide in the chief instigator of the plot.

"After that, all is simple. The good gentleman hands you a bag of imitation diamonds and—clears out with his pal. This morning, when your son did not appear, you would be frantic. The absence of your friend would lead you to believe that he had been kidnaped, too. I gather that they had arranged for someone to go to the villa to-morrow. That person would have discovered your son, and by the time you and he had put your heads together you might have got an inkling of the plot. But by that time the villains would have got an excellent start."

"And now?"

"Oh, now they are safely under lock and key. I arranged for that."

"The villain," said Mrs. Peters, wrathfully remembering her own trustful confidences. "The oily, plausible villain."

"Not at all a nice fellow," agreed Mr. Thompson.

"It beats me how you got on to it," said Willard admiringly. "Pretty smart of you."

The other shook his head deprecatingly. "No, no," he said. "When you are traveling incognito and hear your own name being taken in vain—"

Mrs. Peters stared at him. "Who are you?" she demanded abruptly.

"I am Mr. Parker Pyne," explained that gentleman.

PART II HARLEY QUIN

PRESENTING MR. HARLEY QUIN

The Mr. Quin stories were not written as a series. They were written one at a time at rare intervals. Mr. Quin, I consider, is an epicure's taste.

A set of Dresden figures on my mother's mantelpiece fascinated me as a child and afterward. They represented the Italian commedia dell'arte: Harlequin, Columbine, Pierrot, Pierrette, Punchinello, and Punchinella. As a girl I wrote a series of poems about them, and I rather think that one of the poems, "Harlequin's Song," was my first appearance in print. It was in the *Poetry Review*, and I got a guinea for it!

After I turned from poetry and ghost stories to crime, Harlequin finally reappeared; a figure invisible except when he chose, not quite human, yet concerned with the affairs of human beings and particularly of lovers. He is also the advocate for the dead.

Though each story about him is quite separate, the collection, written over a considerable period of years, outlines in the end the story of Harlequin himself.

With Mr. Quin there has been created little Mr. Satterthwaite, Mr. Quin's friend in this mortal world: Mr. Satterthwaite, the gossip, the looker-on at life, the little man who without ever touching depths of joy and sorrow himself, recognizes drama when he sees it, and is conscious that he has a part to play.

Of the Mr. Quin stories, my favorites are: "World's End," "The Man from the Sea," and "Harlequin's Lane."

—From the introduction to the
1953 Penguin U.K. edition
of *The Mysterious Mr. Quin*

1. THE COMING OF MR. QUIN

It was New Year's Eve.

The elder members of the house party at Royston $ assembled in the big hall.

Mr. Satterthwaite was glad that the young people $ gone to bed. He was not fond of young people in he$ He thought them uninteresting and crude. They lacked $ tlety and as life went he had become increasingly fon$ subtleties.

Mr. Satterthwaite was sixty-two—a little bent, drie$ man with a peering face oddly elflike, and an intense $ inordinate interest in other people's lives. All his life, s$ speak, he had sat in the front row of the stalls watc$ various dramas of human nature unfold before him. His $ had always been that of the onlooker. Only now, with $ age holding him in its clutch, he found himself increasing critical of the drama submitted to him. He demanded $ something a little out of the common.

There was no doubt that he had a flair for these thi$ He knew instinctively when the elements of drama we$ hand. Like a war horse, he sniffed the scent. Since hi$ rival at Royston this afternoon, that strange inner sens$ his had stirred and bid him be ready. Something interes$ was happening or going to happen.

The house party was not a large one. There was $ Evesham, their genial good-humored host, and his se$ political wife who had been before her marriage $ Laura Keene. There was Sir Richard Conway, soldier, traveler and sportsman. There were six or seven young people whose names Mr. Satterthwaite had not grasped, and there were the Portals.

It was the Portals who interested Mr. Satterthwaite.

He had never met Alec Portal before but he knew all about him, had known his father and his grandfather. Alec Portal ran pretty true to type. He was a man of close on forty, fair haired, and blue eyed like all the Portals, fond of sport, good at games, devoid of imagination. Nothing unusual about Alec Portal. The usual good, sound English stock.

But his wife was different. She was, Mr. Satterthwaite knew, an Australian. Portal had been out in Australia two years ago, had met her out there and had married her and brought her home. She had never been to England previous to her marriage. All the same, she wasn't at all like any other Australian woman Mr. Satterthwaite had met.

He observed her now covertly. Interesting woman—very. So still, and yet so—alive. Alive! That was just it! Not exactly beautiful—no, you wouldn't call her beautiful, but there was a kind of calamitous magic about her that you couldn't miss—that no man could miss. The masculine side of Mr. Satterthwaite spoke there, but the feminine side (for Mr. Satterthwaite had a large share of femininity), was equally interested in another question. *Why did Mrs. Portal dye her hair?*

No other man would probably have known that she dyed her hair, but Mr. Satterthwaite knew. He knew all those things. And it puzzled him. Many dark women dye their hair blonde; he had never before come across a fair woman who dyed her hair black.

Everything about her intrigued him. In a queer intuitive way, he felt certain that she was either very happy or very unhappy—but he didn't know which, and it annoyed him not to know. Furthermore there was the curious effect she had upon her husband.

"He adores her," said Mr. Satterthwaite to himself, "but sometimes he's—yes, afraid of her! That's very interesting. That's uncommonly interesting."

Portal drank too much. That was certain. And he had a curious way of watching his wife when she wasn't looking.

"Nerves," said Mr. Satterthwaite. "The fellow's all nerves. She knows it too, but she won't do anything about it."

He felt very curious about the pair of them. Something was going on that he couldn't fathom.

He was roused from his meditations on the subject by the solemn chiming of a big clock.

"Twelve o'clock," said Evesham. "New Year's Day. Happy New Year—everybody. As a matter of fact that clock's five minutes fast. I don't know why the children wouldn't wait up and see the New Year in."

"I don't suppose for a minute they've really gone to bed," said his wife placidly. "They're probably putting hair-brushes or something in our beds. That sort of thing does so amuse them. I can't think why. We should never have been allowed to do such a thing in my young days."

"*Autre temps, autre mœurs*," said Conway, smiling.

He was a tall soldierly-looking man. Both he and Evesham were much of the same type—honest, upright, kindly men with no great pretensions to brains.

"In my young days we all joined hands in a circle and sang 'Auld Lang Syne,'" continued Lady Laura. "'Should Auld acquaintance be forgot'—so touching, I always think the words are."

Evesham moved uneasily.

"Oh! drop it, Laura," he muttered. *"Not here!"*

He strode across the wide hall where they were sitting, and switched on an extra light.

"Very stupid of me," said Lady Laura, *sotta voce*. "Reminds him of poor Mr. Capel, of course. My Dear, is the fire too hot for you?"

Eleanor Portal had made a brusque movement.

"Thank you. I'll move my chair back a little."

What a lovely voice she had—one of those low, murmuring, echoing voices that stay in your memory, thought Mr. Satterthwaite. Her face was in shadow now. What a pity.

From her place in the shadow she spoke again.

"Mr.—Capel?"

"Yes. The man who originally owned this house. He shot himself, you know. Oh! very well, Tom dear, I won't speak of it unless you like. It was a great shock for Tom, of course, because he was here when it happened. So were you, weren't you, Sir Richard?"

"Yes, Lady Laura."

An old grandfather clock in the corner groaned, wheezed, snorted asthmatically, and then struck twelve.

"Happy New Year," grunted Evesham prefunctorily.

Lady Laura wound up her knitting with some deliberation.

"Well, we've seen the New Year in," she observed, and added, looking toward Mrs. Portal, "What do you think, my dear?"

Eleanor Portal rose quickly to her feet.

"Bed, by all means," she said lightly.

"She's very pale," thought Mr. Satterthwaite, as he too rose, and began busying himself with candlesticks. "She's not usually as pale as that."

He lighted her candle and handed it to her with a funny little old fashioned bow. She took it from him with a word of acknowledgment, and went slowly up the stairs.

Suddenly a very odd impulse swept over Mr. Satterthwaite. He wanted to go after her—to reassure her—he had the strangest feeling that she was in danger of some kind.

THE IMPULSE DIED down, and he felt ashamed. *He* was getting nervy too.

She hadn't looked at her husband as she went up the stairs, but now she turned her head over her shoulder and gave him a long searching glance which had a queer intensity in it. It affected Mr. Satterthwaite very oddly.

He found himself saying good night to his hostess in quite a flustered manner.

"I'm sure I hope it *will* be a happy New Year," Lady Laura was saying. "But the political situation seems to me to be fraught with grave uncertainty."

"I'm sure it is," said Mr. Satterthwaite earnestly. "I'm sure it is."

"I only hope," continued Lady Laura, without the least change of manner, "that it will be a dark man who first crosses the threshold. You know that superstition, I suppose, Mr. Satterthwaite? No? You surprise me. To bring luck to the house it must be a dark man who first steps over the door step on New Year's Day. Dear me, I hope I shan't find anything *very* unpleasant in my bed. I never trust the children. They have such very high spirits."

Shaking her head in sad foreboding, Lady Laura moved majestically up the staircase.

With the departure of the women, chairs were pulled in closer round the blazing logs on the big open hearth.

"Say when," said Evesham, hospitably, as he held up the whiskey decanter.

When everybody had said when, the talk reverted to the subject which had been tabooed before.

"You knew Derek Capel, didn't you, Satterthwaite?" asked Conway.

"Slightly—yes."

"And you, Portal?"

"No, I never met him."

So fiercely and defensively did he say it that Mr. Satterthwaite looked up in surprise.

"I always hate it when Laura brings up the subject," said Evesham slowly. "After the tragedy, you know, this place was sold to a big manufacturer fellow. He cleared out after a year—didn't suit him or something. A lot of tommyrot was talked about the place being haunted of course, and it gave the house a bad name. Then, when Laura got me to stand for West Kidleby, of course it meant living up in these parts, and it wasn't so easy to find a suitable house. Royston was going cheap, and—well, in the end I bought it. Ghosts are all tommy-rot, but all the same one doesn't exactly care to be reminded that you're living in a house where one of your own friends shot himself. Poor old Derek—we shall never know why he did it."

"He won't be the first or the last fellow who's shot himself without being able to give a reason," said Alec Portal heavily.

He rose and poured himself out another drink, splashing the whiskey in with a liberal hand.

"There's something very wrong with him," said Mr. Satterthwaite, to himself. "Very wrong indeed. I wish I knew what it was all about."

"Gad!" said Conway. "Listen to the wind. It's a wild night."

"A good night for ghosts to walk," said Portal with a reckless laugh. "All the devils in Hell are abroad tonight."

"According to Lady Laura, even the blackest of them would bring us luck," observed Conway, with a laugh. "Hark to that!"

The wind rose in another terrific wail, and as it died away there came three loud knocks on the big nailed doorway.

Everyone started.

"Who on earth can that be at this time of night?" cried Evesham.

They stared at each other.

"I will open it," said Evesham. "The servants have gone to bed."

He strode across to the door, fumbled a little over the heavy bars, and finally flung it open. An icy blast of wind came sweeping into the hall.

Framed in the doorway stood a man's figure, tall and slender. To Mr. Satterthwaite, watching, he appeared, by some curious effect of the stained glass above the door, to be dressed in every color of the rainbow. Then, as he stepped forward, he showed himself to be a thin dark man dressed in motoring clothes.

"I must really apologize for this intrusion," said the stranger, in a pleasant level voice. "But my car broke down. Nothing much, my chauffeur is putting it to rights, but it will take half an hour or so, and it is so confoundedly cold outside—"

He broke off, and Evesham took up the thread quickly.

"I should think it was. Come in and have a drink. We can't give you any assistance about the car, can we?"

"No, thanks. My man knows what to do. By the way, my name is Quin—Harley Quin."

"Sit down, Mr. Quin," said Evesham. "Sir Richard Conway, Mr. Satterthwaite, Mr. Portal. My name is Evesham."

Mr. Quin acknowledged the introductions, and dropped into the chair that Evesham had hospitably pulled forward. As he sat, some effect of the firelight threw a bar of shadow across his face which gave almost the impression of a mask.

Evesham threw a couple more logs on the fire.

"A drink?"

"Thanks."

Evesham brought it to him and asked as he did so:

"So you know this part of the world well, Mr. Quin?"

"I passed through it some years ago."

"Really?"

"Yes. This house belonged then to a man called Capel."

"Ah! yes," said Evesham. "Poor Derek Capel. You knew him?"

"Yes, I knew him."

Evesham's manner underwent a faint change, almost imperceptible to one who had not studied the English character. Before, it had contained a subtle reserve; now this was laid aside. Mr. Quin had known Derek Capel. He was the friend of a friend, and as such, was vouched for and fully accredited.

"Astounding affair, that," he said confidentially. "We were just talking about it. I can tell you, it went against the grain, buying this place. If there had been anything else suitable, but there wasn't. You see, I was in the house the night he shot himself—so was Conway—and upon my word, I've always expected his ghost to walk."

"A very inexplicable business," said Mr. Quin, slowly and deliberately, and he paused with the air of an actor who has just spoken an important cue.

"You may well say inexplicable," burst in Conway. "The thing's a black mystery—always will be."

"I wonder," said Mr. Quin, noncommittally. "Yes, Sir Richard, you were saying?"

"Astounding—that's what it was. Here's a man in the prime of life, gay, light hearted, without a care in the world. Five or six old pals staying with him. Top of his spirits at dinner, full of plans for the future. And from the dinner table he goes straight upstairs to his room, takes a revolver from a drawer and shoots himself. Why? Nobody ever knew. Nobody ever will know."

"Isn't that rather a sweeping statement, Sir Richard?" asked Mr. Quin smiling.

Conway stared at him.

"What d'you mean? I don't understand."

"A problem is not necessarily unsolvable because it has remained unsolved."

"Oh! Come, man, if nothing came out at the time, it's not likely to come out now—ten years afterward?"

Mr. Quin shook his head gently.

"I disagree with you. The evidence of history is against you. The contemporary historian never writes such a true history as the historian of a later generation. It is a question of getting the true perspective, of seeing things in proportion. If you like to call it so, it is, like everything else, a question of relativity."

Alec Portal leaned forward, his face twitching painfully.

"You are right, Mr. Quin," he cried, "you are right. Time does not dispose of a question—it only presents it anew in a different guise."

Evesham was smiling tolerantly.

"Then you mean to say, Mr. Quin, that if we were to hold, let us say, a Court of Inquiry, tonight, into the circumstances of Derek Capel's death, we are as likely to arrive at the truth as we should have been at the time?"

"*More* likely, Mr. Evesham. The personal equation has largely dropped out, and you will remember facts as facts without seeking to put your own interpretation upon them."

Evesham frowned doubtfully.

"One must have a starting point, of course," said Mr. Quin in his quiet level voice. "A starting point is usually a theory. One of you must have a theory, I am sure. How about you, Sir Richard?"

Conway frowned thoughtfully.

"Well, of course," he said apologetically, "we thought—naturally we all thought—that there must be a woman in it somewhere. It's usually either that or money, isn't it? And it certainly wasn't money. No trouble of that description. So—what else could it have been?"

Mr. Satterthwaite started. He had leaned forward to contribute a small remark of his own and, in the act of doing so, he had caught sight of a woman's figure crouched against the balustrade of the gallery above. She was huddled down against it, invisible from everywhere but where he himself sat, and she was evidently listening with strained attention to what was going on below. So immovable was she that he hardly believed the evidence of his own eyes.

But he recognized the pattern of the dress easily enough—an old-world brocade. It was Eleanor Portal.

And suddenly all the events of the night seemed to fall into pattern—Mr. Quin's arrival, no fortuitous chance, but the appearing of an actor when his cue was given. There was a drama being played in the big hall at Royston tonight—a drama none the less real in that one of the actors was dead. Oh! yes, Derek Capel had a part in the play. Mr. Satterthwaite was sure of that.

And, again suddenly, a new illumination came to him. This was Mr. Quin's doing. It was he who was staging the play—was giving the actors their cues. He was at the heart of the mystery pulling the strings, making the puppets work. He knew everything, even to the presence of the woman crouched against the woodwork upstairs. Yes, he knew.

Sitting well back in his chair, secure in his rôle of audience, Mr. Satterthwaite watched the drama unfold before his eyes. Quietly and naturally, Mr. Quin was pulling the strings, setting his puppets in motion.

"A woman—yes," he murmured thoughtfully. "There was no mention of any woman at dinner?"

"Why, of course," cried Evesham. "He announced his engagement. That's just what made it seem so absolutely mad. Very bucked about it he was. Said it wasn't to be announced just yet—but gave us the hint that he was in the running for the Benedick stakes."

"Of course we all guessed who the lady was," said Conway. "Marjorie Dilke. Nice girl."

It seemed to be Mr. Quin's turn to speak, but he did not do so, and something about his silence seemed oddly provocative. It was as though he challenged the last statement. It had the effect of putting Conway in a defensive position.

"Who else could it have been? Eh, Evesham?"

"I don't know," said Tom Evesham slowly. "What did he say exactly now? Something about being in the running for the Benedick stakes—that he couldn't tell us the lady's name till he had her permission—it wasn't to be announced yet. He said, I remember, that he was a damned lucky fellow. That he wanted his two old friends to know that by that time next year he'd be a happy married man. Of course, we assumed it was Marjorie. They were great friends and he'd been about with her a lot."

"The only thing—" began Conway and stopped.

"What were you going to say, Dick?"

"Well, I mean, it was odd in a way, if it was Marjorie, that the engagement shouldn't be announced at once. I mean, why the secrecy? Sounds more as though it were a married woman—you know someone whose husband had just died, or who was divorcing him."

"That's true," said Evesham. "If that were the case, of course the engagement couldn't be announced at once. And you know, thinking back about it, I don't believe he had been seeing much of Marjorie. All that was the year before. I remember thinking things seemed to have cooled off between them."

"Curious," said Mr. Quin.

"Yes—looked almost as though someone had come between them."

"Another woman," said Conway thoughtfully.

"By jove," said Evesham. "You know, there was something almost indecently hilarious about old Derek that night. He looked almost drunk with happiness. And yet—I can't quite explain what I mean—but he looked oddly defiant too."

"Like a man defying Fate," said Alec Portal heavily.

Was it of Derek Capel he was speaking—or was it of himself?

Mr. Satterthwaite, looking at him, inclined to the latter view. Yes, that was what Alec Portal represented—a man defying Fate.

His imagination, muddled by drink, responded suddenly to that note in the story which recalled his own secret preoccupation.

Mr. Satterthwaite looked up. She was still there. Watching, listening—still motionless, frozen—like a dead woman.

"Perfectly true," said Conway. "Capel *was* excited—curiously so. I'd describe him as a man who has staked heavily and won against well-nigh overwhelming odds."

"Getting up courage, perhaps, for what he's made up his mind to do?" suggested Portal.

And as though moved by an association of ideas, he got up and helped himself to another drink.

"Not a bit of it," said Evesham sharply. "I'd almost swear nothing of that kind was in his mind. Conway's right. A successful gambler who has brought off a long shot and can hardly believe in his own good fortune. That was the attitude."

Conway gave a gesture of discouragement.

"And yet," he said. "Ten minutes later—"

They sat in silence. Evesham brought his hand down with a bang on the table.

"Something must have happened in that ten minutes," he cried. "It must! But what? Let's go over it carefully. We were all talking. In the middle of it Capel got up suddenly and left the room—"

"Why?" said Mr. Quin.

The interruption seemed to disconcert Evesham.

"I beg your pardon?"

"I only said: Why?" said Mr. Quin.

Evesham frowned in an effort of memory.

"It didn't seem vital—at the time. Oh! of course—the post. Don't you remember that jangling bell, and how excited we were? We'd been snowed up for three days, remember. Biggest snowstorm for years and years. All the roads were impassable. No newspapers, no letters. Capel went out to see if something had come through at last, and got a great pile of things, newspapers and letters. He opened the paper to see if there was any news, and then went upstairs with his letters. Three minutes afterward, we heard a shot. Inexplicable—absolutely inexplicable."

"That's not inexplicable," said Portal. "Of course the fellow got some unexpected news in a letter. Obvious, I should have said."

"Oh! Don't think we missed anything so obvious as that. It was one of the Coroner's first questions. *But Capel never opened one of his letters.* The whole pile lay unopened on his dressing table."

Portal looked crestfallen.

"You're sure he didn't open just one of them? He might have destroyed it after reading it?"

"No, I'm quite positive. Of course, that would have been the natural solution. No, every one of the letters was unopened. Nothing burned—nothing torn up. There was no fire in the room."

Portal shook his head.

"Extraordinary."

"It was a ghastly business altogether," said Evesham in a low voice. "Conway and I went up when we heard the shot, and found him. It gave me a shock, I can tell you."

"Nothing to be done but telephone for the police, I suppose?" said Mr. Quin.

"Royston wasn't on the telephone then. I had it put in when I bought the place. No, luckily enough, the local constable happened to be in the kitchen at the time. One of the dogs—you remember poor old Rover, Conway?—had strayed the day before. A passing carter had found it half buried in a snowdrift and had taken it to the police station. They recognized it as Capel's, and a dog he was particularly fond of, and the constable came up with it. He'd just arrived a minute before the shot was fired. It saved us some trouble."

"Gad, that was a snowstorm," said Conway reminiscently. "About this time of year, wasn't it? Early January."

"February, I think. Let me see, we went abroad soon afterward."

"I'm pretty sure it was January. My hunter Ned—you remember Ned?—lamed himself the end of January. That was just after this business."

"It must have been quite the end of January then. Funny how difficult it is to recall dates after a lapse of years."

"One of the most difficult things in the world," said Mr. Quin, conversationally. "Unless you can find a landmark in some big public event—an assassination of a crowned head, or a big murder trial."

"Why, of course," cried Conway, "it was just before the Appleton case."

"Just after, wasn't it?"

"No, no, don't you remember? Capel knew the Appletons—he'd stayed with the old man the previous Spring—just a week before he died. He was talking of him one night—what an old curmudgeon he was, and how awful it must have been for a young and beautiful woman like Mrs. Appleton to be tied to him. There was no suspicion then that she had done away with him."

"By jove, you're right. I remember reading the paragraph in the paper saying an exhumation order had been granted. It would have been that same day—I remember only seeing it with half my mind, you know, the other half wondering about poor old Derek lying dead upstairs."

"A common, but very curious phenomenon, that," observed Mr. Quin. "In moments of great stress, the mind focuses itself upon some quite unimportant matter which is remembered long afterward with the utmost fidelity, driven in, as it were, by the mental stress of the moment. It may be some quite irrelevant detail, like the pattern of a wallpaper, but it will never be forgotten."

"Rather extraordinary, your saying that, Mr. Quin," said Conway. "just as you were speaking, I suddenly felt myself back in Derek Capel's room—with Derek lying dead on the floor. I saw as plainly as possible the big tree outside the window, and the shadow it threw upon the snow outside. Yes, the moonlight, the snow, and the shadow of the tree—I can see them again this minute. By Gad, I believe I could draw them, and yet I never realized I was looking at them at the time."

"His room was the big one over the porch, was it not?" asked Mr. Quin.

"Yes, and the tree was the big beech, just at the angle of the drive."

Mr. Quin nodded, as though satisfied. Mr. Satterthwaite was

curiously thrilled. He was convinced that every word, every reflection of Mr. Quin's voice was pregnant with purpose. He was driving at something—exactly what Mr. Satterthwaite did not know, but he was quite convinced as to whose was the master hand.

There was a momentary pause, and then Evesham reverted to the preceding topic.

"That Appleton case, I remember it very well now. What a sensation it made. She got off, didn't she? Pretty woman, very fair—remarkably fair."

Almost against his will, Mr. Satterthwaite's eyes sought the kneeling figure up above. Was it his fancy, or did he see it shrink a little, as though at a blow? Did he see a hand slide upward to the tablecloth—and then pause?

There was a crash of falling glass. Alec Portal, helping himself to whiskey, had let the decanter slip.

"I say—damn' sorry. Can't think what came over me."

Evesham cut short his apologies.

"Quite all right. Quite all right, my dear fellow. Curious—that smash reminded me. That's what she did, didn't she? Mrs. Appleton? Smashed the port decanter?"

"Yes. Old Appleton has his glass of port—only one—each night. The day after his death, one of the servants saw her take the decanter out and smash it deliberately. That set them talking, of course. They all knew she had been perfectly wretched with him. Rumor grew and grew, and in the end, months later, some of his relatives applied for an exhumation order. And sure enough, the old fellow had been poisoned. Arsenic, wasn't it?"

"No—strychnine, I think. It doesn't much matter. Well, of course, there it was. Only one person was likely to have done it. Mrs. Appleton stood her trial. She was acquitted more through the lack of evidence against her than from any overwhelming proof of innocence. In other words, she was lucky. Yes, I don't suppose there's much doubt she did it right enough. What happened to her afterward?"

"Went out to Canada, I believe. Or was it Australia? She had an uncle or something of the sort out there who offered her a home. Best thing she could do under the circumstances."

Mr. Satterthwaite was fascinated by Alec Portal's right hand as it clasped his glass. How tightly he was gripping it.

"You'll smash that in a minute or two, if you're not careful," thought Mr. Satterthwaite. "Dear me, how interesting all this is."

Evesham rose and helped himself to a drink.

"Well, we're not much nearer to knowing why poor Derek Capel shot himself," he remarked. "The Court of Inquiry hasn't been a great success, has it, Mr. Quin?"

Mr. Quin laughed.

It was a strange laugh, mocking—yet sad. It made everyone jump.

"I beg your pardon," he said. "You are still living in the past, Mr. Evesham. You are still hampered by your preconceived notion. But I, the man from outside, the stranger passing by, see only—facts!"

"Facts?"

"Yes—facts."

"What do you mean?" said Evesham.

"I see a clear sequence of facts, outlined by yourselves, but of which you have not seen the significance. Let us go back ten years and look at what we see—untrammeled by ideas or sentiment."

Mr. Quin had risen. He looked very tall. The fire leaped fitfully behind him. He spoke in a low compelling voice.

"You are at dinner. Derek Capel announces his engagement. You think then it was to Marjorie Dilke. You are not so sure now. He has the restlessly excited manner of a man who has successfully defied Fate—who, in your own words, has pulled off a big coup against overwhelming odds. Then comes the clanging of the bell. He goes out to get the long overdue mail. He doesn't open his letters, but you mention yourselves that *he opened the paper to glance at the news*. It is ten years ago—so we cannot know what the news was that day— a far off earthquake, a near at hand political crisis? The only thing we do know about the contents of that paper is that it contained one small paragraph—*a paragraph stating that the Home Office had given permission to exhume the body of Mr. Appleton three days ago.*"

"What?"

Mr. Quin went on.

"Derek Capel goes up to his room, and there he sees something out of the window. Sir Richard Conway has told us that the curtain was not drawn across it and further that it gave on the drive. What did he see? What could he have seen that forced him to take his life?"

"What do you mean? What did he see?"

"I think," said Mr. Quin, "that he saw a policeman. A policeman who had come about a dog. But Derek Capel didn't know that—he just saw—a policeman."

There was a long silence—as though it took some time to drive the inference home.

"My God!" whispered Evesham at last. "You can't mean that? Appleton? But he wasn't there at the time Appleton died. The old man was alone with his wife—"

"But he may have been there a week earlier. Strychnine is not very soluble unless it is in the form of the hydrochloride. The greater part of it, put into the port, would be taken in the last glass, perhaps a week after he left."

Portal sprang forward. His voice was hoarse and his eyes bloodshot.

"Why did she break the decanter?" he cried. "Why did she break the decanter? Tell me that."

For the first time that evening, Mr. Quin addressed himself to Mr. Satterthwaite.

"You have a wide experience of life, Mr. Satterthwaite. Perhaps you can tell us that."

Mr. Satterthwaite's voice trembled a little. His cue had come at last. He was to speak some of the most important lines in the play. He was an actor now—not a looker on.

"As I see it," he murmured modestly, "she—cared for Derek Capel. She was, I think, a good woman—and she had sent him away. When her husband—died, she suspected the truth. And so, to save the man she loved, she tried to destroy the evidence against him. Later, I think, he persuaded her that her suspicions were unfounded, and she consented to marry him. But even then, she hung back—women, I fancy, have a lot of instinct."

Mr. Satterthwaite had spoken his part.

Suddenly a long trembling sigh filled the air.

"My God!" cried Evesham, starting, "what was that?"

Mr. Satterthwaite could have told him that it was Eleanor Portal in the gallery above, but he was too artistic to spoil a good effect.

Mr. Quin was smiling.

"My car will be ready by now. Thank you for your hospitality, Mr. Evesham. I have, I hope, done something for my friend."

They stared at him in black amazement.

"That aspect of the matter has not struck you? He loved this woman, you know. Loved her enough to commit murder for her sake. When retribution overtook him, as he mistakenly thought, he took his own life. But, unwittingly, he left her to face the music."

"She was acquitted," muttered Evesham.

"Because the case against her could not be proved. I fancy—it may be only a fancy—that she is still—facing the music."

Portal had sunk into a chair, his face buried in his hands.

Quin turned to Satterthwaite.

"Good-by, Mr. Satterthwaite. You are interested in the drama, are you not?"

Mr. Satterthwaite nodded—surprised.

"I must recommend the Harlequinade to your attention. It is dying out nowadays—but it repays attention, I assure you. Its symbolism is a little difficult to follow—but the immortals are always immortal, you know. I wish you all good night."

They saw him stride out into the dark. As before, the colored glass gave the effect of motley.

Mr. Satterthwaite went upstairs. He went to draw down his window, for the air was cold. The figure of Mr. Quin moved down the drive, and from a side door came a woman's figure, running. For a moment they spoke together, then she retraced her steps to the house. She passed just below the window, and Mr. Satterthwaite was struck anew by the vitality of her face. She moved now like a woman in a happy dream.

"Eleanor!"

Alec Portal had joined her.

"Eleanor, forgive me—forgive me. You told me the truth, but God forgive me—I did not quite believe—"

Mr. Satterthwaite was intensely interested in other people's affairs, but he was also a gentleman. It was borne in upon him that he must shut the window. He did so.

But he shut it very slowly.

He heard her voice, exquisite and indescribable.

"I know—I know. You have been in Hell. So was I once. Loving—yet alternately believing and suspecting—thrusting aside one's doubts and having them spring up again with leering faces. I know, Alec, I know. But there is a worse Hell than that, the Hell I have lived in with you. I have seen your doubt—your fear of me—poisoning all our love. That man—that chance passer-by, saved me. I could bear it no longer, you understand. Tonight—tonight I was going to kill myself—Alec—Alec!"

2. THE SHADOW ON
THE GLASS

"Listen to this," said Lady Cynthia Drage.

She read aloud from the journal she held in her hand.

" 'Mr. and Mrs. Unkerton are entertaining a party at Greenways House this week. Among the guests are Lady Cynthia Drage, Mr. and Mrs. Richard Scott, Major Porter, D.S.O., Mrs. Staverton, Captain Allenson and Mr. Satterthwaite.' "

"It's as well," remarked Lady Cynthia, casting away the paper, "to know what we're in for. But they *have* made a mess of things!"

Her companion, that same Mr. Satterthwaite whose name figured at the end of the list of guests, looked at her interrogatively. It had been said that if Mr. Satterthwaite was found at the houses of those rich who had newly arrived, it was a sign either that the cooking was unusually good, or that a drama of human life was to be enacted there. Mr. Satterthwaite was abnormally interested in the comedies and tragedies of his fellow men.

Lady Cynthia, who was a middle-aged woman, with a hard face and a liberal allowance of make-up, tapped him smartly with the newest thing in parasols which lay rakishly across her knee.

"Don't pretend you don't understand me. You do perfectly. What's more I believe you're here on purpose to see the fur fly!"

Mr. Satterthwaite protested vigorously. He didn't know what she was talking about.

"I'm talking about Richard Scott. Do you pretend you've never heard of him?"

"No, of course not. He's the Big Game man, isn't he?"

"That's it—'Great big bears and tigers, etc.,' as the song says. Of course, he's a great lion himself just now—the Unkertons would naturally be mad to get hold of him—*and* the bride! A charming child—oh! quite a charming child—but so naïve, only twenty, you know, and he must be at least forty-five."

"Mrs. Scott seems to me very charming," said Mr. Satterthwaite sedately.

"Yes, poor child."

"Why poor child?"

Lady Cynthia cast him a look of reproach, and went on approaching the point at issue in her own manner.

"Porter's all right—a dull dog, though—another of these African hunters, all sunburn and silence. Second fiddle to Richard Scott and always has been—lifelong friends and all that sort of thing. When I come to think of it, I believe they were together on that trip—"

"Which trip?"

"*The* trip. The Mrs. Staverton trip. You'll be saying next you've never heard of Mrs. Staverton."

"I *have* heard of Mrs. Staverton," said Mr. Satterthwaite, almost with unwillingness.

And he and Lady Cynthia exchanged glances.

"It's so exactly like the Unkertons," wailed the latter; "they are absolutely hopeless—socially, I mean. The idea of asking those two together! Of course they'd heard that Mrs. Staverton was a sportswoman and a traveler and all that, and about her book. People like the Unkertons don't even begin to realize what pitfalls there are! I've been running them, myself, for the last year, and what I've gone through nobody knows. One has to be constantly at their elbow. 'Don't do that! You can't do this!' Thank goodness, I'm through with it now. Not that we've quarreled—oh! no, I never quarrel—but somebody else can take on the job. As I've always said, I can put up with vulgarity, but I can't stand meanness!"

After this somewhat cryptic utterance, Lady Cynthia was silent for a moment, ruminating on the Unkertons' meanness as displayed to herself.

"If I'd still been running the show for them," she went on presently, "I should have said quite firmly and plainly: 'You can't ask Mrs. Staverton with the Richard Scotts. She and he were once—'"

She stopped eloquently.

"But were they once?" asked Mr. Satterthwaite.

"My dear man! It's well known. That trip into the Interior! I'm surprised the woman had the face to accept the invitation."

"Perhaps she didn't know the others were coming," suggested Mr. Satterthwaite.

"Perhaps she did. That's far more likely."

"You think—"

"She's what I call a dangerous woman—the sort of woman who'd stick at nothing. I wouldn't be in Richard Scott's shoes this week-end."

"And his wife knows nothing, you think?"

"I'm certain of it. But I suppose some kind friend will enlighten her sooner or later. Here's Jimmy Allenson. Such a nice boy. He saved my life in Egypt last winter—I was so bored, you know. Hullo, Jimmy, come here at once."

Captain Allenson obeyed, dropping down on the turf beside her. He was a handsome young fellow of thirty, with white teeth and an infectious smile.

"I'm glad somebody wants me," he observed. "The Scotts are doing the turtle dove stunt, two required, not three, Porter's devouring the Field, and I've been in mortal danger of being entertained by my hostess."

He laughed. Lady Cynthia laughed with him. Mr. Satterthwaite, who was in some ways a little old-fashioned, so much so that he seldom made fun of his host and hostess until after he had left their house, remained grave.

"Poor Jimmy," said Lady Cynthia.

"Mine not to reason why, mine but to swiftly fly. I had a narrow escape of being told the family ghost story."

"An Unkerton ghost," cried Lady Cynthia. "How screaming."

"Not an Unkerton ghost," said Mr. Satterthwaite. "A Greenways ghost. They bought it with the house."

"Of course," said Lady Cynthia. "I remember now. But it doesn't clank chains, does it? It's only something to do with a window."

Jimmy Allenson looked up quickly.

"A window?"

But for the moment Mr. Satterthwaite did not answer. He was looking over Jimmy's head at three figures approaching from the direction of the house—a slim girl between two men. There was a superficial resemblance between the men, both were tall and dark with bronzed faces and quick eyes, but looked at more closely the resemblance vanished.

Richard Scott, hunter and explorer, was a man of extraordinarily vivid personality. He had a manner that radiated magnetism. John Porter, his friend and fellow hunter, was a man of squarer build with an impassive, rather wooden face, and very thoughtful gray eyes. He was a quiet man, content always to play second fiddle to his friend.

And between these two walked Moira Scott who, until three months ago, had been Moira O'Connell, a slender figure, big wistful brown eyes, and golden red hair that stood out round her small face like a saint's halo.

"That child mustn't be hurt," said Mr. Satterthwaite to himself. "It would be abominable that a child like that should be hurt."

Lady Cynthia greeted the newcomers with a wave of the latest thing in parasols.

"Sit down, and don't interrupt," she said. "Mr. Satterthwaite is telling us a ghost story."

"I love ghost stories," said Moira Scott. She dropped down on the grass.

"The ghost of Greenways House?" asked Richard Scott

"Yes, you know about it?"

Scott nodded.

"I used to stay here in the old days," he explained. "Before the Elliots had to sell up. The Watching Cavalier, that's it, isn't it?"

"The Watching Cavalier," said his wife softly. "I like that. It sounds interesting. Please go on."

But Mr. Satterthwaite seemed somewhat loath to do so. He assured her that it was not really interesting at all.

"Now you've done it, Satterthwaite," said Richard Scott sardonically. "That hint of reluctance clinches it."

In response to popular clamor, Mr. Satterthwaite was forced to speak.

"It's really very uninteresting," he said apologetically. "I believe the original story centers round a Cavalier ancestor of the Elliot family. His wife had a Roundhead lover. The husband was killed by the lover in an upstairs room, and the guilty pair fled; but, as they fled, they looked back at the house, and saw the face of the dead husband at the window, watching them. That is the legend, but the ghost story is only concerned with a pane of glass in the window of that particular room, on which is an irregular stain, almost imperceptible from near at hand, but which from far away certainly gives the effect of a man's face looking out."

"Which window is it?" asked Mrs. Scott, looking up at the house.

"You can't see it from here," said Mr. Satterthwaite. "It is round the other side, but was boarded up from the inside some years ago—forty years ago, I think, to be accurate."

"What did they do that for? I thought you said the ghost didn't walk."

"It doesn't," Mr. Satterthwaite assured her. "I suppose—well, I suppose there grew to be a superstitious feeling about it, that's all."

Then, deftly enough, he succeeded in turning the conversation. Jimmy Allenson was perfectly ready to hold forth upon Egyptian sand diviners.

"Frauds, most of them. Ready enough to tell you vague things about the past, but won't commit themselves as to the future."

"I should have thought it was usually the other way about," remarked John Porter.

"It's illegal to tell the future in this country, isn't it?" said Richard Scott. "Moira persuaded a gypsy into telling her fortune, but the woman gave her her shilling back, and said there was nothing doing, or words to that effect."

"Perhaps she saw something so frightful that she didn't like to tell it me," said Moira.

"Don't pile on the agony, Mrs. Scott," said Allenson lightly. "I, for one, refuse to believe that an unlucky fate is hanging over you."

"I wonder," thought Mr. Satterthwaite to himself. "I wonder."

Then he looked up sharply. Two women were coming from the house, a short stout woman, with black hair, inappropriately dressed in jade green, and a tall slim figure in creamy white. The first woman was his hostess, Mrs. Unkerton; the second was a woman he had often heard of, but never met.

"Here's Mrs. Staverton," announced Mrs. Unkerton, in a tone of great satisfaction. "All friends here, I think."

"These people have an uncanny gift for saying just the most awful things they can," murmured Lady Cynthia, but Mr. Satterthwaite was not listening. He was watching Mrs. Staverton.

Very easy—very natural. Her careless "Hullo! Richard, ages since we met. Sorry I couldn't come to the wedding. Is this your wife? You must be tired of meeting all your husband's weather-beaten old friends." Moira's response—suitable, rather shy. The elder woman's swift appraising glance that went on lightly to another old friend.

"Hullo, John!" The same easy tone, but with a subtle difference in it—a warming quality that had been absent before.

And then that sudden smile. It transformed her. Lady Cynthia had been quite right. A dangerous woman! Very fair—deep blue eyes—not the traditional coloring of the siren—a face almost haggard in repose. A woman with a slow dragging voice and a sudden dazzling smile.

Iris Staverton sat down. She became naturally and inevitably the center of the group. So, you felt, it would always be.

Mr. Satterthwaite was recalled from his thoughts by Major Porter's suggesting a stroll. Mr. Satterthwaite, who was not, as a gen-

eral rule, much given to strolling, acquiesced. The two men saun-
tered off together across the lawn.

"Very interesting story of yours just now," said the Major.

"I will show you the window," said Mr. Satterthwaite.

He led the way round to the west side of the house. Here there
was a small formal garden—the Privy Garden, it was always called,
and there was some point in the name, for it was surrounded by high
holly hedges, and even the entrance to it ran zigzag between the
same high prickly hedges.

Once inside, it was very charming with an old world charm of
formal flower beds, flagged paths and a low stone seat, exquisitely
carved. When they had reached the center of the garden, Mr. Satterthwaite turned and pointed up at the house. The length of
Greenways House ran north and south. In this narrow west wall
there was only one window, a window on the first floor, almost overgrown by ivy, with grimy panes, and which you could just see was
boarded up on the inside.

"There you are," said Mr. Satterthwaite.

Craning his neck a little, Porter looked up.

"H'm, I can see a kind of discoloration on one of the panes,
nothing more."

"We're too near," said Mr. Satterthwaite. "There's a clearing
higher up in the woods where you get a really good view."

He led the way out of the Privy Garden, and, turning sharply to
the left, struck into the woods. A certain enthusiasm of showman-
ship possessed him, and he hardly noticed that the man at his side
was absent and inattentive.

"They had, of course, to make another window, when they
boarded up this one," he explained. "The new one faces south, overlooking the lawn where we were sitting just now. I rather fancy the
Scotts have the room in question. That is why I didn't want to pursue
the subject. Mrs. Scott might have felt nervous if she had realized
that she was sleeping in what might be called the haunted room.

"Yes. I see," said Porter.

Mr. Satterthwaite looked at him sharply, and realized that the
other had not heard a word of what he was saying.

"Very interesting," said Porter. He slashed with his stick at some tall foxgloves, and, frowning, he said: "She ought not to have come. She ought never to have come."

People often spoke after this fashion to Mr. Satterthwaite. He seemed to matter so little, to have so negative a personality. He was merely a glorified listener.

"No," said Porter, "she ought never to have come."

Mr. Satterthwaite knew instinctively that it was not of Mrs. Scott he spoke.

"You think not?" he asked.

Porter shook his head as though in foreboding.

"I was on that trip," he said abruptly. "The three of us went. Scott and I and Iris. She's a wonderful woman—and a damned fine shot." He paused. "What made them ask her?" he finished abruptly.

Mr. Satterthwaite shrugged his shoulders.

"Ignorance," he said.

"There's going to be trouble," said the other. "We must stand by—and do what we can."

"But surely Mrs. Staverton—"

"I'm talking of Scott." He paused. "You see—there's Mrs. Scott to consider."

Mr. Satterthwaite had been considering her all along, but he did not think it necessary to say so, since the other man had so clearly forgotten her until this minute.

"How did Scott meet his wife?" he asked.

"Last winter, in Cairo. A quick business. They were engaged in three weeks, and married in six."

"She seems to me very charming."

"She is; no doubt about it. And he adores her—but that will make no difference." And again Major Porter repeated to himself, using the pronoun that meant to him one person only: "Hang it all, she shouldn't have come."

Just then they stepped out upon a high grassy knoll at some little distance from the house. With again something of the pride of the showman, Mr. Satterthwaite stretched out his arm.

"Look," he said.

It was fast growing dusk. The window could still be plainly descried, and apparently pressed against one of the panes was a man's face surmounted by a plumed cavalier's hat.

"Very curious," said Porter. "Really very curious. What will happen when that pane of glass gets smashed some day?"

Mr. Satterthwaite smiled.

"That is one of the most interesting parts of the story. That pane of glass has been replaced to my certain knowledge at least eleven times, perhaps oftener. The last time was twelve years ago when the then owner of the house determined to destroy the myth. But it's always the same. *The stain reappears*—not all at once, the discoloration spreads gradually. It takes a month or two as a rule."

For the first time, Porter showed signs of real interest. He gave a sudden quick shiver.

"Damned odd, these things. No accounting for them. What's the real reason of having the room boarded up inside?"

"Well, an idea got about that the room was—unlucky. The Eveshams were in it just before the divorce. Then Stanley and his wife were staying here, and had that room when he ran off with his chorus girl."

Porter raised his eyebrows.

"I see. Danger, not to life, but to morals."

"And now," thought Mr. Satterthwaite to himself, "the Scotts have it. I wonder—"

They retraced their steps in silence to the house. Walking almost noiselessly on the soft turf, each absorbed in his own thoughts, they became unwittingly eavesdroppers. They were rounding the corner of the holly hedge when they heard Iris Staverton's voice, raised fierce and clear from the depths of the Privy Garden:

"You shall be sorry—sorry—for this!"

Scott's voice answered, low and uncertain, so that the words could not be distinguished; and then the woman's voice rose again, speaking words that they were to remember later.

"Jealousy—it drives one to the Devil—it *is* the Devil! It can drive one to black murder. Be careful, Richard; for God's sake, be careful."

And then, on that, she had come out of the Privy Garden, ahead of them, and on round the corner of the house without seeing them, walking swiftly, almost running, like a woman hag ridden and pursued.

Mr. Satterthwaite thought again of Lady Cynthia's words. A dangerous woman. For the first time, he had a premonition of tragedy, coming swift and inexorable, not to be gainsaid.

Yet that evening he felt ashamed of his fears. Everything seemed normal and pleasant Mrs. Staverton, with her easy insouciance, showed no sign of strain. Moira Scott was her charming unaffected self. The two women appeared to be getting on very well. Richard Scott himself seemed to be in boisterous spirits.

The most worried-looking person was stout Mrs. Unkerton. She confided at length in Mr. Satterthwaite.

"Think it silly or not, as you like, there's something giving me the creeps. And I'll tell you frankly, I've sent for the glazier, unbeknown to Ned.

"The glazier?"

"To put a new pane of glass in that window. It's all very well. Ned's proud of it—says it gives the house a tone. I don't like it. I tell you flat. We'll have a nice, plain, modern pane of glass, with no nasty stories attached to it."

"You forget," said Mr. Satterthwaite. "Or perhaps you don't know. The stain comes back."

"That's as it may be," said Mrs. Unkerton. "All I can say is, if it does, it's against nature!"

Mr. Satterthwaite raised his eyebrows, but did not reply.

"And what if it does?" pursued Mrs. Unkerton defiantly. "We're not so bankrupt, Ned and I, that we can't afford a new pane of glass every month—or every week if need be for the matter of that."

Mr. Satterthwaite did not meet the challenge. He had seen too many things crumple and fall before the power of money to believe that even a Cavalier ghost could put up a successful fight. Nevertheless, he was interested by Mrs. Unkerton's manifest uneasiness.

Even she was not exempt from the tension in the atmosphere—only she attributed it to an attenuated ghost story, not to the clash of personalities among her guests.

Mr. Satterthwaite was fated to hear yet another scrap of conversation which threw light upon the situation. He was going up the wide staircase to bed. John Porter and Mrs. Staverton were sitting together in an alcove of the big hall. She was speaking with a faint irritation in her golden voice.

"I hadn't the least idea the Scotts were going to be here. I daresay, if I had known, I shouldn't have come; but I can assure you, my dear John, that now I am here, I'm not going to run away."

Mr. Satterthwaite passed on up the staircase out of earshot. He thought to himself: "I wonder now. How much of that is true? Did she know? I wonder. What's going to come of it?"

He shook his head.

In the clear light of the morning he felt that he had perhaps been a little melodramatic in his imaginings of the evening before. A moment of strain—yet, certainly—inevitable under the circumstances—but nothing more. People adjusted themselves. His fancy that some great catastrophe was pending was nerves—pure nerves—or possibly liver. Yes, that was it, liver. He was due at Carlsbad in another fortnight.

On his own account he proposed a little stroll that evening just as it was growing dusk. He suggested to Major Porter that they should go up to the clearing and see if Mrs. Unkerton had been as good as her word, and had a new pane of glass put in. To himself, he said: "Exercise, that's what I need. Exercise."

The two men walked slowly through the woods. Porter, as usual, was taciturn.

"I can't help feeling," said Mr. Satterthwaite, loquaciously, "that we were a little foolish in our imaginings yesterday. Expecting—er—trouble, you know. After all, people have to behave themselves—swallow their feelings and that sort of thing."

"Perhaps," said Porter. After a minute or two he added: "Civilized people."

"You mean?"

"People who've lived outside civilization a good deal sometimes go back. Revert. Whatever you call it."

They emerged on to the grassy knoll. Mr. Satterthwaite was breathing rather fast. He never enjoyed going up hill.

He looked toward the window. The face was still there, more lifelike than ever.

"Our hostess has repented, I see."

Porter threw it only a cursory glance.

"Unkerton cut up rough, I expect," he said indifferently. "He's the sort of man who is willing to be proud of another family's ghost, and who isn't going to run the risk of having it driven away when he's paid spot cash for it."

He was silent a minute or two, staring, not at the house, but at the thick undergrowth by which they were surrounded.

"Has it ever struck you," he said, "that civilization's damned dangerous?"

"Dangerous?" Such a revolutionary remark shocked Mr. Satterthwaite to the core.

"Yes. There are no safety valves, you see."

He turned abruptly, and they descended the path by which they had come.

"I really am quite at a loss to understand you," said Mr. Satterthwaite, pattering along with nimble steps to keep up with the other's strides. "Reasonable people—"

Porter laughed. A short disconcerting laugh. Then he looked at the correct little gentleman by his side.

"You think it's all bunkum on my part, Mr. Satterthwaite? But there are people, you know, who can tell you when a storm's coming. They feel it beforehand in the air. And other people can foretell trouble. There's trouble coming now, Mr. Satterthwaite, big trouble. It may come any minute. It may—"

He stopped dead, clutching Mr. Satterthwaite's arm. And in that tense minute of silence it came—the sound of two shots and, following them, a cry—a cry in a woman's voice.

"My God!" cried Porter, "it's come."

He raced down the path, Mr. Satterthwaite panting behind him. In a minute they came out onto the lawn, close by the hedge of the Privy Garden. At the same time, Richard Scott and Mr. Unkerton came round the opposite corner of the house. They halted, facing each other, to left and right of the entrance to the Privy Garden.

"It—it came from in there," said Unkerton, pointing with a flabby hand.

"We must see," said Porter. He led the way into the enclosure. As he rounded the last bend of the holly hedge, he stopped dead. Mr. Satterthwaite peered over his shoulder. A loud cry burst from Richard Scott.

There were three people in the Privy Garden. Two of them lay on the grass near the stone seat, a man and a woman. The third was Mrs. Staverton. She was standing quite close to them by the holly hedge, gazing with horror-stricken eyes, and holding something in her right hand.

"Iris," cried Porter. "Iris. For God's sake! What's that you've got in your hand?"

She looked down at it then—with a kind of wonder, an unbelievable indifference.

"It's a pistol," she said wonderingly. And then—after what seemed an interminable time, but was in reality only a few seconds. "I—picked it up."

Mr. Satterthwaite had gone forward to where Unkerton and Scott were kneeling on the turf.

"A doctor," the latter was murmuring. "We must have a doctor."

But it was too late for any doctor. Jimmy Allenson, who had complained that the sand diviners hedged about the future, and Moira Scott, to whom a gypsy had returned a shilling, lay there in the last great stillness.

It was Richard Scott who completed a brief examination. The iron nerve of the man showed in this crisis. After the first cry of agony, he was himself again.

He laid his wife gently down again.

"Shot from behind," he said briefly. "The bullet has passed The right through her."

Then he handled Jimmy Allenson. The wound here was in the breast and the bullet was lodged in the body.

John Porter came toward them.

"Nothing should be touched," he said sternly. "The police must see it all exactly as it is now."

"The police," said Richard Scott. His eyes lit up with a sudden flame as he looked at the woman standing by the holly hedge. He made a step in that direction, but at the same time John Porter also moved, so as to bar his way. For a moment it seemed as though there was a duel of eyes between the two friends.

Porter very quietly shook his head.

"No, Richard," he said. "It looks like it—but you're wrong."

Richard Scott spoke with difficulty, moistening his dry lips.

"Then why—has she got that in her hand?"

And again Iris Staverton said in the same lifeless tone, "I—picked it up."

"The police," said Unkerton, rising. "We must send for the police—at once. You will telephone perhaps, Scott? Someone should stay here—yes, I am sure someone should stay here."

In his quiet gentlemanly manner, Mr. Satterthwaite offered to do so. His host accepted the offer with manifest relief.

"The ladies," he explained. "I must break the news to the ladies, Lady Cynthia and my dear wife."

Mr. Satterthwaite stayed in the Privy Garden looking down on the body of that which had once been Moira Scott.

"Poor child," he said to himself. "Poor child."

He quoted to himself the tag about the evil men do living after them. For was not Richard Scott in a way responsible for his innocent wife's death? They would hang Iris Staverton, he supposed, not that he liked to think of it, but was not it at least a part of the blame he laid at the man's door? The evil that men do—

And the girl, the innocent girl, had paid.

He looked down at her with a very deep pity. Her small face, so white and wistful, a half smile on the lips still. The ruffled golden hair, the delicate ear. There was a spot of blood on the lobe of it. With an inner feeling of being something of a detective, Mr. Satterthwaite deduced an earring, torn away in her fall. He craned his neck forward. Yes, he was right, there was a small pearl drop hanging from the other ear.

Poor child, poor child.

"AND NOW, SIR," said Inspector Winkfield.

They were in the library. The Inspector, a shrewd-looking forceful man of forty odd, was concluding his investigations. He had questioned most of the guests, and had by now pretty well made up his mind on the case. He was listening to what Major Porter and Mr. Satterthwaite had to say. Mr. Unkerton sat heavily in a chair, staring with protruding eyes at the opposite wall.

"As I understand it, gentlemen," said the Inspector, "you'd been for a walk. You were returning to the house by a path that winds round the left side of what they call the Privy Garden. Is that correct?"

"Quite correct, Inspector."

"You heard two shots, and a woman's scream?"

"Yes."

"You then ran as fast as you could, emerged from the woods and made your way to the entrance of the Privy Garden. If anybody had left that garden, they could only do so by the one entrance. The holly hedges are impassable. If anyone had run out of the garden and turned to the right, he would have been met by Mr. Unkerton and Mr. Scott. If he had turned to the left, he could not have done so without being seen by you. Is that right?"

"That is so," said Major Porter. His face was very white.

"That seems to settle it," said the Inspector. "Mr. and Mrs. Unkerton and Lady Cynthia Drage were sitting on the lawn, Mr. Scott was in the billiard room, which opens on to that lawn. At ten minutes past six, Mrs. Staverton came out of the house, spoke a word or two to those sitting there, and went round the corner of the house toward the Privy Garden. Two minutes later the shots were heard. Mr. Scott rushed out of the house and, together with Mr. Unkerton, ran to the Privy Garden. At the same time, you and Mr.—er Satterthwaite arrived from the opposite direction. Mrs. Staverton was in the Privy Garden with a pistol in her hand from which two shots had been fired. As I see it, she shot the lady first from behind, as she was sitting on the bench. Then Captain Allenson sprang up and went for her, and she shot him in the chest as he came toward her. I understand that there had been a—er—previous attachment between her and Mr. Richard Scott—"

"That's a damned lie," said Porter.

His voice rang out hoarse and defiant. The Inspector said nothing, merely shook his head.

"What is her own story?" asked Mr. Satterthwaite.

"She says that she went into the Privy Garden to be quiet for a little. Just before she rounded the last hedge, she heard the shots. She came round the corner, saw the pistol lying at her feet, and picked it up. No one passed her, and she saw no one in the garden but the two victims." The Inspector gave an eloquent pause. "That's what she says—and although I cautioned her, she insisted on making a statement."

"If she said that," said Major Porter, and his face was still deadly white, "she was speaking the truth. I know Iris Staverton."

"Well, sir," said the Inspector, "there'll be plenty of time to go into all that later. In the meantime, I've got my duty to do."

With an abrupt movement, Porter turned to Mr. Satterthwaite.

"You! Can't you help? Can't *you* do something?"

Mr. Satterthwaite could not help feeling immensely flattered. He had been appealed to, he, most insignificant of men, and by a man like John Porter.

He was just about to flutter out a regretful reply, when the butler, Thompson, entered, with a card upon a salver which he took to his master with an apologetic cough. Mr. Unkerton was still sitting huddled up in a chair, taking no part in the proceedings.

"I told the gentleman you would probably not be able to see him, sir," said Thompson, "but he insisted that he had an appointment and that it was most urgent."

Unkerton took the card.

"Mr. Harley Quin," he read. "I remember, he was to see me about a picture. I did make an appointment, but as things are—"

But Mr. Satterthwaite had started forward.

"Mr. Harley Quin, did you say?" he cried. "How extraordinary, how very extraordinary. Major Porter, you asked me if I could help you. I think I can. This Mr. Quin is a friend—or I should say, an acquaintance of mine. He is a most remarkable man."

"One of these amateur solvers of crime, I suppose," remarked the Inspector disparagingly.

"No," said Mr. Satterthwaite. "He is not that kind of man at all. But he has a power—an almost uncanny power—of showing you what you have seen with your own eyes, of making clear to you what you have heard with your own ears. Let us, at any rate, give him an outline of the case, and hear what he has to say."

Mr. Unkerton glanced at the Inspector, who merely Snorted and looked at the ceiling. Then the former gave a short nod to Thompson, who left the room and returned ushering in a tall slim stranger.

"Mr. Unkerton?" The stranger shook him by the hand. "I am sorry to intrude upon you at such a time. We must leave our little picture chat until another time. Ah! my friend, Mr. Satterthwaite. Still as fond of the drama as ever?"

A faint smile played for a minute round the stranger's lips as he said these last words.

"Mr. Quin," said Mr. Satterthwaite impressively. "We have a drama here; we are in the midst of one. I should like, and my friend Major Porter would like, to have your opinion of it."

Mr. Quin sat down. The red-shaded lamp threw a broad hand of colored light over the checked pattern of his overcoat, and left his face in shadow almost as though he wore a mask.

Succinctly, Mr. Satterthwaite recited the main points of the tragedy. Then he paused, breathlessly awaiting the words of the oracle.

But Mr. Quin merely shook his head.

"A sad story," he said. "A very sad and shocking tragedy. The lack of motive makes it very intriguing."

Unkerton stared at him.

"You don't understand," he said. "Mrs. Staverton was heard to threaten Richard Scott. She was bitterly jealous of his wife. Jealousy—"

"I agree," said Mr. Quin. "Jealousy or Demoniac Possession. It's all the same. But you misunderstand me. I was not referring to the murder of Mrs. Scott, but to that of Captain Allenson."

"You're right," cried Porter, springing forward. "There's a flaw there. If Iris had ever contemplated shooting Mrs. Scott, she'd have got her alone somewhere. No, we're on the wrong tack. And I think I see another solution. Only those three people went into the Privy Garden. That is indisputable, and I don't intend to dispute it. But I reconstruct the tragedy differently. Supposing Jimmy Allenson shoots first Mrs. Scott and then himself. That's possible, isn't it? He flings the pistol from him as he falls—Mrs. Staverton finds it lying on the ground and picks it up just as she said. How's that?"

The Inspector shook his head.

"Won't wash, Major Porter. If Captain Allenson had fired that shot close to his body, the cloth would have been singed."

"He might have held the pistol at arm's length."

"Why should he? No sense in it. Besides, there's no motive."

"Might have gone off his head suddenly," muttered Porter, but without any great conviction. He fell to silence again, suddenly rousing himself to say defiantly: "Well, Mr. Quin?"

The latter shook his head.

"I'm not a magician. I'm not even a criminologist. But I will tell you one thing—I believe in the value of impressions. In any time of crisis, there is always one moment that stands out from all the others, one picture that remains when all else has faded. Mr. Satterthwaite is, I think, likely to have been the most unprejudiced observer of those present. Will you cast your mind back, Mr. Satterthwaite, and tell us the moment that made the strongest impression on you? Was it when you heard the shots? Was it when you first saw the dead bodies? Was it when you first observed the pistol in Mrs. Staverton's hand? Clear your mind of any preconceived standard of values, and tell us."

Mr. Satterthwaite fixed his eyes on Mr. Quin's face, rather as a schoolboy might repeat a lesson of which he was not sure.

"No," he said, slowly. "It was not any of these. The moment that I shall always remember was when I stood alone by the bodies—afterward—looking down on Mrs. Scott. She was lying on her side. Her hair was ruffled. There was a spot of blood on her little ear."

And instantly, as he said it, he felt that he had said a terrific, a significant thing.

"Blood on her ear? Yes, I remember," said Unkerton slowly.

"Her earring must have been torn out when she fell," explained Mr. Satterthwaite.

But it sounded a little improbable as he said it.

"She was lying on her left side," said Porter. "I suppose it was that ear?"

"No," said Mr. Satterthwaite quickly. "It was her right ear."

The Inspector coughed.

"I found this in the grass," he vouchsafed. He held up a loop of gold wire.

"But, my God, man," cried Porter. "The thing can't have been wrenched to pieces by a mere fall. It's more as though it had been shot away by a bullet."

"So it was," cried Mr. Satterthwaite. "It was a bullet. It must have been."

"There were only two shots," said the Inspector. "A shot can't have grazed her ear and shot her in the back as well. And if one shot carried away the earring, and the second shot killed her, it can't have killed Captain Allenson as well—not unless he was standing close in front of her—very close—facing her as it might be. Oh! no, not even then, unless, that is—"

"Unless she was in his arms, you were going to say," said Mr. Quin, with a queer little smile. "Well, why not?"

Everyone stared at each other. The idea was so vitally strange to them—Allenson and Mrs. Scott. Mr. Unkerton voiced the same feeling.

"But they hardly knew each other," he said.

"I don't, know," said Mr. Satterthwaite thoughtfully. "They

might have known each other better than we thought. Lady Cynthia said he saved her from being bored in Egypt last winter, and you" he turned to Porter, "you told me that Richard Scott met his wife in Cairo last winter. They might have known each other very well indeed out there."

"They didn't seem to be together much," said Unkerton.

"No—they rather avoided each other. It was almost unnatural, now I come to think of it—"

They all looked at Mr. Quin, as if a little startled at the conclusions at which they had arrived so unexpectedly.

Mr. Quin rose to his feet.

"You see," he said, "what Mr. Satterthwaite's impression has done for us." He turned to Unkerton. "It is your turn now."

"Eh? I don't understand you."

"You were very thoughtful when I came into this room. I should like to know exactly what thought it was that obsessed you. Never mind if it has nothing to do with the tragedy. Never mind if it seems to you—superstitious—" Mr. Unkerton started, ever so slightly. "Tell us."

"I don't mind telling you," said Unkerton. "Though it's nothing to do with the business, and you'll probably laugh at me into the bargain. I was wishing that my Missis had left well alone and not replaced that pane of glass in the haunted window. I feel as though doing that has maybe brought a curse upon us."

He was unable to understand why the two men opposite him stared so.

"But she hasn't replaced it yet," said Mr. Satterthwaite at last.

"Yes, she has. Man came first thing this morning."

"My God!" said Porter, "I begin to understand. That room, it's paneled, I suppose, not papered?"

"Yes, but what does that—"

But Porter had swung out of the room. The others followed him. He went straight upstairs to the Scotts' bedroom. It was a charming room, paneled in cream, with two windows facing South. Porter felt with his hands along the panels on the western wall.

"There's a spring somewhere—must be. Ah!" There was a click, and a section of the paneling rolled back. It disclosed the grimy panes of the haunted window. One pane of glass was clean and new. Porter stooped quickly and picked up something. He held it out on the palm of his hand. It was a fragment of ostrich feather. Then he looked at Mr. Quin. Mr. Quin nodded.

He went across to the hat cupboard in the bedroom. There were several hats in it—the dead woman's hats. He took out one with a large brim and curling feathers—an elaborate Ascot hat.

Mr. Quin began speaking in a gentle, reflective voice.

"Let us suppose," said Mr. Quin, "a man who is by nature intensely jealous, a man who has stayed here in bygone years and knows the secret of the spring in the paneling. To amuse himself he opens it one day, and looks out over the Privy Garden. There, secure as they think from being overlooked, he sees his wife and another man. There can be no possible doubt in his mind as to the relations between them. He is mad with rage. What shall he do? An idea comes to him. He goes to the cupboard and puts on the hat with the brim and feathers. It is growing dusk, and he remembers the story of the stain on the glass. Anyone looking up at the window will see as they think the watching Cavalier. Thus secured he watches them, and at the moment they are clasped in each other's arms, he shoots. He is a good shot—a wonderful shot. As they fall, he fires once more—that shot carries away the earring. He flings the pistol out of the window into the Privy Garden, rushes down stairs and out through the billiard room."

Porter took a step toward him.

"But he let her be accused?" he cried. "He stood by and let her be accused? Why? Why?"

"I think you know why," said Mr. Quin. "I should guess—it's only guesswork on my part, mind—that Richard Scott was once madly in love with Iris Staverton—so madly that even meeting her years afterward stirred up the embers of jealousy again. I should say that Iris Staverton once fancied that she might love him, that she went on a hunting trip with him and another—and that she came back in love with the better man."

"The better man," muttered Porter, dazed. "You mean—"

"Yes," said Mr. Quin, with a faint smile. "I mean you." He paused a minute, and then said: "If I were you—I should go to her now."

"I will," said Porter.

He turned and left the room.

3. AT THE BELLS
AND MOTLEY

Mr. Satterthwaite was annoyed. Altogether it had been an unfortunate day. They had started late; there had been two punctures already; finally they had taken the wrong turning and lost themselves amid the wilds of Salisbury Plain. Now it was close on eight o'clock; they were still a matter of forty miles from Marswick Manor, whither they were bound, and a third puncture had supervened to render matters still more trying.

Mr. Satterthwaite, looking like some small bird whose plumage had been ruffled, walked up and down in front of the village garage while his chauffeur conversed in hoarse undertones with the local expert.

"Half an hour *at* least," said that worthy, pronouncing judgment.

"And lucky at that," supplemented Masters, the chauffeur. "More like three quarters if you ask me."

"What is this—place, anyway?" demanded Mr. Satterthwaite fretfully. Being a little gentleman considerate of the feelings of others, he substituted the word "place" for "God forsaken hole" which had first risen to his lips.

"Kirtlington Mallet."

Mr. Satterthwaite was not much wiser, and yet a faint familiarity seemed to linger round the name. He looked round him disparagingly. Kirtlington Mallet seemed to consist of one straggling street, the garage and the post office on one side of it balanced by three in determinate shops on the other side. Farther down the road, however, Mr. Satterthwaite perceived something that creaked and swung in the wind, and his spirits rose ever so slightly.

"There's an inn here, I see," he remarked.

"Bells and Motley," said the garage man. "That's it—yonder."

"If I might make a suggestion, sir," said Masters. "Why not try it? They would be able to give you some sort of a meal, no doubt— not of course, what you are accustomed to—" He paused apologetically, for Mr. Satterthwaite was accustomed to the best cooking of continental chefs, and had in his own service a *cordon bleu* to whom he paid a fabulous salary.

"We shan't be able to take the road again for another three quarters of an hour, sir. I'm sure of that. And it's already past eight o'-clock. You could ring up Sir George Foster, sir, from the inn, and acquaint him with the cause of our delay."

"You seem to think you can arrange everything, Masters," said Mr. Satterthwaite snappily.

Masters, who did think so, maintained a respectful silence.

Mr. Satterthwaite, in spite of his earnest wish to discountenance any suggestion that might possibly be made to him—he was in that mood—nevertheless looked down the road toward the creaking inn sign with faint inward approval. He was a man of birdlike appetite, an epicure; but even such men can be hungry.

"The Bells and Motley," he said thoughtfully. "That's an odd name for an inn. I don't know that I ever heard it before."

"There's odd folks come to it by all account," said the local man.

He was bending over the wheel, and his voice came muffled and indistinct.

"Odd folks?" queried Mr. Satterthwaite. "Now what do you mean by that?"

The other hardly seemed to know what he meant.

"Folks that come and go. That kind," he said vaguely.

Mr. Satterthwaite reflected that people who come to an inn are almost of necessity those who "come and go." The definition seemed to him to lack precision. But nevertheless his curiosity was stimulated. Somehow or other he had got to put in three quarters of an hour. The Bells and Motley would be as good as anywhere else.

With his usual small, mincing steps he walked away down the road. From afar there came a rumble of thunder. The mechanic looked up and spoke to Masters:

"There's a storm coming over. Thought I could feel it in the air."

"Crikey," said Masters. "And forty miles to go."

"Ah!" said the other. "There's no need to be hurrying over this job. You'll not be wanted to take the road till the storm's passed over. That little boss of yours doesn't look as though he'd relish being out in thunder and lightning."

"Hope they'll do nun well at that place," muttered the chauffeur. "I'll be pushing along there for a bite myself presently."

"Billy Jones is all right," said the garage man. "Keeps a good table."

Mr. William Jones, a big burly man of fifty, and landlord of the Bells and Motley, was at this minute beaming ingratiatingly down on little Mr. Satterthwaite.

"Can do you a nice steak, sir—*and* fried potatoes, and as good a cheese as any gentleman could wish for. This way, sir, in the coffee room. We're not very full at present, the last of the fishing gentlemen just gone. A little later we'll be full again for the hunting. Only one gentleman here at present, name of Quin—"

Mr. Satterthwaite stopped dead.

"Quin?" he said excitedly. "Did you say Quin?"

"That's the name, sir. Friend of yours, perhaps?"

"Yes, indeed. Oh! yes, most certainly." Twittering with excitement, Mr. Satterthwaite hardly realized that the world might contain more than one man of that name. He had no doubts at all. In an odd way, the information fitted in with what the man at the garage had said. "Folks that come and go." A very apt description of Mr. Quin. And the name of the inn too seemed a peculiarly fitting and appropriate one.

"Dear me, dear me," said Mr. Satterthwaite. "What a *very* odd thing. That we should meet like this! Mr. Harley Quin, is it not?"

"That's right, sir. This is the coffee room, sir. Ah! here is the gentleman."

Tall, dark, smiling, the familiar figure of Mr. Quin rose from the table at which he was sitting, and the well-remembered voice spoke.

"Ah! Mr. Satterthwaite, we meet again. An unexpected meeting!"

Mr. Satterthwaite was shaking him warmly by the hand.

"Delighted. Delighted, I'm sure. A lucky breakdown for me. My car, you know. And you are staying here? For long?"

"One night only."

"Then I am indeed fortunate."

Mr. Satterthwaite sat down opposite his friend with a little sigh of satisfaction, and regarded the dark, smiling face opposite him with a pleasurable expectancy.

The other man shook his head gently.

"I assure you," he said, "that I have not a bowl of goldfish or a rabbit to produce from my sleeve."

"Too bad," cried Mr. Satterthwaite, a little taken aback. "Yes, I must confess—I do rather adopt that attitude toward you. A man of magic. Ha, ha. That is how I regard you. A man of magic."

"And yet," said Mr. Quin, "it is you who do the conjuring tricks, not I."

"Ah!" said Mr. Satterthwaite eagerly. "But I cannot do them without you. I lack—shall we say—inspiration?"

Mr. Quin smilingly shook his head.

"That is too big a word. I speak the cue, that is all."

The landlord came in at that minute with bread and a slab of yellow butter. As he set the things on the table there was a vivid flash of lightning, and a clap of thunder almost overhead.

"A wild night, gentlemen."

"On such a night—" began Mr. Satterthwaite, and stopped.

"Funny now," said the landlord, unconscious of the question, "if those weren't just the words I was going to use myself. It was just such a night as this when Captain Harwell brought his bride home, the very day before he disappeared forever."

"Ah!" cried Mr. Satterthwaite, suddenly. "Of course!"

He had got the clue. He knew now why the name Kirtlington Mallet was familiar. Three months before he had read every detail of the astonishing disappearance of Captain Richard Harwell. Like other newspaper readers all over Great Britain he had puzzled over the details of the disappearance, and, also like every other Briton, had evolved his own theories.

"Of course," he repeated. "It was at Kirtlington Mallet it happened."

"It was at this house he stayed for the hunting last winter," said the landlord. "Oh! I knew him well. A main handsome young gentleman and not one that you'd think had a care on his mind. He was done away with—that's my belief. Many's the time I've seen them come riding home together—he and Miss Le Couteau, and all the village saying there'd be a match come of it—and sure enough, so it did. A very beautiful young lady, and well thought of, for all she was a Canadian and a stranger. Ah! there's some dark mystery there. We'll never know the rights of it. It broke her heart. It did, sure enough. You've heard as she's sold the place up and gone abroad; couldn't abear to go on here with everyone staring and pointing after her—through no fault of her own, poor young dear? A black mystery, that's what it is."

He shook his head, then, suddenly recollecting his duties, hurried from the room.

"A black mystery," said Mr. Quin softly.

His voice was provocative in Mr. Satterthwaite's ears.

"Are you pretending that we can solve the mystery where Scotland Yard failed?" he asked sharply.

The other made a characteristic gesture.

"Why not? Time has passed. Three months. That makes a difference."

"That is a curious idea of yours," said Mr. Satterthwaite slowly. "That one sees things better afterward than at the time."

"The longer the time that has elapsed, the more things fall into proportion. One sees them in their true relationship to one another."

There was a silence which lasted for some minutes.

"I am not sure," said Mr. Satterthwaite, in a hesitating voice, "that I remember the facts clearly by now."

"I think you do," said Mr. Quin quietly.

It was all the encouragement Mr. Satterthwaite needed. His general rôle in life was that of listener and looker on. Only in the company of Mr. Quin was the position reversed. There Mr. Quin was the appreciative listener, and Mr. Satterthwaite took the center of the stage.

"It was just over a year ago," he said, "that Ashley Grange passed into the possession of Miss Eleanor Le Couteau. It is a beautiful old house, but it had been neglected and allowed to remain empty for many years. It could not have found a better chatelaine. Miss Le Couteau was a French Canadian, her forbears were *émigrés* from the French Revolution, and had handed down to her a collection of almost priceless French relics and antiques. She was a buyer and a collector also, with a very fine and discriminating taste, so much so that, when she decided to sell Ashley Grange and everything it contained after the tragedy, Mr. Cyrus G. Bradburn, the American millionaire, made no bones about paying the fancy price of sixty thousand pounds for the Grange as it stood."

Mr. Satterthwaite paused.

"I mention these things," he said apologetically, "not because they are relevant to the story—strictly speaking, they are not, but to convey an atmosphere—the atmosphere of young Mrs. Harwell."

Mr. Quin nodded.

"Atmosphere is always valuable," he said gravely.

"So we get a picture of this girl," continued the other. "Just twenty-three, dark, beautiful, accomplished, nothing crude and unfinished about her. And rich—we must not forget that. She was an orphan. A Mrs. St. Clair, a lady of unimpeachable breeding and social standing, lived with her of duenna. But Eleanor Le Couteau had complete control of her own fortune. And fortune hunters are never hard to seek. At least a dozen impecunious young men were to be found dangling round her on all occasions, in the hunting field, in the ballroom, wherever she went. Young Lord Leccan the most eligible party in the country, is reported to have asked her to marry him, but she remained heart-free. That is, until the coming of Captain Richard Harwell.

"Captain Harwell had put up at the local inn for the hunting. He was a dashing rider to hounds, a handsome laughing daredevil of a fellow. You remember the old saying, Mr. Quin? 'Happy the wooing that's not long doing.' The adage was carried out at least in part. At the end of two months, Richard Harwell and Eleanor Le Couteau were engaged.

"The marriage followed three months afterward. The happy pair went abroad for a two weeks' honeymoon, and then returned to take up their residence at Ashley Grange. The landlord has just told us that it was on a night of storm such as this that they returned to their home. An omen, I wonder? Who can tell. Be that as it may, the following morning very early—about half past seven—Captain Harwell was seen walking in the garden by one of the gardeners, John Mathias. He was bareheaded, and was whistling. We have a picture there, a picture of lightheartedness, of careless happiness. And yet from that minute, as far as we know, no one ever set eyes on Captain Richard Harwell again."

Mr. Satterthwaite paused, pleasantly conscious of a dramatic moment. The admiring glance of Mr. Quin gave him the tribute he needed, and he went on.

"The disappearance was remarkable—unaccountable. It was not till the following day that the distracted wife called in the police. As you know, they have not succeeded in solving the mystery."

"There have, I suppose, been theories?" asked Mr. Quin.

"Oh! theories, I grant you. Theory No. 1, that Captain Harwell had been murdered, done away with. But if so, where was the body? It could hardly have been spirited away. And besides, what motive was there? As far as was known, Captain Harwell had not an enemy in the world."

He paused abruptly, as though uncertain. Mr. Quin leaned forward.

"You are thinking," he said softly, "of young Stephen Grant."

"I am," admitted Mr. Satterthwaite. "Stephen Grant, if I remember rightly, had been in charge of Captain Harwell's horses, and had been discharged by his master for some trifling offense. On the morning after the homecoming, very early, Stephen Grant was seen in the vicinity of Ashley Grange, and could give no good account of his presence there. He was detained by the police as being concerned in the disappearance of Captain Harwell, but nothing could be proved against him, and he was eventually discharged. It is true that he might be supposed to bear a grudge against Captain Harwell for his summary dismissal, but the motive was undeniably of the flimsiest. I suppose the police felt they must do something. You see, as I said just now, Captain Harwell had not an enemy in the world."

"As far as was known," said Mr. Quin reflectively.

Mr. Satterthwaite nodded appreciatively.

"We are coming to that. What, after all, *was* known of Captain Harwell? When the police came to look into his antecedents they were confronted with a singular paucity of material. Who was Richard Harwell? Where did he come from? He had appeared, literally out of the blue, as it seemed. He was a magnificent rider, and apparently well off. Nobody in Kirtlington Mallet had bothered to inquire further. Miss Le Couteau had had no parents or guardians to make inquiries into the prospects and standing of her fiancé. She was her own mistress. The police theory at this point was clear enough. A rich girl and an impudent impostor. The old story!"

"But it was not quite that. True, Miss Le Couteau had no parents or guardians, but she had an excellent firm of solicitors in London who acted for her. Their evidence made the mystery deeper. Eleanor Le Couteau had wished to settle a sum outright upon her prospective husband, but he had refused. He himself was well off, he declared. It was proved conclusively that Harwell never had a penny of his wife's money. Her fortune was absolutely intact.

"He was, therefore, no common swindler; but was his object a refinement of the art? Did he propose blackmail at some future date if Eleanor Harwell should wish to marry some other man? I will admit that something of that kind seemed to me the most likely solution. It has always seemed so to me—until tonight."

Mr. Quin leaned forward, prompting him.

"Tonight?"

"Tonight—I am not satisfied with that. How did he manage to disappear so suddenly and completely—at that hour in the morning, with every laborer bestirring himself and tramping to work? Bareheaded, too."

"There is no doubt about that latter point—since the gardener saw him?"

"Yes—the gardener—John Mathias. Was there anything there, I wonder?"

"The police would not overlook him," said Mr. Quin.

"They questioned him closely. He never wavered in his statement. His wife bore him out. He left his cottage at seven to attend to the greenhouses, he returned at twenty minutes to eight. The servants in the house heard the front door slam at about a quarter after seven. That fixes the time when Captain Harwell left the house. Ah! yes, I know what you are thinking."

"Do you, I wonder?" said Mr. Quin.

"I fancy so. Time enough for Mathias to have made away with his master. But why, man, why? And if so, where did he hide the body?"

The landlord came in bearing a tray.

"Sorry to have kept you so long, gentlemen."

He set upon the table a mammoth steak and beside it a dish filled to overflowing with crisp brown potatoes. The odor from the dishes was pleasant to Mr. Satterthwaite's nostrils. He felt gracious.

"This looks excellent," he said. "Most excellent. We have been discussing the disappearance of Captain Harwell. What became of the gardener Mathias?"

"Took a place in Essex, I believe. Didn't care to stay hereabouts. There were some as looked askance at him, you understand. Not that I ever believed he had anything to do with it."

Mr. Satterthwaite helped himself to steak. Mr. Quin followed suit. The landlord seemed disposed to linger and chat. Mr. Satterthwaite had no objection; on the contrary.

"This Mathias now," he said. "What kind of a man was he?"

"Middle-aged chap, must have been a powerful fellow once, but bent and crippled with rheumatism. He had that mortal bad, was laid up many a time with it, unable to do any work. For my part, I think it was sheer kindness on Miss Eleanor's part to keep him on. He'd outgrown his usefulness as a gardener, though his wife managed to make herself useful up at the house. Been a cook, she had, and always willing to lend a hand."

"What sort of a woman was she?" asked Mr. Satterthwaite quickly.

The landlord's answer disappointed him.

"A plain body. Middle-aged, and dour-like in manner. Deaf, too. Not that I ever knew much of them. They'd only been here a month, you understand, when the thing happened. They say he'd been a rare good gardener in his time, though. Wonderful testimonials Miss Eleanor had with him."

"Was she interested in gardening?" asked Mr. Quin softly.

"No, sir, I couldn't say that she was, not like some of the ladies round here who pay good money to gardeners and spend the whole of their time grubbing about on their knees as well. Foolishness I call it. You see, Miss Le Couteau wasn't here very much except in the winter for the hunting. The rest of the time she was up in London and away in those foreign seaside places where they say the French ladies don't so much as put a toe into the water for fear of spoiling their costumes, or so I've heard."

Mr. Satterthwaite smiled.

"There was no—er—woman of any kind mixed up with Captain Harwell?" he asked.

Though his first theory was disposed of, he nevertheless clung to his idea.

Mr. William Jones shook his head.

"Nothing of that sort. Never a whisper of it. No, it's a dark mystery, that's what it is."

"And your theory? What do you yourself think?" persisted Mr. Satterthwaite.

"What do I think?"

"Yes."

"Don't know what to think. It's my belief as how he was done in, but who by I can't say. I'll fetch you gentlemen the cheese."

He stumped from the room bearing empty dishes. The storm, which had been quieting down, suddenly broke out with redoubled vigor. A flash of forked lightning and a great clap of thunder close upon each other made little Mr. Satterthwaite jump, and before the last echoes of the thunder had died away, a girl came into the room carrying the advertised cheese.

She was tall and dark, and handsome in a sullen fashion of her own. Her likeness to the landlord of the Bells and Motley was apparent enough to proclaim her his daughter.

"Good evening, Mary," said Mr. Quin. "A stormy night."

She nodded.

"I hate these stormy nights," she muttered.

"You are afraid of thunder, perhaps?" said Mr. Satterthwaite kindly.

"Afraid of thunder? Not me! There's little that I'm afraid of. No, but the storm sets them off. Talking, talking, the same thing over and over again, like a lot of parrots. Father begins it: 'It reminds me, this does, of the night poor Captain Harwell—' And so on, and so on." She turned on Mr. Quin, "You've heard how he goes on. What's the sense of it? Can't anyone let past things be?"

"A thing is only past when it is done with," said Mr. Quin.

"Isn't this done with? Suppose he wanted to disappear? These fine gentlemen do sometimes."

"You think he disappeared of his own free will?"

"Why not? It would make better sense than to suppose a kind-hearted creature like Stephen Grant murdered him. What should he murder him for, I should like to know? Stephen had had a drop too much one day and spoke to him saucy like, and got the sack for it. But what of it? He got another place just as good. Is that a reason to murder a man in cold blood?"

"But surely," said Mr. Satterthwaite, "the police were quite satisfied of his innocence."

"The police! What do the police matter? When Stephen comes

into the bar of an evening, every man looks at him queer like. They don't really believe he murdered Harwell, but they're not sure, and so they look at him sideways and edge away. Nice life for a man, to see people shrink away from you, as though you were something different from the rest of folks. Why won't Father hear of our getting married, Stephen and I? 'You can take your pigs to a better market, my girl. I've nothing against Stephen, but'—well, we don't know, do we?"

She stopped, her breast heaving with the violence of her resentment.

"It's cruel, cruel, that's what it is," she burst out. "Stephen, that wouldn't hurt a fly! And all through life there'll be people who'll think he did it. It's turning him queer and bitter like. I don't wonder, I'm sure. And me more he's like that, the more people think there must have been something in it."

Again she stopped. Her eyes were fixed on Mr. Quin's face, as though something in it was drawing this outburst from her.

"Can nothing be done?" said Mr. Satterthwaite.

He was genuinely distressed. The thing was, he saw, inevitable. The very vagueness and unsatisfactoriness of the evidence against Stephen Grant made it the more difficult for him to disprove the accusation.

The girl whirled round on him.

"Nothing but the truth can help him," she cried. "If Captain Harwell were to be found, if he was to come back. If the true rights of it were only known—"

She broke off with something very like a sob, and hurried quickly from the room.

"A fine-looking girl," said Mr. Satterthwaite. "A sad case altogether. I wish—I very much wish that something could be done about it."

His kind heart was troubled.

"We are doing what we can," said Mr. Quin. "There is still nearly half an hour before your car can be ready."

Mr. Satterthwaite stared at him.

"You think we can come at the truth just by—talking it over like this?"

"You have seen much of life," said Mr. Quin gravely. "More than most people."

"Life has passed me by," said Mr. Satterthwaite bitterly.

"But in so doing has sharpened your vision. Where others are blind you can see."

"It is true," said Mr. Satterthwaite. "I am a great observer."

He plumed himself complacently. The moment of bitterness was past.

"I look at it like this," he said after a minute or two. "To get at the cause for a thing, we must study the effect."

"Very good," said Mr. Quin approvingly.

"The effect in this case is that Miss Le Couteau—Mrs. Harwell, I mean—is a wife and yet not a wife. She is not free—she cannot marry again. And look at it as we will, we see Richard Harwell as a sinister figure, a man from nowhere with a mysterious past."

"I agree," said Mr. Quin. "You see what all are bound to see, what cannot be missed, Captain Harwell in the limelight, a suspicious figure.

Mr. Satterthwaite looked at him doubtfully. The words seemed somehow to suggest a faintly different picture to his mind.

"We have studied the effect," he said. "Or call it the *result*. We can now pass—"

Mr. Quin interrupted him.

"You have not touched on the result on the strictly material side."

"You are right," said Mr. Satterthwaite, after a moment or two for consideration. "One should do the thing thoroughly. Let us say then that the result of the tragedy is that Mrs. Harwell is a wife and not a wife, unable to marry again, that Mr. Cyrus Bradburn has been able to buy Ashley Grange and its contents for—sixty thousand pounds, was it?—and that somebody in Essex has been able to secure John Mathias as a gardener! For all that, we do not suspect 'somebody in Essex' or Mr. Cyrus Bradburn of having engineered the disappearance of Captain Harwell."

"You are sarcastic," said Mr. Quin.

Mr. Satterthwaite looked sharply at him.

"But surely you agree—"

"Oh! I agree," said Mr. Quin. "The idea is absurd. What next?"

"Let us imagine ourselves back on the fatal day. The disappearance has taken place, let us say, this very morning."

"No, no," said Mr. Quin, smiling. "Since, in our imagination at least, we have power over time, let us turn it the other way. Let us say the disappearance of Captain Harwell took place a hundred years ago. That we, in the year two thousand and twenty-five, are looking back."

"You are a strange man," said Mr. Satterthwaite slowly. "You believe in the past, not the present. Why?"

"You used, not long ago, the word atmosphere. There is no atmosphere in the present."

"That is true perhaps," said Mr. Satterthwaite thoughtfully. "Yes it is true. The present is apt to be—parochial."

"A good word," said Mr. Quin.

Mr. Satterthwaite gave a funny little bow.

"You are too kind," he said.

Let us take—not this present year, that would be too difficult, but say—last year," continued the other. "Sum it up for me, you, who have the gift of the neat phrase."

Mr. Satterthwaite thought for a minute. He was jealous of his reputation.

"A hundred years ago we have the age of powder and patches," he said. "Shall we say that 1924 was the age of crossword puzzles and cat burglars?"

"Very good," approved Mr. Quin. "You mean that nationally, not internationally, I presume?"

"As to crossword puzzles, I must confess that I do not know," said Mr. Satterthwaite. "But the cat burglar had a great inning on the Continent. You remember that series of famous thefts from French Châteaux? It is surmised that one man alone could not have done it. The most miraculous feats were performed to gain admission. There was a theory that a troupe of acrobats were concerned—the Clondinis. I once saw their performance—truly masterly. A mother, son and daughter. They vanished from the stage in a rather mysterious fashion. But we are wandering from our subject."

"Not very far," said Mr. Quin. "Only across the Channel."

"Where the French ladies will not wet their toes according to our worthy host," said Mr. Satterthwaite laughing.

There was a pause. It seemed somehow significant.

"Why did he disappear?" cried Mr. Satterthwaite. "Why? Why? It is incredible, a kind of conjuring trick."

"Yes," said Mr. Quin. "A conjuring trick. That describes it exactly. Atmosphere again, you see. And wherein does the essence of a conjuring trick lie?"

"'The quickness of the hand deceives the eye,'" quoted Mr. Satterthwaite glibly.

"That is everything, is it not? To deceive the eye? Sometimes by the quickness of the eye, sometimes—by other means. There are many devices, the pistol shot, the waving of a red handkerchief, something that seems important, but in reality is not. The eye is diverted from the real business, it is caught by the spectacular action that means nothing—nothing at all."

Mr. Satterthwaite leaned forward, his eyes shining.

"There is something in that. It is an idea."

He went on softly: "The pistol shot. What was the pistol shot in the conjuring trick we are discussing? What is the spectacular moment that holds the imagination?"

He drew in his breath sharply.

"The disappearance," breathed Mr. Satterthwaite. "Take that away, and it leaves nothing."

"Nothing? Suppose things took the same course without that dramatic gesture."

"You mean—supposing Miss Le Couteau were still to sell Ashley Grange to Mr. Bradburn and leave—for no reason?"

"Well."

"Well, why not? It would have aroused talk, I suppose, there would have been a lot of interest displayed in the value of the contents, in—Ah! wait!"

He was silent a minute, then burst out.

"You are right, there is too much limelight, the limelight on Captain Harwell. And because of that, she has been in shadow. Miss Le Couteau! Everyone asking 'Who is Captain Harwell? Where did he come from?' But because she is the injured party, no one makes inquiries about her. Was she really a French Canadian? Were those wonderful heirlooms really handed down to her? You were right when you said just now that we had not wandered far from our subject—only across the Channel. Those so called heirlooms were stolen from the French Chateaux, most of them valuable objet d'art, and in consequence difficult to dispose of. She buys the house—for a mere song, probably—settles down there and pays a good sum to an irreproachable Englishwoman to chaperone her. Then he comes. The plot is laid beforehand. The marriage, the disappearance and the nine days' wonder! What more natural than that a broken-hearted woman should want to sell everything that reminds her of past happiness? The American is a connoisseur, the things are genuine and beautiful, some of them beyond price. He makes an offer, she accepts it. She leaves the neighborhood, a sad and tragic figure. The great coup has come off. The eye of the public has been deceived by the quickness of the hand and the spectacular nature of the trick."

Mr. Satterthwaite paused, flushed with triumph.

"But for you, I should never have seen it," he said with sudden humility. "You have a most curious effect upon me. One says things so often without even seeing what they really mean. You have the knack of showing one. But it is still not quite clear to me. It must have been most difficult for Harwell to disappear as he did. After all, the police all over England were looking for him."

"They were probably looking," said Mr. Quin, "all over England."

"It would have been simplest to remain hidden at the Grange," mused Mr. Satterthwaite. "If it could be managed."

"He was, I think, very near the Grange," said Mr. Quin.

His look of significance was not lost on Mr. Satterthwaite.

"Mathias' cottage?" he exclaimed. "But the police must have searched it?"

"Repeatedly, I should imagine," said Mr. Quin.

"Mathias," said Mr. Satterthwaite, frowning.

"And Mrs. Mathias," said Mr. Quin.

Mr. Satterthwaite stared hard at him.

"If that gang was really the Clondinis," he said dreamily, "there are three of them in it. The two young ones were Harwell and Eleanor Le Couteau. The mother now, was she Mathias? But in that case."

"Mathias suffered from rheumatism, did he not?" said Mr. Quin innocently.

"Oh!" cried Mr. Satterthwaite. "I have it. But could it be done? I believe it could. Listen. Mathias was there a month. During that time, Harwell and Eleanor were away for a fortnight on a honeymoon. For the fortnight before the wedding, they were supposedly in town. A clever man could have doubled the parts of Harwell and Mathias. When Harwell was at Kirtlington Mallet, Mathias was conveniently laid up with rheumatism, with Mrs. Mathias to sustain the fiction. Her part was very necessary. Without her, someone might have suspected the truth. As you say, Harwell was hidden in Mathias' cottage. He *was* Mathias. When at last the plans matured, and Ashley Grange was sold, he and his wife gave out that they were taking a place in Essex. Exit John Mathias and his wife—for ever."

There was a knock at the coffee-room door, and Masters entered.

"The car is at the door, sir," he said.

Mr. Satterthwaite rose. So did Mr. Quin, who went across to the window, pulling the curtains. A beam of moonlight streamed into the room.

"The storm is over," he said.

Mr. Satterthwaite was pulling on his gloves.

"The Commissioner is dining with me next week," he said importantly. "I shall put my theory—ah!—before him."

"It will be easily proved or disproved," said Mr. Quin. "A comparison of the objects at Ashley Grange with a list supplied by the French police—!"

"Just so," said Mr. Satterthwaite. "Rather hard luck on Mr. Bradburn, but—well—"

"He can, I believe, stand the loss," said Mr. Quin.

Mr. Satterthwaite held out his hand.

"Good-by," he said. "I cannot tell you how much I have appreciated this unexpected meeting. You are leaving here tomorrow, I think you said?"

"Possibly tonight. My business here is done. I come and go, you know."

Mr. Satterthwaite remembered hearing those same words earlier in the evening. Rather curious.

He went out to the car and the waiting Masters. From the open door into the bar the landlord's voice floated out, rich and complacent.

"A dark mystery," he was saying. "A dark mystery, that's what it is."

But he did not use the word "dark." The word he used suggested quite a different color. Mr. William Jones was a man of discrimination who suited his adjectives to his company. The company in the bar liked then adjectives full flavored.

Mr. Satterthwaite reclined luxuriously in the comfortable limousine. His breast was swelled with triumph. He saw the girl Mary come out on the steps and stand under the creaking inn sign.

"She little knows," said Mr. Satterthwaite to himself. "She little knows what *I* am going to do!"

The sign of the Bells and Motley swayed gently in the wind.

4. THE SIGN IN THE SKY

The Judge was finishing his charge to the jury.

"Now, gentlemen, I have almost finished what I want to say to you. There is evidence for you to consider as to whether this case is plainly made out against this man so that you may say he is guilty of the murder of Vivien Barnaby. You have had the evidence of the servants as to the time the shot was fired. They have one and all agreed upon it. You have had the evidence of the letter written to the defendant by Vivien Barnaby on the morning of that same day, Friday, September 23rd, a letter which the defense has not attempted to deny. You have had evidence that the prisoner first denied having been at Deering Hill, and later, after evidence had been given by the police, admitted he had. You will draw your own conclusions from that denial. This is not a case of direct evidence. You will have to come to your own conclusions on the subject of motive—of means—of opportunity. The contention of the defense is that some person unknown entered the music room after the defendant had left it, and shot Vivien Barnaby with the gun which by a strange forgetfulness the defendant had left behind him. You have heard the defendant's story of the reason it took him half an hour to get home. If you disbelieve the defendant's story and are satisfied, beyond any reasonable doubt that the defendant did, upon Friday, September 23rd, discharge his gun at close quarters to Vivien Barnaby's head with intent to kill her, then, gentlemen, your verdict must be guilty. If, on the other hand, you have any reasonable doubt, it is your duty to acquit the prisoner. I will now ask you to retire to your room and consider and let me know when you have arrived at a conclusion."

The jury were absent a little under half an hour. They returned the verdict that to everyone had seemed a foregone conclusion, the verdict of "Guilty."

Mr. Satterthwaite left the court after hearing the verdict, with a thoughtful frown on his face.

A mere murder trial, as such, did not attract him. He was of too fastidious a temperament to find interest in the sordid details of the average crime. But the Wylde case had been different. Young Martin Wylde was what is termed a gentleman—and the victim, Sir George Barnaby's young wife, had been personally known to the elderly gentleman.

He was thinking of all this as he walked up Holborn, and then plunged into a tangle of mean streets leading in the direction of Soho. In one of these streets there was a small restaurant, known only to the few, of whom Mr. Satterthwaite was one. It was not cheap—it was on the contrary, exceedingly expensive, since it catered exclusively for the palate of the jaded *gourmet*. It was quiet—no strains of jazz were allowed to disturb the hushed atmosphere—it was rather dark; waiters appeared soft-footed out of the twilight, bearing silver dishes with the air of participating in some holy rite. The name of the restaurant was Arlecchino.

Still thoughtful, Mr. Satterthwaite turned into the Arlecchino and made for his favorite table in a recess in the far corner. Owing to the twilight before mentioned, it was not until he was quite close to it that he saw it was already occupied by a tall, dark man who sat with his face in shadow, and with a play of color from a stained window turning his sober garb to a kind of riotous motley.

Mr. Satterthwaite would have turned back, but just at that moment the stranger moved slightly and the other recognized him.

"God bless my soul," said Mr. Satterthwaite, who was given to old-fashioned expressions. "Why, it's Mr. Quin!"

Three times before he had met Mr. Quin, and each time the meeting had resulted in something a little out of the ordinary. A strange person, this Mr. Quin, with a knack of showing you the things you had known all along in a totally different light.

At once Mr. Satterthwaite felt excited—pleasurably excited. His rôle was that of the looker on, and he knew it, but sometimes when in the company of Mr. Quin, he had the illusion of being an actor—and the principal actor at that.

"This is very pleasant," he said, beaming all over his dried up little face. "Very pleasant indeed. You've no objection to my joining you, I hope?"

"I shall be delighted," said Mr. Quin. "As you see I have not yet begun my meal."

A deferential head waiter hovered up out of the shadows. Mr. Satterthwaite, as befitted a man with a seasoned palate, gave his whole mind to the task of selection. In a few minutes, the head waiter, a slight smile of approbation on his lips, retired, and a young satellite began his ministrations. Mr. Satterthwaite turned to Mr. Quin.

"I have just come from the Old Bailey," he began. "A sad business, I thought."

"He was found guilty?" said Mr. Quin.

"Yes, the jury were out only half an hour."

Mr. Quin bowed his head.

"An inevitable result—on the evidence," he said.

"And yet," began Mr. Satterthwaite—and stopped.

Mr. Quin finished the sentence for him.

"And yet your sympathies were with the accused? Is that what you were going to say?"

"I suppose it was. Martin Wylde is a nice looking young fellow—one can hardly believe it of him. All the same, there have been a good many nice looking young fellows lately who have turned out to be murderers of a particularly cold blooded and repellent type."

"Too many," said Mr. Quin quietly.

"I beg your pardon?" said Mr. Satterthwaite, slightly startled.

"Too many for Martin Wylde. There has been a tendency from the beginning to regard this as just one more of a series of the same type of crime—a man seeking to free himself from one woman in order to marry another."

"Well," said Mr. Satterthwaite, doubtfully. "On the evidence—"

"Ah!" said Mr. Quin quickly, "I am afraid I have not followed all the evidence."

Mr. Satterthwaite's self-confidence came back to him with a rush. He felt a sudden sense of power. He was tempted to be consciously dramatic.

"Let me try and show it to you. I have met the Barnabys, you understand. I know the peculiar circumstances. With me, you will come behind the scenes—you will see the thing from inside."

Mr. Quin leaned forward with his quick encouraging smile.

"If anyone can show me that, it will be Mr. Satterthwaite," he murmured.

Mr. Satterthwaite gripped the table with both hands. He was uplifted, carried out of himself. For the moment, he was an artist pure and simple—an artist whose medium was words.

Swiftly, with a dozen broad strokes, he etched in the picture of life at Deering Hill. Sir George Barnaby, elderly, obese, purse-proud. A man perpetually fussing over the little things of life. A man who wound up his clocks every Friday afternoon, and who paid his own housekeeping books every Tuesday morning, and who always saw to the locking of his own front door every night. A careful man.

And from Sir George he went on to Lady Barnaby. Here his touch was gentler, but none the less sure. He had seen her but once, but his impression of her was definite and lasting. A vivid, defiant creature—pitifully young. A trapped child, that was how he described her.

"She hated him, you understand? She had married him before she knew what she was doing. And now—"

She was desperate—that was how he put it. Turning this way and that. She had no money of her own; she was entirely dependent on this elderly husband. But all the same she was a creature at bay—still unsure of her own powers, with a beauty that was as yet more promise than actuality. And she was greedy. Mr. Satterthwaite affirmed that definitely. Side by side with defiance there ran a greedy streak—a clasping and a clutching at life.

"I never met Martin Wylde," continued Mr. Satterthwaite. "But I heard of him. He lived less than a mile away. Farming, that was his line. And she took an interest in farming—or pretended to. If you ask me, it was pretending. I think that she saw in him her only way of escape—and she grabbed at him, greedily, like a child might have done. Well, there could only be one end to that. We know what that end was, because the letters were read out in court. He kept her letters—she didn't keep his, but from the text of hers one can see that he was cooling off. He admits as much. There was the other girl. She also lived in the village of Deering Vale. Her father was the doctor there. You saw her in court, perhaps? No, I remember, you were not there, you said. I shall have to describe her to you. A fair girl—very fair. Gentle. Perhaps—yes, perhaps a tiny bit stupid. But very restful, you know. And loyal. Above all, loyal."

He looked at Mr. Quin for encouragement, and Mr. Quin gave it him by a slow appreciative smile. Mr. Satterthwaite went on.

"You heard that last letter read—you must have seen it, in the papers, I mean. The one written on the morning of Friday, September 13th. It was full of desperate reproaches and vague threats, and it ended by begging Martin Wylde to come to Deering Hill that same evening at six o'clock. *I will leave the side door open for you, so that no one need know you have been here. I shall be in the music room.* It was sent by hand."

Mr. Satterthwaite paused for a minute or two.

"When he was first arrested, you remember, Martin Wylde denied that he had been to the house at all that evening. His statement was that he had taken his gun and gone out shooting in the woods. But when the police brought forward their evidence, that statement broke down. They had found his finger-prints, you remember, both on the wood of the side door and on one of the two cocktail glasses on the table in the music room. He admitted then that he had come to see Lady Barnaby, that they had had a stormy interview, but that it had ended in his having managed to soothe her down. He swore that he left his gun outside leaning against the wall near the door, and that he left Lady Barnaby alive and well, the time being then a minute or two after a quarter past six. He went straight home, he says, but evidence was called to show that he did not reach his farm until a quarter to seven, and, as I have just mentioned, it is barely a mile away. It would not take half an hour to get there. He forgot all about his gun, he declares. Not a very likely statement—and yet—"

"And yet?" queried Mr. Quin.

"Well," said Mr. Satterthwaite slowly, "it's a possible one, isn't it? Counsel ridiculed the supposition, of course, but I think he was wrong. You see, I've known a good many young men, and these emotional scenes upset them very much—especially the dark nervous type like Martin Wylde. Women, now, can go through a scene like that, and feel positively better for it afterward, with all their wits about them. It acts like a safety valve for them, steadies their nerves down and all that. But I can see Martin Wylde going away with his head in a whirl, sick and miserable, and without a thought of the gun he had left leaning up against the wall."

He was silent for some minutes before he went on.

"Not that it matters. For the next part is only too clear, unfortunately. It was exactly twenty minutes past six when the shot was heard. All the servants heard it, the cook, the kitchen-maid, the butler, the housemaid and Lady Barnaby's own maid. They came rushing to the music room. She was lying huddled over the arm of her chair. The gun had been discharged close to the back of her head, so that the shot hadn't a chance to scatter. At least two of them penetrated the brain."

He paused again and Mr. Quin asked casually:

"The servants.gave evidence, I suppose?"

Mr. Satterthwaite nodded.

"Yes. The butler got there a second or two before the others, but their evidence was practically a repetition of each other's."

"So they *all* gave evidence," said Mr. Quin musingly. "There were no exceptions?"

"Now I remember it," said Mr. Satterthwaite, "the housemaid was only called at the inquest. She's gone to Canada since, I believe."

"I see," said Mr. Quin.

There was a silence, and somehow the air of the little restaurant seemed to be charged with an uneasy feeling. Mr. Satterthwaite felt suddenly as though he were on the defensive.

"Why shouldn't she?" he said abruptly.

"Why should she?" said Mr. Quin with a very slight shrug of the shoulders.

Somehow, the question annoyed Mr. Satterthwaite. He wanted to shy away from it—to get back on familiar ground.

"There couldn't be much doubt who fired the shot. As a matter of fact the servants seemed to have lost their heads a bit. There was no one in the house to take charge. It was some minutes before anyone thought of ringing up the police, and when they did so, they found that the telephone was out of order."

"Oh," said Mr. Quin. "The telephone was out of order."

"It was," said Mr. Satterthwaite—and was struck suddenly by the feeling that he had said something tremendously important. "It might, of course, have been done on purpose," he said slowly. "But there seems no point in that. Death was practically instantaneous."

Mr. Quin said nothing, and Mr. Satterthwaite felt that his explanation was unsatisfactory.

"There was absolutely no one to suspect but young Wylde," he went on. "By his own account, even, he was only out of the house three minutes before the shot was fired. And who else could have fired it? Sir George was at a bridge party a few houses away. He left there at half past six and was met just outside the gate by a servant bringing him the news. The last rubber finished at half past six exactly—no doubt about that. Then there was Sir George's secretary, Henry Thompson. He was in London that day, and actually at a business meeting at the moment the shot was fired. Finally there is Sylvia Dale who, after all, had a perfectly good motive, impossible as it seems that she should have had anything to do with such a crime. She was at the station of Deering Vale seeing a friend off by the 6:28 train. That lets her out. Then the servants. What earthly motive could any one of them have? Besides they all arrived on the spot practically simultaneously. No, it must have been Martin Wylde."

But he said it in a dissatisfied kind of voice.

They went on with their lunch. Mr. Quin was not in a talkative mood, and Mr. Satterthwaite had said all he had to say. But the silence was not a barren one. It was filled with the growing dissatisfaction of Mr. Satterthwaite, heightened and fostered in some strange way by the mere quiescence of the other man.

Mr. Satterthwaite suddenly put down his knife and fork with a clatter.

"Supposing that that young man is really innocent," he said. "He's going to be hanged."

He looked very startled and upset about it. And still Mr. Quin said nothing.

"It's not as though—" began Mr. Satterthwaite, and stopped. "Why shouldn't the woman go to Canada?" he ended inconsequently.

Mr. Quin shook his head.

"I don't even know what part of Canada she went to," continued Mr. Satterthwaite peevishly.

"Could you find out?" suggested the other.

"I suppose I could. The butler, now. He'd know. Or possibly Thompson, the secretary."

He paused again. When he resumed speech, his voice sounded almost pleading.

"It's not as though it were anything to do with me?"

"That a young man is going to be hanged in a little over three weeks?"

"Well, yes—if you put it that way, I suppose. Yes, I see what you mean. Life and death. And that poor girl, too. It's not that I'm hardhearted—but, after all—what good will it do? Isn't the whole thing rather fantastic? Even if I found out where the woman's gone to in Canada—why, it would probably mean that I should have to go out there myself."

Mr. Satterthwaite looked seriously upset.

"And I was thinking of going to the Riviera next week," he said pathetically.

And his glance toward Mr. Quin said as plainly as it could be said: "Do let me off, won't you?"

"You have never been to Canada?"

"Never."

"A very interesting country."

Mr. Satterthwaite looked at him undecidedly.

"You think I ought to go?"

Mr. Quin leaned back in his chair and lighted a cigarette. Between puffs of smoke, he spoke deliberately.

"You are, I believe, a rich man, Mr. Satterthwaite. Not a millionaire, but a man able to indulge a hobby without counting the expense. You have looked on at the dramas of other people. Have you never contemplated stepping in and playing a part? Have you never seen yourself for a minute as the arbiter of other people's destinies— standing in the center of the stage with life and death in your hands?"

Mr. Satterthwaite leaned forward. The old eagerness surged over him.

"You mean—if I go on this wild goose chase to Canada—"

Mr. Quin smiled.

"Oh! it was your suggestion, going to Canada, not mine," he said lightly.

"You can't put me off like that," said Mr. Satterthwaite earnestly. "Whenever I have come across you—" He stopped.

"Well?"

"There is something about you I do not understand. Perhaps I never shall. The last time I met you—"

"On Midsummer Eve."

Mr. Satterthwaite was startled, as though the words held a clue that he did not quite understand.

"Was it Midsummer Eve?" he asked confusedly.

"Yes. But let us not dwell on that. It is unimportant, is it not?"

"Since you say so," said Mr. Satterthwaite courteously. He felt that elusive clue slipping through his fingers. "When I come back from Canada—" he paused a little awkwardly—"I—I should much like to see you again."

"I am afraid I have no fixed address for the moment," said Mr. Quin regretfully. "But I often come to this place. If you also frequent it, we shall no doubt meet before very long."

They parted pleasantly.

Mr. Satterthwaite was very excited. He hurried round to Cook's and inquired about boat sailings. Then he rang up Deering Hill. The voice of a butler, suave and deferential, answered him.

"My name is Satterthwaite. I am speaking for a—er—firm of solicitors. I wished to make a few inquiries about a young woman who was recently housemaid in your establishment."

"Would that be Louisa, sir? Louisa Bullard?"

"That is the name," said Mr. Satterthwaite, very pleased to be told it.

"I regret she is not in this country, sir. She went to Canada six months ago."

"Can you give me her present address?"

The butler was afraid he couldn't. It was a place in the mountains she had gone to—a Scotch name—ah! Banff, that was it. Some of the other young women in the house had been expecting to hear from her, but she had never written or given them any address.

Mr. Satterthwaite thanked him and rang off. He was still undaunted. The adventurous spirit was strong in his breast. He would go to Banff. If this Louisa Bullard was there, he would track her down somehow or other.

To his own surprise, he enjoyed the trip greatly. It was many years since he had taken a long sea voyage. The Riviera, Le Touquet and Deauville, and Scotland had been his usual round. The feeling that he was setting off on an impossible mission added a secret zest to his journey. What an utter fool these fellow travelers of his would think him did they but know the object of his quest! But then—they were not acquainted with Mr. Quin.

In Banff he found his objective easily attained. Louisa Bullard was employed in the large hotel there. Twelve hours after his arrival he was standing face to face with her.

She was a woman of about thirty-five, anemic looking, but with a strong frame. She had pale brown hair inclined to curl, and a pair of honest brown eyes. She was, he thought, slightly stupid, but very trustworthy.

She accepted quite readily his statement that he had been asked to collect a few further facts from her about the tragedy at Deering Hill.

"I saw in the paper that Mr. Martin Wylde had been convicted, sir. Very sad, it is, too."

She seemed, however, to have no doubt as to his guilt.

"A nice young gentleman gone wrong. But though I wouldn't speak ill of the dead, it was her ladyship what led him on. Wouldn't leave him alone, she wouldn't. Well, they've both got their punishment. There's a text used to hang on my wall when I was a child, 'God is not mocked,' and it's very true. I knew something was going to happen that very evening—and sure enough it did."

"How was that?" said Mr. Satterthwaite.

"I was in my room, sir, changing my dress, and I happened to glance out of the window. There was a train going along, and the white smoke of it rose up in the air, and if you'll believe me it formed itself into the sign of a gigantic hand. A great white hand against the crimson of the sky. The fingers were crooked like, as though they were reaching out for something. It fair gave me a turn. 'Did you ever, now?' I said to myself. 'That's a sign of something coming'— and sure enough at that very minute I heard the shot. 'It's come,' I said to myself, and I rushed downstairs and joined Carrie and the others who were in the hall, and we went into the music room and there she was, shot through the head—and the blood and everything. Horrible! I spoke up, I did, and told Sir George how I'd seen the sign beforehand, but he didn't seem to think much of it. An unlucky day, that was; I'd felt it in my bones from early in the morning. Friday, and the 13th—what could you expect?"

She rambled on. Mr. Satterthwaite was patient. Again and again he took her back to the crime, questioning her closely. In the end he was forced to confess defeat. Louisa Bullard had told all she knew, and her story was perfectly simple and straightforward.

Yet he did discover one fact of importance. The post in question had been suggested to her by Mr. Thompson, Sir George's secretary.

The wages attached were so large that she was tempted, and accepted the job, although it involved her leaving England very hurriedly. A Mr. Denman had made all the arrangements to this end and had also warned her not to write to her fellow servants in England, as this might "get her into trouble with the immigration authorities," which statement she had accepted in blind faith.

The amount of the wages, casually mentioned by her, was indeed so large that Mr. Satterthwaite was startled. After some hesitation he made up his mind to approach this Mr. Denman.

He found very little difficulty in inducing Mr. Denman to tell all he knew. The latter had come across Thompson in London, and Thompson had done him a good turn. The secretary had written to him in September saying that for personal reasons Sir George was anxious to get this girl out of England. Could he find her a job? A sum of money had been sent to raise the wages to a high figure.

"Usual trouble, I guess," said Mr. Denman, leaning back nonchalantly in his chair. "Seems a nice quiet girl, too."

Mr. Satterthwaite did not agree that this was the usual trouble. Louisa Bullard, he was sure, was not a cast off fancy of Sir George Barnaby's. For some reason it had been vital to get her out of England. But why? And who was at the bottom of it? Sir George himself, working through Thompson? Or the latter working on his own initiative, and dragging in his employer's name.

Still pondering over these questions, Mr. Satterthwaite made the return journey. He was cast down and despondent. His journey had done no good.

Smarting under a sense of failure, he made his way to the Arlecchino the day after his return. He hardly expected to be successful the first time, but to his satisfaction the familiar figure was sitting at the table in the recess, and the dark face of Mr. Harley Quin smiled a welcome.

"Well," said Mr. Satterthwaite as he helped himself to a pat of butter, "you sent me on a nice wild goose chase."

Mr. Quin raised his eyebrows.

"I sent you?" he objected. "It was your own idea entirely.

"Whose-ever idea it was, it's not succeeded. Louisa Bullard has nothing to tell."

Thereupon Mr. Satterthwaite related the details of his conversation with the housemaid and then went on to his interview with Mr. Denman. Mr. Quin listened in silence.

"In one sense, I was justified," continued Mr. Satterthwaite. "She was deliberately got out of the way. But why? I can't see it."

"No?" said Mr. Quin, and his voice was, as ever, provocative.

Mr. Satterthwaite flushed.

"I daresay you think I might have questioned her more adroitly. I can assure you that I took her over the story again and again. It was not my fault that I did not get what we want."

"Are you sure," said Mr. Quin, "that you did not get what you want?"

Mr. Satterthwaite looked up at him in astonishment, and met that sad mocking gaze he knew so well.

The little man shook his head, slightly bewildered.

There was a silence, and then Mr. Quin said, with a total change of manner:

"You gave me a wonderful picture the other day of the people in this business. In a few words you made them stand out as clearly as though they were etched. I wish you would do something of that kind for the place—you left that in shadow."

Mr. Satterthwaite was flattered.

"The place? Deering Hill? Well, it's a very ordinary sort of house nowadays. Red brick, you know, and bay windows. Quite hideous outside, but very comfortable inside. Not a very large house. About two acres of ground. They're all much the same, those houses round the links. Built for rich men to live in. The inside of the house is reminiscent of a hotel—the bedrooms are like hotel suites. Baths and hot and cold basins in all the bedrooms and a good many gilded electric light fittings. All wonderfully comfortable, but not very country-like. You can tell that Deering Vale is only nineteen miles from London."

Mr. Quin listened attentively.

"The train service is bad, I have heard," he remarked.

"Oh! I don't know about that," said Mr. Satterthwaite, warming to his subject. "I was down there for a bit last summer. I found it quite convenient for town. Of course the trains only go every hour. Forty-eight minutes past the hour from Waterloo—up to 10:48."

"And how long does it take to Deering Vale?"

"Just about three quarters of an hour. Twenty-eight minutes past the hour at Deering Vale.

"Of course," said Mr. Quin with a gesture of vexation. "I should have remembered. Miss Dale saw someone off by the 6:28 that evening, didn't she?"

Mr. Satterthwaite did not reply for a minute or two. His mind had gone back with a rush to his unsolved problem. Presently he said:

"I wish you would tell me what you meant just now when you asked me if I was sure I had not got what I wanted?"

It sounded rather complicated, put that way, but Mr. Quin made no pretense of not understanding.

"I just wondered if you weren't being a little too exacting. After all, you found out that Louisa Bullard was deliberately got out of the country. That being so, there must be a reason. And the reason must lie in what she said to you."

"Well," said Mr. Satterthwaite argumentatively. "What did she say? If she'd given evidence at the trial, what could she have said?"

"She might have told what she saw," said Mr. Quin.

"What did she see?"

"A sign in the sky."

Mr. Satterthwaite stared at him.

"Are you thinking of *that* nonsense? That superstitious notion of its being the hand of God?"

"Perhaps," said Mr. Quin. "For all you and I know it may have been the hand of God, you know."

The other was clearly puzzled at the gravity of his manner.

"Nonsense," he said. "She said herself it was the smoke of the train."

"An up train or a down train, I wonder," murmured Mr. Quin.

"Hardly an up train. They go at ten minutes to the hour. It must have been a down train—the 6:28—no, that won't do. She said the shot came immediately afterward, and we know the shot was fired at twenty minutes past six. The train couldn't have been ten minutes early."

"Hardly, on that line," agreed Mr. Quin.

Mr. Satterthwaite was staring ahead of him.

"Perhaps a goods train," he murmured. "But surely, if so—"

"There would have been no need to get her out of England. I agree," said Mr. Quin.

Mr. Satterthwaite gazed at him, fascinated.

"The 6:28," he said slowly. "But if so, if the shot was fired then, why did everyone say it was earlier."

"Obvious," said Mr. Quin. "The clocks must have been wrong."

"All of them?" said Mr. Satterthwaite doubtfully. "That's a pretty tall coincidence, you know."

"I wasn't thinking of it as a coincidence," said the other. "I was thinking that it was Friday."

"Friday?" said Mr. Satterthwaite.

"You did tell me, you know, that Sir George always wound the clocks on a Friday afternoon," said Mr. Quin apologetically.

"He put them back ten minutes," said Mr. Satterthwaite, almost in a whisper, so awed was he by the discoveries he was making. "Then he went out to bridge. I think he must have opened the note from his wife to Martin Wylde that morning—yes, decidedly he opened it. He left his bridge party at 6:30, found Martin's gun standing by the side door, and went in and shot her from behind. Then he went out again, threw the gun into the bushes where it was found later, and was apparently just coming out of the neighbor's gate when someone came running to fetch him. But the telephone— what about the telephone? Ah! yes, I see. He disconnected it so that a summons could not be sent to the police that way—they might have noted the time it was received. And Wylde's story works out now. The real time he left was five and twenty past six. Walking slowly, he would reach home about a quarter to seven. Yes, I see it all. Louisa was the only danger with her endless talk about her superstitious fancies. Someone might realize the significance of the train and then—good-by to that excellent *alibi*."

"Wonderful," commented Mr. Quin.

Mr. Satterthwaite turned to him, flushed with success.

"The only thing is—how to proceed now?"

"I should suggest Sylvia Dale," said Mr. Quin.

Mr. Satterthwaite looked doubtful.

"I mentioned to you," he said. "She seemed to me a little—er—stupid."

"She has a father and brothers who will take the necessary steps."

"That is true," said Mr. Satterthwaite, relieved.

A very short time afterward he was sitting with the girl, telling her the story. She listened attentively. She put no questions to him but when he had done she rose.

"I must have a taxi—at once."

"My dear child, what are you going to do?"

"I am going to Sir George Barnaby."

"Impossible. Absolutely the wrong procedure. Allow me to—"

He twittered on by her side. But he produced no impression. Sylvia Dale was intent on her own plans. She allowed him to go with her in the taxi, but to all his remonstrances she addressed a deaf ear. She left him in the taxi while she went into Sir George's city office.

It was half an hour later when she came out. She looked exhausted, her fair beauty drooping like a waterless flower. Mr. Satterthwaite received her with concern.

"I've won," she murmured, as she leaned back with half closed eyes.

"What?" he was startled. "What did you do? What did you say?"

She sat up a little.

"I told him that Louisa Bullard had been to the police with her story. I told him that the police had made inquiries and that he had been seen going into his own grounds and out again, a few minutes after half past six. I told him that the game was up. He—he went to pieces. I told him that there was still time for him to get away, that the police weren't coming for another hour to arrest him. I told him that if he'd sign a confession that he'd killed Vivien I'd do nothing, but that if he didn't I'd scream and tell the whole building the truth. He was so panicky that he didn't know what he was doing. He signed the paper without realizing what he was doing."

She thrust it into his hands.

"Take it—take it. You know what to do with it so that they'll set Martin free."

"He actually signed it," cried Mr. Satterthwaite, amazed.

"He is a little stupid, you know," said Sylvia Dale. "So am I," she added as an afterthought. "That is why I know how stupid people behave. We get rattled, you know, and then we do the wrong thing and are sorry afterward."

She shivered and Mr. Satterthwaite patted her hand.

"You need something to pull you together," he said. "Come, we are close to a very favorite resort of mine—the Arlecchino. Have you ever been there?"

She shook her head.

Mr. Satterthwaite stopped the taxi and took the girl into the little restaurant. He made his way to the table in the recess, his heart-beating hopefully. But the table was empty.

Sylvia Dale saw the disappointment in his face.

"What is it?" she asked.

"Nothing," said Mr. Satterthwaite. "That is, I half expected to see a friend of mine here. It doesn't matter. Some day, I expect, I shall see him again."

5. THE SOUL OF THE CROUPIER

Mr. Satterthwaite was enjoying the sunshine on the terrace at Monte Carlo.

Every year regularly, on the second Sunday in January, Mr. Satterthwaite left England for the Riviera. He was far more punctual than any swallow. In the month of April he returned to England. May and June he spent in London, and had never been known to miss Ascot. He left town after the Eton and Harrow match, paying a few country house visits before repairing to Deauville or Le Touquet. Shooting parties occupied most of September and October, and he usually spent a couple of months in town to wind up the year. He knew everybody, and it may safely be said that everybody knew him.

This morning he was frowning. The blue of the sea was admirable, the gardens were, as always, a delight, but the people disappointed him—he thought them an ill-dressed shoddy crowd. Some, of course, were gamblers, doomed souls who could not keep away. Those Mr. Satterthwaite tolerated. They were a necessary background. But he missed the usual leaven of the *élite*—his own people.

"It's the exchange," said Mr. Satterthwaite gloomily. "All sorts of people come here now who could never have afforded it before. And then, of course, I'm getting old. All the young people—the people coming on—they go to these Swiss places."

But there were others that he missed, the well dressed Barons and Counts of foreign diplomacy, the Grand Dukes and the Royal Princes. The only Royal Prince he had seen so far was working a lift in one of the less well-known Hotels. He missed, too, the beautiful and expensive ladies. There were still a few of them, but not nearly so many as there used to be.

Mr. Satterthwaite was an earnest student of the drama called Life, but he liked his material to be highly colored. He felt discouragement sweep over him. Values were changing—and he—was too old to change.

It was at that moment that he observed the Countess Czarnova coming toward him.

Mr. Satterthwaite had seen the Countess at Monte Carlo for many seasons now. The first time he had seen her she had been in the company of a Grand Duke. On the next occasion she was with an Austrian Baron. On successive years her friends had been sallow men wearing rather flamboyant jewelry. For the last year or two she was much seen with very young men, almost boys.

She was walking with a very young man now. Mr. Satterthwaite happened to know him, and he was sorry. Franklin Rudge was a young American, a typical product of one of the Middle West States, eager to register impressions, crude, but lovable, a curious mixture of native shrewdness and idealism. He was in Monte Carlo with a party of other young Americans of both sexes, all much of the same type. It was their first glimpse of the Old World and they were outspoken in criticism and in appreciation.

On the whole they disliked the English people in the hotel, and the English people disliked them. Mr. Satterthwaite, who prided himself on being a cosmopolitan, rather liked them. Their directness and vigor appealed to him, though their occasional solecisms made him shudder.

It occurred to him that the Countess Czarnova was a most unsuitable friend for young Franklin Rudge. He took off his hat politely as they came abreast of him, and the Countess gave him a charming bow and smile.

She was a very tall woman, superbly made. Her hair was black, so were her eyes, and her eyelashes and eyebrows were more superbly black than any Nature had ever fashioned.

Mr. Satterthwaite who knew far more of feminine secrets than it is good for any man to know, rendered immediate homage to the art with which she was made up. Her complexion appeared to be flawless, of a uniform creamy white. The very faint bistre shadows under her eyes were most effective. Her mouth was neither crimson nor scarlet, but a subdued wine color. She was dressed in a very daring creation of black and white, and carried a parasol of the shade of pinky red which is most helpful to the complexion.

Franklin Rudge was looking happy and important.

"There goes a young fool," said Mr. Satterthwaite to himself. "But I suppose it's no business of mine, and anyway he wouldn't listen to me. Well, well, I've bought experience myself in my time."

But he still felt rather worried, because there was a very attractive little American girl in the party, and he was sure that she would not like Franklin Rudge's friendship with the Countess at all.

He was just about to retrace his steps in the opposite direction when he caught sight of the girl in question coming up one of the paths toward him. She wore a well cut tailor made suit with a white muslin shirt waist, she had on good sensible walking shoes, and carried a guidebook. There are some Americans who pass through Paris and emerge clothed as the Queen of Sheba, but Elizabeth Martin was not one of them. She was "doing Europe" in a stern conscientious spirit. She had high ideas of culture and art and she was anxious to get as much as possible for her limited store of money.

It is doubtful if Mr. Satterthwaite thought of her as either cultured or artistic. To him she merely appeared very young.

"Good morning, Mr. Satterthwaite," said Elizabeth. "Have you seen Franklin—Mr. Rudge—anywhere about?"

"I saw him just a few minutes ago."

"With his friend the Countess, I suppose," said the girl sharply.

"Er—with the Countess, yes," admitted Mr. Satterthwaite.

"That Countess of his doesn't cut any ice with me," said the girl in a rather high shrill voice. "Franklin's just crazy about her. *Why* I can't think."

"She's got a very charming manner, I believe," said Mr. Satterthwaite cautiously.

"Do you know her?"

"Slightly."

"I'm right down worried about Franklin," said Miss Martin. "That boy's got a lot of sense as a rule. You'd never think he'd fall for this sort of siren stuff. And he won't hear a thing, he gets madder than a hornet if anyone tries to say a word to him. Tell me, anyway— is she a real Countess?"

"I shouldn't like to say," said Mr. Satterthwaite. "She may be."

"That's the real Ha Ha English manner," said Elizabeth with signs of displeasure. "All I can say is that in Sargon Springs—that's our home town, Mr. Satterthwaite—that Countess would look a mighty queer bird."

Mr. Satterthwaite thought it possible. He forebore to point out that they were not in Sargon Springs but in the principality of Monaco where the Countess happened to synchronize with her environment a great deal better than Miss Martin did.

He made no answer and Elizabeth went on toward the Casino. Mr. Satterthwaite sat on a seat in the sun, and was presently joined by Franklin Rudge. Rudge was full of enthusiasm.

"I'm enjoying myself," he announced with naïve enthusiasm. "Yes, sir! This is what I call seeing life—rather a different kind of life from what we have in the States."

The elder man turned a thoughtful face to him.

"Life is lived very much the same everywhere," he said rather wearily. "It wears different clothes—that's all."

Franklin Rudge stared.

"I don't get you."

"No," said Mr. Satterthwaite. "That's because you've got a long way to travel yet. But I apologize. No elderly man should permit himself to get into the habit of preaching."

"Oh! that's all right." Rudge laughed, displaying the beautiful teeth of all his countrymen. "I don't say, mind you, that I'm not disappointed in the Casino. I thought the gambling would be different—something much more feverish. It seems just rather dull and sordid to me."

"Gambling is life and death to the gambler, but it has no great spectacular value," said Mr. Satterthwaite. "It is more exciting to read about than to see."

The young man nodded his agreement.

"You're rather a big bug socially, aren't you?" he asked, with a diffident candor that made it impossible to take offense. "I mean you know all the Duchesses and Earls and Countesses and things."

"A good many of them," said Mr. Satterthwaite. "And also the Jews and the Portuguese and the Greeks and the Argentines."

"Eh?" said Mr. Rudge.

"I was just explaining," said Mr. Satterthwaite, "that I move in English society."

Franklin Rudge meditated for a moment or two.

"You know the Countess Czarnova, don't you?" he said at length.

"Slightly," said Mr. Satterthwaite, making the same answer he had made to Elizabeth.

"Now there's a woman whom it's been very interesting to meet. One's inclined to think that the aristocracy of Europe is played out and effete. That may be true of the men, but the women are different. Isn't it a pleasure to meet an exquisite creature like the Countess? Witty, charming, intelligent, generations of civilization behind her, an aristocrat to her finger tips!"

"Is she?" asked Mr. Satterthwaite.

"Well, isn't she? You know what her family are?"

"No," said Mr. Satterthwaite. "I'm afraid I know very little about her."

"She was a Radzynski," explained Franklin Rudge. "One of the oldest families in Hungary. She's had the most extraordinary life. You know that great rope of pearls she wears?"

Mr. Satterthwaite nodded.

"That was given her by the King of Bosnia. She smuggled some secret papers out of the kingdom for him."

"I heard," said Mr. Satterthwaite, "that the pearls had been given her by the King of Bosnia."

The fact was indeed a matter of common gossip, it being reported that the lady had been a *chère amie* of His Majesty's in days gone by.

"Now I'll tell you something more."

Mr. Satterthwaite listened, and the more he listened the more he admired the fertile imagination of the Countess Czarnova. No vulgar "siren stuff" (as Elizabeth Martin had put it) for her. The young man was shrewd enough in that way, clean living and idealistic. No, the Countess moved austerely through a labyrinth of diplomatic intrigues. She had enemies, detractors—naturally! It was a glimpse, so the young American was to feel, into the life of the old régime with the Countess as the central figure, aloof, aristocratic, the friend of counselors and princes, a figure to inspire romantic devotion.

"And she's had any amount to contend against," ended the young man warmly. "It's an extraordinary thing, but she's never found a woman who would be a real friend to her. Women have been against her all her life."

"Probably," said Mr. Satterthwaite.

"Don't you call it a scandalous thing?" demanded Rudge hotly.

"N-no," said Mr. Satterthwaite thoughtfully. "I don't know that I do. Women have got their own standards, you know. It's no good our mixing ourselves up in their affairs. They must run their own show."

"I don't agree with you," said Rudge earnestly. "It's one of the worst things in the world today, the unkindness of woman to woman. You know Elizabeth Martin? Now she agrees with me in theory absolutely. We've often discussed it together. She's only a kid, but her ideas are all right. But the moment it comes to a practical test—why, she's as bad as any of them. Got a real down on the Countess without knowing a darned thing about her, and won't listen when I try to tell her things. It's all *wrong*, Mr. Satterthwaite. I believe in democracy—and—what's that but brotherhood between men and sisterhood between women?"

He paused earnestly. Mr. Satterthwaite tried to think of any circumstances in which a sisterly feeling might arise between the Countess and Elizabeth Martin and failed.

"Now the Countess, on the other hand," went on Rudge, "admires Elizabeth immensely, and thinks her charming in every way. Now what does that show?"

"It shows," said Mr. Satterthwaite dryly, "that the Countess has lived a considerable time longer than Miss Martin has."

Franklin Rudge went off unexpectedly at a tangent.

"Do you know how old she is? She told me. Rather sporting of her. I should have guessed her to be twenty-nine, but she told me of her own accord that she was thirty-five. She doesn't look it, does she?"

Mr. Satterthwaite, whose private estimate of the lady's age was between forty-five and forty-nine, merely raised his eyebrows.

"I should caution you against believing all you are told at Monte Carlo," he murmured.

He had enough experience to know the futility of arguing with the lad. Franklin Rudge was at a pitch of white hot chivalry when he would have disbelieved any statement that was not backed with authoritative proof.

"Here is the Countess," said the boy, rising.

She came up to them with the languid grace that so became her. Presently they all three sat down together. She was very charming to Mr. Satterthwaite, but in rather an aloof manner. She deferred to him prettily, asking his opinion, and treating him as an authority on the Riviera.

The whole thing was cleverly managed. Very few minutes had elapsed before Franklin Rudge found himself gracefully but unmistakably dismissed, and the Countess and Mr. Satterthwaite were left *tête-à-tête*.

She put down her parasol and began drawing patterns with it in the dust.

"You are interested in that nice American boy, Mr. Satterthwaite, are you not?"

Her voice was low with a caressing note in it.

"He's a nice young fellow," said Mr. Satterthwaite noncommittally.

"I find him sympathetic, yes," said the Countess reflectively. "I have told him much of my life."

"Indeed," said Mr. Satterthwaite.

"Details such as I have told to few others," she continued dreamily. "I have had an extraordinary life, Mr. Satterthwaite. Few would credit the amazing things that have happened to me."

Mr. Satterthwaite was shrewd enough to penetrate her meaning. After all, the stories that she had told to Franklin Rudge *might* be the truth. It was extremely unlikely, and in the last degree improbable, but it was *possible*. No one could definitely say "This is not so."

He did not reply, and the Countess continued to look out dreamily across the bay. And suddenly Mr. Satterthwaite had a strange and new impression of her. He saw her no longer as a harpy, but as a desperate creature at bay, fighting tooth and nail. He stole a sideways glance at her. The parasol was down, he could see the little haggard lines at the corners of her eyes. In one temple a pulse was beating.

It flowed through him again and again—that increasing certitude. She was a creature desperate and driven. She would be merciless to him or to anyone who stood between her and Franklin Rudge. But he still felt he hadn't got the hang of the situation. Clearly she had plenty of money. She was always beautifully dressed, and her jewels were marvelous. There could be no real urgency of that kind. Was it love? Women of her age did, he well knew, fall in love with boys. It might be that. There was, he felt sure, something out of the common about the situation.

Her *tête-à-tête* with him was, he recognized, a throwing down of the gauntlet. She had singled him out as her chief enemy. He felt sure that she hoped to goad him into speaking slightingly of her to Franklin Rudge. Mr. Satterthwaite smiled to himself. He was too old a bird for that. He knew when it was wise to hold one's tongue.

He watched her that night in the Cercle Privé, as she tried her fortunes at roulette.

Again and again she staked, only to see her stake swept away. She bore her losses well, with the stoical *sang froid* of the old *habitué*. She staked *en plein* once or twice, put the maximum on red, won a little on the middle dozen and then lost it again, finally she backed *manque* six times and lost every time. Then with a little graceful shrug of the shoulders she turned away.

She was looking unusually striking in a dress of gold tissue with an underlying note of green. The famous Bosnian pearls were looped round her neck and long pearl earrings hung from her ears.

Mr. Satterthwaite heard two men near him appraise her.

"The Czarnova," said one. "She wears well, does she not? The Crown jewels of Bosnia look fine on her."

The other, a small man, stared curiously after her.

"So those are the pearls of Bosnia, are they?" he asked. "*En vérité*. That is odd."

He chuckled softly to himself.

Mr. Satterthwaite missed hearing more, for at the moment he turned his head and was overjoyed to recognize an old friend.

"My dear Mr. Quin." He shook him warmly by the hand. "The last place I should ever have dreamed of seeing you."

Mr. Quin smiled, his dark attractive face lighting up.

"It should not surprise you," he said. "It is Carnival time. I am often here in Carnival time."

"Really? Well, this is a great pleasure. Are you anxious to remain in the rooms? I find them rather warm."

"It will be pleasanter outside," agreed the other. "We will walk in the gardens."

The air outside was sharp, but not chill. Both men drew deep breaths.

"That is better," said Mr. Satterthwaite.

"Much better," agreed Mr. Quin. "And we can talk freely. I am sure that there is much that you want to tell me."

"There is indeed."

Speaking eagerly, Mr. Satterthwaite unfolded his perplexities. As usual he took pride in his power of conveying atmosphere. The

Countess, young Franklin, uncompromising Elizabeth—he sketched them all in with a deft touch.

"You have changed since I first knew you," said Mr. Quin, smiling, when the recital was over.

"In what way?"

"You were content then to look on at the dramas that life offered. Now—you want to take part—to act."

"It is true," confessed Mr. Satterthwaite. "But in this case I do not know what to do. It is all very perplexing. Perhaps—" he hesitated. "Perhaps you will help me?"

"With pleasure," said Mr. Quin. "We will see what we can do."

Mr. Satterthwaite had an odd sense of comfort and reliance.

The following day he introduced Franklin Rudge and Elizabeth Martin to his friend Mr. Harley Quin. He was pleased to see that they got on together. The Countess was not mentioned, but at lunch time he heard news that aroused his attention.

"Mirabelle is arriving in Monte this evening," he confided excitedly to Mr. Quin.

"The Parisian Stage favorite?"

"Yes. I daresay you know—it's common property—she is the King of Bosnia's latest craze. He has showered jewels on her, I believe. They say she is the most exacting and extravagant woman in Paris."

"It should be interesting to see her and the Countess Czarnova meet tonight."

"Exactly what I thought."

Mirabelle was a tall thin creature with a wonderful head of dyed fair hair. Her complexion was a pale mauve with orange lips. She was amazingly chic. She was dressed in something that looked like a glorified bird of paradise, and she wore chains of jewels hanging down her bare back. A heavy bracelet set with immense diamonds clasped her left ankle.

She created a sensation when she appeared in the Casino.

"Your friend the Countess will have a difficulty in outdoing this," murmured Mr. Quin in Mr. Satterthwaite's ear.

The latter nodded. He was curious to see how the Countess comported herself.

She came late, and a low murmur ran round as she walked unconcernedly to one of the center roulette tables.

She was dressed in white—a mere straight slip of marocain, such as a debutante might have worn, and her gleaming white neck and arms were unadorned. She wore not a single jewel.

"It is clever, that," said Mr. Satterthwaite with instant approval. "She disdains rivalry and turns the tables on her adversary."

He himself walked over and stood by the table. From time to time he amused himself by placing a stake. Sometimes he won, more often he lost.

There was a terrific run on the last dozen. The numbers 31 and 34 turned up again and again. Stakes flocked to the bottom of the cloth.

With a smile Mr. Satterthwaite made his last stake for the evening, and placed the maximum on Number 5.

The Countess in her turn leaned forward and placed the maximum on Number 6.

"*Faites vos jeux,*" called the croupier hoarsely. "*Rien ne va plus. Plus rien.*"

The ball spun, humming merrily. Mr. Satterthwaite thought to himself: *This means something different to each of us. Agonies of hope and despair, boredom, idle amusement, life and death."*

Click!

The croupier bent forward to see.

"*Numero cinque, rouge, impair et manque.*"

Mr. Satterthwaite had won!

The croupier, having raked in the other stakes, pushed forward Mr. Satterthwaite's winnings. He put out his hand to take them. The Countess did the same. The croupier looked from one to the other of them.

"A *Madame,*" he said brusquely.

The Countess picked up the money. Mr. Satterthwaite drew back. He remained a gentleman. The Countess looked him full in the face and he returned her glance. One or two of the people round pointed out to the croupier that he had made a mistake, but the man shook his head impatiently. He had decided. That was the end. He raised his raucous cry.

"*Faites vos jeux, Messieurs et Mesdames.*"

Mr. Satterthwaite rejoined Mr. Quin. Beneath his impeccable demeanor, he was feeling extremely indignant. Mr. Quin listened sympathetically.

"Too bad," he said, "but these things happen. We are to meet your friend Franklin Rudge later. I am giving a little supper party."

The three met at midnight, and Mr. Quin explained his plan.

"It is what is called a 'Hedges and Highways' party," he explained. "We choose our meeting place, then each one goes out and is bound in honor to invite the first person he meets."

Franklin Rudge was amused by the idea.

"Say, what happens if they won't accept?"

"You must use your utmost powers of persuasion."

"Good. And where's the meeting place?"

"A somewhat Bohemian café—where one can take strange guests. It is called Le Caveau."

He explained its whereabouts, and the three parted. Mr. Satterthwaite was so fortunate as to run straight into Elizabeth Martin and he claimed her joyfully. They reached Le Caveau and descended into a kind of cellar where they found a table spread for supper and lit by old-fashioned candles in candlesticks.

"We are the first," said Mr. Satterthwaite. "Ah! here comes Franklin—"

He stopped abruptly. With Franklin was the Countess. It was an awkward moment. Elizabeth displayed less graciousness than she might have done. The Countess, as a woman of the world, retained the honors.

Last of all came Mr. Quin. With him was a small dark man, neatly dressed, whose face seemed familiar to Mr. Satterthwaite. A moment later he recognized him. It was the croupier who earlier in the evening had made such a lamentable mistake.

"Let me introduce you to the company, M. Pierre Vaucher," said Mr. Quin.

The little man seemed confused. Mr. Quin performed the necessary introductions easily and lightly. Supper was brought—an excellent supper. Wine came—very excellent wine. Some of the frigidity went out of the atmosphere. The Countess was very silent, so was Elizabeth. Franklin Rudge became talkative. He told various stories—not humorous stories, but serious ones. And quietly and assiduously Mr. Quin passed round the wine.

"I'll tell you—and this is a true story—about a man who made good," said Franklin Rudge impressively. For one coming from a prohibition country he had shown no lack of appreciation of champagne.

He told his story—perhaps at somewhat unnecessary length. It was, like many true stories, greatly inferior to fiction.

As he uttered the last word, Pierre Vaucher, opposite him, seemed to wake up. He also had done justice to the champagne. He leaned forward across the table.

"I, too, will tell you a story," he said thickly. "But mine is the story of a man who did not make good. It is the story of a man who went, not up, but down the hill. And, like yours, it is a true story."

"Pray tell it to us, monsieur," said Mr. Satterthwaite courteously.

Pierre Vaucher leaned back in his chair and looked at the ceiling.

"It is in Paris that the story begins. There was a man there, a working jeweler. He was young and light hearted and industrious in his profession. They said there was a future before him. A good marriage was already arranged for him, the bride not too bad looking, the dowry most satisfactory. And then, what would you think? One morning he sees a girl. Such a miserable little wisp of a girl, Messieurs. Beautiful? Yes, perhaps, if she were not half starved. But anyway, for this young man, she has a magic that he cannot resist. She has been struggling to find work, she is virtuous—or at least that is what she tells him. I do not know if it was true."

The Countess's voice came suddenly out of the semidarkness.

"Why should it not be true? There are many like that."

"Well, as I say, the young man believed her. And he married her—an act of folly! His family would have no more to say to him. He had outraged their feelings. He married—I will call her Jeanne—

it was a good action. He told her so. He felt that she should be very grateful to him. He had sacrificed much for her sake."

"A charming beginning for the poor girl," observed the Countess sarcastically.

"He loved her, yes, but from the beginning she maddened him. She had moods—tantrums—she would be cold to him one day—passionate the next. At last he saw the truth. She had never loved him. She had married him so as to keep body and soul together. That truth hurt him, it hurt him horribly, but he tried his utmost to let nothing appear on the surface. And he still felt he deserved gratitude and obedience to his wishes. They quarreled. She reproached him—Mon Dieu, what did she not reproach him with?

"You can see the next step, can you not? The thing that was bound to come. She left him. For two years he was alone, working in his little shop with no news of her. He had one friend—absinthe. The business did not prosper so well.

"And then one day he came into the shop to find her sitting there. She was beautifully dressed. She had rings on her hands. He stood considering her. His heart was beating—but beating! He was at a loss what to do. He would have liked to have beaten her; to have clasped her in his arms, to have thrown her down on the floor and trampled on her, to have thrown himself at her feet. He did none of these things. He took up his pincers and went on with his work. 'Madame desires?' he asked formally.

"That upset her. She did not look for that, see you. 'Pierre,' she said, 'I have come back.' He laid aside his pincers and looked at her. 'You wish to be forgiven,' he said. 'You want me to take you back? You are sincerely repentant?' 'Do you want me back?' she murmured. Oh! very softly she said it.

"He knew she was laying a trap for him. He longed to seize her in his arms, but he was too clever for that. He pretended indifference.

" 'I am a Christian man,' he said. 'I try to do what the Church directs.' 'Ah!' he thought, 'I will humble her, humble her to her knees.'

"But Jeanne, that is what I will call her, flung back her head and laughed. Evil laughter it was. 'I mock myself at you, little Pierre,' she said. 'Look at these rich clothes, these rings and bracelets. I came to show myself to you. I thought I would make you take me in your arms and when you did so, then—*then* I would spit in your face and tell you how I hated you!'

"And on that she went out of the shop. Can you believe, Messieurs, that a woman could be as evil as all that—to come back only to torment me?"

"No," said the Countess. "I would not believe it, and any man who was not a fool would not believe it either. But all men are blind fools."

Pierre Vaucher took no notice of her. He went on.

"And so that young man of whom I tell you sank lower lower. He drank more absinthe. The little shop was sold over his head. He became of the dregs, of the gutter. Then came the war. Ah! it was good, the war. It took that man out of the gutter and taught him to be a brute beast no longer. It drilled him—and sobered him. He endured cold and pain and the fear of death—but he did not die, and when the war ended, he was a man again.

"It was then, Messieurs, that he came South. His lungs had been affected by the gas; they said he must find work in the South. I will not weary you with all the things he did. Suffice it to say that he ended up as a croupier, and there—there in the Casino one evening, he saw again—the woman who had ruined his life. She did not recognize him, but he recognized her. She appeared to be rich and to lack for nothing—but, Messieurs, the eyes of a croupier are sharp. There came an evening when she placed her last stake in the world on the table. Ask me not how I know—I do know—one feels these things. Others might not believe. She still had rich clothes—why not pawn them, one would say? But to do that—pah! your credit is gone at once. Her jewels? Ah, no! Was I not a jeweler in my time? Long ago the real jewels have gone. The pearls of a King sold one by one, and replaced with false. And meantime one must eat and pay one's hotel bill. Yes, and the rich men—well, they have seen one about for many years. Bah! they say—she is over fifty! A younger chicken for my money."

A long shuddering sigh came out of the windows where the Countess leaned back.

"Yes. It was a great moment, that. Two nights I have watched her. Lose, lose, and lose again. And now the end. She puts all on one number. Beside her, an English milord stakes the maximum also—on the next number. The ball rolls; the moment has come; she has lost.

"Her eyes meet mine. What do I do? I jeopardize my place in the Casino. I rob the English milord. 'A Madame,' I say, and pay over the money."

"Ah!" there was a crash, as the Countess sprang to her feet and leaned across the table, sweeping her glass onto the floor.

"Why?" she cried, "That's what I want to know, why did you do it?"

There was a long pause, a pause that seemed interminable, and still those two facing each other across the table looked and looked. It was like a duel.

A mean little smile crept across Pierre Vaucher's face. He raised his hands.

"Madame," he said. "There is such a thing as pity."

"Ah!"

She sank down again.

"I see."

She was calm, smiling, herself again.

"An interesting story, M.—Vaucher, is it not? Permit me to give you a light for your cigarette."

She deftly rolled up a spill, lighted it at the candle and held it toward him. He leaned forward till the flame caught the tip of the cigarette he held between his lips.

Then she rose unexpectedly to her feet.

"And now I must leave you all. Please—I need no one to escort me."

Before one could realize it she was gone. Mr. Satterthwaite would have hurried out after her, but he was arrested by a startled oath from the Frenchman.

"*A thousand thunders!*"

He was staring at the half-burned spill which the Countess had dropped on the table. He unrolled it.

"*Mon Dieu!*" he muttered. "A fifty thousand franc bank note. You understand? Her winnings tonight. All that she has in the world. And she lighted my cigarette with it! Because she was too proud to accept—pity. Ah! proud, she was always proud as the Devil. She is unique—wonderful."

He sprang up from his seat and darted out. Mr. Satterthwaite and Mr. Quin had also risen. The waiter approached Franklin Rudge.

"*La note, Monsieur,*" he observed unemotionally.

Mr. Quin rescued it from him quickly.

"I feel kind of lonesome, Elizabeth," remarked Franklin Rudge. "These foreigners—they beat the band! I don't understand them. What's it all mean, anyhow?"

He looked across at her.

"Gee, it's good to look at anything so hundred percent American as you." His voice took on the plaintive note of a small child. "These foreigners are so *odd.*"

They thanked Mr. Quin and went out into the night together. Mr. Quin picked up his change and smiled across at Mr. Satterthwaite, who was preening himself like a contented bird.

"Well," said the latter. "That's all gone off splendidly. Our pair of love birds will be all right now."

"Which ones?" asked Mr. Quin.

"Oh," said Mr. Satterthwaite, taken aback, "Oh! yes, well, I suppose you are right, allowing for the Latin point of view and all that—"

He looked dubious.

Mr. Quin smiled, and a stained glass panel behind him invested him for just a moment in a motley garment of colored light.

6. THE WORLD'S END

Mr. Satterthwaite had come to Corsica because of the Duchess. It was out of his beat. On the Riviera he was sure of his comforts, and to be comfortable meant a lot to Mr. Satterthwaite. But though he liked his comfort, he also liked a Duchess. In his way, a harmless, gentlemanly, old-fashioned way, Mr. Satterthwaite was a snob. He liked the best people. And the Duchess of Leith was a very authentic Duchess. There were no Chicago pork butchers in her ancestry. She was the daughter of a duke as well as the wife of one.

For the rest, she was rather a shabby looking old lady, a good deal given to black bead trimmings on her clothes. She had quantities of diamonds in old-fashioned settings, and she wore them as her mother before her had worn them: pinned all over her indiscriminately. Someone had suggested once that the Duchess stood in the middle of the room while her maid flung brooches at her haphazard. She subscribed generously to charities, and looked well after her tenants and dependents, but was extremely mean over small sums. She cadged lifts from her friends, and did her shopping in bargain basements.

The Duchess was seized with a whim for Corsica. Cannes bored her, and she had had a bitter argument with the hotel proprietor over the price of her rooms.

"And you shall go with me, Satterthwaite," she said firmly. "We needn't be afraid of scandal at our time of life."

Mr. Satterthwaite was delicately flattered. No one had ever mentioned scandal in connection with him before. He was far too insignificant. Scandal—and a Duchess—delicious.

"Picturesque, you know," said the Duchess. "Brigands—all that sort of thing. And extremely cheap, so I've heard. Manuelli was positively impudent this morning. These hotel proprietors need putting in their place. They can't expect to get the best people if they go on like this. I told him so plainly."

"I believe," said Mr. Satterthwaite, "that one can fly over quite comfortably. Prom Antibes."

"They probably charge you a pretty penny for it," said the Duchess sharply. "Find out, will you?"

"Certainly, Duchess."

Mr. Satterthwaite was still in a flutter of gratification, despite the fact that his rôle was clearly to be that of a glorified courier.

When she learned the price of a passage by *avion*, the Duchess turned it down promptly.

"They needn't think I'm going to pay a ridiculous sum like that to go in one of their nasty dangerous things."

So they went by boat, and Mr. Satterthwaite endured ten hours of acute discomfort. To begin with, as the boat sailed at seven, he took it for granted that there would be dinner on board. But there was no dinner. The boat was small and the sea was rough. Mr. Satterthwaite was decanted at Ajaccio in the early hours of the morning more dead than alive.

The Duchess, on the contrary, was perfectly fresh. She never minded discomfort, if she could feel she was saving money. She waxed enthusiastic over the scene on the quay, with me palm trees and the rising sun. The whole population seemed to have turned out to watch the arrival of the boat, and the launching of the gangway was attended with excited cries and directions.

"On dirait," said a stout Frenchman who stood beside that, *"que jamais avant on n'a fait cette manœuvre la!"*

"That maid of mine has been sick all night," said the Duchess. "The girl's a perfect fool."

Mr. Satterthwaite smiled in a pallid fashion.

"A waste of good food, I call it," continued the Duchess robustly.

"Did she get any food?" asked Mr. Satterthwaite enviously.

"I happened to bring some biscuits and a stick of chocolate on board with me," said the Duchess. "When I found there was no dinner to be got, I gave the lot to her. The lower classes always make such a fuss about going without their meals."

With a cry of triumph the launching of the gangway was accomplished. A musical comedy chorus of brigands rushed aboard and wrested hand luggage from the passengers by main force.

"Come on, Satterthwaite," said the Duchess. "I want a hot bath and some coffee."

So did Mr. Satterthwaite. He was not wholly successful, however. They were received at the hotel by a bowing manager and were shown to their rooms. The Duchess's had a bathroom attached. Mr. Satterthwaite, however, was directed to a bath that appeared to be situated in somebody else's bedroom. To expect the water to be hot at that hour in the morning was, perhaps, unreasonable. Later he drank intensely black coffee, served in a pot without a lid. The shutters and the window of his room had been flung open, and the crisp morning air came in fragrantly. A day of dazzling blue and green.

The waiter waved his hand with a flourish to call attention to the view.

"Ajaccio," he said solemnly. *"Le plus beau port du monde!"*

And he departed abruptly.

Looking out over the deep blue of the bay, with the snow mountains beyond, Mr. Satterthwaite was almost inclined to agree with him. He finished his coffee, and lying down on the bed, fell fast asleep.

At *déjeuner* the Duchess was in great spirits.

"This is just what will be good for you, Satterthwaite," she said. "Get you out of all those fussy little old maidish ways of yours." She swept a lorgnette around the room. "Upon my word, there's Naomi Carlton-Smith."

She indicated a girl sitting by herself at a table in the window, a round shouldered girl, who slouched as she sat. Her dress appeared to be made of some kind of brown sacking. She had black hair, untidily bobbed.

"An artist?" asked Mr. Satterthwaite.

He was always good at placing people.

"Quite right," said the Duchess. "Calls herself one, anyway. I knew she was mouching around in some queer quarter of the globe. Poor as a church mouse, proud as Lucifer, and a bee in her bonnet like all the Carlton-Smiths. Her mother was my first cousin."

"She's one of the Knowlton lot then?

The Duchess nodded.

"Been her own worst enemy," she volunteered. "Clever girl too. Mixed herself up with a most undesirable young man. One of that Chelsea crowd. Wrote plays or poems or something unhealthy. Nobody took 'em, of course. Then he stole somebody's jewels and got caught out. I forget what they gave him. Five years, I think. But you must remember? It was last winter."

"Last winter I was in Egypt," explained Mr. Satterthwaite. "I had flu very badly the end of January, and the doctors insisted on Egypt afterward. I missed a lot."

His voice rang with a note of real regret.

"That girl seems to me to be moping," said the Duchess, raising her lorgnette once more. "I can't allow that."

On her way out, she stopped by Miss Carlton-Smith's table and tapped the girl on the shoulder.

"Well, Naomi, you don't seem to remember me?"

Naomi rose rather unwillingly to her feet.

"Yes, I do, Duchess. I saw you come in. I thought it quite likely you mightn't recognize me."

She drawled the words lazily, with a complete indifference of manner.

"When you've finished your lunch, come and talk to me on the terrace," ordered the Duchess.

"Very well."

Naomi yawned.

"Shocking manners," said the Duchess to Mr. Satterthwaite, as she resumed her progress. "All the Carlton-Smiths have."

They had their coffee outside in the sunshine. They had been there about six minutes when Naomi Carlton-Smith lounged out from the hotel and joined them. She let herself fall slackly onto a chair with her legs stretched out ungracefully in front of her.

An odd face, with its jutting chin and deep-set gray eyes. A clever, unhappy face—a face that only just missed being beautiful.

"Well, Naomi," said the Duchess briskly. "And what are you doing with yourself?"

"Oh! I dunno. Just marking time."

"Been painting?"

"A bit."

"Show me your things."

Naomi grinned. She was not cowed by the autocrat. She was amused. She went into the hotel and came out again with a portfolio.

"You won't like 'em, Duchess," she said warningly. "Say what you like. You won't hurt my feelings."

Mr. Satterthwaite moved his chair a little nearer. He was interested. In another minute he was more interested still. The Duchess was frankly unsympathetic.

"I can't even see which way up the things ought to be," she complained. "Good gracious, child, there was never a sky that color—or a sea either."

"That's the way I see 'em," said Naomi placidly.

"Ugh!" said the Duchess, inspecting another. "This gives me the creeps."

"It's meant to," said Naomi. "You're paying me a compliment without knowing it."

It was a queer vorticist study of prickly pear—just recognizable as such. Gray green with splodges of violent color where the fruit glittered like jewels. A swirling mass of evil, fleshy—festering. Mr. Satterthwaite shuddered and turned his head aside.

He found Naomi looking at him and nodding her head in comprehension.

"I know," she said. "But it *is* beastly."

The Duchess cleared her throat.

"It seems quite easy to be an artist nowadays," she observed witheringly. "There's no attempt to copy things. You just shovel on some paint—I don't know what with, not a brush, I'm sure—"

"Palette knife," interposed Naomi, smiling broadly once more.

"A good deal at a time," continued the Duchess. "In lumps. And there you are! Everyone says: 'How clever.' Well, I've no patience with that sort of thing. Give me—"

"A nice picture of a dog and a horse, by Edward Landseer."

"And why not?" demanded the Duchess. "What's wrong with Landseer?"

"Nothing," said Naomi. "He's all right. And you're all right. The tops of things are always nice and shiny and smooth. I respect you, Duchess; you've got force; you've met life fair and square and you've come out on top. But the people who are underneath see the under side of things. And that's interesting in a way."

The Duchess stared at her.

"I haven't the faintest idea what you're talking about," she declared.

Mr. Satterthwaite was still examining the sketches. He realized, as the Duchess could not, the perfection of technique behind them. He was startled and delighted. He looked up at the girl.

"Will you sell me one of these, Miss Carlton-Smith?" he asked.

"You can have any one you like for five guineas," said the girl indifferently.

Mr. Satterthwaite hesitated a minute or two and then he selected a study of prickly pear and aloe. In the foreground was a vivid blur of yellow mimosa, the scarlet of the aloe flower danced in and out of the picture, and inexorable, mathematically underlying the whole, was the oblong pattern of the prickly pear and the sword motif of the aloe.

He made a little bow to the girl.

"I am very happy to have secured this, and I think I have made a bargain. Some day, Miss Carlton-Smith, I shall be able to sell this sketch at a very good profit—if I want to!"

The girl leaned forward to see which one he had taken. He saw a new look come into her eyes. For the first time she was really aware of his existence, and there was respect in the quick glance she gave him.

"You have chosen the best," she said. "I—I am glad."

"Well, I suppose you know what you're doing," said the Duchess. "And I daresay you're right. I've heard that you're quite a connoisseur. But you can't tell me that all this new stuff is art, because it isn't. Still, we needn't go into that. Now I'm only going to be here a few days and I want to see something of the island. You've got a car, I suppose, Naomi?"

The girl nodded.

"Excellent," said the Duchess. "We'll make a trip somewhere tomorrow."

"It's only a two-seater."

"Nonsense, there's a dicky, I suppose, that will do for Mr. Satterthwaite?"

A shuddering sigh went through Mr. Satterthwaite. He had observed the Corsican roads that morning. Naomi was regarding him thoughtfully.

"I'm afraid my car will be no good to you," she said. "It's a terribly battered old bus. I bought it secondhand for a mere song. It will just get me up the hills—with coaxing. But I can't take passengers. There's quite a good garage, though, in the town. You can hire a car there."

"Hire a car," said the Duchess, scandalized. "What an idea. Who's that nice looking man, rather yellow, who drove up in a four-seater just before lunch?"

"I expect you mean Mr. Tomlinson. He's a retired Indian judge."

"That accounts for the yellowness," said the Duchess. "I was afraid it might be jaundice. He seems quite a decent sort of man. I shall talk to him."

That evening, on coming down to dinner, Mr. Satterthwaite found the Duchess, resplendent in black beads and diamonds, talking earnestly to the owner of the four-seater car. She beckoned authoritatively.

"Come here, Mr. Satterthwaite. Mr. Tomlinson is telling me the most interesting things, and what do you think? He is actually going to take us on an expedition tomorrow in his car."

Mr. Satterthwaite regarded her with admiration.

"We must go into dinner," said the Duchess. "Do come and sit at our table, Mr. Tomlinson, and then you can go on with what you were telling me."

"Quite a decent sort of man," the Duchess pronounced later.

"With quite a decent sort of car," retorted Mr. Satterthwaite.

"Naughty," said the Duchess, and gave him a resounding blow on the knuckles with the dingy black fan she always carried. Mr. Satterthwaite winced with pain.

"Naomi is coming too," said the Duchess. "In her car. That girl wants taking out of herself. She's very selfish. Not exactly self-centered, but totally indifferent to everyone and everything. Don't you agree?"

"I don't think that's possible," said Mr. Satterthwaite slowly. "I mean, everyone's interest must go *somewhere*. There are, of course, the people who revolve round themselves—but I agree with you, she's not one of that kind. She's totally uninterested in herself. And yet she's got a strong character—there must be *something*. I thought at first it was her art—but it isn't. I've never met anyone so detached from life. That's—dangerous."

"Dangerous? What do you mean?"

"Well, you see—it must be an obsession of some kind, and obsessions are always dangerous."

"Satterthwaite," said the Duchess, "don't be a fool. And listen to me. About tomorrow—"

Mr. Satterthwaite listened. It was very much his rôle in life.

They started early the following morning, taking their lunch with them. Naomi, who had been six months on the island, was to

THE WORLD'S END 277

be the pioneer. Mr. Satterthwaite went over to her as she sat waiting to start.

"You are sure that—I can't come with you," he said wistfully.

She shook her head.

"You'll be much more comfortable in the back of the other car. Nicely padded seats and all that. This is a regular old rattle trap. You'd leap in the air going over the bumps."

"And then of course the hills."

Naomi laughed.

"Oh! I only said that to rescue you from the dickey. The Duchess could perfectly well afford to have hired a car. She's the meanest woman in England. All the same, the old thing is rather a sport, and I can't help liking her."

"Then I could come with you after all," said Mr. Satterthwaite, eagerly.

She looked at him curiously.

"Why are you so anxious to come with me?"

"Can you ask?" Mr. Satterthwaite made his funny old-fashioned bow.

She smiled, but shook her head.

"That isn't the reason," she said thoughtfully. "It's odd. But you can't come with me—not today."

"Another day, perhaps," suggested Mr. Satterthwaite politely.

"Oh! another day!" she laughed suddenly, a very queer laugh Mr. Satterthwaite thought. "Another day! Well, we'll see."

They started. They drove through the town, and then round the long curve of the bay, winding inland to cross a river and then back to the coast with its hundreds of little sandy coves. And then they began to climb. In and out, round nerve shattering curves, upward, ever upward on the tortuous winding road. The blue bay was far below them and, on the other side of it, Ajaccio sparkled in the sun, white like a fairy city.

In and out, in and out, with a precipice first one side of them, then the other. Mr. Satterthwaite felt slightly giddy, he also felt slightly sick. The road was not very wide. And still they climbed.

It was cold now. The wind came to them straight off the snow peaks. Mr. Satterthwaite turned up his coat collar and buttoned it tightly under his chin.

It was very cold. Across the water Ajaccio was still bathed in sunlight, but up here thick gray clouds came drifting across the face of the sun. Mr. Satterthwaite ceased to admire the view. He yearned for a steam-heated hotel and a comfortable armchair.

Ahead of them Naomi's little two-seater drove steadily forward. Up, still up. They were on top of the world now. On either side of them were lower hills, hills sloping down to valleys. They looked straight across to the snow peaks. And the wind came tearing over them, sharp, like a knife.

Suddenly Naomi's car stopped, and she looked back.

"We've arrived," she said. "At the world's end. And I don't think it's an awfully good day for it."

They all got out. They had arrived in a tiny village, half a dozen stone cottages. An imposing name was printed in letters a foot high.

"Coti Chiaveeri."

Naomi shrugged her shoulders.

"That's its official name, but I prefer to call it the world's end."

She walked on a few steps, and Mr. Satterthwaite joined her. They were beyond the houses now. The road stopped. As Naomi had said, this was the end, the back of beyond, the beginning of nowhere. Behind them the white ribbon of the road, in front of them—nothing. Only far, far below, the sea.

Mr. Satterthwaite drew a deep breath.

"It's an extraordinary place. One feels that anything might happen here, that one might meet—anyone—"

He stopped, for just in front of them a man was sitting on a boulder, his face turned to the sea. They had not seen him till this moment, and his appearance had the suddenness of a conjuring trick. He might have sprung from the surrounding landscape.

"I wonder—" began Mr. Satterthwaite.

But at that minute the stranger turned, and Mr. Satterthwaite saw his face.

"Why, Mr. Quin! How extraordinary. Miss Carlton-Smith, I

want to introduce my friend Mr. Quin to you. He's the most amazing fellow. You are, you know. You always turn up in the nick of time—"

He stopped, with the feeling that he had said something awkwardly significant, and yet for the life of him he could not think what it was.

Naomi had shaken hands with Mr. Quin in her usual abrupt style.

"We're here for a picnic," she said. "And it seems to me we shall be pretty well frozen to the bone."

Mr. Satterthwaite shivered.

"Perhaps," he said uncertainly. "We shall find a sheltered spot?"

"Which this isn't," agreed Naomi. "Still, it's worth seeing, isn't it?"

"Yes, indeed." Mr. Satterthwaite turned to Mr. Quin. "Miss Carlton-Smith calls this place the world's end. Rather a good name, eh?"

Mr. Quin nodded his head slowly several times.

"Yes—a very suggestive name. I suppose one only comes once in one's life to a place like that—a place where one can't go on any longer."

"What do you mean?" asked Naomi sharply.

He turned to her.

"Well, usually, there's a choice, isn't there? To the right or to the left. Forward or back. Here—there's the road behind you, and in front of you—nothing."

Naomi stared at him. Suddenly she shivered and began to retrace her steps toward the others. The two men fell in beside her. Mr. Quin continued to talk, but his tone was now easily conversational.

"Is the small car yours, Miss Carlton-Smith?"

"Yes."

"You drive yourself? One needs, I think, a good deal of nerve to do that round here. The turns are rather appalling. A moment of inattention, a brake that failed to hold, and—over the edge—down—down—down. It would be—very easily done."

They had joined the others. Mr. Satterthwaite introduced his friend. He felt a tug at his arm. It was Naomi. She drew him apart from the others.

"Who is he?" she demanded fiercely.

Mr. Satterthwaite gazed at her in astonishment.

"Well, I hardly know. I mean, I have known him for some years now—we have run across each other from time to time, but in the sense of knowing actually—"

He stopped. These were futilities that he was uttering, and the girl by his side was not listening. She was standing with her head bent down, her hands clenched by her sides.

"He knows things," she said. "He knows things. How does he know?"

Mr. Satterthwaite had no answer. He could only look at her dumbly, unable to comprehend the storm that shook her.

"I'm afraid," she muttered.

"Afraid of Mr. Quin?"

"I'm afraid of his eyes. He sees things."

Something cold and wet fell on Mr. Satterthwaite's cheek. He looked up.

"Why, it's snowing," he exclaimed in great surprise.

"A nice day to have chosen for a picnic," said Naomi.

She had regained control of herself with an effort.

What was to be done? A babel of suggestions broke out. The snow came down fast and thick. Mr. Quin made a suggestion and everyone welcomed it. There was a little stone Cassecroute at the end of the row of houses. There was a stampede toward it.

"You have your provisions," said Mr. Quin, "and they will probably be able to make you some coffee."

It was a tiny place, rather dark, for the one little window did little toward lighting it, but from one end came a grateful glow of warmth. An old Corsican woman was just throwing a handful of branches on the fire. It blazed up and by its light the newcomers realized that others were before them.

Three people were sitting at the end of a bare wooden table. There was something unreal about the scene to Mr. Satterthwaite's eye; there was something even more unreal about the people.

The woman who sat at the end of the table looked like a duchess—that is she looked like the popular conception of a duchess. She was the ideal stage *grande dame*. Her aristocratic head was held high, her exquisitely dressed hair was of a snowy white. She was dressed in gray—soft draperies that fell about her in artistic folds. One long white hand supported her chin, the other was holding a roll spread with *pâté de foie gras*. On her right was a man with a very white face, very black hair, and horn-rimmed spectacles. He was marvelously and beautifully dressed. At the moment his head was thrown back, and his left arm was thrown out, as though he were about to declaim something.

On the left of the white haired lady was a jolly looking little man with a bald head. After the first glance, nobody looked at him.

There was just a moment of uncertainty, and then the Duchess (the authentic Duchess) took charge.

"Isn't this storm too dreadful," she said pleasantly, coming forward, and smiling a purposeful and efficient smile that she had found very useful when serving on welfare and other committees. "I suppose you've been caught in it just like we have? But Corsica is a marvelous place. I only arrived this morning."

The man with the black hair got up, and the Duchess with a gracious smile slipped into his seat.

The white haired lady spoke:

"We have been here a week," she said.

Mr. Satterthwaite started. Could anyone who had once heard that voice ever forget it? It echoed round the stone room, charged with emotion—with exquisite melancholy. It seemed to him that she had said something wonderful, memorable, full of meaning. She had spoken from her heart.

He spoke in a hurried aside to Mr. Tomlinson.

"The man in spectacles is Mr. Vyse—the producer, you know."

The retired Indian judge was looking at Mr. Vyse with a good deal of dislike.

"What does he produce?" he asked. "Children?"

"Oh! dear me, no," said Mr. Satterthwaite, shocked by the mere mention of anything so crude in connection with Mr. Vyse. "Plays."

"I think," said Naomi, "I'll go out again. It's too hot in here."

Her voice, strong and harsh, made Mr. Satterthwaite jump. She made, almost blindly, as it seemed, for the door, brushing Mr. Tom-linson aside. But in the doorway itself she came face to face with Mr. Quin, and he barred her way.

"Go back and sit down," he said.

His voice was authoritative. To Mr. Satterthwaite's surprise the girl hesitated a minute and then obeyed. She sat down at the foot of the table as far from the others as possible.

Mr. Satterthwaite bustled forward and buttonholed the producer.

"You may not remember me," he began, "my name is Satterth-waite."

"Of course!" A long bony hand shot out and envelop the other's in a painful grip. "My dear man. Fancy meeting you here. You know Miss Nunn, of course?"

Mr. Satterthwaite jumped. No wonder that voice had been fa-miliar. Thousands, all over England, had thrilled to those wonderful emotion-laden tones. Rosina Nunn! England's greatest emotional actress. Mr. Satterthwaite too had lain under her spell. No one like her for interpreting a part—for bringing out the finer shades of meaning. He had thought of her always as an intellectual actress, one who comprehended and got inside the soul of her part.

He might be excused for not recognizing her. Rosina Nunn was volatile in her tastes. For twenty-five years of her life she had been a blonde. After a tour in the States, she had returned with the locks of the raven, and she had taken up tragedy in earnest. This "French Marquise" effect was her latest whim.

"Oh! by the way, Mr. Judd—Miss Nunn's husband," said Vyse, carelessly introducing the man with the bald head.

Rosina Nunn had had several husbands, Mr. Satterthwaite knew. Mr. Judd was evidently the latest.

Mr. Judd was busily unwrapping packages from a hamper at his side. He addressed his wife.

"Some more *pâté*, dearest. That last wasn't as thick as you like it."

Rosina Nunn surrendered her roll to him, as she murmured simply:

"Henry thinks of the most enchanting meals. I always leave the commissariat to him."

"Feed the brute," said Mr. Judd, and laughed. He patted his wife on the shoulder.

"Treats her just as though she were a dog," murmured the melancholy voice of Mr. Vyse in Mr. Satterthwaite's ear. "Cuts up her food for her. Odd creatures, women."

Mr. Satterthwaite and Mr. Quin between them unpacked lunch. Hard boiled eggs, cold ham and Gruyere cheese were distributed round the table. The Duchess and Miss Nunn appeared to be deep in murmured confidences. Fragments came along in the actress's deep contralto.

"The bread must be very lightly toasted, you understand? Then just a *very* thin layer of marmalade. Rolled up and put in the oven for one minute—not more. Simply delicious."

"That woman lives for food," murmured Mr. Vyse. "Simply lives for it. She can't think of anything else. I remember in *Riders to the Sea*—you know 'and it's the fine, quiet time I'll be having.' I could *not* get the effect I wanted. At last I told her to think of peppermint creams—she's very fond of peppermint creams. I got the effect at once—a sort of far away look that went to your very soul."

Mr. Satterthwaite was silent. He was remembering.

Mr. Tomlinson opposite cleared his throat preparatory to entering into conversation.

"You produce plays, I hear, eh? I'm fond of a good play myself. *Jim the Penman*, now; that was a play."

"My God," said Mr. Vyse, and shivered down all the long length of him.

"A tiny clove of garlic," said Miss Nunn to the Duchess. "You tell your cook. It's wonderful."

She sighed happily and turned to her husband.

"Henry," she said plaintively, "I've never even *seen* the caviare."

"You're as near as nothing to sitting on it," returned Mr. Judd cheerfully. "You put it behind you on the chair."

Rosina Nunn retrieved it hurriedly, and beamed round the table.

"Henry is too wonderful. I'm so terribly absent minded. I never know where I've put anything."

"Like the day you packed your pearls in your sponge bag," said

Henry jocosely. "And then left it behind at the hotel. My word, I did a bit of wiring and phoning that day."

"They were insured," said Miss Nunn dreamily. "Not like my opal."

A spasm of exquisite heart-rending grief flitted across her face.

Several times, when in the company of Mr. Quin, Mr. Satterthwaite had had the feeling of taking part in a play. This illusion was with him very strongly now. This was a dream. Everyone had his part. The words "my opal" were his own cue. He leaned forward.

"Your opal, Miss Nunn?"

"Have you got the butter, Henry? Thank you. Yes, my opal. It was stolen, you know. And I never got it back."

"Do tell us," said Mr. Satterthwaite.

"Well—I was born in October—so it's lucky for me to wear opals, and because of that I wanted a real beauty. I waited a long time for it. They said it was one of the most perfect ones known. Not very large—about the size of a two shilling piece—but oh! the color and the fire."

She sighed. Mr. Satterthwaite observed that the Duchess was fidgetting and seemed uncomfortable, but nothing could stop Miss Nunn now. She went on, and the exquisite inflections of her voice made the story sound like some mournful saga of old.

"It was stolen by a young man called Alec Gerard. He wrote plays."

"Very good plays," put in Mr. Vyse professionally. "Why, I once kept one of his plays six months."

"Did you produce it?" asked Mr. Tomlinson.

"Oh! no," said Mr. Vyse, shocked at the idea. "But do you know, at one time, I actually thought of doing so?"

"It had a wonderful part in it for me," said Miss Nunn. "*Rachel's Children,* it was called—though there wasn't anyone called Rachel in the play. He came to talk to me about it—at the theater. I liked him. He was nice looking—and very shy, poor boy. I remember—" a beautiful faraway look stole over her face—"he brought me some peppermint creams. The opal was lying on the dressing table. He'd been out in Australia, and he knew something about opals. He took it over to the light to look at it. I suppose he must have slipped it into his pocket then. I missed it as soon as he'd gone. There *was* a to-do. You remember?"

She turned to Mr. Vyse.

"Oh! I remember," said Mr. Vyse with a groan.

"They found the empty case in his rooms," continued the actress. "He'd been terribly hard up, but the very next day he was able to pay a large sum into his bank. He pretended to account for it by saying that a friend of his had put some money on a horse for him, but he couldn't produce the friend. He said he must have put the case in his pocket by mistake. I think that was a terribly weak thing to say, don't you? He might have thought of something better than that. I had to go and give evidence. There were pictures of me in all the papers. My press agent said it was very good publicity—but I'd much rather have had my opal back."

She shook her head sadly.

"Have some preserved pineapple?" said Mr. Judd.

Miss Nunn brightened up.

"Where is it?"

"I gave it to you just now."

Miss Nunn looked behind her and in front of her, eyed her gray silk *pochette,* and then slowly drew up a large purple silk bag that was reposing on the ground beside her. She began to turn the contents out slowly on the table, much to Mr. Satterthwaite's interest.

There was a powder puff, a lip-stick, a small jewel case, a skein of wool, another powder puff, two handkerchiefs, a box of chocolate creams, an enameled paper knife, a mirror, a little dark brown wooden box, five letters, a walnut, a small square of mauve crêpe de chine, a piece of ribbon and the end of a *croissant.* Last of all came the preserved pineapple.

"*Eureka,*" murmured Mr. Satterthwaite softly.

"I beg your pardon?"

"Nothing," said Mr. Satterthwaite hastily. "What a charming paper knife."

"Yes, isn't it? Somebody gave it to me. I can't remember who."

"That's an Indian box," remarked Mr. Tomlinson. "Ingenious little things, aren't they?"

"Somebody gave me that too," said Miss Nunn. "I've had it a long time. It used always to stand on my dressing table at the theater. I don't think it's very pretty, though, do you?"

The box was of plain dark brown wood. It pushed open from the side. On the top of it were two plain flaps of wood that could be turned round and round.

"Not pretty perhaps," said Mr. Tomlinson with a chuckle. "But I'll bet you've never seen one like it."

Mr. Satterthwaite leaned forward. He had an excited feeling.

"Why did you say it was ingenious?" he demanded.

"Well, isn't it?"

The judge appealed to Miss Nunn. She looked at him blankly.

"I suppose I mustn't show them the trick of it—eh?'

Miss Nunn still looked blank.

"What trick?" asked Mr. Judd.

"God bless my soul, don't you know?"

He looked round the inquiring faces.

"Fancy that now. May I have the box a minute? Thank you."

He pushed it open.

"Now then, can anyone give me something to put in it—not too big. Here's a small piece of Gru;aayre cheese. That will do capitally. I place it inside, shut the box."

He fumbled for a minute or two with his hands.

"Now see—"

He opened the box again. It was empty.

"Well I never," said Mr. Judd. "How do you do it?"

"It's quite simple. Turn the box upside down, and move the left hand flap half way round, then shut the right hand flap. Now to bring our piece of cheese back again we must reverse that. The right hand flap halfway round, and the left one closed, still keeping the box upside down. And now—Hey Presto!"

The box slid open. A gasp went round the table. The cheese was there—but so was something else. A round thing that blinked forth every color of the rainbow.

"My opal!"

It was a clarion note. Rosina Nunn stood upright, her hands clasped to her breast.

"My opal! But how did it get there?"

Henry Judd cleared his throat.

"I—er—I rather think, Rosy, my girl, you must have put it there yourself."

Someone got up from the table and blundered out into the air. It was Naomi Carlton-Smith. Mr. Quin followed her.

"But when? Do you mean—"

Mr. Satterthwaite watched her while the truth dawned on her. It took over two minutes before she got it.

"You mean last year—at the theater."

"You know," said Henry apologetically. "You *do* fiddle with things, Rosy. Look at you with the caviare today."

Miss Nunn was painfully following out her mental processes.

"I just slipped it in without thinking, and then I suppose I turned the box about and did the thing by accident, but then—but then—" At last it came. "But then Alec Gerard didn't steal it after all. Oh!"—a full-throated cry, poignant, moving—"How dreadful!"

"Well," said Mr. Vyse, "that can be put right now."

"Yes, but he's been in prison a year." And then she startled them. She turned sharply on the Duchess. "Who is that girl—that girl who has just gone out?"

"Miss Carlton-Smith," said the Duchess, "was engaged to Mr. Gerard. She—took the thing very hard."

Mr. Satterthwaite stole softly away. The snow had stopped. Naomi was sitting on the stone wall. She had a sketch book in her hand, and some colored crayons were scattered round. Mr. Quin was standing beside her.

She held out the sketch book to Mr. Satterthwaite. It was a very rough affair—but it had genius. A kaleidoscopic whirl of snowflakes with a figure in the center.

"Very good," said Mr. Satterthwaite.

Mr. Quin looked up at the sky.

"The storm is over," he said. "The roads will be slippery, but I do not think there will be any accident—now."

"There will be no accident," said Naomi. Her voice was charged with some meaning that Mr. Satterthwaite did not understand. She turned and smiled at him—a sudden dazzling smile. "Mr. Satterthwaite can drive back with me if he likes."

He knew then to what length desperation had driven her.

"Well," said Mr. Quin, "I must bid you good-by."

He moved away.

"Where is he going?" said Mr. Satterthwaite, staring after him.

"Back where he came from, I suppose," said Naomi in an odd voice.

"But—but there isn't anything there," said Mr. Satterthwaite, for Mr. Quin was making for that spot on the edge of the cliff where they had first seen him. "You know you said yourself it was the World's End."

He handed back the sketchbook.

"It's very good," he said. "A very good likeness. But why—er— why did you put him in fancy dress?"

Her eyes met his for a brief second.

"I see him like that," said Naomi Carlton-Smith.

7. THE VOICE IN
THE DARK

I

I am a little worried about Margery," said Lady Stranleigh. "My girl,
you know," she added.

She sighed pensively.

"It makes one feel terribly old to have a grown-up daughter."

Mr. Satterthwaite, who was the recipient of these condences,
rose to the occasion gallantly.

"No one could believe it possible," he declared with a little bow.

"Flatterer," said Lady Stranleigh, but she said it vaguely and it
was clear that her mind was elsewhere.

Mr. Satterthwaite looked at the slender white clad figure $
some admiration. The Cannes sunshine was searching, but Lady
Stranleigh came through the test very well. At a distance the youthful effect was really extraordinary. One almost wondered if she
were grown up or not. Mr. Satterthwaite, who knew everything,
knew that it was perfectly possible for Lady Stranleigh to have
grown-up grandchildren. She represented the extreme triumph of
art over nature. Her figure was marvelous, her complexion was mar-

velous. She had enriched many beauty parlors and certainly the result was astounding. Lady Stranleigh lit a cigarette, crossed her
beautiful legs, encased in the finest $f nude silk stockings, and
murmured:

"Yes, I really am rather worried about Margery."

"Dear me," said Mr. Satterthwaite, "what is the trouble?"

Lady Stranleigh turned her beautiful blue eyes upon him.

"You have never met her, have you? She is Charles's daughter,"
she added helpfully.

If entries in *Who's Who* were strictly truthful, the entry concerning Lady Stranleigh might have ended as follows: *hobbies: getting married.* She had floated through life shedding husbands as she
went. She had lost three by divorce and one by death.

"If she had been Rudolf's child I could have understood it,"
mused Lady Stranleigh. "You remember Rudolf? He was always temperamental. Six months after we married I had to apply for those
queer things—what do they call them? Conjugal what nots, you know
what I mean. Thank goodness it is all much simpler nowadays. I remember I had to write him the silliest kind of letter—my lawyer practically dictated it to me. Asking him to come back, you know, and that
I would do all I could, etc., etc., but you never could count on Rudolf,
he was so temperamental. He came rushing home at once, which was
quite the wrong thing to do, and not at all what the lawyers meant."

She sighed.

"About Margery?" suggested Mr. Satterthwaite, tactfully leading
her back to the subject under discussion.

"Of course. I was just going to tell you, wasn't I? Margery has
been seeing things, or hearing them. Ghosts, you know, and all that.
I should never have thought that Margery could be so imaginative.
She is a dear good girl, always has been, but just a shade—dull."

"Impossible," murmured Mr. Satterthwaite with a confused idea
of being complimentary.

"In fact very dull," said Lady Stranleigh. "Doesn't care for dancing, or cocktails or any of the things a young girl ought to care about.
She much prefers staying at home to hunt instead of coming out
here with me."

"Dear, dear," said Mr. Satterthwaite. "She wouldn't come out with you, you say?"

"Well, I didn't exactly press her. Daughters have a depressing effect upon one, I find."

Mr. Satterthwaite tried to think of Lady Stranleigh accompanied by a serious-minded daughter and failed.

"I can't help wondering if Margery is going off her head," continued Margery's mother in a cheerful voice. "Hearing voices is a very bad sign, so they tell me. It is not as though Abbot's Mede were haunted. The old building was burned to the ground in 1836, and they put up a kind of early Victorian château which simply cannot be haunted. It is much too ugly and commonplace."

Mr. Satterthwaite coughed. He was wondering why he was being told all this.

"I thought perhaps," said Lady Stranleigh, smiling brilliantly upon him, "that *you* might be able to help me."

"I?"

"Yes. You are going back to England tomorrow, aren't you?"

"I am. Yes, that is so," admitted Mr. Satterthwaite cautiously.

"And you know all these psychical research people. Of course you do, you know everybody."

Mr. Satterthwaite smiled a little. It was one of his weaknesses to know everybody.

"So what can be simpler?" continued Lady Stranleigh. "I never get on with that sort of person. You know—earnest men with beards and usually spectacles. They bore me terribly and I am quite at my worst with them."

Mr. Satterthwaite was rather taken aback. Lady Stranleigh continued to smile at him brilliantly.

"So that is all settled, isn't it?" she said brightly. "You will go down to Abbot's Mede and see Margery, and make all the arrangements. I shall be terribly grateful to you. Of course if Margery is *really* going off her head, I will come home. Ah! here is Bimbo."

Her smile from being brilliant became dazzling.

A young man in white tennis flannels was approaching them. He was about twenty-five years of age and extremely good-looking.

The young man said simply:

"I have been looking for you everywhere, Babs."

"What has the tennis been like?"

"Septic."

Lady Stranleigh rose. She turned her head over her shoulder and murmured in dulcet tones to Mr. Satterthwaite:

"It is simply marvelous of you to help me. I shall never forget it."

Mr. Satterthwaite looked after the retreating couple.

"I wonder," he mused to himself, "if Bimbo is going to be No. 5."

II

The conductor of the Train de Luxe was pointing out to Mr. Satterthwaite where an accident on the line had occurred a few years previously. As he finished his spirited narrative, the other looked up and saw a wellknown face smiling at him over the conductor's shoulder.

"My dear Mr. Quin," said Mr. Satterthwaite.

His little withered face broke into smiles.

"What a coincidence! That we should both be returning to England on the same train. You are going there, I suppose."

"Yes," said Mr. Quin. "I have business there of rather an important nature. Are you taking the first service of dinner?"

"I always do so. Of course it is an absurd time—half past six, but one runs less risk with the cooking."

Mr. Quin nodded comprehendingly.

"I also," he said. "We might perhaps arrange to sit together."

Half past six found Mr. Quin and Mr. Satterthwaite established opposite each other at a small table in the dining car. Mr. Satterthwaite gave due attention to the wine list and then turned to his companion.

"I have not seen you since—Ah, yes,—not since Corsica, You left very suddenly that day."

Mr. Quin shrugged his shoulders.

"Not more so than usual. I come and go, you know. I come and go."

The words seemed to awake some echo of remembrance in Mr. Satterthwaite's mind. A little shiver passed down his spine—not a disagreeable sensation, quite the contrary. He was conscious of a pleasurable sense of anticipation.

Mr. Quin was holding up a bottle of red wine, examining me label on it. The bottle was between him and the light but for a minute or two a red glow enveloped his person.

Mr. Satterthwaite felt again that sudden stir of excitement.

"I too have a kind of mission in England," he remarked, smiling broadly at the remembrance. "You know Lady Stranleigh perhaps?"

Mr. Quin shook his head. •

"It is an old title," said Mr. Satterthwaite, "a very old title. One of the few that can descend in the female line. She is a baroness in her own right. Rather a romantic history really."

Mr. Quin settled himself more comfortably in his chair. A waiter, flying down the swinging car, desposited cups of soup before them as if by a miracle. Mr. Quin sipped it cautiously.

"You are about to give me one of those wonderful descriptive portraits of yours," he murmured, "that is so, is it not?"

Mr. Satterthwaite beamed on him.

"She is really a marvelous woman," he said. "Sixty, you know— yes, I should say at least sixty. I knew them as girls, she and her sister. Beatrice, that was the name of the elder one. Beatrice and Barbara. I remember them as the Barron girls. Both good-looking and, in those days, very hard up. That was a great many years ago— why, dear me, I was a young man myself then." Mr. Satterthwaite sighed. "There were several lives then between them and the title. Old Lord Stranleigh was a first cousin once removed, I think. Lady Stranleigh's life has been quite a romantic affair. Three unexpected deaths—two of the old man's brothers and a nephew. Then there was the *Uralia*. You remember the wreck of the *Uralia*? She went down off the coast of New Zealand. The Barron girls were on board. Beatrice was drowned. This one, Barbara, was among the few survivors. Six months later, old Stranleigh died and she succeeded to the title and came into a considerable fortune. Since then she has lived for one thing only—herself! She has always been the same, beautiful, unscrupulous, completely callous, interested solely in herself. She has had four husbands, and I have no doubt could get a fifth in a minute."

He went on to describe the mission with which he had been entrusted by Lady Stranleigh.

"I thought of running down to Abbot's Mede to see the young lady," he explained. "I—I feel that something ought to be done about the matter. It is impossible to think of Lady Stranleigh as an ordinary mother." He stopped, looking across the table at Mr. Quin.

"I wish you would come with me," he said wistfully. "Would it not be possible?"

"I am afraid not," said Mr. Quin, "but, let me see—Abbot's Mede is in Wiltshire is it not?"

Mr. Satterthwaite nodded.

"I thought as much. As it happens, I shall be staying not far from Abbot's Mede, at a place you and I both know."

He smiled. "You remember that little inn, The Bells and Motley?"

"Of course," cried Mr. Satterthwaite, "you will be there?"

Mr. Quin nodded. "For a week or ten days, possibly longer. If you will come and look me up one day, I shall be delighted to see you."

And somehow or other Mr. Satterthwaite felt strangely comforted by the assurance.

III

"My dear Miss—er—Margery," said Mr. Satterthwaite, "I assure you that I should not dream of laughing at you."

Margery Gale frowned a little. They were sitting in the large comfortable hall of Abbot's Mede. Margery Gale was a big, squarely built girl. She bore no resemblance to her mother, but took entirely after her father's side of the family, a line of hard riding country squires. She looked fresh and wholesome and the picture of sanity. Nevertheless, Mr. Satterthwaite was reflecting to himself that the Barrons as a family were all inclined to mental instability. Margery might have inherited her physical appearance from her father and at the same time have inherited some mental kink from her mother's side of the family.

"I wish," said Margery, "that I could get rid of that Casson woman. I don't believe in spiritualism, and I don't like it. She is one of these silly women that run a craze to death. She is always bothering me to have a medium down here."

Mr. Satterthwaite coughed, fidgetted a little in his chair and then said in a judicial manner:

"Let me be quite sure that I have all the facts. The first of the—er—phenomena occurred two months ago, I understand."

"About that," agreed the girl. "Sometimes it was a whisper and sometimes it was quite a clear voice, but it always said much the same thing."

"Which was?"

"*Give back what is not yours. Give back what you have stolen.* On each occasion I switched on the light, but the room was quite empty and there was no one there. In the end I got so nervous that I got Clayton, Mother's maid, to sleep on the sofa in my room."

"And the voice came just the same?"

"Yes, but—and this is what frightens me—Clayton did not hear it."

Mr. Satterthwaite reflected for a minute or two.

"Did it come loudly or softly that evening?"

"It was almost a whisper," admitted Margery, "if Clayton was sound asleep I suppose she would not really have heard it. She wanted me to see a doctor." The girl laughed bitterly.

"But since last night even Clayton believes," she continued.

"What happened last night?"

"I am just going to tell you. I have told no one as yet. I had been out hunting yesterday and we had had a long run. I was dead tired, and slept very heavily. I dreamed—a horrible dream—that I had fallen over some iron railings and that one of the spikes was entering slowly into my throat. I woke to find that it was true—there was some sharp point pressing into the side of my neck and at the same time a voice was murmuring softly: *'You have stolen what is mine. This is death.'*

"I screamed," continued Margery, "and clutched at the air but there was nothing there. Clayton heard me scream from the room next door where she was sleeping. She came rushing in, and she distinctly felt something brushing past her in the darkness, but she says that, whatever that something was, it was not anything human."

Mr. Satterthwaite stared at her. The girl was obviously very shaken and upset. He noticed on the left side of her throat a small square of sticking plaster. She caught the direction of his gaze and nodded.

"Yes," she said, "it was not imagination, you see."

Mr. Satterthwaite put a question almost apologetically, it sounded so melodramatic.

"You don't know of anyone—er—who has a grudge against you?" he asked.

"Of course not," said Margery, "what an idea."

Mr. Satterthwaite started on another line of attack.

"What visitors have you had during the last two months?"

"You don't mean just people for week-ends, I suppose? Marcia Keane has been with me all along. She is my best friend and just as keen on horses as I am. Then my cousin Roley Vavasour has been here a good deal."

Mr. Satterthwaite nodded. He suggested that he should see Clayton, the maid.

"She has been with you a long time, I suppose?" he asked.

"Donkey's years," said Margery. "She was Mother's and Aunt Beatrice's maid when they were girls. That is why Mother has kept her on, I suppose, although she has got a French maid for herself. Clayton does sewing and pottering little odd jobs."

She took him upstairs and presently Clayton came to them. She was a tall, thin old woman with gray hair neatly parted, and looked the acme of respectability.

"No, sir," she said in answer to Mr. Satterthwaite's inquiries, "I have never heard anything of the house being haunted. To tell you the truth, sir, I thought it was all Miss Margery's imagination until last night. But I actually felt something—brushing by me in the darkness. And I can tell you this, sir, *it was not anything human.* And then there is that wound in Miss Margery's neck. She didn't do that herself, poor lamb."

But her words were suggestive to Mr. Satterthwaite. Was it possible that Margery could have inflicted that wound herself? He had heard of strange cases where girls apparently just as 'sane and well balanced as Margery had done the most amazing things.

"It win soon heal up," said Clayton. "It's not like this scar of mine."

She pointed to a mark on her own forehead.

"That was done forty years ago, sir, I still bear the mark of it."

"It was the time the *Uralia* went down," put in Margery. "Clayton was hit on the head by a spar, weren't you, Clayton?"

"Yes, miss."

"What do you think yourself, Clayton?" asked Mr. Satterthwaite. "What do you think was the meaning of this attack on Miss Margery?"

"I really should not like to say, sir."

Mr. Satterthwaite read this correctly as the reserve of the well trained servant.

"What do you really think, Clayton?" he said persuasively.

"I think, sir, that something very wicked must have been done in this house, and that until that is wiped out there won't be any peace."

The woman spoke gravely, and her faded blue eyes met his steadily.

Mr. Satterthwaite went downstairs rather disappointed. Clayton evidently held the orthodox view, a deliberate "haunting" as a consequence of some evil deed in the past. Mr. Satterthwaite himself was not so easily satisfied. The phenomena had only taken place in the last two months. Had only taken place since Marcia Keane and Roley Vavasour had been there. He must find out something about these two. It was possible that the whole thing was a practical joke. But he shook his head, dissatisfied with that solution. The thing was more sinister than that. The post had just come in and Margery was

opening and reading her letters. Suddenly she gave an exclamation.
"Mother is too absurd," she said. "Do read this." She handed the
letter to Mr. Satterthwaite.

It was an epistle typical of Lady Stranleigh.

DARLING MARGERY, [SHE WROTE],

> I am so glad you have that nice little Mr. Satterthwaite
> there. He is awfully clever and knows all the big wig spook
> people. You must have them all down and investigate things
> thoroughly. I am sure you will have a perfectly marvelous
> time and I only wish I could be there, but I have really been
> quite ill the last few days. The hotels are so careless about
> the food they give one. The doctor says it is some kind of
> poisoning. I was really *very* ill.
>
> Sweet of you to send me the chocolates, darling, but
> surely just a wee bit silly, wasn't it? I mean, there's such
> wonderful confectionery out here.
>
> Bye Bye, darling, and have a lovely time laying the fam-
> ily ghosts. Bimbo says my tennis is coming on marvelously.
> Oceans of love,

> Yours,
> BARBARA.

"Mother always wants me to call her Barbara," said Margery.
"Simply silly, I think."

Mr. Satterthwaite smiled a little. He realized that the stolid con-
servatism of her daughter must on occasions be very trying to Lady
Stranleigh. The contents of her letter struck him in a way in which
obviously they did not strike Margery.

"Did you send your mother a box of chocolates?" he asked.

Margery shook her head. "No, I didn't, it must have been someone else."

Mr. Satterthwaite looked grave. Two things struck him as of significance. Lady Stranleigh had received a gift of a box of chocolates

and she was suffering from a severe attack of poisoning. Apparently she had not connected these two things. Was there a connection? He himself was inclined to think there was.

A tall dark girl lounged out of the morning room and joined them. She was introduced to Mr. Satterthwaite as Marcia Keane. She smiled on the little man in an easy good-humored fashion.

"Have you come down to hunt Margery's pet ghost?" she asked in a drawling voice. "We all rot her about that ghost. Hello, here's Roley."

A car had just drawn up at the front door. Out of it tumbled a tall young man with fair hair and an eager boyish manner.

"Hello, Margery," he cried, "Hello, Marcia! I have brought down reinforcements." He turned to the two women who were just entering the hall. Mr. Satterthwaite recognized in the first one of the two the Mrs. Casson of whom Margery had spoken just now.

"You must forgive me, Margery dear," she drawled, smiling broadly. "Mr. Vavasour told us that it would be quite all right. It was really his idea that I should bring down Mrs. Lloyd with me."

She indicated her companion with a slight gesture of the hand.

"This is Mrs. Lloyd," she said in a tone of triumph. "Simply the most wonderful medium that ever existed."

Mrs. Lloyd uttered no modest protest; she bowed and remained with her hands crossed in front of her. She was a highly colored young woman of commonplace appearance. Her clothes were unfashionable but rather ornate. She wore a chain of moonstones and several rings.

Margery Gale, as Mr. Satterthwaite could see, was not too pleased at this intrusion. She threw an angry look at Roley Vavasour, who seemed quite unconscious of the offense he had caused.

"Lunch is ready, I think," said Margery.

"Good," said Mrs. Casson, "we will hold a *séance* immediately afterward. Have you got some fruit for Mrs. Lloyd? She never eats a solid meal before a *séance*."

They all went into the dining room. The medium ate two bananas and an apple, and replied cautiously and briefly to the various polite remarks which Margery addressed to her from time to time. Just before they rose from table, she flung back her head suddenly and sniffed the air.

"There is something very wrong in this house, I feel it."

"Isn't she wonderful," said Mrs. Casson in a low delighted voice.

"Oh! undoubtedly," said Mr. Satterthwaite dryly.

The *séance* was held in the library. The hostess was, as Mr. Satterthwaite could see, very unwilling; only the obvious delight of her guests in the proceedings reconciled her to the ordeal.

The arrangements were made with a good deal of care by Mrs. Casson, who was evidently well up in those matters. The chairs were set round in a circle, the curtains were drawn, and presently the medium announced herself ready to begin.

"Six people," she said, looking round the room. "That is bad. We must have an uneven number. Seven is ideal. I get my best results out of a circle of seven."

"One of the servants," suggested Roley. He rose. "I will rout out the butler."

"Let's have Clayton," said Margery.

Mr. Satterthwaite saw a look of annoyance pass over Roley Vavasour's good-looking face.

"But why Clayton?" he demanded.

"You don't like Clayton," said Margery slowly.

Roley shrugged his shoulders. "Clayton doesn't like me," he said whimsically, "in fact she hates me like poison." He waited a minute or two but Margery did not give way. "All right," he said, "have her down."

The circle was formed. There was a period of silence, broken by the usual coughs and fidgettings. Presently a succession of raps were heard and then the voice of the medium's control, a Red Indian called Cherokee.

"Indian Brave says you good evening ladies and gentlemen. Someone here very anxious speak. Someone here very anxious give message to young lady. I go now. The spirit say what she come to say."

A pause and then a new voice, that of a woman, said softly:

"Is Margery here?"

Roley Vavasour took it upon himself to answer.

"Yes," he said, "she is. Who is that speaking?"

"I am Beatrice."

"Beatrice? Who is Beatrice?"

To everyone's annoyance the voice of the Red Indian Cherokee was heard once more.

"I have message for all of you people. Life here very bright and beautiful. We all work very hard. Help those who have not yet passed over."

Again a silence and then the woman's voice was heard once more.

"This is Beatrice speaking."

"Beatrice who?"

"Beatrice Barron."

Mr. Satterthwaite leaned forward. He was very excited.

"Beatrice Barron who was drowned in the *Uralia?*"

"Yes, that is right. I remember the *Uralia*. I have a message—for this house—*Give back what is not yours.*"

"I don't understand," said Margery helplessly, "I—oh, are you really Aunt Beatrice?"

"Yes, I am your aunt."

"Of course she is," said Mrs. Casson reproachfully, "how can you be so suspicious? The spirits don't like it."

And suddenly Mr. Satterthwaite thought of a very simple test. His voice quivered a little as he spoke.

"Do you remember Mr. Bottacetti?" he asked.

Immediately there came a ripple of laughter.

"Poor old Boatupsetty. Of course."

Mr. Satterthwaite was dumbfounded. The test had succeeded. It was an incident of over forty years ago, which had happened when he and the Barron girls had found themselves at the same seaside resort. A young Italian acquaintance of theirs had gone out in a boat and capsized, and Beatrice Barron had jestingly named him Boatupsetty. It seemed impossible that anyone in the room could know of this incident except himself.

The medium stirred and groaned.

"She is coming out," said Mrs. Casson; "that is all we will get out of her today, I am afraid."

The daylight shone once more on the room full of people, two of whom at least were badly scared.

Mr. Satterthwaite saw by Margery's white face that she was deeply perturbed. When they had got rid of Mrs. Casson and the medium, he sought a private interview with his hostess.

"I want to ask you one or two questions, Miss Margery. If you and your mother were to die who succeeds to the title and estates?"

"Roley Vavasour, I suppose. His mother was mother's first cousin."

Mr. Satterthwaite nodded.

"He seems to have been here a lot this winter," he said gently. "You will forgive me asking—but is he—fond of you?"

"He asked me to marry him three weeks ago," said Margery quietly. "I said no."

"Please forgive me, but are you engaged to anyone else?"

He saw the color sweep over her face.

"I am," she said emphatically. "I am going to marry Noel Barton. Mother laughs and says it is absurd. She seems to think it is ridiculous to be engaged to a curate. Why, I should like to know? There are curates and curates! You should see Noel on a horse."

"Oh, quite so," said Mr. Satterthwaite. "Oh, undoubtedly."

A footman entered with a telegram on a salver. Margery tore it open. "Mother is arriving home tomorrow," she said. "Bother. I wish to goodness she would stay away."

Mr. Satterthwaite made no comment on this filial sentiment. Perhaps he thought it justified. "In that case," he murmured, "I think I am returning to London."

IV

Mr. Satterthwaite was not quite pleased with himself. He felt that he had left this particular problem in an unfinished state. True that, on Lady Stranleigh's return, his responsibility was ended; yet he felt assured that he had not heard the last of the Abbot's Mede mystery.

But the next development, when it came, was so serious in its character that it found him totally unprepared. He learned of it in the pages of his morning paper. "Baroness dies in her Bath," as the *Daily Megaphone* had it. The other papers were more restrained and delicate in their language, but the fact was the same. Lady Stranleigh had been found dead in her bath, and her death was due to drowning. She had, it was assumed, lost consciousness and while in that state her head had slipped below the water.

But Mr. Satterthwaite was not satisfied with that explanation. Calling for his valet, he made his toilet with less than his usual care and ten minutes later his big Rolls Royce was carrying him out of London as fast as it could travel.

But strangely enough it was not for Abbot's Mede he was bound, but for a small inn some fifteen miles distant which bore the rather unusual name of The Bells and Motley. It was with great relief that he heard that Mr. Harley Quin was still staying there. In another minute he was face to face with his friend.

Mr. Satterthwaite clasped him by the hand and began to speak at once in an agitated manner.

"I am terribly upset. You must help me. Already I have a dreadful feeling that it may be too late—that that nice girl may be the next to go; for she is a nice girl, nice through and through."

"If you will tell me," said Mr. Quin, smiling, "what it is all about?"

Mr. Satterthwaite looked at him reproachfully.

"You know. I am perfectly certain that you know. But I will tell you."

He poured out the story of his stay at Abbot's Mede and, as always with Mr. Quin, he found himself taking pleasure in his narrative. He was eloquent and subtle and meticulous as to detail.

"So you see," he ended, "there must be an explanation."

He looked hopefully at Mr. Quin, as a dog looks at his master.

"But it is you who must solve the problem, not I," said Mr. Quin. "I do not know these people. You do."

"I knew the Barron girls forty years ago," said Mr. Satterthwaite with pride.

Mr. Quin nodded and looked sympathetic, so much so that the other went on dreamily.

"That time at Brighton now, Bottacetti-Boatupsetty, quite a silly joke but how we laughed. Dear, dear, I was young then. Did a lot of foolish things. I remember the maid they had with them. Alice, her name was, a little bit of a thing—very ingenuous. I kissed her in the passage of the hotel I remember, and one of the girls nearly caught me doing it. Dear, dear, how long ago that all was."

He shook his head again and sighed. Then he looked at Mr. Quin.

"So you can't help me?" he said wistfully. "On other occasions—"

"On other occasions you have proved successful owing entirely to your own efforts," said Mr. Quin gravely. "I think it will be the same this time. If I were you, I should go to Abbot's Mede now."

"Quite so, quite so," said Mr. Satterthwaite. "As a matter of fact, that is what I thought of doing. I can't persuade you to come with me?"

Mr. Quin shook his head.

"No," he said, "my work here is done. I am leaving almost immediately."

At Abbot's Mede, Mr. Satterthwaite was taken at once to Margery Gale. She was sitting dry-eyed at a desk in the morning-room on which was strewn various papers. Something in her greeting touched him. She seemed so very pleased to see him.

"Roley and Marcia have just left. Mr. Satterthwaite, it is not as the doctors think. I am convinced, absolutely convinced, that Mother was pushed under the water and held there. She was murdered, and whoever murdered her wants to murder me too. I am sure of that. That is why—" She indicated the document in front of her.

"I have been making my will," she explained. "A lot of the money and some of the property does not go with the title, and there is my father's money as well. I am leaving everything I can to Noel. I know he will make a good use of it, and I do not trust Roley; he has always been out for what he can get. Will you sign it as a witness?"

"My dear young lady," said Mr. Satterthwaite, "you should sign a will in the presence of two witnesses, and they should then sign themselves at the same time."

Margery brushed aside this legal pronouncement.

"I don't see that it matters in the least," she declared. "Clayton saw me sign and then she signed her name. I was going to ring for the butler, but you will do instead."

Mr. Satterthwaite uttered no fresh protest; he unscrewed his fountain pen and then, as he was about to append his signature, he paused suddenly. The name, written just above his own recalled a flow of memories. Alice Clayton.

Something seemed to be struggling very hard to get through to him. Alice Clayton; there was some significance about that. Something to do with Mr. Quin was mixed up with it. Something he had said to Mr. Quin only a very short time ago.

Ah, he had it now. Alice Clayton, that was her name. *The little bit of a thing.* People changed—yes, *but not like that.* And the Alice Clayton he knew had had brown eyes. The room seemed whirling round him. He felt for a chair and presently, as though from a great distance, he heard Margery's voice speaking to him anxiously.

"Are you ill? Oh, what is it? I am sure you are ill!"

He was himself again. He took her hand.

"My dear, I see it all now. You must prepare yourself for a great shock. The woman upstairs whom you call Clayton is not Clayton at all. The real Alice Clayton was drowned on the *Uralia*."

Margery was staring at him. "Who—who is she then?"

"I am not mistaken; I cannot be mistaken. The woman you call Clayton is your mother's sister, Beatrice Barron. You remember telling me that she was struck on the head by a spar? I should imagine that that blow destroyed her memory and that being the case, your mother saw the chance—"

"Of pinching the title you mean?" asked Margery bitterly. "Yes she would do that. It seems dreadful to say that, now she is dead, but she was like that."

"Beatrice was the elder sister," said Mr. Satterthwaite. "By your uncle's death she would inherit everything and your mother would get nothing. Your mother claimed the wounded girl as her *maid*, not as her *sister*. The girl recovered from the blow and believed of course what was told her, that she was Alice Clayton, your mother's maid. I should imagine that, just lately, her memory has begun to return, but that the blow on the head, given all these years ago, has at last caused mischief on the brain."

Margery was looking at him with eyes of horror.

"She killed Mother and she wanted to kill me," she breathed.

"It seems so," said Mr. Satterthwaite. "In her brain there was just one muddled idea—that her inheritance had been stolen and was being kept from her by you and your mother."

"But—but Clayton is so old."

Mr. Satterthwaite was silent for a minute as a vision rose up before him—the faded old woman with gray hair and the radiant golden haired creature sitting in the sunshine at Cannes. Sisters! Could it really be so? He remembered the Barron girls and their likeness to each other. Just because two lives had developed on different tracks—

He shook his head sharply, obsessed by the wonder and pity of life.

He turned to Margery and said gently, "We had better go upstairs and see her."

They found Clayton sitting in the little workroom where she sewed. She did not turn her head as they came in, for a reason that Mr. Satterthwaite soon found out.

"Heart failure," he murmured, as he touched the cold rigid shoulder. "Perhaps it is best that way."

8. THE FACE OF HELEN

I

Mr. Satterthwaite was at the opera and sat alone in his big box on the first tier. Outside the door was a printed card bearing his name. An appreciator and a connoisseur of all the arts, Mr. Satterthwaite was especially fond of good music, and was a regular subscriber to Covent Garden every year, reserving a box for Tuesdays and Fridays throughout the season.

But it was not often that he sat in it alone. He was a gregarious little gentleman, and he liked filling his box with the élite of the great world to which he belonged, and also with the aristocracy of the artistic world, in which he was equally at home. He was alone tonight because a countess had disappointed him. The Countess, besides being a beautiful and celebrated woman, was also a good mother. Her children had been attacked by that common and distressing disease, the mumps, and the Countess remained at home in tearful confabulation with exquisitely starched nurses. Her husband, who had supplied her with the aforementioned children and a title, but who was otherwise a complete nonentity, had seized at the chance to escape. Nothing bored him more than music.

So Mr. Satterthwaite sat alone. *Cavalleria Rusticana* and *Pagliacci* were being given that night, and, since the first had never appealed to him, he arrived just after the curtain went down on Santuzza's death agony, in time to glance round the house with a practiced eye, before everyone streamed out, bent on paying visits or fighting for coffee or lemonade. Mr. Satterthwaite adjusted his opera glasses, looked round the house, marked down his prey and sallied forth with a well mapped out plan of campaign ahead of him, a plan, however, which he did not put into execution, for just outside his box he cannoned into a tall, dark man, and recognized him with a pleasurable thrill of excitement.

"Mr. Quin," cried Mr. Satterthwaite.

He seized his friend warmly by the hand, clutching him as though he feared any minute to see him vanish into thin air.

"You must share my box," said Mr. Satterthwaite determinedly. "You are not with a party?"

"No, I am sitting by myself in the stalls," responded Mr. Quin with a smile.

"Then that is settled," said Mr. Satterthwaite with a sigh of relief.

His manner was almost comic, had there been anyone to observe it.

"You are very kind," said Mr. Quin.

"Not at all. It is a pleasure. I didn't know you were fond of music?"

"There are reasons why I am attracted to *Pagliacci*."

"Ah! of course," said Mr. Satterthwaite, nodding sapiently, though, if put to it, he would have found it hard to explain just why he had used that expression. "Of course, you would be."

They went back to the box at the first summons of the bell, and, leaning over the front of it, they watched the people returning to the stalls.

"That's a beautiful head," observed Mr. Satterthwaite suddenly.

He indicated with his glasses a spot immediately beneath them in the stalls circle. A girl sat there whose face they could not see— only the pure gold of her hair that fitted with the closeness of a cap till it merged into the white neck.

"A Greek head," said Mr. Satterthwaite reverently. "Pure

Greek." He sighed happily. "It's a remarkable thing when you come to think of it—how very few people have hair that *fits* them. It's more noticeable now that everyone is shingled."

"You are so observant," said Mr. Quin.

"I see things," admitted Mr. Satterthwaite. "I do see things. For instance, I picked out that head at once. We must have a look at her face sooner or later. But it won't match, I'm sure. That would be a chance in a thousand."

Almost as the words left his lips, the lights flickered and went down, the sharp rap of the conductor's baton was heard, and the opera began. A new tenor, said to be a second Caruso, was singing that night. He had been referred to by the newspapers as a Jugo-Slav, a Czech, an Albanian, a Magyar, and a Bulgarian, with a beautiful impartiality. He had given an extraordinary concert at the Albert Hall, a program of the folk songs of his native hills, with a specially tuned orchestra. They were in strange half tones, and the would-be musical had pronounced them "too marvelous." Real musicians had reserved judgment, realizing that the ear had to be specially trained and attuned before any criticism was possible. It was quite a relief to some people to find this evening that Yoaschbim could sing in ordinary Italian with all the traditional sobs and quivers.

The curtain went down on the first act, and applause burst out vociferously. Mr. Satterthwaite turned to Mr. Quin. He realized that the latter was waiting for him to pronounce judgment, and plumed himself a little. After all, he *knew*. As a critic he was well-nigh infallible.

Very slowly he nodded his head.

"It is the real thing," he said.

"You think so?"

"As fine a voice as Caruso's. People will not recognize that it is so at first, for his technique is not yet perfect. There are ragged edges, a lack of certainty in the attack. But the voice is there—magnificent."

"I went to his concert at the Albert Hall," said Mr. Quin.

"Did you? I could not go."

"He made a wonderful hit with a shepherd's song."

"I read about it," said Mr. Satterthwaite. "The refrain ends each time with a high note—a kind of cry. A note midway between A and B flat. Very curious."

Yoaschbim had taken three calls, bowing and smiling. The lights went up and the people began to file out. Mr. Satterthwaite leaned over to watch the girl with the golden head. She rose, adjusted her scarf, and turned.

Mr. Satterthwaite caught his breath. There were, he knew, such faces in the world—faces that made history—

The girl moved to the gangway, her companion, a young man, beside her. And Mr. Satterthwaite noticed how every man in the vicinity looked—and continued to look covertly.

"Beauty!" said Mr. Satterthwaite to himself. "There is such a thing. Not charm, nor attraction, nor magnetism, nor any of the things we talk about so glibly—just sheer beauty. The shape of a face, the line of an eyebrow, the curve of a jaw." He quoted softly under his breath: "*The face that launched a thousand ships.*" And for the first time he realized the meaning of those words.

He glanced across at Mr. Quin who was watching him in what seemed such perfect comprehension that Mr. Satterthwaite felt there was no need for words.

"I've always wondered," he said simply, "what such women were really like."

"You mean?"

"The Helens, the Cleopatras, the Mary Stuarts."

Mr. Quin nodded thoughtfully.

"If we go out," he suggested, "we may—see."

They went out together, and their quest was successful. The pair they were in search of were seated on a lounge halfway up the staircase. For the first time, Mr. Satterthwaite noted the girl's companion, a dark young man, not handsome, but with a suggestion of restless fire about him. A face full of strange angles; jutting cheekbones, a forceful, slightly crooked jaw, deep-set eyes that were curiously light under the dark, overhanging brows.

"An interesting face," said Mr. Satterthwaite to himself. "A real face. It means something."

The young man was leaning forward talking earnestly. The girl was listening. Neither of them belonged to Mr. Satterthwaite's world. He took them to be of the "Arty" class. The girl wore a rather shapeless garment of cheap green silk. Her shoes were of soiled, white satin. The young man wore his evening clothes with an air of being uncomfortable in them.

The two men passed and repassed several times. The fourth time they did so, the couple had been joined by a third—a fair young man with a suggestion of the clerk about him. With his coming a certain tension had set in. The newcomer was fidgetting with his tie and seemed ill at ease; the girl's beautiful face was turned gravely up toward him, and her companion was scowling furiously.

"The usual story," said Mr. Quin very softly, as they passed.

"Yes," said Mr. Satterthwaite with a sigh. "It's inevitable, I suppose. The snarling of two dogs over a bone always has been, it always will be. And yet, one could wish for something different. Beauty—" He stopped. Beauty to Mr. Satterthwaite, meant something very wonderful. He found it difficult to speak of it. He looked at Mr. Quin, who nodded his head gravely in understanding.

They went back to their seats for the second act.

At the close of the performance, Mr. Satterthwaite turned eagerly to his friend.

"It is a wet night. My car is here. You must allow me to drive you—er—somewhere."

The last word was Mr. Satterthwaite's delicacy coming into play. "To drive you home" would, he felt, have savored of curiosity. Mr. Quin had always been singularly reticent. It was extraordinary how little Mr. Satterthwaite knew about him.

"But perhaps," continued the little man, "you have your own car waiting?"

"No," said Mr. Quin. "I have no car waiting."

"Then—"

But Mr. Quin shook his head.

"You are most kind," he said, "but I prefer to go my own way. Besides," he said with a rather curious smile, "if anything should—happen, it will be for you to act. Good night, and thank you. Once again we have seen the drama together."

He had gone so quickly that Mr. Satterthwaite had no time to protest, but he was left with a faint uneasiness stirring in his mind. To what drama did Mr. Quin refer? *Pagliacci* or another?

Masters, Mr. Satterthwaite's chauffeur, was in the habit of waiting in a side street. His master disliked the long delay while the cars drew up in turn before the opera house. Now, as on previous occasions, he walked rapidly round the corner and along the street toward where he knew he should find Masters awaiting him. Just in front of him were a girl and a man, and even as he recognized them, another man joined them.

It all broke out in a minute. A man's voice, angrily uplifted. Another man's voice in injured protest. And then the scuffle. Blows, angry breathing, more blows, the form of a policeman appearing majestically from nowhere—and in another minute Mr. Satterthwaite was beside the girl where she shrank back against the wall.

"Allow me," he said. "You must not stay here."

He took her by the arm and marshalled her swiftly down the street. Once she looked back.

"Oughtn't I—?" she began uncertainly.

Mr. Satterthwaite shook his head.

"It would be very unpleasant for you to be mixed up in it. You would probably be asked to go along to the police station with them. I am sure neither of your—friends would wish that."

He stopped.

"This is my car. If you will allow me to do so, I shall have much pleasure in driving you home."

The girl looked at him searchingly. The staid respectability of Mr. Satterthwaite impressed her favorably. She bent her head.

"Thank you," she said, and got into the car, the door of which Masters was holding open.

In reply to a question from Mr. Satterthwaite, she gave an address in Chelsea, and he got in beside her.

The girl was upset and not in the mood for talking, and Mr. Satterthwaite was too tactful to intrude upon her thoughts. Presently, however, she turned to him and spoke of her own accord.

"I wish," she said pettishly, "people wouldn't be so silly."

"It is a nuisance," agreed Mr. Satterthwaite.

His matter-of-fact manner put her at her ease, and she went on as though feeling the need of confiding in someone.

"It wasn't as though—I mean, well, it was like this. Mr. Eastney and I have been friends for a long time—ever since I came to London. He's taken no end of trouble about my voice, and got me some very good introductions, and he's been more kind to me than I can say. He's absolutely music mad. It was very good of him to take me tonight. I'm sure he can't really afford it. And then Mr. Burns came up and spoke to us—quite nicely, I'm sure, and Phil, Mr. Eastney, got sulky about it. I don't know why he should. It's a free country, I'm sure. And Mr. Burns is always pleasant, and good tempered. Then just as we were walking to the Tube, he came up and joined us, and he hadn't so much as said two words before Philip flew out at him like a madman. And—Oh! I don't like it."

"Don't you?" asked Mr. Satterthwaite very softly.

She blushed, but very little. There was none of the conscious siren about her. A certain measure of pleasurable excitement in being fought for there must be—that was only nature—but Mr. Satterthwaite decided that a worried perplexity lay uppermost, and he had the clue to it in another moment when she observed inconsequently:

"I do hope he hasn't hurt him."

"Now which is 'him'?" thought Mr. Satterthwaite, smiling to himself in the darkness.

He backed his own judgment and said:

"You hope Mr.—er—Eastney hasn't hurt Mr. Burns?"

She nodded.

"Yes, that's what I said. It seems so dreadful. I wish I knew."

The car was drawing up.

"Are you on the telephone?" he asked.

"Yes."

"If you like, I will find out exactly what has happened, and then telephone to you."

The girl's face brightened.

"Oh! that would be very kind of you. Are you sure it's not too much bother?"

"Not in the least."

She thanked him again and gave him her telephone number, adding with a touch of shyness:

"My name is Gillian West."

As he was driven through the night, bound on his errand, a curious smile came to Mr. Satterthwaite's lips.

He thought: "So that is all it is—The shape of a face, the curve of a jaw!'"

But he fulfilled his promise.

II

The following Sunday afternoon, Mr. Satterthwaite went to Kew Gardens to admire the rhododendrons. Very long ago (incredibly long ago, it seemed to Mr. Satterthwaite) he had driven down to Kew Gardens with a certain young lady to see the bluebells. Mr. Satterthwaite had arranged very carefully beforehand in his own mind exactly what he was going to say, and the precise words he would use in asking the young lady for her hand in marriage. He was just conning them over in his mind, and responding to her raptures about the bluebells a little absent-mindedly, when the shock came. The young lady stopped exclaiming at the bluebells and suddenly confided in Mr. Satterthwaite (as a true friend) her love for another. Mr. Satterthwaite put away the little set speech he had prepared, and hastily rummaged for sympathy and friendship in the bottom drawer of his mind.

Such was Mr. Satterthwaite's romance—a rather tepid early Victorian one, but it had left him with a romantic attachment to Kew Gardens, and he would often go there to see the bluebells, or, if he had been abroad later than usual, the rhododendrons, and would sigh to himself, and feel rather sentimental, and really enjoy himself very much indeed in an old-fashioned, romantic way.

This particular afternoon he was strolling back past the tea houses when he recognized a couple sitting at one of the small tables on the grass. They were Gillian West and the fair young man, and at that same moment they recognized him. He saw the girl flush and speak eagerly to her companion. In another minute he was shaking hands with them both in his correct, rather prim fashion, and had accepted the shy invitation proffered him to have tea with them.

"I can't tell you, sir," said Mr. Burns, "how grateful I am to you for looking after Gillian the other night. She told me all about it."

"Yes, indeed," said the girl. "It was ever so kind of you."

Mr. Satterthwaite felt pleased and interested in the pair. Their naïveté and sincerity touched him. Also, it was to him a peep into a world with which he was not well acquainted. These people were of a class unknown to him.

In his little dried-up way, Mr. Satterthwaite could be very sympathetic. Very soon he was hearing all about his new friends. He noted that Mr. Burns had become Charlie, and he was not unprepared for the statement that the two were engaged.

As a matter of fact," said Mr. Burns with refreshing candor, "it just happened this afternoon, didn't it, Gil?"

Burns was a clerk in a shipping firm. He was making a fair salary, had a little money of his own, and the two proposed to be married quite soon.

Mr. Satterthwaite listened, and nodded, and congratulated.

"An ordinary young man," he thought to himself, "a very ordinary young man. Nice, straightforward young chap, plenty to say for himself, good opinion of himself without being conceited, nice-looking without being unduly handsome. Nothing remarkable about him and will never set the Thames on fire. And the girl loves him."

Aloud he said, "And Mr. Eastney—"

He purposely broke off, but he had said enough to produce an effect for which he was not unprepared. Charlie Burns' face darkened, and Gillian looked troubled. More than troubled, he thought. She looked afraid.

"I don't like it," she said in a low voice. Her words were addressed to Mr. Satterthwaite, as though she knew by instinct that he would understand a feeling incomprehensible to her lover. "You see—he's done a lot for me. He's encouraged me to take up singing, and—and helped me with it. But I've known all the time that my voice wasn't really good—not first-class. Of course, I've had engagements—"

She stopped.

"You've had a bit of trouble too," said Burns. "A girl wants someone to look after her. Gillian's had a lot of unpleasantness, Mr. Satterthwaite. Altogether she's had a lot of unpleasantness. She's a good-looker, as you can see, and—well, that often leads to trouble for a girl."

Between them, Mr. Satterthwaite became enlightened as to various happenings which were vaguely classed by Burns under the heading of "unpleasantness." The young man who had shot himself, the extraordinary conduct of the Bank Manager (who was a married man!), the violent stranger (who must have been balmy!), the wild behavior of the elderly artist. A trail of violence and tragedy that Gillian West had left in her wake, recited in the commonplace tones of Charles Burns. "And it's my opinion," he ended, "that this fellow Eastney is a bit cracked. Gillian would have had trouble with him if I hadn't turned up to look after her."

His laugh sounded a little fatuous to Mr. Satterthwaite, and no responsive smile came to the girl's face. She was looking earnestly at Mr. Satterthwaite.

"Phil's all right," she said slowly. "He cares for me, I know, and I care for him like a friend—but—but not anything more. I don't know how he'll take the news about Charlie. I'm sure. He—I'm so afraid he'll be—"

She stopped, inarticulate in face of the dangers she vaguely sensed.

"If I can help you in any way," said Mr. Satterthwaite warmly, "pray command me."

He fancied Charlie Burns looked vaguely resentful, but Gillian said at once: "Thank you."

Mr. Satterthwaite left his new friends after having promised to take tea with Gillian on the following Thursday.

When Thursday came, Mr. Satterthwaite felt a little thrill of pleasurable anticipation. He thought: "I'm an old man—but not too old to be thrilled by a face. A face—" Then he shook his head with a sense of foreboding.

Gillian was alone. Charlie Burns was to come in later. She looked much happier, Mr. Satterthwaite thought, as though a load had been lifted from her mind. Indeed, she frankly admitted as much.

"I dreaded telling Phil about Charlie. It was silly of me. I ought to have known Phil better. He was upset, of course, but no one could have been sweeter. Really sweet he was. Look what he sent me this morning—a wedding present. Isn't it magnificent?"

It was indeed rather magnificent for a young man in Philip Eastney's circumstances. A four valve wireless set, of the latest type.

"We both love music so much, you see," explained the girl. "Phil said that when I was listening to a concert on this, I should always think of him a little. And I'm sure I shall. Because we have been such friends."

"You must be proud of your friend," said Mr. Satterthwaite gently. "He seems to have taken the blow like a true sportsman."

Gillian nodded. He saw the quick tears come into her eyes.

"He asked me to do one thing for him. Tonight is the anniversary of the day we first met. He asked me if I would stay at home quietly this evening and listen to the wireless program—not go out with Charlie anywhere. I said of course I would, and that I was very touched, and that I would think of him with a lot of gratitude and affection."

Mr. Satterthwaite nodded, but he was puzzled. He was seldom at fault in his delineation of character, and he would have judged Philip Eastney quite incapable of such a sentimental request. The young man must be of a more banal order than he supposed. Gillian evidently thought the idea quite in keeping with her rejected lover's character. Mr. Satterthwaite was a little—just a little—disappointed. He was sentimental himself, and knew it, but he expected better things of the rest of the world. Besides, sentiment belonged to his age. It had no part to play in the modern world.

He asked Gillian to sing and she complied. He told her her voice was charming, but he knew quite well in his own mind that it was distinctly second-class. Any success that could have come to her in the profession she had adopted would have been won by her face, not her voice.

He was not particularly anxious to see young Burns again, so presently he rose to go. It was at that moment that his attention was attracted by an ornament on the mantelpiece which stood out among the other rather gimcrack objects like a jewel on a dust heap.

It was a curving beaker of thin green glass, long-stemmed and graceful, and poised on the edge of it was what looked like a gigantic soap-bubble, a ball of iridescent glass. Gillian noticed his absorption.

"That's an extra wedding present from Phil. It's rather pretty, I think. He works in a sort of glass factory."

"It is a beautiful thing," said Mr. Satterthwaite reverently. "The glass blowers of Murano might have been proud of that."

He went away with his interest in Philip Eastney strangely stimulated. An extraordinarily interesting young man. And yet the girl with the wonderful face preferred Charlie Burns. What a strange and inscrutable universe!

It had just occurred to Mr. Satterthwaite that, owing to the remarkable beauty of Gillian West, his evening with Mr. Quin had somehow missed fire. As a rule, every meeting with that mysterious individual had resulted in some strange and unforeseen happening. It was with the hope of perhaps running against the man of mystery that Mr. Satterthwaite bent his steps toward the Arlecchino Restaurant where once, in the days gone by, he had met Mr. Quin and which Mr. Quin had said he often frequented.

Mr. Satterthwaite went from room to room at the Arlechino, looking hopefully about him, but there was no sign of Mr. Quin's dark, smiling face. There was, however, somebody else. Sitting at a small table alone was Philip Eastney.

The place was crowded and Mr. Satterthwaite took his seat opposite the young man. He felt a sudden strange sense of exultation, as though he were caught up and made part of a shimmering pattern of events. He was in this thing—whatever it was. He knew now what Mr. Quin had meant that evening at the opera. There was a

drama going on, and in it was a part, an important part for Mr. Satterthwaite. He must not fail to take his cue and speak his lines.

He sat down opposite Philip Eastney with the sense of accom-
plishing the inevitable. It was easy enough to get into conversation.
Eastney seemed anxious to talk. Mr. Satterthwaite was, as always,
an encouraging and sympathetic listener. They talked of the war, of
explosives, of poison gases. Eastney had a lot to say about these last,
for during the greater part of the war he had been engaged in their
manufacture. Mr. Satterthwaite found him really interesting.

There was one gas, Eastney said, that had never been tried. The
Armistice had come too soon. Great things had been hoped for it.
One whiff of it was deadly. He warmed to animation as he spoke.

Having broken the ice, Mr. Satterthwaite gently turned the conversation to music. Eastney's thin face lit up. He spoke with the passion and abandon of the real music lover. They discussed
Yoaschbim, and the young man was enthusiastic. Both he and Mr.
Satterthwaite agreed that nothing on earth could surpass a really
fine tenor voice. Eastney as a boy had heard Caruso, and he had
never forgotten it.

"Do you know that he could sing to a wine glass and shatter it?"
he demanded.

"I always thought that was a fable," said Mr. Satterthwaite,
smiling.

"No, it's gospel truth, I believe. The thing's quite possible. It's a
question of resonance."

He went off into technical details. His face was flushed and his
eyes shone. The subject seemed to fascinate him, and Mr. Satterthwaite noted that he seemed to have a thorough grasp of what he was
talking about. The older man realized that he was talking to an ex-
ceptional brain, a brain that might almost be described as that of a
genius. Brilliant, erratic, undecided as yet as to the true channel to
give it outlet, but undoubtedly genius.

And he thought of Charlie Burns and wondered at Gillian West.

It was with quite a start that he realized how late it was getting,
and he called for his bill. Eastney looked slightly apologetic.

"I'm ashamed of myself—running on so," he said. "But it was a lucky chance sent you along here tonight. I—I needed someone to talk to this evening."

He ended his speech with a curious little laugh. His eyes were still blazing with some subdued excitement. Yet there was something tragic about him.

"It has been quite a pleasure," said Mr. Satterthwaite. "Our conversation has been most interesting and instructive to me."

He then made his funny, courteous little bow and passed out of the restaurant. The night was a warm one and as he walked slowly down the street a very odd fancy came to him. He had the feeling that he was not alone—that someone was walking by his side. In vain he told himself that the idea was a delusion—it persisted. Someone was walking beside him down that dark, quiet street, someone whom he could not see. He wondered what it was that brought the figure of Mr. Quin so clearly before his mind. He felt exactly as though Mr. Quin were there walking beside him, and yet he had only to use his eyes to assure himself that it was not so, that he was alone.

But the thought of Mr. Quin persisted, and with it came something else; a need, an urgency of some kind, an oppressive foreboding of calamity. There was something he must do—and do quickly. There was something very wrong, and it lay in his hands to put it right.

So strong was the feeling that Mr. Satterthwaite forebore to fight against it. Instead, he shut his eyes and tried to bring that mental image of Mr. Quin nearer. If he could only have asked Mr. Quin—but even as the thought flashed through his mind he knew it was wrong. It was never any use asking Mr. Quin anything. "The threads are all in your hands"—that was the kind of thing Mr. Quin would say.

The threads. Threads of what? He analyzed his own feeling and impressions carefully. That presentiment of danger, now. Whom did it threaten?

At once a picture rose up before his eyes, the picture of Gillian West sitting alone listening to the wireless.

Mr. Satterthwaite flung a penny to a passing newspaper boy, and snatched at a paper. He turned at once to the London Radio program. Yoaschbim was broadcasting tonight, he noted with interest. He was singing "Salve Dimora," from "Faust" and afterward a selection of his folk songs. "The Shepherd's Song," "The Fish," "The Little Deer," etc.

Mr. Satterthwaite crumpled the paper together. The knowledge of what Gillian was listening to seemed to make the picture of her clearer. Sitting there alone—

An odd request, that, of Philip Eastney's. Not like the man, not like him at all. There was no sentimentality in Eastney. He was a man of violent feeling, a dangerous man, perhaps—

Again his thoughts brought up with a jerk. A *dangerous man*— that meant something. *"The threads are all in your hands."* That meeting with Philip Eastney tonight—rather odd. A lucky chance, Eastney had said. Was it chance? Or was it part of that interwoven design of which Mr. Satterthwaite had once or twice been conscious this evening?

He cast his mind back. There must be *something* in Eastney's conversation, some clue there. There must, or else why this strange feeling of urgency? What had he talked about? Singing, war work, Caruso.

Caruso—Mr. Satterthwaite's thoughts went off at a tangent. Yoaschbim's voice was very nearly equal to that of Caruso. Gillian would be sitting listening to it now as it rang out true and powerful, echoing round the room, setting glasses ringing—

He caught his breath. Glasses ringing! Caruso, singing to a wine glass and the wine glass breaking. Yoaschbim singing in the London studio and in a room over a mile away the crash and tinkle of glass— not a wine glass, a thin, green, glass beaker. A crystal soap bubble falling, a soap bubble that perhaps was not empty—

It was at that moment that Mr. Satterthwaite as judged by passers-by suddenly went mad. He tore open the newspaper once more, took a brief glance at the wireless announcements and then began to run for his life down the quiet street. At the end of it he found a crawling taxi, and jumping into it, he yelled an address to the driver and the information that it was life or death to get there quickly. The driver, judging him mentally afflicted but rich, did his utmost.

Mr. Satterthwaite lay back, his head a jumble of fragmentary thoughts, forgotten bits of science learned at school, phrases used by Eastney that night. Resonance—natural periods—if the period of the force coincides with the natural period—there was something about a suspension bridge, soldiers marching over it and the swing of their stride being the same as the period of the bridge. Eastney had studied the subject. Eastney knew. And Eastney was a genius.

At 10:45 Yoaschbim was to broadcast. It was that now. Yes, but the "Faust" had to come first. It was the "Shepherd's Song," with the great shout after the refrain, that would—that would—do what?

His mind went whirling round again. Tones, over-tones, half-tones. He didn't know much about these things—but Eastney knew. Pray heaven he would be in time!

The taxi stopped. Mr. Satterthwaite flung himself out and raced up the stone stairs to a second floor like a young athlete. The door of the flat was ajar. He pushed it open and the great tenor voice welcomed him. The words of the "Shepherd's Song" were familiar to him in a less unconventional setting.

"Shepherd, see thy horse's flowing mane—"

He was in time then. He burst open the sitting room door. Gillian was sitting there in a tall chair by the fireplace.

'Barya Mischa's daughter is to wed today:
To the wedding I must haste away."

She must have thought him mad. He clutched at her, crying out something incomprehensible, and half pulled, half dragged her out till they stood upon the stairway.

"To the wedding I must haste away—
Ya-ha!"

A wonderful high note, full-throated, powerful, hit full in the middle, a note any singer might be proud of. And with it another sound, the faint tinkle of broken glass.

A stray cat darted past them and in through the flat door. Gillian made a movement, but Mr. Satterthwaite held her back, speaking incoherently.

"No, no—it's deadly: no smell, nothing to warn you. A mere whiff, and it's all over. Nobody knows quite how deadly it would be. It's unlike anything that's ever been tried before."

He was repeating the things that Philip Eastney had told him over the table at dinner.

Gillian stared at him uncomprehendingly.

III

Philip Eastney drew out his watch and looked at it. It was just half past eleven. For the last three quarters of an hour he had been pacing up and down the Embankment. He looked out over the Thames and then turned—to look into the face of his dinner companion.

"That's odd," he said, and laughed. "We seem fated to run into each other tonight.

"If you call it Fate," said Mr. Satterthwaite.

Philip Eastney looked at him more attentively and his own expression changed.

"Yes?" he said quietly.

Mr. Satterthwaite went straight to the point.

"I have just come from Miss West's flat."

"Yes?"

The same voice, with the same deadly quiet.

"We have—taken a dead cat out of it."

There was silence, then Eastney said:

"Who are you?"

Mr. Satterthwaite spoke for some time. He recited the whole history of events.

"So you see, I was in time," he ended up. He paused and added quite gently:

"Have you anything to—say?"

He expected something, some outburst, some wild justification. But nothing came.

"No," said Philip Eastney quietly, and turned on his heel and walked away.

Mr. Satterthwaite looked after him till his figure was swallowed up in the gloom. In spite of himself, he had a strange fellow feeling for Eastney, the feeling of an artist for another artist, of a sentimentalist for a real lover, of a plain man for a genius.

At last he roused himself with a start and began to walk in the same direction as Eastney. A fog was beginning to come up. Presently he met a policeman who looked at him suspiciously.

"Did you hear a kind of splash just now?" asked the policeman.

"No," said Mr. Satterthwaite.

The policeman was peering out over the river.

"Another of these suicides, I expect," he grunted disconsolately. "They will do it."

"I suppose," said Mr. Satterthwaite, "that they have their reasons."

"Money, mostly," said the policeman. "Sometimes it's a woman," he said, as he prepared to move away. "It's not always their fault, but some women cause a lot of trouble."

"Some women," agreed Mr. Satterthwaite softly.

When the policeman had gone on, he sat down on a seat with the fog coming up all around him, and thought about Helen of Troy, and wondered if she were a nice, ordinary woman, blessed or cursed with a wonderful face.

9. THE DEAD HARLEQUIN

Mr. Satterthwaite walked slowly up Bond Street enjoying the sunshine. He was, as usual, carefully and beautifully dressed, and was bound for the Harchester Galleries where there was an exhibition of the paintings of one Frank Bristow, a new and hitherto unknown artist who showed signs of suddenly becoming the rage. Mr. Satterthwaite was a patron of the arts.

As Mr. Satterthwaite entered the Harchester Galleries he was greeted at once with a smile of pleased recognition.

"Good morning, Mr. Satterthwaite, I thought we should see you before long. You know Bristow's work? Fine—very fine indeed. Quite unique of its kind."

Mr. Satterthwaite purchased a catalog and stepped through the open archway into the long room where the artist's work was displayed. They were water colors, executed with such extraordinary technique and finish that they resembled colored etchings. Mr. Satterthwaite walked slowly round the walls scrutinizing and on the whole approving. He thought that this young man deserved to arrive. Here were originality, vision, and a most severe and exacting technique. There were crudities, of course. That was only to be expected but—this was also something closely allied to genius. Mr. Satterthwaite paused before a little masterpiece representing Westminster Bridge with it crowd of buses, trams and hurrying pedestrians. A tiny thing and wonderfully perfect. It was called, he noted, "The Ant Heap." He passed on and quite suddenly drew in his breath with a gasp, his imagination held and rivetted.

The picture was called "The Dead Harlequin." The forefront of it represented a floor of inlaid squares of black and white marble. In the middle of the floor lay Harlequin on his back with his arms out-stretched in his motley of black and red. Behind him was a window and outside that window, gazing in at the figure on the floor, was what appeared to be the same man silhouetted against the red glow of the setting sun.

The picture excited Mr. Satterthwaite for two reasons, the first reason was that he recognized, or thought that he recognized, the face of the man in the picture. It bore a distinct resemblance to a certain Mr. Quin, an acquaintance whom Mr. Satterthwaite had en-countered once or twice under somewhat mystifying circumstances.

"Surely I can't be mistaken," he murmured. "If it *is* so—what does it mean?"

For it had been Mr. Satterthwaite's experience that every ap-pearance of Mr. Quin had some distinct significance attaching to it.

There was, as already mentioned, a second reason for Mr. Sat-terthwaite's interest. He recognized the scene of the picture.

"The Terrace Room at Charnley," said Mr. Satterthwaite, "curi-ous—and very interesting."

He looked with more attention at the picture, wondering what exactly had been in the artist's mind. One Harlequin dead on the floor, another Harlequin looking through the window—or was it the same Harlequin? He moved slowly along the walls gazing at other pictures with unseeing eyes, with his mind always busy on the same subject. He was excited. Life, which had seemed a little drab this morning, was drab no longer. He knew quite certainly that he was on the threshold of exciting and interesting events. He crossed to the table where sat Mr. Cobb, a dignitary of the Harchester Galleries, whom he had known for many years.

"I have a fancy for buying No. 39," he said, "if it is not already sold."

Mr. Cobb consulted a ledger.

"The pick of the bunch," he murmured, "quite a little gem, isn't it? No, it is not sold." He quoted a price. "It is a good investment, Mr. Satterthwaite. You will have to pay three times as much for it this time next year."

"That is always said on these occasions," said Mr. Satterthwaite smiling.

"Well, and haven't I been right?" demanded Mr. Cobb. "I don't believe, if you were to sell your collection, Mr. Satterthwaite, that a single picture would fetch less than you gave for it."

"I will buy this picture," said Mr. Satterthwaite. "I will give you a check now."

"You won't regret it. We believe in Bristow."

"He is a young man?"

"Twenty-seven or eight, I should say."

"I should like to meet him," said Mr. Satterthwaite. "Perhaps he will come and dine with me one night?"

"I can give you his address. I am sure he would leap at the chance. Your name stands for a good deal in the artistic world."

"You flatter me," said Mr. Satterthwaite, and was going on when Mr. Cobb interrupted.

"Here he is now. I will introduce you to him right away."

He rose from behind his table. Mr. Satterthwaite accompanied him to where a big clumsy young man was leaning against the wall surveying the world at large from behind the barricade of a ferocious scowl.

Mr. Cobb made the necessary introductions and Mr. Satterthwaite made a formal and gracious little speech.

"I have just had the pleasure of acquiring one of your pictures, 'The Dead Harlequin.'"

"Oh! Well! You won't lose by it," said Mr. Bristow, ungraciously. "It's a bit of damned good work, although I say it."

"I can see that," said Mr. Satterthwaite. "Your work interests me very much, Mr. Bristow. It is extraordinarily mature for so young a man. I wonder if you would give me the pleasure of dining with me one night? Are you engaged this evening?"

"As a matter of fact, I am not," said Mr. Bristow, still with no overdone appearance of graciousness.

"Then shall we say eight o'clock?" said Mr. Satterthwaite. "Here is my card with the address on it."

"Oh, all right," said Mr. Bristow. "Thanks," he added, as a somewhat obvious afterthought.

"A young man who has a poor opinion of himself and is afraid that the world should share it."

Such was Mr. Satterthwaite's summing up as he stepped out into the sunshine of Bond Street, and Mr. Satterthwaite's judgment of his fellow men was seldom far astray.

Frank Bristow arrived about five minutes past eight to find his host and another guest awaiting him. The other guest was introduced as a Colonel Monckton. They went into dinner almost immediately. There was a fourth place laid at the oval mahogany table and Mr. Satterthwaite uttered a word of explanation.

"I half expected my friend Mr. Quin might drop in," he said. "I wonder if you have ever met him. Mr. Harley Quin?"

"I never meet people," growled Bristow.

Colonel Monckton stared at the artist with the detached interest he might have accorded to a new species of jelly fish. Mr. Satterthwaite exerted himself to keep the ball of conversation rolling amicably.

"I took a special interest in that picture of yours because I thought I recognized the scene of it as being the Terrace Room at Charnley. Was I right?" As the artist nodded, he went on. "That is very interesting. I have stayed at Charnley several times myself in the past. Perhaps you know some of the family."

"No, I don't!" said Bristow. "That sort of family wouldn't care to know me. I went there in a charabanc."

"Dear me," said Colonel Monckton for the sake of saying something. "In a charabanc! Dear me!"

Frank Bristow scowled at him.

"Why not?" he demanded ferociously.

Poor Colonel Monckton was taken aback. He looked reproachfully at Mr. Satterthwaite as though to say:

"These primitive forms of life may be interesting to you as a nat-
uralist, but why drag *me* in?"

"Oh, beastly things, charabancs!" he said. "They jolt you so going
over the bumps."

"If you can't afford a Rolls Royce you have got to go in charabancs," said Bristow fiercely.

Colonel Monckton stared at him. Mr. Satterthwaite thought:

"Unless I can soon manage to put this young man at his ease we
are going to have a very distressing evening."

"Charnley always fascinated me," he said. "I have been there
only once since the tragedy. A grim house—and a ghostly one."

"That's true," said Bristow.

"There are actually two authentic ghosts," said Monckton. "They
say that Charles I walks up and down the terrace with his head under his arm—I have forgotten why, I'm sure. Then there is the
Weeping Lady with the Silver Ewer who is always seen after one of
the Charnleys dies."

"Tosh," said Bristow scornfully.

"They have certainly been a very ill-fated family," said Mr. Satterthwaite hurriedly. "Four holders of the title have died a violent
death, and the late Lord Charnley committed suicide."

"A ghastly business," said Monckton. "I was there when it happened."

"Let me see, that must be fourteen years ago," said Mr. Satterthwaite, "the house has been shut up ever since."

"I don't wonder at that," said Monckton. "It must have been a
terrible shock for a young girl. They had been married a month, just
home from their honeymoon. Big fancy dress ball to celebrate their
home-coming. Just as the guests were starting to arrive Charnley
locked himself into the Oak Parlor and shot himself. That sort of
thing isn't done. I beg your pardon?"

He turned his head sharply to the left and looked across at Mr. Satterthwaite with an apologetic laugh.

"I am beginning to get the jimjams, Satterthwaite. I thought for a moment there was someone sitting in that empty chair and that he said something to me."

"Yes," he went on after a minute or two. "It was a pretty ghastly shock to Alix Charnley. She was one of the prettiest girls you could see anywhere and cram full of what people call the joy of living, and now they say she is like a ghost herself. Not that I have seen her for years. I believe she lives abroad most of the time."

"And the boy?"

"The boy is at Eton. What he will do when he comes of age I don't know. I don't think, somehow, that he will reopen the old place."

"It would make a good People's Pleasure Park," said Bristow.

Colonel Monckton looked at him with cold abhorrence.

"No, no, you don't really mean that," said Mr. Satterthwaite. "You wouldn't have painted that picture if you did. Tradition and atmosphere are intangible things. They take centuries to build up and if you destroyed them you couldn't rebuild them again in twenty-four hours."

He rose. "Let us go into the smoking room. I have some photographs there of Charnley which I should like to show you."

One of Mr. Satterthwaite's hobbies was amateur photography. He was also the proud author of a book, *Homes of My Friends*. The friends in question were all rather exalted, and the book itself showed Mr. Satterthwaite forth in rather a more snobbish light than was really fair to him.

"That is a photograph I took of the Terrace Room last year," he said. He handed it to Bristow. "You see it is taken at almost the same angle as is shown in your picture. That is rather a wonderful rug—it is a pity that photographs can't show coloring."

"I remember it," said Bristow, "a marvelous bit of color. It glowed like a flame. All the same it looked a bit incongruous there. The wrong size for that big room with its black and white squares.

There is no rug anywhere else in the room. It spoils the whole effect—it was like a gigantic blood stain."

"Perhaps that gave you your idea for your picture?" said Mr. Satterthwaite.

"Perhaps it did," said Bristow thoughtfully. "On the face of it, one would naturally stage a tragedy in the little paneled room leading out of it."

"The Oak Parlor," said Monckton. "Yes, that is the haunted room right enough. There is a Priests' hiding hole there—a movable panel by the fireplace. Tradition has it that Charles I was concealed there once. There were two deaths from duelling in that room. And it was there, as I say, that Reggie Charnley shot himself."

He took the photograph from Bristow's hand.

"Why, that is the Bokhara rug," he said, "worth a couple of thousand pounds, I believe. When I was there it was in the Oak Parlor—the right place for it. It looks silly on that great expanse of marble flags."

Mr. Satterthwaite was looking at the empty chair which he had drawn up beside his. Then he said thoughtfully, "I wonder when it was moved?"

"It must have been recently. Why, I remember having a conversation about it on the very day of the tragedy. Charnley was saying it really ought to be kept under glass."

Mr. Satterthwaite shook his head. "The house was shut up immediately after the tragedy and everything was left exactly as it was."

Bristow broke in with a question. He had laid aside his aggressive manner.

"Why did Lord Charnley shoot himself?" he asked.

Colonel Monckton shifted uncomfortably in his chair.

"No one ever knew," he said vaguely.

"I suppose," said Mr. Satterthwaite slowly, "that it *was* suicide."

The Colonel looked at him in blank astonishment.

"Suicide," he said, "why, of course it was suicide. My dear fellow, I was there in the house myself."

Mr. Satterthwaite looked toward the empty chair at his side and, smiling to himself as though at some hidden joke the others could not see, he said quietly:

"Sometimes one sees things more clearly years afterward than one could possibly at the time."

"Nonsense," spluttered Monckton, "arrant nonsense! How can you possibly see things better when they are vague in your memory instead of clear and sharp?"

But Mr. Satterthwaite was reinforced from an unexpected quarter.

"I know what you mean," said the artist. "I should say that possibly you were right. It is a question of proportion, isn't it? And more than proportion probably. Relativity and all that sort of thing."

"If you ask me," said the Colonel, "all this Einstein business is a lot of dashed nonsense. So are spiritualists and the spook of one's grandmother!" He glared round fiercely.

"Of course it was suicide," he went on. "Didn't I practically see the thing happen with my own eyes?"

"Tell us about it," said Mr. Satterthwaite, "so that we shall see it with our eyes also."

With a somewhat mollified grunt the Colonel settled himself more comfortably in his chair.

"The whole thing was extraordinarily unexpected," he began. "Charnley had been his usual normal self. There was a big party staying in the house for this ball. No one could ever have guessed he would go and shoot himself just as the guests began arriving."

"It would have been better taste if he had waited until they had gone," said Mr. Satterthwaite.

"Of course it would. Damned bad taste—to do a thing like that."

"Uncharacteristic," said Mr. Satterthwaite.

"Yes," admitted Monckton, "it wasn't like Charnley."

"And yet it *was* suicide?"

"Of course it was suicide. Why there were three or four of us there at the top of the stairs. Myself, the Ostrander girl, Algie Darcy—oh, and one or two others. Charnley passed along the hall below and went into the Oak Parlor. The Ostrander girl said there was a ghastly look on his face and his eyes were staring—but of course that is nonsense—she couldn't even see his face from where we were—but he did walk in a hunched up way as if he had the weight of the world on his shoulders. One of the girls called to him—she was somebody's governess, I think, whom Lady Charnley had included in the party out of kindness. She was looking for him with a message. She called out 'Lord Charnley, Lady Charnley wants to know—' He paid no attention and went into the Oak Parlor and slammed the door and we heard the key turn in the lock. Then, one minute after, we *heard the shot.*

"We rushed down to the hall. There is another door from the Oak Parlor leading into the Terrace Room. We tried that but it was locked too. In the end we had to break the door down. Charnley was lying on the floor—dead—with a pistol close beside his right hand. Now what could that have been but suicide? Accident? Don't tell me. There is only one other possibility—murder—and you can't have murder without a murderer. You admit that, I suppose."

"The murderer might have escaped," suggested Mr. Satterthwaite.

"That is impossible. If you have a bit of paper and a pencil I will draw a plan of the place. There are two doors into the Oak Parlor, one into the hall and one into the Terrace Room. Both these doors were locked on the inside *and the keys were in the locks.*"

"The window?"

"Shut, and the shutters fastened across it."

There was a pause.

"So that is that," said Colonel Monckton triumphantly.

"It certainly seems to be," said Mr. Satterthwaite sadly.

"Mind you," said the Colonel, "although I was laughing just now at the spiritualists, I don't mind admitting that there was a deuced rummy atmosphere about the place—about that room in particular. There are several bullet holes in the panels of the walls, the result of the duels that took place in that room, and there is a queer stain on the floor, that always comes back though they have replaced the wood several times. I suppose there will be another blood stain on the floor now—poor Charnley's blood."

"Was there much blood?" asked Mr. Satterthwaite.

"Very little—curiously little—so the doctor said."

"Where did he shoot himself, through the head?"

"No, through the heart."

"That is not the easy way to do it," said Bristow. "Frightfully difficult to know where one's heart is. I should never do it that way myself."

Mr. Satterthwaite shook his head. He was vaguely dissatisfied. He had hoped to get at something—he hardly knew what. Colonel Monckton went on.

"It is a spooky place, Charnley. Of course I didn't see anything."

"You didn't see the Weeping Lady with the Silver Ewer?"

"No, I did not, sir," said the Colonel emphatically, "but I expect every servant in the place swore they did."

"Superstition was the curse of the Middle Ages," said Bristow. "There are still traces of it here and there, but thank goodness, we are getting free from it."

"Superstition," mused Mr. Satterthwaite, his eyes turned again to the empty chair. "Sometimes, don't you think—it might be useful?"

Bristow stared at him.

"Useful, that's a queer word."

"Well, I hope you are convinced now, Satterthwaite," said the Colonel.

"Oh, quite," said Mr. Satterthwaite. "On the face of it, it seems odd—so purposeless for a newly married man, young, rich, happy, celebrating his home-coming—curious—but I agree there is no getting away from the facts." He repeated softly "the facts" and frowned.

"I suppose the interesting thing is a thing we none of us will ever know," said Monckton, "the story behind it all. Of course there were rumors—all sorts of rumors. You know the kind of things people say."

"But no one *knew* anything," said Mr. Satterthwaite thoughtfully.

"It's not a best seller mystery, is it?" remarked Bristow. "No one gained by the man's death."

"No one except an unborn child," said Mr. Satterthwaite.

Monckton gave a sharp chuckle. "Rather a blow to poor Hugo Charnley," he observed. "As soon as it was known that there was going to be a child he had the graceful task of sitting tight and waiting to see if it would be a girl or boy. Rather an anxious wait for his creditors too. In the end a boy it was and a disappointment for the lot of them."

"Was the widow very disconsolate?" asked Bristow.

"Poor child," said Monckton, "I shall never forget her. She didn't cry or break down or anything. She was like something—frozen. As I say, she shut up the house shortly afterward and as far as I know it has never been reopened since."

"So we are left in the dark as to motive," said Bristow with a slight laugh. "Another man or another woman, it must have been one or the other, eh?"

"It seems like it," said Mr. Satterthwaite.

"And the betting is strongly on another woman," continued Bristow, "since the fair widow has not married again. I hate women," he added dispassionately.

Mr. Satterthwaite smiled a little and Frank Bristow saw the smile and pounced upon it.

"You may smile," he said, "but I do. They upset everything. They interfere. They get between you and your work. They—I only once met a woman who was—well interesting."

"I thought there would be one," said Mr. Satterthwaite.

"Not in the way you mean. I—I just met her casually. As a matter of fact—it was in a train. After all," he added defiantly, "why shouldn't one meet people in trains?"

"Certainly, certainly," added Mr. Satterthwaite soothingly, "a train is as good a place as anywhere else."

"It was coming down from the North. We had the carriage to ourselves. I don't know why, but we began to talk. I don't know her name and I don't suppose I shall ever meet her again. I don't know that I want to. It might be—a pity." He paused struggling to express himself. "She wasn't quite real, you know. Shadowy. Like one of the people who come out of the hills in Gaelic fairy tales."

Mr. Satterthwaite nodded gently. His imagination pictured the scene easily enough. The very positive and realistic Bristow and a figure that was silvery and ghostly—shadowy, as Bristow had said.

"I suppose if something very terrible had happened, so terrible as to be almost unbearable, one might get like that. One might run away from reality into a half world of one's own and then, of course, after a time, one wouldn't be able to get back."

"Was that what had happened to her?" asked Mr. Satterthwaite curiously.

"I don't know," said Bristow. "She didn't tell me anything, I am only guessing. One has to guess if one is going to get anywhere."

"Yes," said Mr. Satterthwaite slowly. "One has to guess."

He looked up as the door opened. He looked up quickly and expectantly but the butler's words disappointed him.

"A lady, sir, has called to see you on very urgent business. Miss Aspasia Glen."

Mr. Satterthwaite rose in some astonishment. He knew the name of Aspasia Glen. Who in London did not. First advertised as the Woman with the Scarf she had given a series of matinées single handed that had taken London by storm. With the aid of her scarf she had rapidly impersonated various characters. In turn the scarf had been the coif of a nun, the shawl of a mill worker, the headdress of a peasant and a hundred other things, and in each impersonation Aspasia Glen had been totally and utterly different. As an artist Mr. Satterthwaite paid full reverence to her. As it happened he had never made her acquaintance. A call upon him at this unusual hour intrigued him greatly. With a few words of apology to the others he left the room and crossed the hall to the drawing room.

Miss Glen was sitting in the very center of a large settee upholstered in gold brocade. So poised she dominated the room. Mr. Satterthwaite perceived at once that she meant to dominate the situation. Curiously enough his first feeling was one of repulsion. He had been a sincere admirer of Aspasia Glen's art. Her personality, as conveyed to him over the footlights, had been appealing and sympathetic. Her effects there had been wistful and suggestive rather than commanding. But now, face to face with the woman herself, he received a totally different impression. There was something hard—bold—forceful about her. She was tall and dark, possibly about thirty-five years of age. She was undoubtedly very good-looking and she clearly relied upon the fact.

"You must forgive me this unconventional call, Mr. Satterthwaite," she said. Her voice was full and rich and seductive.

"I won't say that I have wanted to know you for a long time, but I *am* glad of the excuse. As for coming tonight—" she laughed, "well, when I want a thing, I simply can't wait. When I want a thing, I simply *must* have it."

"Any excuse that has brought me such a charming lady guest must be welcomed by me," said Mr. Satterthwaite in an old-fashioned gallant manner.

"How nice you are to me," said Aspasia Glen.

"My dear lady," said Mr. Satterthwaite, "may I thank you here and now for the pleasure you have so often given me—in my seat in the stalls."

She smiled delightfully at him.

"I am coming straight to the point. I was at the Harchester Galleries today. I saw a picture there I simply couldn't live without. I wanted to buy it and I couldn't because you had already bought it. So—" she paused. "I do want it so," she went on. "Dear Mr. Satterthwaite, I simply *must* have it. I brought my checkbook." She looked at him hopefully. "Everyone tells me you are so frightfully kind. People *are* kind to me, you know. It is very bad for me—but there it is."

So these were Aspasia Glen's methods. Mr. Satterthwaite was inwardly coldly critical of this ultrafemininity and of this spoiled child pose. It ought to appeal to him, he supposed, but it didn't. Aspasia Glen had made a mistake. She had judged him as an elderly dilettante, easily flattered by a pretty woman. But Mr. Satterthwaite behind his gallant manner had a shrewd and critical mind. He saw people pretty well as they were, not as they wished to appear to him. He saw before him not a charming woman, pleading for a whim, but a ruthless egoist determined to get her own way for some reason which was obscure to him. And he knew quite certainly that Aspasia

Glen was not going to get her own way. He was not going to give up the picture of "The Dead Harlequin" to her. He sought rapidly in his mind for the best way of circumventing her without overt rudeness.

"I am sure," he said, "that everyone gives you your own way as often as they can and is only too delighted to do so."

"Then you are really going to let me have the picture?"

Mr. Satterthwaite shook his head slowly and regretfully.

"I am afraid that is impossible. You see—" he paused. "I bought that picture for a lady. It is a present."

"Oh! but surely—"

The telephone on the table rang sharply. With a murmured word of excuse Mr. Satterthwaite took up the receiver. A voice spoke to him, a small cold voice that sounded very far away.

"Can I speak to Mr. Satterthwaite, please?"

"It is Mr. Satterthwaite speaking."

"I am Lady Charnley, Alix Charnley. I daresay you don't remember me, Mr. Satterthwaite; it is a great many years since we met."

"My dear Alix. Of course I remember you."

"There is something I wanted to ask you. I was at the Harchester Galleries at an exhibition of pictures today. There was one called "The Dead Harlequin," perhaps you recognized it—it was the Terrace Room at Charnley. I—I want to have that picture. It was sold to you." She paused. "Mr. Satterthwaite, for reasons of my own I want that picture. Will you resell it to me?"

Mr. Satterthwaite thought to himself, "Why, this is a miracle." As he spoke into the receiver he was thankful that Aspasia Glen could only hear one side of the conversation. "If you will accept my gift, dear lady, it will make me very happy." He heard a sharp exclamation behind him and hurried on. "I bought it for you. I did indeed. But listen, my dear Alix, I want to ask you to do me a great favor if you will."

"Of course. Mr. Satterthwaite, I am so *very* grateful."

He went on. "I want you to come round now to my house, at once."

There was a slight pause and then she answered quietly, "I will come at once."

Mr. Satterthwaite put down the receiver and turned to Miss Glen.

She said quickly and angrily, "That was the picture you were talking about?"

"Yes," said Mr. Satterthwaite, "the lady to whom I am presenting it is coming round to this house in a few minutes."

Suddenly Aspasia Glen's face broke once more into smiles. "You will give me a chance of persuading her to turn the picture over to me?"

"I will give you a chance of persuading her."

Inwardly he was strangely excited. He was in the midst of a drama that was shaping itself to some foredoomed end. He, the looker on, was playing a star part. He turned to Miss Glen.

"Will you come into the other room with me? I should like you to meet some friends of mine."

He held the door open for her and crossing the hall opened the door of the smoking room.

"Miss Glen," he said, "let me introduce to you an old friend of mine, Colonel Monckton. Mr. Bristow, the painter of the picture you admire so much." Then he started as a third figure rose from the chair which he had left empty beside his own.

"I think you expected me this evening," said Mr. Quin. "During your absence I introduced myself to your friends. I am so glad I was able to drop in."

"My dear friend," said Mr. Satterthwaite, "I—I have been carrying on as well as I am able but—" he stopped before the slight sardonic glance of Mr. Quin's dark eyes. "Let me introduce you. Mr. Harley Quin, Miss Aspasia Glen."

Was it his fancy—or did she shrink back slightly. A curious expression flitted over her face. Suddenly Bristow broke in boisterously, "I have got it."

"Got what?"

"Got hold of what was puzzling me. There is a likeness, there is a distinct likeness." He was staring curiously at Mr. Quin. "You see it?" he turned to Mr. Satterthwaite, "don't you see a distinct likeness to the Harlequin of my picture—the man looking in through the window?"

It was no fancy this time. He distinctly heard Miss Glen draw in her breath sharply and even saw that she stepped back one pace.

"I told you that I was expecting someone," said Mr. Satterthwaite. He spoke with an air of triumph. "I must tell you that my friend Mr. Quin is a most extraordinary person. He can unravel mysteries. He can make you see things."

"Are you a medium, sir?" demanded Colonel Monckton, eyeing Mr. Quin doubtfully.

The latter smiled and slowly shook his head.

"Mr. Satterthwaite exaggerates," he said quietly. "Once or twice when I have been with him he has done some extraordinary good deductive work. Why he puts the credit down to me I can't say. His modesty I suppose."

"No, no," said Mr. Satterthwaite excitedly. "It isn't. You make me see things—things that I ought to have seen all along—that I actually have seen—but without knowing that I saw them."

"It sounds to me deuced complicated," said Colonel Monckton.

"Not really," said Mr. Quin, "the trouble is that we are not content just to see things—we will tack the wrong interpretation on to the things we see."

Aspasia Glen turned to Frank Bristow.

"I want to know," she said nervously, "what put the idea of painting that picture into your head?"

Bristow shrugged his shoulders. "I don't quite know," he confessed. "Something about the place—about Charnley, I mean—took hold of my imagination. The big empty room, the terrace outside, the idea of ghosts and things, I suppose. I have just been hearing the tale of the last Lord Charnley who shot himself. Supposing you are dead, and your spirit lives on? It must be odd, you know. You might stand outside on the terrace looking in at the window at your own dead body and you would see everything."

"What do you mean?" said Aspasia Glen. "*See* everything?"

"Well, you would see what happened. You would see—"

The door opened and the butler announced Lady Charnley.

Mr. Satterthwaite went to meet her. He had not seen her for nearly thirteen years. He remembered her as she once was, an eager glowing girl. And now he saw—a Frozen Lady. Very fair, very pale, with an air of drifting rather than walking, a snowflake driven at random by an icy breeze. Something unreal about her. So cold, so far away.

"It was very good of you to come," said Mr. Satterthwaite.

He led her forward. She made a half gesture of recognition toward Miss Glen and then paused as the other made no response.

"I am so sorry," she murmured, "but surely I have met you somewhere, haven't I?"

"Over the footlights perhaps," said Mr. Satterthwaite. "This is Miss Aspasia Glen, Lady Charnley."

"I am very pleased to meet you, Lady Charnley," said Aspasia Glen.

Her voice had suddenly a slight transatlantic tinge to it. Mr. Satterthwaite was reminded of one of her various stage impersonations.

"Colonel Monckton you know," continued Mr. Satterthwaite, "and this is Mr. Bristow."

He saw a sudden faint tinge of color in her cheeks.

"Mr. Bristow and I have met too," she said and smiled a little. "In a train."

"And Mr. Harley Quin."

He watched her closely, but this time there was no flicker of recognition. He set a chair for her and then seating himself he cleared his throat and spoke a little nervously. "I—this is rather an unusual little gathering. It centers round this picture. I—I think that if we liked we could—clear things up."

"You are not going to hold a *séance*, Satterthwaite?" asked Colonel Monckton. "You are very odd this evening."

"No," said Mr. Satterthwaite, "not exactly a *séance*. But my friend, Mr. Quin, believes, and I agree, that one can by looking back over the past see things as they were and not as they appeared to be."

"The past?" said Lady Charnley.

"I am speaking of your husband's suicide, Alix. I know it hurts you—"

"No," said Alix Charnley, "it doesn't hurt me. Nothing hurts me now."

Mr. Satterthwaite thought of Frank Bristow's words. *"She was not quite real you know. Shadowy. Like one of the people who come out of the hills in Gaelic fairy tales."*

"Shadowy," he had called her. That described her exactly. A shadow, a reflection of something else. Where then was the real Alix? And his mind answered quickly—*"In the Past. Divided from us by fourteen years of time."*

"My dear," he said, "you frighten me. You are like the Weeping Lady with the Silver Ewer."

Crash! The coffee cup on the table by Aspasia Glen's elbow fell shattered to the floor. Mr. Satterthwaite waved aside her apologies. He thought: "We are getting nearer, we are getting nearer every minute—but nearer to what?"

"Let us take our minds back to that night fourteen years ago," he said. "Lord Charnley killed himself. For what reason? No one knows." Lady Charnley stirred slightly in her chair.

"Lady Charnley knows," said Frank Bristow abruptly.

"Nonsense," said Colonel Monckton, then stopped, frowning at her curiously.

She was looking across at the artist. It was as though he drew the words out of her: She spoke, nodding her head slowly, and her voice was like a snowflake, cold and soft.

"Yes, you are quite right. I *know*. That is why as long as I live I can never go back to Charnley. That is why when my boy Dick wants me to open the place up and live there again I tell him it can't be done."

"Will you tell us the reason, Lady Charnley?" asked Mr. Quin.

She looked at him. Then, as though hypnotized, she spoke as quietly and naturally as a child.

"I will tell you if you like. Nothing seems to matter very much now. I found a letter among his papers and I destroyed it."

"What letter?" said Mr. Quin.

"The letter from the girl—from that poor child. She was the

Merriams' nursery governess. He had—he had made love to her—
yes, while he was engaged to me, just before we were married. And
she—she was going to have a child too. She wrote saying so, and that
she was going to tell me about it. So, you see, he shot himself."

She looked round at them wearily and dreamily, like a child who
has repeated a lesson it knows too well.

Colonel Monckton blew his nose.

"My God," he said, "so that was it. Well, that explains things
with a vengeance."

"Does it?" said Mr. Satterthwaite. "It doesn't explain one thing.
It doesn't explain why Mr. Bristow painted that picture."

"What do you mean?"

Mr. Satterthwaite looked across at Mr. Quin as though for encouragement and apparently got it, for he proceeded.

"Yes, I know I sound mad to all of you, but that picture is the focus of the whole thing. We are all here tonight because of that picture. That picture *had* to be painted—that is what I mean."

"You mean the uncanny influence of the Oak Parlor," began Colonel Monckton.

"No," said Mr. Satterthwaite. "Not the Oak Parlor. The Terrace
Room. That is it! The spirit of me dead man standing outside the
window and looking in and seeing his own dead body on the floor."

"Which he couldn't have done," said the Colonel, "because the
body was in the Oak Parlor."

"Supposing it wasn't," said Mr. Satterthwaite, "supposing it was
exactly where Mr. Bristow saw it, saw it imaginatively, I mean, on
the black and white flags in front of the window."

"You are talking nonsense," said Colonel Monckton, "if it was
there we shouldn't have found it in the Oak Parlor."

"Not unless someone carried it there," said Mr. Satterthwaite.

"And in that case how could we have seen Charnley going in at
the door of the Oak Parlor," inquired Colonel Monckton.

"Well, you didn't see his face, did you?" asked Mr. Satterthwaite.
"What I mean is, you saw a man going into the Oak Parlor in fancy
dress, I suppose."

"Brocade things and a wig," said Monckton.

"Just so, and you thought it was Lord Charnley because the girl called out to him as Lord Charnley."

"And because when we broke in a few minutes later there was only Lord Charnley there dead. You can't get away from that, Satterthwaite."

"No," said Mr. Satterthwaite, discouraged. "No—unless there was a hiding place of some kind."

"Weren't you saying something about there being a Priests' hole in that room?" put in Frank Bristow.

"Oh!" cried Mr. Satterthwaite. "Supposing—" he waved a hand for silence and sheltered his forehead with his other hand and then spoke slowly and hesitatingly.

"I have got an idea—it may be just an idea but I think it hangs together. Supposing someone shot Lord Charnley. Shot him in the Terrace Room. Then he—and another person—dragged the body into the Oak Parlor. They laid it down there with the pistol by its right hand. Now we go on to the next step. It must seem absolutely certain that Lord Charnley has committed suicide. I think that could be done very easily. The man in his brocade and wig passes along the hall by the Oak Parlor door and someone, to make sure of things, calls out to him as Lord Charnley from the top of the stairs. He goes in and locks both doors and fires a shot into the woodwork. There were bullet holes already in that room if you remember, one more wouldn't be noticed. He then hides quietly in the secret chamber. The doors are broken open and people rush in. It seems certain that Lord Charnley has committed suicide. No other hypothesis is even entertained."

"Well, I think that is balderdash," said Colonel Monckton. "You forget that Charnley had a motive right enough for suicide."

"A letter found afterward," said Mr. Satterthwaite. "A lying, cruel letter written by a very clever and unscrupulous little actress who meant one day to be Lady Charnley herself."

"You mean?"

"I mean the girl in league with Hugo Charnley," said Mr. Satterthwaite. "You know, Monckton, everyone knows, that that man was a blackguard. He thought that he was certain to come into the title." He turned sharply to Lady Charnley. "What was the name of the girl who wrote that letter?"

"Monica Ford," said Lady Charnley.

"Was it Monica Ford, Monckton, who called out to Lord Charnley from the top of the stairs?"

"Yes, now you come to speak of it, I believe it was."

"Oh, it's impossible," said Lady Charnley, "I—I went to her about it. She told me it was all true. I only saw her that once afterward but surely she couldn't have been acting the whole time."

Mr. Satterthwaite looked across the room at Aspasia Glen.

"I think she could," he said quietly. "I think she had in her the makings of a very accomplished actress."

"There is one thing you haven't got over," said Frank Bristow. "There would be blood on the floor of the Terrace Room. Bound to be. They couldn't clear that up in a hurry."

"No," admitted Mr. Satterthwaite, "but there is one thing they could do—a thing that would only take a second or two—they could throw over the blood stains the Bokhara rug. Nobody ever saw the Bokhara rug in the Terrace Room before that night."

"I believe you are right," said Monckton, "but all the same those blood stains would have to be cleared up some time?"

"Yes," said Mr. Satterthwaite, "in the middle of the night. A woman with a jug and basin could go down the stairs and clear up the blood stains quite easily."

"But supposing someone saw her?"

"It wouldn't matter," said Mr. Satterthwaite. "I am speaking now of things as they *are*. I said a woman with a jug and basin. But if I had said a Weeping Lady with a Silver Ewer that is what they would have *appeared* to be." He got up and went across to Aspasia Glen. "That is what you did, wasn't it?" he said. "They call you the Woman with the Scarf now but it was that night you played your first part, the Weeping Lady with the Silver Ewer. That is why you knocked the coffee cup off that table just now. You were afraid when you saw that picture. You thought someone knew."

Lady Charnley stretched out a white accusing hand.

"Monica Ford," she breathed. "I recognize you now.

Aspasia Glen sprang to her feet with a cry. She pushed little Mr. Satterthwaite aside with a shove of the hand and stood shaking in front of Mr. Quin.

"So I was right Someone *did* know! Oh, I haven't been deceived by this tomfoolery. This pretense of working things out." She pointed at Mr. Quin. "*You* were there. *You* were there outside the window looking in. You saw what we did, Hugo and I. I *knew* there was someone looking in, I felt it all the time. And yet when I looked up there was nobody there. I knew someone was watching us. I thought once I caught a glimpse of a face at the window. It has frightened me all these years. And then I saw that picture with you standing at the window and I recognized your face. You have known all these years. Why did you break silence now? That is what I want to know."

"Perhaps so that the dead may rest in peace," said Mr. Quin.

Suddenly Aspasia Glen made a rush for the door and stood there flinging a few defiant words over her shoulder.

"Do what you like. God knows there are witnesses enough to what I have been saying. I don't care, I don't care. I loved Hugo and I helped him with the ghastly business and he chucked me afterward. He died last year. You can set the police on my tracks if you like but, as that little dried up fellow there said, 'I am a pretty good actress.' They will find it hard to find me." She crashed the door behind her and a moment later they heard the slam of the front door also.

"Reggie," cried Lady Charnley, "Reggie." The tears were streaming down her face. "Oh, my dear, my dear, I can go back to Charnley now. I can live there with Dickie. I can tell him what his father was, me finest, the most splendid man in all the world."

"We must consult very seriously as to what must be done in the matter," said Colonel Monckton. "Alix, my dear, if you will let me take you home I shall be glad to have a few words with you on the subject."

Lady Charnley rose. She came across to Mr. Satterthwaite and laying both hands on his shoulders she kissed him very gently.

"It is so wonderful to be alive again after being so long dead," she said. "It was like being dead, you know. Thank you, dear Mr. Satterthwaite." She went out of the room with Colonel Monckton. Mr. Satterthwaite gazed after them. A grunt from Frank Bristow, whom he had forgotten, made him turn sharply round.

"She is a lovely creature," said Bristow moodily. "But she's not nearly so interesting as she was," he said gloomily.

"There speaks the artist," said Mr. Satterthwaite.

"Well, she isn't," said Mr. Bristow. "I suppose I should only get the cold shoulder if I ever went butting in at Charnley. I don't want to go where I am not wanted."

"My dear young man," said Mr. Satterthwaite, "if you will think a little less of the impression you are making on other people, you will, I think, be wiser and happier. You would also do well to disabuse your mind of some very old-fashioned notions, one of which is that birth has any significance at all in our modern conditions. You are one of those large proportioned young men whom women always consider good-looking, and you have possibly, if not certainly, genius. Just say that over to yourself ten times before you go to bed every night and in three months' time go and call on Lady Charnley at Charnley. That is my advice to you, and I am an old man with considerable experience of the world."

A very charming smile suddenly spread over the artist's face.

"You have been thunderingly good to me," he said suddenly. He seized Mr. Satterthwaite's hand and wrung it in a powerful grip. "I am no end grateful. I must be off now. Thanks very much for one of the most extraordinary evenings I have ever spent."

He looked round as though to say good-by to someone else and then started.

"I say, sir, your friend has gone. I never saw him go. He is rather a queer bird, isn't he?"

"He goes and comes very suddenly," said Mr. Satterthwaite. "That is one of his characteristics. One doesn't always see him come and go."

"Like Harlequin," said Frank Bristow, "he is invisible," and laughed heartily at his own joke.

10. THE BIRD WITH THE BROKEN WING

Mr. Satterthwaite looked out of the window. It was raining steadily. He shivered. Very few country houses, he reflected, were really properly heated. It cheered him to think that in a few hours' time he would be speeding toward London. Once one had passed sixty years of age, London was really much the best place.

He was feeling a little old and pathetic. Most of the members of the house party were so young. Four of them had just gone off into the library to do table turning. They had invited him to accompany them but he had declined. He failed to derive any amusement from the monotonous counting of the letters of the alphabet and the usual meaningless jumble of letters that resulted.

Yes, London was the best place for him. He was glad that he had declined Madge Keeley's invitation when she had rung up to invite him over to Laidell half an hour ago. An adorable young person, certainly, but London was best.

Mr. Satterthwaite shivered again and remembered that the fire in the library was usually a good one. He opened the door and adventured cautiously into the darkened room.

"If I'm not in the way—"

"Was that N or M? We shall have to count again. No, of course not, Mr. Satterthwaite. Do you know, the most exciting things have been happening. The spirit says her name is Ada Spiers and John here is going to marry someone called Gladys Bun almost immediately."

Mr. Satterthwaite sat down in a big easy chair in front of the fire. His eyelids drooped over his eyes and he dozed. From time to time he returned to consciousness, hearing fragments of speech.

"It can't be P A B Z L—not unless he's a Russian. John, you're shoving. I *saw* you. I believe it's a new spirit come."

Another interval of dozing. Then a name jerked him wide awake.

"Q U I N. Is that right?" "Yes, it's rapped once for Yes."

"Quin. Have you a message for someone here? Yes. For me? For John? For Sarah? For Evelyn? No—but there's no one else. Oh! it's for Mr. Satterthwaite, perhaps? It says 'Yes.' Mr. Satterthwaite, it's a message for you."

"What does it say?"

Mr. Satterthwaite was broad awake now, sitting taut and erect in his chair, his eyes shining.

The table rocked and one of the girls counted.

"L A I—it can't be—that doesn't make sense. No word begins L A I."

"Go on," said Mr. Satterthwaite, and the command in his voice was so sharp that he was obeyed without question.

"L A I D E L—and another L—Oh! that seems to be all."

"Go on."

"Tell us some more, please."

A pause.

"There doesn't seem to be any more. The table's gone quite dead. How silly."

"No," said Mr. Satterthwaite thoughtfully. "I don't think it's silly."

He rose and left the room. He went straight to the telephone. Presently he was through.

"Can I speak to Miss Keeley? Is that you, Madge, my dear? I want to change my mind, if I may, and accept your kind invitation. It

is not so urgent as I thought that I should get back to town. Yes—
yes—I will arrive in time for dinner."

He hung up the receiver, a strange flush on his withered cheeks.
Mr. Quin—the mysterious Mr. Harley Quin. Mr. Satterthwaite
counted over on his fingers the times he had been brought into contact with that man of mystery. Where Mr. Quin was concerned—
things happened! What had happened or was going to happen—at
Laidell?

Whatever it was, there was work for him, Mr. Satterthwaite, to
do. In some ways or other, he would have an active part to play. He
was sure of that.

Laidell was a large house. Its owner, David Keeley, was one of
those quiet men with indeterminate personalities who seem to
count as part of the furniture. Their inconspicuousness has nothing
to do with brain power—David Keeley was a most brilliant mathematician and had written a book totally incomprehensible to ninety-
nine hundredths of humanity. But like so many men of brilliant
intellect, he radiated no bodily vigor or magnetism. It was a standing
joke that David Keeley was a real "invisible man." Footmen passed
him by with the vegetables, and guests forgot to say how do you do
or good-by.

His daughter Madge was very different. A fine upstanding
young woman, bursting with energy and life. Thorough, healthy and
normal, and extremely pretty.

It was she who received Mr. Satterthwaite when he arrived.

"How nice of you to come—after all."

"Very delightful of you to let me change my mind. Madge, my
dear, you're looking very well."

"Oh! I'm always well."

"Yes, I know. But it's more than that. You look—well, blooming
is the word I have in mind. Has anything happened, my dear?
Anything—well—special."

She laughed—blushed a little.

"It's too bad, Mr. Satterthwaite. You always guess things."

He took her hand.

"So it's that, is it? Mr. Right has come along?"

It was an old-fashioned term, but Madge did not object to it. She rather liked Mr. Satterthwaite's old-fashioned ways.

"I suppose so—yes. But nobody's supposed to know. It's a secret. But I don't really mind your knowing, Mr. Satterthwaite. You're always so nice and sympathetic."

Mr. Satterthwaite thoroughly enjoyed romance at second hand. He was sentimental and Victorian.

"I mustn't ask who the lucky man is? Well, then all I can say is that I hope he is worthy of the honor you are conferring on him."

Rather a duck, old Mr. Satterthwaite, thought Madge.

"Oh! we shall get on awfully well together, I think," she said. "You see, we like doing the same things, and that's so awfully important, isn't it? We've really got a lot in common—and we know all about each other and all that. It's really been coming on for a long time. That gives one such a nice safe feeling, doesn't it?"

"Undoubtedly," said Mr. Satterthwaite. "But in my experience one can never really know all about anyone else. That is part of the interest and charm of life."

"Oh! I'll risk it," said Madge, laughing, and they went up to dress for dinner.

Mr. Satterthwaite was late. He had not brought a valet, and having his things unpacked for him by a stranger always flurried him a little. He came down to find everyone assembled, and in the modern style Madge merely said:

"Oh! here's Mr. Satterthwaite. I'm starving. Let's go in."

She led the way with a tall gray haired woman—a woman of striking personality. She had a very clear, rather incisive, voice and her face was clear cut and rather beautiful.

"How d'you do, Satterthwaite," said Mr. Keeley.

Mr. Satterthwaite jumped.

"How do you do," he said. "I'm afraid I didn't see you."

"Nobody does," said Mr. Keeley sadly.

They went in. The table was a low oval of mahogany. Mr. Satterthwaite was placed between his young hostess and a short dark girl—a very hearty girl with a loud voice and a ringing determined laugh that expressed more the determination to be cheerful at all costs than any real mirth. Her name seemed to be Doris and she was the type of young woman Mr. Satterthwaite most disliked. She had, he considered, no artistic justification for existence.

On Madge's other side was a man of about thirty whose likeness to the gray haired woman proclaimed them mother and son.

Next to him—

Mr. Satterthwaite caught his breath.

He didn't know what it was exactly. It was not beauty. It was something else—something much more elusive and intangible than beauty.

She was listening to Mr. Keeley's rather ponderous dinner table conversation, her head bent a little sideways. She was there, it seemed to Mr. Satterthwaite—and yet she was not there! She was, somehow, a great deal less substantial than anyone else seated round the oval table. Something in the droop of her body sideways was beautiful—was more than beautiful. She looked up—her eyes met Mr. Satterthwaite's for the moment across the table—and the word he wanted leaped to his mind.

Enchantment—that was it. She had the quality of enchantment. She might have been one of those creatures who are only half human—one of the Hidden People from the Hollow Hills. She made everyone else look rather too real.

But at the same time, in a queer way, she stirred his pity. It was as though semi-humanity handicapped her. He sought for a phrase and found it.

"A bird with a broken wing," said Mr. Satterthwaite.

Satisfied, he turned his mind back to the subject of Girl Guides and hoped that the girl Doris had not noticed his abstraction. When she turned to the man on the other side of her—a man Mr. Satterthwaite had hardly noticed—he himself turned to Madge.

"Who is the lady sitting next to your father?" he asked in a low voice.

"Mrs. Graham? Oh! no, you mean Mabelle. Don't you know her? Mabelle Annesley. She was a Clydesley—one of the ill-fated Clydesleys."

He started. The ill-fated Clydesleys. He remembered. A brother had shot himself, a sister had been drowned, another had perished in an earthquake. A queer doomed family. This girl must be the youngest of them.

His thoughts were recalled suddenly. Madge's hand touched his under the table. Everyone else was talking. She gave a faint inclination of her head to her left.

"That's him," she murmured ungrammatically.

Mr. Satterthwaite nodded quickly in comprehension. So this young Graham was the man of Madge's choice. Well, she could hardly have done better as far as appearances went—and Mr. Satterthwaite was a shrewd observer. A pleasant, likeable, rather matter-of-fact young fellow. They'd make a nice pair—no nonsense about either of them—good healthy sociable young folk.

Laidell was run on old-fashioned lines. The ladies left the dining room first. Mr. Satterthwaite moved up to Graham and began to talk to him. His estimate of the young man was confirmed, yet there was something that struck him as being not quite true to type. Roger Graham was distrait, his mind seemed far away, his hand shook as he replaced the glass on the table.

"He's got something on his mind," thought Mr. Satterthwaite acutely. "Not nearly as important as he thinks it is, I daresay. All the same, I wonder what it is."

Mr. Satterthwaite was in the habit of swallowing a couple of digestive pastilles after meals. Having neglected to bring them down with him, he went up to his room to fetch them.

On his way down to the drawing room, he passed along the long corridor on the ground floor. About halfway along it was a room known as the terrace room. As Mr. Satterthwaite looked through the open doorway in passing, he stopped short.

Moonlight was streaming into the room. The latticed panes gave it a queer rhythmic pattern. A figure was sitting on the low window sill, drooping a little sideways and softly twanging the strings of a ukulele—not in a jazz rhythm, but in a far older rhythm, the beat of fairy horses riding on fairy hills.

Mr. Satterthwaite stood fascinated. She wore a dress of dull dark blue chiffon, ruched and pleated so that it looked like the feathers of a bird. She bent over the instrument crooning to it.

He came into the room—slowly, step by step. He was close to her when she looked up and saw him. She didn't start, he noticed, or seem surprised.

"I hope I'm not intruding," he began.

"Please—sit down."

He sat near her on a polished oak chair. She hummed softly under her breath.

"There's a lot of magic about tonight," she said. "Don't you think so?"

Yes, there was a lot of magic about.

"They wanted me to fetch my uke," she explained. "And as I passed here, I thought it would be so lovely to be alone here—in the dark and the moon."

"Then I—" Mr. Satterthwaite half rose, but she stopped him.

"Don't go. You—you fit in, somehow. It's queer, but you do."

He sat down again.

"It's been a queer sort of evening," she said. "I was out in the woods late this afternoon, and I met a man—such a strange sort of man—tall and dark, like a lost soul. The sun was setting, and the light of it through the trees made him look like a kind of Harlequin."

"Ah!" Mr. Satterthwaite leaned forward—his interest quickened.

"I wanted to speak to him—he—he looked so like somebody I know. But I lost him in the trees."

"I think I know him," said Mr. Satterthwaite.

"Do you? He is interesting, isn't he?"

"Yes, he is interesting."

There was a pause. Mr. Satterthwaite was perplexed. There was something, he felt, that he ought to do—and he didn't know what it was. But surely—surely, it had to do with this girl. He said rather clumsily:

"Sometimes—when one is unhappy—one wants to get away—"

"Yes. That's true." She broke off suddenly. "Oh! I see what you mean. But you're wrong. It's just the other way round. I wanted to be alone because I'm happy."

"Happy?"

"Terribly happy."

She spoke quite quietly, but Mr. Satterthwaite had a sudden sense of shock. What this strange girl meant by being happy wasn't the same as Madge Keeley would have meant, by the same words. Happiness, for Mabelle Annesley, meant some kind of intense and vivid ecstasy—something that was not only human, but more than human. He shrank back a little.

"I—didn't know," he said clumsily.

"Of course you couldn't. And it's not—the actual thing—I'm not happy yet—but I'm going to be." She leaned forward. "Do you know what it's like to stand in a wood—a big wood with dark shadows and trees very close all round you—a wood you might never get out of—and then, suddenly—just in front of you, you see the country of your dreams—shining and beautiful—you've only got to step out from the trees and the darkness and you've found it?"

"So many things look beautiful," said Mr. Satterthwaite, "before we've reached them. Some of the ugliest things in the world look the most beautiful."

There was a step on the floor. Mr. Satterthwaite turned his head. A fair man with a stupid, rather wooden, face stood there. He was the man Mr. Satterthwaite had hardly noticed at the dinner table.

"They're waiting for you, Mabelle," he said.

She got up; the expression had gone out of her face; her voice was flat and calm.

"I'm coming, Gerard," she said. "I've been talking to Mr. Satterthwaite."

She went out of the room, Mr. Satterthwaite following. He turned his head over his shoulder as he went and caught the expression on her husband's face, a hungry despairing look.

"Enchantment," thought Mr. Satterthwaite. "He feels it right enough. Poor fellow—poor fellow."

The drawing room was well lighted. Madge and Doris Coles were vociferous in reproaches.

"Mabelle, you little beast—you've been ages."

She sat on a low stool, tuned the ukulele and sang. They all joined in.

"Is it possible," thought Mr. Satterthwaite, "that so many idiotic songs could have been written about My Baby."

But he had to admit that the syncopated wailing tunes were stirring. Though, of course, they weren't a patch on the old-fashioned waltz.

The air got very smoky. The syncopated rhythm went on.

"No conversation," thought Mr. Satterthwaite. "No good music. No *peace*." He wished the world had not become definitely so noisy.

Suddenly Mabelle Annesley broke off, smiling across the room at him, and began to sing a song of Grieg's.

"My swan—my fair one—"

It was a favorite of Mr. Satterthwaite's. He liked the note of ingenuous surprise at the end.

"Wert only a swan then? A swan then?"

After that, the party broke up. Madge offered drinks, while her father picked up the discarded ukulele and began twanging it absent-mindedly. The party exchanged good nights, drifted nearer and nearer to the door. Everyone talked at once. Gerard Annesley slipped away unostentatiously, leaving the others.

Outside the drawing room door, Mr. Satterthwaite bade Mrs. Graham a ceremonious good night. There were two staircases, one close at hand, the other at the end of a long corridor. It was by the latter that Mr. Satterthwaite reached his room. Mrs. Graham and her son passed up the stairs near at hand where the quiet Gerard Annesley had already preceded them.

"You'd better get your ukulele, Mabelle," said Madge. "You'll forget it in the morning if you don't. You've got to make such an early start."

"Come on, Mr. Satterthwaite," said Doris Coles, seizing him boisterously by one arm. "Early to bed—etcetera."

Madge took him by the other arm and all three ran down the

corridor to peals of Doris's laughter. They paused at the end to wait for David Keeley, who was following at a much more sedate pace, turning out electric lights as he came. The four of them went upstairs together.

MR. SATTERTHWAITE WAS JUST preparing to descend to the dining room for breakfast on the following morning when there was a light tap on the door and Madge Keeley entered. Her face was dead white and she was shivering all over.

"Oh! Mr. Satterthwaite."

"My dear child, what's happened?" He took her hand.

"Mabelle—Mabelle Annesley—"

"Yes?"

What had happened? What? Something terrible—he knew that. Madge could hardly get the words out.

"She—she hanged herself last night. On the back of her door. Oh! it's too horrible." She broke down—sobbing.

Hanged herself. Impossible. Incomprehensible!

He said a few soothing old-fashioned words to Madge, and hurried downstairs. He found David Keeley looking perplexed and incompetent.

"I've telephoned to the police, Satterthwaite. Apparently that's got to be done. So the doctor said. He's just finished examining the—the—Good Lord, it's a beastly business. She must have been desperately unhappy—to do it that way. Queer that song last night. Swan Song, eh? She looked rather like a swan—a black swan."

Yes.

"Swan Song," repeated Keeley. "Shows it was in her mind, eh?"

"It would seem so—yes, certainly it would seem so."

He hesitated, then asked if he might see—if, that is—

His host comprehended the stammering request.

"If you want to—I'd forgotten you have a *penchant* for human tragedies."

He led the way up the broad staircase. Mr. Satterthwaite followed him. At the head of the stairs was the room occupied by Roger Graham, and opposite it, on the other side of the passage, his mother's room. The latter door was ajar and a faint wisp of smoke floated through it.

A momentary surprise invaded Mr. Satterthwaite's mind. He had not judged Mrs. Graham to be a woman who smoked so early in the day. Indeed, he had had the idea that she did not smoke at all.

They went along the passage to the end door but one. David Keeley entered the room and Mr. Satterthwaite followed him.

The room was not a very large one and showed signs of a man's occupation. A door in the wall led into a second room. A bit of cut rope still dangled from a hook high up on the door. On the bed—

Mr. Satterthwaite stood for a minute looking down on the heap of huddled chiffon. He noticed that it was ruched and pleated like the plumage of a bird. At the face, after one glance, he did not look again.

He glanced from the door with its dangling rope to the communicating door through which they had come.

"Was that open?"

"Yes. At least the maid says so."

"Annesley slept in there? Didn't he hear anything?"

"He says—nothing."

"Almost incredible," murmured Mr. Satterthwaite. He looked back at the form on the bed.

"Where is he?"

"Annesley? He's downstairs with the doctor."

They went downstairs to find an Inspector of police had arrived. Mr. Satterthwaite was agreeably surprised to recognize in him an old acquaintance, Inspector Winkfield. The Inspector went upstairs with the doctor and a few minutes later a request came that all members of the house party should assemble in the drawing room.

The blinds had been drawn and the whole room had a funereal aspect. Doris Coles looked frightened and subdued. Every now and then she dabbed her eyes with a hand-kerchief. Madge was resolute and alert, her feelings fully under control by now. Mrs. Graham was composed, as always, her face grave and impassive. The tragedy seemed to have affected her son more keenly than anyone. He looked a positive wreck this morning. David Keeley, as usual, had subsided into the background.

The bereaved husband sat alone, a little apart from the others. There was a queer dazed look about him, as though he could hardly realize what had taken place.

Mr. Satterthwaite, outwardly composed, was inwardly seething with the importance of a duty shortly to be performed.

Inspector Winkfield, followed by Doctor Morris, came in and shut the door behind him. He cleared his throat and spoke.

"This is a very sad occurrence—very sad, I'm sure. It's necessary, under the circumstances, that I should ask everybody a few questions. You'll not object, I'm sure. I'll begin with Mr. Annesley. You'll forgive my asking, sir, but had your good lady ever threatened to take her life?"

Mr. Satterthwaite opened his lips impulsively, then closed them again. There was plenty of time. Better not speak too soon.

"I—no, I don't think so."

His voice was so hesitating, so peculiar, that everyone shot a covert glance at him.

"You're not sure, sir?"

"Yes—I'm—quite sure. She didn't."

"Ah! Were you aware that she was unhappy in any way?"

"No, I—No, I wasn't."

"She said nothing to you? About feeling depressed, for instance?"

"I—no, nothing."

Whatever the Inspector thought, he said nothing. Instead he proceeded to his next point.

"Will you describe to me briefly the events of last night?"

"We—all went up to bed. I fell asleep immediately and heard nothing. The housemaid's scream aroused me this morning. I rushed into the adjoining room and found my wife—and found her—"

His voice broke. The Inspector nodded.

"Yes, yes, that's quite enough. We needn't go into that. When did you last see your wife the night before?"

"I—downstairs."

"Downstairs?"

"Yes, we all left the drawing room together. I went straight up, leaving the others talking in the hall."

"And did you see your wife again? Didn't she say good night when she came up to bed?"

"I was asleep when she came up."

"But she only followed you a few minutes later. That's right, isn't it, sir?" He looked at David Keeley who nodded.

"She hadn't come up half an hour later."

Annesley spoke stubbornly. The Inspector's eyes strayed gently to Mrs. Graham.

"She didn't stay in your room talking, Madam?"

Did Mr. Satterthwaite fancy it, or was there a slight pause before Mrs. Graham said, with her customary quiet decision of manner:

"No, I went straight into my room and closed the door. I heard nothing."

"And you say, sir," the Inspector had shifted his attention back to Annesley, "that you slept and heard nothing. The communicating door was open, was it not?"

"I—I believe so. But my wife would have entered her room by the other door from the corridor."

"Even so, sir, there would have been certain sounds—a choking noise, a drumming of heels on the door—"

"No."

It was Mr. Satterthwaite who spoke, impetuously, unable to stop himself. Every eye turned toward him in surprise. He himself became nervous, stammered, and turned pink.

"I—I beg your pardon, Inspector. But I must speak. You are on the wrong tack—the wrong tack altogether. Mrs. Annesley did not kill herself—I am sure of it. She was murdered."

There was a dead silence, then Inspector Winkfield said quietly:

"What leads you to say that, sir?"

"I—it is a feeling. A very strong feeling."

"But I think, sir, there must be more than that to it. There must be some particular reason."

Well, of course there *was* a particular reason. There was the mysterious message from Mr. Quin. But you couldn't tell a police inspector that. Mr. Satterthwaite cast about desperately, and found something.

"Last night—when we were talking together, she said she was very happy. Very happy—just that. That wasn't like a woman thinking of committing suicide."

He was triumphant. He added:

"She went back to the drawing room to fetch her ukulele, so that she wouldn't forget it in the morning. That didn't look like suicide either."

"No," admitted the Inspector. "No, perhaps it didn't." He turned to David Keeley. "Did she take the ukulele upstairs with her?"

The mathematician tried to remember.

"I think—yes, she did. She went upstairs carrying it in her hand. I remember seeing it just as she turned the corner of the staircase before I turned off the light down here."

"Oh!" cried Madge. "But it's here now."

She pointed dramatically to where the ukulele lay on a table.

"That's curious," said the Inspector. He stepped swiftly across and rang the bell.

A brief order sent the butler in search of the housemaid whose business it was to do the rooms in the morning. She came and was quite positive in her answer. The ukulele had been there first thing that morning when she had dusted.

Inspector Winkfield dismissed her and then said curtly.

"I would like to speak to Mr. Satterthwaite in private, please. Everyone else may go. But no none is to leave the house."

Mr. Satterthwaite twittered into, speech as soon as the door had closed behind the others.

"I—I am sure, Inspector, that you have the case excellently in hand. Excellently. I just felt that—having, as I say, a very strong feeling—"

The Inspector arrested further speech with an upraised hand.

"You're quite right, Mr. Satterthwaite. The lady was murdered."

"You knew it?" Mr. Satterthwaite was chagrined.

"There were certain things that puzzled Dr. Morris." He looked across at the doctor who had remained, and the doctor assented to his statement with a nod of the head. "We made a thorough examination. The rope that was round her neck wasn't the rope that she was strangled with—it was something much thinner that did the job, something more like a wire. It had cut right into the flesh. The mark of the rope was superimposed on it. She was strangled and then hung up on that door afterward to make it look like suicide."

"But who—?"

"Yes," said the Inspector. "Who? That's the question. What about the husband sleeping next door, who never said good night to his wife and who heard nothing? I should say we hadn't far to look. Must find out what terms they were on. That's where you can be useful to us, Mr. Satterthwaite. You've the *ongtray* here, and you can get the hang of things in a way we can't. Find out what relations there were between the two."

"I hardly like—" began Mr. Satterthwaite, stiffening.

"It won't be the first murder mystery you've helped us with. I remember the case of Mrs. Strangeways. You've got a *flair* for that sort of thing, sir. An absolute *flair*."

Yes, it was true—he *had* a *flair*. He said quietly:

"I will do my best, Inspector."

Had Gerard Annesley killed his wife? Had he? Mr. Satterthwaite recalled that look of misery last night. He loved her—and he was suffering. Suffering will drive a man to strange deeds.

But there was something else—some other factor. Mabelle had spoken of herself as coming out of a wood—she was looking forward to happiness—not a quiet rational happiness—but a happiness that was irrational—a wild ecstasy—

If Gerard Annesley had spoken the truth, Mabelle had not come to her room till at least half an hour later than he had done. Yet David Keeley had seen her going up those stairs. There were two other rooms occupied in that wing. There was Mrs. Graham's and there was her son's.

Her son's. But he and Madge—

Surely Madge would have guessed. But Madge wasn't the guessing kind. All the same, no smoke without fire—

Smoke!

Ah! he remembered. *A wisp of smoke curling out through Mrs. Graham's bedroom door.*

He acted on impulse. Straight up the stairs he went and into her room. It was empty. He closed the door behind him and locked it.

He went across to the grate. A heap of charred fragments. Very gingerly he raked them over with his finger. His luck was in. In the very center were some unburned fragments—fragments of letters.

Very disjointed fragments, but they told him something of value.

"Life can be wonderful, Roger darling. I never knew—" "all my life has been a dream till I met you, Roger—" "—Gerard knows, I think— I am sorry, but what can I do. Nothing is real to me but you, Roger. We shall be together, soon.

"What are you going to tell him at Laidell, Roger? You write strangely—but I am not afraid—"

Very carefully, Mr. Satterthwaite put the fragments into an envelope from the writing table. He went to the door, unlocked it and opened it to find himself face to face with Mrs. Graham.

It was an awkward moment, and Mr. Satterthwaite was momentarily out of countenance. He did what was, perhaps, the best thing, attacked the situation with simplicity.

"I have been searching your room, Mrs. Graham. I have found something—a packet of letters imperfectly burned."

A wave of alarm passed over her face. It was gone in a flash but it had been there.

"Letters from Mrs. Annesley to your son."

She hesitated for a minute, then said quietly.

"That is so. I thought they would be better burned."

"For what reason?"

"My son is engaged to be married. These letters—if they had been brought into publicity through the poor girl's suicide—might have caused much pain and trouble."

"Your son could burn his own letters."

She had no answer ready for that. Mr. Satterthwaite pursued his advantage.

"You found these letters in his room, brought them into your room and burned them. Why? You were afraid, Mrs. Graham."

"I am not in the habit of being afraid, Mr. Satterthwaite."

"No—but this was a desperate case."

"Desperate?"

"Your son might have been in danger of arrest—for murder."

"Murder!"

He saw her face go white; he went on quickly:

"You heard Mrs. Annesley go into your son's room last night. Had he told her of his engagement? No, I see he hadn't. He told her then. They quarreled, and he—"

"That's a lie!"

They had been so absorbed in their duel of words that they had not heard approaching footsteps. Roger Graham had come up behind them unperceived by either.

"It's all right, Mother. Don't—worry. Come into my room, Mr. Satterthwaite."

Mr. Satterthwaite followed him into his room. Mrs. Graham had turned away and did not attempt to follow them. Roger Graham shut the door.

"Listen, Mr. Satterthwaite. You think I killed Mabelle. You think I strangled her—here—and took her along and hung her up on that door—later—when everyone was asleep?"

Mr. Satterthwaite stared at him. Then he said surprisingly:

"No, I do not think so."

"Thank God for that. I couldn't have killed Mabelle. I—I loved her. Or didn't I? I don't know. It's a tangle that I can't explain. I'm fond of Madge—I always have been. And she's such a good sort. We suit each other. But Mabelle was different. It was—I can't explain it—a sort of enchantment. I was, I think, afraid of her."

Mr. Satterthwaite nodded.

"It was madness—a kind of bewildering ecstasy. But it was impossible. It wouldn't have worked. That sort of thing—doesn't last. I know what it means now to have a spell cast over you."

"Yes, it must have been like that," said Mr. Satterthwaite thoughtfully.

"I—I wanted to get out of it all. I was going to tell Mabelle—last night."

"But you didn't?"

"No, I didn't," said Graham slowly. "I swear to you, Mr. Satterthwaite, that I never saw her after I said good night downstairs.

"I believe you," said Mr. Satterthwaite.

He got up. It was not Roger Graham who had killed Mabelle Annesley. He could have fled from her, but he could not have killed her. He had been afraid of her, afraid of that wild intangible fairylike quality of hers. He had known enchantment—and turned his back on it. He had gone for the safe sensible thing that he had known "would work" and had relinquished the intangible dream that might lead him he knew not where.

He was a sensible young man, and, as such, uninteresting to Mr. Satterthwaite, who was an artist and a connoisseur in life.

He left Roger Graham in his room and went downstairs. The drawing room was empty. Mabelle's ukulele lay on a stool by the window. He took it up and twanged it absent-mindedly. He knew nothing of the instrument, but his ear told him that it was abominably out of tune. He turned a key experimentally.

Doris Coles came into the room. She looked at him reproachfully. "Poor Mabelle's uke," she said.

Her clear condemnation made Mr. Satterthwaite feel obstinate. "Tune it for me," he said, and added: "If you can."

"Of course I can," said Doris, wounded at the suggestion of incompetence in any direction.

She took it from him, twanged a string, turned a key briskly— and the string snapped.

"Well, I never. Oh! I see—but how extraordinary. It's the wrong string—a size too big. It's an A string. How stupid to put that on. Of course it snaps when you try to tune it up. How stupid people are."

"Yes," said Mr. Satterthwaite. "They are—even when they try to be clever."

His tone was so odd that she stared at him. He took the ukulele from her and removed the broken string. He went out of the room holding it in his hand. In the library he found David Keeley.

"Here," he said.

He held out the string. Keeley took it.

"What's this?"

"A broken ukulele string." He paused and then went on: "*What did you do with the other one?*"

"The other one?"

"*The one you strangled her with.* You were very clever, weren't you? It was done very quickly—just in that moment we were all laughing and talking in the hall.

"Mabelle came back into this room for her ukulele. You had taken the string off as you fiddled with it just before. You caught her round the throat with it and strangled her. Then you came out and locked the door and joined us. Later, in the dead of night, you came down and—and disposed of the body by hanging it on the door of her room. And you put another string on the ukulele—*but it was the wrong string*, that's why you were stupid."

There was a pause.

"But why did you do it," said Mr. Satterthwaite. "In God's name, *why?*"

Mr. Keeley laughed, a funny giggling little laugh that made Mr. Satterthwaite feel rather sick.

"It was so very simple," he said. "That's why! And then—nobody ever noticed me. Nobody ever noticed what I was doing. I thought— I thought I'd have the laugh on them."

And again he gave that furtive little giggle and looked at Mr. Satterthwaite with mad eyes.

Mr. Satterthwaite was glad that at that moment Inspector Winkfield came into the room.

.   .   .

IT WAS TWENTY-FOUR hours later, on his way to London, that Mr. Satterthwaite awoke from a doze to find a tall dark man sitting opposite to him in the railway carriage. He was not altogether surprised.

"My dear Mr. Quin!"

"Yes—I am here."

Mr. Satterthwaite said slowly:

"I can hardly face you. I am ashamed. I failed."

"Are you so sure of that?"

"I did not save her."

"But you discovered the truth?"

"Yes, that is true. One or other of those young men might have been accused—might even have been found guilty. So, at any rate, I saved a man's life. But she—she—that strange enchanting creature—" His voice broke off.

Mr. Quin looked at him.

"Is death the greatest evil that can happen to anyone?"

"I—well—perhaps—No."

Mr. Satterthwaite remembered—Madge and Roger Graham—Mabelle's face in the moonlight—its serene unearthly happiness—

"No," he admitted. "No—perhaps death is not the greatest evil."

He remembered the ruffled blue chiffon of her dress that had seemed to him like the plumage of a bird, a bird with a broken wing.

When he looked up, he found himself alone. Mr. Quin was no longer there. But he had left something behind.

On the seat was a roughly carved bird fashioned out of some dim blue stone. It had, possibly, no great artistic merit. But it had something else.

It had the vague quality of enchantment.

So said Mr. Satterthwaite—and Mr. Satterthwaite was a connoisseur.

11. THE MAN FROM THE SEA

Mr. Satterthwaite was feeling old. That might not have been surprising since, in the estimation of many people, he was old. Careless youths said to their partners: "Old Satterthwaite? Oh! he must be a hundred—or at any rate about eighty." And even the kindest of girls said indulgently, "Oh! Satterthwaite. Yes, he's quite old. He must be sixty." Which was almost worse, since he was sixty-nine.

In his own view, however, he was not old. Sixty-nine was an interesting age—an age of infinite possibilities—an age when at last the experience of a lifetime was beginning to tell. But to feel old—that was different—a tired discouraged state of mind when one was inclined to ask oneself depressing questions. What was he after all? A little dried up, elderly man, with neither chick nor child, with no human belongings, only a valuable art collection which seemed at the moment strangely unsatisfying. No one to care whether he lived or died—

At this point in his meditations Mr. Satterthwaite pulled himself up short. What he was thinking was morbid and unprofitable. He knew well enough, who better, that the chances were that a wife would have hated him or, alternatively, that he would have hated her, that children would have been a constant source of worry and anxiety and that demand upon his time and affection would have worried him considerably.

To be safe and comfortable, said Mr. Satterthwaite firmly—that was the thing.

The last thought reminded him of a letter he had received that morning. He drew it from his pocket and reread it, savoring its contents pleasurably. To begin with, it was from a duchess, and Mr. Satterthwaite liked hearing from duchesses. It is true that the letter began by demanding a large subscription for charity and but for that would probably never have been written, but the terms in which it was couched were so agreeable that Mr. Satterthwaite was able to gloss over the first fact.

"So you've deserted the Riviera," wrote the Duchess. "What is this island of yours like? Cheap? Cannotti put up his prices shamefully this year, and I shan't go to the Riviera again. I might try your island next year if you report favorably, though I should hate five days on a boat. Still anywhere you recommend is sure to be pretty comfortable—too much so. You'll get to be one of those people who do nothing but coddle themselves and think of their comfort. There's only one thing that will save you, Satterthwaite, and that is your inordinate interest in other people's affairs—"

As Mr. Satterthwaite folded the letter, a vision came up vividly before him of the duchess. Her meannesses, her unexpected and alarming kindness, her caustic tongue, her indomitable spirit.

Spirit! Everyone needed spirit. He drew out another letter with a German stamp upon it—written by a young singer in whom he had interested himself. It was a grateful affectionate letter.

"How can I thank you, dear Mr. Satterthwaite? It seems too wonderful to think that in a few days I shall be singing Isolde—"

A pity that she was to make her debut as Isolde. A charming, hardworking child, Olga, with a beautiful voice, but no temperament. He hummed to himself. *"Nay order him! Pray understand it! I command it. I, Isolde."* No, the child hadn't got it in her—the spirit— the indomitable will—all expressed in that final "Ich Isolde!"

Well, at any rate he had done something for somebody. This island depressed him—why, oh! why had he deserted the Riviera which he knew so well, and where he was so well known? Nobody here took any interest in him. Nobody seemed to realize that here was *the* Mr. Satterthwaite—the friend of duchesses and countesses and singers and writers. No one in the island was of any social importance or of any artistic importance either. Most people had been there seven, fourteen, or twenty-one years running, and valued themselves and were valued accordingly. ·

With a deep sigh Mr. Satterthwaite proceeded down from the hotel to the small straggling harbor below. His way lay between an avenue of bougainvillæaa—a vivid mass of flaunting scarlet, that made him feel older and grayer than ever.

"I'm getting old," he murmured. "I'm getting old and tired."

He was glad when he had passed the bougainvillæaa and was walking down the white street with the blue sea at the end of it. A disreputable dog was standing in the middle of the road, yawning and stretching himself in the sun. Having prolonged his stretch to the utmost limits of ecstasy, he sat down and treated himself to a really good scratch. He then rose, shook himself, and looked round for any other good things that life might have to offer.

There was a dump of rubbish by the side of the road and to this he went sniffing in pleasurable anticipation. True enough, his nose had not deceived him! A smell of such rich putrescence that it surpassed even his anticipations! He sniffed with growing appreciation, then, suddenly abandoning himself, he lay on his back and rolled frenziedly on the delicious dump. Clearly the world this morning was a dog paradise!

Tiring at last, he regained his feet and strolled out once more into the middle of the road. And then, without the least warning, a ramshackle car careened wildly round the corner, caught him full and square and passed on unheeding.

The dog rose to his feet, stood a minute regarding Mr. Satterthwaite, a vague dumb reproach in its eyes, then fell over. Mr. Satterthwaite went up to him and bent down. The dog was dead. He went on his way, wondering at the sadness and cruelty of life. What a queer dumb look of reproach had been in the dog's eyes. "Oh! World," it seemed to say. "Oh! Wonderful World in which I have trusted. Why have you done this to me?"

Mr. Satterthwaite went on, past the palm trees and the straggling white houses, past the black lava beach where the surf thundered and where once, long ago, a well known English swimmer had been carried out to sea and drowned, past the rock pools where children and elderly ladies bobbed up and down and called it bathing, along the steep road that winds upward to the top of the cliff. For there on the edge of the cliff was a house, appropriately named La Paz. A white house with faded green shutters tightly closed, a tangled beautiful garden, and a walk between cypresss trees that led to a plateau on the edge of the cliff where you looked down—down—down—to the deep blue sea below.

It was to this spot that Mr. Satterthwaite was bound. He had developed a great love for the garden of La Paz. He had never entered the villa. It seemed always to be empty. Manuel, the Spanish gardener, wished one good morning with a flourish, and gallantly presented ladies with a bouquet and gentlemen with a single flower as a buttonhole, his dark face wreathed in smiles.

Sometimes Mr. Satterthwaite made up stories in his own mind about the owner of the villa. His favorite was a Spanish dancer, once world famed for her beauty, who hid herself here so that the world should never know that she was no longer beautiful.

He pictured her coming out of the house at dusk and walking through the garden. Sometimes he was tempted to ask Manuel for the truth, but he resisted the temptation. He preferred his fancies.

After exchanging a few words with Manuel and graciously accepting an orange rosebud Mr. Satterthwaite passed on down the cypress walk to the sea. It was rather wonderful sitting there—on the edge of nothing—with that sheer drop below one. It made him think of Tristan and Isolde, of the beginning of the third act with Tristan and Kurwenal—that lonely waiting, and of Isolde rushing up from the sea and Tristan dying in her arms. (No, little Olga would never make an Isolde. Isolde of Cornwall, that royal hater and royal lover—) He shivered. He felt old, chilly, alone. What had he had out of life? Nothing—nothing. Not as much as that dog in the street.

It was an unexpected sound that roused him from his reverie. Footsteps coming along the cypress walk were inaudible; the first he knew of somebody's presence was the English monosyllable "Damn."

He looked round to find a young man staring at him in obvious surprise and disappointment: Mr. Satterthwaite recognized him at once as an arrival of the day before who had more or less intrigued him. Mr. Satterthwaite called him a young man—because in comparison to most of the diehards in the hotel he *was* a young man, but he would certainly never see forty again and was probably drawing appreciably near to his half century. Yet, in spite of that, the term young man fitted him—Mr. Satterthwaite was usually right about such things—there was an impression of immaturity about him. As there is a touch of puppyhood about many a full grown dog, so it was with the stranger.

Mr. Satterthwaite thought: "This chap has really never grown up—not properly, that is."

And yet there was nothing Peter Pannish about him. He was sleek—almost plump, he had the air of one who has always done himself exceedingly well in the material sense and denied himself no pleasure or satisfaction. He had brown eyes—rather round—fair hair turning gray—a little mustache and rather a florid face.

The thing that had puzzled Mr. Satterthwaite was what had brought him to the island. He could imagine him shooting things, hunting things, playing polo or golf or tennis, making love to pretty women. But in the island there was nothing to hunt or shoot, no games except golf croquet, and the nearest approach to a pretty woman was represented by elderly Miss Baba Kindersley. There were, of course, artists, to whom the beauty of the scenery made appeal, but Mr. Satterthwaite was quite certain that the young man was not an artist. He was clearly marked with the stamp of the Philistine.

While he was revolving these things in his mind, the other spoke, realizing somewhat belatedly that his single ejaculation so far might be open to criticism.

"I beg your pardon," he said with some embarrassment. "As a matter of fact, I was—well, startled. I didn't expect anyone to be here."

He smiled disarmingly. He had a charming smile—friendly—appealing.

"It is rather a lonely spot," agreed Mr. Satterthwaite, and he moved politely a little further up the bench. The other accepted the mute invitation and sat down.

"I don't know about lonely," he said. "There always seems to be *someone* here."

There was a tinge of latent resentment in his voice. Mr. Satterthwaite wondered why. He read the other as a friendly soul. Why this insistence on solitude? A rendezvous, perhaps? No—not that. He looked again with carefully veiled scrutiny at his companion. Where had he seen that particular expression before quite lately? That look of dumb bewildered resentment.

"You've been up here before then?" said Mr. Satterthwaite, more for the sake of saying something than for anything else.

"I was up here last night—after dinner."

"Really? I thought the gates were always locked."

There was a moment's pause and then, almost sullenly, the young man said:

"I climbed over the wall."

Mr. Satterthwaite looked at him with real attention now. He had a sleuthlike habit of mind and he was aware that his companion had only arrived on the preceding afternoon. He had had little time to discover the beauties of the villa by daylight and he had so far spoken to nobody. Yet after dark he had made straight for La Paz. Why? Almost involuntarily Mr. Satterthwaite turned his head to look at the green shuttered villa, but it was as ever serenely lifeless, close shuttered. No, the solution of the mystery was not there.

"And you actually found someone here then?"

The other nodded.

"Yes. Must have been from the other Hotel. He had on fancy dress."

"Fancy dress?"

"Yes. A kind of Harlequin rig."

"What?"

The query fairly burst from Mr. Satterthwaite's lips. His companion turned to stare at him in surprise.

"They often do have fancy dress shows at the hotels, I suppose?"

"Oh! quite," said Mr. Satterthwaite. "Quite, quite, quite."

He paused breathlessly, then added:

"You must excuse my excitement. Do you happen to know anything about catalyzis?"

The young man stared at him.

"Never heard of it. What is it?"

Mr. Satterthwaite quoted gravely: *"A chemical reaction depending for its success on the presence of a certain substance which itself remains unchanged."*

"Oh!" said the young man uncertainly.

"I have a certain friend—his name is Mr. Quin, and he can best be described in the terms of catalyzis. His presence is a sign that things are going to happen; because he is there strange revelations come to light, discoveries are made. And yet—he himself takes no part in the proceedings. I have a feeling that it was my friend you met here last might."

"He's a very sudden sort of chap then. He gave me quite a shock. One minute he wasn't there and the next minute he was! Almost as though he came up out of the sea."

Mr. Satterthwaite looked along the little plateau and down the sheer drop below.

"That's nonsense, of course," said the other. "But it's the feeling he gave me. Of course, really, there isn't the foothold for a fly." He looked over the edge. "A straight clear drop. If you went over—well, that would be the end right enough."

"An ideal spot for a murder, in fact," said Mr. Satterthwaite pleasantly.

. The other stared at him, almost as though for the moment he did not follow. Then he said vaguely: "Oh! yes—of course." .

He sat there, making little dabs at the ground with his stick and frowning. Suddenly Mr. Satterthwaite got the resemblance he had been seeking. That dumb bewildered questioning. *So had the dog looked who was run over.* His eyes and this young man's eyes asked the same pathetic question with the same reproach. *"Oh! world that I have trusted—what have you done to me?"*

He saw other points of resemblance between the two, the same pleasure-loving, easygoing existence, the same joyous abandon to the delights of life, the same absence of intellectual questioning. Enough for both to live in the moment—the world was a good place, a place of carnal delights—sun, sea, sky—a discreet garbage heap. And then—what? A car had hit the dog. What had hit the man?

The subject of these cogitations broke in at this point, speaking, however, more to himself than to Mr. Satterthwaite.

"One wonders," he said, "what it's all for."

Familiar words—words that usually brought a smile to Mr. Satterthwaite's lips, with their unconscious betrayal of the innate egoism of humanity which insists on regarding every manifestation of life as directly designed for its delight or its torment. He did not answer, and presently the stranger said with a slight, rather apologetic laugh:

"I've heard it said that every man should build a house, plant a tree and have a son." He paused and then added: "I believe I planted an acorn once—"

Mr. Satterthwaite stirred slightly. His curiosity was aroused— that ever present interest in the affairs of other people of which the duchess had accused him was roused. It was not difficult. Mr. Satterthwaite had a very feminine side to his nature; he was as good a listener as any woman, and he knew the right moment to put in a prompting word. Presently he was hearing the whole story.

Anthony Cosdon, that was the stranger's name, and his life had been much as Mr. Satterthwaite had imagined it. He was a bad hand at telling a story but his listener supplied the gaps easily enough. A very ordinary life—an average income, a little soldiering, a good deal of sport whenever sport offered, plenty of friends, plenty of pleasant things to do, a sufficiency of women. The kind of life that practically inhibits thought of any description and substitutes sensation. To speak frankly, an animal's life. "But there are worse things than that," thought Mr. Satterthwaite from the depths of his experience. "Oh! many worse things than that." This world had seemed a very good place to Anthony Cosdon. He had grumbled because everyone always grumbled, but it had never been a serious grumble. And then—*this*.

He came to it at last—rather vaguely and incoherently. Hadn't felt quite the thing—nothing much. Saw his doctor, and the doctor had persuaded him to go to a Harley Street man. And then—the incredible truth. They'd tried to hedge about it—spoke of great care— a quiet life, but they hadn't been able to disguise that that was all eyewash—letting him down lightly. It boiled down to this—six months. That's what they gave him. Six months.

He turned those bewildered brown eyes on Mr. Satterthwaite. It was, of course, rather a shock to a fellow. One didn't—one didn't somehow, know what to *do*.

Mr. Satterthwaite nodded gravely and understandingly.

It was a bit difficult to take in all at once, Anthony Cosdon went on. How to put in the time. Rather a rotten business waiting about to get pipped. He didn't feel really ill—not yet. Though that might come later, so the specialist had said—in fact it was bound to. It seemed such nonsense to be going to die when one didn't in the least want to. The best thing, he had thought, would be to carry on as usual. But somehow that hadn't worked.

Here Mr. Satterthwaite interrupted him. Wasn't there, he hinted delicately, any woman?

But apparently there wasn't. There were women, of course, but not that kind. His crowd was a very cheery crowd. They didn't, so he implied, like corpses. He didn't wish to make a kind of walking funeral of himself. It would have been embarrassing for everybody. So he had come abroad.

"You came to these islands? But why?" Mr. Satterthwaite was hunting for something, something intangible but delicate that eluded him and yet which he was sure was there. "You've been here before, perhaps?"

"Yes." He admitted it almost unwillingly. "Years ago when I was a youngster."

And suddenly, almost unconsciously so it seemed, he shot a quick glance backward over his shoulder in the direction of the villa.

"I remembered this place," he said, nodding at the sea. *"One step to eternity!"*

"And that is why you came up here last night," finished Mr. Satterthwaite calmly.

Anthony Cosdon shot him a dismayed glance.

"Oh! I say—really—" he protested.

"Last night you found someone here. This afternoon you have found me. Your life has been saved—twice."

"You may put it that way if you like—but damn it all, it's *my* life. I've a right to do what I like with it."

"That is a *cliché*," said Mr. Satterthwaite wearily.

"Of course I see your point," said Anthony Cosdon generously. "Naturally you've got to say what you can. I'd try to dissuade a fellow myself, even though I knew deep down that he was right. And you know that I'm right. A clean, quick end is better than a lingering one—causing trouble and expense and bother to all. In any case it's not as though I had anyone in the world belonging to me—"

"If you had?" asked Mr. Satterthwaite sharply.

Cosdon drew a deep breath.

"I don't know. Even then, I think, this way would be best. But anyway—I haven't—"

He stopped abruptly. Mr. Satterthwaite eyed him curiously. Incurably romantic, he suggested again that there was, somewhere, some woman. But Cosdon negatived it. He oughtn't, he said, to complain. He had had on the whole, a very good life. It was a pity it was going to be over so soon, that was all. But at any rate he had had, he supposed, everything worth having. Except a son. He would have liked a son. He would like to know now that he had a son living after him. Still, he reiterated the fact, he had had a very good life.

It was at this point that Mr. Satterthwaite lost patience. Nobody, he pointed out, who was still in the larval stage, could claim to know anything of life at all. Since the words *larval stage* clearly meant nothing at all to Cosdon, he proceeded to make his meaning clearer.

"You have not begun to live yet. You are still at the beginning of life."

Cosdon laughed.

"Why, my hair's gray. I'm forty—"

Mr. Satterthwaite interrupted him.

"That has nothing to do with it. Life is a compound of physical and mental experience. I, for instance, am sixty-nine, and I am really sixty-nine. I have known, either at first or second hand, nearly all the experiences life has to offer. You are like a man who talks of a full year and has seen nothing but snow and ice! The flowers of Spring, the languorous days of Summer, the falling leaves of Autumn—he knows nothing of them—not even that there are such things. And you are going to turn your back on even the opportunity of knowing them."

"You seem to forget," said Anthony Cosdon dryly, "that in any case, I have only six months."

"Time, like everything else, is relative," said Mr. Satterthwaite. "That six months might be the longest and most varied experience of your whole life."

Cosdon looked unconvinced.

"In my place," he said, "you would do the same." Mr. Satterthwaite shook his head.

"No," he said simply. "In the first place, I doubt if I should have the courage. It needs courage, and I am not at all a brave individual. And in the second place—"

"Well?"

"I always want to know what is going to happen tomorrow."

Cosdon rose suddenly with a laugh.

"Well, sir, you've been very good in letting me talk to you. I hardly know why—Anyway, there it is. I've said a lot too much. Forget it."

"And tomorrow, when an accident is reported, I am to leave it at that? To make no suggestions of suicide?"

"That's as you like. I'm glad you realize one thing—that you can't prevent me."

"My dear young man," said Mr. Satterthwaite placidly, "I can hardly attach myself to you like the proverbial limpet. Sooner or later you would give me the slip and accomplish your purpose. But you are frustrated at any rate for this afternoon. You would hardly like to go to your death leaving me under the possible imputation of having pushed you over."

"That is true," said Cosdon. "If you insist on remaining here—"

"I do," said Mr. Satterthwaite firmly.

Cosdon laughed good-humoredly.

"Then the plan must be deferred for the moment. In which case I will go back to the hotel. See you later perhaps."

Mr. Satterthwaite was left looking at the sea.

"And now," he said to himself softly, "what next? There must be a next. I wonder—"

He got up. For a while he stood at the edge of the plateau looking down at the dancing water beneath. But he found no inspiration there, and turning slowly he walked back along the path between the cypresses and into the quiet garden. He looked at the shuttered peaceful house and he wondered as he had often wondered before who had lived there and what had taken place within those placid walls. On a sudden impulse he walked up some crumbling stone steps and laid a hand on one of the faded green shutters.

To his surprise it swung back at his touch. He hesitated a moment, then pushed it boldly open. The next minute he stepped back with a little exclamation of dismay. A woman stood in the window facing him. She wore black and had a black lace mantilla draped over her head.

Mr. Satterthwaite floundered wildly in Italian interspersed with German—the nearest he could get in the hurry of the moment to

Spanish. He was desolated and ashamed, he explained haltingly. The Signora must forgive. He thereupon retreated hastily, the woman not having spoken one word.

He was halfway across the courtyard when she spoke—two sharp words like a pistol crack.

"Come back!"

It was a barked out command such as might have been addressed to a dog, yet so absolute was the authority it conveyed that Mr. Satterthwaite had swung round hurriedly and trotted back to the window almost automatically before it occurred to him to feel any resentment. He obeyed like a dog. The woman was still standing motionless at the window. She looked him up and down appraising him with perfect calmness.

"You are English," she said. "I thought so."

Mr. Satterthwaite started off on a second apology.

"If I had known you were English," he said, "I could have expressed myself better just now. I offer my most sincere apologies for my rudeness in trying the shutter. I am afraid I can plead no excuse save curiosity. I had a great wish to see what the inside of this charming house was like."

She laughed suddenly, a deep rich laugh.

"If you really want to see it," she said, "you had better come in."

She stood aside, and Mr. Satterthwaite, feeling pleasurably excited, stepped into the room. It was dark, since the shutters of the other windows were closed, but he could see that it was scantily and rather shabbily furnished and that the dust lay thick everywhere.

"Not here," she said "I do not use this room."

She led the way and he followed her, out of the room across a passage and into a room the other side. Here the windows gave on the sea and the sun streamed in. The furniture like that of the other room was poor in quality, but there were some worn rugs that had been good in their time, a large screen of Spanish leather and bowls of fresh flowers.

"You will have tea with me," said Mr. Satterthwaite's hostess. She added, reassuringly, "It is perfectly good tea and will be made with boiling water."

She went out of the door and called out something in Spanish, then she returned and sat down on a sofa opposite her guest. For the first time, Mr. Satterthwaite was able to study her appearance.

The first effect she had upon him was to make him feel even more gray and shriveled and elderly than usual by contrast with her own forceful personality. She was a tall woman, very sunburned, dark and handsome, though no longer young. When she was in the room the sun seemed to be shining twice as brightly as when she was out of it, and presently a curious feeling of warmth and aliveness began to steal over Mr. Satterthwaite. It was as though he stretched out thin shriveled hands to a reassuring flame. He thought: "She's so much vitality herself that she's got a lot left over for other people."

He recalled the command in her voice when she had stopped him and wished that his protégée Olga could be imbued with a little of that force. He thought: "What an Isolde she'd make! And yet she probably hasn't got the ghost of a singing voice. Life is badly arranged." He was, all the same, a little afraid of her. He did not like domineering women.

She had clearly been considering him as she sat with her chin in her hands, making no pretense about it. At last she nodded as though she had made up her mind.

"I am glad you came," she said at last. "I needed someone very badly to talk to this afternoon. And you are used to that, aren't you?"

"I don't quite understand."

"I meant people tell you things. You knew what I meant! Why pretend?"

"Well—perhaps—"

She swept on, regardless of anything he had been going to say.

"One could say anything to you. That is because you are half a woman. You know what we feel—what we think—the queer, queer things we do."

Her voice died away. Tea was brought by a large smiling Spanish girl. It was good tea—China—Mr. Satterthwaite sipped it appreciatively.

"You live here?" he inquired conversationally.

"Yes."

"But not altogether. The house is usually shut up, is it not? At least so I have been told."

"I am here a good deal, more than anyone knows. I only use these rooms."

"You have had the house long?"

"It has belonged to me for twenty-two-years—and I lived here for a year before that."

Mr. Satterthwaite said rather inanely, or so he felt, "That is a very long time."

"The year? Or the twenty-two years?"

His interest stirred, Mr. Satterthwaite said gravely: "That depends."

She nodded.

"Yes, it depends. They are two separate periods. They have nothing to do with each other. Which is long? Which is short? Even now I cannot say."

She was silent for a minute, brooding. Then she said with a little smile:

"It is such a long time since I have talked with anyone—such a long time! I do not apologize. You came to my shutter. You wished to look through my window. And that is what you are always doing, is it not? Pushing aside the shutter and looking through the window into the truth of people's lives. If they will let you. And often if they will not let you! It would be difficult to hide anything from you. You would guess—and guess right."

Mr. Satterthwaite had an odd impulse to be perfectly sincere.

"I am sixty-nine," he said. "Everything I know of life I know at second hand. Sometimes that is very bitter to me. And yet, because of it, I know a good deal."

She nodded thoughtfully.

"I know. Life is very strange. I cannot imagine what it must be like to be that—always a looker on."

Her tone was wondering. Mr. Satterthwaite smiled.

"No, you would not know. Your place is in the center of the stage. You will always be the Prima Donna."

"What a curious thing to say."

"But I am right. Things have happened to you—will always happen to you. Sometimes, I think, there have been tragic things. Is that so?"

Her eyes narrowed. She looked across at him.

"If you are here long, somebody will tell you of the English swimmer who was drowned at the foot of this cliff. They will tell you how young and strong he was, how handsome, and they will tell you that his young wife looked down from the top of the cliff and saw him drowning."

"Yes, I have already heard that story."

"That man was my husband. This was his villa. He brought me out here with him when I was eighteen, and a year later, he died—driven by the surf on the black rocks, cut and bruised and mutilated, battered to death."

Mr. Satterthwaite gave a shocked exclamation. She leaned forward, her burning eyes focused on his face.

"You spoke of a tragedy. Can you imagine a greater tragedy than that? For a young wife, only a year married, to stand helpless while the man she loved fought for his life—and lost it—horribly."

"Terrible," said Mr. Satterthwaite. He spoke with real emotion. "Terrible. I agree with you. Nothing in life could be so dreadful."

Suddenly she laughed. Her head went back.

"You are wrong," she said. "There is something more terrible. And that is for a young wife to stand there and hope and long for her husband to drown."

"But, good God," cried Mr. Satterthwaite, "you don't mean—"

"Yes, I do. That's what it was really. I knelt there—knelt down on the cliff and prayed. The Spanish servants thought I was praying for his life to be saved. I wasn't. I was praying that I might wish him to be spared. I was saying one thing over and over again, 'God, help me not to wish him dead. God, help me not to wish him dead.' But it wasn't any good. All the time I hoped—hoped—and my hope came true."

She was silent for a minute or two and then she said, very gently, in quite a different voice:

"That is a terrible thing, isn't it? It's the sort of thing one can't forget. I was so terribly happy when I knew he was really dead and couldn't come back to torture me any more."

"My child," said Mr. Satterthwaite, shocked.

"I know. I was too young to have that happen to me. Those things should happen to one when one is older—when one is more prepared for—for beastliness. Nobody knew, you know, what he was really like. I thought he was wonderful when I first met him and was so happy and proud when he asked me to marry him. But things went wrong almost at once. He was angry with me—nothing I could do pleased him—and yet I tried so hard. And then he began to like hurting me. And above all to terrify me. That's what he enjoyed most. He thought out all sort of things—dreadful things. I won't tell you. I suppose, really, he must have been a little mad. I was alone here, in his power, and cruelty began to be his hobby." Her eyes widened and darkened. "The worst was my baby. I was going to have a baby. Because of some of the things he did to me—it was born dead. My little baby. I nearly died too—but I didn't. I wished I had."

Mr. Satterthwaite made an inarticulate sound.

"And then I was delivered—in the way I've told you. Some girls who were staying at the hotel dared him. That's how it happened. All the Spaniards told him it was madness to risk the sea just there. But he was very vain—he wanted to show off. And I—I saw him drown—and was glad. God oughtn't to let such things happen."

Mr. Satterthwaite stretched out his little dry hand and took hers. She squeezed it hard as a child might have done. The maturity had fallen away from her face. He saw her without difficulty as she had been at nineteen.

"At first it seemed too good to be true. The house was mine and I could live in it. And no one could hurt me any more! I was an orphan, you know, I had no near relations, no one to care what became of me. That simplified things. I lived on here—in this villa—and it seemed like Heaven. Yes, like Heaven. I've never been so happy since, and never shall again. Just to wake up and know that everything was all right—no pain, no terror, no wondering what he was going to do to me next. Yes, it was Heaven."

"And then?"

"I suppose human beings aren't ever satisfied. At first, just being free was enough. But after a while I began to get—well, lonely, I suppose. I began to think about my baby that died. If only I had had my baby! I wanted it as a baby, and also as a plaything. I wanted dreadfully something or someone to play with. It sounds silly and childish, but there it was."

"I understand," said Mr. Satterthwaite gravely.

"It's difficult to explain the next bit. It just—well, happened, you see. There was a young Englishman staying at the hotel. He strayed into the garden by mistake. I was wearing Spanish dress and he took me for a Spanish girl. I thought it would be rather fun to pretend I was one, so I played up. His Spanish was very bad but he could just manage a little. I told him the villa belonged to an English lady who was away. I said she had taught me a little English, and I pretended to speak broken English. It was such fun—such fun—even now I can remember what fun it was. He began to make love to me. We agreed to pretend that the villa was our home, that we were just married and coming to live there. I suggested that we should try one of the shutters—the one you tried this evening. It was open and inside the room was dusty and uncared for. We crept in. It was exciting and wonderful. We pretended it was our own house."

She broke off suddenly, looked appealingly at Mr. Satterthwaite.

"It all seemed lovely—like a fairy tale. And the lovely thing about it, to me, was that it wasn't true. It wasn't real."

Mr. Satterthwaite nodded. He saw her, perhaps, more clearly than she saw herself—that frightened lonely child entranced with her make believe that was so safe because it wasn't real.

"He was, I suppose, a very ordinary young man. Out for adventure, but quite sweet about it. We went on pretending."

She stopped, looked at Mr. Satterthwaite and said again:

"You understand? We went on pretending—"

She went on again in a minute.

"He came up again the next morning to the villa. I saw him from my bedroom through the shutter. Of course he didn't dream I was inside. He still thought I was a little Spanish peasant girl. He stood there looking about him. He'd asked me to meet him. I'd said I would but I never meant to.

"He just stood there looking worried. I think he was worried about me. It was nice of him to be worried about me. He *was* nice—"

She paused again.

"The next day he left. I've never seen him again."

"My baby was born nine months later. I was wonderfully happy all the time. To be able to have a baby so peacefully with no one to hurt you or make you miserable. I wished I'd remembered to ask my English boy his Christian name. I would have called the baby after him. It seemed unkind not to. It seemed rather unfair. He'd given me the thing I wanted most in the world, and he would never even know about it! But of course I told myself that he wouldn't look at it that way—that to know would probably only worry and annoy him. I had been just a passing amusement for him, that was all."

"And the baby?" asked Mr. Satterthwaite.

"He was splendid. I called him John. Splendid. I wish you could see him now. He's twenty. He's going to be a mining engineer. He's been the best and dearest son in the world to me. I told him his father had died before he was born."

Mr. Satterthwaite stared at her. A curious story. And somehow, a story that was not completely told. There was, he felt sure, something else.

"Twenty years is a long time," he said thoughtfully. "You've never contemplated marrying again?"

She shook her head. A slow burning blush spread over her tanned cheeks.

"The child was enough for you—always?"

She looked at him. Her eyes were softer than he had yet seen them.

"Such queer things happen!" she murmured. "Such queer, queer things. You wouldn't believe them—No, I'm wrong, *you* might, perhaps. I didn't love John's father, not at the time. I don't think I even knew what love was. I assumed as a matter of course, that the child would be like me. But he wasn't. He mightn't have been my child at all. He was like his father—he was like no one but his father. I learned to know that man—through his child. Through the child, I learned to love him. I love him now. I always shall love him. You may say that it's imagination, that I've built up an ideal, but it isn't so. I love the man, the real human man. I'd know him if I saw him tomorrow—even though it's over twenty years we met. Loving him has made me into a woman. I love him as a woman loves a man. For twenty years I've lived loving him. I shall die loving him."

She stopped abruptly—then challenged her listener.

"Do you think I'm mad—to say these strange things?"

"Oh! my dear," said Mr. Satterthwaite. He took her hand again. "You do understand?"

"I think I do. But there's something more, isn't there? Something that you haven't yet told me?"

Her brow clouded over.

"Yes, there's something. It was clever of you to guess. I knew at once you weren't the sort one can hide things from. But I don't want to tell you—and the reason I don't want to tell you is because it's best for you not to know."

He looked at her. Her eyes met his bravely and defiantly.

He said to himself: "This is the test. All the clues are in my hand. I ought to be able to know. If I reason rightly I shall know."

There was a pause, then he said slowly:

"Something's gone wrong." He saw her eyelids give the faintest quiver and knew himself to be on the right track.

"Something's gone wrong—suddenly—after all these years." He felt himself groping—groping—in the dark recesses of her mind where she was trying to hide her secret from him.

"The boy—it's to do with him. You wouldn't mind about anything else."

He heard the very faint gasp she gave and knew he had probed correctly. A cruel business but necessary. It was her will against his. She had got a dominant ruthless will, but he too had a will hidden beneath his meek manner. And he had behind him the Heaven sent assurance of a man who is doing his proper job. He felt a passing contemptuous pity for men whose business it was to track down such crudities as crime. This detective business of the mind, this assembling of clues, this delving for the truth, this wild joy as one drew nearer to the goal—Her very passion to keep the truth from him helped him. He felt her stiffen defiantly as he drew nearer and nearer.

"It is better for me not to know, you say. Better for *me?* But you are not a very considerate woman. You would not shrink from putting a stranger to a little temporary inconvenience. It is more than that, then? If you tell me you make me an accomplice before the fact. That sounds like crime. Fantastic! I could not associate crime with you. Or only one sort of crime. A crime against yourself."

Her lids drooped in spite of herself, veiled her eyes. He leaned forward and caught her wrist.

"It *is* that, then! You are thinking of taking your life."

She gave a low cry.

"How did you know? How did you know?"

"But why? You are not tired of life. I never saw a woman less tired of it—more radiantly alive."

She got up, went to the window, pushing back a strand of her dark hair as she did so.

"Since you have guessed so much I might as well tell you the truth. I should not have let you in this evening. I might have known that you would see too much. You are that kind of man. You were right about the cause. It's the boy. He knows nothing. But last time he was home, he spoke tragically of a friend of his, and I discovered something. If he finds out that he is illegitimate it will break his heart. He is proud—horribly proud! There is a girl. Oh! I won't go into details. But he is coming very soon—and he wants to know all about his father—he wants details. The girl's parents naturally want to know. When he discovers the truth, he will break with her, exile himself, ruin his life. Oh! I know the things you would say. He is young, foolish, wrong headed to take it like that! All true perhaps. But does it matter what people ought to be? They are what they are. *It will break his heart.* But if, before he comes, there has been an accident, everything will be swallowed up in grief for me. He will look through my papers, find nothing, and be annoyed that I told him so little. But he will not suspect the truth. It is the best way. One must pay for happiness, and I have had so much—oh! so much happiness. And in reality the price will be easy too A little courage—to take the leap—perhaps a moment of so of anguish."

"But, my dear child—"

"Don't argue with me." She flared round on him. "I won't listen to conventional arguments. My life is my own. Up to now, it has been needed—for John. But he needs it no longer. He wants a mate—a companion—he will turn to her all the more willingly because I am no longer there. My life is useless, but my death will be of use. And I have the right to do what I like with my own life."

"Are you sure?"

The sternness of his tone surprised her. She stammered slightly.

"If it is no good to anyone—and I am the best judge of that—"

He interrupted her again.

"Not necessarily."

"What do you mean?"

"Listen. I will put a case to you. A man comes to a certain place—to commit suicide, shall we say? But by chance he finds another man there, so he fails in his purpose and goes away—to live. The second man has saved the first man's life, not by being necessary to him or prominent in his life but just by the mere physical fact of having been in a certain place at a certain moment. You take your life today and perhaps, some five, six, seven years hence, someone will go to death or disaster simply for lack of your presence in a given spot or place. It may be a runaway horse coming down a street that swerved aside at sight of you and so fails to trample a child that is playing in the gutter. That child may live to grow up and be a great musician, or discover a cure for cancer. Or it may be less melodramatic than that. He may just grow up to ordinary everyday happiness."

She stared at him.

"You are a strange man. These things you say—I have never thought of them."

"You say your life is your own," went on Mr. Satterthwaite. "But can you dare to ignore the chance that you are taking part in a gigantic drama under the orders of a divine Producer? Your cue may not come till the end of the play—it may be totally unimportant, a mere walking on part, but upon it may hang the issues of the play, if you do not give the cue to another player. The whole edifice may crumple. You as you, may not matter to anyone in the world, but you as a person in a particular place may matter unimaginably."

She sat down, still staring.

"What do you want me to do?" she said simply.

It was Mr. Satterthwaite's moment of triumph. He issued orders.

"I want you at least to promise me one thing—to do nothing rash for twenty-four hours."

She was silent a moment or two and then she said, "I promise."

"There is one other thing—a favor."

"Yes!"

"Leave the shutter of the room I came in by unfastened, and keep vigil there tonight."

She looked at him curiously, but nodded assent.

"And now," said Mr. Satterthwaite, slightly conscious of anti-climax, "I really must be going. God bless you, my dear."

He made a rather embarrassed exit. The stalwart Spanish girl met him in the passage and opened a side door for him, staring curiously at him the while.

It was just growing dark as he reached the hotel. There was a solitary figure sitting on the terrace. Mr. Satterthwaite made straight for it. He was excited and his heart was beating quite fast. He felt that tremendous issues lay in his hands. One false move—

But he tried to conceal his agitation and to speak naturally and casually to Anthony Cosdon.

"A warm evening," he observed. "I quite lost count of time sitting up there on the cliff."

"Have you been up there all this time?"

Mr. Satterthwaite nodded. The swing door into the hotel opened to let someone through, and a beam of light fell suddenly on the other's face, illuminating its look of dull suffering, of uncomprehending dumb endurance.

Mr. Satterthwaite thought to himself: "It's worse for him than it would be for me. Imagination, conjecture, speculation—they can do a lot for you. You can, as it were, ring the changes upon pain. The uncomprehending blind suffering of an animal—that's terrible."

Cosdon spoke suddenly in a harsh voice.

"I'm going for a stroll after dinner. You—you understand? The third time's lucky. For God's sake don't interfere. I know your interference will be well meaning and all that—but take it from me, it's useless."

Mr. Satterthwaite drew himself up.

"I never interfere," he said, thereby giving the lie to the whole purpose and object of his existence.

"I know what you think—" went on Cosdon, but he was interrupted.

"You must excuse me, but there I beg to differ from you," said Mr. Satterthwaite. "Nobody knows what another person is thinking. They may imagine they do, but they are nearly always wrong."

"Well, perhaps that's so." Cosdon was doubtful, slightly taken aback.

"Your life is your own," said Mr. Satterthwaite. "Nobody can alter or influence the use you mean to make of it. Let us talk of a less painful subject. That old villa, for instance. It has a curious charm, withdrawn, sheltered from the world, shielding heaven knows what mystery. It tempted me to do a doubtful action. I tried one of the shutters."

"You did?" Cosdon turned his head sharply. "But it was fastened, of course?"

"No," said Mr. Satterthwaite. "It was open." He added gently: "The third shutter from the end."

"Why," Cosdon burst out, "that was the one—"

He broke off suddenly, but Mr. Satterthwaite had seen the light that had sprung up in his eyes. He rose—satisfied.

Some slight tinge of anxiety still remained with him. Using his favorite metaphor of a drama, he hoped that he had spoken his few lines correctly. For they were very important lines.

But thinking it over, his artistic judgment was satisfied. On his way up to the cliff, Cosdon would try that shutter. It was not in human nature to resist. A memory of twenty odd years ago had brought him to this spot, the same memory would take him to the shutter. And afterward?

"I shall know in the morning," said Mr. Satterthwaite, and proceeded to change methodically for his evening meal.

It was somewhere round ten o'clock that Mr. Satterthwaite set foot once more in the garden of La Paz. Manuel bade him a smiling "Good morning," and handed him a single rosebud which Mr. Satterthwaite put carefully into his buttonhole. Then he went on to the house. He stood there for some minutes looking up at the peaceful white walls, the trailing orange creeper, and the faded green shutters. So silent, so peaceful. Had the whole thing been a dream?

But at that moment one of the windows opened and the lady who occupied Mr. Satterthwaite's thoughts came out. She came straight to him with a buoyant swaying walk, like someone carried on a great wave of exultation. Her eyes were shining, her color high. She looked like a figure of joy on a frieze. There was no hesitation about her, no doubt or tremors. Straight to Mr. Satterthwaite she came, put her hands on his shoulders and kissed him—not once but many times. Large, dark, red roses, very velvety—that is how he thought of it afterward. Sunshine, Summer, birds singing—that was the atmosphere into which he felt himself caught up. Warmth, joy and tremendous vigor.

"I'm so happy," she said. "You darling! How did you know? How *could* you know? You're like the good magician in the fairy tales."

She paused, a sort of breathlessness of happiness upon her.

"We're going over today—to the Consul—to get married. When John comes, his father will be here. We'll tell him there was some misunderstanding in the past. Oh! he won't ask questions. Oh! I'm so happy—so happy—so happy."

Happiness did indeed surge from her like a tide. It lapped round Mr. Satterthwaite in a warm exhilarating flood.

"It's so wonderful to Anthony to find he has a son. I never dreamed he'd mind or care." She looked confidently into Mr. Satterthwaite's eyes. "Isn't it strange how things come right and end all beautifully?"

He had his clearest vision of her yet. A child—still a child—with her love of make believe—her fairy tales that ended beautifully with two people "living happily ever afterward."

He said gently:

"If you bring this man of yours happiness in these last months, you will indeed have done a very beautiful thing."

Her eyes opened wide—surprised.

"Oh!" she said. "You don't think I'd let him die, do you? After all these years—when he's come to me. I've known lots of people whom doctors have given up and who are alive today. Die? Of course he's not going to die!"

He looked at her—her strength, her beauty, her vitality—her indomitable courage and will. He too had known doctors to be mistaken. The personal factor—you never knew how much and how little it counted.

She said again, with scorn and amusement in her voice:

"You don't think I'd let him die, do you?"

"No," said Mr. Satterthwaite at last very gently. "Somehow, my dear, I don't think you will."

Then, at last, he walked down the cypress path to the bench overlooking the sea and found there the person he was expecting to see. Mr. Quin rose and greeted him—the same as ever, dark, saturnine, smiling and sad.

"You expected me?" he asked.

And Mr. Satterthwaite answered, "Yes, I expected you."

They sat together on the bench.

"I have an idea that you have been playing Providence once more to judge by your expression," said Mr. Quin presently.

Mr. Satterthwaite looked at him reproachfully.

"As if you didn't know all about it."

"You always accuse me of omniscience," said Mr. Quin, smiling.

"If you know nothing, why were you here the night before last—waiting?" countered Mr. Satterthwaite.

"Oh! that—"

"Yes, that."

"I had a—commission to perform."

"For whom?"

"You have sometimes fancifully named me an advocate for the dead."

"The dead," said Mr. Satterthwaite, a little puzzled. "I don't understand."

Mr. Quin pointed a long lean finger down at the blue depths below.

"A man was drowned down there twenty-two years ago."

"I know—but I don't see—"

"Supposing that, after all, that man loved his young wife. Love can make devils of men as well as angels. She had a girlish adoration for him, but he could never touch the womanhood in her—and that drove him mad. He tortured her because he loved her. Such things happen. You know that as well as I do."

"Yes," admitted Mr. Satterthwaite. "I have seen such things—but rarely—very rarely."

"And you have also seen, more commonly, that there is such a thing as remorse—the desire to make amends—at all costs to make amends."

"Yes, but death came too soon."

"Death!" There was contempt in Mr. Quin's voice. "You believe in a life after death, do you not? And who are you to say that the same wishes, the same desires, may not operate in that other life? If the desire is strong enough—a messenger may be found."

His voice trailed away.

Mr. Satterthwaite got up, trembling a little.

"I must get back to the hotel," he said. "If you are going that way—"

But Mr. Quin shook his head.

"No," he said. "I shall go back the way I came."

When Mr. Satterthwaite looked back over his shoulder, he saw his friend walking toward the edge of the cliff.

12. HARLEQUIN'S LANE

Mr. Satterthwaite was never quite sure what took him to stay with the Denmans. They were not of his kind—that is to say, they belonged neither to the great world, nor to the more interesting artistic circles. They were Philistines, and dull Philistines at that. Mr. Satterthwaite had met them first at Biarritz, had accepted an invitation to stay with them, had come, had been bored, and yet strangely enough had come again and yet again.

Why? He was asking himself that question on this twenty-first of June, as he sped out of London in his Rolls Royce.

John Denman was a man of forty, a solid well-established figure, respected in the business world. His friends were not Mr. Satterthwaite's friends, his ideas even less so. He was a man clever in his own line but devoid of imagination outside it.

"Why am I doing this thing?" Mr. Satterthwaite asked himself once more—and the only answer that came seemed to him so vague and so inherently preposterous that he almost put it aside. For the only reason that presented itself was the fact that one of the rooms in the house (a comfortable well-appointed house), stirred his curiosity. That room was Mrs. Denman's own sitting room.

It was hardly an expression of her personality because, so far as Mr. Satterthwaite could judge, she had no personality. He had never met a woman so completely expressionless. She was, he knew, a Russian by birth. John Denman had been in Russia at the outbreak of the European War; he had fought with the Russian troops, had narrowly escaped with his life on the outbreak of the revolution, and had brought this Russian girl with him, a penniless refugee. In face of strong disapproval from his parents he had married her.

Mrs. Denman's room was in no way remarkable. It was well and solidly furnished with good Hepplewhite furniture—a trifle more masculine than feminine in atmosphere. But in it there was one incongruous item: a Chinese lacquer screen—a thing of creamy yellow and pale rose. Any museum might have been glad to own it. It was a collector's piece, rare and beautiful.

It was out of place against that solid English background. It should have been the keynote of the room with everything arranged to harmonize subtly with it. And yet Mr. Satterthwaite could not accuse the Denmans of lack of taste. Everything else in the house was in perfectly blended accord.

He shook his head. The thing, trivial though it was—puzzled him. Because of it, so he verily believed, he had come again and again to the house. It was, perhaps, a woman's fantasy—but that solution did not satisfy him as he thought of Mrs. Denman—a quiet hard featured woman, speaking English so correctly that no one would ever have guessed her a foreigner.

The car drew up at his destination and he got out, his mind still dwelling on the problem of the Chinese screen. The name of the Denmans' house was Ashmead, and it occupied some five acres of Melton Heath, which is thirty miles from London, stands five hundred feet above sea level and is, for the most part, inhabited by those who have ample incomes.

The butler received Mr. Satterthwaite suavely. Mr. and Mrs. Denman were both out—at a rehearsal—they hoped Mr. Satterthwaite would make himself at home until they returned.

Mr. Satterthwaite nodded and proceeded to carry out these injunctions by stepping into the garden. After a cursory examination of the flower beds, he strolled down a shady walk and presently came to a door in the wall. It was unlocked and he passed through it and came out into a narrow lane.

Mr. Satterthwaite looked to left and right. A very charming lane, shady and green, with high hedges—a rural lane that twisted and turned in good old-fashioned style. He remembered the stamped address: ASHMEAD, HARLEQUIN'S LANE—remembered too, a local name for it that Mrs. Denman had once told him.

"Harlequin's Lane," he murmured to himself softly. "I wonder—"

He turned a corner.

Not at the time, but afterward, he wondered why this time he felt no surprise at meeting that elusive friend of his: Mr. Harley Quin. The two men clasped hands.

"So *you're* down here," said Mr. Satterthwaite.

"Yes," said Mr. Quin. "I'm staying in the same house as you are."

"Staying there?"

"Yes. Does it surprise you?"

"No," said Mr. Satterthwaite slowly. "Only—well, you never stay anywhere for long, do you?"

"Only as long as is necessary," said Mr. Quin gravely.

"I see," said Mr. Satterthwaite.

They walked on in silence for some minutes.

"This lane," began Mr. Satterthwaite, and stopped.

"Belongs to me," said Mr. Quin.

"I thought it did," said Mr. Satterthwaite. "Somehow, I thought it must. There's the other name for it, too, the local name. They call it the 'Lovers' Lane' You know that?"

Mr. Quin nodded.

"But surely" he said gently, "there is a 'Lovers Lane' in every village."

"I suppose so," said Mr. Satterthwaite, and he sighed a little.

He felt suddenly rather old and out of things, a little dried up wizen old fogey of a man. Each side of him were the hedges, very green and alive.

"Where does this lane end, I wonder?" he asked suddenly.

"It ends—*here*," said Mr. Quin.

They came round a last bend. The lane ended in a piece of waste ground, and almost at their feet a great pit opened. In it were tin cans gleaming in the sun, and other cans that were too red with rust to gleam, old boots, fragments of newspapers, a hundred and one odds and ends that were no longer of account to anybody.

"A rubbish heap," exclaimed Mr. Satterthwaite, and breathed deeply and indignantly.

"Sometimes there are very wonderful things on a rubbish heap," said Mr. Quin.

"I know, I know," cried Mr. Satterthwaite, and quoted with just a trace of self-consciousness: "'Bring the the two most beautiful things in the city, said God.' You know how it goes, eh?"

Mr. Quin nodded.

Mr. Satterthwaite looked up at the ruins of a small cottage perched on the brink of the wall of cliff.

"Hardly a pretty view for a house," he remarked.

"I fancy this wasn't a rubbish heap in those days," said Mr. Quin. "I believe the Denmans lived there when they were first married. They moved into the big house when the old people died. The cottage was pulled down when they began to quarry the rock here—but nothing much was done, as you can see."

They turned and began retracing their steps.

"I suppose," said Mr. Satterthwaite, smiling, "that many couples come wandering down this lane on these warm summer evenings."

"Probably."

"Lovers," said Mr. Satterthwaite. He repeated the word thoughtfully and quite without the normal embarrassment of the Englishman. Mr. Quin had that effect upon him. "Lovers. You have done a lot for lovers, Mr. Quin."

The other bowed his head without replying.

"You have saved them from sorrow—from worse than sorrow, from death. You have been an advocate for the dead themselves."

"You are speaking of yourself—of what *you* have done—not of me."

"It is the same thing," said Mr. Satterthwaite. "You know it is," he urged, as the other did not speak. "You have acted—through me. For some reason or other you do not act directly—yourself."

"Sometimes I do," said Mr. Quin.

His voice held a new note. In spite of himself Mr. Satterthwaite shivered a little. The afternoon, he thought, must be growing chilly. And yet the sun seemed as bright as ever.

At that moment a girl turned the corner ahead of them and came into sight. She was a very pretty girl, fair haired and blue eyed, wearing a pink cotton frock. Mr. Satterthwaite recognized her as Molly Stanwell whom he had met down here before.

She waved a hand in welcome to him.

"John and Anna have just gone back," she cried. "They thought you must have come, but they simply had to be at the rehearsal."

"Rehearsal of what?" inquired Mr. Satterthwaite.

"This masquerade thing—I don't quite know what you'd call it. There is singing and dancing and all sorts of things in it. Mr. Manly (do you remember him down here?), he has quite a good tenor voice, is to be Pierrot, and I am Pierrette. Two professionals are coming down for the dancing—Harlequin and Columbine, you know. And then there is a-big chorus of girls. Lady Roscheimer is so keen on training village girls to sing. She's really getting the thing up for that. The music is rather lovely—but very modern—next to no tune anywhere. Claude Wickam. Perhaps you know him?"

Mr. Satterthwaite nodded, for, as has been mentioned before, it was his *métier* to know everybody. He knew about that aspiring genius Claude Wickam, and about Lady Roscheimer, who was fat and had a *penchant* for young men of the artistic persuasion. And he knew all about Sir Leopold Roscheimer who liked his wife to be happy and, most rare among husbands, did not mind her being happy in her own way.

They found Claude Wickam at tea with the Denmans, cramming his mouth indiscriminately with anything handy, talking rapidly, and waving long white hands that had a double-jointed appearance. His short-sighted eyes peered through large horn rimmed spectacles.

John Denman, upright, slightly florid with the faintest possible tendency to sleekness, listened with an air of bored attention. On the appearance of Mr. Satterthwaite, the musician transferred his remarks to him. Anna Denman sat behind the tea things, quiet and expressionless as usual.

Mr. Satterthwaite stole a covert glance at her. Tall, gaunt, very thin, with the skin tightly stretched over high cheek bones, black hair parted in the middle, a skin that was weather beaten. An out of door woman who cared nothing for the use of cosmetics. A Dutch Doll of a woman, wooden, lifeless—and yet—

He thought: "There *should* be meaning behind that face, and yet there isn't. That's what's all wrong. Yes, all wrong." And to Claude Wickam he said: "I beg your pardon? You were saying?"

Claude Wickam, who liked the sound of his own voice, began all over again. Russia, he said, that was the only country in the world worth being interested in. They experimented. With lives, if you like, but still they experimented. "Magnificent!" He crammed a sandwich into his mouth with one hand, and added a bite of the chocolate éclair he was waving about in the other. "Take," he said (with his mouthful), "the Russian Ballet." Remembering his hostess, he turned to her. What did *she* think of the Russian Ballet?

The question was obviously only a prelude to the important point—what Claude Wickam thought of the Russian Ballet—but her answer was unexpected and threw him completely out of his stride.

"I have never seen it."

"What?" He gazed at her open mouthed. "But—surely—"

Her voice went on level and emotionless.

"Before my marriage, I was a dancer. So now—"

"A busman's holiday," said her husband.

"Dancing." She shrugged her shoulders. "I know all the tricks of it. It does not interest me."

"Oh!"

It took but a moment for Claude to recover his aplomb. His voice went on.

"Talking of lives," said Mr. Satterthwaite, "and experimenting in them, the Russian nation made one costly experiment."

Claude Wickam swung round on him.

"I know what you are going to say," he cried. "Kharsanova! The immortal, the only Kharsanova! You saw her dance?"

"Three times," said Mr. Satterthwaite. "Twice in Paris, once in London. I shall—not forget it."

He spoke in an almost reverent voice.

"I saw her too," said Claude Wickam. "I was ten years old. An uncle took me. God! I shall never forget it."

He threw a piece of bun fiercely into a flower bed.

"There is a statuette of her in a museum in Berlin," said Mr. Satterthwaite. "It is marvelous. That impression of fragility—as though you could break her with a flip of the thumb nail. I have seen her as Columbine, in the Swan, as the dying Nymph." He paused, shaking his head. "There was genius. It will be long years before such another is born. She was young too. Destroyed ignorantly and wantonly in the first days of the Revolution."

"Fools! Madmen! Apes!" said Claude Wickam. He choked with a mouthful of tea.

"I studied with Kharsanova," said Mrs. Denman. "I remember her well."

"She was wonderful?" said Mr. Satterthwaite.

"Yes," said Mrs. Denman quietly. "She was wonderful."

Claude Wickam departed, and John Denman drew a deep sigh of relief, at which his wife laughed.

Mr. Satterthwaite nodded. "I know what you think. But in spite of everything, the music that that boy writes *is* music."

"I suppose it is," said Denman.

"Oh! undoubtedly. How long it will be—well, that is different."

John Denman looked at him curiously.

"You mean?"

"I mean that success has come early. And that is dangerous. Always dangerous." He looked across at Mr. Quin. "You agree with me?"

"You are always right," said Mr. Quin.

"We will come upstairs to my room," said Mrs. Denman. "It is pleasant there."

She led the way, and they followed her. Mr. Satterthwaite drew a deep breath as he caught sight of the Chinese screen. He looked up to find Mrs. Denman watching him.

"You are the man who is always right," she said, nodding her head slowly at him. "What do you make of my screen?"

He felt that in some way the words were a challenge to him, and he answered almost haltingly, stumbling over the words a little.

"Why, it's—it's beautiful. More, it's unique."

"You're right." Denman had come up behind him. "We bought it early in our married life. Got it for about a tenth of its value, but even then—well, it crippled us for over a year. You remember, Anna?"

"Yes," said Mrs. Denman, "I remember."

"In fact, we'd no business to buy it at all—not then. Now, of course, it's different. There was some very good lacquer going at Christie's the other day. Just what we need to make this room perfect. All Chinese together. Clear out the other stuff. Would you believe it, Satterthwaite, my wife wouldn't hear of it?"

"I like this room as it is," said Mrs. Denman.

There was a curious look on her face. Again Mr. Satterthwaite felt challenged and defeated. He looked round him, and for the first time he noticed the absence of all personal touch. There were no photographs, no flowers, no nicknacks. It was not like a woman's room at all. Save for that one incongruous factor of the Chinese screen, it might have been a sample room shown at some big furnishing house.

He found her smiling at him.

"Listen," she said. She bent forward, and for a moment she seemed less English, more definitely foreign. "I speak to you, for you will understand. We bought that screen with more than money— with love. For love of it, because it was beautiful and unique, we went without other things, things we needed and missed. These other Chinese pieces my husband speaks of, those we should buy with money only, we should not pay away anything of ourselves."

Her husband laughed.

"Oh! have it your own way," he said, but with a trace of irritation in his voice. "But it's all wrong against this English background. This other stuff, it's good enough of its kind, genuine solid, no fake about it—but mediocre. Good plain late Hepplewhite."

She nodded.

"Good, solid, genuine English," she murmured softly.

Mr. Satterthwaite stared at her. He caught a meaning behind these words. The English room—the flaming beauty of the Chinese screen—No, it was gone again.

"I met Miss Stanwell in the lane," he said conversationally. "She tells me she is going to be Pierrette in this show tonight."

"Yes," said Denman. "And she's awfully good, too."

"She has clumsy feet," said Anna.

"Nonsense," said her husband. "All women are alike, Satterthwaite. Can't bear to hear another women praised. Molly is a very good-looking girl, and so of course every woman has to have their knife into her."

"I spoke of dancing," said Anna Denman. She sounded faintly surprised. "She is very pretty, yes, but her feet move clumsily. You cannot tell me anything else, because I know about dancing."

Mr. Satterthwaite intervened tactfully.

"You have two professional dancers coming down, I understand?"

"Yes. For the ballet proper. Prince Oranoff is bringing them down in his car."

"Sergius Oranoff?"

The question came from Anna Denman. Her husband turned and looked at her.

"You know him?"

"I used to know him—in Russia."

Mr. Satterthwaite thought that John Denman looked disturbed.

"Will he know you?"

"Yes. He will know me."

She laughed—a low almost triumphant laugh. There was nothing of the Dutch Doll about her face now. She nodded reassuringly at her husband.

"Serge. So he is bringing down the two dancers. He was always interested in dancing."

"I remember."

John Denman spoke abruptly, then turned and left the room. Mr. Quin followed him. Anna Denman crossed to the telephone and asked for a number. She arrested Mr. Satterthwaite with a gesture as he was about to follow the example of the other two men.

"Can I speak to Lady Roscheimer? Oh! it is you. This is Anna Denman speaking. Has Prince Oranoff arrived yet? What? *What?* Oh! my dear! But how ghastly."

She listened for a few moments longer, then replaced the receiver. She turned to Mr. Satterthwaite.

"There has been an accident. There would be with Sergius Ivanovitch driving. Oh! he has not altered in all these years. The girl was not badly hurt, but bruised and shaken, too much to dance tonight. The man's arm is broken. Serge Ivanovitch himself is unhurt. The devil looks after his own, perhaps."

"And what about tonight's performance?"

"Exactly, my friend. Something must be done about it."

She sat thinking. Presently she looked at him.

"I am a bad hostess, Mr. Satterthwaite. I do not entertain you."

"I assure you that it is not necessary. There's one thing though, Mrs. Denman, that I would very much like to know."

"Yes?"

"How did you come across Mr. Quin?"

"He is often down here," she said slowly. "I think he owns land in this part of the world."

"He does, he does. He told me so this afternoon," said Mr. Satterthwaite.

"He is—" she paused. Her eyes met Mr. Satterthwaite's. "I think you know what he is better than I do," she finished.

"I?"

"Is it not so?"

He was troubled. His neat little soul found her disturbing. He felt that she wished to force him further than he was prepared to go, that she wanted him to put into words that which he was not prepared to admit to himself.

"*You* know!" she said. "I think you know most things, Mr. Satterthwaite."

Here was incense, yet for once it failed to intoxicate him. He shook his head in unwonted humility.

"What can anyone know?" he asked. "So little—so very little."

She nodded in assent. Presently she spoke again, in a queer brooding voice, without looking at him.

"Supposing I were to tell you something—you would not laugh? No, I do not think you would laugh. Supposing, then, that to carry on one's"—she paused—"one's trade, one's profession, one were to make use of a fantasy—one were to pretend to oneself something that did not exist—that one were to imagine a certain person. It is a pretense, you understand, a make believe—nothing more. But one day—"

"Yes?" said Mr. Satterthwaite.

He was keenly interested.

"The fantasy came true! The thing one imagined—the impossible thing, the thing that could not be—was real! Is that madness? Tell me, Mr. Satterthwaite. Is that madness—or do you believe it too?"

"I—" Queer how he could not get the words put. How they seemed to stick somewhere at the back of his throat.

"Folly," said Anna Denman. "Folly."

She swept out of the room and left Mr. Satterthwaite with his confession of faith unspoken.

He came down to dinner to find Mrs. Denman entertaining a guest, a tall dark man approaching middle age.

"Prince Oranoff—Mr. Satterthwaite."

The two men bowed. Mr. Satterthwaite had the feeling that some conversation had been broken off on his entry which would not be resumed. But there was no sense of strain. The Russian conversed easily and naturally on those subjects which were nearest to Mr. Satterthwaite's heart. He was a man of very fine artistic taste, and they soon found that they had many friends in common. John Denman joined them, and the talk became localized. Oranoff expressed regret for the accident.

"It was not my fault. I like to drive fast—yes, but I am a good driver. It was Fate—chance—" he shrugged his shoulders—"the masters of all of us."

"There speaks the Russian in you, Sergius Ivanovitch," said Mrs. Denman.

"And finds an echo in you, Anna Mikalovna," he threw back quickly.

Mr. Satterthwaite looked from one to the other of the three of them. John Denman, fair, aloof, English, and the other two, dark, thin, strangely alike. Something rose in his mind—what was it? Ah! he had it now. The first act of the Walkure. Siegmund and Sieglinde—so alike—and the alien Hunding. Conjectures began to stir in his brain. Was this the meaning of the presence of Mr. Quin? One thing he believed in firmly—wherever Mr. Quin showed himself—there lay drama. Was this it here—the old hackneyed three cornered tragedy?

He was vaguely disappointed? He had hoped for better things.

"What's been arranged, Anna?" asked Denman. "The thing will have to be put off, I suppose. I heard you ringing the Roscheimers up."

She shook her head.

"No—there is no need to put it off."

"But you can't do it without the ballet?"

"You certainly couldn't have a Harlequinade without Harlequin and Columbine," agreed Anna Denman dryly. "I'm going to be Columbine, John."

"You?" He was astonished—disturbed, Mr. Satterthwaite thought.

She nodded composedly.

"You need not be afraid, John. I shall not disgrace you. You forget—it was my profession once."

Mr. Satterthwaite thought: "What an extraordinary thing a voice is. The things it says—and the things it leaves unsaid and means! I wish I knew—"

"Well," said John Denman grudgingly. "That solves one half of the problem. What about the other? Where will you find Harlequin?"

"I *have* found him—there!"

She gestured toward the open doorway where Mr. Quin had just appeared. He smiled back at her.

"Good Lord, Quin," said John Denman. "Do you know anything of this game? I should never have imagined it."

"Mr. Quin is vouched for by an expert," said his wife. "Mr. Satterthwaite will answer for him."

She smiled at Mr. Satterthwaite, and the little man found himself murmuring:

"Oh! yes, I—I answer for Mr. Quin."

Denman turned his attention elsewhere.

"You know there's to be a fancy dress dance business afterward. Great nuisance. We'll have to rig you up, Satterthwaite."

Mr. Satterthwaite shook his head very decidedly.

"My years will excuse me." A brilliant idea struck him. "A table napkin under the arm. There I am, an elderly waiter who has seen better days."

He laughed.

"An interesting profession," said Mr. Quin. "One sees so much."

"I've got to put on some fool Pierrot thing," said Denman gloomily. "It's cool anyway, that's one thing. What about you?" He looked at Oranoff.

"I have a Harlequin costume," said the Russian. His eyes wandered for a minute to his hostess's face.

Mr. Satterthwaite wondered if he was mistaken in fancying that there was just a moment of constraint.

"There might have been three of us," said Denman, with a laugh. "I've got an old Harlequin costume my wife made me when we were first married for some show or other." He paused, looking down on his broad shirt front. "I don't suppose I could get into it now."

"No," said his wife, "you couldn't get into it now."

And again her voice said something more than mere words.

She glanced up at the clock.

"If Molly doesn't turn up soon, we won't wait for her."

But at that moment the girl was announced. She was already wearing her Pierrette dress of white and green, and very charming she looked in it, so Mr. Satterthwaite reflected.

She was full of excitement and enthusiasm over the forthcoming performance.

"I'm getting awfully nervous, though," she announced, as they drank coffee after dinner. "I know my voice will wobble, and I shall forget the words."

"Your voice is very charming," said Anna. "I should not worry about it if I were you."

"Oh! but I do. The other I don't mind about—the dancing, I mean. That's sure to go all right. I mean, you can't go very far wrong with your feet, can you?"

She appealed to Anna, but the older woman did not respond. Instead she said:

"Sing something now to Mr. Satterthwaite. You will find that he will reassure you."

Molly went over to the piano. Her voice rang out, fresh and tuneful in an old Irish ballad.

"Sheila, dark Sheila, what is it that you're seeing?
What is it that you're seeing, that you're seeing in the fire?
'I see a lad that loves me—and I see a lad that leaves me and
a third lad, a Shadow Lad—and he's the lad that grieves
me.'"

The song went on. At the end, Mr. Satterthwaite nodded vigorous approval.

"Mrs. Denman is right. Your voice is charming. Not, perhaps, very fully trained, but delightfully natural, and with that unstudied quality of youth in it."

"That's right," agreed John Denman. "You go ahead, Molly, and don't be downed by stage fright. We'd better be getting over to the Roscheimers' now."

The party separated to don cloaks. It was a glorious night and they proposed to walk over, the house being only a few hundred yards down the road.

Mr. Satterthwaite found himself by his friend.

"It's an odd thing," he said, "but that song made me think of you.

*A third lad—a Shadow Lad—*there's mystery there, and wherever there's mystery I—well, think of you."

"Am I so mysterious?" smiled Mr. Quin.

Mr. Satterthwaite nodded vigorously.

"Yes, indeed. Do you know, until tonight, I had no idea that you were a professional dancer."

"Really?" said Mr. Quin.

"Listen," said Mr. Satterthwaite. He hummed the love motif from the Walkure. "That is what has been ringing in my head all through dinner as I looked at those two."

"Which two?"

"Prince Oranoff and Mrs. Denman. Don't you see the difference in her tonight? It's as though—as though a shutter had suddenly been opened and you see the glow within."

"Yes," said Mr. Quin. "Perhaps so."

"The same old drama," said Mr. Satterthwaite. "I am right, am I not? Those two belong together. They are of the same world, think the same thoughts, dream the same dreams. One sees how it has come about. Ten years ago Denman must have been very good-looking, young, dashing, a figure of romance. And he saved her life. All quite natural. But now—what is he, after all? A good fellow—prosperous, successful—but—well, mediocre. Good honest English stuff—very much like that Hepplewhite furniture upstairs. As English—and as ordinary—as that pretty English girl with her fresh untrained voice. Oh! you may smile, Mr. Quin, but you cannot deny what I am saying."

"I deny nothing. In what you see you are always right. And yet—"

"Yet what?"

Mr. Quin leaned forward. His dark melancholy eyes searched those of Mr. Satterthwaite.

"Have you learned so little of life?" he breathed.

He left Mr. Satterthwaite vaguely disquieted, such a prey to meditation that he found the others had started without him, owing to his delay in selecting a scarf for his neck. He went out by the garden, and through the same door as in the afternoon. The lane was bathed in moonlight, and even as he stood in the doorway, he saw a couple enlaced in each other's arms.

For a moment he thought—

And then he saw. *John Denman and Molly Stanwell.* Denman's voice came to him, hoarse and anguished.

"I can't live without you. What are we to do?"

Mr. Satterthwaite turned to go back the way he had come, but a hand stayed him. Someone else stood in the doorway beside him, someone else whose eyes had also seen.

Mr. Satterthwaite had only to catch one glimpse of her face to know how wildly astray all his conclusions had been.

Her anguished hand held him there until those other two had passed up the lane and disappeared from sight. He heard himself speaking to her, saying foolish little things meant to be comforting, and ludicrously inadequate to the agony he had divined. She only spoke once.

"Please," she said, "don't leave me."

He found that oddly touching. He was, then, of use to someone. And he went on saying those things that meant nothing at all, but which were, somehow, better than silence. They went that way to the Roscheimers'. Now and then her hand tightened on his shoulder, and he understood that she was glad of his company. She only took it away when they finally came to their destination. She stood very erect, her head held high.

"Now," she said, "I shall dance! Do not be afraid for me, my friend. I shall dance."

She left him abruptly. He was seized upon by Lady Roscheimer, much bediamonded and very full of lamentations. By her he was passed on to Claude Wickam.

"Ruined! Completely ruined. The sort of thing that always happens to me. All these country bumpkins think they can dance. I was never even consulted—"

His voice went on—went on interminably. He had found a sympathetic listener, a man who *knew.* He gave himself up to an orgy of self-pity. It only ended when the first strains of music began.

Mr. Satterthwaite came out of his dream. He was alert once more, the critic. Wickam was an unutterable ass, but he could write music—delicate gossamer stuff, intangible as a fairy web—yet with nothing of the pretty pretty about it.

The scenery was good. Lady Roscheimer never spared expense when aiding her protégées. A glade of Arcady with lighting effects that gave it the proper atmosphere of unreality.

Two figures dancing as they had danced through time immemorial. A slender Harlequin flashing spangles in the moonlight with magic wand and masked face, a white Columbine pirouetting like some immortal dream—

Mr. Satterthwaite sat up. He had lived through this before. Yes, surely—

Now his body was far away from Lady Roscheimer's drawing room. It was in a Berlin Museum gazing it a statuette of an immortal Columbine.

Harlequin and Columbine danced on. The wide world was theirs to dance in.

Moonlight—and a human figure. Pierrot wandering through the wood, singing to the moon. Pierrot who has seen Columbine and knows no rest. The immortal two vanish, but Columbine looks back. She has heard the song of a human heart.

Pierrot wandering on through the wood—darkness—his voice dies away in the distance.

The village green—dancing of village girls—pierrots and pierrettes. Molly as Pierrette. No dancer—Anna Denman was right there—but a fresh tuneful voice as she sings her song, "Pierrette dancing on the green."

A good tune—Mr. Satterthwaite nodded approval. Wickam wasn't above writing a tune when there was need for it. The majority of the village girls made him shudder, but he realized that Lady Roscheimer was determinedly philanthropical.

They press Pierrot to join the dance. He refuses. With white face he wanders on—the eternal lover seeking his ideal. Evening falls. Harlequin and Columbine, invisible, dance in and out of the unconscious throng. The place is deserted, only Pierrot, weary, falls asleep on a grassy bank. Harlequin and Columbine dance round him. He

wakes and sees Columbine. He woos her in vain, pleads, beseeches—
She stands uncertain. Harlequin beckons to her to begone. But
she sees him no longer. She is listening to Pierrot, to his song of love
outpoured once more. She falls into his arms, and the curtain
comes down.

The second act is Pierrot's cottage. Columbine sits on his
hearth. She is pale, weary. She listens—for what? Pierrot sings to
her—woos her back to thoughts of him once more. The evening
darkens. Thunder is heard. Columbine puts aside her spinning
wheel. She is eager, stirred. She listens no longer to Pierrot. It is her
own music that is in the air, the music of Harlequin and Columbine.
She is awake. She remembers.

A crash of thunder! Harlequin stands in the doorway. Pierrot
cannot see him, but Columbine springs up with a glad laugh. Children come running, but she pushes them aside. With another crash
of thunder the walls fall, and Columbine dances out into the wild
night with Harlequin.

Darkness, and through it the tune that Pierrette has sung. Light
comes slowly. The cottage once more. Pierrot and Pierrette grown
old and gray sit in front of the fire in two armchairs. The music is
happy, but subdued. Pierrette nods in her chair. Through the window comes a shaft of moonlight, and with it the motif of Pierrot's
long forgotten song. He stirs in his chair.

Faint music—fairy music—Harlequin and Columbine outside.
The door swings open and Columbine dances in. She leans over the
sleeping Pierrot, kisses him on the lips.

Crash! A peal of thunder. She is outside again. In the center of
the stage is the lighted window and through it are seen the two figures of Harlequin and Columbine dancing slowly away, growing
fainter and fainter . . .

A log falls. Pierrette jumps up angrily, rushes across to the window and pulls the blind. So it ends, on a sudden discord.

Mr. Satterthwaite sat very still among the applause and vocifer-
ations. At last he got up and made his way outside. He came upon
Molly Stanwell, flushed and eager, receiving compliments. He saw

John Denman, pushing and elbowing his way through the throng, his eyes alight with a new flame. Molly came toward him, but, almost unconsciously, he put her aside. It was not her he was seeking.

"My wife? Where is she?"

"I think she went out in the garden."

It was, however, Mr. Satterthwaite who found her, sitting on a stone seat under a cypress tree. When he came up to her, he did an odd thing. He knelt down and raised her hand to his lips.

"Ah!" she said. "You think I danced well?"

"You danced—as you always danced, Madame Kharsanova."

She drew in her breath sharply.

"So—you have guessed."

"There is only one Kharsanova. No one could see you dance and forget. But why—why?"

"What else was possible?"

"You mean?"

She had spoken very simply. She was just as simple now.

"Oh! but you understand. You are of the world. A great dancer—she can have lovers, yes—but a husband, that is different. And he—he did not want the other. He wanted me to belong to him as—as Kharsanova could never have belonged."

"I see," said Mr. Satterthwaite. "I see. So you gave it up?"

She nodded.

"You must have loved him very much," said Mr. Satterthwaite gently.

"To make such a sacrifice?" She laughed.

"Not quite that. To make it so light-heartedly."

"Ah! yes—perhaps—you are right."

"And now?" asked Mr. Satterthwaite.

Her face grew grave.

"Now?" She paused, then raised her voice and spoke into the shadows.

"Is that you, Sergius Ivanovitch?"

Prince Oranoff came out into the moonlight. He took her hand and smiled at Mr. Satterthwaite without self-consciousness.

"Ten years ago I mourned the death of Anna Kharsanova," he said simply. "She was to me as my other self. Today I have found her again. We shall part no more."

"At the end of the lane in ten minutes," said Anna. "I shall not fail you."

Oranoff nodded and went off again. The dancer turned to Mr. Satterthwaite. A smile played about her lips.

"Well—you are not satisfied, my friend?"

"Do you know," said Mr. Satterthwaite abruptly, "that your husband is looking for you?"

He saw the tremor that passed over her face, but her voice was steady enough.

"Yes," she said gravely. "That may well be."

"I saw his eyes. They—" he stopped abruptly.

She was still calm.

"Yes, perhaps. For an hour. An hour's magic, born of past memories, of music, of moonlight. That is all."

"Then there is nothing that I can say?" He felt old, dispirited.

"For ten years I have lived with the man I love," said Anna Kharsanova. "Now I am going to the man who for ten years has loved me."

Mr. Satterthwaite said nothing. He had no arguments left. Besides it really seemed the simplest solution. Only—

Only, somehow, it was not the solution he wanted. He felt her hand on his shoulder.

"I know, my friend, I know. But there is no third way. Always one looks for one thing—the lover, the perfect, the eternal lover. It is the music of Harlequin one hears. No lover ever satisfies one, for all lovers are mortal. And Harlequin is only a myth, an invisible presence—unless—"

"Yes," said Mr. Satterthwaite. "Yes?"

"Unless—his name is—Death!"

Mr. Satterthwaite shivered. She moved away from him, was swallowed up in the shadows.

He never knew quite how long he sat on there, but suddenly he started up with the feeling that he had been wasting valuable time. He hurried away, impelled in a certain direction almost in spite of himself.

As he came out into the lane, he had a strange feeling of unreality. Magic—magic and moonlight. And two figures coming toward him.

Oranoff in his Harlequin dress. So he thought at first. Then as they passed him he knew his mistake. That lithe swaying figure belonged to one person only—Mr. Quin.

They went on down the lane—their feet light as though they were treading on air. Mr. Quin turned his head and looked back, and Mr. Satterthwaite had a shock, for it was not the face of Mr. Quin as he had ever seen it before. It was the face of a stranger—no, not quite a stranger. Ah! he had it now, it was the face of John Denman as it might have looked before life went too well with him! Eager, adventurous, the face at once of a boy and of a lover.

Her laugh floated down to him, clear and happy. . . . He looked after them and saw in the distance the lights of a little cottage. He gazed after them like a man in a dream.

He was rudely awakened by a hand that fell on his shoulder and he was jerked round to face Sergius Oranoff. The man looked white and distracted.

"Where is she? Where is she? She promised—and she has not come."

"Madame has just gone up the lane—alone."

It was Mrs. Denman's maid who spoke from the shadow of the door behind them. She had been waiting with her mistress's wraps.

"I was standing here and saw her pass," she added.

Mr. Satterthwaite threw one harsh word at her.

"Alone? Alone, did you say?"

The maid's eyes widened in surprise,

"Yes, sir. Didn't you see her?"

Mr. Satterthwaite clutched at Oranoff.

"Quickly," he muttered. "I'm—I'm afraid."

They hurried down the lane together, the Russian talking in quick disjointed sentences.

"She is a wonderful creature. Ah! how she danced tonight. And that friend of yours. Who is he? Ah! but he is wonderful—unique. In the old days, when she danced the Columbine of Rimsky Korsakoff, she never found the perfect Harlequin. Mordroff, Kassnine—none of them were quite perfect. She had her own little fancy. She told me of it once. Always she danced with a dream Harlequin—a man who was not really there. It was Harlequin himself, she said, who came to dance with her. It was that fancy of hers that made her Columbine so wonderful."

Mr. Satterthwaite nodded. There was only one thought in his head.

"Hurry," he said. "We must be in time. Oh! we must be in time."

They came round the last corner—came to the deep pit and to something lying in it that had not been there before, the body of a woman lying in a wonderful pose, arms flung wide and head thrown back. A dead face and body that were triumphant and beautiful in the moonlight.

Words came back to Mr. Satterthwaite dimly—Mr. Quin's words:—"*wonderful things on a rubbish heap . . .*" He understood them now.

Oranoff was murmuring broken phrases. The tears were streaming down his face.

"I loved her. Always I loved her." He used almost the same words that had occurred to Mr. Satterthwaite earlier in the day. "We were of the same world, she and I. We had the same thoughts, the same dreams. I would have loved her always—"

"How do you know?"

The Russian stared at him—at the fretful peevishness of the tone.

"How do you know?" went on Mr. Satterthwaite. "It is what all lovers think—what all lovers say. There is only one lover—"

He turned and almost ran into Mr. Quin. In an agitated manner, Mr. Satterthwaite caught him by the arm and drew him aside.

"It was *you*," he said. "It was *you* who were with her just now?"

Mr. Quin waited a minute and then said gently, "You can put it that way, if you like."

"And the maid didn't see you?"

"The maid didn't see me."

"But *I* did. Why was that?"

"Perhaps, as a result of the price you have paid, you see things that other people—do not."

Mr. Satterthwaite looked at him uncomprehendingly for a minute or two. Then he began suddenly to quiver all over like an aspen leaf.

"What is this place?" he whispered. "What is this place?"

"I told you earlier today. It is *My* lane."

"A Lovers' Lane," murmured Mr. Satterthwaite. "And people pass along it."

"Most people, sooner or later."

"And at the end of it—what do they find?"

Mr. Quin smiled. His voice was very gentle. He pointed at the ruined cottage above them.

"The house of their dreams—or a rubbish heap—who shall say?"

Mr. Satterthwaite looked up at him suddenly. A wild rebellion surged over him. He felt cheated, defrauded.

"But I—" his voice shook. "*I* have never passed down your lane."

"And do you regret?"

Mr. Satterthwaite quailed. Mr. Quin seemed to have loomed to enormous proportions. Mr. Satterthwaite had a vista of something at once menacing and terrifying. Joy, Sorrow, Despair.

And his comfortable little soul shrank back appalled.

"Do you regret?" Mr. Quin repeated his question. There was something terrible about him.

"No," Mr. Satterthwaite stammered. "N-no."

And then suddenly he rallied.

"But I see things," he cried. "I may have been only a looker on at Life—but I see things that other people do not. You said so yourself, Mr. Quin."

But Mr. Quin had vanished.

13. THE LOVE DETECTIVES

Little Mr. Satterthwaite looked thoughtfully across at his host. The friendship between these two men was an odd one. The colonel was a simple country gentleman whose passion in life was sport. The few weeks that he spent perforce in London, he spent unwillingly. Mr. Satterthwaite, on the other hand, was a town bird. He was an authority on French cooking, on ladies' dress, and on all the latest scandals. His passion was observing human nature, and he was an expert in his own special line—that of an onlooker at life.

It would seem, therefore, that he and Colonel Melrose would have little in common, for the colonel had no interest in his neighbors' affairs and a horror of any kind of emotion. The two men were friends mainly because their fathers before them had been friends. Also they knew the same people and had reactionary views about *nouveaux riches*.

It was about half past seven. The two men were sitting in the colonel's comfortable study, and Melrose was describing a run of the previous winter with a keen hunting man's enthusiasm. Mr. Satterthwaite, whose knowledge of horses consisted chiefly of the time-honored Sunday-morning visit to the stables which still obtains in old-fashioned country houses, listened with his invariable politeness.

The sharp ringing of the telephone interrupted Melrose. He crossed to the table and took up the receiver.

"Hello, yes—Colonel Melrose speaking. What's that?" His whole demeanor altered—became stiff and official. It was the magistrate speaking now, not the sportsman.

He listened for some moments, then said laconically, "Right, Curtis. I'll be over at once." He replaced the receiver and turned to his guest. "Sir James Dwighton has been found in his library—murdered."

"What?"

Mr. Satterthwaite was startled—thrilled.

"I must go over to Alderway at once. Care to come with me?"

Mr. Satterthwaite remembered that the colonel was chief constable of the county.

"If I shan't be in the way—" He hesitated.

"Not at all. That was Inspector Curtis telephoning. Good, honest fellow, but no brains. I'd be glad if you would come with me, Satterthwaite. I've got an idea this is going to turn out a nasty business."

"Have they got the fellow who did it?"

"No," replied Melrose shortly.

Mr. Satterthwaite's trained ear detected a nuance of reserve behind the curt negative. He began to go over in his mind all that he knew of the Dwightons.

A pompous old fellow, the late Sir James, brusque in his manner. A man that might easily make enemies. Veering on sixty, with grizzled hair and a florid face. Reputed to be tightfisted in the extreme.

His mind went on to Lady Dwighton. Her image floated before him, young, auburn-haired, slender. He remembered various rumors, hints, odd bits of gossip. So that was it—that was why Melrose looked so glum. Then he pulled himself up—his imagination was running away with him.

Five minutes later Mr. Satterthwaite took his place beside his host in the latter's little two seater, and they drove off together into the night.

The colonel was a taciturn man. They had gone quite a mile and a half before he spoke. Then he jerked out abruptly. "You know 'em, I suppose?"

"The Dwightons? I know all about them, of course." Who was there Mr. Satterthwaite didn't know all about? "I've met him once, I think, and her rather oftener."

"Pretty woman," said Melrose.

"Beautiful!" declared Mr. Satterthwaite.

"Think so?"

"A pure Renaissance type," declared Mr. Satterthwaite, warming up to his theme. "She acted in those theatricals—the charity matinee, you know, last spring. I was very much struck. Nothing modern about her—a pure survival. One can imagine her in the doge's palace, or as Lucrezia Borgia."

The colonel let the car swerve slightly, and Mr. Satterthwaite came to an abrupt stop. He wondered what fatality had brought the name of Lucrezia Borgia to his tongue. Under the circumstances—

"Dwighton was not poisoned, was he?" he asked abruptly.

Melrose looked at him sideways, somewhat curiously. "Why do you ask that, I wonder?" he said.

"Oh, I—I don't know." Mr. Satterthwaite was flustered. "I—It just occurred to me."

"Well, he wasn't," said Melrose gloomily. "If you want to know, he was crashed on the head."

"With a blunt instrument," murmured Mr. Satterthwaite, nodding his head sagely.

"Don't talk like a damned detective story, Satterthwaite. He was hit on the head with a bronze figure."

"Oh," said Satterthwaite, and relapsed into silence.

"Know anything of a chap called Paul Delangua?" asked Melrose after a minute or two.

"Yes. Good-looking young fellow."

"I daresay women would call him so," growled the colonel.

"You don't like him?"

"No, I don't."

"I should have thought you would have. He rides very well."

"Like a foreigner at the horse show. Full of monkey tricks."

Mr. Satterthwaite suppressed a smile. Poor old Melrose was so very British in his outlook. Agreeably conscious himself of a cosmopolitan point of view, Mr. Satterthwaite was able to deplore the insular attitude toward life.

"Has he been down in this part of the world?" he asked.

"He's been staying at Alderway with the Dwightons. The rumor goes that Sir James kicked him out a week ago."

"Why?"

"Found him making love to his wife, I suppose. What the hell—"

There was a violent swerve, and a jarring impact.

"Most dangerous crossroads in England," said Melrose. "All the same, the other fellow should have sounded his horn. We're on the main road. I fancy we've damaged him rather more than he has damaged us."

He sprang out. A figure alighted from the other car and joined him. Fragments of speech reached Satterthwaite.

"Entirely my fault, I'm afraid," the stranger was saying. "But I do not know this part of the country very well, and there's absolutely no sign of any kind to show you're coming onto the main road."

The colonel, mollified, rejoined suitably. The two men bent together over the stranger's car, which a chauffeur was already examining. The conversation became highly technical.

"A matter of half an hour, I'm afraid," said the stranger. "But don't let me detain you. I'm glad your car escaped injury as well as it did."

"As a matter of fact—" the colonel was beginning, but he was interrupted.

Mr. Satterthwaite, seething with excitement, hopped out of the car with a birdlike action, and seized the stranger warmly by the hand.

"It *is*! I thought I recognized the voice," he declared excitedly. "What an extraordinary thing. What a very extraordinary thing."

"Eh?" said Colonel Melrose.

"Mr. Harley Quin. Melrose, I'm sure you've heard me speak many times of Mr. Quin?"

Colonel Melrose did not seem to remember the fact, but he assisted politely at the scene while Mr. Satterthwaite was chirruping gaily on. "I haven't seen you—let me see—"

"Since the night at the Bells and Motley," said the other quietly.

"The Bells and Motley, eh?" said the colonel.

"An inn," explained Mr. Satterthwaite.

"What an odd name for an inn."

"Only an old one," said Mr. Quin. "There was a time, remember, when bells and motley were more common in England than they are nowadays."

"I suppose so; yes, no doubt you are right," said Melrose vaguely. He blinked. By a curious effect of light—the headlights of one car and the red taillight of the other—Mr. Quin seemed for a moment to be dressed in motley himself. But it was only the light.

"We can't leave you here stranded on the road," continued Mr. Satterthwaite. "You must come along with us. There's plenty of room for three, isn't there, Melrose?"

"Oh rather." But the colonel's voice was a little doubtful. "The only thing is," he remarked, "the job we're on. Eh, Satterthwaite?"

Mr. Satterthwaite stood stock-still. Ideas leaped and flashed over him. He positively shook with excitement.

"No," he cried. "No, I should have known better! There is no chance where you are concerned, Mr. Quin. It was not an accident that we all met tonight at the crossroads."

Colonel Melrose stared at his friend in astonishment. Mr. Satterthwaite took him by the arm.

"You remember what I told you—about our friend Derek Capel? The motive for his suicide, which no one could guess? It was Mr. Quin who solved that problem—and there have been others since. He shows you things that are there all the time, but which you haven't seen. He's marvelous."

"My dear Satterthwaite, you are making me blush," said Mr. Quin, smiling. "As far as I can remember, these discoveries were all made by you, not by me."

"They were made because you were there," said Mr. Satterthwaite with intense conviction.

"Well," said Colonel Melrose, clearing his throat uncomfortably. "We mustn't waste any more time. Let's get on."

He climbed into the driver's seat. He was not too well pleased at having the stranger foisted upon him through Mr. Satterthwaite's enthusiasm, but he had no valid objection to offer, and he was anxious to get on to Alderway as fast as possible.

Mr. Satterthwaite urged Mr. Quin in next, and himself took the outside seat. The car was a roomy one and took three without undue squeezing.

"So you are interested in crime, Mr. Quin?" said the colonel, doing his best to be genial.

"No, not exactly in crime."

"What, then?"

Mr. Quin smiled. "Let us ask Mr. Satterthwaite. He is a very shrewd observer."

"I think," said Satterthwaite slowly, "I may be wrong, but I think—that Mr. Quin is interested in—lovers."

He blushed as he said the last word, which is one no Englishman can pronounce without self-consciousness. Mr. Satterthwaite brought it out apologetically, and with an effect of inverted commas.

"By gad!" said the colonel, startled and silenced.

He reflected inwardly that this seemed to be a very rum friend of Satterthwaite's. He glanced at him sideways. The fellow looked all right—quite a normal young chap. Rather dark, but not at all foreign-looking.

"And now," said Satterthwaite importantly, "I must tell you all about the case."

He talked for some ten minutes. Sitting there in the darkness, rushing through the night, he had an intoxicating feeling of power. What did it matter if he were only a looker-on at life? He had words at his command, he was master of them, he could string them to a pattern—a strange Renaissance pattern composed of the beauty of Laura Dwighton, with her white arms and red hair—and the shadowy dark figure of Paul Delangua, whom women found handsome.

Set that against the background of Alderway—Alderway that

had stood since the days of Henry VII and, some said, before that. Alderway that was English to the core, with its clipped yew and its old beak barn and the fishpond, where monks had kept their carp for Fridays.

In a few deft strokes he had etched in Sir James, a Dwighton who was a true descendant of the old De Wittons, who long ago had wrung money out of the land and locked it fast in coffers, so that whoever else had fallen on evil days, the masters of Alderway had never become impoverished.

At last Mr. Satterthwaite ceased. He was sure, had been sure all along, of the sympathy of his audience. He waited now the word of praise which was his due. It came.

"You are an artist, Mr. Satterthwaite."

"I—I do my best." The little man was suddenly humble.

They had turned in at the lodge gates some minutes ago. Now the car drew up in front of the doorway, and a police constable came hurriedly down the steps to meet them.

"Good evening, sir. Inspector Curtis is in the library."

"Right."

Melrose ran up the steps followed by the other two. As the three of them passed across the wide hall, an elderly butler peered from a doorway apprehensively. Melrose nodded to him.

"Evening, Miles. This is a sad business."

"It is indeed," the other quavered. "I can hardly believe it, sir; indeed I can't. To think that anyone should strike down the master."

"Yes, yes," said Melrose, cutting him short. "I'll have a talk with you presently."

He strode on to the library. There a big, soldierly-looking inspector greeted him with respect.

"Nasty business, sir. I have not disturbed things. No fingerprints on the weapon. Whoever did it knew his business."

Mr. Satterthwaite looked at the bowed figure sitting at the big writing-table, and looked hurriedly away again. The man had been struck down from behind, a smashing blow that had crashed in the skull. The sight was not a pretty one.

The weapon lay on the floor—a bronze figure about two feet

high, the base of it stained and wet. Mr. Satterthwaite bent over it curiously.

"A Venus," he said softly. "So he was struck down by Venus."

He found food for poetic meditation in the thought.

"The windows," said the inspector, "were all closed and bolted on the inside."

He paused significantly.

"Making an inside job of it," said the chief constable reluctantly. "Well—well, we'll see."

The murdered man was dressed in golf clothes, and a bag of golf clubs had been flung untidily across a big leather couch.

"Just come in from the links," explained the inspector, following the chief constable's glance. "At five-fifteen, that was. Had tea brought here by the butler. Later he rang for his valet to bring him down a pair of soft slippers. As far as we can tell, the valet was the last person to see him alive."

Melrose nodded, and turned his attention once more to the writing-table.

A good many of the ornaments had been overturned and broken. Prominent among these was a big dark enamel clock, which lay on its side in the very center of the table.

The inspector cleared his throat.

"That's what you might call a piece of luck, sir," he said. "As you see, it's stopped. *At half past six*. That gives us the time of the crime. Very convenient."

The colonel was staring at the clock.

"As you say," he remarked. "Very convenient." He paused a minute, and then added, "Too damned convenient! I don't like it, Inspector."

He looked around at the other two. His eye sought Mr. Quin's with a look of appeal in it.

"Damn it all," he said. "It's too neat. You know what I mean. Things don't happen like that."

"You mean," murmured Mr. Quin, "that clocks don't fall like that?"

Melrose stared at him for a moment, then back at the clock,

which had that pathetic and innocent look familiar to objects which have been suddenly bereft of their dignity. Very carefully Colonel Melrose replaced it on its legs again. He struck the table a violent blow. The clock rocked, but it did not fall. Melrose repeated the action, and very slowly, with a kind of unwillingness, the clock fell over on its back.

"What time was the crime discovered?" demanded Melrose sharply.

"Just about seven o'clock, sir."

"Who discovered it?"

"The butler."

"Fetch him in," said the chief constable. "I'll see him now. Where is Lady Dwighton, by the way?"

"Lying down, sir. Her maid says that she's prostrated and can't see anyone."

Melrose nodded, and Inspector Curtis went in search of the butler. Mr. Quin was looking thoughtfully into the fireplace. Mr. Satterthwaite followed his example. He blinked at the smoldering logs for a minute or two, and then something bright lying in the grate caught his eye. He stooped and picked up a little sliver of curved glass.

"You wanted me, sir?"

It was the butler's voice, still quavering and uncertain. Mr. Satterthwaite slipped the fragment of glass into his waistcoat pocket and turned round.

The old man was standing in the doorway.

"Sit down," said the chief constable kindly. "You're shaking all over. It's been a shock to you, I expect."

"It has indeed, sir."

"Well I shan't keep you long. Your master came in just after five, I believe?"

"Yes, sir. He ordered tea to be brought to him here. Afterward, when I came to take it away, he asked for Jennings to be sent to him—that's his valet, sir."

"What time was that?"

"About ten minutes past six, sir."

"Yes—well?"

"I sent word to Jennings, sir. And it wasn't till I came in here to shut the windows and draw the curtains at seven o'clock that I saw—"

Melrose cut him short. "Yes, yes, you needn't go into all that. You didn't touch the body, or disturb anything, did you?"

"Oh! No indeed, sir! I went as fast as I could go to the telephone to ring up the police."

"And then?"

"I told Janet—her ladyship's maid, sir—to break the news to her ladyship."

"You haven't seen your mistress at all this evening?"

Colonel Melrose put the question casually enough, but Mr. Satterthwaite's keen ears caught anxiety behind the words.

"Not to speak to, sir. Her ladyship has remained in her own apartments since the tragedy."

"Did you see her before?"

The question came sharply, and everyone in the room noted the hesitation before the butler replied.

"I—I just caught a glimpse of her, sir, descending the staircase."

"Did she come in here?"

Mr. Satterthwaite held his breath.

"I—I think so, sir."

"What time was that?"

You might have heard a pin drop. Did the old man know, Mr. Satterthwaite wondered, what hung on his answer?

"It was just upon half past six, sir."

Colonel Melrose drew a deep breath. "That will do, thank you. Just send Jennings, the valet, to me, will you?"

Jennings answered the summons with promptitude. A narrow-faced man with a catlike tread. Something sly and secretive about him.

A man, thought Mr. Satterthwaite, who would easily murder his master if he could be sure of not being found out.

He listened eagerly to the man's answers to Colonel Melrose's questions. But his story seemed straightforward enough. He had brought his master down some soft hide slippers and removed the brogues.

"What did you do after that, Jennings?"

"I went back to the stewards' room, sir."

"At what time did you leave your master?"

"It must have been just after a quarter past six, sir."

"Where were you at half past six, Jennings?"

"In the stewards' room, sir."

Colonel Melrose dismissed the man with a nod. He looked across at Curtis inquiringly.

"Quite correct, sir, I checked that up. He was in the stewards' room from about six-twenty until seven o'clock."

"Then that lets him out," said the chief constable a trifle regretfully. "Besides, there's no motive."

They looked at each other.

There was a tap at the door.

"Come in," said the colonel.

A scared-looking lady's maid appeared.

"If you please, her ladyship has heard that Colonel Melrose is here and she would like to see him."

"Certainly," said Melrose. "I'll come at once. Will you show me the way?"

But a hand pushed the girl aside. A very different figure now stood in the doorway. Laura Dwighton looked like a visitor from another world.

She was dressed in a clinging medieval tea gown of dull-blue brocade. Her auburn hair was parted in the middle and brought down over her ears. Conscious of the fact she had a style of her own, Lady Dwighton had never had her hair cut. It was drawn back into a simple knot on the nape of her neck. Her arms were bare.

One of them was outstretched to steady herself against the frame of the doorway, the other hung down by her side, clasping a book. *She looks,* Mr. Satterthwaite thought, *like a Madonna from an early Italian canvas.*

She stood there, swaying slightly from side to side. Colonel Melrose sprang toward her.

"I've come to tell you—to tell you—"

Her voice was low and rich. Mr. Satterthwaite was so entranced with the dramatic value of the scene that he had forgotten its reality.

"Please, Lady Dwighton—" Melrose had an arm round her, supporting her. He took her across the hall into a small anteroom, its walls hung with faded silk. Quin and Satterthwaite followed. She sank down on the low settee, her head resting back on a rust-colored cushion, her eyelids closed. The three men watched her. Suddenly she opened her eyes and sat up. She spoke very quietly.

"*I killed him,*" she said. "*That's what I came to tell you. I killed him!*"

There was a moment's agonized silence. Mr. Satterthwaite's heart missed a beat.

"Lady Dwighton," said Melrose. "You've had a great shock—you're unstrung. I don't think you quite know what you're saying."

Would she draw back now—while there was yet time?

"I know perfectly what I'm saying. It was I who shot him."

Two of the men in the room gasped, the other made no sound. Laura Dwighton leaned still farther forward.

"Don't you understand? I came down and shot him. I admit it."

The book she had been holding in her hand clattered to the floor. There was a paper cutter in it, a thing shaped like a dagger with a jeweled hilt. Mr. Satterthwaite picked it up mechanically and placed it on the table. As he did so he thought, *That's a dangerous toy. You could kill a man with that.*

"Well—" Laura Dwighton's voice was impatient—"what are you going to do about it? Arrest me? Take me away?"

Colonel Melrose found his voice with difficulty.

"What you have told me is very serious, Lady Dwighton. I must ask you to go to your room till I have—er—made arrangements."

She nodded and rose to her feet. She was quite composed now, grave and cold.

As she turned toward the door, Mr. Quin spoke. "What did you do with the revolver, Lady Dwighton?"

A flicker of uncertainty passed across her face. "I—I dropped it there on the floor. No, I think I threw it out of the window—oh! I can't remember now. What does it matter? I hardly knew what I was doing. It doesn't matter, does it?"

"No," said Mr. Quin. "I hardly think it matters."

She looked at him in perplexity with a shade of something that might have been alarm. Then she flung back her head and went imperiously out of the room. Mr. Satterthwaite hastened after her. She might, he felt, collapse at any minute. But she was already halfway up the staircase, displaying no sign of her earlier weakness. The scared-looking maid was standing at the foot of the stairway, and Mr. Satterthwaite spoke to her authoritatively.

"Look after your mistress," he said.

"Yes, sir." The girl prepared to ascend after the blue-robed figure. "Oh, please, sir, they don't suspect him, do they?"

"Suspect whom?"

"Jennings, sir. Oh! Indeed, sir, he wouldn't hurt a fly."

"Jennings? No, of course not. Go and look after your mistress."

"Yes, sir."

The girl ran quickly up the staircase. Mr. Satterthwaite returned to the room he had just vacated.

Colonel Melrose was saying heavily, "Well, I'm jiggered. There's more in this than meets the eye. It—it's like those dashed silly things heroines do in many novels."

"It's unreal," agreed Mr. Satterthwaite. "It's like something on the stage."

Mr. Quin nodded. "Yes, you admire the drama, do you not? You are a man who appreciates good acting when you see it."

Mr. Satterthwaite looked hard at him.

In the silence that followed a far-off sound came to their ears.

"Sounds like a shot," said Colonel Melrose. "One of the keepers, I daresay. That's probably what she heard. Perhaps she went down to see. She wouldn't go close or examine the body. She'd leap at once to the conclusion—"

"Mr. Delangua, sir." It was the old butler who spoke, standing apologetically in the doorway.

"Eh?" said Melrose. "What's that?"

"Mr. Delangua is here, sir, and would like to speak to you if he may."

Colonel Melrose leaned back in his chair. "Show him in," he said grimly.

A moment later Paul Delangua stood in the doorway. As Colonel Melrose had hinted, there was something un-English about him— the easy grace of his movements, the dark, handsome face, the eyes set a little too near together. There hung about him the air of the Renaissance. He and Laura Dwighton suggested the same atmosphere.

"Good evening, gentlemen," said Delangua. He made a little theatrical bow.

"I don't know what your business may be, Mr. Delangua," said Colonel Melrose sharply, "but if it is nothing to do with the matter at hand—"

Delangua interrupted him with a laugh. "On the contrary," he said, "it has everything to do with it."

"What do you mean?"

"I mean," said Delangua quietly, "that I have come to give myself up for the murder of Sir James Dwighton."

"You know what you are saying?" said Melrose gravely.

"Perfectly."

The young man's eyes were riveted to the table.

"I don't understand—"

"Why I give myself up? Call it remorse—call it anything you please. I stabbed him, right enough—you may be quite sure of that." He nodded toward the table. "You've got the weapon there, I see. A very handy little tool. Lady Dwighton unfortunately left it lying around in a book, and I happened to snatch it up."

"One minute," said Colonel Melrose. "Am I to understand that you admit stabbing Sir James with this?" He held the dagger aloft.

"Quite right. I stole in through the window, you know. He had his back to me. It was quite easy. I left the same way."

"Through the window?"

"Through the window, of course."

"And what time was this?

Delangua hesitated. "Let me see—I was talking to the keeper

fellow—that was at a quarter past six. I heard the church tower chime. It must have been—well, say somewhere about half past."

A grim smile came to the colonel's lips.

"Quite right, young man," he said. "Half past six was the time. Perhaps you've heard that already? But this is altogether a most peculiar murder!"

"Why?"

"So many people confess to it," said Colonel Melrose.

They heard the sharp intake of the other's breath.

"Who else has confessed to it?" he asked in a voice that he vainly strove to render steady.

"Lady Dwighton."

Delangua threw back his head and laughed in rather a forced manner. "Lady Dwighton is apt to be hysterical," he said lightly. "I shouldn't pay any attention to what she says if I were you."

"I don't think I shall," said Melrose. "But there's another odd thing about this murder."

"What's that?"

"Well," said Melrose, "Lady Dwighton has confessed to having shot Sir James, and you have confessed to having stabbed him. But luckily for both of you, he wasn't shot or stabbed, you see. His skull was smashed in."

"My God!" cried Delangua. "But a woman couldn't possibly do that—"

He stopped, biting his lip. Melrose nodded with the ghost of a smile.

"Often read of it," he volunteered. "Never seen it happen."

"What?"

"Couple of young idiots each accusing themselves because they thought the other had done it," said Melrose. "Now we've got to begin at the beginning."

"The valet," cried Mr. Satterthwaite. "That girl just now—I wasn't paying any attention at the time." He paused, striving for coherence. "She was afraid of our suspecting him. There must be some motive that he had and which we don't know, but she does."

Colonel Melrose frowned, then he rang the bell. When it was

answered, he said, "Please ask Lady Dwighton if she will be good enough to come down again."

They waited in silence until she came. At sight of Delangua she started and stretched out a hand to save herself from falling. Colonel Melrose came quickly to the rescue.

"It's quite all right, Lady Dwighton. Please don't be alarmed."

"I don't understand. What is Mr. Delangua doing here?"

Delangua came over to her, "Laura—Laura—why did you do it?"

"Do it?"

"I know. It was for me—because you thought that I—After all, it was natural, I suppose. But, oh! You angel!"

Colonel Melrose cleared his throat. He was a man who disliked emotion and had a horror of anything approaching a "scene."

"If you'll allow me to say so, Lady Dwighton, both you and Mr. Delangua have had a lucky escape. He had just arrived in his turn to 'confess' to the murder—oh, it's quite all right, he didn't do it! But what we want to know is the truth. No more shillyshallying. The butler says you went into the library at half past six—is that so?"

Laura looked at Delangua. He nodded.

"The truth, Laura," he said. "That is what we want now."

She breathed a deep sigh. "I will tell you."

She sank down on a chair that Mr. Satterthwaite had hurriedly pushed forward.

"I did come down. I opened the library door and I saw—"

She stopped and swallowed. Mr. Satterthwaite leaned forward and patted her hand encouragingly.

"Yes," he said. "Yes. You saw?"

"My husband was lying across the writing-table. I saw his head—the blood—oh!"

She put her hands to her face. The chief constable leaned forward.

"Excuse me, Lady Dwighton. You thought Mr. Delangua had shot him?"

She nodded. "Forgive me, Paul," she pleaded. "But you said—you said—"

"That I'd shoot him like a dog," said Delangua grimly. "I remember. That was the day I discovered he'd been ill-treating you."

The chief constable kept sternly to the matter in hand.

"Then I am to understand, Lady Dwighton, that you went upstairs again and—er—said nothing. We needn't go into your reason. You didn't touch the body or go near the writing-table?"

She shuddered.

"No, no. I ran straight out of the room."

"I see, I see. And what time was this exactly? Do you know?"

"It was just half past six when I got back to my bedroom."

"Then at—say five-and-twenty past six, Sir James was already dead." The chief constable looked at the others. "That clock—it was faked, eh? We suspected that all along. Nothing easier than to move the hands to whatever time you wished, but they made a mistake to lay it down on its side like that. Well, that seems to narrow it down to the butler or the valet, and I can't believe it's the butler. Tell me, Lady Dwighton, did this man Jennings have any grudge against your husband?"

Laura lifted her face from her hands. "Not exactly a grudge, but—well James told me only this morning that he'd dismissed him. He'd found him pilfering."

"Ah! Now we're getting at it. Jennings would have been dismissed without a character. A serious matter for him."

"You said something about a clock," said Laura Dwighton. "There's just a chance—if you want to fix the time—James would have been sure to have his little golf watch on him. Mightn't that have been smashed, too, when he fell forward?"

"It's an idea," said the colonel slowly. "But I'm afraid—Curtis!"

The inspector nodded in quick comprehension and left the room. He returned a minute later. On the palm of his hand was a silver watch marked like a golf ball, the kind that are sold for golfers to carry loose in a pocket with balls.

"Here it is, sir," he said, "but I doubt if it will be any good. They're tough, these watches."

The colonel took it from him and held it to his ear.

"It seems to have stopped, anyway," he observed.

He pressed with his thumb, and the lid of the watch flew open. Inside the glass was cracked across.

"Ah!" he said exultantly.

The hand pointed to exactly a quarter past six.

"A VERY GOOD glass of port, Colonel Melrose," said Mr. Quin.

It was half past nine, and the three men had just finished a belated dinner at Colonel Melrose's house. Mr. Satterthwaite was particularly jubilant.

"I was quite right," he chuckled. "You can't deny it, Mr. Quin. You turned up tonight to save two absurd young people who were both bent on putting their heads into a noose."

"Did I?" said Mr. Quin. "Surely not. I did nothing at all."

"As it turned out, it was not necessary," agreed Mr. Satterthwaite. "But it might have been. It was touch and go, you know. I shall never forget the moment when Lady Dwighton said, 'I killed him.' I've never seen anything on the stage half as dramatic."

"I'm inclined to agree with you," said Mr. Quin.

"Wouldn't have believed such a thing could happen outside a novel," declared the colonel, for perhaps the twentieth time that night.

"Does it?" asked Mr. Quin.

The colonel stared at him, "Damn it, it happened tonight."

"Mind you," interposed Mr. Satterthwaite, leaning back and sipping his port, "Lady Dwighton was magnificent, quite magnificent, but she made one mistake. She shouldn't have leaped to the conclusion that her husband had been shot. In the same way Delangua was a fool to assume that he had been stabbed just because the dagger happened to be lying on the table in front of us. It was a mere coincidence that Lady Dwighton should have brought it down with her."

"Was it?" asked Mr. Quin.

"Now if they'd only confined themselves to saying that they'd

THE LOVE DETECTIVES 437

killed Sir James, without particularizing how—" went on Mr. Satterthwaite—"what would have been the result?"

"They might have been believed," said Mr. Quin with an odd smile.

"The whole thing was exactly like a novel," said the colonel.

"That's where they got the idea from, I daresay," said Mr. Quin.

"Possibly," agreed Mr. Satterthwaite. "Things one has read do come back to one in the oddest way." He looked across at Mr. Quinn. "Of course," he said, "the clock really looked suspicious from the first. One ought never to forget how easy it is to put the hands of a clock or watch forward or back."

Mr. Quin nodded and repeated the words. "Forward," he said, and paused. "Or back."

There was something encouraging in his voice. His bright, dark eyes were fixed on Mr. Sattertliwaite.

"The hands of the clock were put forward," said Mr. Satterthwaite. "We know that."

"Were they?" asked Mr. Quin.

Mr. Satterthwaite stared at him. "Do you mean," he said slowly, "that it was the watch which was put back? But that doesn't make sense. It's impossible."

"Not impossible," murmured Mr. Quin.

"Well—absurd. To whose advantage could that be?"

"Only, I suppose, to someone who had an *alibi* for that time."

"By gad!" cried the colonel. "That's the time young Delangua said he was talking to the keeper."

"He told us that very particularly," said Mr. Satterthwaite.

They looked at each other. They had an uneasy feeling as of solid ground failing beneath their feet. Facts went spinning round, turning new and unexpected faces. And in the center of the kaleidoscope was the dark, smiling face of Mr. Quin.

"But in that case—" began Melrose—"in that case—"

Mr. Satterthwaite, nimble-witted, finished his sentence for him. "It's all the other way round. A plant just the same—but a plant against the valet. Oh, but it can't be! It's impossible. Why each of them accused themselves of the crime."

"Yes," said Mr. Quin. "Up till then you suspected them, didn't you?" His voice went on, placid and dreamy. "Just like something out of a book, you said, colonel. They got the idea there. It's what the innocent hero and heroine do. Of course it made you think them innocent—there was the force of tradition behind them. Mr. Satterthwaite has been saying all along it was like something on the stage. You were both right. It wasn't real. You've been saying so all along without knowing what you were saying. They'd have told a much better story than that if they'd wanted to be believed."

The two men looked at him helplessly.

"It would be clever," said Mr. Satterthwaite slowly. "It would be diabolically clever. And I've thought of something else. The butler said he went in at seven to shut the windows—so he must have expected them to be open."

"That's the way Delangua came in," said Mr. Quin. "He killed Sir James with one blow, and he and she together did what they had to do—"

He looked at Mr. Satterthwaite, encouraging him to reconstruct the scene. He did so, hesitatingly.

"They smashed the clock and put it on its side. Yes. They altered the watch and smashed it. Then he went out of the window, and she fastened it after him. But there's one thing I don't see. Why bother with the watch at all? Why not simply put back the hands of the clock?"

"The clock was always a little obvious," said Mr. Quin.

"Anyone might have seen through a rather transparent device like that."

"But surely the watch was too farfetched. Why, it was pure chance that we ever thought of the watch."

"Oh, no," said Mr. Quin. "It was the lady's suggestion, remember."

Mr. Satterthwaite stared at him, fascinated.

"And yet, you know," said Mr. Quin dreamily, "the one person who wouldn't be likely to overlook the watch would be the valet. Valets know better than anyone what their masters carry in their pockets. If he altered the clock, the valet would have altered the watch, too. They don't understand human nature, those two. They are not like Mr. Satterthwaite."

Mr. Satterthwaite shook his head.

"I was all wrong," he murmured humbly. "I thought that you had come to save them."

"So I did," said Mr. Quin. "Oh! Not those two—the others. Perhaps you didn't notice the lady's maid? She wasn't wearing blue brocade, or acting a dramatic part. But she's really a very pretty girl, and I think she loves that man Jennings very much. I think that between you you'll be able to save her man from getting hanged."

"We've no proof of any kind," said Colonel Melrose heavily.

Mr. Quin smiled. "Mr. Satterthwaite has."

"I?" Mr. Satterthwaite was astonished.

Mr. Quin went on. "You've got a proof that that watch wasn't smashed in Sir James's pocket. You can't smash a watch like that without opening the case. Just try it and see. Someone took the watch out and opened it, set back the hands, smashed the glass, and then shut it and put it back. They never noticed that a fragment of glass was missing."

"Oh!" cried Mr. Satterthwaite. His hand flew to his waistcoat pocket. He drew out a fragment of curved glass.

It was his moment.

"With this," said Mr. Satterthwaite importantly, "I shall save a man from death."

PART III HERCULE POIROT

1. THE THIRD-
FLOOR FLAT

"Bother!" said Pat.

With a deepening frown she rummaged wildly in the silken trifle she called an evening bag. Two young men and another girl watched her anxiously. They were all standing outside the closed door of Patricia Garnett's flat.

"It's no good," said Pat. "It's not there. And now what shall we do?"

"What is life without a latchkey?" murmured Jimmy Faulkener.

He was a short, broad-shouldered young man, with good-tempered blue eyes.

Pat turned on him angrily. "Don't make jokes, Jimmy. This is serious."

"Look again, Pat," said Donovan Bailey. "It must be there somewhere."

He had a lazy, pleasant voice that matched his lean, dark figure.

"If you ever brought it out," said the other girl, Mildred Hope.

"Of course I brought it out," said Pat. "I believe I gave it to one of you two." She turned on the man accusingly. "I told Donovan to take it for me."

But she was not to find a scapegoat so easily. Donovan put in a firm disclaimer, and Jimmy backed him up.

"I saw you put it in your bag, myself," said Jimmy.

"Well, then, one of you dropped it out when you picked up my bag. I've dropped it once or twice."

"Once or twice!" said Donovan. "You've dropped it a dozen times at least, besides leaving it behind on every possible occasion."

"I can't see why everything on earth doesn't drop out of it the whole time," said Jimmy.

"The point is—how are we going to get in?" said Mildred.

She was a sensible girl, who kept to the point, but she was not nearly so attractive as the impulsive and troublesome Pat.

All four of them regarded the closed door blankly.

"Couldn't the porter help?" suggested Jimmy. "Hasn't he got a master key or something of that kind?"

Pat shook her head. There were only two keys. One was inside the flat hung up in the kitchen and the other was—or should be—in the maligned bag.

"If only the flat were on the ground floor," wailed Pat. "We could have broken open a window or something. Donovan, you wouldn't like to be a cat burglar, would you?"

Donovan declined firmly but politely to be a cat burglar.

"A flat on the fourth floor is a bit of an undertaking," said Jimmy.

"How about a fire escape?" suggested Donovan.

"There isn't one."

"There should be," said Jimmy. "A building five stories high ought to have a fire escape."

"I daresay," said Pat. "But what should be doesn't help us. How am I ever to get into my flat?"

"Isn't there a sort of thingummybob?" said Donovan. "A thing the tradesmen send up chops and Brussels sprouts in?"

"The service lift," said Pat. "Oh, yes, but it's only a sort of wire-basket thing. Oh! wait—I know. What about the coal lift?"

"Now that," said Donovan, "is an idea."

Mildred made a discouraging suggestion. "It'll be bolted," she said. "In Pat's kitchen, I mean, on the inside."

But the idea was instantly negatived.

"Don't you believe it," said Donovan.

"Not in *Pat's* kitchen," said Jimmy. "Pat never locks and bolts things."

"I don't think it's bolted," said Pat. "I took the dustbin off this morning, and I'm sure I never bolted it afterward, and I don't think I've been near it since."

"Well," said Donovan, "that fact's going to be very useful to us tonight, but, all the same, young Pat, let me point out to you that these slack habits are leaving you at the mercy of burglars—nonfeline—every night."

Pat disregarded these admonitions.

"Come on," she cried, and began racing down the four flights of stairs. The others followed her. Pat led them through a dark recess, apparently full to overflowing of perambulators, and through another door into the well of the flats, and guided them to the right lift. There was, at the moment, a dustbin on it. Donovan lifted it off and stepped gingerly onto the platform in its place. He wrinkled up his nose.

"A little noisome," he remarked. "But what of that? Do I go alone on this venture or is anyone coming with me?"

"I'll come, too," said Jimmy.

He stepped on by Donovan's side.

"I suppose the lift will bear me," he added doubtfully.

"You can't weigh much more than a ton of coal," said Pat, who had never been particularly strong on her weights-and-measures table.

"And, anyway, we shall soon find out," said Donovan cheerfully, as he hauled on the rope.

With a grinding noise they disappeared from sight.

"This thing makes an awful noise," remarked Jimmy, as they passed up through blackness. "What will the people in the other flats think?"

"Ghosts or burglars, I expect," said Donovan. "Hauling this rope is quite heavy work. The porter of Friars Mansions does more work than I ever suspected. I say, Jimmy, old son, are you counting the floors?"

"Oh, Lord! No. I forgot about it."

"Well, I have, which is just as well. That's the third we're passing now. The next is ours."

"And now, I suppose," grumbled Jimmy, "we shall find that Pat did bolt the door after all."

But these fears were unfounded. The wooden door swung back at a touch, and Donovan and Jimmy stepped out into the inky blackness of Pat's kitchen.

"We ought to have a torch for this wild night work," explained Donovan. "If I know Pat, everything's on the floor, and we shall smash endless crockery before I can get to the light switch. Don't move about, Jimmy, till I get the light on."

He felt his way cautiously over the floor, uttering one fervent "Damn!" as a corner of the kitchen table took him unawares in the ribs. He reached the switch, and in another moment another "Damn!" floated out of the darkness.

"What's the matter?" asked Jimmy.

"Light won't come on. Dud bulb, I suppose. Wait a minute. I'll turn the sitting-room light on."

The sitting-room was the door immediately across the passage. Jimmy heard Donovan go out of the door, and presently fresh muffled curses reached him. He himself edged his way cautiously across the kitchen.

"What's the matter?"

"I don't know. Rooms get bewitched at night, I believe. Everything seems to be in a different place. Chairs and tables where you least expected them. Oh, hell! Here's another!"

But at this moment Jimmy fortunately connected with the electric-light switch and pressed it down. In another minute two young men were looking at each other in silent horror.

This room was not Pat's sitting-room. They were in the wrong flat.

To begin with, the room was about ten times more crowded than Pat's, which explained Donovan's pathetic bewilderment at repeatedly cannoning into chairs and tables. There was a large round table in the center of the room covered with a baize cloth, and there was an aspidistra in the window. It was, in fact, the kind of room whose owner, the young men felt sure, would be difficult to explain to. With silent horror they gazed down at the table, on which lay a little pile of letters.

"Mrs. Ernestine Grant," breathed Donovan, picking them up and reading the name. "Oh, help! Do you think she's heard us?"

"It's a miracle she hasn't heard you," said Jimmy. "What with your language and the way you've been crashing into the furniture. Come on, for the Lord's sake, let's get out of here quickly."

They hastily switched off the light and retraced their steps on tiptoe to the lift. Jimmy breathed a sigh of relief as they regained the fastness of its depths without further incident.

"I do like a woman to be a good, sound sleeper," he said approvingly. "Mrs. Ernestine Grant has her points."

"I see it now," said Donovan; "why we made the mistake in the floor, I mean. Out in that well we started up from the basement." He heaved on the rope, and the lift shot up. "We're right this time."

"I devoutly trust we are," said Jimmy as he stepped out into another inky void. "My nerves won't stand many more shocks of this kind."

But no further nerve strain was imposed. The first click of the light showed them Pat's kitchen, and in another minute they were opening the front door and admitting the two girls who were waiting outside.

"You have been a long time," grumbled Pat. "Mildred and I have been waiting here ages."

"We've had an adventure," said Donovan. "We might have been hauled off to the police station as dangerous malefactors."

Pat had passed on into the sitting-room, where she switched on the light and dropped her wrap on the sofa. She listened with lively interest to Donovan's account of his adventures.

"I'm glad she didn't catch you," she commented. "I'm sure she's an old curmudgeon. I got a note from her this morning—wanted to see me sometime—something she had to complain about—my piano, I suppose. People who don't like pianos over their heads shouldn't come and live in flats. I say, Donovan, you've hurt your hand. It's all over blood. Go and wash it under the tap."

Donovan looked down at his hand in surprise. He went out of the room obediently and presently his voice called to Jimmy.

"Hullo," said the other, "what's up? You haven't hurt yourself badly, have you?"

"I haven't hurt myself at all."

There was something so queer in Donovan's voice that Jimmy stared at him in surprise. Donovan held out his washed hand and Jimmy saw that there was no mark or cut of any kind on it.

"That's odd," he said, frowning. "There was quite a lot of blood. Where did it come from?" And then suddenly he realized what his quicker-witted friend had already seen. "By Jove," he said. "It must have come from that flat." He stopped, thinking over the possibilities his words implied. "You're sure it was—er—blood?" he said. "Not paint?"

Donovan shook his head. "It was blood, all right," he said, and shivered.

They looked at each other. The same thought was clearly in each of their minds. It was Jimmy who voiced it first.

"I say," he said awkwardly. "Do you think we ought to—well—go down again—and have—a—a look around? See it's all right, you know?"

"What about the girls?"

"We won't say anything to them. Pat's going to put on an apron and make us an omelet. We'll be back by the time they wonder where we are."

"Oh, well, come on," said Donovan. "I suppose we've got to go through with it. I daresay there isn't anything really wrong."

But his tone lacked conviction. They got into the lift and descended to the floor below. They found their way across the kitchen without much difficulty and once more switched on the sitting-room light.

"It must have been in here," said Donovan, "that—that I got the stuff on me. I never touched anything in the kitchen."

He looked round him. Jimmy did the same, and they both frowned. Everything looked neat and commonplace and miles removed from any suggestion of violence or gore.

Suddenly Jimmy started violently and caught his companion's arm.

"Look!"

Donovan followed the pointing finger, and in his turn uttered an exclamation. From beneath the heavy rep curtains there protruded a foot—a woman's foot in a gaping patent-leather shoe.

Jimmy went to the curtains and drew them sharply apart. In the recess of the window a woman's huddled body lay on the floor, a sticky dark pool beside it. She was dead, there was no doubt of that. Jimmy was attempting to raise her up when Donovan stopped him.

"You'd better not do that. She oughtn't to be touched till the police come."

"The police. Oh! Of course. I say, Donovan, what a ghastly business. Who do you think she is? Mrs. Ernestine Grant?"

"Looks like it. At any rate, if there's anyone else in the flat they're keeping jolly quiet."

"What do we do next?" asked Jimmy. "Run out and get a policeman or ring up from Pat's flat?"

"I should think ringing up would be best. Come on, we might as well go out the front door. We can't spend the whole night going up and down in that evil-smelling lift."

Jimmy agreed. Just as they were passing through the door he hesitated. "Look here; do you think one of us ought to stay—just to keep an eye on things—till the police come?"

"Yes, I think you're right. If you'll stay I'll run up and telephone."

He ran quickly up the stairs and rang the bell of the flat above. Pat came to open it, a very pretty Pat with a flushed face and a cooking apron on. Her eyes widened in surprise.

"You? But how—Donovan, what is it? Is anything the matter?"

He took both her hands in his. "It's all right, Pat—only we've made rather an unpleasant discovery in the flat below. A woman—dead."

"Oh!" She gave a little gasp. "How horrible. Has she had a fit or something?"

"No. It looks—well—it looks rather as though she had been murdered."

"Oh, Donovan!"

"I know. It's pretty beastly."

Her hands were still in his. She had left them there—was even clinging to him. Darling Pat—how he loved her. Did she care at all for him? Sometimes he thought she did. Sometimes he was afraid that Jimmy Faulkener—remembrances of Jimmy waiting patiently below made him start guiltily.

"Pat, dear, we must telephone to the police."

"Monsieur is right," said a voice behind him. "And in the meantime, while we are waiting their arrival, perhaps I can be of some slight assistance."

They had been standing in the doorway of the flat, and now they peered out onto the landing. A figure was standing on the stairs a little way above them. It moved down and into their range of vision.

They stood staring at a little man with a very fierce mustache and an egg-shaped head. He wore a resplendent dressing-gown and embroidered slippers. He bowed gallantly to Patricia.

"Mademoiselle!" he said. "I am, as perhaps you know, the tenant of the flat above. I like to be up high—the air—the view over London. I take the flat in the name of Mr. O'Connor. But I am not an Irishman. I have another name. That is why I venture to put myself at your service. Permit me." With a flourish he pulled out a card and handed it to Pat. She read it.

"M. Hercule Poirot. Oh!" She caught her breath. "*The* M. Poirot? The great detective? And you will really help?"

"That is my intention, mademoiselle. I nearly offered my help earlier in the evening."

Pat looked puzzled.

"I heard you discussing how to gain admission to your flat. Me, I am very clever at picking locks. I could, without doubt, have opened your door for you, but I hesitated to suggest it. You would have had the grave suspicions of me."

Pat laughed.

"Now, monsieur," said Poirot to Donovan. "Go in, I pray of you, and telephone to the police. I will descend to the flat below."

Pat came down the stairs with him. They found Jimmy on guard, and Pat explained Poirot's presence. Jimmy, in his turn, explained to Poirot his and Donovan's adventures. The detective listened attentively.

"The lift door was unbolted, you say? You emerged into the kitchen, but the light it would not turn on."

He directed his footsteps to the kitchen as he spoke. His fingers pressed the switch.

"*Tiens! Voilà ce qui est curieux!*" he said as the light flashed on. "It functions perfectly now. I wonder—"

He held up a finger to insure silence and listened. A faint sound broke the stillness—the sound of an unmistakable snore.

"Ah!" said Poirot "*La chambre de domestique.*"

He tiptoed across the kitchen into a little pantry, out of which led a door. He opened the door and switched on the light. The room was the kind of dog kennel designed by the builders of flats to accommodate a human being. The floor space was almost entirely occupied by the bed. In the bed was a rosy-cheeked girl lying on her back with her mouth wide-open, snoring placidly.

Poirot switched off the light and beat a retreat.

"She will not wake," he said. "We will let her sleep till the police come."

He went back to the sitting-room. Donovan had joined them.

"The police will be here almost immediately, they say," he said breathlessly. "We are to touch nothing."

Poirot nodded. "We will not touch," he said. "We will look, that is all."

He moved into the room. Mildred had come down with Donovan, and all four young people stood in the doorway and watched him with breathless interest.

"What I can't understand, sir, is this," said Donovan. "I never went near the window—how did the blood come on my hand?"

"My young friend, the answer to that stares you in the face. Of what color is the tablecloth? Red, is it not? And doubtless you did put your hand on the table."

"Yes, I did. Is that—" He stopped.

Poirot nodded. He was bending over the table. He indicated with his hand a dark patch on the red.

"It was here that the crime was committed," he said solemnly. "The body was moved afterward."

Then he stood upright and looked slowly round the room. He did not move, he handled nothing, but nevertheless the four watching felt as though every object in that rather frowsty place gave up its secret to his observant eye.

Hercule Poirot nodded his head as though satisfied. A little sigh escaped him. "I see," he said.

"You see what?" asked Donovan curiously.

"I see," said Poirot, "what you doubtless felt—that the room is overfull of furniture."

Donovan smiled ruefully. "I did go barging about a bit," he confessed. "Of course, everything was in a different place to Pat's room, and I couldn't make it out."

"Not everything," said Poirot.

Donovan looked at him inquiringly.

"I mean," said Poirot apologetically, "that certain things are always fixed. In a block of flats the door, the window, the fireplace—they are in the same place in the rooms which are below each other."

"Isn't that rather splitting hairs?" asked Mildred. She was looking at Poirot with faint disapproval.

"One should always speak with absolute accuracy. That is a little—how do you say?—fad of mine."

There was the noise of footsteps on the stairs, and three men came in. They were a police inspector, a constable, and the divisional surgeon. The inspector recognized Poirot and greeted him in an almost reverential manner. Then he turned to the others.

"I shall want statements from everyone," he began, "but in the first place—"

Poirot interrupted. "A little suggestion. We will go back to the flat upstairs and mademoiselle here shall do what she was planning to do—make us an omelet. Me, I have a passion for the omelets. Then, *M. l'Inspecteur*, when you have finished here, you will mount to us and ask questions at your leisure."

It was arranged accordingly, and Poirot went up with them.

"M. Poirot," said Pat, "I think you're a perfect dear. And you shall have a lovely omelet. I really make omelets frightfully well."

"That is good. Once, mademoiselle, I loved a beautiful young English girl, who resembled you greatly— but alas!—she could not cook. So perhaps everything was for the best."

There was a faint sadness in his voice, and Jimmy Faulkener looked at him curiously.

Once in the flat, however, he exerted himself to please and amuse. The grim tragedy below was almost forgotten.

The omelet had been consumed and duly praised by the time that Inspector Rice's footsteps were heard. He came in accompanied by the doctor, having left the constable below.

"Well, Monsieur Poirot," he said. "It all seems clear and aboveboard—not much in your line, though we may find it hard to catch the man. I'd just like to hear how the discovery came to be made."

Donovan and Jimmy between them recounted the happenings of the evening. The inspector turned reproachfully to Pat.

"You shouldn't leave your lift door unbolted, miss. You really shouldn't."

"I shan't again," said Pat, with a shiver. "Somebody might come in and murder me like that poor woman below."

"Ah! but they didn't come in that way, though," said the inspector.

"You will recount to us what you have discovered, yes?" said Poirot.

"I don't know as I ought to—but seeing it's you, M. Poirot—"

"*Précisément*," said Poirot. "And these young people—they will be discreet."

"The newspapers will get hold of it, anyway, soon enough," said the inspector. "There's no real secret about the matter. Well, the dead woman's Mrs. Grant, all right. I had the porter up to identify her. Woman of about thirty-five. She was sitting at the table, and she was shot with an automatic pistol of small caliber, probably by someone sitting opposite her at table. She fell forward, and that's how the bloodstain came on the table."

"But wouldn't someone have heard the shot?" asked Mildred.

"The pistol was fitted with a silencer. No, you wouldn't hear anything. By the way, did you hear the screech the maid let out when we told her her mistress was dead? No. Well, that just shows how unlikely it was that anyone would hear the other."

"Has the maid no story to tell?" asked Poirot.

"It was her evening out. She's got her own key. She came in about ten o'clock. Everything was quiet. She thought her mistress had gone to bed."

"She did not look in the sitting-room, then?"

"Yes, she took the letters in there which had come by the evening post, but she saw nothing unusual—any more than Mr. Faulkener and Mr. Bailey did. You see, the murderer had concealed the body rather neatly behind the curtains."

"But it was a curious thing to do, don't you think?"

Poirot's voice was very gentle, yet it held something that made the inspector look up quickly.

"Didn't want the crime discovered till he'd had time to make his getaway."

"Perhaps—perhaps—But continue with what you were saying."

"The maid went out at five o'clock. The doctor here puts the time of death as—roughly—about four to five hours ago. That's right, isn't it?"

The doctor, who was a man of few words, contented himself with jerking his head affirmatively.

"It's a quarter to twelve now. The actual time can, I think, be narrowed down to a fairly definite hour."

He took out a crumpled sheet of paper.

"We found this in the pocket of the dead woman's dress. You needn't be afraid of handling it. There are no fingerprints on it."

Poirot smoothed out the sheet. Across it some words were printed in small, prim capitals.

I WILL COME TO SEE YOU THIS EVENING AT HALF PAST SEVEN.—J.F.

"A compromising document to leave behind," commented Poirot, as he handed it back.

"Well, he didn't know she'd got it in her pocket," said the inspector. "He probably thought she'd destroyed it. We've evidence that he was a careful man, though. The pistol she was shot with we found under the body—and there again no fingerprints. They'd been wiped off very carefully with a silk handkerchief."

"How do you know," said Poirot, "that it was a silk handkerchief?"

"Because we found it," said the inspector triumphantly. "At the last, as he was drawing the curtains, he must have let it fall unnoticed."

He handed across a big white silk handkerchief—good-quality handkerchief. It did not need the inspector's finger to draw Poirot's attention to the mark on it in the center. It was neatly marked and quite legible. Poirot read the name out.

"John Fraser."

"That's it," said the inspector. "John Fraser—J.F. in the note. We know the name of the man we have to look for, and I daresay when we find out a little about the dead woman, and her relations come forward, we shall soon get a line on him."

"I wonder," said Poirot. "No, *mon cher,* somehow I do not think he will be easy to find, your John Fraser. He is a strange man—careful, since he marks his handkerchiefs and wipes the pistol with which he has committed the crime—yet careless since he loses his handkerchief and does not search for a letter that might incriminate him."

"Flurried, that's what he was," said the inspector.

"It is possible," said Poirot. "Yes, it is possible. And he was not seen entering the building?"

"There are all sorts of people going in and out at that time. These are big blocks. I suppose none of you"—he addressed the four collectively—"saw anyone coming out of the flat?"

Pat shook her head. "We went out earlier—about seven o'clock."

"I see." The inspector rose. Poirot accompanied him to the door. "As a little favor, may I examine the flat below?"

"Why, certainly, M. Poirot. I know what they think of you at headquarters. I'll leave you a key. I've got two. It will be empty. The maid cleared out to some relatives, too scared to stay there alone."

"I thank you," said M. Poirot. He went back into the flat, thoughtful.

"You're not satisfied, M. Poirot?" said Jimmy.

"No," said Poirot. "I am not satisfied."

Donovan looked at him curiously. "What is it that—well, worries you?"

Poirot did not answer. He remained silent for a minute or two, frowning, as though in thought, then he made a sudden impatient movement of his shoulders.

"I will say good night to you, mademoiselle. You must be tired. You have had much cooking to do—eh?"

Pat laughed. "Only the omelet. I didn't do dinner. Donovan and Jimmy came and called for us, and we went out to a little place in Soho."

"And then without doubt, you went to a theater?"

"Yes. 'The Brown Eyes of Caroline.'"

"Ah!" said Poirot. "It should have been blue eyes—the blue eyes of mademoiselle."

He made a sentimental gesture, and then once more wished Pat good night, also Mildred, who was staying the night by special request, as Pat admitted frankly that she would get the horrors if left alone on this particular night.

The two young men accompanied Poirot. When the door was shut, and they were preparing to say good-by to him on the landing, Poirot forestalled them.

"My young friends, you heard me say that I was not satisfied? *Eh bien*, it is true—I am not. I go now to make some little investigations of my own. You would like to accompany me—yes?"

An eager assent greeted this proposal. Poirot led the way to the flat below and inserted the key the inspector had given him in the lock. On entering, he did not, as the others had expected, enter the sitting-room. Instead he went straight to the kitchen. In a little recess which served as a scullery a big iron bin was standing. Poirot uncovered this and, doubling himself up, began to rootle in it with the energy of a ferocious terrier.

Both Jimmy and Donovan stared at him in amazement.

Suddenly with a cry of triumph he emerged. In his hand he held aloft a small stoppered bottle.

"Voilà!" he said. "I find what I seek." He sniffed at it delicately, "Alas! I am *enrhumé*—I have the cold in the head."

Donovan took the bottle from him and sniffed in his turn, but could smell nothing. He took out the stopper and held the bottle to his nose before Poirot's warning cry could stop him.

Immediately he fell like a log. Poirot, by springing forward, partly broke his fall.

"Imbecile!" he cried. "The idea. To remove the stopper in that foolhardy manner! Did he not observe how delicately I handled it? Monsieur—Faulkener—is it not? Will you be so good as to get me a little brandy? I observed a decanter in the sitting-room."

Jimmy hurried off, but by the time he returned, Donovan was sitting up and declaring himself quite all right again. He had to listen to a short lecture from Poirot on the necessity of caution in sniffing at possibly poisonous substances.

"I think I'll be off home," said Donovan, rising shakily to his feet. "That is, if I can't be any more use here. I feel a bit wonky still."

"Assuredly," said Poirot. "That is the best thing you can do. M. Faulkener, attend me here a little minute. I will return on the instant."

He accompanied Donovan to the door and beyond. They remained outside on the landing talking for some minutes. When Poirot at last re-entered the flat he found Jimmy standing in the sitting-room gazing round him with puzzled eyes.

"Well, M. Poirot," he said, "what next?"

"There is nothing next. The case is finished."

"What?"

"I know everything—now."

Jimmy stared at him. "That little bottle you found?"

"Exactly. That little bottle."

Jimmy shook his head. "I can't make head or tail of it. For some reason or other I can see you are dissatisfied with the evidence against this John Fraser, whoever he may be."

"Whoever he may be," repeated Poirot softly. "If he is anyone at all—well, I shall be surprised."

"I don't understand."

"He is a name—that is all—a name carefully marked on a handkerchief!"

"And the letter?"

"Did you notice that it was printed? Now, why? I will tell you. Handwriting might be recognized, and a typewritten letter is more easily traced than you would imagine—but if a real John Fraser wrote that letter those two points would not have appealed to him! No, it was written on purpose, and put in the dead woman's pocket for us to find. There is no such person as John Fraser."

Jimmy looked at him inquiringly.

"And so," went on Poirot, "I went back to the point that first struck me. You heard me say that certain things in a room were always in the same place under given circumstances. I gave three instances. I might have mentioned a fourth—the electric-light switch, my friend."

Jimmy still stared uncomprehendingly. Poirot went on.

"Your friend Donovan did not go near the window—it was by resting his hand on this table that he got it covered in blood! But I asked myself at once—why did he rest it there? What was he doing groping about this room in darkness? For remember, my friend, the electric-light switch is always in the same place—by the door. Why, when he came to this room, did he not at once feel for the light and turn it on? That was the natural, the normal thing to do. According to him, he tried to turn on the light in the kitchen, but failed. Yet when I tried the switch it was in perfect working order. Did he, then, not wish the light to go on just then? If it had gone on you would both have seen at once that you were in the wrong flat. There would have been no reason to come into this room."

"What are you driving at, M. Poirot? I don't understand. What do you mean?"

"I mean—this."

Poirot held up a Yale door key.

"The key of this flat?"

"No, *mon ami*, the key of the flat above. Mademoiselle Patricia's key, which M. Donovan Bailey abstracted from her bag sometime during the evening."

"But why—why?"

"*Parbleu!* so that he could do what he wanted to do—gain admission to this flat in a perfectly unsuspicious manner. He made sure that the lift door was unbolted earlier in the evening."

"Where did you get the key?"

Poirot's smile broadened. "I found it just now—where I looked for it—in M. Donovan's pocket. See you, that little bottle I pretended to find was a ruse. M. Donovan is taken in. He does what I knew he would do—unstoppers it and sniffs. And in that little bottle is ethyl chloride, a very powerful instant anesthetic. It gives me just the moment or two of unconsciousness I need. I take from his pocket the two things that I knew would be there. This key was one of them—the other—"

He stopped and then went on.

"I questioned at the time the reason the inspector gave for the body being concealed behind the curtain. To gain time? No, there was more than that. And so I thought of just one thing—the post, my friend. The evening post that comes at half past nine or thereabouts. Say the murderer does not find something he expects to find, but that something may be delivered by post later. Clearly, then, he must come back. But the crime must not be discovered by the maid when she comes in, or the police would take possession of the flat, so he hides the body behind the curtain. And the maid suspects nothing and lays the letters on the table as usual."

"The letters?"

"Yes, the letters." Poirot drew something from his pocket. "This is the second article I took from M. Donovan when he was unconscious." He showed the superscription—a typewritten envelope addressed to Mrs. Ernestine Grant. "But I will ask you one thing first, M. Faulkener, before we look at the contents of this letter. Are you or are you not in love with Mademoiselle Patricia?"

"I care for Pat damnably—but I've never thought I had a chance."

"You thought that she cared for M. Donovan? It may be that she had begun to care for him—but it was only a beginning, my friend. It is for you to make her forget—to stand by her in her trouble."

"Trouble?" said Jimmy sharply.

"Yes, trouble. We will do all we can to keep her name out of it, but it will be impossible to do so entirely. She was, you see, the motive."

He ripped open the envelope that he held. An enclosure fell out. The covering letter was brief, and was from a firm of solicitors. ˙

Dear Madam,

The document you enclose is quite in order, and the fact of the marriage having taken place in a foreign country does not invalidate it in any way.

Yours truly, etc.

Poirot spread out the enclosure. It was a certificate of marriage between Donovan Bailey and Ernestine Grant, dated eight years ago.

"Oh, my God!" said Jimmy. "Pat said she'd had a letter from the woman asking to see her, but she never dreamed it was anything important."

Poirot nodded. "M. Donovan knew—he went to see his wife this evening before going to the flat above—a strange irony, by the way, that led the unfortunate woman to come to this building where her rival lived—he murdered her in cold blood—and then went on to his evening's amusement. His wife must have told him that she had sent the marriage certificate to her solicitors and was expecting to hear from them. Doubtless he himself had tried to make her believe that there was a flaw in the marriage."

"He seemed in quite good spirits, too, all the evening. M. Poirot, you haven't let him escape?" Jimmy shuddered.

"There is no escape for him," said Poirot gravely. "You need not fear."

"It's Pat I'm thinking about mostly," said Jimmy. "You don't think—she really cared."

"*Mon ami,* that is your part," said Poirot gently. "To make her turn to you and forget. I do not think you will find it very difficult!"

2. THE ADVENTURE OF JOHNNIE WAVERLY

You can understand the feelings of a mother," said Mrs. Waverly for perhaps the sixth time.

She looked appealingly at Poirot. My little friend, always sympathetic to motherhood in distress, gesticulated reassuringly.

"But yes, but yes, I comprehend perfectly. Have faith in Papa Poirot."

"The police—" began Mr. Waverly.

His wife waved the interruption aside, "I won't have anything more to do with the police. We trusted to them and look what happened! But I'd heard so much of M. Poirot and the wonderful things he'd done, that I felt he might possibly be able to help us. A mother's feelings—"

Poirot hastily stemmed the reiteration with an eloquent gesture. Mrs. Waverly's emotion was obviously genuine, but it assorted strangely with her shrewd, rather hard type of countenance. When I heard later that she was the daughter of a prominent steel manufacturer of Birmingham who had worked his way up in the world from an office boy to his present eminence, I realized that she had inherited many of the paternal qualities.

Mr. Waverly was a big, florid, jovial-looking man. He stood with his legs straddled wide apart and looked the type of the country squire.

"I suppose you know all about this business, M. Poirot?"

The question was almost superfluous. For some days past the paper had been full of the sensational kidnaping of little Johnnie Waverly, the three-year-old son and heir of Marcus Waverly, Esq., of Waverly Court, Surrey, one of the oldest families in England.

"The main facts I know, of course, but recount to me the whole story, monsieur. I beg of you. And in detail if you please."

"Well, I suppose the beginning of the whole thing was about ten days ago when I got an anonymous letter—beastly things, anyway—that I couldn't make head or tail of. The writer had the impudence to demand that I should pay him twenty-five thousand pounds—twenty-five thousand pounds, M. Poirot! Failing my agreement, he threatened to kidnap Johnnie. Of course I threw the thing into the wastepaper basket without more ado. Thought it was some silly joke. Five days later I got another letter. 'Unless you pay, your son will be kidnaped on the twenty-ninth.' That was on the twenty-seventh. Ada was worried, but I couldn't bring myself to treat the matter seriously. Damn it all, we're in England. Nobody goes about kidnaping children and holding them up to ransom."

"It is not a common practice, certainly," said Poirot. "Proceed, monsieur."

"Well, Ada gave me no peace, so—feeling a bit of a fool—I laid the matter before Scotland Yard. They didn't seem to take the thing very seriously—inclined to my view that it was some silly joke. On the twenty-eighth I got a third letter. 'You have not paid. Your son will be taken from you at twelve o'clock noon tomorrow, the twenty-ninth. It will cost you fifty thousand pounds to recover him.' Up I drove to Scotland Yard again. This time they were more impressed. They inclined to the view that the letters were written by a lunatic, and that in all probability an attempt of some kind would be made at the hour stated. They assured me that they would take all due precautions. Inspector McNeil and a sufficient force would come down to Waverly on the morrow and take charge.

"I went home much relieved in my mind. Yet we already had the feeling of being in a state of siege. I gave orders that no stranger was to be admitted, and that no one was to leave the house. The evening passed off without any untoward incident, but on the following morning my wife was seriously unwell. Alarmed by her condition, I sent for Doctor Dakers. Her symptoms appeared to puzzle him. While hesitating to suggest that she had been poisoned, I could see that that was what was in his mind. There was no danger, he assured me, but it would be a day or two before she would be able to get about again. Returning to my own room, I was startled and amazed to find a note pinned to my pillow. It was in the same handwriting as the others and contained just three words: 'At twelve o'clock.'

"I admit, M. Poirot, that then I saw red! Someone in the house was in this—one of the servants. I had them all up, blackguarded them right and left. They never split on each other; it was Miss Collins, my wife's companion, who informed me that she had seen Johnnie's nurse slip down the drive early that morning. I taxed her with it, and she broke down. She had left the child with the nursery maid and stolen out to meet a friend of hers—a man! Pretty goings on! She denied having pinned the note to my pillow—she may have been speaking the truth, I don't know. I felt I couldn't take the risk of the child's own nurse being in the plot. One of the servants was implicated—of that I was sure. Finally I lost my temper and sacked the whole bunch, nurse and all. I gave them an hour to pack their boxes and get out of the house."

Mr. Waverly's red face was quite two shades redder as he remembered his just wrath.

"Was not that a little injudicious, monsieur?" suggested Poirot. "For all you know, you might have been playing into the enemy's hands."

Mr. Waverly stared at him. "I don't see that. Send the whole lot packing, that was my idea. I wired to London for a fresh lot to be sent down that evening. In the meantime, there'd be only people I could trust in the house, my wife's secretary, Miss Collins, and Tredwell, the butler, who has been with me since I was a boy."

"And this Miss Collins, how long has she been with you?"

"Just a year," said Mrs. Waverly. "She has been invaluable to me as a secretary-companion, and is also a very efficient housekeeper."

"The nurse?"

"She has been with me six months. She came to me with excellent references. All the same I never really liked her, although Johnnie was quite devoted to her."

"Still, I gather she had already left when the catastrophe occurred. Perhaps, Monsieur Waverly, you will be so kind as to continue."

Mr. Waverly resumed his narrative.

"Inspector McNeil arrived about ten-thirty. The servants had all left by then. He declared himself quite satisfied with the internal arrangements. He had various men posted in the park outside, guarding all the approaches to the house, and he assured me that if the whole thing were not a hoax, we should undoubtedly catch my mysterious correspondent.

"I had Johnnie with me, and he and I and the inspector went together into a room we call the Council Chamber. The inspector locked the door. There is a big grandfather clock there, and as the hands drew near to twelve I don't mind confessing that I was as nervous as a cat. There was a whirring sound, and the clock began to strike. I clutched Johnnie. I had a feeling a man might drop from the skies. The last stroke sounded, and as it did so, there was a great commotion outside—shouting and running. The inspector flung up the window, and a constable came running up.

"'We've got him, sir,' he panted. 'He was sneaking up through the bushes. He's got a whole dope outfit on him.'

"We hurried out on the terrace where two constables were holding a ruffianly-looking fellow in shabby clothes, who was twisting and turning in a vain endeavor to escape. One of the policemen held out an unrolled parcel which they had wrested from their captive. It contained a pad of cotton wool and a bottle of chloroform. It made my blood boil to see it. There was a note, too, addressed to me. I tore it open. It bore the following words: 'You should have paid up. To ransom your son will now cost you fifty thousand. In spite of all your precautions he has been abducted at twelve o'clock on the twenty-ninth as I said.'

"I gave a great laugh, the laugh of relief, but as I did so I heard the hum of a motor and a shout. I turned my head. Racing down the drive toward the south lodge at a furious speed was a low, long gray car. It was the man who drove it who had shouted, but that was not what gave me a shock of·horror. It was the sight of Johnnie's flaxen curls. The child was in the car beside him.

"'The inspector ripped out an oath.

"'The child was here not a minute ago,' he cried. His eyes swept over us. We were all there, myself, Tredwell, Miss Collins. 'When did you see him last, Mr. Waverly?'

"I cast my mind back, trying to remember. When the constable had called us, I had run out with the inspector, forgetting all about Johnnie.

"And then there came a sound that startled us, the chiming of a church clock from the village. With an exclamation the inspector pulled out his watch. It was exactly twelve o'clock. With one common accord we ran to the Council Chamber, the clock there marked the hour as ten minutes past. Someone must have deliberately tampered with it, for I have never known it gain or lose before. It is a perfect timekeeper."

Mr. Waverly paused. Poirot smiled to himself and straightened a little mat which the anxious father had pushed askew.

"A pleasing little problem, obscure and charming," murmured Poirot. "I will investigate it for you with pleasure. Truly it was planned à merveille."

Mrs. Waverly looked at him reproachfully. "But my boy," she wailed.

Poirot hastily composed his face and looked the picture of earnest sympathy again. "He is safe, madame, he is unharmed. Rest assured, these miscreants will take the greatest care of him. Is he not to them the turkey—no, the goose—that lays the golden eggs?"

"M. Poirot, I'm sure there's only one thing to be done—pay up. I was all against it at first—but now! A mother's feelings—"

"But we have interrupted monsieur in his history," cried Poirot hastily.

"I expect you know the rest pretty well from the papers," said Mr. Waverly. "Of course, Inspector McNeil got onto the telephone immediately. A description of the car and the man was circulated all round, and it looked at first as though everything was going to turn out all right. A car, answering to the description, with a man and a small boy, had passed through various villages, apparently making for London. At one place they had stopped, and it was noticed that the child was crying and obviously afraid of his companion. When Inspector McNeil announced that the car had been stopped and the man and boy detained, I was almost ill with relief. You know the sequel. The boy was not Johnnie, and the man was an ardent motorist, fond of children, who had picked up a small child playing in the streets of Edenswell, a village about fifteen miles from us, and was kindly giving him a ride. Thanks to the cocksure blundering of the police, all traces have disappeared. Had they not persistently followed the wrong car, they might by now have found the boy."

"Calm yourself, monsieur. The police are a brave and intelligent force of men. Their mistake was a very natural one. And altogether it was a clever scheme. As to the man they caught in the grounds, I understand that his defense has consisted all along of a persistent denial. He declares that the note and parcel were given to him to deliver at Waverly Court. The man who gave them to him handed him a ten-shilling note and promised him another if it were delivered at exactly ten minutes to twelve. He was to approach the house through the grounds and knock at the side door."

"I don't believe a word of it," declared Mrs. Waverly hotly. "It's all a parcel of lies."

"*En vérité,* it is a thin story," said Poirot reflectively. "But so far they have not shaken it. I understand, also, that he made a certain accusation?"

His glance interrogated Mr. Waverly. The latter got rather red again.

"The fellow had the impertinence to pretend that he recognized in Tredwell the man who gave him the parcel. 'Only the bloke has shaved off his mustache.' Tredwell, who was born on the estate!"

Poirot smiled a little at the country gentleman's indignation. "Yet you yourself suspect an inmate of the house to have been accessory to the abduction."

"Yes, but not Tredwell."

"And you, madame?" asked Poirot, suddenly turning to her.

"It could not have been Tredwell who gave this tramp the letter and parcel—if anybody ever did, which I don't believe—It was given him at ten o'clock, he says. At ten o'clock, Tredwell was with my husband in the smokingroom."

"Were you able to see the face of the man in the car, monsieur? Did it resemble that of Tredwell in any way?"

"It was too far away for me to see his face."

"Has Tredwell a brother, do you know?"

"He had several, but they are all dead. The last one was killed in the war."

"I am not yet clear as to the grounds of Waverly Court. The car was heading for the south lodge. Is there another entrance?"

"Yes, what we call the east lodge. It can be seen from the other side of the house."

"It seems to me strange that nobody saw the car entering the grounds."

"There is a right of way through, and access to a small chapel. A good many cars pass through. The man must have stopped the car in a convenient place and run up to the house just as the alarm was given and attention attracted elsewhere."

"Unless he was already inside the house," mused Poirot. "Is there any place where he could have hidden?"

"Well, we certainly didn't make a thorough search of the house beforehand. There seemed no need. I suppose he might have hidden himself somewhere, but who would have let him in?"

"We shall come to that later. One thing at a time—let us be methodical. There is no special hiding-place in the house? Waverly Court is an old place, and there are sometimes 'priest's holes' as they call them."

"By gad, there *is* a priest's hole. It opens from one of the panels in the hall."

"Near the Council Chamber?"

"Just outside the door."

"*Voilà!*"

"But nobody knows of its existence except my wife and myself."

"Tredwell?"

"Well—he might have heard of it."

"Miss Collins?"

"I have never mentioned it to her."

Poirot reflected for a minute.

"Well, monsieur, the next thing is for me to come down to Waverly Court. If I arrive this afternoon, will it suit you?"

"Oh, as soon as possible, please, Monsieur Poirot!" cried Mrs. Waverly. "Read this once more."

She thrust into his hands the last missive from the enemy which had reached the Waverlys that morning and which had sent her posthaste to Poirot. It gave clever and explicit directions for the paying over of the money, and ended with a threat that the boy's life would pay for any treachery. It was clear that a love of money warred with the essential mother love of Mrs. Waverly, and that the latter was at last gaining the day.

Poirot detained Mrs. Waverly for a minute behind her husband.

"Madame, the truth, if you please. Do you share your husband's faith in the butler, Tredwell?"

"I have nothing against him, Monsieur Poirot, I cannot see how he can have been concerned in this, but—well, I have never liked him—never!"

"One other thing, madame, can you give me the address of the child's nurse?"

"149 Netherall Road, Hammersmith. You don't imagine—"

"Never do I imagine. Only—I employ the little gray cells. And sometimes, just sometimes, I have a little idea."

Poirot came back to me as the door closed.

"So madame has never liked the butler. It is interesting, that, eh, Hastings?"

I refused to be drawn. Poirot has deceived me so often that I now go warily. There is always a catch somewhere.

After completing an elaborate outdoor toilet, we set off for Netherall Road. We were fortunate enough to find Miss Jessie Withers at home. She was a pleasant-faced woman of thirty-five, capable and superior. I could not believe that she could be mixed up in the affair. She was bitterly resentful of the way she had been dismissed, but admitted that she had been in the wrong. She was engaged to be married to a painter and decorator who happened to be in the neighborhood, and she had run out to meet him. The thing seemed natural enough. I could not quite understand Poirot. All his questions seemed to me quite irrelevant. They were concerned mainly with the daily routine of her life at Waverly Court. I was frankly bored and glad when Poirot took his departure.

"Kidnaping is an easy job, *mon ami*," he observed, as he hailed a taxi in the Hammersmith Road and ordered it to drive to Waterloo. "That child could have been abducted with the greatest ease any day for the last three years."

"I don't see that that advances us much," I remarked coldly.

"*Au contraire*, it advances us enormously, but enormously! If you must wear a tie pin, Hastings, at least let it be in the exact center of your tie. At present it is at least a sixteenth of an inch too much to the right."

Waverly Court was a fine old place and had recently been restored with taste and care. Mr. Waverly showed us the Council Chamber, the terrace, and all the various spots connected with the case. Finally, at Poirot's request, he pressed a spring in the wall, a panel slid aside, and a short passage led us into the priest's hole.

"You see," said Waverly. "There is nothing here."

The tiny room was bare enough, there was not even the mark of a footstep on the floor. I joined Poirot where he was bending attentively over a mark in the corner.

"What do you make of this, my friend?"

There were four imprints close together.

"A dog," I cried.

"A very small dog, Hastings."

"A Pom."

"Smaller than a Pom."

"A griffon?" I suggested doubtfully.

"Smaller even than a griffon. A species unknown to the Kennel Club."

I looked at him. His face was alight with excitement and satisfaction.

"I was right," he murmured. "I knew I was right. Come, Hastings."

As we stepped out into the hall and the panel closed behind us, a young lady came out of a door farther down the passage. Mr. Waverly presented her to us.

"Miss Collins."

Miss Collins was about thirty years of age, brisk and alert in manner. She had fair, rather dull hair, and wore pince-nez.

At Poirot's request, we passed into a small morning room, and he questioned her closely as to the servants and particularly as to Tredwell. She admitted that she did not like the butler.

"He gives himself airs," she explained.

They then went into the question of the food eaten by Mrs. Waverly on the night of the 28th. Miss Collins declared that she had partaken of the same dishes upstairs in her sitting-room and had felt no ill effects. As she was departing I nudged Poirot.

"The dog," I whispered.

"Ah, yes, the dog!" He smiled broadly. "Is there a dog kept here by any chance, mademoiselle?"

"There are two retrievers in the kennels outside."

"No, I mean a small dog, a toy dog."

"No—nothing of the kind."

Poirot permitted her to depart. Then, pressing the bell, he remarked to me, "She lies, that Mademoiselle Collins. Possibly I should, also, in her place. Now for the butler."

Tredwell was a dignified individual. He told his story with perfect aplomb, and it was essentially the same as that of Mr. Waverly. He admitted that he knew the secret of the priest's hole.

When he finally withdrew, pontifical to the last, I met Poirot's quizzical eyes.

"What do you make of it all, Hastings?"

"What do you?" I parried.

"How cautious you become. Never, never will the gray cells function unless you stimulate them. Ah, but I will not tease you! Let us make our deductions together. What points strike us specially as being difficult?"

"There is one thing that strikes me," I said. "Why did the man who kidnaped the child go out by the south lodge instead of by the east lodge where no one would see him?"

"That is a very good point, Hastings, an excellent one. I will match it with another. Why warn the Waverlys beforehand? Why not simply kidnap the child and hold him to ransom?"

"Because they hoped to get the money without being forced into action."

"Surely it was very unlikely that the money would be paid on a mere threat?"

"Also they wanted to focus attention on twelve o'clock, so that when the tramp man was seized, the other could emerge from his hiding-place and get away with the child unnoticed."

"That does not alter the fact that they were making a thing difficult that was perfectly easy. If they do not specify a time or date, nothing would be easier than to wait their chance, and carry off the child in a motor one day when he is out with his nurse."

"Ye-es," I admitted doubtfully.

"In fact, there is a deliberate playing of the farce! Now let us approach the question from another side. Everything goes to show that there was an accomplice inside the house. Point number one, the mysterious poisoning of Mrs. Waverly. Point number two, the letter pinned to the pillow. Point number three, the putting on of the clock ten minutes—all inside jobs. And an additional fact that you may not have noticed. There was no dust in the priest's hole. It had been swept out with a broom.

"Now, then, we have four people in the house. We can exclude the nurse, since she could not have swept out the priest's hole, though she could have attended to the other three points. Four people. Mr. and Mrs. Waverly, Tredwell, the butler, and Miss Collins.

We will take Miss Collins first. We have nothing much against her, except that we know very little about her, that she is obviously an intelligent young woman, and that she has only been here a year."

· "She lied about the dog, you said," I reminded him.

"Ah, yes, the dog." Poirot gave a peculiar smile. "Now let us pass to Tredwell. There are several suspicious facts against him. For one thing, the tramp declares that it was Tredwell who gave him the parcel in the village."

"But Tredwell can prove an alibi on that point."

"Even then, he could have poisoned Mrs. Waverly, pinned the note to the pillow, put on the clock, and swept out the priest's hole. On the other hand, he has been born and bred in the service of the Waverlys. It seems unlikely in the last degree that he should connive at the abduction of the son of the house. It is not in the picture!"

"Well, then?"

"We must proceed logically—however absurd it may seem. We will briefly consider Mrs. Waverly. But she is rich, the money is hers. It is her money which has restored this impoverished estate. There would be no reason for her to kidnap her son and pay over her money to herself. Her husband, now, is in a different position. He has a rich wife. It is not the same thing as being rich himself—in fact I have a little idea that the lady is not very fond of parting with her money, except on a very good pretext. But Mr. Waverly, you can see at once, he is *bon viveur*."

"Impossible," I spluttered.

"Not at all. Who sends away the servants? Mr. Waverly. He can write the notes, drug his wife, put on the hands of the clock, and establish an excellent alibi for his faithful retainer Tredwell. Tredwell has never liked Mrs. Waverly. He is devoted to his master and is willing to obey his orders implicitly. There were three of them in it. Waverly, Tredwell, and some friend of Waverly. That is the mistake the police made, they made no further inquiries about the man who drove the gray car with the wrong child in it. He was the third man. He picks up a child in a village near by, a boy with flaxen curls. He drives in through the east lodge and passes out through the south lodge just at the right moment, waving his hand and shouting. They cannot see his face or the number of the car, so obviously they cannot see the child's face, either. Then he lays a false trail to London, In the meantime, Tredwell has done his part in arranging for the parcel and note to be delivered by a rough-looking gentleman. His master can provide an alibi in the unlikely case of the man recognizing him, in spite of the false mustache he wore. As for Mr. Waverly, as soon as the hullabaloo occurs outside, and the inspector rushes out, he quickly hides the child in the priest's hole, and follows him out. Later in the day, when the inspector is gone and Miss Collins is out of the way, it will be easy enough to drive him off to some safe place in his own car."

"But what about the dog?" I asked. "And Miss Collins lying?"

"That was my little joke. I asked her if there were any toy dogs in the house, and she said no—but doubtless there are some—in the nursery! You see, Mr. Waverly placed some toys in the priest's hole to keep Johnnie amused and quiet."

"M. Poirot." Mr. Waverly entered the room. "Have you discovered anything? Have you any clue to where the boy has been taken?"

Poirot handed him a piece of paper. "Here is the address."

"But this is a blank sheet."

"Because I am waiting for you to write it down for me."

"What the—" Mr. Waverly's face turned purple.

"I know everything, monsieur. I give you twenty-four hours to return the boy. Your ingenuity will be equal to the task of explaining his reappearance. Otherwise, Mrs. Waverly will be informed of the exact sequence of events."

Mr. Waverly sank down in a chair and buried his face in his hands. "He is with my old nurse, ten miles away. He is happy and well cared for."

"I have no doubt of that. If I did not believe you to be a good father at heart, I should not be willing to give you another chance."

"The scandal—"

"Exactly. Your name is an old and honored one. Do not jeopardize it again. Good evening, Mr. Waverly. Ah! by the way, one word of advice. Always sweep in the corners!"

3. FOUR AND TWENTY BLACKBIRDS

Hercule Poirot was dining with his friend, Henry Bonnington, at the Gallant Endeavor in the King's Road, Chelsea.

Mr. Bonnington was fond of the Gallant Endeavor. He liked the leisurely atmosphere, he liked the food which was "plain" and "English" and "not a lot of made-up messes."

Molly, the sympathetic waitress, greeted him as an old friend. She prided herself on remembering her customers' likes and dislikes in the way of food.

"Good evening, sir," she said as the two men took their seats at a corner table. "You're in luck today—turkey stuffed with chestnuts—that's your favorite, isn't it? And ever such a nice Stilton we've got! Will you have soup first or fish?"

The question of food and wine settled, Mr. Bonnington leaned back with a sigh and unfolded his napkin as Molly sped away.

"Good girl, that!" he said approvingly. "Was quite a beauty once—artists used to paint her. She knows about food, too—and that's a great deal more important. Women are very unsound on food as a rule. There's many a woman, if she goes out with a fellow she fancies, won't even notice what she eats. She'll just order the first thing she sees."

Hercule Poirot shook his head. "*C'est terrible.*"

"Men aren't like that, thank goodness!" said Mr. Bonnington complacently.

"Never?" There was a twinkle in Hercule Poirot's eye.

"Well, perhaps when they're very young," conceded Mr. Bonnington. "Young puppies! Young fellows nowadays are all the same— no guts—no stamina. I've no use for the young—and they," he added with strict impartiality, "have no use for me. Perhaps they're right! But to hear some of these young fellows talk you'd think no man had a right to be *alive* after sixty! From the way they go on, you'd wonder more of them didn't help their elderly relations out of the world."

"It is possible," said Hercule Poirot, "that they do."

"Nice mind you've got, Poirot, I must say. All this police work saps your ideals."

Hercule Poirot smiled. "Nevertheless," he said, "it would be interesting to make a table of accidental deaths over the age of sixty. I assure you it would raise some curious speculations in your mind. But tell me, my friend, of your own affairs. How does the world go with you?"

"Mess!" said Mr. Bonnington. "That's what's the matter with the world nowadays. Too much mess. And too much fine language. The fine language helps to conceal the mess. Like a highly flavored sauce concealing the fact that the fish underneath it is none of the best! Give me an honest fillet of sole and no messy sauce over it."

It was given him at that moment by Molly, and he grunted approval.

"You know just what I like, my girl," he said.

"Well, you come here pretty regular, don't you, sir? So I ought to know."

Hercule Poirot said, "Do people, then, always like the same things? Do not they like a change sometimes?"

"Not gentlemen, sir. Ladies like variety—gentlemen always like the same thing."

"What did I tell you?" grunted Bonnington. "Women are fundamentally unsound where food is concerned!"

He looked around the restaurant.

"The world's a funny place. See that odd-looking old fellow with a beard in the corner? Molly'll tell you he's always here Tuesday and Thursday nights. He has come here for close on ten years now—he's a kind of landmark in the place. Yet nobody here knows his name or where he lives or what his business is. It's odd when you come to think of it."

When the waitress brought the portions of turkey he said, "I see you've still got Old Father Time over there."

"That's right, sir. Tuesdays and Thursdays, his days are. Not but what he came in here on a *Monday* last week! It quite upset me! I felt I'd got my dates wrong and that it must be Tuesday without my knowing it! But he came in the next night as well—so the Monday was just a kind of extra, so to speak."

"An interesting deviation from habit," murmured Poirot. "I wonder what the reason was?"

"Well, sir, if you ask me, I think he'd had some kind of upset or worry."

"Why did you think that? His manner?"

"No, sir—not his manner exactly. He was very quiet as he always is. Never says much except 'Good evening' when he comes and goes. No, it was his *order*."

"His order?"

"I daresay you gentlemen will laugh at me." Molly flushed. "But when a gentleman has been here for ten years, you get to know his likes and dislikes. He never could bear suet pudding or blackberries, and I've never known him to take thick soup—but on that Monday night he ordered thick tomato soup, beefsteak and kidney pudding, and blackberry tart! Seemed as though he just didn't notice *what* he ordered!"

"Do you know," said Hercule Poirot, "I find that extraordinarily interesting."

Molly looked gratified and departed.

"Well, Poirot," said Henry Bonnington with a chuckle, Let's have a few deductions from you. All in your best manner."

"I would prefer to hear yours, first."

"Want me to be Watson, eh? Well, old fellow went to a doctor, and the doctor changed his diet."

"To thick tomato soup, steak and kidney pudding, and blackberry tart? I cannot imagine any doctor doing that."

"Don't you believe it, old boy. Doctors will put you onto anything."

"That is the only solution that occurs to you?"

Henry Bonnington said, "Well, seriously, I suppose there's only one explanation possible. Our unknown friend was in the grip of some powerful mental emotion. He was so perturbed by it that he literally did not notice what he was ordering or eating." He paused a minute, and then said, "You'll be telling me next that you know just *what* was on his mind. You'll say, perhaps, that he was making up his mind to commit a murder."

He laughed at his own suggestion.

Hercule Poirot did not laugh.

He has admitted that at that moment he was seriously worried. He claims that he ought then to have had some inkling of what was likely to occur.

His friends assure him that such an idea is quite fantastic.

IT WAS SOME three weeks later that Hercule Poirot and Bonnington met again—this time their meeting was in the subway.

They nodded to each other, swaying about, hanging onto adjacent straps. Then at Piccadilly Circus there was a general exodus, and they found seats right at the forward end of the car—a peaceful spot, since nobody passed in or out that way.

"By the way," said Mr. Bonnington. "Do you remember that old boy we noticed at the Gallant Endeavor? I shouldn't wonder if he'd hopped it to a better world. He's not been there for a whole week. Molly's quite upset about it."

Hercule Poirot sat up. His eyes flashed.

"Indeed?" he said. "Indeed?"

Bonnington said, "D'you remember I suggested he'd been to a

doctor and been put on a diet? Diet's nonsense, of course—but I shouldn't wonder if he had consulted a doctor about his health and what the doctor said gave him a bit of a jolt. That would account for him ordering things off the menu without noticing what he was doing. Quite likely the jolt he got hurried him out of the world sooner than he would have gone otherwise. Doctors ought to be careful what they tell a chap."

"They usually are," said Hercule Poirot.

"This is my station," said Mr. Bonnington. "By-by. Don't suppose we shall ever know now who the old boy was—not even his name. Funny world!"

He hurried out of the carriage.

Hercule Poirot, sitting frowning, looked as though he did not think it was such a funny world. He went home and gave certain instructions to his faithful valet, George.

HERCULE POIROT RAN his finger down a list of names. It was a record of deaths within a certain area.

Poirot's finger stopped.

"Henry Gascoigne. Sixty-nine. I might try him first."

Later in the day Hercule Poirot was sitting in Dr. MacAndrew's surgery just off the King's Road. MacAndrew was a tall, red-haired Scotsman with an intelligent face.

"Gascoigne?" he said. "Yes, that's right. Eccentric old bird. Lived alone in one of those derelict old houses that are being cleared away in order to build a block of modern flats. I hadn't attended him before, but I'd seen him about and I knew who he was. It was the dairy people got the wind up first. The milk bottles began to pile up outside. In the end the people next door sent word to the police, and they broke the door in and found him. He'd pitched down the stairs and broken his neck. Had on an old dressing-gown with a ragged cord—might easily have tripped himself up with it."

"I see," said Hercule Poirot. "It was quite simple—an accident."

"That's right."

"Had he any relations?"

"There's a nephew. Used to come along and see his uncle about once a month. Ramsey, his name is, George Ramsey. He's a medico himself. Lives at Wimbledon."

"How long had Mr. Gascoigne been dead when you saw him?"

"Ah!" said Dr. MacAndrew. "This is where we get official. Not less than forty-eight hours and not more than seventy-two hours. He was found on the morning of the sixth. Actually, we got closer than that. He had a letter in the pocket of his dressing-gown—written on the third—posted in Wimbledon that afternoon—would have been delivered somewhere around nine-twenty p.m. That puts the time of death at after nine-twenty on the evening of the third. That agrees with the contents of the stomach and the processes of digestion. He had had a meal about two hours before death. I examined him on the morning of the sixth, and his condition was quite consistent with death having occurred about sixty hours previously—around about ten p.m. on the third."

"It all seems very consistent. Tell me, when was he last seen alive?"

"He was seen in the King's Road about seven o'clock that same evening, Thursday the third, and he dined at the Gallant Endeavor restaurant at seven-thirty. It seems he always dined there on Thursdays."

"He had no other relations? Only this nephew?"

"There was a twin brother. The whole story is rather curious. They hadn't seen each other for years. As a young man Henry was by way of being an artist, you know. An extremely bad one. It seems the other brother, Anthony Gascoigne, married a very rich woman and gave up art—and the brothers quarreled over it. Hadn't seen each other since, I believe. But oddly enough, *they died on the same day.* The elder twin passed away at one o'clock on the afternoon of the third. Once before I've known a case of twins dying on the same day—in different parts of the world! Probably just a coincidence—but there it is."

"Is the other brother's wife alive?"

"No, she died some years ago."

"Where did Anthony Gascoigne live?"

"He had a house on Kingston Hill. He was, I believe, from what Doctor Ramsey tells me, very much of a recluse."

Hercule Poirot nodded thoughtfully.

The Scotsman looked at him keenly. "What exactly have you got in your mind, M. Poirot?" he asked bluntly. "I've answered your questions—as was my duty, seeing the credentials you brought. But I'm in the dark as to what it's all about."

Poirot said slowly, "A simple case of accidental death, that's what you said. What I have in mind is equally simple—a simple push."

Dr. MacAndrew looked startled.

"In other words, murder! Have you any grounds for that belief?"

"No," said Poirot. "It is a mere supposition."

"There must be something—" persisted the other.

Poirot did not speak.

MacAndrew said, "If it's the nephew, Ramsey, you suspect, I don't mind telling you here and now that you are barking up the wrong tree. Ramsey was playing bridge in Wimbledon from eight-thirty till midnight. That came out at the inquest."

Poirot murmured, "And presumably it was verified. The police are careful."

The doctor said, "Perhaps you know something against him?"

"I didn't know that there was such a person until you mentioned him."

"Then you suspect somebody else?"

"No, no. It is not that at all. It's a case of the routine habits of the human animal. That is very important. And the dead M. Gascoigne does not fit in. It is all wrong, you see."

"I really don't understand."

Hercule Poirot smiled. He rose, and the doctor rose, also.

"You know," said MacAndrew, "honestly, I can't see anything the least bit suspicious about the death of Henry Gascoigne."

The little man spread out his hands. "I'm an obstinate man—a man with a little idea—and nothing to support it! By the way, Doctor MacAndrew, did Henry Gascoigne have false teeth?"

"No, his own teeth were in excellent preservation. Very creditable indeed at his age."

"He looked after them well—they were white and well-brushed?"

"Yes I noticed them particularly."

"Not discolored in any way?"

"No. I don't think he was a smoker if that is what you mean."

"I did not mean that precisely—it was just a long shot—which probably will not come off! Good-by, Doctor MacAndrew, and thank you for your kindness."

He shook the doctor's hand and departed.

"And now," he said, "for the long shot."

AT THE GALLANT Endeavor, he sat down at the same table that he had shared with Bonnington. The girl who served him was not Molly. Molly, the girl told him, was away on a holiday.

It was just seven, and Hercule Poirot found no difficulty in entering into conversation with the girl on the subject of old Mr. Gascoigne.

"Yes," she said, "He'd been here for years and years. But none of us girls ever knew his name. We saw about the inquest in the paper, and there was a picture of him. 'There,' I said to Molly, 'if that isn't our Old Father Time,' as we used to call him."

"He dined here on the evening of his death, did he not?"

"That's right. Thursday, the third. He was always here on a Thursday. Tuesdays and Thursdays—punctual as a clock."

"You don't remember, I suppose, what he had for dinner?"

"Now let me see, it was mulligatawny soup, that's right, and beefsteak pudding, or was it the mutton? No, pudding, that's right, and blackberry-and-apple pie and cheese. And then to think of him going home and falling down those stairs that very same evening. A frayed dressing-gown cord they said it was as caused it. Of course, his clothes were always something awful—old-fashioned and put on anyhow, and all tattered, and yet he *had* a kind of air, all the same, as though he was *somebody!* Oh, we get all sorts of interesting customers here."

She moved off.
Hercule Poirot ate his sole.

ARMED WITH INTRODUCTIONS from a certain influential quarter, Hercule Poirot found no difficulty at all in dealing with the coroner for the district.

"A curious figure, the deceased man Gascoigne," he observed. "A lonely, eccentric old fellow. But his decease seems to arouse an unusual amount of attention." He looked with some curiosity at his visitor as he spoke.

Hercule Poirot chose his words carefully. "There are circumstances connected with it, monsieur, which make investigation desirable."

"Well, how can I help you?"

"It is, I believe, within your province to order documents produced in your court to be destroyed, or to be impounded—as you think fit. A certain letter was found in the pocket of Henry Gascoigne's dressing gown, was it not?"

"That is so."

"A letter from his nephew, Doctor George Ramsey?"

"Quite correct. The letter was produced at the inquest as helping to fix the time of death."

"Is that letter still available?"

Hercule Poirot waited rather anxiously for the reply. When he heard that the letter was still available for examination he drew a sigh of relief. When it was finally produced he studied it with some care. It was written in a slightly cramped handwriting with a stylographic pen. It ran as follows:

Dear Uncle Henry:

I am sorry to tell you that I have had no success as regards Uncle Anthony. He showed no enthusiasm for a visit from you and would give me no reply to your request that he would let bygones be bygones. He is, of course, extremely ill, and his mind is inclined to wander. I should fancy that the end is very near. He seemed hardly to remember who you were.

I am sorry to have failed you, but I can assure you that I did my best.

Your affectionate nephew,
George Ramsey.

The letter itself was dated 3rd November. Poirot glanced at the envelope's postmark—4:30 P.M.

He murmured, "It is beautifully in order, is it not?"

Kingston Hill was his next objective. After a little trouble, with the exercise of good-humored pertinacity, he obtained an interview with Amelia Hill, cook-housekeeper to the late Anthony Gascoigne.

Mrs. Hill was inclined to be stiff and suspicious at first, but the charming geniality of this strange-looking foreigner soon had its effect. Mrs. Amelia Hill began to unbend.

She found herself, as had so many other women before her, pouring out her troubles to a really sympathetic listener.

For fourteen years she had had charge of Mr. Gascoigne's household—*not* an easy job! No, indeed! Many a woman would have quailed under the burdens *she* had to bear! Eccentric the poor gentleman was and no denying it. Remarkably close with his money—a kind of mania with him it was—and he as rich a gentleman as might be! But Mrs. Hill had served him faithfully and put up with his ways, and naturally she'd expected at any rate a *remembrance*. But no— nothing at all! Just an old will that left all his money to his wife and if she predeceased him then everything to his brother, Henry. A will made years ago. It didn't seem fair!

Gradually Hercule Poirot detached her from her main theme of unsatisfied cupidity. It was indeed a heartless injustice! Mrs. Hill could not be blamed for feeling hurt and surprised. It was well known that Mr. Gascoigne was tightfisted about money. It had even been said that the dead man had refused his only brother assistance. Mrs. Hill probably knew all about that.

"Was it that that Doctor Ramsey came to see him about?" asked Mrs. Hill. "I knew it was something about his brother, but I thought it was just that his brother wanted to be reconciled. They'd quarreled years ago."

"I understand," said Poirot, "that Mr. Gascoigne refused absolutely?"

"That's right enough," said Mrs. Hill with a nod. "'Henry?' he says, rather weaklike. 'What's this about Henry? Haven't seen him for years and don't want to. Quarrelsome fellow, Henry.' Just that."

The conversation then reverted to Mrs. Hill's own special grievances, and the unfeeling attitude of the late Mr. Gascoigne's solicitor.

With some difficulty Hercule Poirot took his leave without breaking off the conversation too abruptly.

And so, just after the dinner hour, he came to Elmcrest, Dorset Road, Wimbledon, the residence of Dr. George Ramsey.

The doctor was in. Hercule Poirot was shown into the surgery and there presently Dr. George Ramsey came to him, obviously just risen from the dinner table.

"I'm not a patient, doctor," said Hercule Poirot. "And my coming here is, perhaps, somewhat of an impertinence—but I believe in plain and direct dealing. I do not care for lawyers and their long-winded, roundabout methods."

He had certainly aroused Ramsey's interest. The doctor was a clean-shaven man of middle height. His hair was brown, but his eyelashes were almost white, which gave his eyes a pale, boiled appearance. His manner was brisk and not without humor.

"Lawyers?" he said raising his eyebrows. "Hate the fellows! You rouse my curiosity, my dear sir. Pray sit down."

Poirot did so and then produced one of his professional cards which he handed to the doctor. George Ramsey's white eyelashes blinked.

Poirot leaned forward confidentially. "A good many of my clients are women," he said.

"Naturally," said Dr. George Ramsey, with a slight twinkle.

"As you say, naturally," agreed Poirot. "Women distrust the official police. They prefer private investigations. They do not want to have their troubles made public. An elderly woman came to consult me a few days ago. She was unhappy about a husband she'd quarreled with many years before. This husband of hers was your uncle, the late Mr. Gascoigne."

George Ramsey's face went purple. "My uncle? Nonsense! His wife died many years ago."

"Not your uncle, Mr. *Anthony* Gascoigne. Your uncle, Mr. *Henry* Gascoigne."

"Uncle Henry? But *he* wasn't married!"

"Oh, yes, he was," said Hercule Poirot, lying un-blushingly. "Not a doubt of it. The lady even brought along her marriage certificate."

"It's a lie!" cried George Ramsey. His face was now as purple as a plum. "I don't believe it. You're an impudent liar."

"It is too bad, is it not?" said Poirot. "You have committed murder for nothing."

"Murder?" Ramsey's voice quavered. His pale eyes bulged with terror.

"By the way," said Poirot, "I see you have been eating blackberry tart again. An unwise habit. Blackberries are said to be full of vitamins, but they may be deadly in other ways. On this occasion I rather fancy they have helped to put a rope around a man's neck— your neck, Doctor Ramsey."

"YOU SEE, *MON ami,* where you went wrong was over your fundamental assumption." Hercule Poirot, beaming placidly across the table at his friend, waved an expository hand. "A man under severe mental stress doesn't choose that time to do something that he's never done before. His reflexes just follow the track of least resistance. A man who is upset about something might conceivably come down to dinner dressed in his pajamas—but they will be his *own* pajamas—not somebody else's.

"A man who dislikes thick soup, suet pudding, and blackberries suddenly orders all three one evening. *You* say because he is thinking of something else. But *I say that a man who has got something on his mind will order automatically the dish he has ordered most often before.*

"*Eh bien,* then, what other explanation could there be? I simply could not think of a reasonable explanation. And I was worried! The incident was all wrong.

"Then you told me that the man had disappeared. He had missed a Tuesday and a Thursday the first time for years. I liked that even less. A queer hypothesis sprang up in my mind. If I were right about it *the man was dead.* I made inquiries. The man *was* dead. And he was very neatly and tidily dead. In other words the bad fish was covered up with the sauce!

"He had been seen in the King's Road at seven o'clock. He had had dinner here at seven-thirty—two hours before he died. It all fitted in—the evidence of the stomach contents, the evidence of the letter. Much too much sauce! You couldn't see the fish at all!

"Devoted nephew wrote the letter, devoted nephew had beautiful alibi for time of death. Death very simple—a fall down the stairs. Simple accident? Or murder? Everyone says the former.

"Devoted nephew only surviving relative. Devoted nephew will inherit—but is there anything *to* inherit? Uncle notoriously poor.

"But there is a brother. And brother in his time had married a rich wife. And brother lives in a big rich house on Kingston Hill, so it would seem that rich wife must have left him all her money. You see the sequence—rich wife leaves money to Anthony, Anthony leaves money to Henry, Henry's money goes to George—a complete chain."

"All very pretty in theory," said Mr. Bonnington. "But what did you do?"

"Once you *know*—you can usually get hold of what you want. Henry had died two hours after a *meal*—that is all the inquest really bothered about. But supposing that meal was not dinner, but *lunch.* Put yourself in George's place. George wants money—badly. Anthony Gascoigne is dying—but his death is no good to George. His money goes to Henry, and Henry Gascoigne may live for years. So Henry must die, too—and the sooner the better—but his death must take place *after* Anthony's, and at the same time George must have an alibi. Henry's habit of dining regularly at a restaurant on two evenings of the week suggests an alibi to George. Being a cautious fellow, he tries his plan out first. *He impersonates his uncle one Monday evening at the restaurant in question.*

"It goes without a hitch. Everyone there accepts him as his uncle. He is satisfied. He has only to wait till Uncle Anthony shows definite signs of pegging out. The time comes. He mails a letter to his uncle on the afternoon of the second of November but dates it the third. He comes up to town on the afternoon of the third, calls on his uncle, and carries his scheme into action. A sharp shove and down the stairs goes Uncle Henry.

"George hunts about for the letter he has written, and shoves it in the pocket of his uncle's dressing-gown. At seven-thirty he is at the Gallant Endeavor, beard, bushy eyebrows, all complete. Undoubtedly Mr. Henry Gascoigne is alive at seven-thirty. Then a rapid metamorphosis in a lavatory and back full speed in his car to Wimbledon and an evening of bridge. The perfect alibi."

Mr. Bonnington looked at him. "But the postmark on the letter?"

"Oh, that was very simple. The postmark was smudgy. Why? It had been altered with lampblack from November second to November third. You would not notice it *unless you were looking for it.* And finally there were the blackbirds."

"Blackbirds?"

"Four-and-twenty blackbirds baked in a pie! Or blackberries if you prefer to be literal! George, you comprehend, was, after all, not quite a good enough actor. He *looked* like his uncle and *walked* like his uncle and *spoke* like his uncle and had his uncle's beard and eyebrows, but he forgot to *eat* like his uncle. He ordered the dishes that he himself liked.

"Blackberries discolor the teeth. The corpse's teeth were not discolored, and yet Henry Gascoigne ate blackberries at the Gallant Endeavor that night. But there were no blackberries in the stomach. I asked this morning. And George had been fool enough to keep the beard and the rest of the makeup. Oh! Plenty of evidence once you look for it. I called on George and rattled him. That finished it! He

had been eating blackberries again, by the way. A greedy fellow—
cared a lot about his food. *Eh bien,* greed will hang him, all right, unless I am very much mistaken."

A waitress brought them two portions of blackberry-and-apple
tart.

"Take it away," said Mr. Bonnington. "One can't be too careful.
Bring me a small helping of sago pudding."

4. THE DOUBLE CLUE

But above everything—no publicity," said Mr. Marcus Hardman for perhaps the fourteenth time.

The word *publicity* occurred throughout his conversation with the regularity of a leitmotif. Mr. Hardman was a small man, delicately plump, with exquisitely manicured hands and a plaintive tenor voice. In his way, he was somewhat of a celebrity and the fashionable life was his profession. He was rich, but not remarkably so, and he spent his money zealously in the pursuit of social pleasure. His hobby was collecting. He had the collector's soul. Old lace, old fans, antique jewelry—nothing crude or modern for Marcus Hardman.

Poirot and I, obeying an urgent summons, had arrived to find the little man writhing in an agony of indecision. Under the circumstances, to call in the police was abhorrent to him. On the other hand, not to call them in was to acquiesce in the loss of some of the gems of his collection. He hit upon Poirot as a compromise.

"My rubies, Monsieur Poirot, and the emerald necklace—said to have belonged to Catherine de Medici. Oh, the emerald necklace!"

"If you will recount to me the circumstances of their disappearance?" suggested Poirot gently.

"I am endeavoring to do so. Yesterday afternoon I had a little tea party—quite an informal affair, some half a dozen people or so. I have given one or two of them during the season, and though perhaps I should not say so, they have been quite a success. Some good music—Nacora, the pianist, and Katherine Bird, the Australian contralto—in the big studio. Well, early in the afternoon, I was showing my guests my collection of medieval jewels. I keep them in the small wall safe over there. It is arranged like a cabinet inside, with colored velvet background, to display the stones. Afterward we inspected the fans—in that case on the wall. Then we all went to the studio for music. It was not until after everyone had gone that I discovered the safe rifled! I must have failed to shut it properly, and someone had seized the opportunity to denude it of its contents. The rubies, Monsieur Poirot, the emerald necklace—the collection of a lifetime! What would I not give to recover them! But there must be no publicity! You fully understand that, do you not, Monsieur Poirot? My own guests, my personal friends! It would be a horrible scandal!"

"Who was the last person to leave this room when you went to the studio?"

"Mr. Johnston. You may know him? The South African millionaire. He has just rented the Abbotburys' house in Park Lane. He lingered behind a few moments, I remember. But surely, oh, surely it could not be he!"

"Did any of your guests return to this room during the afternoon on any pretext?"

"I was prepared for that question, Monsieur Poirot. Three of them did so. Countess Vera Rossakoff, Mr. Bernard Parker, and Lady Runcorn."

"Let us hear about them."

"The Countess Rossakoff is a very charming Russian lady, a member of the old régime. She has recently come to this country. She had bade me goodbye, and I was therefore somewhat surprised to find her in this room apparently gazing in rapture at my cabinet of fans. You know, Monsieur Poirot, the more I think of it, the more suspicious it seems to me. Don't you agree?"

"Extremely suspicious; but let us hear about the others."

"Well, Parker simply came here to fetch a case of miniatures that I was anxious to show to Lady Runcorn."

"And Lady Runcorn herself?"

"As I daresay you know, Lady Runcorn is a middle-aged woman of considerable force of character who devotes most of her time to various charitable committees. She simply returned to fetch a handbag she had laid down somewhere."

"*Bien, monsieur.* So we have four possible suspects. The Russian countess, the English *grand dame*, the South African millionaire, and Mr. Bernard Parker. Who *is* Mr. Parker, by the way?"

The question appeared to embarrass Mr. Hardman considerably.

"He is—er—he is a young fellow. Well, in fact, a young fellow I know."

"I had already deduced as much," replied Poirot gravely. "What does he do, this Mr. Parker?"

"He is a young man about town—not, perhaps, quite in the swim, if I may so express myself."

"How did he come to be a friend of yours, may I ask?"

"Well—er—on one or two occasions he has—performed certain little commissions for me."

"Continue, monsieur," said Poirot.

Hardman looked piteously at him. Evidently the last thing he wanted to do was to continue. But as Poirot maintained an inexorable silence, he capitulated.

"You see, Monsieur Poirot—it is well known that I am interested in antique jewels. Sometimes there is a family heirloom to be disposed of—which, mind you, would never be sold in the open market or to a dealer. But a private sale to me is a very different matter. Parker arranges the details of such things, he is in touch with both sides, and thus any little embarrassment is avoided. He brings anything of that kind to my notice. For instance, the Countess Rossakoff has brought some family jewels with her from Russia. She is anxious to sell them. Bernard Parker was to have arranged the transaction."

"I see," said Poirot thoughtfully. "And you trust him implicitly?"

"I have had no reason to do otherwise."

"Mr. Hardman, of these four people, which do you yourself suspect?"

"Oh, Monsieur Poirot, what a question! They are my friends, as I told you. I suspect none of them—or all of them, whichever way you like to put it."

"I do not agree. You suspect one of those four. It is not Countess Rossakoff. It is not Mr. Parker. Is it Lady Runcorn or Mr. Johnston?"

"You drive me into a corner, Monsieur Poirot, you do indeed. I am most anxious to have no scandal. Lady Runcorn belongs to one of the oldest families in England; but it is true, it is most unfortunately true, that her aunt, Lady Caroline, suffered from a most melancholy affliction. It was understood, of course, by all her friends, and her maid returned the teaspoons, or whatever it was, as promptly as possible. You see my predicament!"

"So Lady Runcorn had an aunt who was a kleptomaniac? Very interesting. You permit that I examine the safe?"

Mr. Hardman assenting, Poirot pushed back the door of the safe and examined the interior. The empty velvet-lined shelves gaped at us.

"Even now the door does not shut properly," murmured Poirot, as he swung it to and fro. "I wonder why? Ah, what have we here? A glove, caught in the hinge. A man's glove."

He held it out to Mr. Hardman.

"That's not one of my gloves," the latter declared.

"Aha! Something more!" Poirot bent deftly and picked up a small object from the floor of the safe. It was a flat cigarette case made of black moiré.

"My cigarette case!" cried Mr. Hardman.

"Yours? Surely not, monsieur. Those are not your initials."

He pointed to an entwined monogram of two letters executed in platinum.

Hardman took it in his hand.

"You are right," he declared. "It is very like mine, but the initials are different. A 'P' and a 'B.' Good heavens—Parker!"

"It would seem so," said Poirot. "A somewhat careless young

man—especially if the glove is his also. That would be a double clue, would it not?"

"Bernard Parker!" murmured Hardman. "What a relief! Well, Monsieur Poirot, I leave it to you to recover the jewels. Place the matter in the hands of the police if you think fit—that is, if you are quite sure that it is he who is guilty."

"SEE YOU, MY FRIEND," said Poirot to me, as we left the house together, "he has one law for the titled, and another law for the plain, this Mr. Hardman. Me, I have not yet been ennobled, so I am on the side of the plain. I have sympathy for this young man. The whole thing was a little curious, was it not? There was Hardman suspecting Lady Run-corn; there was I, suspecting the Countess and Johnston; and all the time, the obscure Mr. Parker was our man."

"Why did you suspect the other two?"

"*Parbleu!* It is such a simple thing to be a Russian refugee or a South African millionaire. Any woman can call herself a Russian countess; anyone can buy a house in Park Lane and call himself a South African millionaire. Who is going to contradict them? But I observe that we are passing through Bury Street. Our careless young friend lives here. Let us, as you say, strike while the iron is in the fire."

Mr. Bernard Parker was at home. We found him reclining on some cushions, clad in an amazing dressing gown of purple and orange. I have seldom taken a greater dislike to anyone than I did to this particular young man with his white, effeminate face and affected lisping speech.

"Good morning, monsieur," said Poirot briskly. "I come from Mr. Hardman. Yesterday, at the party, somebody has stolen all his jewels. Permit me to ask you, monsieur—is this your glove?"

Mr. Parker's mental processes did not seem very rapid. He stared at the glove, as though gathering his wits together.

"Where did you find it?" he asked at last.

"Is it your glove, monsieur?"

Mr. Parker appeared to make up his mind.

"No, it isn't," he declared.

"And this cigarette case, is that yours?"

"Certainly not. I always carry a silver one."

"Very well, monsieur. I go to put matters in the hands of the police."

"Oh, I say, I wouldn't do that, if I were you," cried Mr. Parker in some concern. "Beastly unsympathetic people, the police. Wait a bit. I'll go round and see old Hardman. Look here—oh, stop a minute."

But Poirot beat a determined retreat.

"We have given him something to think about, have we not?" he chuckled. "Tomorrow we will observe what has occurred."

But we were destined to have a reminder of the Hardman case that afternoon. Without the least warning the door flew open, and a whirlwind in human form invaded our privacy, bringing with her a swirl of sables (it was as cold as only an English June day can be) and a hat rampant with slaughtered ospreys. Countess Vera Rossakoff was a somewhat disturbing personality.

"You are Monsieur Poirot? What is this that you have done? You accuse that poor boy! It is infamous. It is scandalous. I know him. He is a chicken, a lamb—never would he steal. He has done everything for me. Will I stand by and see him martyred and butchered?"

"Tell me, madame, is this his cigarette case?" Poirot held out the black moiré case.

The Countess paused for a moment while she inspected it.

"Yes, it is his. I know it well. What of it? Did you find it in the room? We were all there; he dropped it then, I suppose. Ah, you policemen, you are worse than the Red Guards—"

"And is this his glove?"

"How should I know? One glove is like another. Do not try to stop me—he must be set free. His character must be cleared. You shall do it. I will sell my jewels and give you much money."

"Madame—"

"It is agreed, then? No, no, do not argue. The poor boy! He

came to me, the tears in his eyes. 'I will save you,' I said. 'I will go to this man—this ogre, this monster! Leave it to Vera. Now it is settled, I go."

With as little ceremony as she had come, she swept from the room, leaving an overpowering perfume of an exotic nature behind her.

"What a woman!" I exclaimed. "And what furs!"

"Ah, yes, *they* were genuine enough! Could a spurious countess have real furs? My little joke, Hastings. . . . No, she is truly Russian, I fancy. Well, well, so Master Bernard went bleating to her."

"The cigarette case is his. I wonder if the glove is also—"

With a smile Poirot drew from his pocket a second glove and placed it by the first. There was no doubt of their being a pair.

"Where did you get the second one, Poirot?"

"It was thrown down with a stick on the table in the hall in Bury Street. Truly, a very careless young man, Monsieur Parker. Well, well, *mon ami*—we must be thorough. Just for the form of the thing, I will make a little visit to Park Lane."

Needless to say, I accompanied my friend. Johnston was out, but we saw his private secretary. It transpired that Johnston had only recently arrived from South Africa. He had never been in England before.

"He is interested in precious stones, is he not?" hazarded Poirot.

"Gold mining is nearer the mark," laughed the secretary.

Poirot came away from the interview thoughtful. Late that evening, to my utter surprise, I found him earnestly studying a Russian grammar.

"Good heavens, Poirot!" I cried. "Are you learning Russian in order to converse with the Countess in her own language?"

"She certainly would not listen to my English, my friend!"

"But surely, Poirot, well-born Russians invariably speak French?"

"You are a mine of information, Hastings! I will cease puzzling over the intricacies of the Russian alphabet."

He threw the book from him with a dramatic gesture. I was not entirely satisfied. There was a twinkle in his eye which I knew of old. It was an invariable sign that Hercule Poirot was pleased with himself.

"Perhaps," I said sapiently, "you doubt her being really a Russian. You are going to test her?"

"Ah, no, no, she is Russian all right."

"Well, then—"

"If you really want to distinguish yourself over this case, Hastings, I recommend 'First Steps in Russian' as an invaluable aid."

Then he laughed and would say no more. I picked up the book from the floor and dipped into it curiously, but could make neither head nor tail of Poirot's remarks.

The following morning brought us no news of any kind, but that did not seem to worry my little friend. At breakfast, he announced his intention of calling upon Mr. Hardman early in the day. We found the elderly society butterfly at home, and seemingly a little calmer than on the previous day.

"Well, Monsieur Poirot, any news?" he demanded eagerly.

Poirot handed him a slip of paper.

"That is the person who took the jewels, monsieur. Shall I put matters in the hands of the police? Or would you prefer me to recover the jewels without bringing the police into the matter?"

Mr. Hardman was staring at the paper. At last he found his voice.

"Most astonishing. I should infinitely prefer to have no scandal in the matter. I give you *carte blanche*, Monsieur Poirot. I am sure you will be discreet."

Our next procedure was to hail a taxi, which Poirot ordered to drive to the Carlton. There he inquired for Countess Rossakoff. In a few minutes we were ushered up into the lady's suite. She came to meet us with outstretched hands, arrayed in a marvelous negligee of barbaric design.

"Monsieur Poirot!" she cried. "You have succeeded? You have cleared that poor infant?"

"Madame la Comtesse, your friend Mr. Parker is perfectly safe from arrest."

"Ah, but you are the clever little man! Superb! And so quickly too."

"On the other hand, I have promised Mr. Hardman that the jewels shall be returned to him today."

"So?"

"Therefore, madame, I should be extremely obliged if you would place them in my hands without delay. I am sorry to hurry you, but I am keeping a taxi—in case it should be necessary for me to go on to Scotland Yard; and we Belgians, madame, we practice the thrift."

The Countess had lighted a cigarette. For some seconds she sat perfectly still, blowing smoke rings, and gazing steadily at Poirot. Then she burst into a laugh, and rose. She went across to the bureau, opened a drawer, and took out a black silk handbag. She tossed it lightly to Poirot Her tone, when she spoke, was perfectly light and unmoved.

"We Russians, on the contrary, practice prodigality," she said. "And to do that, unfortunately, one must have money. You need not look inside. They are all there."

Poirot arose.

"I congratulate you, madame, on your quick intelligence and your promptitude."

"Ah! But since you were keeping your taxi waiting, what else could I do?"

"You are too amiable, madame. You are remaining long in London?"

"I am afraid not—owing to you."

"Accept my apologies."

"We shall meet again elsewhere, perhaps."

"I hope so."

"And I—do not!" exclaimed the Countess with a laugh. "It is a great compliment that I pay you there—there are very few men in the world whom I fear. Goodbye, Monsieur Poirot."

"Goodbye, Madame la Comtesse. Ah—pardon me, I forgot! Allow me to return you your cigarette case."

And with a bow he handed to her the little black moiré case we had found in the safe. She accepted it without any change of expression—just a lifted eyebrow and a murmured: "I see!"

"WHAT A WOMAN!" cried Poirot enthusiastically as we descended the stairs. "*Man Dieu, quelle femme!* Not a word of argument—of protestation, of bluff! One quick glance, and she had sized up the position correctly. I tell you, Hastings, a woman who can accept defeat like that—with a careless smile—will go far! She is dangerous; she has the nerves of steel; she—" He tripped heavily.

"If you can manage to moderate your transports and look where you're going, it might be as well," I suggested. "When did you first suspect the Countess?"

"*Mon ami,* it was the glove *and* the cigarette case—the double clue, shall we say?—that worried me. Bernard Parker might easily have dropped one or the other—but hardly both. Ah, no, that would have been *too* careless! In the same way, if someone else had placed them there to incriminate Parker, one would have been sufficient— the cigarette case *or* the glove—again not both. So I was forced to the conclusion that one of the two things did *not* belong to Parker. I imagined at first that the case was his, and that the glove was not. But when I discovered the fellow to the glove, I saw that it was the other way about. Whose, then, was the cigarette case? Clearly, it could not belong to Lady Runcorn. The initials were wrong. Mr. Johnston? Only if he were here under a false name. I interviewed his secretary, and it was apparent at once that everything was clear and aboveboard. There was no reticence about Mr. Johnston's past. The Countess, then? She was supposed to have brought jewels with her from Russia; she had only to take the stones from their settings, and it was extremely doubtful if they could ever be identified. What could be easier for her than to pick up one of Parker's gloves from the hall that day and thrust it into the safe? But, *bien sûr,* she did not intend to drop her own cigarette case."

"But if the case was hers, why did it have 'B.P.' on it? The Countess' initials are V. R."

Poirot smiled gently upon me.

"Exactly, *mon ami;* but in the Russian alphabet, *B* is *V* and *P* is *R.*"

"Well, you couldn't expect me to guess that. I don't know Russian."

"Neither do I, Hastings. That is why I bought my little book— and urged it on your attention."

He sighed.

"A remarkable woman. I have a feeling, my friend—a very decided feeling—I shall meet her again. Where, I wonder?"

5. DOUBLE SIN

I had called in at my friend Poirot's rooms to find him sadly overworked. So much had he become the rage that every rich woman who had mislaid a bracelet or lost a pet kitten rushed to secure the services of the great Hercule Poirot. My little friend was a strange mixture of Flemish thrift and artistic fervor. He accepted many cases in which he had little interest owing to the first instinct being predominant.

He also undertook cases in which there was a little or no monetary reward sheerly because the problem involved interested him. The result was that, as I say, he was overworking himself. He admitted as much himself, and I found little difficulty in persuading him to accompany me for a week's holiday to that well-known South Coast resort, Ebermouth.

We had spent four very agreeable days when Poirot came to me, an open letter in his hand.

"*Mon ami,* you remember my friend Joseph Aarons, the theatrical agent?"

I assented after a moment's thought. Poirot's friends are so many and so varied, and range from dustmen to dukes.

"*Eh bien,* Hastings, Joseph Aarons finds himself at Charlock

Bay. He is far from well, and there is a little affair that it seems is worrying him. He begs me to go over and see him. I think, *mon ami*, that I must accede to his request. He is a faithful friend, the good Joseph Aarons, and has done much to assist me in the past."

"Certainly, if you think so," I said. "I believe Charlock Bay is a beautiful spot, and as it happens I've never been there."

"Then we combine business with pleasure," said Poirot. "You will inquire the trains, yes?"

"It will probably mean a change or two," I said with a grimace. "You know what these cross-country lines are. To go from the South Devon coast to the North Devon coast is sometimes a day's journey."

However, on inquiry, I found that the journey could be accomplished by only one change at Exeter and that the trains were good. I was hastening back to Poirot with the information when I happened to pass the offices of the Speedy cars and saw written up:

Tomorrow. All-day excursion to
Charlock Bay. Starting 8:30 through
some of the most beautiful scenery in Devon.

I inquired a few particulars and returned to the hotel full of enthusiasm. Unfortunately, I found it hard to make Poirot share my feelings.

"My friend, why this passion for the motor coach? The train, see you, it is sure? The tires, they do not burst; the accidents, they do not happen. One is not incommoded by too much air. The windows can be shut and no drafts admitted."

I hinted delicately that the advantage of fresh air was what attracted me most to the motor-coach scheme.

"And if it rains? Your English climate is so uncertain."

"There's a hood and all that. Besides, if it rains badly, the excursion doesn't take place."

"Ah!" said Poirot. "Then let us hope that it rains."

"Of course, if you feel like that and . . ."

"No, no, *mon ami*. I see that you have set your heart on the trip. Fortunately, I have my great coat with me and two mufflers." He sighed. "But shall we have sufficient time at Charlock Bay?"

"Well, I'm afraid it means staying the night there. You see, the tour goes round by Dartmoor. We have lunch at Monkhampton. We arrive at Charlock Bay about four o'clock, and the coach starts back at five, arriving here at ten o'clock."

"So!" said Poirot. "And there are people who do this for pleasure! We shall, of course, get a reduction of the fare since we do not make the return journey?"

"I hardly think that's likely."

"You must insist."

"Come now, Poirot, don't be mean. You know you're coining money."

"My friend, it is not the meanness. It is the business sense. If I were a millionaire, I would pay only what was just and right."

As I had foreseen, however, Poirot was doomed to fail in this respect. The gentleman who issued tickets at the Speedy office was calm and unimpassioned but adamant. His point was that we ought to return. He even implied that we ought to pay extra for the privilege of leaving the coach at Charlock Bay.

Defeated, Poirot paid over the required sum and left the office.

"The English, they have no sense of money," he grumbled. "Did you observe a young man, Hastings, who paid over the full fare and yet mentioned his intention of leaving the coach at Monkhampton?"

"I don't think I did. As a matter of fact . . ."

"You were observing the pretty young lady who booked No. 5, the next seat to ours. Ah! Yes, my friend, I saw you. And that is why when I was on the point of taking seats No. 13 and 14—which are in the middle and as well sheltered as it is possible to be—you rudely pushed yourself forward and said that 3 and 4 would be better."

"Really, Poirot," I said, blushing.

"Auburn hair—always the auburn hair!"

"At any rate, she was more worth looking at than an odd young man."

"That depends upon the point of view. To me, the young man was interesting."

Something rather significant in Poirot's tone made me look at him quickly. "Why? What do you mean?"

"Oh! Do not excite yourself. Shall I say that he interested me because he was trying to grow a mustache and as yet the result is poor." Poirot stroked his own magnificent mustache tenderly. "It is an art," he murmured, "the growing of the mustache! I have sympathy for all who attempt it."

It is always difficult with Poirot to know when he is serious and when he is merely amusing himself at one's expense. I judged it safest to say no more.

The following morning dawned bright and sunny. A really glorious day! Poirot, however, was taking no chances. He wore a woolly waistcoat, a mackintosh, a heavy overcoat, and two mufflers, in addition to wearing his thickest suit. He also swallowed two tablets of "Antigrippe" before starting and packed a further supply.

We took a couple of small suitcases with us. The pretty girl we had noticed the day before had a small suitcase, and so did the young man whom I gathered to have been the object of Poirot's sympathy. Otherwise, there was no luggage. The four pieces were stowed away by the driver, and we all took our places.

Poirot, rather maliciously, I thought, assigned me the outside place as "I had the mania for the fresh air" and himself occupied the seat next to our fair neighbor. Presently, however, he made amends. The man in seat 6 was a noisy fellow, inclined to be facetious and boisterous, and Poirot asked the girl in a low voice if she would like to change seats with him. She agreed gratefully, and, the change having been effected, she entered into conversation with us and we were soon all three chattering together merrily.

She was evidently quite young, not more than nineteen, and as ingenuous as a child. She soon confided to us the reason of her trip. She was going, it seemed, on business for her aunt who kept a most interesting antique shop in Ebermouth.

This aunt had been left in very reduced circumstances on the death of her father and had used her small capital and a houseful of beautiful things which her father had left to start in business. She had been extremely successful and had made quite a name for herself in the trade. This girl, Mary Durrant, had come to be with her aunt and learn the business and was very excited about it—much preferring it to the other alternative—becoming a nursery governess or companion.

Poirot nodded interest and approval to all this.

"Mademoiselle will be successful, I am sure," he said gallantly. "But I will give her a little word of advice. Do not be too trusting, mademoiselle. Everywhere in the world there are rogues and vagabonds, even it may be on this very coach of ours. One should always be on the guard, suspicious!"

She stared at him open-mouthed, and he nodded sapiently.

"But yes, it is as I say. Who knows? Even I who speak to you may be a malefactor of the worst description."

And he twinkled more than ever at her surprised face.

We stopped for lunch at Monkhampton, and, after a few words with the waiter, Poirot managed to secure us a small table for three close by the window. Outside, in a big courtyard, about twenty *char-a-bancs* were parked—*char-a-bancs* which had come from all over the county. The hotel dining room was full, and the noise was rather considerable.

"One can have altogether too much of the holiday spirit," I said with a grimace.

Mary Durrant agreed. "Ebermouth is quite spoiled in the summers nowadays. My aunt says it used to be quite different. Now one can hardly get along the pavements for the crowd."

"But it is good for business, mademoiselle."

"Not for ours particularly. We sell only rare and valuable things. We do not go in for cheap bric-a-brac. My aunt has clients all over England. If they want a particular period table or chair, or a certain piece of china, they write to her, and, sooner or later, she gets it for them. That is what has happened in this case."

We looked interested and she went on to explain. A certain American gentleman, Mr. J. Baker Wood, was a connoisseur and collector of miniatures. A very valuable set of miniatures had recently come into the market, and Miss Elizabeth Penn—Mary's aunt—had purchased them. She had written to Mr. Wood describing the miniatures and naming a price. He had replied at once, saying that he was prepared to purchase if the miniatures were as represented and asking that someone should be sent with them for him to see where he was staying at Charlock Bay. Miss Durrant had accordingly been dispatched, acting as representative for the firm.

"They're lovely things, of course," she said. "But I can't imagine anyone paying all that money for them. Five hundred pounds! Just think of it! They're by Cosway. Is it Cosway I mean? I get so mixed up in these things."

Poirot smiled. "You are not yet experienced, eh, mademoiselle?"

"I've had no training," said Mary ruefully. "We weren't brought up to know about old things. It's a lot to learn."

She sighed. Then suddenly, I saw her eyes widen in surprise. She was sitting facing the window, and her glance now was directed out of that window, into the courtyard. With a hurried word, she rose from her seat and almost ran out of the room. She returned in a few moments, breathless and apologetic.

"I'm so sorry rushing off like that. But I thought I saw a man taking my suitcase out of the coach. I went flying after him, and it turned out to be his own. It's one almost exactly like mine. I felt like such a fool. It looked as though I were accusing him of stealing it."

She laughed at the idea.

Poirot, however, did not laugh. "What man was it, mademoiselle? Describe him to me."

"He had on a brown suit. A thin weedy young man with a very indeterminate mustache."

"Aha," said Poirot. "Our friend of yesterday, Hastings. You know this young man, mademoiselle. You have seen him before?"

"No, never. Why?"

"Nothing. It is rather curious—that is all."

He relapsed into silence and took no further part in the conversation until something Mary Durrant said caught his attention.

"Eh, mademoiselle, what is that you say?"

"I said that on my return journey I should have to be careful of 'malefactors,' as you call them. I believe Mr. Wood always pays for things in cash. If I have five hundred pounds in notes on me, I shall be worth some malefactor's attention."

She laughed but again Poirot did not respond. Instead, he asked her what hotel she proposed to stay at in Charlock Bay.

"The Anchor Hotel. It is small and not expensive, but quite good."

"So!" said Poirot. "The Anchor Hotel. Precisely where Hastings here has made up his mind to stay. How odd!"

He twinkled at me.

"You are staying long in Charlock Bay?" asked Mary.

"One night only. I have business there. You could not guess, I am sure, what my profession is, mademoiselle?"

I saw Mary consider several possibilities and reject them— probably from a feeling of caution. At last, she hazarded the suggestion that Poirot was a conjurer. He was vastly entertained.

"Ah! But it is an idea, that! You think I take the rabbits out of the hat? No, mademoiselle. Me, I am the opposite of a conjurer. The conjurer, he makes things disappear. Me, I make things that have disappeared, reappear." He leaned forward dramatically so as to give the words full effect. "It is a secret, mademoiselle, but I will tell you, I am a detective!"

He leaned back in his chair pleased with the effect he had created. Mary Durrant stared at him spellbound. But any further conversation was barred for the braying of various horns outside announced that the road monsters were ready to proceed.

As Poirot and I went out together I commented on the charm of our luncheon companion. Poirot agreed.

"Yes, she is charming. But, also rather silly?"

"Silly?"

"Do not be outraged. A girl may be beautiful and have auburn hair and yet be silly. It is the height of foolishness to take two strangers into her confidence as she has done."

"Well, she could see we were all right."

"That is imbecile, what you say, my friend. Anyone who knows his job—naturally he will appear 'all right.' That little one she talked of being careful when she would have five hundred pounds in money with her. But she has five hundred pounds with her now."

"In miniatures."

"Exactly. In miniatures. And between one and the other, there is no great difference, *mon ami.*"

"But no one knows about them except us."

"And the waiter and the people at the next table. And, doubtless, several people in Ebermouth! Mademoiselle Durrant, she is charming, but, if I were Miss Elizabeth Penn, I would first of all instruct my new assistant in the common sense." He paused and then said in a different voice: "You know, my friend, it would be the easiest thing in the world to remove a suitcase from one of those *char-a-bancs* while we were all at luncheon."

"Oh! Come, Poirot, somebody will be sure to see."

"And what would they see? Somebody removing his luggage. It would be done in an open and aboveboard manner, and it would be nobody's business to interfere."

"Do you mean—Poirot, are you hinting—But that fellow in the brown suit—it was his own suitcase?"

Poirot frowned. "So it seems. All the same, it is curious, Hastings, that he should have not removed his suitcase before, when the car first arrived. He has not lunched here, you notice."

"If Miss Durrant hadn't been sitting opposite the window, she wouldn't have seen him," I said slowly.

"And since it was his own suitcase, that would not have mattered," said Poirot. "So let us dismiss it from our thoughts, *mon ami.*"

Nevertheless, when we had resumed our places and were speeding along once more, he took the opportunity of giving Mary Durrant a further lecture on the dangers of indiscretion which she received meekly enough but with the air of thinking it all rather a joke.

We arrived at Charlock Bay at four o'clock and were fortunate enough to be able to get rooms at the Anchor Hotel—a charming old-world inn in one of the side streets.

Poirot had just unpacked a few necessaries and was applying a little cosmetic to his mustache preparatory to going out to call upon Joseph Aarons when there came a frenzied knocking at the door. I called "Come in," and, to my utter amazement, Mary Durrant appeared, her face white and large tears standing in her eyes.

"I do beg your pardon—but—but the most awful thing has happened. And you did say you were a detective?" This to Poirot.

"What has happened, mademoiselle?"

"I opened my suitcase. The miniatures were in a crocodile dispatch case—locked, of course. Now, look!"

She held out a small square crocodile-covered case. The lid hung loose. Poirot took it from her. The case had been forced; great strength must have been used. The marks were plain enough. Poirot examined it and nodded.

"The miniatures?" he asked, though we both knew the answer well enough.

"Gone. They've been stolen. Oh! What shall I do?"

"Don't worry," I said. "My friend is Hercule Poirot. You must have heard of him. He'll get them back for you if anyone can."

"Monsieur Poirot. The great Monsieur Poirot."

Poirot was vain enough to be pleased at the obvious reverence in her voice. "Yes, my child," he said. "It is I, myself. And you can leave your little affair in my hands. I will do all that can be done. But I fear—I much fear—that it will be too late. Tell me, was the lock of your suitcase forced also?"

She shook her head.

"Let me see it, please."

We went together to her room, and Poirot examined the suitcase closely. It had obviously been opened with a key.

"Which is simple enough. These suitcase locks are all much of the same pattern. *Eh, bien,* we must ring up the police and we must also get in touch with Mr. Baker Wood as soon as possible. I will attend to that myself."

I went with him and asked what he meant by saying it might be too late. "*Mon cher,* I said today that I was the opposite of the conjurer—that I make the disappearing things reappear—but suppose someone has been beforehand with me. You do not understand? You will in a minute."

He disappeared into the telephone box. He came out five minutes later looking very grave. "It is as I feared. A lady called upon Mr. Wood with the miniatures half an hour ago. She represented herself as coming from Miss Elizabeth Penn. He was delighted with the miniatures and paid for them forthwith."

"Half an hour ago—before we arrived here."

Poirot smiled rather enigmatically "The Speedy cars are quite speedy, but a fast motor from say, Monkhampton would get here a good hour ahead of them at least."

"And what do we do now?"

"The good Hastings—always practical. We inform the police, do all we can for Miss Durrant, and—yes, I think decidedly, we have an interview with Mr. J. Baker Wood."

We carried out this program. Poor Mary Durrant was terribly upset, fearing her aunt would blame her.

"Which she probably will," observed Poirot, as we set out for the Seaside Hotel where Mr. Wood was staying. "And with perfect justice. The idea of leaving five hundred pounds' worth of valuables in a suitcase and going to lunch! All the same, *mon ami,* there are one or two curious points about the case. That dispatch box, for instance, why was it forced?"

"To get out the miniatures."

"But was not that a foolishness? Say our thief is tampering with the luggage at lunch time under the pretext of getting out his own. Surely it is much simpler to open the suitcase, transfer the dispatch case unopened to his own suitcase, and get away, than to waste the time forcing the lock?"

"He had to make sure the miniatures were inside."

Poirot did not look convinced, but, as we were just being shown into Mr. Wood's suite, we had no time for more discussion.

I took an immediate dislike to Mr. Baker Wood.

He was a large vulgar man, very much overdressed and wearing a diamond solitaire ring. He was blustering and noisy.

Of course, he'd not suspected anything amiss? Why should he? The woman said she had the miniatures all right. Very fine specimens, too! Had he the numbers of the notes? No, he hadn't. And who was Mr.—er—Poirot, anyway, to come asking him all these questions?

"I will not ask you anything more, monsieur, except for one

thing. A description of the woman who called upon you. Was she young and pretty?"

"No, sir, she was not. Most emphatically not. A tall woman, middle-aged, gray hair, blotchy complexion and a budding mustache. A siren? Not on your life."

"Poirot," I cried, as we took our departure. "A mustache. Did you hear?"

"I have the use of my ears, thank you, Hastings."

"But what a very unpleasant man."

"He has not the charming manner, no."

"Well, we ought to get the thief all right," I remarked. "We can identify him."

"You are of such a naive simplicity, Hastings. Do you not know that there is such a thing as an alibi?"

"You think he will have an alibi?"

Poirot replied unexpectedly: "I sincerely hope so."

"The trouble with you is," I said, "that you like a thing to be difficult."

"Quite right, *mon ami*. I do not like—how do you say it—the bird who sits!"

Poirot's prophecy was fully justified. Our traveling companion in the brown suit turned out to be a Mr. Norton Kane. He had gone straight to the Gorge Hotel at Monkhampton and had been there during the afternoon. The only evidence against him was that of Miss Durrant who declared that she had seen him getting out his luggage from the car while we were at lunch.

"Which in itself is not a suspicious act," said Poirot meditatively.

After that remark, he lapsed into silence and refused to discuss the matter any further, saying when I pressed him, that he was thinking of mustaches in general, and that I should be well advised to do the same.

I discovered, however, that he had asked Joseph Aarons—with whom he spent the evening—to give him every detail possible about Mr. Baker Wood. As both men were staying at the same hotel, there was a chance of gleaning some stray crumbs of information. Whatever Poirot learned, he kept to himself, however.

Mary Durrant, after various interviews with the police, had returned to Ebermouth by an early morning train. We lunched with Joseph Aarons, and, after lunch, Poirot announced to me that he had settled the theatrical agent's problem satisfactorily, and that we could return to Ebermouth as soon as we liked. "But not by road, *mon ami;* we go by rail this time."

"Are you afraid of having your pocket picked, or of meeting another damsel in distress?"

"Both those affairs, Hastings, might happen to me on the train. No, I am in haste to be back in Ebermouth, because I want to proceed with our case."

"Our case?"

"But, yes, my friend. Mademoiselle Durrant appealed to me to help her. Because the matter is now in the hands of the police, it does not follow that I am free to wash my hands of it. I came here to oblige an old friend, but it shall never be said of Hercule Poirot that he deserted a stranger in need!" And he drew himself up grandiloquently.

"I think you were interested before that," I said shrewdly. "In the office of cars, when you first caught sight of that young man, though what drew your attention to him I don't know."

"Don't you, Hastings? You should. Well, well, that must remain my little secret."

We had a short conversation with the police inspector in charge of the case before leaving. He had interviewed Mr. Norton Kane, and told Poirot in confidence that the young man's manner had not impressed him favorably. He had blustered, denied, and contradicted himself.

"But just how the trick was done, I don't know," he confessed. "He could have handed the stuff to a confederate who pushed off at once in a fast car. But that's just theory. We've got to find the car and the confederate and pin the thing down."

Poirot nodded thoughtfully.

"Do you think that was how it was done?" I asked him, as we were seated in the train.

"No, my friend, that was not how it was done. It was cleverer than that."

"Won't you tell me?"

"Not yet. You know—it is my weakness—I like to keep my little secrets till the end."

"Is the end going to be soon?"

"Very soon now."

We arrived in Ebermouth a little after six and Poirot drove at once to the shop which bore the name "Elizabeth Penn." The establishment was closed, but Poirot rang the bell, and presently Mary herself opened the door, and expressed surprise and delight at seeing us.

"Please come in and see my aunt," she said.

She led us into a back room. An elderly lady came forward to meet us; she had white hair and looked rather like a miniature herself with her pink-and-white skin and her blue eyes. Round her rather bent shoulders she wore a cape of priceless old lace.

"Is this the great Monsieur Poirot?" she asked in a low charming voice. "Mary has been telling me. I could hardly believe it. And you will really help us in our trouble. You will advise us?"

Poirot looked at her for a moment, then bowed.

"Mademoiselle Penn—the effect is charming. But you should really grow a mustache."

Miss Penn gave a gasp and drew back.

"You were absent from business yesterday, were you not?"

"I was here in the morning. Later I had a bad headache and went directly home."

"Not home, mademoiselle. For your headache you tried the change of air, did you not? The air of Charlock Bay is very bracing, I believe."

He took me by the arm and drew me toward the door. He paused there and spoke over his shoulder.

"You comprehend, I know everything. This little—farce—it must cease."

There was a menace in his tone. Miss Penn, her face ghastly white, nodded mutely. Poirot turned to the girl.

"Mademoiselle," he said gently, "you are young and charming. But participating in these little affairs will lead to that youth and charm being hidden behind prison walls—and I, Hercule Poirot, tell you that that will be a pity."

Then he stepped out into the street and I followed him, bewildered.

"From the first, *mon ami,* I was interested. When that young man booked his place as far as Monkhampton only, I saw the girl's attention suddenly riveted on him. Now why? He was not of the type to make a woman look at him for himself alone. When we started on that coach, I had a feeling that something would happen. Who saw the young man tampering with the luggage? Mademoiselle and mademoiselle only, and remember she chose that seat—a seat facing the window—a most unfeminine choice.

"And then she comes to us with the tale of robbery—the dispatch box forced which makes not the common sense, as I told you at the time.

"And what is the result of it all? Mr. Baker Wood has paid over good money for stolen goods. The miniatures will be returned to Miss Penn. She will sell them and will have made a thousand pounds instead of five hundred. I make the discreet inquiries and learn that her business is in a bad state—touch and go. I say to myself—the aunt and niece are in this together."

"Then you never suspected Norton Kane?"

"*Mon ami!* With that mustache? A criminal is either clean shaven or he has a proper mustache that can be removed at will. But what an opportunity for the clever Miss Penn—a shrinking elderly lady with a pink-and-white complexion as we saw her. But if she holds herself erect, wears large boots, alters her complexion with a few unseemly blotches and—crowning touch—adds a few sparse hairs to her upper lip. What then? A masculine woman, says Mr. Wood, and—'a man in disguise' say we at once."

"She really went to Charlock yesterday?"

"Assuredly. The train, as you may remember telling me, left here at eleven and got to Charlock Bay at two o'clock. Then the return train is even quicker—the one we came by. It leaves Charlock at four:five and gets here at six:fifteen. Naturally, the miniatures were never in the dispatch case at all. That was artistically forced before being packed. Mademoiselle Mary has only to find a couple of mugs who will be sympathetic to her charm and champion beauty in distress. But one of the mugs was no mug—he was Hercule Poirot!"

I hardly liked the inference. I said hurriedly:

"Then, when you said you were helping a stranger, you were willfully deceiving me. That's exactly what you were doing."

"Never do I deceive you, Hastings. I only permit you to deceive yourself. I was referring to Mr. Baker Wood—a stranger to these shores." His face darkened. "Ah! When I think of that imposition, that iniquitous overcharge; the same fare single to Charlock as return, my blood boils to protect the visitor! Not a pleasant man, Mr. Baker Wood, not, as you would say, sympathetic. But a visitor! And we visitors, Hastings, must stand together. Me, I am all for the visitors!"

6. WASPS' NEST

Out of the house came John Harrison and stood a moment on the terrace looking out over the garden. He was a big man with a lean, cadaverous face. His aspect was usually somewhat grim but when as now, the rugged features softened into a smile, there was something very attractive about him.

John Harrison loved his garden, and it had never looked better than it did on this August evening, summery and languorous. The rambler roses were still beautiful; sweet peas scented the air.

A well-known creaking sound made Harrison turn his head sharply. Who was coming in through the garden gate? In another minute, an expression of utter astonishment came over his face, for the dandified figure coming up the path was the last he expected to see in this part of the world.

"By all that's wonderful," cried Harrison. "Monsieur Poirot!"

It was, indeed, the famous Hercule Poirot whose renown as a detective had spread over the whole world.

"Yes," he said, "it is I. You said to me once: 'If you are ever in this part of the world, come and see me.' I take you at your word. I arrive."

"And I'm delighted," said Harrison heartily. "Sit down and have a drink."

With a hospitable hand, he indicated a table on the veranda bearing assorted bottles.

"I thank you," said Poirot, sinking down into a basket chair. "You have, I suppose, no syrup? No, no, I thought not. A little plain soda water then—no whiskey." And he added in a feeling voice as the other placed the glass beside him: "Alas: My mustaches are limp. It is this heat!"

"And what brings you into this quiet spot?" asked Harrison as he dropped into another chair. "Pleasure?"

"No, *mon ami,* business."

"Business? In this out-of-the-way place?"

Poirot nodded gravely. "But yes, my friend, all crimes are not committed in crowds, you know?"

The other laughed. "I suppose that was rather an idiotic remark of mine. But what particular crime are you investigating down here, or is that a thing I mustn't ask?"

"You may ask," said the detective. "Indeed, I would prefer that you asked."

Harrison looked at him curiously. He sensed something a little unusual in the other's manner. "You are investigating a crime, you say?" he advanced rather hesitatingly. "A serious crime?"

"A crime of the most serious there is."

"You mean . . ."

"Murder."

So gravely did Hercule Poirot say that word that Harrison was quite taken aback. The detective was looking straight at him and again there was something so unusual in his glance that Harrison hardly knew how to proceed. At last, he said: "But I have heard of no murder."

"No," said Poirot, "you would not have heard of it."

"Who has been murdered?"

"As yet," said Hercule Poirot, "nobody."

"What?"

"That is why I said you would not have heard of it. I am investigating a crime that has not yet taken place."

"But look here, that is nonsense."

"Not at all. If one can investigate a murder before it has happened, surely that is very much better than afterward. One might even—a little idea—prevent it."

Harrison stared at him. "You are not serious, Monsieur Poirot."

"But yes, I am serious."

"You really believe that a murder is going to be committed? Oh, it's absurd!"

Hercule Poirot finished the first part of the sentence without taking any notice of the exclamation.

"Unless we can manage to prevent it. Yes, *mon ami*, that is what I mean."

"We?"

"I said we. I shall need your cooperation."

"Is that why you came down here?"

Again Poirot looked at him, and again an indefinable something made Harrison uneasy.

"I came here, Monsieur Harrison because I—well—like you."

And then he added in an entirely different voice: "I see, Monsieur Harrison, that you have a wasps' nest there. You should destroy it."

The change of subject made Harrison frown in a puzzled way. He followed Poirot's glance and said in rather a bewildered voice: "As a matter of fact, I'm going to. Or rather, young Langton is. You remember Claude Langton? He was at the same dinner where I met you. He's coming over this evening to take the nest. Rather fancies himself at the job."

"Ah!" said Poirot. "And how is he going to do it?"

"Petrol and the garden syringe. He's bringing his own syringe over; it's a more convenient size than mine."

"There is another way, is there not?" asked Poirot. "With cyanide of potassium?"

Harrison looked a little surprised. "Yes, but that's rather dangerous stuff. Always a bit of risk having it about the place."

Poirot nodded gravely. "Yes, it is deadly poison." He waited a minute and then repeated in a grave voice. "Deadly poison."

"Useful if you want to do away with your mother-in-law, eh?" said Harrison with a laugh.

But Hercule Poirot remained grave. "And you are quite sure, Monsieur Harrison, that it is with petrol that Monsieur Langton is going to destroy your wasps' nest?"

"Quite sure. Why?"

"I wondered. I was at the chemist's in Barchester this afternoon. For one of my purchases I had to sign the poison book. I saw the last entry. It was for cyanide of potassium and it was signed for by Claude Langton."

Harrison stared. "That's odd," he said. "Langton told me the other day that he'd never dream of using the stuff; in fact, he said it oughtn't to be sold for the purpose."

Poirot looked out over the roses. His voice was very quiet as he asked a question. "Do you like Langton?"

The other started. The question somehow seemed to find him quite unprepared. "I—I—well, I mean—of course, I like him. Why shouldn't I?"

"I only wondered," said Poirot placidly, "whether you did."

And as the other did not answer, he went on. "I also wondered if he liked you?"

"What are you getting at, Monsieur Poirot? There's something in your mind I can't fathom."

"I am going to be very frank. You are engaged to be married, Monsieur Harrison. I know Miss Molly Deane. She is a very charming, a very beautiful girl. Before she was engaged to you, she was engaged to Claude Langton. She threw him over for you."

Harrison nodded.

"I do not ask what her reasons were; she may have been justified. But I tell you this, it is not too much to suppose that Langton has not forgotten or forgiven."

"You're wrong, Monsieur Poirot. I swear you're wrong. Langton's been a sportsman; he's taken things like a man. He's been amazingly decent to me—gone out of his way to be friendly."

"And that does not strike you as unusual? You use the word 'amazingly,' but you do not seem to be amazed."

"What do you mean, M. Poirot?"

"I mean," said Poirot, and his voice had a new note in it, "that a man may conceal his hate till the proper time comes."

"Hate?" Harrison shook his head and laughed.

"The English are very stupid," said Poirot. "They think that they can deceive anyone but that no one can deceive them. The sportsman—the good fellow—never will they believe evil of him. And because they are brave, but stupid, sometimes they die when they need not die."

"You are warning me," said Harrison in a low voice. "I see it now—what has puzzled me all along. You are warning me against Claude Langton. You came here today to warn me . . ."

Poirot nodded. Harrison sprang up suddenly. "But you are mad, Monsieur Poirot. This is England. Things don't happen like that here. Disappointed suitors don't go about stabbing people in the back and poisoning them. And you're wrong about Langton. That chap wouldn't hurt a fly."

"The lives of flies are not my concern," said Poirot placidly. "And although you say Monsieur Langton would not take the life of one, yet you forget that he is even now preparing to take the lives of several thousand wasps."

Harrison did not at once reply. The little detective in his turn sprang to his feet. He advanced to his friend and laid a hand on his shoulder. So agitated was he that he almost shook the big man, and, as he did so, he hissed into his ear: "Rouse yourself, my friend, rouse yourself. And look—look where I am pointing. There on the bank, close by that tree root. See you, the wasps returning home, placid at the end of the day? In a little hour, there will be destruction, and they know it not. There is no one to tell them. They have not, it seems, a Hercule Poirot. I tell you, Monsieur Harrison, I am down here on business. Murder is my business. And it is my business before it has happened as well as afterward. At what time does Monsieur Langton come to take this wasps' nest?"

"Langton would never . . ."

"At what time?"

"At nine o'clock. But I tell you, you're all wrong. Langton would never . . ."

"These English!" cried Poirot in a passion. He caught up his hat and stick and moved down the path, pausing to speak over his shoulder. "I do not stay to argue with you. I should only enrage myself. But you understand, I return at nine o'clock?"

Harrison opened his mouth to speak, but Poirot did not give him the chance. "I know what you would say: 'Langton would never,' et cetera. Ah, Langton would never! But all the same I return at nine o'clock. But, yes, it will amuse me—put it like that—it will amuse me to see the taking of a wasps' nest. Another of your English sports!"

He waited for no reply but passed rapidly down the path and out through the door that creaked. Once outside on the road, his pace slackened. His vivacity died down, his face became grave and troubled. Once he drew his watch from his pocket and consulted it. The hands pointed to ten minutes past eight. "Over three quarters of an hour," he murmured. "I wonder if I should have waited."

His footsteps slackened; he almost seemed on the point of returning. Some vague foreboding seemed to assail him. He shook it off resolutely, however, and continued to walk in the direction of the village. But his face was still troubled, and once or twice he shook his head like a man only partly satisfied.

It was still some minutes of nine when he once more approached the garden door. It was a clear, still evening; hardly a breeze stirred the leaves. There was, perhaps, something a little sinister in the stillness, like the lull before a storm.

Poirot's footsteps quickened ever so slightly. He was suddenly alarmed—and uncertain. He feared he knew not what.

And at that moment the garden door opened and Claude Langton stepped quickly out into the road. He started when he saw Poirot.

"Oh—er—good evening."

"Good evening, Monsieur Langton. You are early."

Langton stared at him. "I don't know what you mean."

"You have taken the wasps' nest?"

"As a matter of fact, I didn't."

"Oh!" said Poirot softly. "So you did not take the wasps' nest. What did you do then?"

"Oh, just sat and yarned a bit with old Harrison. I really must hurry along now, Monsieur Poirot. I'd no idea you were remaining in this part of the world."

"I had business here, you see."

"Oh! Well, you'll find Harrison on the terrace. Sorry I can't stop."

He hurried away. Poirot looked after him. A nervous young fellow, good looking with a weak mouth!

"So I shall find Harrison on the terrace," murmured Poirot. "I wonder." He went in through the garden door and up the path. Harrison was sitting in a chair by the table. He sat motionless and did not even turn his head as Poirot came up to him.

"Ah! *Mon ami,*" said Poirot. "You are all right, eh?"

There was a long pause and then Harrison said in a queer, dazed voice, "What did you say?"

"I said—are you all right?"

"All right? Yes, I'm all right. Why not?"

"You feel no ill effects? That is good."

"Ill effects? From what?"

"Washing soda."

Harrison roused himself suddenly. "Washing soda? What do you mean?"

Poirot made an apologetic gesture. "I infinitely regret the necessity, but I put some in your pocket."

"You put some in my pocket? What on earth for?"

Harrison stared at him. Poirot spoke quietly and impersonally like a lecturer coming down to the level of a small child.

"You see, one of the advantages, or disadvantages, of being a detective is that it brings you into contact with the criminal classes. And the criminal classes, they can teach you some very interesting and curious things. There was a pickpocket once—I interested myself in him because for once in a way he has not done what they say he has done—and so I get him off. And because he is grateful he pays me in the only way he can think of—which is to show me the tricks of his trade.

"And so it happens that I can pick a man's pocket if I choose without his ever suspecting the fact. I lay one hand on his shoulder, I excite myself, and he feels nothing. But all the same I have managed to transfer what is in his pocket to my pocket and leave washing soda in its place.

"You see," continued Poirot dreamily, "if a man wants to get at some poison quickly to put in a glass, unobserved, he positively must keep it in his righthand coat pocket; there is nowhere else. I knew it would be there."

He dropped his hand into his pocket and brought out a few white, lumpy crystals. "Exceedingly dangerous," he murmured, "to carry it like that—loose."

Calmly and without hurrying himself, he took from another pocket a wide-mouthed bottle. He slipped in the crystals, stepped to the table and filled up the bottle with plain water. Then carefully corking it, he shook it until all the crystals were dissolved. Harrison watched him as though fascinated.

Satisfied with his solution, Poirot stepped across to the nest. He uncorked the bottle, turned his head aside, and poured the solution into the wasps' nest, then stood back a pace or two watching.

Some wasps that were returning alighted, quivered a little and then lay still. Other wasps crawled out of the hole only to die. Poirot watched for a minute or two and then nodded his head and came back to the veranda.

"A quick death," he said. "A very quick death."

Harrison found his voice. "How much do you know?"

Poirot looked straight ahead. "As I told you, I saw Claude Langton's name in the book. What I did not tell you was that almost immediately afterward, I happened to meet him. He told me he had been buying cyanide of potassium at your request—to take a wasps' nest. That struck me as a little odd, my friend, because I remember that at that dinner of which you spoke, you held forth on the superior merits of petrol and denounced the buying of cyanide as dangerous and unnecessary."

"Go on."

"I knew something else. I had seen Claude Langton and Molly Deane together when they thought no one saw them. I do not know what lovers' quarrel it was that originally parted them and drove her into your arms, but I realized that misunderstandings were over and that Miss Deane was drifting back to her love."

"Go on."

"I knew something more, my friend. I was in Harley Street the other day, and I saw you come out of a certain doctor's house. I know that doctor and for what disease one consults him, and I read the expression on your face. I have seen it only once or twice in my lifetime, but it is not easily mistaken. It was the face of a man under sentence of death. I am right, am I not?"

"Quite right. He gave me two months."

"You did not see me, my friend, for you had other things to think about. I saw something else on your face—the thing that I told you this afternoon men try to conceal. I saw hate there, my friend. You did not trouble to conceal it, because you thought there were none to observe."

"Go on," said Harrison.

"There is not much more to say. I came down here, saw Langton's name by accident in the poison book as I tell you, met him, and came here to you. I laid traps for you. You denied having asked Langton to get cyanide, or rather you expressed surprise at his having done so. You were taken aback at first at my appearance, but presently, you saw how well it would fit in and you encouraged my suspicions. I knew from Langton himself that he was coming at half past eight. You told me nine o'clock, thinking I should come and find everything over. And so I knew everything."

"Why did you come?" cried Harrison. "If only you hadn't come!"

Poirot drew himself up. "I told you," he said, "murder is my business."

"Murder? Suicide, you mean."

"No." Poirot's voice rang out sharply and clearly. "I mean murder. Your death was to be quick and easy, but the death you planned for Langton was the worst death any man can die. He bought the poison; he comes to see you, and he is alone with you. You die suddenly, and the cyanide is found in your glass, and Claude Langton hangs. That was your plan."

Again Harrison moaned.

"Why did you come? Why did you come?"

"I have told you, but there is another reason. I liked you. Listen, *mon ami*, you are a dying man; you have lost the girl you loved, but there is one thing that you are not: you are not a murderer. Tell me now: are you glad or sorry that I came?"

There was a moment's pause and then Harrison drew himself up. There was a new dignity in his face—the look of a man who has conquered his own baser self. He stretched out his hand across the table.

"Thank goodness you came," he cried. "Oh! Thank goodness you came."

7. THE THEFT OF
THE ROYAL RUBY

I regret exceedingly . . ." said M. Hercule Poirot. He was interrupted. Not rudely interrupted. The interruption was suave, dexterous, persuasive rather than contradictory.

"Please don't refuse offhand, Monsieur Poirot. There are grave issues of State. Your cooperation will be appreciated in the highest quarters."

"You are too kind." Hercule Poirot waved a hand, "But I really cannot undertake to do as you ask. At this season of the year . . ."

Again Mr. Jesmond interrupted. "Christmas time," he said, persuasively. "An old-fashioned Christmas in the English countryside."

Hercule Poirot shivered. The thought of the English countryside at this season of the year did not attract him.

"A good old-fashioned Christmas!" Mr. Jesmond stressed it.

"Me—I am not an Englishman," said Hercule Poirot. "In my country, Christmas, it is for the children. The New Year, that is what we celebrate."

"Ah," said Mr. Jesmond, "but Christmas in England is a great institution and I assure you at Kings Lacey you would see it at its best. It's a wonderful old house, you know. Why, one wing of it dates from the fourteenth century."

Again Poirot shivered. The thought of a fourteenth-century English manor house filled him with apprehension. He had suffered too often in the historic country houses of England. He looked round appreciatively at his comfortable modern flat with its radiators and the latest patent devices for excluding any kind of draft.

"In the winter," he said firmly, "I do not leave London."

"I don't think you quite appreciate, Monsieur Poirot, what a very serious matter this is." Mr. Jesmond glanced at his companion and then back at Poirot.

Poirot's second visitor had up to now said nothing but a polite and formal "How do you do." He sat now, gazing down at his well-polished shoes, with an air of the utmost dejection on his coffee-colored face. He was a young man, not more than twenty-three, and he was clearly in a state of complete misery.

"Yes, yes," said Hercule Poirot. "Of course the matter is serious. I do appreciate that. His Highness has my heartfelt sympathy."

"The position is one of the utmost delicacy," said Mr. Jesmond.

Poirot transferred his gaze from the young man to his older companion. If one wanted to sum up Mr. Jesmond in a word, the word would have been discretion. Everything about Mr. Jesmond was discreet. His well-cut but inconspicuous clothes, his agreeable, well-bred voice which rarely soared out of an agreeable monotone, his light-brown hair just thinning a little at the temples, his pale serious face. It seemed to Hercule Poirot that he had known not one Mr. Jesmond but a dozen Mr. Jesmonds in his time, all using sooner or later the same phrase—"a position of the utmost delicacy."

"The police," said Hercule Poirot, "can be very discreet, you know."

Mr. Jesmond shook his head firmly.

"Not the police," he said. "To recover the—er—what we want to recover will almost inevitably involve taking proceedings in the law courts and we know so little. We *suspect,* but we do not *know.*"

"You have my sympathy," said Hercule Poirot again.

If he imagined that his sympathy was going to mean anything to his two visitors, he was wrong. They did not want sympathy, they wanted practical help. Mr. Jesmond began once more to talk about the delights of an English Christmas.

"It's dying out, you know," he said, "the real old-fashioned type of Christmas. People spend it at hotels nowadays. But an English Christmas with all the family gathered round, the children and their stockings, the Christmas tree, the turkey and plum pudding, the crackers. The snow-man outside the window . . ."

In the interests of exactitude, Hercule Poirot intervened.

"To make a snow-man one has to have the snow," he remarked severely. "And one cannot have snow to order, even for an English Christmas."

"I was talking to a friend of mine in the meteorological office only today," said Mr. Jesmond, "and he tells me that it is highly probable there *will* be snow this Christmas."

It was the wrong thing to have said. Hercule Poirot shuddered more forcefully than ever.

"Snow in the country!" he said. "That would be still more abominable. A large, cold, stone manor house."

"Not at all," said Mr. Jesmond. "Things have changed very much in the last ten years or so. Oil-fired central heating."

"They have oil-fired central heating at Kings Lacey?" asked Poirot. For the first time he seemed to waver.

Mr. Jesmond seized his opportunity. "Yes, indeed," he said, "and a splendid hot water system. Radiators in every bedroom. I assure you, my dear Monsieur Poirot, Kings Lacey is comfort itself in the winter time. You might even find the house *too* warm."

"That is most unlikely," said Hercule Poirot.

With practiced dexterity Mr. Jesmond shifted his ground a little.

"You can appreciate the terrible dilemma we are in," he said, in a confidential manner.

Hercule Poirot nodded. The problem was, indeed, not a happy one. A young potentate-to-be, the only son of the ruler of a rich and important native State had arrived in London a few weeks ago. His country had been passing through a period of restlessness and discontent. Though loyal to the father whose way of life had remained persistently Eastern, popular opinion was somewhat dubious of the younger generation. His follies had been Western ones and as such looked upon with disapproval.

Recently, however, his betrothal had been announced. He was to marry a cousin of the same blood, a young woman who, though educated at Cambridge, was careful to display no Western influences in her own country. The wedding day was announced and the young prince had made a journey to England, bringing with him some of the famous jewels of his house to be reset in appropriate modern settings by Cartier. These had included a very famous ruby which had been removed from its cumbersome old-fashioned necklace and had been given a new look by the famous jewelers. So far so good, but after this came the snag. It was not to be supposed that a young man possessed of much wealth and convivial tastes, should not commit a few follies of the pleasanter type. As to that there would have been no censure. Young princes were supposed to amuse themselves in this fashion. For the prince to take the girl friend of the moment for a walk down Bond Street and bestow upon her an emerald bracelet or a diamond clip as a reward for the pleasure she had afforded him would have been regarded as quite natural and suitable, corresponding in fact to the Cadillac cars which his father invariably presented to his favorite dancing girl of the moment.

But the prince had been far more indiscreet than that. Flattered by the lady's interest, he had displayed to her the famous ruby in its new setting, and had finally been so unwise as to accede to her request to be allowed to wear it—just for one evening!

The sequel was short and sad. The lady had retired from their supper table to powder her nose. Time passed. She did not return. She had left the establishment by another door and since then had disappeared into space. The important and distressing thing was that the ruby in its new setting had disappeared with her.

These were the facts that could not possibly be made public without the most dire consequences. The ruby was something more than a ruby, it was a historical possession of great significance, and the circumstances of its disappearance were such that any undue publicity about them might result in the most serious political consequences.

Mr. Jesmond was not the man to put these facts into simple language. He wrapped them up, as it were, in a great deal of verbiage. Who exactly Mr. Jesmond was, Hercule Poirot did not exactly know. He had met other Mr. Jesmonds in the course of his career. Whether he was connected with the Home Office, the Foreign Office or some more discreet branch of public service was not specified. He was acting in the interests of the Commonwealth. The ruby must be recovered.

M. Poirot, so Mr. Jesmond delicately insisted, was the man to recover it.

"Perhaps—yes," Hercule Poirot admitted, "but you can tell me so little. Suggestion—suspicion—all that is not very much to go upon."

"Come now, Monsieur Poirot, surely it is not beyond your powers. Ah, come now."

"I do not always succeed."

But this was mock modesty. It was clear enough from Poirot's tone that for him to undertake a mission was almost synonymous with succeeding in it.

"His Highness is very young," Mr. Jesmond said. "It will be sad if his whole life is to be blighted for a mere youthful indiscretion."

Poirot looked kindly at the downcast young man. "It is the time for follies, when one is young," he said encouragingly, "and for the ordinary young man it does not matter so much. The good papa, he pays up; the family lawyer, he helps to disentangle the inconvenience; the young man, he learns by experience and all ends for the best. In a position such as yours, it is hard indeed. Your approaching marriage . . ."

"That is it. That is it exactly." For the first time words poured from the young man. "You see she is very, very serious. She takes life very seriously. She has acquired at Cambridge many very serious ideas. There is to be education in my country. There are to be schools. There are to be many things. All in the name of progress, you understand, of democracy. It will not be, she says, like it was in my father's time. Naturally she knows that I will have diversions in London, but not the scandal. No! It is the scandal that matters. You see it is very, very famous, this ruby. There is a long trail behind it, a history. Much bloodshed—many deaths!"

"Deaths," said Hercule Poirot thoughtfully. He looked at Mr. Jesmond. "One hopes," he said, "it will not come to that?"

Mr. Jesmond made a peculiar noise rather like a hen who has decided to lay an egg and then thought better of it.

"No, no, indeed," he said, sounding rather prim. "There is no question, I am sure, of anything of *that* kind."

"You cannot be sure," said Hercule Poirot. "Whoever has the ruby now, there may be others who want to gain possession of it, and who will not stick at a trifle, my friend."

"I really don't think," said Mr. Jesmond, sounding more prim than ever, "that we need enter into speculations of that kind. Quite unprofitable."

"Me," said Hercule Poirot, suddenly becoming very foreign, "me, I explore all the avenues, like the politicians."

Mr. Jesmond looked at him doubtfully. Pulling himself together, he said, "Well, I can take it that it is settled, Monsieur Poirot? You will go to Kings Lacey?"

"And how do I explain myself there?" asked Hercule Poirot.

Mr. Jesmond smiled with confidence.

"That, I think, can be arranged very easily," he said. "I can assure you that it will all seem quite natural. You will find the Laceys most charming. Delightful people."

"And you do not deceive me about the oil-fired central heating?"

"No, no, indeed." Mr. Jesmond sounded quite pained. "I assure you you will find every comfort."

"*Tout confort moderne,*" murmured Poirot to himself, reminiscently. "*Eh bien,*" he said, "I accept."

THE TEMPERATURE IN the long drawing-room at Kings Lacey was a comfortable sixty-eight as Hercule Poirot sat talking to Mrs. Lacey by one of the big mullioned windows. Mrs. Lacey was engaged in needlework. She was not doing *petit point* or embroidering flowers upon silk. Instead, she appeared to be engaged in the prosaic task of hemming dishcloths. As she sewed she talked in a soft reflective voice that Poirot found very charming.

"I hope you will enjoy our Christmas party here, Monsieur Poirot. It's only the family, you know. My granddaughter and a grandson and a friend of his and Bridget who's my great-niece, and Diana who's a cousin and David Welwyn who is a very old friend. Just a family party. But Edwina Morecombe said that that's what you really wanted to see. An old-fashioned Christmas. Nothing could be more old-fashioned than we are! My husband, you know, absolutely lives in the past. He likes everything to be just as it was when he was a boy of twelve years old, and used to come here for his holidays." She smiled to herself. "All the same old things, the Christmas tree and the stockings hung up and the oyster soup and the turkey—two turkeys, one boiled and one roast—and the plum pudding with the ring and the bachelor's button and all the rest of it in it. We can't have sixpences nowadays because they're not pure silver any more. But all the old desserts, the Elvas plums and Carlsbad plums and almonds and raisins, and crystallized fruit and ginger. Dear me, I sound like a catalog from Fortnum and Mason!"

"You arouse my gastronomic juices, madame."

"I expect we'll all have frightful indigestion by tomorrow evening," said Mrs. Lacey. "One isn't used to eating so much nowadays, is one?"

She was interrupted by some loud shouts and whoops of laughter outside the window. She glanced out.

"I don't know what they're doing out there. Playing some game or other, I suppose. I've always been so afraid, you know, that these young people would be bored by our Christmas here. But not at all, it's just the opposite. Now my own son and daughter and their friends, they used to be rather sophisticated about Christmas. Say it was all nonsense and too much fuss and it would be far better to go out to a hotel somewhere and dance. But the younger generation seem to find all this terribly attractive. Besides," added Mrs. Lacey practically, "schoolboys and schoolgirls are always hungry, aren't they? I think they must starve them at these schools. After all, one does know children of that age each eat about as much as three strong men."

Poirot laughed and said, "It is most kind of you and your husband, madame, to include me in this way in your family party."

"Oh, we're both delighted, I'm sure," said Mrs. Lacey. "And if you find Horace a little gruff," she continued, "pay no attention. It's just his manner, you know."

What her husband, Colonel Lacey, had actually said was: "Can't think why you want one of these damned foreigners here cluttering up Christmas? Why can't we have him some other time? Can't stick foreigners! All right, all right, so Edwina Morecombe wished him on us. What's it got to do with *her*, I should like to know? Why doesn't *she* have him for Christmas?"

"Because you know very well," Mrs. Lacey had said, "that Edwina always goes to Claridge's."

Her husband had looked at her piercingly and said, "Not up to something, are you, Em?"

"Up to something?" said Em, opening very blue eyes. "Of course not. Why should I be?"

Old Colonel Lacey laughed, a deep, rumbling laugh. "I wouldn't put it past you, Em," he said. "When you look your most innocent is when you *are* up to something."

Revolving these things in her mind, Mrs. Lacey went on: "Edwina said she thought perhaps you might help us. . . . I'm sure I don't know quite how, but she said that friends of yours had once found you very helpful in—in a case something like ours. I—well, perhaps you don't know what I'm talking about?"

Poirot looked at her encouragingly. Mrs. Lacey was close on seventy, as upright as a ramrod, with snow-white hair, pink cheeks, blue eyes, a ridiculous nose and a determined chin.

"If there is anything I can do I shall only be too happy to do it," said Poirot. "It is, I understand, a rather unfortunate matter of a young girl's infatuation."

Mrs. Lacey nodded. "Yes. It seems extraordinary that I should— well, want to talk to you about it. After all, you *are* a perfect stranger. . . ."

"*And* a foreigner," said Poirot, in an understanding manner.

"Yes," said Mrs. Lacey, "but perhaps that makes it easier, in a way. Anyhow, Edwina seemed to think that you might perhaps know something—how shall I put it—something useful about this young Desmond Lee-Wortley."

Poirot paused a moment to admire the ingenuity of Mr. Jesmond and the ease with which he had made use of Lady Morecombe to further his own purposes.

"He has not, I understand, a very good reputation, this young man?" he began delicately.

"No, indeed, he hasn't! A very bad reputation! But that's no help so far as Sarah is concerned. It's never any good, is it, telling young girls that men have a bad reputation? It—it just spurs them on!"

"You are so very right," said Poirot.

"In my young day," went on Mrs. Lacey. "(Oh dear, that's a very long time ago!) We used to be warned, you know, against certain young men, and of course it *did* heighten one's interest in them, and if one could possibly manage to dance with them, or to be alone with them in a dark conservatory . . ." she laughed. "That's why I wouldn't let Horace do any of the things he wanted to do."

"Tell me," said Poirot, "exactly what it is that troubles you?"

"Our son was killed in the war," said Mrs. Lacey. "My daughter-in-law died when Sarah was born so that she has always been with us, and we've brought her up. Perhaps we've brought her up unwisely—I don't know. But we thought we ought always to leave her as free as possible."

"That is desirable, I think," said Poirot. "One cannot go against the spirit of the times."

"No," said Mrs. Lacey, "that's just what I felt about it. And, of course, girls nowadays do do these sort of things."

Poirot looked at her inquiringly.

"I think the way one expresses it," said Mrs. Lacey, "is that Sarah has got in with what they call the coffeebar set. She won't go to dances or come out properly or be a deb or anything of that kind. Instead she has two rather unpleasant rooms in Chelsea down by the river and wears these funny clothes that they like to wear, and black stockings or bright green ones. Very thick stockings. (So prickly, I always think!) And she goes about without washing or combing her hair."

"*Ça, c'est tout à fait naturelle,*" said Poirot. "It is the fashion of the moment. They grow out of it."

"Yes, I know," said Mrs. Lacey. "I wouldn't worry about *that* sort of thing. But you see she's taken up with this Desmond Lee-Wortley and he really has a *very* unsavory reputation. He lives more or less on well-to-do girls. They seem to go quite mad about him. He very nearly married the Hope girl, but her people got her made a ward in court or something. And of course that's what Horace wants to do. He says he must do it for her protection. But I don't think it's really a good idea, Monsieur Poirot. I mean, they'll just run away together and go to Scotland or Ireland or the Argentine or somewhere and either get married or else live together without getting married. And although it may be contempt of court and all that—well, it isn't really an answer, is it, in the end? Especially if a baby's coming. One has to give in then, and let them get married. And then, nearly always, it seems to me, after a year or two there's a divorce. And then the girl comes home and usually after a year or two she marries someone so nice he's almost dull and settles down. But it's particularly sad, it seems to me, if there is a child, because it's not the same thing, being brought up by a stepfather, however nice. No, I think it's much better if we did as we did in my young days. I mean the first young man one fell in love with was *always* someone undesirable. I remember I had a horrible passion for a young man called— now what was his name now?—how strange it is, I can't remember his Christian name at all! Tibbitt, that was his surname. Young Tibbitt. Of course, my father more or less forbade him the house, but he used to get asked to the same dances, and we used to dance together. And sometimes we'd escape and sit out together and occasionally friends would arrange picnics to which we both went. Of course, it was all very exciting and forbidden and one enjoyed it enormously. But one didn't go to the—well, to the *lengths* that girls go nowadays. And so, after a while, the Mr. Tibbitts faded out. And do you know, when I saw him four years later I was surprised what I could *ever* have seen in him! He seemed to be such a *dull* young man. Flashy, you know. No interesting conversation."

"One always thinks the days of one's own youth are best," said Poirot, somewhat sententiously.

"I know," said Mrs. Lacey. "It's tiresome, isn't it? I mustn't be tiresome. But all the same I *don't* want Sarah, who's a dear girl really, to marry Desmond Lee-Wortley. She and David Welwyn, who is staying here, were always such friends and so fond of each other, and we did hope, Horace and I, that they would grow up and marry. But of course she just finds him dull now, and she's absolutely infatuated with Desmond."

"I do not quite understand, madame," said Poirot. "You have him here now, staying in the house, this Desmond Lee-Wortley?"

"That's *my* doing," said Mrs. Lacey. "Horace was all for forbidding her to see him and all that. Of course, in Horace's day, the father or guardian would have called round at the young man's lodgings with a horse whip! Horace was all for forbidding the fellow the house, and forbidding the girl to see him. I told him that was quite the wrong attitude to take. 'No,' I said. 'Ask him down here. We'll have him down for Christmas with the family party.' Of course, my husband said I was mad! But I said, 'At any rate, dear, let's *try* it. Let her see him in *our* atmosphere and *our* house and we'll be very nice to him and very polite, and perhaps then he'll seem less interesting to her'!"

"I think, as they say, you *have* something there, madame," said Poirot. "I think your point of view is very wise. Wiser than your husband's."

"Well, I hope it is," said Mrs. Lacey doubtfully. "It doesn't seem to be working much yet. But of course he's only been here a couple of days." A sudden dimple showed in her wrinkled cheek. "I'll confess something to you, Monsieur Poirot. I myself can't help liking him. I don't mean I *really* like him, with my *mind*, but I can feel the charm all right. Oh yes, I can see what Sarah sees in him. But I'm an old enough woman and have enough experience to know that he's absolutely no good. Even if I *do* enjoy his company. Though I do think," added Mrs. Lacey, rather wistfully, "he has *some* good points.

He asked if he might bring his sister here, you know. She's had an operation and was in hospital. He said it was so sad for her being in a nursing home over Christmas and he wondered if it would be too much trouble if he could bring her with him. He said he'd take all her meals up to her and all that. Well now, I do think that *was* rather nice of him, don't you, Monsieur Poirot?"

"It shows a consideration," said Poirot, thoughtfully, "which seems almost out of character."

"Oh, I don't know. You can have family affections at the same time as wishing to prey on a rich young girl. Sarah will be *very* rich, you know, not only with what we leave her—and of course that won't be very much because most of the money goes with the place to Colin, my grandson. But her mother was a very rich woman and Sarah will inherit all her money when she's twenty-one. She's only twenty now. No, I do think it was nice of Desmond to mind about his sister. And he didn't pretend she was anything very wonderful or that. She's a shorthand typist, I gather—does secretarial work in London. And he's been as good as his word and does carry up trays to her. Not all the time, of course, but quite often. So I think he has some nice points. But all the same," said Mrs. Lacey with great decision, "I don't want Sarah to marry him."

"From all I have heard and been told," said Poirot, "that would indeed be a disaster."

"Do you think it would be possible for you to help us in any way?" asked Mrs. Lacey.

"I think it is possible, yes," said Hercule Poirot, "but I do not wish to promise too much. For the Mr. Desmond Lee-Wortleys of this world are clever, madame. But do not despair. One can, perhaps, do a little something. I shall at any rate, put forth my best endeavors, if only in gratitude for your kindness in asking me here for this Christmas festivity." He looked round him. "And it cannot be so easy these days to have Christmas festivities."

"No, indeed," Mrs. Lacey sighed. She leaned forward. "Do you know, Monsieur Poirot, what I really dream of—what I would love to have?"

"But tell me, madame."

"I simply long to have a small, modern bungalow. No, perhaps not a bungalow exactly, but a small, modern, easy to run house built somewhere in the park here, and live in it with an absolutely up-to-date kitchen and no long passages. Everything easy and simple."

"It is a very practical idea, madame."

"It's not practical for me," said Mrs. Lacey. "My husband *adores* this place. He *loves* living here. He doesn't mind being slightly uncomfortable, he doesn't mind the inconveniences and he would hate, simply *hate*, to live in a small modern house in the park!"

"So you sacrifice yourself to his wishes?"

Mrs. Lacey drew herself up. "I do not consider it a sacrifice, Monsieur Poirot," she said. "I married my husband with the wish to make him happy. He has been a good husband to me and made me very happy all these years, and I wish to give happiness to him."

"So you will continue to live here," said Poirot.

"It's not really too uncomfortable," said Mrs. Lacey.

"No, no," said Poirot, hastily. "On the contrary, it is most comfortable. Your central heating and your bath water are perfection."

"We spent a lot of money in making the house comfortable to live in," said Mrs. Lacey. "We were able to sell some land. Ripe for development, I think they call it. Fortunately right out of sight of the house on the other side of the park. Really rather an ugly bit of ground with no nice view, but we got a very good price for it. So that we have been able to have as many improvements as possible."

"But the service, madame?"

"Oh, well, that presents less difficulty than you might think. Of course, one cannot expect to be looked after and waited upon as one used to be. Different people come in from the village. Two women in the morning, another two to cook lunch and wash it up, and different ones again in the evening. There are plenty of people who want to come and work for a few hours a day. Of course for Christmas we are very lucky. My dear Mrs. Ross always comes in every Christmas. She is a wonderful cook, really first-class. She retired about ten years ago, but she comes in to help us in any emergency. Then there is dear Peverell."

"Your butler?"

"Yes. He is pensioned off and lives in the little house near the lodge, but he is so devoted, and he insists on coming to wait on us at Christmas. Really, I'm terrified, Monsieur Poirot, because he's so old and so shaky that I feel certain that if he carries anything heavy he will drop it. It's really an agony to watch him. And his heart is not good and I'm afraid of his doing too much. But it would hurt his feelings dreadfully if I did not let him come. He hems and hahs and makes disapproving noises when he sees the state our silver is in and within three days of being here, it is all wonderful again. Yes. He is a dear faithful friend." She smiled at Poirot. "So you see, we are all set for a happy Christmas. A white Christmas, too," she added as she looked out of the window. "See? It is beginning to snow. Ah, the children are coming in. You must meet them, Monsieur Poirot."

Poirot was introduced with due ceremony. First, to Colin and Michael, the schoolboy grandson and his friend, nice polite lads of fifteen, one dark, one fair. Then to their cousin, Bridget, a black-haired girl of about the same age with enormous vitality.

"And this is my granddaughter, Sarah," said Mrs. Lacey.

Poirot looked with some interest at Sarah, an attractive girl with a mop of red hair; her manner seemed to him nervy and a trifle defiant, but she showed real affection for her grandmother.

"And this is Mr. Lee-Wortley."

Mr. Lee-Wortley wore a fisherman's jersey and tight black jeans; his hair was rather long and it seemed doubtful whether he had shaved that morning. In contrast to him was a young man introduced as David Welwyn, who was solid and quiet, with a pleasant smile, and rather obviously addicted to soap and water. There was one other member of the party, a handsome, rather intense looking girl who was introduced as Diana Middleton.

Tea was brought in. A hearty meal of scones, crumpets, sandwiches and three kinds of cake. The younger members of the party appreciated the tea. Colonel Lacey came in last, remarking in a noncommittal voice:

"Hey, tea? Oh yes, tea."

He received his cup of tea from his wife's hand, helped himself to two scones, cast a look of aversion at Desmond Lee-Wortley and sat down as far away from him as he could. He was a big man with bushy eyebrows and a red, weather-beaten face. He might have been taken for a farmer rather than the lord of the manor.

"Started to snow," he said. "It's going to be a white Christmas all right."

After tea the party dispersed.

"I expect they'll go and play with their tape recorders now," said Mrs. Lacey to Poirot. She looked indulgently after her grandson as he left the room. Her tone was that of one who says "The children are going to play with their toy soldiers."

"They're frightfully technical, of course," she said, "and very grand about it all."

The boys and Bridget, however, decided to go along to the lake and see if the ice on it was likely to make skating possible.

"I thought we could have skated on it this morning," said Colin. "But old Hodgkins said no. He's always so terribly careful."

"Come for a walk, David," said Diana Middleton, softly. David hesitated for half a moment, his eyes on Sarah's red head. She was standing by Desmond Lee-Wortley, her hand on his arm, looking up into his face.

"All right," said David Welwyn, "yes, let's."

Diana slipped a quick hand through his arm and they turned toward the door into the garden. Sarah said:

"Shall we go, too, Desmond? It's fearfully stuffy in the house."

"Who wants to walk?" said Desmond. "I'll get my car out. We'll go along to the Speckled Boar and have a drink."

Sarah hesitated for a moment before saying:

"Let's go to Market Ledbury to the White Hart. It's much more fun."

Though for all the world she would not have put it into words, Sarah had an instinctive revulsion from going down to the local pub with Desmond. It was, somehow, not in the tradition of Kings Lacey. The women of Kings Lacey had never frequented the bar of the Speckled Boar. She had an obscure feeling that to go there would be to let old Colonel Lacey and his wife down. And why not? Desmond Lee-Wortley would have said. For a moment of exasperation Sarah felt that he ought to know why not! One didn't upset such old darlings as Grandfather and dear old Em unless it was necessary. They'd been very sweet, really, letting her lead her own life, not understanding in the least why she wanted to live in Chelsea in the way she did, but accepting it. That was due to Em of course. Grandfather would have kicked up no end of a row.

Sarah had no illusions about her grandfather's attitude. It was not his doing that Desmond had been asked to stay at Kings Lacey. That was Em, and Em was a darling and always had been.

When Desmond had gone to fetch his car, Sarah popped her head into the drawing-room again.

"We're going over to Market Ledbury," she said. "We thought we'd have a drink there at the White Hart."

There was a slight amount of defiance in her voice, but Mrs. Lacey did not seem to notice it.

"Well, dear," she said, "I'm sure that will be very nice. David and Diana have gone for a walk, I see. I'm so glad. I really think it was a brainwave on my part to ask Diana here. So sad being left a widow so young—only twenty-two—I do hope she marries again *soon.*"

Sarah looked at her sharply. "What are you up to, Em?"

"It's my little plan," said Mrs. Lacey gleefully. "I think she's just right for David. Of course I know he was terribly in love with *you,* Sarah dear, but you'd no use for him and I realize that he isn't your type. But I don't want him to go on being unhappy, and I think Diana will really suit him."

"What a matchmaker you are, Em," said Sarah.

"I know," said Mrs. Lacey. "Old women always are. Diana's quite keen on him already, I think. Don't you think she'd be just right for him?"

"I shouldn't say so," said Sarah. "I think Diana's far too—well, too intense, too serious. I should think David would find it terribly boring being married to her."

"Well, we'll see," said Mrs. Lacey. "Anyway, *you* don't want him, do you, dear?"

"No, indeed," said Sarah, very quickly. She added, in a sudden rush, "You *do* like Desmond, don't you, Em?"

"I'm sure he's very nice indeed," said Mrs. Lacey.

"Grandfather doesn't like him," said Sarah.

"Well, you could hardly expect him to, could you?" said Mrs. Lacey reasonably, "but I dare say he'll come round when he gets used to the idea. You mustn't rush him, Sarah dear. Old people are very slow to change their minds and your grandfather *is* rather obstinate."

"I don't care what Grandfather thinks or says," said Sarah. "I shall get married to Desmond whenever I like!"

"I know, dear, I know. But do try and be realistic about it. Your grandfather could cause a lot of trouble, you know. You're not of age yet. In another year you can do as you please. I expect Horace will have come round long before that."

"You're on my side aren't you, darling?" said Sarah. She flung her arms round her grandmother's neck and gave her an affectionate kiss.

"I want you to be happy," said Mrs. Lacey. "Ah! there's your young man bringing his car round. You know, I like these very tight trousers these young men wear nowadays. They look so smart—only, of course, it does accentuate knock knees."

Yes, Sarah thought, Desmond *had* got knock knees, she had never noticed it before. . . .

"Go on, dear, enjoy yourself," said Mrs. Lacey.

She watched her go out to the car, then, remembering her foreign guest, she went along to the library. Looking in, however, she saw that Hercule Poirot was taking a pleasant little nap, and smiling to herself, she went across the hall and out into the kitchen to have a conference with Mrs. Ross.

"Come on, beautiful," said Desmond. "Your family cutting up rough because you're coming out to a pub? Years behind the times here, aren't they?"

"Of course they're not making a fuss," said Sarah sharply as she got into the car.

"What's the idea of having that foreign fellow down? He's a detective, isn't he? What needs detecting here?"

"Oh, he's not here professionally," said Sarah. "Edwina Morecombe, my godmother, asked us to have him. I think he's retired from professional work long ago."

"Sounds like a broken-down old cab horse," said Desmond.

"He wanted to see an old-fashioned English Christmas, I believe," said Sarah vaguely.

Desmond laughed scornfully. "Such a lot of tripe, that sort of thing," he said. "How you can stand it I don't know."

Sarah's red hair was tossed back and her aggressive chin shot up.

"I enjoy it!" she said defiantly.

"You can't, baby. Let's cut the whole thing tomorrow. Go over to Scarborough or somewhere."

"I couldn't possibly do that."

"Why not?"

"Oh, it would hurt their feelings."

"Oh, bilge! You know you don't enjoy this childish sentimental bosh."

"Well, not really perhaps, but . . ." Sarah broke off. She realized with a feeling of guilt that she was looking forward a good deal to the Christmas celebration. She enjoyed the whole thing, but she was ashamed to admit that to Desmond. It was not the thing to enjoy Christmas and family life. Just for a moment she wished that Desmond had not come down there at Christmas time. In fact, she almost wished that Desmond had not come down here at all. It was much more fun seeing Desmond in London than here at home.

In the meantime the boys and Bridget were walking back from the lake, still discussing earnestly the problems of skating. Flecks of snow had been falling, and looking up at the sky it could be prophesied that before long there was going to be a heavy snowfall.

"It's going to snow all night," said Colin. "Bet you by Christmas morning we have a couple of feet of snow."

The prospect was a pleasurable one.

"Let's make a snow-man," said Michael.

"Good lord," said Colin, "I haven't made a snow-man since— well, since I was about four years old."

"I don't believe it's a bit easy to do," said Bridget. "I mean, you have to know how."

"We might make an effigy of Monsieur Poirot," said Colin. "Give it a big black mustache. There is one in the dressing-up box."

"I don't see, you know," said Michael thoughtfully, "how Monsieur Poirot could ever have been a detective. I don't see how he'd ever be able to disguise himself."

"I know," said Bridget, "and one can't imagine him running about with a microscope and looking for clues or measuring footprints."

"I've got an idea," said Colin. "Let's put on a show for him!"

"What do you mean, a show?" asked Bridget.

"Well, arrange a murder for him."

"What a gorgeous idea," said Bridget. "Do you mean a body in the snow—that sort of thing?"

"Yes. It would make him feel at home, wouldn't it?"

Bridget giggled.

"I don't know that I'd go as far as that."

"If it snows," said Colin, "we'll have the perfect setting. A body and footprints—we'll have to think that out rather carefully and pinch one of Grandfather's daggers and make some blood."

They came to a halt and oblivious to the rapidly falling snow, entered into an excited discussion.

"There's a paintbox in the old schoolroom. We could mix up some blood—crimson-lake, I should think."

"Crimson-lake's a bit too pink, I think," said Bridget. "It ought to be a bit browner."

"Who's going to be the body?" asked Michael.

"I'll be the body," said Bridget quickly.

"Oh, look here," said Colin, "I thought of it."

"Oh, no, no," said Bridget, "it must be me. It's got to be a girl. It's more exciting. Beautiful girl lying lifeless in the snow."

"Beautiful girl! Ah-ha," said Michael in derision.

"I've got black hair, too," said Bridget.

"What's that got to do with it?"

"Well, it'll show up so well on the snow and I shall wear my red pajamas."

"If you wear red pajamas, they won't show the bloodstains," said Michael in a practical manner.

"But they'd look so effective against the snow," said Bridget, "and they've got white facings, you know, so the blood could be on that. Oh, won't it be gorgeous? Do you think he will really be taken in?"

"He will if we do it well enough," said Michael. "We'll have just your footprints in the snow and one other person's going to the body and coming away from it—a man's, of course. He won't want to disturb them, so he won't know that you're not really dead. You don't think," Michael stopped, struck by a sudden idea. The others looked at him. "You don't think he'll be *annoyed* about it?"

"Oh, I shouldn't think so," said Bridget, with facile optimism. "I'm sure he'll understand that we've just done it to entertain him. A sort of Christmas treat."

"I don't think we ought to do it on Christmas Day," said Colin reflectively. "I don't think Grandfather would like that very much."

"Boxing Day then," said Bridget.

"Boxing Day would be just right," said Michael.

"And it'll give us more time, too," pursued Bridget. "After all, there are a lot of things to arrange. Let's go and have a look at all the props."

They hurried into the house.

THE EVENING WAS a busy one. Holly and mistletoe had been brought in in large quantities and a Christmas tree had been set up at one end of the dining-room. Everyone helped to decorate it, to put up the branches of holly behind pictures and to hang mistletoe in a convenient position in the hall.

"I had no idea anything so archaic still went on," murmured Desmond to Sarah with a sneer.

"We've always done it," said Sarah, defensively.

"What a reason!"

"Oh, don't be tiresome, Desmond. *I* think it's fun."

"Sarah my sweet, you *can't!*"

"Well, not—not really perhaps but—I do in a way."

"Who's going to brave the snow and go to midnight mass?" asked Mrs. Lacey at twenty minutes to twelve.

"Not me," said Desmond. "Come on, Sarah."

With a hand on her arm he guided her into the library and went over to the record case.

"There are limits, darling," said Desmond. "Midnight mass!"

"Yes," said Sarah. "Oh yes."

With a good deal of laughter, donning of coats and stamping of feet, most of the others got off. The two boys, Bridget, David and Diana set out for the ten minutes' walk to the church through the falling snow. Their laughter died away in the distance.

"Midnight mass!" said Colonel Lacey, snorting. "Never went to midnight mass in my young days. *Mass,* indeed! Popish, that is! Oh, I beg your pardon, Monsieur Poirot."

Poirot waved a hand. "It is quite all right. Do not mind me."

"Matins is good enough for anybody, I should say," said the colonel. "Proper Sunday morning service. 'Hark the herald angels sing,' and all the good old Christmas hymns. And then back to Christmas dinner. That's right, isn't it, Em?"

"Yes, dear," said Mrs. Lacey. "That's what *we* do. But the young ones enjoy the midnight service. And it's nice, really, that they *want* to go."

"Sarah and that fellow don't want to go."

"Well, there dear, I think you're wrong," said Mrs. Lacey. "Sarah, you know, *did* want to go, but she didn't like to say so."

"Beats me why she cares what that fellow's opinion is."

"She's very young, really," said Mrs. Lacey placidly. "Are you going to bed, Monsieur Poirot? Good night. I hope you'll sleep well."

"And you, madame? Are you not going to bed yet?"

"Not just yet," said Mrs. Lacey. "I've got the stockings to fill, you see. Oh, I know they're all practically grown up, but they do *like* their stockings. One puts jokes in them! Silly little things. But it all makes for a lot of fun."

"You work very hard to make this a happy house at Christmas time," said Poirot. "I honor you."

He raised her hand to his lips in a courtly fashion.

"Hm," grunted Colonel Lacey, as Poirot departed. "Flowery sort of fellow. Still—he appreciates you."

Mrs. Lacey dimpled up at him. "Have you noticed, Horace, that I'm standing under the mistletoe?" she asked with the demureness of a girl of nineteen.

Hercule Poirot entered his bedroom. It was a large room well provided with radiators. As he went over toward the big four poster bed he noticed an envelope lying on his pillow. He opened it and drew out a piece of paper. On it was a shakily printed message in capital letters.

DON'T EAT NONE OF THE PLUM PUDDING. ONE AS WISHES YOU WELL.

Hercule Poirot stared at it. His eyebrows rose. "Cryptic," he murmured, "and most unexpected."

CHRISTMAS DINNER TOOK place at two o'clock and was a feast indeed. Enormous logs crackled merrily in the wide fireplace and above their crackling rose the babel of many tongues talking together. Oyster soup had been consumed, two enormous turkeys had come and gone, mere carcasses of their former selves. Now, the supreme moment, the Christmas pudding was brought in, in state! Old Peverell, his hands and his knees shaking with the weakness of eighty years, permitted no one but himself to bear it in. Mrs. Lacey sat, her hands pressed together in nervous apprehension. One Christmas, she felt sure, Peverell would fall down dead. Having either to take the risk of letting him fall down dead or of hurting his feelings to such an extent that he would probably prefer to be dead than alive, she had so far chosen the former alternative. On a silver dish the Christmas pudding reposed in its glory. A large football of a pudding, a piece of holly stuck in it like a triumphant flag and glorious flames of blue and red rising round it. There was a cheer and cries of "Ooh-ah."

One thing Mrs. Lacey had done: prevailed upon Peverell to place the pudding in front of her so that she could help it rather than hand it in turn round the table. She breathed a sigh of relief as it was deposited safely in front of her. Rapidly the plates were passed round, flames still licking the portions.

"Wish, Monsieur Poirot," cried Bridget. "Wish before the flame goes. Quick, Gran darling, quick."

Mrs. Lacey leaned back with a sigh of satisfaction. Operation Pudding had been a success. In front of everyone was a helping with flames still licking it. There was a momentary silence all round the table as everyone wished hard.

There was nobody to notice the rather curious expression on the face of Monsieur Poirot as he surveyed the portion of pudding on his plate. *"Don't eat none of the plum pudding."* What on earth did that sinister warning mean? There could be nothing different about his portion of plum pudding from that of everyone else! Sighing as he admitted himself baffled—and Hercule Poirot never liked to admit himself baffled—he picked up his spoon and fork.

"Hard sauce, Monsieur Poirot?"

Poirot helped himself appreciatively to hard sauce.

"Swiped my best brandy again, eh, Em?" said the colonel good-humoredly from the other end of the table. Mrs. Lacey twinkled at him.

"Mrs. Ross insists on having the best brandy, dear," she said. "She says it makes all the difference."

"Well, well," said Colonel Lacey, "Christmas comes but once a year and Mrs. Ross is a great woman. A great woman and a great cook."

"She is indeed," said Colin. "Smashing plum pudding, this. Mmmm." He filled an appreciative mouth.

Gently, almost gingerly, Hercule Poirot attacked his portion of pudding. He ate a mouthful. It was delicious! He ate another. Something tinkled faintly on his plate. He investigated with a fork. Bridget, on his left, came to his aid.

"You've got something, Monsieur Poirot," she said. "I wonder what it is."

Poirot detached a little silver object from the surrounding raisins that clung to it.

"Oooh," said Bridget, "it's the bachelor's button! Monsieur Poirot's got the bachelor's button!"

Hercule Poirot dipped the small silver button into the finger-bowl of water that stood by his plate, and washed it clear of pudding crumbs.

"It is very pretty," he observed.

"That means you're going to be a bachelor, Monsieur Poirot," explained Colin helpfully.

"That is to be expected," said Poirot gravely. "I have been a bachelor for many long years and it is unlikely that I shall change that status now."

"Oh, never say die," said Michael. "I saw in the paper that someone of ninety-five married a girl of twenty-two the other day."

"You encourage me," said Hercule Poirot.

Colonel Lacey uttered a sudden exclamation. His face became purple and his hand went to his mouth.

"Confound it, Emmeline," he roared, "why on earth do you let the cook put glass in the pudding?"

"Glass!" cried Mrs. Lacey, astonished.

Colonel Lacey withdrew the offending substance from his mouth. "Might have broken a tooth," he grumbled. "Or swallowed the damn' thing and had appendicitis."

He dropped the piece of glass into the finger-bowl, rinsed it and held it up.

"God bless my soul," he ejaculated. "It's a red stone out of one of the cracker brooches." He held it aloft.

"You permit?"

Very deftly Monsieur Poirot stretched across his neighbor, took it from Colonel Lacey's fingers and examined it attentively. As the squire had said, it was an enormous red stone the color of a ruby. The light gleamed from its facets as he turned it about. Somewhere around the table a chair was pushed back and then drawn in again.

"Phew!" cried Michael. "How wizard it would be if it was *real*."

"Perhaps it is real," said Bridget hopefully.

"Oh, don't be an ass, Bridget. Why a ruby of that size would be worth thousands and thousands and thousands of pounds. Wouldn't it, Monsieur Poirot?"

"It would indeed," said Poirot.

"But what *I* can't understand," said Mrs. Lacey, "is how it got into the pudding."

"Oooh," said Colin, diverted by his last mouthful, "I've got the pig. It isn't fair."

Bridget chanted immediately, "Colin's got the pig! Colin's got the pig! Colin is the greedy guzzling *Pig!*"

"I've got the ring," said Diana in a clear, high voice.

"Good for you, Diana. You'll be married first, of us all."

"I've got the thimble," wailed Bridget.

"Bridget's going to be an old maid," chanted the two boys. "Yah, Bridget's going to be an old maid."

"Who's got the money?" demanded David. "There's a real ten shilling piece, gold, in this pudding. I know. Mrs. Ross told me so."

"I think I'm the lucky one," said Desmond Lee-Wortley.

Colonel Lacey's two next door neighbors heard him mutter, "Yes, you would be."

"*I've* got a ring, too," said David. He looked across at Diana. "Quite a coincidence, isn't it?"

The laughter went on. Nobody noticed that Monsieur Poirot carelessly, as though thinking of something else, had dropped the red stone into his pocket.

Mince-pies and Christmas dessert followed the pudding. The older members of the party then retired for a welcome siesta before the tea-time ceremony of the lighting of the Christmas tree. Hercule Poirot, however, did not take a siesta. Instead, he made his way to the enormous old-fashioned kitchen.

"It is permitted," he asked, looking round and beaming, "that I congratulate the cook on this marvelous meal that I have just eaten?"

There was a moment's pause and then Mrs. Ross came forward in a stately manner to meet him. She was a large woman, nobly built with all the dignity of a stage duchess. Two lean gray-haired women were beyond in the scullery washing up and a tow-haired girl was moving to and fro between the scullery and the kitchen. But these were obviously mere myrmidons. Mrs. Ross was the queen of the kitchen quarters.

"I am glad you enjoyed it, sir," she said graciously.

"Enjoyed it!" cried Hercule Poirot. With an extravagant foreign gesture he raised his hand to his lips, kissed it, and wafted the kiss to the ceiling. "But you are a genius, Mrs. Ross! A genius! *Never* have I tasted such a wonderful meal. The oyster soup . . ." he made an expressive noise with his lips. "—and the stuffing. The chestnut stuffing in the turkey, that was quite unique in my experience."

"Well, it's funny that you should say that, sir," said Mrs. Ross graciously. "It's a very special recipe, that stuffing. It was given me by an Austrian chef that I worked with many years ago. But all the rest," she added, "is just good, plain English cooking."

"And is there anything better?" demanded Hercule Poirot.

"Well, it's nice of you to say so, sir. Of course, you being a foreign gentleman might have preferred the continental style. Not but what I can't manage continental dishes, too."

"I am sure, Mrs. Ross, you could manage anything! But you must know that English cooking—*good* English cooking, not the cooking one gets in the second-class hotels or the restaurants—is much appreciated by *gourmets* on the continent, and I believe I am correct in saying that a special expedition was made to London in the early eighteen hundreds, and a report sent back to France of the wonders of the English puddings. 'We have nothing like that in France,' they wrote. 'It is worth making a journey to London just to taste the varieties and excellencies of the English puddings.' And above all puddings," continued Poirot, well launched now on a kind of rhapsody, "is the Christmas plum pudding, such as we have eaten today. That was a home-made pudding, was it not? Not a bought one?"

"Yes, indeed, sir. Of my own making and my own recipe such as I've made for many, many years. When I came here Mrs. Lacey said that she'd ordered a pudding from a London store to save me the trouble. But no, madame, I said, that may be kind of you but no bought pudding from a store can equal a home-made Christmas one. Mind you," said Mrs. Ross, warming to her subject like the artist she was, "it was made too soon before the day. A good Christmas pudding should be made some weeks before and allowed to wait The longer they're kept, within reason, the better they are. I mind now that when I was a child and we went to church every Sunday, we'd start listening for the collect that begins 'Stir up O Lord we beseech thee' because that collect was the signal, as it were, that the puddings should be made that week. And so they always were. We had the collect on the Sunday, and that week sure enough my mother would make the Christmas puddings. And so it should have been here this year. As it was, that pudding was only made three days ago, the day before you arrived, sir. However, I kept to the old custom. Everyone in the house had to come out into the kitchen and have a stir and make a wish. That's an old custom, sir, and I've always held to it."

"Most interesting," said Hercule Poirot. "Most interesting. And so everyone came out into the kitchen?"

"Yes, sir. The young gentlemen, Miss Bridget and the London gentleman who's staying here, and his sister and Mr. David and Miss Diana—Mrs. Middleton, I should say . . . All had a stir, they did."

"How many puddings did you make? Is this the only one?"

"No, sir, I made four. Two large ones and two smaller ones. The other large one I planned to serve on New Year's Day and the smaller ones were for Colonel and Mrs. Lacey when they're alone like and not so many in the family."

"I see, I see," said Poirot.

"As a matter of fact, sir," said Mrs. Ross, "it was the wrong pudding you had for lunch today."

"The wrong pudding?" Poirot frowned. "How is that?"

"Well, sir, we have a big Christmas mold. A china mold with a pattern of holly and mistletoe on top and we always have the Christmas Day pudding boiled in that. But there was a most unfortunate accident. This morning, when Annie was getting it down from the shelf in the larder, she slipped and dropped it and it broke. Well, sir, naturally I couldn't serve that, could I? There might have been splinters in it. So we had to use the other one—the New Year's Day one, which is in a plain bowl. It makes a nice round but it's not so decorative as the Christmas mold. Really, where we'll get another mold like that I don't know. They don't make things in that size nowadays. All tiddly bits of things. Why, you can't even buy a breakfast dish that'll take a proper eight to ten eggs and bacon. Ah, things aren't what they were."

"No, indeed," said Poirot. "But today that is not so. This Christmas Day has been like the Christmas Days of old, is that not true?"

Mrs. Ross sighed. "Well, I'm glad you say so, sir, but of course I haven't the *help* now that I used to have. Not skilled help, that is. The girls nowadays . . ." she lowered her voice slightly, "—they mean very well and they're very willing but they've not been *trained,* sir, if you understand what I mean."

"Times change, yes," said Hercule Poirot. "I, too, find it sad sometimes."

"This house, sir," said Mrs. Ross, "it's too large, you know, for the mistress and the colonel. The mistress, she knows that. Living in a corner of it as they do, it's not the same thing at all. It only comes alive, as you might say, at Christmas time when all the family come."

"It is the first time, I think, that Mr. Lee-Wortley and his sister have been here?"

"Yes, sir." A note of slight reserve crept into Mrs. Ross's voice, "A very nice gentleman he is but, well—it seems a funny friend for Miss Sarah to have, according to our ideas. But there—London ways are different! It's sad that his sister's so poorly. Had an operation, she had. She seemed all right the first day she was here, but that very day, after we'd been stirring the puddings, she was took bad again and she's been in bed ever since. Got up too soon after her operation, I expect. Ah, doctors nowadays, they have you out of hospital before you can hardly stand on your feet. Why, my very own nephew's wife . . ." And Mrs. Ross went into a long and spirited tale of hospital treatment as accorded to her relations, comparing it unfavorably with the consideration that had been lavished upon them in older times.

Poirot duly commiserated with her. "It remains," he said, "to thank you for this exquisite and sumptuous meal. You permit a little acknowledgment of my appreciation?" A crisp five pound note passed from his hand into that of Mrs. Ross who said perfunctorily:

"You really shouldn't do *that*, sir."

"I insist. I insist."

"Well, it's very kind of you indeed, sir." Mrs. Ross accepted the tribute as no more than her due. "And I wish you, sir, a very happy Christmas and a prosperous New Year."

The end of Christmas Day was like the end of most Christmas Days. The tree was lighted, a splendid Christmas cake came in for tea, was greeted with approval but was partaken of only moderately. There was cold supper.

Both Poirot and his host and hostess went to bed early.

"Good night, Monsieur Poirot," said Mrs. Lacey. "I hope you've enjoyed yourself."

"It has been a wonderful day, madame, wonderful."

"You're looking very thoughtful," said Mrs. Lacey.

"It is the English pudding that I consider."

"You found it a little heavy, perhaps?" asked Mrs. Lacey delicately.

"No, no, I do not speak gastronomically. I consider its significance."

"It's traditional, of course," said Mrs. Lacey. "Well, good night, Monsieur Poirot, and don't dream too much of Christmas puddings and mincepies."

"Yes," murmured Poirot to himself as he undressed. "It is a problem certainly, that Christmas plum pudding. There is here something that I do not understand at all." He shook his head in a vexed manner. "Well—we shall see."

After making certain preparations, Poirot went to bed, but not to sleep.

It was some two hours later that his patience was rewarded. The door of his bedroom opened very gently. He smiled to himself. It was as he had thought it would be. His mind went back fleetingly to the cup of coffee so politely handed him by Desmond Lee-Wortley. A little later, when Desmond's back was turned, he had laid the cup down for a few moments on a table. He had then apparently picked it up again and Desmond had had the satisfaction, if satisfaction it was, of seeing him drink the coffee to the last drop. But a little smile lifted Poirot's mustache as he reflected that it was not he but someone else who was sleeping a good sound sleep tonight. "That pleasant young David," said Poirot to himself, "he is worried, unhappy. It will do him no harm to have a night's really sound sleep. And now, let us see what will happen?"

He lay quite still, breathing in an even manner with occasionally a suggestion, but the very faintest suggestion, of a snore.

Someone came up to the bed and bent over him. Then, satisfied, that someone turned away and went to the dressing-table. By the light of a tiny torch the visitor was examining Poirot's belongings neatly arranged on top of the dressing-table, Fingers explored the wallet, gently pulled open the drawers of the dressing-table, then extended the search to the pockets of Poirot's clothes. Finally the visitor approached the bed and with great caution slid his hand under the pillow. Withdrawing his hand, he stood for a moment or two as though uncertain what to do next. He walked round the room looking inside ornaments, went into the adjoining bathroom from whence he presently returned. Then, with a faint exclamation of disgust, he went out of the room.

"Ah," said Poirot, under his breath. "You have a disappointment. Yes, yes, a serious disappointment. Bah! To imagine, even, that Hercule Poirot would hide something where you could find it!" Then, turning over on his other side, he went peacefully to sleep.

He was aroused next morning by an urgent soft tapping on his door.

"*Qui est là?* Come in, come in."

The door opened. Breathless, red-faced, Colin stood upon the threshold. Behind him stood Michael.

"Monsieur Poirot, Monsieur Poirot."

"But yes?" Poirot sat up in bed. "It is the early tea? But no. It is you, Colin. What has occurred?"

Colin was, for a moment, speechless. He seemed to be under the grip of some strong emotion. In actual fact it was the sight of the nightcap that Hercule Poirot wore that affected for the moment his organs of speech. Presently he controlled himself and spoke.

"I think—Monsieur Poirot, could you help us? Something rather awful has happened."

"Something has happened? But what?"

"It's—it's Bridget. She's out there in the snow. I think—she doesn't move or speak and—oh, you'd better come and look for yourself. I'm terribly afraid—she may be *dead*."

"What?" Poirot cast aside his bed covers. "Mademoiselle Bridget—dead!"

"I think—I think somebody's killed her. There's—there's blood and—oh do come!"

"But certainly. But certainly. I come on the instant."

With great practicality Poirot inserted his feet into his outdoor shoes and pulled a fur-lined overcoat over his pajamas.

"I come," he said. "I come on the moment. You have aroused the house?"

"No. No, so far I haven't told anyone but you. I thought it would be better. Grandfather and Gran aren't up yet. They're laying breakfast downstairs, but I didn't say anything to Peverell. She—Bridget—she's round the other side of the house, near the terrace and the library window."

"I see. Lead the way. I will follow."

Turning away to hide his delighted grin, Colin led the way downstairs. They went out through the side door. It was a clear morning with the sun not yet high over the horizon. It was not snowing now, but it had snowed heavily during the night and everywhere around was an unbroken carpet of thick snow. The world looked very pure and white and beautiful.

"There!" said Colin breathlessly. "I—it's—*there!*" He pointed dramatically.

The scene was indeed dramatic enough. A few yards away Bridget lay in the snow. She was wearing scarlet pajamas and a white wool wrap thrown round her shoulders. The white wool wrap was stained with crimson. Her head was turned aside and hidden by the mass of her outspread black hair. One arm was under her body, the other lay flung out, the fingers clenched, and standing up in the center of the crimson stain was the hilt of a large curved Kurdish knife which Colonel Lacey had shown to his guests only the evening before.

"*Mon Dieu!*" ejaculated M. Poirot. "It is like something on the stage!"

There was a faint choking noise from Michael. Colin thrust himself quickly into the breach.

"I know," he said. "It—it doesn't seem *real* somehow, does it? Do you see those footprints—I suppose we mustn't disturb them?"

"Ah yes, the footprints. No, we must be careful not to disturb those footprints."

"That's what I thought," said Colin. "That's why I wouldn't let anyone go near her until we got you. I thought you'd know what to do."

"All the same," said Hercule Poirot briskly, "first, we must see if she is still alive? Is not that so?"

"Well—yes—of course," said Michael, a little doubtfully, "but you see, we thought—I mean, we didn't like . . ."

"Ah, you have the prudence! You have read the detective stories. It is most important that nothing should be touched and that the body should be left as it is. But we cannot be sure as yet if it *is* a body, can we? After all, though prudence is admirable, common humanity comes first. We must think of the doctor, must we not, before we think of the police?"

"Oh yes. Of course," said Colin, still a little taken aback.

"We only thought—I mean—we thought we'd better get you before we did anything," said Michael hastily.

"Then you will both remain here," said Poirot. "I will approach from the other side so as not to disturb these footprints. Such excellent footprints, are they not—so very clear? The footprints of a man and a girl going out together to the place where she lies. And then the man's footsteps come back but the girl's—do not."

"They must be the footprints of the murderer," said Colin, with bated breath.

"Exactly," said Poirot. "The footprints of the murderer. A long narrow foot with rather a peculiar type of shoe. Very interesting. Easy, I think, to recognize. Yes, those footprints will be very important."

At that moment Desmond Lee-Wortley came out of the house with Sarah and joined them.

"What on earth are you all doing here?" he demanded in a somewhat theatrical manner. "I saw you from my bedroom window. What's up? Good lord, what's this? It—it looks like . . ."

"Exactly," said Hercule Poirot. "It looks like murder, does it not?"

Sarah gave a gasp, then shot a quick suspicious glance at the two boys.

"You mean someone's killed the girl—what's-her-name—Bridget?" demanded Desmond. "Who on earth would want to kill her? It's unbelievable!"

"There are many things that are unbelievable," said Poirot. "Especially before breakfast, is it not? That is what one of your classics says. Six impossible things before breakfast." He added: "Please wait here, all of you."

Carefully making a circuit, he approached Bridget and bent for a moment down over the body. Colin and Michael were now both shaking with suppressed laughter. Sarah joined them, murmuring, "What have you two been up to?"

"Good old Bridget," whispered Colin. "Isn't she wonderful? Not a twitch!"

"I've never seen anything look so dead as Bridget does," whispered Michael.

Hercule Poirot straightened up again.

"This is a terrible thing," he said. His voice held an emotion it had not held before.

Overcome by mirth, Michael and Colin both turned away. In a choked voice Michael said:

"What—what must we do?"

"There is only one thing to do," said Poirot. "We must send for the police. Will one of you telephone or would you prefer me to do it?"

"I think," said Colin, "I think—what about it, Michael?"

"Yes," said Michael, "I think the jig's up now." He stepped forward. For the first time he seemed a little unsure of himself. "I'm aw-fully sorry," he said, "I hope you won't mind too much. It—er—it was a sort of joke for Christmas and all that, you know. We thought we'd—well, lay on a murder for you."

"You thought you would lay on a murder for me? Then this—then this . . ."

"It's just a show we put on," explained Colin, "to—to make you feel at home, you know."

"Aha," said Hercule Poirot. "I understand. You make of me the April fool, is that it? But today is not April the first, it is December the twenty-sixth."

"I suppose we oughtn't to have done it really," said Colin, "but—but—you don't mind very much, do you, Monsieur Poirot? Come on, Bridget," he called, "get up. You must be half-frozen to death already."

The figure in the snow, however, did not stir.

"It is odd," said Hercule Poirot, "she does not seem to hear you." He looked thoughtfully at them. "It is a joke, you say? You are sure this is a joke?"

"Why, yes." Colin spoke uncomfortably. "We—we didn't mean any harm."

"But why then does Mademoiselle Bridget not get up?"

"I can't imagine," said Colin.

"Come on, Bridget," said Sarah impatiently. "Don't go on lying there playing the fool."

"We really are very sorry, Monsieur Poirot," said Colin appre-hensively. "We do really apologize."

"You need not apologize," said Poirot, in a peculiar tone.

"What do you mean?" Colin stared at him. He turned again. "Bridget! Bridget! What's the matter? Why doesn't she get up? Why does she go on lying there?"

Poirot beckoned to Desmond. "*You,* Mr. Lee-Wortley. Come here . . ."

Desmond joined him.

"Feel her pulse," said Poirot.

Desmond Lee-Wortley bent down. He touched the arm—the wrist.

"There's no pulse . . ." he stared at Poirot. "Her arm's stiff. Good God, she really *is* dead!"

Poirot nodded. "Yes, she is dead," he said. "Someone has turned the comedy into a tragedy."

"Someone—who?"

"There is a set of footprints going and returning. A set of footprints that bears a strong resemblance to the footprints *you* have just made, Mr. Lee-Wortley, coming from the path to this spot."

Desmond Lee-Wortley wheeled round.

"What on earth . . . Are you accusing me? ME? You're crazy! Why on earth should I want to kill the girl?"

"Ah—why? I wonder . . . Let us see. . . ."

He bent down and very gently prised open the stiff fingers of the girl's clenched hand.

Desmond drew a sharp breath. He gazed down unbelievingly. In the palm of the dead girl's hand was what appeared to be a large ruby.

"It's that damn' thing out of the pudding!" he cried.

"Is it?" said Poirot. "Are you sure?"

"Of course it is."

With a swift movement Desmond bent down and plucked the red stone out of Bridget's hand.

"You should not do that," said Poirot reproachfully. "Nothing should have been disturbed."

"I haven't disturbed the body, have I? But this thing might—might get lost and it's evidence. The great thing is to get the police here as soon as possible. I'll go at once and telephone."

He wheeled round and ran sharply toward the house. Sarah came swiftly to Poirot's side.

"I don't understand," she whispered. Her face was dead white. "I don't *understand*." She caught at Poirot's arm. "What did you mean about—about the footprints?"

"Look for yourself, mademoiselle."

The footprints that led to the body and back again were the

same as the ones just made accompanying Poirot to the girl's body and back.

"You mean—that it was Desmond? Nonsense!"

Suddenly the noise of a car came through the clear air. They wheeled round. They saw the car clearly enough driving at a furious pace down the drive and Sarah recognized what car it was.

"It's Desmond," she said. "It's Desmond's car. He—he must have gone to fetch the police instead of telephoning."

Diana Middleton came running out of the house to join them.

"What's happened?" she cried in a breathless voice. "Desmond just came rushing into the house. He said something about Bridget being killed and then he rattled the telephone but it was dead. He couldn't get any answer. He said the wires must have been cut. He said the only thing was to take a car and go for the police. Why the police? . . ."

Poirot made a gesture.

"Bridget?" Diana stared at him. "But surely—isn't it a joke of some kind? I heard something—something last night. I thought that they were going to play a joke on you, Monsieur Poirot?"

"Yes," said Poirot, "that was the idea—to play a joke on me. But now come into the house, all of you. We shall catch our deaths of cold here and there is nothing to be done until Mr. Lee-Wortley returns with the police."

"But look here," said Colin, "we can't—we can't leave Bridget here alone."

"You can do her no good by remaining," said Poirot gently. "Come, it is a sad, a very sad tragedy, but there is nothing we can do any more to help Mademoiselle Bridget. So let us come in and get warm and have perhaps a cup of tea or of coffee."

They followed him obediently into the house. Peverell was just about to ring the gong. If he thought it extraordinary for most of the household to be outside and for Poirot to make an appearance in pajamas and an overcoat, he displayed no sign of it. Peverell in his old age was still the perfect butler. He noticed nothing that he was not asked to notice. They went into the dining-room and sat down.

When they all had a cup of coffee in front of them and were sipping it, Poirot spoke.

"I have to recount to you," he said, "a little history. I cannot tell you all the details, no. But I can give you the main outline. It concerns a young princeling who came to this country. He brought with him a famous jewel which he was to have reset for the lady he was going to marry, but unfortunately before that he made friends with a very pretty young lady. This pretty young lady did not care very much for the man, but she did care for his jewel—so much so that one day she disappeared with this historic possession which had belonged to his house for generations. So the poor young man, he is in a quandary, you see. Above all he cannot have a scandal. Impossible to go to the police. Therefore he comes to me, to Hercule Poirot. 'Recover for me,' he says, 'my historic ruby.' *Eh bien*, this young lady, she has a friend and the friend, he has put through several very questionable transactions. He has been concerned with blackmail and he has been concerned with the sale of jewelry abroad. Always he has been very clever. He is suspected, yes, but nothing can be proved. It comes to my knowledge that this very clever gentleman, he is spending Christmas here in this house. It is important that the pretty young lady, once she has acquired the jewel, should disappear for a while from circulation, so that no pressure can be put upon her, no questions can be asked her. It is arranged, therefore, that she comes here to Kings Lacey, ostensibly as the sister of the clever gentleman . . ."

Sarah drew a sharp breath.

"Oh, no. Oh, no, not *here*! Not with me here!"

"But so it is," said Poirot. "And by a little manipulation I, too, become a guest here for Christmas. This young lady, she is supposed to have just come out of hospital. She is much better when she arrives here. But then comes the news that I, too, arrive, a detective— a well-known detective. At once she has what you call the wind up. She hides the ruby in the first place she can think of, and then very quickly she has a relapse and takes to her bed again. She does not want that I should see her, for doubtless I have a photograph and I shall recognize her. It is very boring for her, yes, but she has to stay in her room and her brother, he brings her up the trays."

"And the ruby?" demanded Michael.

"I think," said Poirot, "that at the moment it is mentioned I arrive, the young lady was in the kitchen with the rest of you, all laughing and talking and stirring the Christmas puddings. The Christmas puddings are put into bowls and the young lady she hides the ruby, pressing it down into one of the pudding bowls. Not the one that we are going to have on Christmas Day. Oh no, that one she knows is in a special mold. She puts it in the other one, the one that is destined to be eaten on New Year's Day. Before then she will be ready to leave, and when she leaves no doubt that Christmas pudding will go with her. But see how fate takes a hand. On the very morning of Christmas Day there is an accident. The Christmas pudding in its fancy mold is dropped on the stone floor and the mold is shattered to pieces. So what can be done? The good Mrs. Ross, she takes the other pudding and sends it in."

"Good lord," said Colin, "do you mean that on Christmas Day when Grandfather was eating his pudding that that was a *real* ruby he'd got in his mouth?"

"Precisely," said Poirot, "and you can imagine the emotions of Mr. Desmond Lee-Wortley when he saw that. *Eh bien,* what happens next? The ruby is passed round. I examine it and I manage unobtrusively to slip it in my pocket. In a careless way as though I were not interested. But one person at least observes what I have done. When I lie in bed that person searches my room. He searches me. He does not find the ruby. Why?"

"Because," said Michael breathlessly, "you had given it to Bridget. That's what you mean. And so that's why—but I don't understand quite—I mean . . . Look here, what *did* happen?"

Poirot smiled at him.

"Come now into the library," he said, "and look out of the window and I will show you something that may explain the mystery."

He led the way and they followed him.

"Consider once again," said Poirot, "the scene of the crime."

He pointed out of the window. A simultaneous gasp broke from the lips of all of them. There was no body lying on the snow, no trace of the tragedy seemed to remain except a mass of scuffled snow.

"It wasn't all a dream, was it?" said Colin faintly. "I—has some-one taken the body away?"

"Ah," said Poirot. "You see? The Mystery of the Disappearing Body." He nodded his head and his eyes twinkled gently.

"Good lord," cried Michael. "Monsieur Poirot, you are—you haven't—oh, look here, he's been having us on all this time!"

Poirot twinkled more than ever.

"It is true, my children, I also have had my little joke. I knew about your little plot, you see, and so I arranged a counter-plot of my own. Ah, *voilà* Mademoiselle Bridget. None the worse, I hope, for your exposure in the snow? Never should I forgive myself if you *attrapped une fluxion de poitrine*."

Bridget had just come into the room. She was wearing a thick skirt and a woolen sweater. She was laughing.

"I sent a *tisane* to your room," said Poirot severely. "You have drunk it?"

"One sip was enough!" said Bridget. "I'm all right. Did I do it well, Monsieur Poirot? Goodness, my arm hurts still after that tourniquet you made me put on it."

"You were splendid, my child," said Poirot. "Splendid. But see, all the others are still in the fog. Last night I went to Mademoiselle Bridget. I told her that I knew about your little *complot* and I asked her if she would act a part for me. She did it very cleverly. She made the footprints with a pair of Mr. Lee-Wortley's shoes."

Sarah said in a harsh voice:

"But what's the point of it all, Monsieur Poirot? What's the point of sending Desmond off to fetch the police? They'll be very angry when they find out it's nothing but a hoax."

Poirot shook his head gently.

"But I do not think for one moment, Mademoiselle, that Mr. Lee-Wortley went to fetch the police," he said. "Murder is a thing in which Mr. Lee-Wortley does not want to be mixed up. He lost his nerve badly. All he could see was his chance to get the ruby. He snatched that, he pretended the telephone was out of order and he rushed off in a car on the pretense of fetching the police. I think myself it is the last you will see of him for some time. He has, I understand, his own ways of getting out of England. He has his own plane, has he not, mademoiselle?"

Sarah nodded. "Yes," she said. "We were thinking of . . ." She stopped.

"He wanted you to elope with him that way, did he not? *Eh bien,* that is a very good way of smuggling a jewel out of the country. When you are eloping with a girl, and that fact is publicized, then you will not be suspected of also smuggling a historic jewel out of the country. Oh yes, that would have made a very good *camouflage.*"

"I don't believe it," said Sarah. "I don't believe a word of it!"

"Then ask his sister," said Poirot, gently nodding his head over her shoulder. Sarah turned her head sharply.

A platinum blonde stood in the doorway. She wore a fur coat and was scowling. She was clearly in a furious temper.

"Sister my foot!" she said, with a short unpleasant laugh. "That swine's no brother of mine! So he's beaten it, has he, and left me to carry the can? The whole thing was *his* idea! *He* put me up to it! Said it was money for jam. They'd never prosecute because of the scandal. I could always threaten to say that Ali had *given* me his historic jewel. Des and I were to have shared the swag in Paris—and now the swine runs out on me! I'd like to murder him!" She switched abruptly. "The sooner I get out of here . . . Can someone telephone for a taxi?"

"A car is waiting at the front door to take you to the station, mademoiselle," said Poirot.

"Think of everything, don't you?"

"Most things," said Poirot complacently.

But Poirot was not to get off so easily. When he returned to the dining-room after assisting the spurious Miss Lee-Wortley into the waiting car, Colin was waiting for him.

There was a frown on his boyish face.

"But look here, Monsieur Poirot. *What about the ruby?* Do you mean to say you've let him get away with it?"

Poirot's face fell. He twirled his mustaches. He seemed ill at ease.

"I shall recover it yet," he said weakly. "There are other ways. I shall still . . ."

"Well, I do think!" said Michael. "To let that swine get away with the ruby!"

Bridget was sharper.

"He's having us on again," she cried. "You are, aren't you, Monsieur Poirot?"

"Shall we do a final conjuring trick, Mademoiselle? Feel in my left-hand pocket."

Bridget thrust her hand in. She drew it out again with a scream of triumph and held aloft a large ruby blinking in crimson splendor.

"You comprehend," explained Poirot, "the one that was clasped in your hand was a paste replica. I brought it from London in case it was possible to make a substitution. You understand? We do not want the scandal. Monsieur Desmond will try and dispose of that ruby in Paris or in Belgium or wherever it is that he has his contacts, and then it will be discovered that the stone is not real! What could be more excellent? All finishes happily. The scandal is avoided, my princeling receives his ruby back again, he returns to his country and makes a sober and we hope a happy marriage. All ends well."

"Except for me," murmured Sarah under her breath.

She spoke so low that no one heard her but Poirot. He shook his head gently.

"You are in error, Mademoiselle Sarah, in what you say there. You have gained experience. All experience is valuable. Ahead of you I prophesy there lies happiness."

"That's what *you* say," said Sarah.

"But look here, Monsieur Poirot," Colin was frowning. "How did you know about the show we were going to put on for you?"

"It is my business to know things," said Hercule Poirot. He twirled his mustache.

"Yes, but I don't see how you could have managed it. Did someone split—did someone come and tell you?"

"No, no, not that."

"Then how? Tell us how?"

They all chorused, "Yes, tell us how."

"But no," Poirot protested. "But not. If I tell you how I deduced that, you will think nothing of it. It is like the conjuror who shows how his tricks are done!"

"Tell us, Monsieur Poirot! Go on. Tell us, tell us!"

"You really wish that I should solve for you this last mystery?"

"Yes, go on. Tell us."

"Ah, I do not think I can. You will be so disappointed."

"Now, come on, Monsieur Poirot, tell us. *How did you know?*"

"Well, you see, I was sitting in the library by the window in a chair after tea the other day and I was reposing myself. I had been asleep and when I awoke you were discussing your plans just outside the window close to me, and the window was open at the top."

"Is that all?" cried Colin, disgusted. "How simple!"

"Is it not?" cried Hercule Poirot, smiling. "You see? You *are* disappointed!"

"Oh well," said Michael, "at any rate we know everything now."

"Do we?" murmured Hercule Poirot to himself. "*I* do not. *I,* whose business it is to know things."

He walked out into the hall, shaking his head a little. For perhaps the twentieth time he drew from his pocket a rather dirty piece of paper. "DON'T EAT NONE OF THE PLUM PUDDING. ONE AS WISHES YOU WELL."

Hercule Poirot shook his head reflectively. He who could explain everything could not explain this! Humiliating. Who had written it? *Why* had it been written? Until he found that out he would never know a moment's peace. Suddenly he came out of his reverie to be aware of a peculiar gasping noise. He looked sharply down. On the floor, busy with a dustpan and brush was a tow-headed creature in a flowered overall. She was staring at the paper in his hand with large round eyes.

"Oh sir," said this apparition. "Oh, *sir. Please,* sir."

"And who may you be, *mon enfant?*" inquired Poirot genially.

"Annie Bates, sir, please sir. I come here to help Mrs. Ross. I didn't mean, sir, I didn't mean to—to do anything what I shouldn't do. I did mean it well, sir. For your good, I mean."

Enlightenment came to Poirot. He held out the dirty piece of paper.

"Did you write that, Annie?"

"I didn't mean any harm, sir. Really I didn't."

"Of course you didn't, Annie." He smiled at her. "But tell me about it. Why did you write this?"

"Well, it was them two, sir. Mr. Lee-Wortley and his sister. Not that she *was* his sister, I'm sure. None of us thought so! And she wasn't ill a bit. We could all tell *that*. We thought—we all thought— something queer was going on. I'll tell you straight, sir. I was in her bathroom taking in the clean towels, and I listened at the door. *He* was in her room and they were talking together. I heard what they said plain as plain. 'This detective,' he was saying. 'This fellow Poirot who's coming here. We've got to do something about it. We've got to get him out of the way as soon as possible.' And then he says to her in a nasty, sinister sort of way, lowering his voice, 'Where did you put it?' And she answered him, '*In the pudding*.' Oh, sir, my heart gave such a leap I thought it would stop beating. I thought they meant to poison you in the Christmas pudding. I didn't know *what* to do! Mrs. Ross, she wouldn't listen to the likes of me. Then the idea came to me as I'd write you a warning. And I did and I put it on your pillow where you'd find it when you went to bed." Annie paused breathlessly.

Poirot surveyed her gravely for some minutes.

"You see too many sensational films, I think, Annie," he said at last, "or perhaps it is the television that affects you? But the important thing is that you have the good heart and a certain amount of ingenuity. When I return to London I will send you a present."

"Oh thank you, sir. Thank you very much, sir."

"What would you like, Annie, as a present?"

"Anything I like, sir? Could I have anything I like?"

"Within reason," said Hercule Poirot prudently, "yes."

"Oh sir, could I have a vanity box? A real posh slap up vanity box like the one Mr. Lee-Wortley's sister, wot wasn't his sister, had?"

"Yes," said Poirot, "yes, I think that could be managed.

"It is interesting," he mused. "I was in a museum the other day observing some antiquities from Babylon or one of those places, thousands of years old—and among them were cosmetics boxes. The heart of woman does not change."

"Beg your pardon, sir?" said Annie.

"It is nothing," said Poirot, "I reflect you shall have your vanity box, child."

"Oh, thank you, sir. Oh, thank you very much indeed, sir."

Annie departed ecstatically. Poirot looked after her, nodding his head in satisfaction.

"Ah," he said to himself. "And now—I go. There is nothing more to be done here."

A pair of arms slipped round his shoulders unexpectedly.

"If you *will* stand just under the mistletoe . . ." said Bridget.

HERCULE POIROT ENJOYED it. He enjoyed it very much. He said to himself that he had had a very good Christmas.

8. THE SECOND GONG

Joan Ashby came out of her bedroom and stood a moment on the landing outside her door. She was half turning as if to go back into the room when, below her feet as it seemed, a gong boomed out.

Immediately Joan started forward almost at a run. So great was her hurry that at the top of the big staircase she collided with a young man arriving from the opposite direction.

"Hullo, Joan! Why the wild hurry?"

"Sorry, Harry. I didn't see you."

"So I gathered," said Harry Dalehouse dryly. "But as I say, why the wild haste?"

"It was the gong."

"I know. But it's only the first gong."

"No, it's the second."

"First."

"Second."

Thus arguing they had been descending the stairs. They were now in the hall, where the butler, having replaced the gongstick, was advancing toward them at a grave and dignified pace.

"It is the second," persisted Joan. "I know it is. Well, for one thing, look at the time."

Harry Dalehouse glanced up at the grandfather clock.

"Just twelve minutes past eight," he remarked. "Joan, I believe you're right, but I never heard the first one. Digby," he addressed the butler, "is this the first gong or the second?"

"The first, sir."

"At twelve minutes past eight? Digby, somebody will get the sack for this."

A faint smile showed for a minute on the butler's face.

"Dinner is being served ten minutes later tonight, sir. The master's orders."

"Incredible!" cried Harry Dalehouse. "Tut, tut! Upon my word, things are coming to a pretty pass! Wonders will never cease. What ails my revered uncle?"

"The seven o'clock train, sir, was half an hour late, and as——"

The butler broke off, as a sound like the crack of a whip was heard.

"What on earth——" said Harry. "Why, that sounded exactly like a shot."

A dark handsome man of thirty-five came out of the drawing-room on their left.

"What was that?" he asked. "It sounded exactly like a shot."

"It must have been a car backfiring, sir," said the butler. "The road runs quite close to the house this side and the upstairs windows are open."

"Perhaps," said Joan doubtfully. "But that would be over there." She waved a hand to the right. "And I thought the noise came from here." She pointed to the left.

The dark man shook his head.

"I don't think so. I was in the drawing-room. I came out here because I thought the noise came from this direction." He nodded his head in front of him in the direction of the gong and the front door.

"East, west, and south, eh?" said the irrepressible Harry. "Well, I'll make it complete, Keene. North for me. I thought it came from behind us. Any solutions offered?"

"Well, there's always murder," said Geoffrey Keene, smiling. "I beg your pardon, Miss Ashby."

"Only a shiver," said Joan. "It's nothing. A what-do-you-call-it walking over my grave."

"A good thought—murder," said Harry. "But, alas! No groans, no blood. I fear the solution is a poacher after a rabbit."

"Seems tame, but I suppose that's it," agreed the other. "But it sounded so near. However, let's come into the drawing-room."

"Thank goodness, we're not late," said Joan fervently. "I was simply hareing it down the stairs thinking that was the second gong."

All laughing, they went into the big drawing-room.

Lytcham Close was one of the most famous old houses in England. Its owner, Hubert Lytcham Roche, was the last of a long line, and his more distant relatives were apt to remark that "Old Hubert, you know, really ought to be certified. Mad as a hatter, poor old bird."

Allowing for the exaggeration natural to friends and relatives, some truth remained. Hubert Lytcham Roche was certainly eccentric. Though a very fine musician, he was a man of ungovernable temper and had an almost abnormal sense of his own importance. People staying in the house had to respect his prejudices or else they were never asked again.

One such prejudice was his music. If he played to his guests, as he often did in the evening, absolute silence must obtain. A whispered comment, a rustle of a dress, a movement even—and he would turn round scowling fiercely, and good-bye to the unlucky guest's chances of being asked again.

Another point was absolute punctuality for the crowning meal of the day. Breakfast was immaterial—you might come down at noon if you wished. Lunch also—a simple meal of cold meats and stewed fruit. But dinner was a rite, a festival, prepared by a *cordon bleu* whom he had tempted from a big hotel by the payment of a fabulous salary.

A first gong was sounded at five minutes past eight. At a quarter-past eight a second gong was heard, and immediately after the door was flung open, dinner announced to the assembled guests, and a solemn procession wended its way to the dining room. Anyone who had the temerity to be late for the second gong was henceforth excommunicated—and Lytcham Close shut to the unlucky diner forever.

Hence the anxiety of Joan Ashby, and also the astonishment of Harry Dalehouse, at hearing that the sacred function was to be delayed ten minutes on this particular evening. Though not very intimate with his uncle, he had been to Lytcham Close often enough to know what a very unusual occurrence that was.

Geoffrey Keene, who was Lytcham Roche's secretary, was also very much surprised.

"Extraordinary," he commented. "I've never known such a thing happen. Are you sure?"

"Digby said so."

"He said something about a train," said Joan Ashby. "At least I think so."

"Queer," said Keene thoughtfully. "We shall hear all about it in due course, I suppose. But it's very odd."

Both men were silent for a moment or two, watching the girl. Joan Ashby was a charming creature, blue-eyed and golden-haired, with an impish glance. This was her first visit to Lytcham Close and her invitation was at Harry's prompting.

The door opened and Diana Cleves, the Lytcham Roches' adopted daughter, came into the room.

There was a daredevil grace about Diana, a witchery in her dark eyes and her mocking tongue. Nearly all men fell for Diana and she enjoyed her conquests. A strange creature, with her alluring suggestion of warmth and her complete coldness.

"Beaten the Old Man for once," she remarked. "First time for weeks he hasn't been here first, looking at his watch and tramping up and down like a tiger at feeding time."

The young men had sprung forward. She smiled entrancingly at them both—then turned to Harry. Geoffrey Keene's dark cheek flushed as he dropped back.

He recovered himself, however, a moment later as Mrs. Lytcham Roche came in. She was a tall, dark woman, naturally vague in manner, wearing floating draperies of an indeterminate shade of green. With her was a middle-aged man with a beaklike nose and a determined chin—Gregory Barling. He was a somewhat prominent figure in the financial world and, well bred on his mother's side, he had for some years been an intimate friend of Hubert Lytcham Roche.

Boom!

The gong resounded imposingly. As it died away, the door was flung open and Digby announced:

"Dinner is served."

Then, well-trained servant though he was, a look of complete astonishment flashed over his impassive face. For the first time in his memory, his master was not in the room!

That his astonishment was shared by everybody was evident. Mrs. Lytcham Roche gave a little uncertain laugh.

"Most amazing. Really—I don't know what to do. . . ."

Everybody was taken aback. The whole tradition of Lytcham Close was undermined. What could have happened? Conversation ceased. There was a strained sense of waiting.

At last the door opened once more; a sigh of relief went round only tempered by a slight anxiety as to how to treat the situation. Nothing must be said to emphasize the fact that the host had himself transgressed the stringent rule of the house.

But the newcomer was not Lytcham Roche. Instead of the big, bearded, vikinglike figure, there advanced into the long drawing-room a very small man, palpably a foreigner, with an egg-shaped head, a flamboyant mustache, and most irreproachable evening clothes.

His eyes twinkling, the newcomer advanced toward Mrs. Lytcham Roche.

"My apologies, madame," he said. "I am, I fear, a few minutes late."

"Oh, not at all!" murmured Mrs. Lytcham Roche vaguely. "Not at all, Mr.——" She paused.

"Poirot, madame. Hercule Poirot."

He heard behind him a very soft "Oh"—a gasp rather than an articulate word—a woman's ejaculation. Perhaps he was flattered.

"You knew I was coming?" he murmured gently. "*N'est-ce pas, madame?* your husband told you."

"Oh—oh, yes," said Mrs. Lytcham Roche, her manner unconvincing in the extreme. "I mean, I suppose so. I am so terribly unpractical, M. Poirot. I never remember anything. But fortunately Digby sees to everything."

"My train, I fear, was late," said M. Poirot. "An accident on the line in front of us."

"Oh," cried Joan, "so that's why dinner was put off."

His eye came quickly round to her—a most uncannily discerning eye.

"That is something out of the usual—eh?"

"I really can't think——" began Mrs. Lytcham Roche, and then stopped. "I mean," she went on confusedly, "it's so odd. Hubert never——"

Poirot's eyes swept rapidly round the group.

"M. Lytcham Roche is not down yet?"

"No, and it's so extraordinary——" She looked appealingly at Geoffrey Keene.

"Mr. Lytcham Roche is the soul of punctuality," explained Keene. "He has not been late for dinner for—well, I don't know that he was ever late before."

To a stranger the situation must have been ludicrous—the perturbed faces and the general consternation.

"I know," said Mrs. Lytcham Roche with the air of one solving a problem; "I shall ring for Digby."

She suited the action to the word.

The butler came promptly.

"Digby," said Mrs. Lytcham Roche, "your master. Is he——"

As was customary with her, she did not finish her sentence. It was clear that the butler did not expect her to do so. He replied promptly and with understanding.

"Mr. Lytcham Roche came down at five minutes to eight and went into the study, madam."

"Oh!" She paused. "You don't think—I mean—he heard the gong?"

"I think he must have—the gong is immediately outside the study door."

"Yes, of course, of course," said Mrs. Lytcham Roche more vaguely than ever.

"Shall I inform him, madam, that dinner is ready?"

"Oh, thank you, Digby. Yes, I think—yes, yes, I should."

"I don't know," said Mrs. Lytcham Roche to her guests as the butler withdrew, "what I would do without Digby!"

A pause followed.

Then Digby reëntered the room. His breath was coming a little faster than is considered good form in a butler.

"Excuse me, madam—the study door is locked."

It was then that M. Hercule Poirot took command of the situation.

"I think," he said, "that we had better go to the study."

He led the way and everyone followed. His assumption of authority seemed perfectly natural. He was no longer a rather comic-looking guest. He was a personality and master of the situation.

He led the way out into the hall, past the staircase, past the great clock, past the recess in which stood the gong. Exactly opposite that recess was a closed door.

He tapped on it, first gently, then with increasing violence. But there was no reply. Very nimbly he dropped to his knees and applied his eye to the keyhole. He rose and looked round.

"Messieurs," he said, "we must break open this door. Immediately!"

As before no one questioned his authority. Geoffrey Keene and Gregory Barling were the two biggest men. They attacked the door under Poirot's directions. It was no easy matter. The doors of Lytcham Close were solid affairs—no modern jerry-building here. It resisted the attack valiantly, but at last it gave before the united attack of the men and crashed inward.

The house party hesitated in the doorway. They saw what they had subconsciously feared to see. Facing them was the window. On the left, between the door and the window, was a big writing table. Sitting, not at the table, but sideways to it, was a man—a big man—

slouched forward in the chair. His back was to them and his face to the window, but his position told the tale. His right hand hung limply down and below it, on the carpet, was a small shining pistol.

Poirot spoke sharply to Gregory Barling:

"Take Mrs. Lytcham Roche away—and the other two ladies."

The other nodded comprehendingly. He laid a hand on his hostess' arm. She shivered.

"He has shot himself," she murmured. "Horrible!" With another shiver she permitted him to lead her away. The two girls followed.

Poirot came forward into the room, the two young men behind him.

He knelt down by the body, motioning them to keep back a little.

He found the bullet hole on the right side of the head. It had passed out the other side and had evidently struck a mirror hanging on the left-hand wall, since this was shivered. On the writing table was a sheet of paper, blank save for the word "SORRY" scrawled across it in hesitating, shaky writing.

Poirot's eyes darted back to the door.

"The key is not in the lock," he said. "I wonder——"

His hand slid into the dead man's pocket.

"Here it is," he said. "At least I think so. Have the goodness to try it, monsieur?"

Geoffrey Keene took it from him and tried it in the lock.

"That's it, all right."

"And the window?"

Harry Dalehouse strode across to it.

"Shut."

"You permit?" Very swiftly, Poirot scrambled to his feet and joined the other at the window. It was a long French window. Poirot opened it, stood a minute scrutinizing the grass just in front of it, then closed it again.

"My friends," he said, "we must telephone for the police. Until they have come and satisfied themselves that it is truly suicide nothing must be touched. Death can only have occurred about a quarter of an hour ago."

"I know," said Harry hoarsely. "We heard the shot."

"*Comment?* What is that you say?"

Harry explained with the help of Geoffrey Keene. As he finished speaking, Barling reappeared.

Poirot repeated what he had said before, and while Keene went off to telephone, Poirot requested Barling to give him a few minutes' interview.

They went into a small morning room, leaving Digby on guard outside the study door, while Harry went off to find the ladies.

"You were, I understand, an intimate friend of M. Lytcham Roche," began Poirot. "It is for that reason that I address myself to you primarily. In etiquette, perhaps, I should have spoken first to madame, but at the moment I do not think that is *pratique.*"

He paused.

"I am, see you, in a delicate situation. I will lay the facts plainly before you. I am, by profession, a private detective."

The financier smiled a little.

"It is not necessary to tell me that, M. Poirot. Your name is, by now, a household word."

"Monsieur is too amiable," said Poirot, bowing. "Let us, then, proceed. I receive, at my London address, a letter from this M. Lytcham Roche. In it he says that he has reason to believe that he is being swindled of large sums of money. For family reasons, so he puts it, he does not wish to call in the police, but he desires that I should come down and look into the matter for him. Well, I agree. I come. Not quite so soon as M. Lytcham Roche wishes—for after all I have other affairs, and M. Lytcham Roche, he is not quite the King of England, though he seems to think he is."

Barling gave a wry smile.

"He did think of himself that way."

"Exactly. Oh, you comprehend—his letter showed plainly enough that he was what one calls an eccentric. He was not insane, but he was unbalanced, *n'est-ce pas?*"

"What he's just done ought to show that."

"Oh, monsieur, but suicide is not always the act of the unbalanced. The coroner's jury, they say so, yes, but that is to spare the feelings of those left behind."

"Hubert was not a normal individual," said Barling decisively. "He was given to ungovernable rages, was a monomaniac on the subject of family pride, and had a bee in his bonnet in more ways than one. But for all that he was a shrewd man."

"Precisely. He was sufficiently shrewd to discover that he was being robbed."

"Does a man commit suicide because he's being robbed?" Barling asked.

"As you say, monsieur. Ridiculous. And that brings me to the need for haste in the matter. For family reasons—that was the phrase he used in his letter. *Eh, bien,* monsieur, you are a man of the world, you know that it is for precisely that—family reasons—that a man does commit suicide."

"You mean?"

"That it looks—on the face of it—as if *ce pauvre* monsieur had found out something further—and was unable to face what he had found out. But you perceive, I have a duty. I am already employed—commissioned—I have accepted the task. This 'family reason,' the dead man did not want it to get to the police. So I must act quickly. I must learn the truth."

"And when you have learned it?"

"Then—I must use my discretion. I must do what I can."

"I see," said Barling. He smoked for a minute or two in silence, then he said: "All the same I'm afraid I can't help you. Hubert never confided anything to me. I know nothing."

"But tell me, monsieur, who, should you say, had a chance of robbing this poor gentleman?"

"Difficult to say. Of course, there's the agent for the estate. He's a new man."

"The agent?"

"Yes. Marshall. Captain Marshall. Very nice fellow, lost an arm in the war. He came here a year ago. But Hubert liked him, I know, and trusted him too."

"If it were Captain Marshall who was playing him false, there would be no family reasons for silence."

"N-no."

The hesitation did not escape Poirot.

"Speak, monsieur. Speak plainly, I beg of you."

"It may be gossip."

"I implore you, speak."

"Very well, then, I will. Did you notice a very attractive-looking young woman in the drawing-room?"

"I noticed two very attractive-looking young women."

"Oh, yes, Miss Ashby. Pretty little thing. Her first visit. Harry Dalehouse got Mrs. Lytcham Roche to ask her. No, I mean a dark girl—Diana Cleves."

"I noticed her," said Poirot. "She is one that all men would notice, I think."

"She's a little devil," burst out Barling. "She's played fast and loose with every man for twenty miles round. Someone will murder her one of these days."

He wiped his brow with a handkerchief, oblivious of the keen interest with which the other was regarding him.

"And this young lady is——"

"She's Lytcham Roche's adopted daughter. A great disappointment when he and his wife had no children. They adopted Diana Cleves—she was some kind of cousin. Hubert was devoted to her, simply worshiped her."

"Doubtless he would dislike the idea of her marrying?" suggested Poirot.

"Not if she married the right person."

"And the right person was—you, monsieur?"

Barling started and flushed.

"I never said——"

"*Mais, non, mais non!* You said nothing. But it was so, was it not?"

"I fell in love with her—yes. Lytcham Roche was pleased about it. It fitted in with his ideas for her."

"And mademoiselle herself?"

"I told you—she's the devil incarnate."

"I comprehend. She has her own ideas of amusement, is it not so? But Captain Marshall, where does he come in?"

"Well, she's been seeing a lot of him. People talked. Not that I think there's anything in it. Another scalp, that's all."

Poirot nodded.

"But supposing that there had been something in it—well, then, it might explain why M. Lytcham Roche wanted to proceed cautiously."

"You do understand, don't you, that there's no earthly reason for suspecting Marshall of defalcation."

"*Oh, parfaitement, parfaitement!* It might be an affair of a forged check with someone in the household involved. This young Mr. Dalehouse, who is he?"

"A nephew."

"He will inherit, yes?"

"He's a sister's son. Of course he might take the name—there's not a Lytcham Roche left."

"I see."

"The place isn't actually entailed, though it's always gone from father to son. I've always imagined that he'd leave the place to his wife for her lifetime and then perhaps to Diana if he approved of her marriage. You see, her husband could take the name."

"I comprehend," said Poirot ."You have been most kind and help-ful to me, monsieur. May I ask of you one thing further—to explain to Madame Lytcham Roche all that I have told you, and to beg of her that she accord me a minute?"

Sooner than he had thought likely, the door opened and Mrs. Lytcham Roche entered. She floated to a chair.

"Mr. Barling has explained everything to me," she said. "We mustn't have any scandal, of course. Though I do feel really it's fate, don't you? I mean with the mirror and everything."

"*Comment*—the mirror?"

"The moment I saw it—it seemed a symbol. Of Hubert! A curse, you know. I think old families have a curse very often. Hubert was always very strange. Lately he has been stranger than ever."

"You will forgive me for asking, madame, but you are not in any way short of money?"

"Money? I never think of money."

"Do you know what they say, madame? Those who never think of money need a great deal of it."

He ventured a tiny laugh. She did not respond. Her eyes were far away.

"I thank you, madame," he said, and the interview came to an end.

Poirot rang and Digby answered.

"I shall require you to answer a few questions," said Poirot. "I am a private detective sent for by your master before he died."

"A detective!" the butler gasped. "Why?"

"You will please answer my questions. As to the shot now——"

He listened to the butler's account.

"So there were four of you in the hall?"

"Yes, sir; Mr. Dalehouse and Miss Ashby and Mr. Keene came from the drawing-room."

"Where were the others?"

"The others, sir?"

"Yes, Mrs. Lytcham Roche, Miss Cleves, and Mr. Barling."

"Mrs. Lytcham Roche and Mr. Barling came down later, sir."

"And Miss Cleves?"

"I think Miss Cleves was in the drawing-room, sir."

Poirot asked a few more questions, then dismissed the butler with the command to request Miss Cleves to come to him.

She came immediately, and he studied her attentively in view of Barling's revelations. She was certainly beautiful in her white satin frock with the rosebud on the shoulder.

He explained the circumstances which had brought him to Lytcham Close, eyeing her very closely, but she showed only what seemed to be genuine astonishment, with no signs of uneasiness. She spoke of Marshall indifferently with tepid approval. Only at mention of Barling did she approach animation.

"That man's a crook," she said sharply. "I told the Old Man so, but he wouldn't listen—went on putting money into his rotten concerns."

"Are you sorry, mademoiselle, that your—father is dead?"

She stared at him.

"Of course. I'm modern, you know, M. Poirot. I don't indulge in sob stuff. But I was fond of the Old Man. Though, of course, it's best for him."

"Best for him?"

"Yes. One of these days he would have had to be locked up. It was growing on him—this belief that the last Lytcham Roche of Lytcham Close was omnipotent."

Poirot nodded thoughtfully.

"I see, I see—yes, decided signs of mental trouble. By the way, you permit that I examine your little bag? It is charming—all these silk rosebuds. . . . What was I saying? Oh, yes, did you hear the shot?"

"Oh, yes! But I thought it was a car or a poacher, or something."

"You were in the drawing-room?"

"No. I was out in the garden."

"I see. Thank you, mademoiselle. Next I would like to see M. Keene, is it not?"

"Geoffrey? I'll send him along."

Keene came in, alert and interested.

"Mr. Barling has been telling me of the reason for your being down here. I don't know that there's anything I can tell you, but if I can——"

Poirot interrupted him.

"I only want to know one thing, Monsieur Keene. What was it that you stooped and picked up just before we got to the study door this evening?"

"I——" Keene half sprang up from his chair, then subsided again. "I don't know what you mean," he said lightly.

"Oh, I think you do, monsieur. You were behind me, I know, but a friend of mine he says I have eyes in the back of my head. You picked up something and you put it in the right-hand pocket of your dinner jacket."

There was a pause. Indecision was written plainly on Keene's handsome face. At last he made up his mind.

"Take your choice, M. Poirot," he said, and leaning forward he turned his pockets inside out. There was a cigarette holder, a hand-kerchief, a tiny silk rosebud, and a little gold match box.

A moment's silence and then Keene said, "As a matter of fact it was this." He picked up the match box. "I must have dropped it earlier in the evening."

"I think not," said Poirot.

"What do you mean?"

"What I say. I, monsieur, am a man of tidiness, of method, of order. A match box on the ground, I should see it and pick it up—a match box of this size, assuredly I should see it! No, monsieur, I think it was something very much smaller—such as this, perhaps."

He picked up the little silk rosebud.

"From Miss Cleves' bag, I think?"

There was a moment's pause, then Keene admitted it with a laugh.

"Yes, that's so. She—gave it to me last night."

"I see," said Poirot, and at the moment the door opened and a tall fair-haired man in a lounge suit strode into the room.

"Keene—what's all this? Lytcham Roche shot himself? Man, I can't believe it. It's incredible."

"Let me introduce you," said Keene, "to M. Hercule Poirot." The other started. "He will tell you all about it." And he left the room, banging the door.

"M. Poirot"—John Marshall was all eagerness—"I'm most awfully pleased to meet you. It is a bit of luck your being down here. Lytcham Roche never told me you were coming. I'm a most frightful admirer of yours, sir."

A disarming young man, thought Poirot—not so young, either, for there was gray hair at the temples and lines in the forehead. It was the voice and manner that gave the impression of boyishness.

"The police——"

"They are here now, sir. I came up with them on hearing the news. They don't seem particularly surprised. Of course he was mad as a hatter, but even then——"

"Even then you are surprised at his committing suicide?"

"Frankly, yes. I shouldn't have thought that—well, that Lytcham Roche could have imagined the world getting on without him."

"He has had money troubles of late, I understand?"

Marshall nodded.

"He speculated. Wildcat schemes of Barling's."

Poirot said quietly: "I will be very frank. Had you any reason to suppose that Mr. Lytcham Roche suspected you of tampering with your accounts?"

Marshall stared at Poirot in a kind of ludicrous bewilderment. So ludicrous was it that Poirot was forced to smile.

"I see that you are utterly taken aback, Captain Marshall."

"Yes, indeed. The idea's ridiculous."

"Ah! Another question. He did not suspect you of robbing him of his adopted daughter?"

"Oh, so you know about me and Di?" He laughed in an embarrassed fashion.

"It is so, then?"

Marshall nodded.

"But the old man didn't know anything about it. Di wouldn't have him told. I suppose she was right. He'd have gone up like a—a basketful of rockets. I should have been chucked out of a job, and that would have been that."

"And instead what was your plan?"

"Well, upon my word, sir, I hardly know. I left things to Di. She said she'd fix it. As a matter of fact I was looking out for a job. If I could have got one I would have chucked this up."

"And mademoiselle would have married you? But M. Lytcham Roche might have stopped her allowance. Mademoiselle Diana is, I should say, fond of money."

Marshall looked rather uncomfortable.

"I'd have tried to make it up to her, sir."

Geoffrey Keene came into the room. "The police are just going and would like to see you, M. Poirot."

"*Merci.* I will come."

In the study were a stalwart inspector and the police surgeon. "Mr. Poirot?" said the inspector. "We've heard of you, sir. I'm Inspector Reeves."

"You are most amiable," said Poirot, shaking hands. "You do not need my cooperation, no?" He gave a little laugh.

"Not this time, sir. All plain sailing."

"The case is perfectly straightforward, then?" demanded Poirot.

"Absolutely. Door and window locked, key of door in dead man's pocket. Manner very strange the past few days. No doubt about it."

"Everything quite—natural?"

The doctor grunted.

"Must have been sitting at a damned queer angle for the bullet to have hit that mirror. But suicide's a queer business."

"You found the bullet?"

"Yes, here." The doctor held it out. "Near the wall below the mirror. Pistol was Mr. Roche's own. Kept it in the drawer of the desk always. Something behind it all, I daresay, but what that is we shall never know."

Poirot nodded.

The body had been carried to a bedroom. The police now took their leave. Poirot stood at the front door looking after them. A sound made him turn. Harry Dalehouse was close behind him.

"Have you, by any chance, a strong flashlight, my friend?" asked Poirot.

"Yes, I'll get it for you."

When he returned with it Joan Ashby was with him.

"You may accompany me if you like," said Poirot graciously.

He stepped out of the front door and turned to the right, stopping before the study window. About six feet of grass separated it from the path. Poirot bent down, playing the flashlight on the grass. He straightened himself and shook his head.

"No," he said, "not there."

Then he paused and slowly his figure stiffened. On either side of the grass was a deep flower border. Poirot's attention was focused on the right-hand border, full of Michaelmas-daisies and dahlias. His torch was directed on the front of the bed. Distinct on the soft mold were footprints.

"Four of them," murmured Poirot. "Two going toward the window, two coming from it."

"A gardener," suggested Joan.

"But no, mademoiselle, but no. Employ your eyes. These shoes are small, dainty, high-heeled, the shoes of a woman. Mademoiselle Diana mentioned having been out in the garden. Do you know if she went downstairs before you did, mademoiselle?"

Joan shook her head.

"I can't remember. I was in such a hurry because the gong went, and I thought I'd heard the first one. I do seem to remember that her room door was open as I went past, but I'm not sure. Mrs. Lytcham Roche's was shut, I know."

"I see," said Poirot.

Something in his voice made Harry look up sharply, but Poirot was merely frowning gently to himself.

In the doorway they met Diana Cleves.

"The police have gone," she said. "It's all—over."

She gave a deep sigh.

"May I request one little word with you, mademoiselle?"

She led the way into the morning room and Poirot followed, shutting the door.

"Well?" She looked a little surprised.

"One little question, mademoiselle. Were you tonight at any time in the flower border outside the study window?"

"Yes." She nodded. "About seven o'clock and again just before dinner."

"I do not understand," he said.

"I can't see that there is anything to 'understand,' as you call it," she said coldly. "I was picking Michaelmas-daisies—for the table. I always do the flowers. That was about seven o'clock."

"And afterward—later?"

"Oh, that! As a matter of fact I dropped a spot of hair oil on my dress—just on the shoulder here. It was just as I was ready to come down. I didn't want to change the dress. I remembered I'd seen a late rose in bud in the border. I ran out and picked it and pinned it in. See——" She came close to him and lifted the head of the rose. Poirot saw the minute grease spot. She remained close to him, her shoulder almost brushing his.

"And what time was this?"

"Oh, about ten minutes past eight, I suppose."

"You did not—try the window?"

"I believe I did. Yes, I thought it would be quicker to go in that way. But it was fastened."

"I see." Poirot drew a deep breath. "And the shot," he said, "where were you when you heard that? Still in the flower border?"

"Oh, no; it was two or three minutes later, just before I came in by the side door."

"Do you know what this is, mademoiselle?"

On the palm of his hand he held out the tiny silk rosebud. She examined it coolly.

"It looks like a rosebud off my little evening bag. Where did you find it?"

"It was in Mr. Keene's pocket," said Poirot dryly.

"Did you give it to him, mademoiselle?"

"Did he tell you I gave it to him?"

Poirot smiled.

"When did you give it to him, mademoiselle?"

"Last night."

"Did he warn you to say that, mademoiselle?"

"What do you mean?" she asked angrily.

But Poirot did not answer. He strode out of the room and into the drawing-room. Barling, Keene, and Marshall were there. He went straight up to them.

"Messieurs," he said brusquely, "will you follow me to the study?"

He passed out into the hall and addressed Joan and Harry.

"You, too, I pray of you. And will somebody request madame to come? I thank you. Ah! and here is the excellent Digby. Digby, a little question, a very important little question. Did Miss Cleves arrange some Michaelmas-daisies before dinner?"

The butler looked bewildered.

"Yes, sir, she did."

"You are sure?"

"Quite sure, sir."

"*Très bien.* Now—come, all of you."

Inside the study he faced them.

"I have asked you to come here for a reason. The case is over, the police have come and gone. They say Mr. Lytcham Roche has shot himself. All is finished." He paused. "But I, Hercule Poirot, say that it is not finished."

As startled eyes turned to him the door opened and Mrs. Lytcham Roche floated into the room.

"I was saying, madame, that this case is not finished. It is a matter of the psychology. Mr. Lytcham Roche, he had the *manie de grandeur,* he was a king. Such a man does not kill himself. No, no, he may go mad, but he does not kill himself. Mr. Lytcham Roche did not kill himself." He paused. "He was killed."

"Killed?" Marshall gave a short laugh. "Alone in a room with the door and window locked?"

"All the same," said Poirot stubbornly, "he was killed."

"And got up and locked the door or shut the window afterward, I suppose," said Diana cuttingly.

"I will show you something," said Poirot, going to the window. He turned the handle of the French windows and then pulled gently.

"See, they are open. Now I close them, but without turning the handle. Now the window is closed but not fastened. Now!"

He gave a short jarring blow and the handle turned, shooting the bolt down into its socket.

"You see?" said Poirot softly. "It is very loose, this mechanism. It could be done from outside quite easily."

He turned, his manner grim.

"When that shot was fired at twelve minutes past eight, there were four people in the hall. Four people have an alibi. Where were the other three? You, madame? In your room. You, Monsieur Barling. Were you, too, in your room?"

"I was."

"And you, mademoiselle, were in the garden. So you have admitted."

"I don't see——" began Diana

"Wait." He turned to Mrs. Lytcham Roche. "Tell me, madame, have you any idea of how your husband left his money?"

"Hubert read me his will. He said I ought to know. He left me three thousand a year chargeable on the estate, and the dower house or the town house, whichever I preferred. Everything else he left to Diana, on condition that if she married her husband must take the name."

"Ah!"

"But then he made a codicil thing—a few weeks ago, that was."

"Yes, madame?"

"He still left it all to Diana, but on condition that she married Mr. Barling. If she married anyone else, it was all to go to his nephew, Harry Dalehouse."

"But the codicil was only made a few weeks ago," purred Poirot. "Mademoiselle may not have known of that." He stepped forward accusingly. "Mademoiselle Diana, you want to marry Captain Marshall, do you not? Or is it Mr. Keene?"

She walked across the room and put her arm through Marshall's sound one.

"Go on," she said.

"I will put the case against you, mademoiselle. You loved Captain Marshall. You also loved money. Your adopted father he would never have consented to your marrying Captain Marshall, but if he dies you are fairly sure that you get everything. So you go out, you step over the flower border to the window which is open, you have with you the pistol which you have taken from the writing-table drawer. You go up to your victim talking amiably. You fire. You drop the pistol by his hand, having wiped it and then pressed his fingers on it. You go out again, shaking the window till the bolt drops. You come into the house. Is that how it happened? I am asking you, mademoiselle?"

"No," Diana screamed. "No—no!"

He looked at her, then he smiled.

"No," he said, "it was not like that. It might have been so—it is plausible—it is possible—but it cannot have been like that for two reasons. The first reason is that you picked Michaelmas-daisies at seven o'clock, the second arises from something that mademoiselle here told me." He turned toward Joan, who stared at him in bewilderment. He nodded encouragement.

"But yes, mademoiselle. You told me that you hurried downstairs because you thought it was the second gong sounding, having already heard the first."

He shot a rapid glance round the room.

"You do not see what that means?" he cried. "You do not see. Look! Look!" He sprang forward to the chair where the victim had sat. "Did you notice how the body was? Not sitting square to the desk—no, sitting sideways to the desk, facing the window. Is that a natural way to commit suicide? *Jamais, jamais!* You write your apologia 'sorry' on a piece of paper—you open the drawer, you take out the pistol, you hold it to your head and you fire. That is the way of suicide. But now consider murder! The victim sits at his desk, the murderer stands beside him—talking. And talking still—fires. Where does the bullet go then?" He paused. "Straight through the head, through the door if it is open, and so—hits the gong.

"Ah! you begin to see? That was the first gong—heard only by mademoiselle, since her room is above.

"What does our murderer do next? Shuts the door, locks it, puts the key in the dead man's pocket, then turns the body sideways in the chair, presses the dead man's fingers on the pistol and then drops it by his side, cracks the mirror on the wall as a final spectacular touch—in short, 'arranges' his suicide. Then out through the window, the bolt is shaken home, the murderer steps not on the grass, where footprints must show, but on the flower bed, where they can be smoothed out behind him, leaving no trace. Then back into the house, and at twelve minutes past eight, when he is alone in the drawing-room, he fires a service revolver out of the drawing-room window and dashes out into the hall. Is that how you did it, Mr. Geoffrey Keene?"

Fascinated, the secretary stared at the accusing figure drawing nearer to him. Then, with a gurgling cry, he fell to the ground.

"I think I am answered," said Poirot. "Captain Marshall, will you ring up the police?" He bent over the prostrate form. "I fancy he will be still unconscious when they come."

"Geoffrey Keene," murmured Diana. "But what motive had he?"

"I fancy that as secretary he had certain opportunities accounts—checks. Something awakened Mr. Lytcham Roche's suspicions. He sent for me."

"Why for you? Why not for the police?"

"I think, mademoiselle, you can answer that question. Monsieur suspected that there was something between you and that young man. To divert his mind from Captain Marshall, you had flirted shamelessly with Mr. Keene. But yes, you need not deny! Mr. Keene gets wind of my coming and acts promptly. The essence of his scheme is that the crime must seem to take place at 8:12, when he has an alibi. His one danger is the bullet, which must be lying somewhere near the gong and which he has not had time to retrieve. When we are all on our way to the study he picks that up. At such a tense moment he thinks no one will notice. But me, I notice everything! I question him. He reflects a little minute and then he plays the comedy! He insinuates that what he picked up was the silk rosebud, he plays the part of the young man in love shielding the lady he loves. Oh, it was very clever, and if you had not picked Michaelmas-daisies——"

"I don't understand what they have to do with it."

"You do not? Listen—there were only four footprints in the bed, but when you were picking the flowers you must have made many more than that. So in between your picking the flowers and your coming to get the rosebud someone must have smoothed over the bed. Not a gardener—no gardener works after seven. Then it must be someone guilty—it must be the murderer . . . the murder was committed before the shot was heard."

"But why did nobody hear the real shot?" asked Harry.

"A silencer. They will find that and the revolver thrown into the shrubbery."

"What a risk!"

"Why a risk? Everyone was upstairs dressing for dinner. It was a very good moment. The bullet was the only contretemps, and even that, as he thought, passed off well."

Poirot picked it up. "He threw it under the mirror when I was examining the window with Mr. Dalehouse."

"Oh!" Diana wheeled on Marshall. "Marry me, John, and take me away."

Barling coughed. "My dear Diana, under the terms of my friend's will——"

"I don't care," the girl cried. "We can draw pictures on pavements."

"There's no need to do that," said Harry. "We'll go halves, Di. I'm not going to bag things because Uncle had a bee in his bonnet."

Suddenly there was a cry. Mrs. Lytcham Roche had sprung to her feet.

"M. Poirot—the mirror—he—he must have deliberately smashed it."

"Yes, madame."

"Oh!" she stared at him. "But it is unlucky to break a mirror."

"It has proved very unlucky for Mr. Geoffrey Keene," said Poirot cheerfully.

PART IV

MISS JANE MARPLE

1. STRANGE JEST

And this," said Jane Helier, completing her introductions, "is Miss Marple!"

Being an actress, she was able to make her point. It was clearly the climax, the triumphant finale! Her tone was equally compounded of reverent awe and triumph.

The odd part of it was that the object thus proudly proclaimed was merely a gentle, fussy-looking, elderly spinster. In the eyes of the two young people who had just, by Jane's good offices, made her acquaintance, there showed incredulity and a tinge of dismay. They were nice-looking people; the girl, Charmian Stroud, slim and dark—the man, Edward Rossiter, a fair-haired, amiable young giant.

Charmian said a little breathlessly, "Oh! We're awfully pleased to meet you." But there was doubt in her eyes. She flung a quick, questioning glance at Jane Helier.

"Darling," said Jane, answering the glance, "she's absolutely *marvelous*. Leave it all to her. I told you I'd get her here and I have." She added to Miss Marple, "*You'll* fix it for them, I know. It will be easy for *you*."

Miss Marple turned her placid, china-blue eyes toward Mr. Rossiter. "Won't you tell me," she said, "what all this is about?"

"Jane's a friend of ours," Charmian broke in impatiently. "Edward and I are in rather a fix. Jane said if we would come to her party, she'd introduce us to someone who was—who would—who could—"

Edward came to the rescue. "Jane tells us you're the last word in sleuths, Miss Marple!"

The old lady's eyes twinkled, but she protested modestly. "Oh, no, no! Nothing of the kind. It's just that living in a village as I do, one gets to know so much about human nature. But really you have made me quite curious. Do tell me your problem."

"I'm afraid it's terribly hackneyed—just buried treasure," said Edward.

"Indeed? But that sounds most exciting!"

"I know. Like *Treasure Island*. But our problem lacks the usual romantic touches. No point on a chart indicated by a skull and crossbones, no directions like 'four paces to the left, west by north.' It's horribly prosaic—just where we ought to dig."

"Have you tried at all?"

"I should say we'd dug about two solid square acres! The whole place is ready to be turned into a market garden. We're just discussing whether to grow vegetable marrows or potatoes."

Charmian said rather abruptly, "May we really tell you all about it?"

"But, of course, my dear."

"Then let's find a peaceful spot. Come on, Edward." She led the way out of the overcrowded and smoke-laden room, and they went up the stairs, to a small sitting-room on the second floor.

When they were seated, Charmian began abruptly. "Well, here goes! The story starts with Uncle Mathew, uncle—or rather, great great-uncle—to both of us. He was incredibly ancient. Edward and I were his only relations. He was fond of us and always declared that when he died he would leave his money between us. Well, he died last March and left everything he had to be divided equally between Edward and myself. What I've just said sounds rather callous—I don't mean that it was right that he died—actually we were very fond of him. But he'd been ill for some time.

"The point is that the 'everything' he left turned out to be practically nothing at all. And that, frankly, was a bit of a blow to us both, wasn't it, Edward?"

The amiable Edward agreed. "You see," he said, "we'd counted on it a bit. I mean, when you know a good bit of money is coming to you, you don't—well—buckle down and try to make it yourself. I'm in the army—not got anything to speak of outside my pay—and Charmian herself hasn't got a bean. She works as a stage manager in a repertory theater—quite interesting, and she enjoys it—but no money in it. We'd counted on getting married, but weren't worried about the money side of it because we both knew we'd be jolly well off some day."

"And now, you see, we're not!" said Charmian. "What's more, Ansteys—that's the family place, and Edward and I both love it—will probably have to be sold. And Edward and I feel we just can't bear that! But if we don't find Uncle Mathew's money, we shall have to sell."

Edward said, "You know, Charmian, we still haven't come to the vital point."

"Well, you talk, then."

Edward turned to Miss Marple. "It's like this, you see. As Uncle Mathew grew older, he got more and more suspicious. He didn't trust anybody."

"Very wise of him," said Miss Marple. "The depravity of human nature is unbelievable."

"Well, you may be right. Anyway, Uncle Mathew thought so. He had a friend who lost his money in a bank, and another friend who was ruined by an absconding solicitor, and he lost some money himself in a fraudulent company. He got so that he used to hold forth at great length that the only safe and sane thing to do was to convert your money into solid bullion and bury it."

"Ah," said Miss Marple. "I begin to see."

"Yes. Friends argued with him, pointed out that he'd get no interest that way, but he held that that didn't really matter. The bulk of your money, he said, should be 'kept in a box under the bed or buried in the garden.' Those were his words."

Charmian went on. "And when he died, he left hardly anything at all in securities, though he was very rich. So we think that that's what he must have done."

Edward explained. "We found that he had sold securities and drawn out large sums of money from time to time, and nobody knows what he did with them. But it seems probable that he lived up to his principles, and that he did buy gold and bury it."

"He didn't say anything before he died? Leave any paper? No letter?"

"That's the maddening part of it. He didn't. He'd been unconscious for some days, but he rallied before he died. He looked at us both and chuckled—a faint, weak little chuckle. He said, 'You'll be all right, my pretty pair of doves.' And then he tapped his eye—his right eye—and winked at us. And then—he died. Poor old Uncle Mathew."

"He tapped his eye," said Miss Marple thoughtfully.

Edward said eagerly, "Does that convey anything to you? It made me think of an Arsene Lupin story where there was something hidden in a man's glass eye. But Uncle Mathew didn't have a glass eye."

Miss Marple shook her head. "No—I can't think of anything at the moment."

Charmian said disappointedly, "Jane told us you'd say *at once* where to dig!"

Miss Marple smiled, "I'm not quite a conjurer, you know. I didn't know your uncle, or what sort of man he was, and I don't know the house or the grounds."

Charmian said, "If you did know them?"

"Well, it must be quite simple really, mustn't it?" said Miss Marple.

"Simple!" said Charmian. "You come down to Ansteys and see if it's simple!"

It is possible that she did not mean the invitation to be taken seriously, but Miss Marple said briskly, "Well, really, my dear, that's very kind of you. I've always wanted to have the chance of looking for buried treasure. And," she added, looking at them with a beaming, late-Victorian smile, "with a love interest, too!"

. . .

"YOU SEE!" SAID Charmian, gesturing dramatically.

They had just completed a grand tour of Ansteys. They had been round the kitchen garden—heavily trenched. They had been through the little woods, where every important tree had been dug round, and had gazed sadly on the pitted surface of the once smooth lawn. They had been up to the attic, where old trunks and chests had been rifled of their contents. They had been down to the cellars, where flagstones had been heaved unwillingly from their sockets. They had measured and tapped walls, and Miss Marple had been shown every antique piece of furniture that contained or could be suspected of containing a secret drawer.

On a table in the morning room there was a heap of papers— all the papers that the late Mathew Stroud had left. Not one had been destroyed, and Charmian and Edward were wont to return to them again and again, earnestly perusing bills, invitations, and business correspondence in the hope of spotting a hitherto unnoticed clue.

"Can you think of anywhere we haven't looked?" demanded Charmian hopefully.

Miss Marple shook her head. "You seem to have been very thorough, my dear. Perhaps, if I may say so, just a little *too* thorough. I always think, you know, that one should have a plan. It's like my friend, Mrs. Eldritch; she had such a nice little maid, polished linoleum beautifully, but she was so thorough that she polished the bathroom floor too much, and as Mrs. Eldritch was stepping out of the bath the cork mat slipped from under her, and she had a very nasty fall and actually broke her leg! Most awkward, because the bathroom door was locked, of course, and the gardener had to get a ladder and come in through the window—terribly distressing to Mrs. Eldritch, who had always been a very modest woman."

Edward moved restlessly.

Miss Marple said quickly, "Please forgive me. So apt, I know, to fly off at a tangent. But one thing does remind one of another. And sometimes that is helpful. All I was trying to say was that perhaps if we tried to sharpen our wits and think of a likely place—"

Edward said crossly, "You think of one, Miss Marple. Charmian's brains and mine are now only beautiful blanks!"

"Dear, dear. Of course—most tiring for you. If you don't mind I'll just look through all this." She indicated the papers on the table. "That is, if there's nothing private—I don't want to appear to pry."

"Oh, that's all right. But I'm afraid you won't find anything."

She sat down by the table and methodically worked through the sheaf of documents. As she replaced each one, she sorted them automatically into tidy little heaps. When she had finished she sat staring in front of her for some minutes.

Edward asked, not without a touch of malice, "Well, Miss Marple?"

Miss Marple came to herself with a little start. "I beg your pardon. Most helpful."

"You've found something relevant?"

"Oh, no, nothing like that, but I do believe I know what sort of man your Uncle Mathew was. Rather like my own Uncle Henry, I think. Fond of rather obvious jokes. A bachelor, evidently—I wonder why—perhaps an early disappointment? Methodical up to a point, but not very fond of being tied up—so few bachelors are!"

Behind Miss Marple's back, Charmian made a sign to Edward. It said, *She's ga-ga.*

Miss Marple was continuing happily to talk of her deceased Uncle Henry. "Very fond of puns, he was. And to some people, puns are most annoying. A mere play upon words may be very irritating. He was a suspicious man, too. Always was convinced the servants were robbing him. And sometimes, of course, they were, but not always. It grew upon him, poor man. Toward the end he suspected them of tampering with his food, and finally refused to eat anything but boiled eggs! Said nobody could tamper with the inside of a boiled egg. Dear Uncle Henry, he used to be such a merry soul at one time—very fond of his coffee after dinner. He always used to say, 'This coffee is very Moorish,' meaning, you know, that he'd like a little more."

Edward felt that if he heard any more about Uncle Henry he'd go mad.

"Fond of young people, too," went on Miss Marple, "but inclined to tease them a little, if you know what I mean. Used to put bags of sweets where a child just couldn't reach them."

Casting politeness aside, Charmian said, "I think he sounds horrible!"

"Oh, no, dear, just an old bachelor, you know, and not used to children. And he wasn't at all stupid, really. He used to keep a good deal of money in the house, and he had a safe put in. Made a great fuss about it—and how very secure it was. As a result of his talking so much, burglars broke in one night and actually cut a hole in the safe with a chemical device."

"Served him right," said Edward.

"Oh, but there was nothing in the safe," said Miss Marple. "You see, he really kept the money somewhere else—behind some volumes of sermons in the library, as a matter of fact. He said people never took a book of that kind out of the shelf!"

Edward interrupted excitedly. "I say, that's an idea. What about the library?"

But Charmian shook a scornful head. "Do you think I hadn't thought of that? I went through all the books Tuesday of last week, when you went off to Portsmouth. Took them all out, shook them. Nothing there."

Edward sighed. Then, rousing himself, he endeavored to rid himself tactfully of their disappointing guest. "It's been awfully good of you to come down as you have and try to help us. Sorry it's been all a washout. Feel we trespassed a lot on your time. However—I'll get the car out, and you'll be able to catch the three-thirty—"

"Oh," said Miss Marple, "but we've got to find the money, haven't we? You mustn't give up, Mr. Rossiter. 'If at first you don't succeed, try, try, try again.'"

"You mean you're going to go—on trying?"

"Strictly speaking," said Miss Marple, "I haven't begun yet. 'First catch your hare—' as Mrs. Beeton says in her cookery book—a wonderful book but terribly expensive; most of the recipes begin, 'Take a quart of cream and a dozen eggs.' Let me see, where was I? Oh, yes. Well, we have, so to speak, caught our hare—the hare being, of course, your Uncle Mathew, and we've only got to decide now where he would have hidden the money. It ought to be quite simple."

"Simple?" demanded Charmian.

"Oh, yes, dear. I'm sure he would have done the obvious thing. A secret drawer—that's my solution."

Edward said dryly, "You couldn't put bars of gold in a secret drawer."

"No, no, of course not. But there's no reason to believe the money is in gold."

"He always used to say—"

"So did say Uncle Henry about his safe! So I should strongly suspect that that was just a simple blind. Diamonds—now they could be in a secret drawer quite easily."

"But we've looked in all the secret drawers. We had a cabinet-maker over to examine the furniture."

"Did you, dear? That was clever of you. I should suggest your uncle's own desk would be the most likely. Was it the tall escritoire against the wall there?"

"Yes. And I'll show you." Charmian went over to it. She took down the flap. Inside were pigeonholes and little drawers. She opened a small door in the center and touched a spring inside the left-hand drawer. The bottom of the center recess clicked and slid forward. Charmian drew it out, revealing a shallow well beneath. It was empty.

"Now isn't that a coincidence?" exclaimed Miss Marple. "Uncle Henry had a desk just like this, only his was burr walnut and this is mahogany."

"At any rate," said Charmian, "there's nothing there, as you can see."

"I expect," said Miss Marple, "your cabinetmaker was a young man. He didn't know everything. People were very artful when they made hiding-places in those days. There's such a thing as a secret inside a secret."

She extracted a hairpin from her neat bun of gray hair. Straightening it out, she stuck the point into what appeared to be a tiny wormhole in one side of the secret recess. With a little difficulty she pulled out a small drawer. In it was a bundle of faded letters and a folded paper.

Edward and Charmian pounced on the find together. With trembling fingers Edward unfolded the paper. He dropped it with an exclamation of disgust.

"A damned cookery recipe. Baked ham!"

Charmian was untying a ribbon that held the letters together. She drew one out and glanced at it. "Love letters!"

Miss Marple reacted with Victorian gusto. "How interesting! Perhaps the reason your uncle never married."

Charmian read aloud:

My ever dear Mathew, I must confess that the time seems long indeed since I received your last letter. I try to occupy myself with the various tasks allotted to me, and often say to myself that I am indeed fortunate to see so much of the globe, though little did I think when I went to America that I should voyage off to these far islands!

Charmian broke off. "Where is it from? Oh! Hawaii!" She went on:

Alas, these natives are still far from seeing the light. They are in an unclothed and savage state and spend most of their time swimming and dancing, adorning themselves with garlands of flowers. Mr. Gray has made some converts but it is uphill work, and he and Mrs. Gray get sadly discouraged. I try to do all I can to cheer and encourage him, but I, too, am often sad for a reason you can guess, dear Mathew. Alas, absence is a severe trial to a loving heart. Your renewed vows and protestations of affection cheered me greatly. Now and always you have my faithful and devoted heart, dear Mathew, and I remain—

Your true love,
Betty Martin.

P.S.—*I address my letter under cover to our mutual friend, Matilda Graves, as usual. I hope heaven will pardon this little subterfuge.*

Edward whistled, "A female missionary! So that was Uncle Mathew's romance. I wonder why they never married?"

"She seems to have gone all over the world," said Charmian, looking through the letters. "Mauritius—all sorts of places. Probably died of yellow fever or something."

A gentle chuckle made them start. Miss Marple was apparently much amused. "Well, well," she said. "Fancy that, now!"

She was reading the recipe for baked ham. Seeing their inquiring glances, she read out: "'Baked ham with spinach. Take a nice piece of gammon, stuff with cloves, and cover with brown sugar. Bake in a slow oven. Serve with a border of puréed spinach.' What do you think of that, now?"

"I think it sounds filthy," said Edward.

"No, no, actually it would be very good—but what do you think of *the whole thing?*"

A sudden ray of light illuminated Edward's face. "Do you think it's a code-cryptogram of some kind?" He seized it. "Look here, Charmian, it might be, you know! No reason to put a cooking-recipe in a secret drawer otherwise."

"Exactly," said Miss Marple. "Very, very significant."

Charmian said, "I know what it might be—invisible ink! Let's heat it. Turn on the electric fire."

Edward did so, but no signs of writing appeared under the treatment.

Miss Marple coughed. "I really think, you know, that you're making it rather *too* difficult. The recipe is only an indication, so to speak. It is, I think, the letters that are significant."

"The letters?"

"Especially," said Miss Marple, "the signature."

But Edward hardly heard her. He called excitedly, "Charmian! Come here! She's right, See—the envelopes are old, right enough, but the letters themselves were written much later."

"Exactly," said Miss Marple.

"They're only fake old. I bet anything old Uncle Mat faked them himself—"

"Precisely," said Miss Marple.

"The whole thing's a sell. There never was a female missionary. It must be a code."

"My dear, dear children—there's really no need to make it all so difficult. Your uncle was really a very simple man. He had to have his little joke, that was all."

For the first time they gave her their full attention.

"Just exactly what do you mean, Miss Marple?" asked Charmian.

"I mean, dear, that you're actually holding the money in your hand this minute."

Charmian stared down.

"The signature, dear. That gives the whole thing away. The recipe is just an indication. Shorn of all the cloves and brown sugar and the rest of it, what is it *actually*? Why, gammon and spinach to be sure! *Gammon and spinach!* Meaning—nonsense! So it's clear that it's the letters that are important. And then, if you take into consideration what your uncle did just before he died. He tapped his eye, you said. Well, there you are—that gives you the clue, you see."

Charmian said, "Are we mad, or are you?"

"Surely, my dear, you must have heard the expression meaning that something is not a true picture, or has it quite died out nowadays? 'All my eye and Betty Martin'."

Edward gasped, his eyes falling to the letter in his hand. "Betty Martin—"

"Of course, Mr. Rossiter. As you have just said, there isn't—there wasn't any such person. The letters were written by your uncle, and I daresay he got a lot of fun out of writing them! As you say, the writing on the envelopes is much older—in fact, the envelopes couldn't belong to the letters, anyway, because the postmark of the one you are holding is 1851."

She paused. She made it very emphatic. "1851. And that explains everything, doesn't it?"

"Not to me," said Edward.

"Well, of course," said Miss Marple, "I daresay it wouldn't to me if it weren't for my great-nephew Lionel. Such a dear little boy and a passionate stamp collector. Knows all about stamps. It was he who told me about rare and expensive stamps and that a wonderful new find had come up for auction. And I actually remember his mentioning one stamp—an 1851 *blue two-cent*. It realized something like $25,000, I believe. Fancy! I should imagine that the other stamps are something also rare and expensive. No doubt your uncle bought through dealers and was careful to 'cover his tracks,' as they say in detective stories."

Edward groaned. He sat down and buried his face in his hands.

"What's the matter!" demanded Charmian.

"Nothing. It's only the awful thought that, but for Miss Marple, we might have burned these letters in a decent, gentlemanly way!"

"Ah," said Miss Marple, "that's just what these old gentlemen who are fond of their joke never realize. My Uncle Henry, I remember, sent a favorite niece a five-pound note for a Christmas present. He put it inside a Christmas card, gummed the card together, and wrote on it, 'Love and best wishes. Afraid this is all I can manage this year.'

"She, poor girl, was annoyed at what she thought was his meanness and threw it all straight into the fire. So then, of course, he had to give her another."

Edward's feelings toward Uncle Henry had suffered an abrupt and complete change.

"Miss Marple," he said, "I'm going to get a bottle of champagne. We'll all drink the health of your Uncle Henry."

2. TAPE-MEASURE MURDER

Miss Politt took hold of the knocker and rapped politely on the cottage door. After a discreet interval she knocked again. The parcel under her left arm shifted a little as she did so, and she readjusted it. Inside the parcel was Mrs. Spenlow's new green winter dress, ready for fitting. From Miss Politt's left hand dangled a bag of black silk, containing a tape measure, a pincushion, and a large, practical pair of scissors.

Miss Politt was tall and gaunt, with a sharp nose, pursed lips, and meager iron-gray hair. She hesitated before using the knocker for the third time. Glancing down the street, she saw a figure rapidly approaching. Miss Hartnell, jolly, weather-beaten, fifty-five, shouted out in her usual loud bass voice, "Good afternoon, Miss Politt!"

The dressmaker answered, "Good afternoon, Miss Hartnell." Her voice was excessively thin and genteel in its accents. She had started life as a lady's maid. "Excuse me," she went on, "but do you happen to know if by any chance Mrs. Spenlow isn't at home?"

"Not the least idea," said Miss Hartnell.

"It's rather awkward, you see. I was to fit on Mrs. Spenlow's new dress this afternoon. Three-thirty, she said."

Miss Hartnell consulted her wrist watch. "It's a little past the half-hour now."

"Yes. I have knocked three times, but there doesn't seem to be any answer, so I was wondering if perhaps Mrs. Spenlow might have gone out and forgotten. She doesn't forget appointments as a rule, and she wants the dress to wear the day after tomorrow."

Miss Hartnell entered the gate and walked up the path to join Miss Politt outside the door of Laburnam Cottage.

"Why doesn't Gladys answer the door?" she demanded. "Oh, no, of course, it's Thursday—Gladys's day out. I expect Mrs. Spenlow has fallen asleep. I don't expect you've made enough noise with this thing."

Seizing the knocker, she executed a deafening *rat-a-tat-tat,* and in addition thumped upon the panels of the door. She also called out in a stentorian voice, "What ho, within there!"

There was no response.

Miss Politt murmured, "Oh, I think Mrs. Spenlow must have forgotten and gone out. I'll call round some other time." She began edging away down the path.

"Nonsense," said Miss Hartnell firmly. "She can't have gone out. I'd have met her. I'll just take a look through the windows and see if I can find any signs of life."

She laughed in her usual hearty manner, to indicate that it was a joke, and applied a perfunctory glance to the nearest windowpane— perfunctory because she knew quite well that the front room was seldom used, Mr. and Mrs. Spenlow preferring the small back sitting-room.

Perfunctory as it was, though, it succeeded in its object. Miss Hartnell, it is true, saw no signs of life. On the contrary, she saw, through the window, Mrs. Spenlow lying on the hearthrug—dead.

"Of course," said Miss Hartnell, telling the story afterward, "I managed to keep my head. That Politt creature wouldn't have had the least idea of what to do. 'Got to keep our heads,' I said to her. '*You* stay here, and I'll go for Constable Palk.' She said something about not wanting to be left, but I paid no attention at all. One has to be firm with that sort of person. I've always found they enjoy making a fuss. So I was just going off when, at that very moment, Mr. Spenlow came round the corner of the house."

Here Miss Hartnell made a significant pause. It enabled her audience to ask breathlessly, "Tell me, how did he *look?*"

Miss Hartnell would then go on, "Frankly, *I* suspected something at once! He was *far* too calm. He didn't seem surprised in the least. And you may say what you like, it isn't natural for a man to hear that his wife is dead and display no emotion whatever."

Everybody agreed with this statement.

The police agreed with it, too. So suspicious did they consider Mr. Spenlow's detachment, that they lost no time in ascertaining how that gentleman was situated as a result of his wife's death. When they discovered that Mrs. Spenlow had been the monied partner, and that her money went to her husband under a will made soon after their marriage, they were more suspicious than ever.

Miss Marple, that sweet-faced—and, some said, vinegar-tongued—elderly spinster who lived in the house next to the rectory, was interviewed very early—within half an hour of the discovery of the crime. She was approached by Police Constable Palk, importantly thumbing a notebook. "If you don't mind, ma'am, I've a few questions to ask you."

Miss Marple said, "In connection with the murder of Mrs. Spenlow?"

Palk was startled. "May I ask, madam, how you got to know of it?"

"The fish," said Miss Marple.

The reply was perfectly intelligible to Constable Palk. He assumed correctly that the fishmonger's boy had brought it, together with Miss Marple's evening meal.

Miss Marple continued gently. "Lying on the floor in the sitting-room, strangled—possibly by a very narrow belt. But whatever it was, it was taken away."

Palk's face was wrathful. "How that young Fred gets to know everything—"

Miss Marple cut him short adroitly. She said, "There's a pin in your tunic."

Constable Palk looked down, startled. He said, "They do say, 'See a pin and pick it up, all the day you'll have good luck.'"

"I hope that will come true. Now what is it you want me to tell you?"

Constable Palk cleared his throat, looked important, and consulted his notebook. "Statement was made to me by Mr. Arthur Spenlow, husband of the deceased. Mr. Spenlow says that at two-thirty, as far as he can say, he was rung up by Miss Marple, and asked if he would come over at a quarter past three as she was anxious to consult him about something. Now, ma'am, is that true?"

"Certainly not," said Miss Marple.

"You did not ring up Mr. Spenlow at two-thirty?"

"Neither at two-thirty nor any other time."

"Ah," said Constable Palk, and sucked his mustache with a good deal of satisfaction.

"What else did Mr. Spenlow say?"

"Mr. Spenlow's statement was that he came over here as requested, leaving his own house at ten minutes past three; that on arrival here he was informed by the maidservant that Miss Marple was 'not at 'ome.'"

"That part of it is true," said Miss Marple. "He did come here, but I was at a meeting at the Women's institute."

"Ah," said Constable Palk again.

Miss Marple exclaimed, "Do tell me, Constable, do you suspect Mr. Spenlow?"

"It's not for me to say at this stage, but it looks to me as though somebody, naming no names, had been trying to be artful."

Miss Marple said thoughtfully, "Mr. Spenlow?"

She liked Mr. Spenlow. He was a small, spare man, stiff and conventional in speech, the acme of respectability. It seemed odd that he should have come to live in the country, he had so clearly lived in towns all his life. To Miss Marple he confided the reason. He said, "I have always intended, ever since I was a small boy, to live in the country some day and have a garden of my own. I have always been very much attached to flowers. My wife, you know, kept a flower shop. That's where I saw her first."

A dry statement, but it opened up a vista of romance. A younger, prettier Mrs. Spenlow, seen against a background of flowers.

Mr. Spenlow, however, really knew nothing about flowers. He had no idea of seeds, of cuttings, of bedding out, of annuals or perennials, He had only a vision—a vision of a small cottage garden thickly planted with sweet-smelling, brightly colored blossoms. He had asked, almost pathetically, for instruction, and had noted down Miss Marple's replies to questions in a little book.

He was a man of quiet method. It was, perhaps, because of this trait, that the police were interested in him when his wife was found murdered. With patience and perseverance they learned a good deal about the late Mrs. Spenlow—and soon all St. Mary Mead knew it, too.

The late Mrs. Spenlow had begun life as a between-maid in a large house. She had left that position to marry the second gardener, and with him had started a flower shop in London. The shop had prospered. Not so the gardener, who before long had sickened and died.

His widow carried on the shop and enlarged it in an ambitious way. She had continued to prosper. Then she had sold the business at a handsome price and embarked upon matrimony for the second time—with Mr. Spenlow, a middle-aged jeweler who had inherited a small and struggling business. Not long afterward, they had sold the business and come down to St. Mary Mead.

Mrs. Spenlow was a well-to-do woman. The profits from her florist's establishment she had invested—"under spirit guidance," as she explained to all and sundry. The spirits had advised her with unexpected acumen.

All her investments had prospered, some in quite a sensational fashion. Instead, however, of this increasing her belief in spiritualism, Mrs. Spenlow basely deserted mediums and sittings, and made a brief but wholehearted plunge into an obscure religion with Indian affinities which was based on various forms of deep breathing. When, however, she arrived at St. Mary Mead, she had relapsed into a period of orthodox Church-of-England beliefs. She was a good deal at the vicarage, and attended church services with assiduity.

She patronized the village shops, took an interest in the local happenings, and played village bridge.

A humdrum, everyday life. And—suddenly—murder.

COLONEL MELCHETT, THE chief constable, had summoned Inspector Slack.

Slack was a positive type of man. When he had made up his mind, he was sure. He was quite sure now. "Husband did it, sir," he said.

"You think so?"

"Quite sure of it. You've only got to look at him. Guilty as hell. Never showed a sign of grief or emotion. He came back to the house knowing she was dead."

"Wouldn't he at least have tried to act the part of the distracted husband?"

"Not him, sir. Too pleased with himself. Some gentlemen can't act. Too stiff."

"Any other woman in his life?" Colonel Melchett asked.

"Haven't been able to find any trace of one. Of course, he's the artful kind. He'd cover his tracks. As I see it, he was just fed up with his wife. She'd got the money, and I should say was a trying woman to live with—always taking up some 'ism' or other. He cold-bloodedly decided to do away with her and live comfortably on his own."

"Yes, that could be the case, I suppose."

"Depend upon it, that was it. Made his plans careful. Pretended to get a phone call—"

Melchett interrupted him. "No call been traced?"

"No, sir. That means either that he lied, or that the call was put through from a public telephone booth. The only two public phones in the village are at the station and the post office. Post office it certainly wasn't. Mrs. Blade sees everyone who comes in. Station it might be. Train arrives at two twenty-seven and there's a bit of a bustle then. But the main thing is *he* says it was Miss Marple who called him up, and that certainly isn't true. The call didn't come from her house, and she herself was away at the Institute."

"You're not overlooking the possibility that the husband was deliberately got out of the way—by someone who wanted to murder Mrs. Spenlow?"

"You're thinking of young Ted Gerard, aren't you, sir? I've been working on him—what we're up against there is lack of motive. He doesn't stand to gain anything."

"He's an undesirable character, though. Quite a pretty little spot of embezzlement to his credit."

"I'm not saying he isn't a wrong 'un. Still, he did go to his boss and own up to that embezzlement. And his employers weren't wise to it."

"An Oxford Grouper," said Melchett.

"Yes, sir. Became a convert and went off to do the straight thing and own up to having pinched money. I'm not saying, mind you, that it mayn't have been astuteness. He may have thought he was suspected and decided to gamble on honest repentance."

"You have a skeptical mind, Slack," said Colonel Melchett. "By the way, have you talked to Miss Marple at all?"

"What's *she* got to do with it, sir?"

"Oh, nothing. But she hears things, you know. Why don't you go and have a chat with her? She's a very sharp old lady."

Slack changed the subject. "One thing I've been meaning to ask you, sir. That domestic-service job where the deceased started her career—Sir Robert Abercrombie's place. That's where that jewel robbery was—emeralds—worth a packet. Never got them. I've been looking it up—must have happened when the Spenlow woman was there, though she'd have been quite a girl at the time. Don't think she was mixed up in it, do you, sir? Spenlow, you know, was one of those little tuppenny-ha'penny jewelers—just the chap for a fence."

Melchett shook his head. "Don't think there's anything in that. She didn't even know Spenlow at the time. I remember the case. Opinion in police circles was that a son of the house was mixed up in it—Jim Abercrombie—awful young waster. Had a pile of debts, and just after the robbery they were all paid off—some rich woman, so they said, but I don't know—Old Abercrombie hedged a bit about the case—tried to call the police off."

"It was just an idea, sir," said Slack.

MISS MARPLE RECEIVED Inspector Slack with gratification, especially when she heard that he had been sent by Colonel Melchett.

"Now, really, that is very kind of Colonel Melchett. I didn't know he remembered me."

"He remembers you, all right. Told me that what you didn't know of what goes on in St. Mary Mead isn't worth knowing."

"Too kind of him, but really I don't know anything at all. About this murder, I mean."

"You know what the talk about it is."

"Oh, of course—but it wouldn't do, would it, to repeat just idle talk?"

Slack said, with an attempt at geniality, "This isn't an official conversation, you know. It's in confidence, so to speak."

"You mean you really want to know what people are saying? Whether there's any truth in it or not?"

"That's the idea."

"Well, of course, there's been a great deal of talk and speculation. And there are really two distinct camps, if you understand me. To begin with, there are the people who think that the husband did it. A husband or a wife is, in a way, the natural person to suspect, don't you think so?"

"Maybe," said the inspector cautiously.

"Such close quarters, you know. Then, so often, the money angle. I hear that it was Mrs. Spenlow who had the money, and therefore Mr. Spenlow does benefit by her death. In this wicked world I'm afraid the most uncharitable assumptions are often justified."

"He comes into a tidy sum, all right."

"Just so. It would seem quite plausible, wouldn't it, for him to strangle her, leave the house by the back, come across the fields to my house, ask for me and pretend he'd had a telephone call from me, then go back and find his wife murdered in his absence—hoping, of course, that the crime would be put down to some tramp or burglar."

The inspector nodded. "What with the money angle and if they'd been on bad terms lately—"

But Miss Marple interrupted him. "Oh, but they hadn't."

"You know that for a fact?"

"Everyone would have known if they'd quarreled! The maid, Gladys Brent—she'd have soon spread it round the village."

The inspector said feebly, "She mightn't have known—" and received a pitying smile in reply.

Miss Marple went on. "And then there's the other school of thought. Ted Gerard. A good-looking young man. I'm afraid, you know, that good looks are inclined to influence one more than they should. Our last curate but one—quite a magical effect! All the girls came to church—evening service as well as morning. And many older women became unusually active in parish work—and the slippers and scarfs that were made for him! Quite embarrassing for the poor young man.

"But let me see, where was I? Oh, yes, this young man, Ted Gerard. Of course, there has been talk about him. He's come down to see her so often. Though Mrs. Spenlow told me herself that he was a member of what I think they call the Oxford Group. A religious movement. They are quite sincere and very earnest, I believe, and Mrs. Spenlow was impressed by it all."

Miss Marple took a breath and went on. "And I'm sure there was no reason to believe that there was anything more in it than that, but you know what people are. Quite a lot of people are convinced that Mrs. Spenlow was infatuated with the young man, and that she'd lent him quite a lot of money. And it's perfectly true that he was actually seen at the station that day. In the train—the two twenty-seven down train. But of course it would be quite easy, wouldn't it, to slip out of the other side of the train and go through the cutting and over the fence and round by the hedge and never come out of the station entrance at all. So that he need not have been seen going to the cottage. And, of course, people do think that what Mrs. Spenlow was wearing was rather peculiar."

"Peculiar?"

"A kimono. Not a dress." Miss Marple blushed. "That sort of thing, you know, is, perhaps, rather suggestive to some people."

"You think it was suggestive?"

"Oh, no, *I* don't think so. I think it was perfectly natural."

"You think it was natural?"

"Under the circumstances, yes." Miss Marple's glance was cool and reflective.

Inspector Slack said, "It might give us another motive for the husband. Jealousy."

"Oh, no, Mr. Spenlow would never be jealous. He's not the sort of man who notices things. If his wife had gone away and left a note on the pincushion, it would be the first he'd know of anything of that kind."

Inspector Slack was puzzled by the intent way she was looking at him. He had an idea that all her conversation was intended to hint at something he didn't understand. She said now, with some emphasis, "Didn't *you* find any clues, Inspector—on the spot?"

"People don't leave fingerprints and cigarette ash nowadays, Miss Marple."

"But this, I think," she suggested, "was an old-fashioned crime—"

Slack said sharply, "Now what do you mean by that?"

Miss Marple remarked slowly, "I think, you know, that Constable Palk could help you. He was the first person on the—on the 'scene of the crime,' as they say."

MR. SPENLOW WAS SITTING in a deck chair. He looked bewildered. He said, in his thin, precise voice, "I may, of course, be imagining what occurred. My hearing is not as good as it was. But I distinctly think I heard a small boy call after me, 'Yah, who's a Crippen?' It—it conveyed the impression to me that he was of the opinion that I had—had killed my dear wife."

Miss Marple, gently snipping off a dead rose head, said, "That was the impression he meant to convey, no doubt."

"But what could possibly have put such an idea into a child's head?"

Miss Marple coughed. "Listening, no doubt, to the opinions of his elders."

"You—you really mean that other people think that, also?"

"Quite half the people in St. Mary Mead."

"But—my dear lady—what can possibly have given rise to such an idea? I was sincerely attached to my wife. She did not, alas, take to living in the country as much as I had hoped she would do, but perfect agreement on every subject is an impossible ideal. I assure you I feel her loss very keenly."

"Probably. But if you will excuse my saying so, you don't sound as though you do."

Mr. Spenlow drew his meager frame up to its full height. "My dear lady, many years ago I read of a certain Chinese philosopher who, when his dearly loved wife was taken from him, continued calmly to beat a gong in the street—a customary Chinese pastime, I presume—exactly as usual. The people of the city were much impressed by his fortitude."

"But," said Miss Marple, "the people of St. Mary Mead react rather differently. Chinese philosophy does not appeal to them."

"But you understand?"

Miss Marple nodded. "My Uncle Henry," she explained, "was a man of unusual self-control. His motto was 'Never display emotion.' He, too, was very fond of flowers."

"I was thinking," said Mr. Spenlow with something like eagerness, "that I might, perhaps, have a pergola on the west side of the cottage. Pink roses and, perhaps, wisteria. And there is a white starry flower, whose name for the moment escapes me—"

In the tone in which she spoke to her grand-nephew, aged three, Miss Marple said, "I have a very nice catalog here, with pictures. Perhaps you would like to look through it—I have to go up to the village."

Leaving Mr. Spenlow sitting happily in the garden with his catalog, Miss Marple went up to her room, hastily rolled up a dress in a piece of brown paper, and, leaving the house, walked briskly up to the post office. Miss Politt, the dressmaker, lived in rooms over the post office.

But Miss Marple did not at once go through the door and up the stairs. It was just two-thirty, and, a minute late, the Much Benham bus drew up outside the post-office door. It was one of the events of the day in St. Mary Mead. The post-mistress hurried out with parcels, parcels connected with the shop side of her business, for the post office also dealt in sweets, cheap books, and children's toys.

For some four minutes Miss Marple was alone in the post office.

Not till the postmistress returned to her post did Miss Marple go upstairs and explain to Miss Politt that she wanted her old gray crepe altered and made more fashionable if that were possible. Miss Politt promised to see what she could do.

THE CHIEF CONSTABLE was rather astonished when Miss Marple's name was brought to him. She came in with many apologies. "So sorry—so very sorry to disturb you. You are so busy, I know, but then you have always been so very kind, Colonel Melchett, and I felt I would rather come to you instead of to Inspector Slack. For one thing, you know, I should hate Constable Palk to get into any trouble. Strictly speaking, I suppose he shouldn't have touched anything at all."

Colonel Melchett was slightly bewildered. He said, "Palk? That's the St. Mary Mead constable, isn't it? What has he been doing?"

"He picked up a pin, you know. It was in his tunic. And it occurred to me at the time that it was quite probable he had actually picked it up in Mrs. Spenlow's house."

"Quite, quite. But after all, you know, what's a pin? Matter of fact he did pick the pin up just by Mrs. Spenlow's body. Came and told Slack about it yesterday—you put him up to that, I gather? Oughtn't to have touched anything, of course, but as I said, what's a pin? It was only a common pin. Sort of thing any woman might use."

"Oh, no, Colonel Melchett, that's where you're wrong. To a man's eye, perhaps, it looked like an ordinary pin, but it wasn't. It was a special pin, a very thin pin, the kind you buy by the box, the kind used mostly by dressmakers."

Melchett stared at her, a faint light of comprehension breaking in on him. Miss Marple nodded her head several times, eagerly.

"Yes, of course. It seems to me so obvious. She was in her kimono because she was going to try on her new dress, and she went into the front room, and Miss Politt just said something about measurements and put the tape measure round her neck—and then all she'd have to do was to cross it and pull—quite easy, so I've heard. And then, of course, she'd go outside and pull the door to and stand there knocking as though she'd just arrived. But the pin shows she'd *already been in the house.*"

"And it was Miss Politt who telephoned to Spenlow?"

"Yes. From the post office at two-thirty—just when the bus comes and the post office would be empty."

Colonel Melchett said, "But my dear Miss Marple, why? In heaven's name, why? You can't have a murder without a motive."

"Well, I think, you know, Colonel Melchett, from all I've heard, that the crime dates from a long time back. It reminds me, you know, of my two cousins, Antony and Gordon. Whatever Antony did always went right for him, and with poor Gordon it was just the other way about. Race horses went lame, and stocks went down, and property depreciated. As I see it, the two women were in it together."

"In what?"

"The robbery. Long ago. Very valuable emeralds, so I've heard. The lady's maid and the tweeny. Because one thing hasn't been explained—how, when the tweeny married the gardener, did they have enough money to set up a flower shop?

"The answer is, it was her share of the—the swag, I think is the right expression. Everything she did turned out well. Money made money. But the other one, the lady's maid, must have been unlucky. She came down to being just a village dressmaker. Then they met again. Quite all right at first, I expect, until Mr. Ted Gerard came on the scene.

"Mrs. Spenlow, you see, was already suffering from conscience and was inclined to be emotionally religious. This young man no doubt urged her to 'face up' and to 'come clean' and I daresay she was strung up to do so. But Miss Politt didn't see it that way. All she saw was that she might go to prison for a robbery she had committed years ago. So she made up her mind to put a stop to it all. I'm afraid, you know, that she was always rather a wicked woman. I don't believe she'd have turned a hair if that nice, stupid Mr. Spenlow had been hanged."

Colonel Melchett said slowly, "We can—er—verify your theory—up to a point. The identity of the Politt woman with the lady's maid at the Abercrombies', but—"

Miss Marple reassured him. "It will be all quite easy. She's the kind of woman who will break down at once when she's taxed with the truth. And then, you see, I've got her tape measure. I—er—abstracted it yesterday when I was trying on. When she misses it and thinks the police have got it—well, she's quite an ignorant woman and she'll think it will prove the case against her in some way."

She smiled at him encouragingly. "You'll have no trouble, I can assure you." It was the tone in which his favorite aunt had once assured him that he could not fail to pass his entrance examination into Sandhurst.

And he had passed.

3. THE CASE OF THE PERFECT MAID

Oh, if you please, Madam, could I speak to you a moment?"

It might be thought that this request was in the nature of an absurdity, since Edna, Miss Marple's little maid, was actually speaking to her mistress at the moment.

Recognizing the idiom, however, Miss Marple said promptly, "Certainly, Edna, come in and shut the door. What is it?"

Obediently shutting the door, Edna advanced into the room, pleated the corner of her apron between her fingers, and swallowed once or twice.

"Yes, Edna?" said Miss Marple encouragingly.

"Oh, please, Ma'am, It's my cousin, Gladdie."

"Dear me," said Miss Marple, her mind leaping to the worst—and, alas, the most usual conclusion. "Not—not in trouble?"

Edna hastened to reassure her. "Oh, no, ma'am, nothing of that kind. Gladdie's not that kind of girl. It's just that she's upset. You see, she's lost her place."

"Dear me, I am sorry to hear that. She was at Old Hall, wasn't she, with the Miss—Misses—Skinner?"

"Yes, ma'am, that's right, ma'am. And Gladdie's very upset about it—very upset indeed."

"Gladys has changed places rather often before, though, hasn't she?"

"Oh, yes, ma'am. She's always one for a change. Gladdie is. She never seems to get really settled, if you know what I mean. But she's always been the one to give the notice, you see!"

"And this time it's the other way round?" asked Miss Marple dryly.

"Yes, ma'am, and it's upset Gladdie something awful."

Miss Marple looked slightly surprised. Her recollection of Gladys, who had occasionally come to drink tea in the kitchen on her 'days out,' was a stout, giggling girl of unshakably equable temperament.

Edna went on. "You see, ma'am, it's the way it happened—the way Miss Skinner looked."

"How," inquired Miss Marple patiently, "did Miss Skinner look?"

This time Edna got well away with her news bulletin.

"Oh, ma'am, it was ever such a shock to Gladdie. You see, one of Miss Emily's brooches was missing, and such a hue and cry for it as never was, and of course nobody likes a thing like that to happen; it's upsetting, ma'am, if you know what I mean. And Gladdie's helped search everywhere, and there was Miss Lavinia saying she was going to the police about it, and then it turned up again, pushed right to the back of a drawer in the dressing-table, and very thankful Gladdie was.

"And the very next day as ever was a plate got broken, and Miss Lavinia she bounced out right away and told Gladdie to take a month's notice. And what Gladdie feels is it couldn't have been the plate and that Miss Lavinia was just making an excuse of that, and that it must be because of the brooch and they think as she took it and put it back when the police was mentioned, and Gladdie wouldn't do such a thing, not never she wouldn't, and what she feels is as it will get round and tell against her and it's a very serious thing for a girl, as you know, ma'am."

Miss Marple nodded. Though having no particular liking for the bouncing, self-opinioned Gladys, she was quite sure of the girl's intrinsic honesty and could well imagine that the affair must have upset her.

Edna said wistfully, "I suppose, ma'am, there isn't anything you could do about it? Gladdie's in ever such a taking."

"Tell her not to be silly," said Miss Marple crisply. "If she didn't take the brooch—which I'm sure she didn't—then she has no cause to be upset."

"It'll get about," said Edna dismally.

Miss Marple said, "I—er—am going up that way this afternoon. I'll have word with the Misses Skinner."

"Oh, thank you, madam," said Edna.

OLD HALL WAS a big Victorian house surrounded by woods and park land. Since it had been proved unlettable and unsalable as it was, an enterprising speculator had divided it into four flats with a central hot water system, and the use of 'the grounds' to be held in common by the tenants. The experiment had been satisfactory. A rich and eccentric old lady and her maid occupied one flat. The old lady had a passion for birds and entertained a feathered gathering to meals every day. A retired Indian judge and his wife rented a second. A very young couple, recently married, occupied the third, and the fourth had been taken only two months ago by two maiden ladies of the name of Skinner. The four sets of tenants were only on the most distant terms with each other, since none of them had anything in common. The landlord had been heard to say that this was an excellent thing. What he dreaded were friendships followed by estrangements and subsequent complaints to him.

Miss Marple was acquainted with all the tenants, though she knew none of them well. The elder Miss Skinner, Miss Lavinia, was what might be termed the working member of the firm. Miss Emily, the younger, spent most of her time in bed suffering from various complaints which, in the opinion of St. Mary Mead, were largely imaginary. Only Miss Lavinia believed devoutly in her sister's martyrdom and patience under affliction, and willingly ran errands and trotted up and down to the village for things that "my sister had suddenly fancied."

It was the view of St. Mary Mead that if Miss Emily suffered half as much as she said she did, she would have sent for Doctor Haydock long ago. But Miss Emily, when this was hinted to her, shut her eyes in a superior way and murmured that her case was not a simple one—the best specialists in London had been baffled by it—and that a wonderful new man had put her on a most revolutionary course of treatment and that she really hoped her health would improve under it. No humdrum G.P. could possibly understand her case.

"And it's my opinion," said the outspoken Miss Hartnell, "that she's very wise not to send for him. Dear Doctor Haydock, in that breezy manner of his, would tell her that there, was nothing the matter with her and to get up and not make a fuss! Do her a lot of good!"

Failing such arbitrary treatment, however, Miss Emily continued to lie on sofas, to surround herself with strange little pill boxes, and to reject nearly everything that had been cooked for her and ask for something else—usually something difficult and inconvenient to get.

THE DOOR WAS opened to Miss Marple by "Gladdie," looking more depressed than Miss Marple had ever thought possible. In the sitting-room (a quarter of the late drawing-room, which had been partitioned into a dining-room, drawing-room, bathroom, and housemaid's cupboard), Miss Lavinia rose to greet Miss Marple.

Lavinia Skinner was a tall, gaunt, bony female of fifty. She had a gruff voice and an abrupt manner.

"Nice to see you," she said. "Emily's lying down—feeling low today, poor dear. Hope she'll see you, it would cheer her up, but there are times when she doesn't feel up to seeing anybody. Poor dear, she's wonderfully patient."

Miss Marple responded politely. Servants were the main topic of conversation in St. Mary Mead, so it was not difficult to lead the conversation in that direction. Miss Marple said she had heard that that nice girl, Gladys Holmes, was leaving.

Miss Lavinia nodded. "Wednesday week. Broke things, you know. Can't have that."

Miss Marple sighed and said we all had to put up with things nowadays. It was so difficult to get girls to come to the country. Did Miss Skinner really think it was wise to part with Gladys?

"Know it's difficult to get servants," admitted Miss Lavinia. "The Devereuxs haven't got anybody—but then, I don't wonder—always quarreling, jazz on all night—meals any time—that girl knows nothing of housekeeping, I pity her husband! Then the Larkins have just lost their maid. Of course, what with the judge's Indian temper and his wanting chota hazri, as he calls it, at six in the morning and Mrs. Larkin always fussing, I don't wonder at that, either. Mrs. Carmichael's Janet is a fixture, of course—though in my opinion she's the most disagreeable woman, and absolutely bullies the old lady."

"Then don't you think you might reconsider your decision about Gladys? She really is a nice girl. I know all her family; very honest and superior."

Miss Lavinia shook her head.

"I've got my reasons," she said importantly.

Miss Marple murmured, "You missed a brooch, I understand—"

"Now, who has been talking? I suppose the girl has. Quite frankly, I'm almost certain she took it. And then got frightened and put it back—but, of course, one can't say anything unless one is sure." She changed the subject. "Do come and see Miss Emily, Miss Marple. I'm sure it would do her good."

Miss Marple followed meekly to where Miss Lavinia knocked on a door, was bidden enter, and ushered her guest into the best room in the flat, most of the light of which was excluded by half-drawn blinds. Miss Emily was lying in bed, apparently enjoying the half-gloom and her own indefinite sufferings.

The dim light showed her to be a thin, indecisive-looking creature, with a good deal of grayish-yellow hair untidily wound around her head and erupting into curls, the whole thing looking like a bird's nest of which no self-respecting bird could be proud. There was a smell in the room of Eau de Cologne, stale biscuits, and camphor.

With half-closed eyes and in a thin, weak voice, Emily Skinner explained that this was "one of her bad days."

"The worst of ill health is," said Miss Emily in a melancholy tone, "that one knows what a burden one is to everyone around one.

"Lavinia is very good to me. Lavvie dear, I do so hate giving trouble but if my hot-water bottle could only be filled in the way I like it—too full it weighs on me so—on the other hand, if it is not sufficiently filled, it gets cold immediately!"

"I'm sorry, dear. Give it to me. I will empty a little out."

"Perhaps, if you're doing that, it might be refilled. There are no rusks in the house, I suppose—no, no, it doesn't matter. I can do without. Some weak tea and a slice of lemon—no lemons? No, really, I couldn't drink tea without lemon. I think the milk was slightly turned this morning. It has put me right against milk in my tea. It doesn't matter. I can do without my tea. Only I do feel so weak. Oysters, they say, are nourishing. I wonder if I could fancy a few? No, no, too much bother to get hold of them so late in the day. I can fast until tomorrow."

Lavinia left the room murmuring something incoherent about bicycling down to the village.

Miss Emily smiled feebly at her guest and remarked that she did hate giving anyone any trouble.

Miss Marple told Edna that evening that she was afraid her embassy had met with no success.

She was rather troubled to find that rumors as to Gladys's dishonesty were already going around the village.

In the post office, Miss Wetherby tackled her, "My dear Jane, they gave her a written reference saying she was willing and sober and respectable, but saying nothing about honesty. That seems to me most significant! I hear there was some trouble about a brooch. I think there must be something in it, you know, because one doesn't let a servant go nowadays unless it's something rather grave. They'll find it most difficult to get anyone else. Girls simply will not go to Old Hall. They're nervous coming home on their days out. You'll see, the Skinners won't find anyone else, and then, perhaps that dreadful hypochondriac sister will have to get up and do something!"

Great was the chagrin of the village when it was made known that the Misses Skinner had engaged, from an agency, a new maid who, by all accounts, was a perfect paragon.

"A three years' reference recommending her most warmly, she prefers the country, and actually asks less wages than Gladys. I really feel we have been most fortunate."

"Well, really," said Miss Marple, to whom these details were imparted by Miss Lavinia in the fish-monger's shop. "It does seem too good to be true."

It then became the opinion of St. Mary Mead that the paragon would cry off at the last minute and fail to arrive.

None of these prognostications came true, however, and the village was able to observe the domestic treasure, by name, Mary Higgins, driving through the village in Reed's taxi to Old Hall. It had to be admitted that her appearance was good. A most respectable-looking woman, very neatly dressed.

When Miss Marple next visited Old Hall, on the occasion of recruiting stall-holders for the vicarage fete, Mary Higgins opened the door. She was certainly a most superior-looking maid, at a guess forty years of age, with neat black hair, rosy cheeks, a plump figure discreetly arrayed in black with a white apron and cap—"quite the good, old-fashioned type of servant," as Miss Marple explained afterward, and with the proper, inaudible, respectful voice, so different from the loud but adenoidal accents of Gladys.

Miss Lavinia was looking far less harassed than usual and, although she regretted that she could not take a stall owing to her preoccupation with her sister, she nevertheless tendered a handsome monetary contribution, and promised to produce a consignment of penwipers and babies' socks.

Miss Marple commented on her air of well-being.

"I really feel I owe a great deal to Mary. I am so thankful I had the resolution to get rid of that other girl. Mary is really invaluable. Cooks nicely and waits beautifully and keeps our little flat scrupulously clean—mattresses turned over every day. And she is really wonderful with Emily!"

Miss Marple hastily inquired after Emily.

"Oh, poor dear, she has been very much under the weather lately. She can't help it, of course, but it really makes things a little difficult sometimes. Wanting certain things cooked and then, when they come, saying she can't eat now—and then wanting them again half an hour later and everything spoiled and having to be done again. It makes, of course, a lot of work—but fortunately Mary does not seem to mind at all. She's used to waiting on invalids, she says, and understands them. It is such a comfort."

"Dear me," said Miss Marple. "You are fortunate."

"Yes, indeed. I really feel Mary has been sent to us as an answer to prayer."

"She sounds to me," said Miss Marple, "almost too good to be true. I should—well, I should be a little careful if I were you."

Lavinia Skinner failed to perceive the point of this remark. She said, "Oh! I assure you I do all I can to make her comfortable. I don't know what I should do if she left."

"I don't expect she'll leave until she's ready to leave," said Miss Marple and stared very hard at her hostess.

Miss Lavinia said, "If one has no domestic worries, it takes such a load off one's mind, doesn't it? How is your little Edna shaping?"

"She's doing quite nicely. Not much ahead, of course. Not like your Mary. Still I do know all about Edna because she's a village girl."

As she went out into the hall she heard the invalid's voice fretfully raised. "This compress has been allowed to get quite dry—Doctor Allerton particularly said moisture continually renewed. There, there, leave it. I want a cup of tea and a boiled egg—boiled only three minutes and a half, remember, and send Miss Lavinia to me."

The efficient Mary emerged from the bedroom and, saying to Lavinia, "Miss Emily is asking for you, madam," proceeded to open the door for Miss Marple, helping her into her coat and handing her her umbrella in the most irreproachable fashion.

Miss Marple took the umbrella, dropped it, tried to pick it up, and dropped her bag, which flew open. Mary politely retrieved various odds and ends—a handkerchief, an engagement book, an old-fashioned leather purse, two shillings, three pennies, and a striped piece of peppermint rock.

Miss Marple received the last with some signs of confusion.

"Oh, dear, that must have been Mrs. Clement's little boy. He was sucking it, I remember, and he took my bag to play with. He must have put it inside. It's terribly sticky, isn't it?"

"Shall I take it, madam?"

"Oh, would you? Thank you so much."

Mary stooped to retrieve the last item, a small mirror upon recovering which Miss Marple exclaimed fervently, "How lucky, now, that that isn't broken."

She thereupon departed, Mary standing politely by the door holding a piece of striped rock with a completely expressionless face.

FOR TEN DAYS longer St. Mary Mead had to endure hearing of the excellencies of Miss Lavinia's and Miss Emily's treasure.

On the eleventh day, the village awoke to its big thrill.

Mary, the paragon, was missing! Her bed had not been slept in, and the front door was found ajar. She had slipped out quietly during the night.

And not Mary alone was missing! Two brooches and five rings of Miss Lavinia's; three rings, a pendant, a bracelet and four brooches of Miss Emily's were missing, also!

It was the beginning of a chapter of catastrophe.

Young Mrs. Devereux had lost her diamonds which she kept in an unlocked drawer and also some valuable furs given to her as a wedding present. The judge and his wife also had had jewelry taken and a certain amount of money. Mrs. Carmichael was the greatest sufferer. Not only had she some very valuable jewels but she also kept in the flat a large sum of money which had gone. It had been Janet's evening out, and her mistress was in the habit of walking round the gardens at dusk calling to the birds and scattering crumbs. It seemed clear that Mary, the perfect maid, had had keys to fit all the flats!

There was, it must be confessed, a certain amount of ill-natured pleasure in St. Mary Mead. Miss Lavinia had boasted so much of her marvelous Mary.

"And all the time, my dear, just a common thief!"

Interesting revelation followed. Not only had Mary disappeared into the blue, but the agency who had provided her and vouched for her credentials was alarmed to find that the Mary Higgins who had applied to them and whose references they had taken up had, to all intents and purposes, never existed. It was the name of a bona fide servant who had lived with the bona fide sister of a dean, but the real Mary Higgins was existing peacefully in a place in Cornwall.

"Damned clever, the whole thing," Inspector Slack was forced to admit. "And, if you ask me, that woman works in with a gang. There was a case of much the same kind in Northumberland a year ago. Stuff was never traced, and they never caught her. However, we'll do better than that in Much Ben-ham!"

Inspector Slack was always a confident man.

Nevertheless, weeks passed, and Mary Higgins remained triumphantly at large. In vain Inspector Slack redoubled that energy that so belied his name.

Miss Lavinia remained tearful. Miss Emily was so upset, and felt so alarmed by her condition that she actually sent for Doctor Haydock.

The whole of the village was terribly anxious to know what he thought of Miss Emily's claims to ill health, but naturally could not ask him. Satisfactory data came to hand on the subject, however, through Mr. Meek, the chemist's assistant, who was walking out with Clara, Mrs. Price-Ridley's maid. It was then known that Doctor Haydock had prescribed a mixture of asafetida and valerian which, according to Mr. Meek, was the stock remedy for malingerers in the army!

Soon afterward it was learned that Miss Emily, not relishing the medical attention she had had, was declaring that in the state of her health she felt it her duty to be near the specialist in London who understood her case. It was, she said, only fair to Lavinia.

The flat was put up for subletting.

· · ·

IT WAS A few days after that that Miss Marple, rather pink and flustered, called at the police station in Much Benham and asked for Inspector Slack.

Inspector Slack did not like Miss Marple. But he was aware that the chief constable, Colonel Melchett, did not share that opinion. Rather grudgingly, therefore, he received her.

"Good afternoon, Miss Marple, what can I do for you?"

"Oh, dear," said Miss Marple, "I'm afraid you're in a hurry."

"Lots of work on," said Inspector Slack, "but I can spare a few moments."

"Oh, dear," said Miss Marple. "I hope I shall be able to put what I say properly. So difficult, you know, to explain oneself, don't you think? No, perhaps you don't. But you see, not having been educated in the modern style—just a governess, you know, who taught one the dates of the kings of England and general knowledge— Doctor Brewer—three kinds of diseases of wheat—blight, mildew—now what was the third—was it smut?"

"Do you want to talk about smut?" asked Inspector Slack and then blushed.

"Oh, no, no." Miss Marple hastily disclaimed any wish to talk about smut. "Just an illustration, you know. And how needles are made, and all that. Discursive, you know, but not teaching one to keep to the point. Which is what I want to do. It's about Miss Skinner's maid, Gladys, you know."

"Mary Higgins," said Inspector Slack.

"Oh, yes, the second maid. But it's Gladys Holmes I mean— rather an impertinent girl and far too pleased with herself but really strictly honest, and it's so important that that should be recognized."

"No charge against her so far as I know," said the Inspector.

"No, I know there isn't a charge—but that makes it worse. Because, you see, people go on thinking things. Oh, dear—I knew I should explain badly. What I really mean is that the important thing is to find Mary Higgins."

"Certainly," said Inspector Slack. "Have you any ideas on the subject?"

"Well, as a matter of fact, I have," said Miss Marple. "May I ask you a question? Are fingerprints of no use to you?"

"Ah," said Inspector Slack, "that's where she was a bit too artful for us. Did most of her work in rubber gloves or housemaid's gloves, it seems. And she'd been careful—wiped off everything in her bedroom and on the sink. Couldn't find a single fingerprint in the place!"

"If you did have her fingerprints, would it help?"

"It might, madam. They may be known at the Yard. This isn't her first job, I'd say!"

Miss Marple nodded brightly. She opened her bag and extracted a small cardboard box. Inside it, wedged in cotton wool, was a small mirror.

"From my handbag," said Miss Marple. "The maid's prints are on it. I think they should be satisfactory—she touched an extremely sticky substance a moment previously."

Inspector Slack stared. "Did you get her fingerprints on purpose?"

"Of course."

"You suspected her then?"

"Well, you know it did strike me that she was a little too good to be true. I practically told Miss Lavinia so. But she simply wouldn't take the hint! I'm afraid, you know, Inspector, that I don't believe in paragons. Most of us have our faults—and domestic service shows them up very quickly!"

"Well," said Inspector Slack, recovering his balance, "I'm obliged to you, I'm sure. We'll send these up to the Yard and see what they have to say."

He stopped. Miss Marple had put her head a little on one side and was regarding him with a good deal of meaning.

"You wouldn't consider, I suppose, Inspector, looking a little nearer home?"

"What do you mean, Miss Marple?"

"It's very difficult to explain, but when you come across a peculiar thing you notice it. Although, often, peculiar things may be the merest trifles. I've felt that all along, you know; I mean about Gladys and the brooch. She's an honest girl; she didn't take that brooch. Then why did Miss Skinner think she did? Miss Skinner's not a fool;

far from it! Why was she so anxious to let a girl go who was a good servant when servants are hard to get? It was peculiar, you know. So I wondered. I wondered a good deal. And I noticed another peculiar thing! Miss Emily's a hypochondriac, but she's the first hypochondriac who hasn't sent for some doctor or other at once. Hypochondriacs love doctors. Miss Emily didn't!"

"What are you suggesting, Miss Marple?"

"Well, I'm suggesting, you know, that Miss Lavinia and Miss Emily are peculiar people. Miss Emily spends nearly all her time in a dark room. And if that hair of hers isn't a wig I—I'll eat my own back switch! And what I say is this—it's perfectly possible for a thin, pale, gray-haired, whining woman to be the same as a black-haired, rosy-cheeked, plump woman. And nobody that I can find ever saw Miss Emily and Mary Higgins at one and the same time.

"Plenty of time to get impressions of all the keys, plenty of time to find out all about the other tenants, and then—get rid of the local girl. Miss Emily takes a brisk walk across country one night and arrives at the station as Mary Higgins next day. And then, at the right moment, Mary Higgins disappears, and off goes the hue and cry after her. I'll tell you where you'll find her, Inspector. On Miss Emily Skinner's sofa! Get her fingerprints if you don't believe me, but you'll find I'm right! A couple of clever thieves, that's what the Skinners are—and no doubt in league with a clever post and rails or fence or whatever you call it. But they won't get away with it this time! I'm not going to have one of our village girl's character for honesty taken away like that! Gladys Holmes is as honest as the day, and everybody's going to know it! Good afternoon!"

Miss Marple had stalked out before Inspector Slack had recovered.

"Whew!" he muttered. "I wonder if she's right?"

He soon found out that Miss Marple was right again.

Colonel Melchett congratulated Slack on his efficiency, and Miss Marple had Gladys come to tea with Edna and spoke to her seriously on settling down in a good situation when she got one.

4. THE CASE OF THE CARETAKER

Well, demanded Doctor Haydock of his patient. "And how goes it today?"

Miss Marple smiled at him wanly from pillows.

"I suppose, really, that I'm better," she admitted, "but I feel so terribly depressed. I can't help feeling how much better it would have been if I had died. After all, I'm an old woman. Nobody wants me or cares about me."

Doctor Haydock interrupted with his usual brusqueness. "Yes, yes, typical afterreaction to this type of flu. What you need is something to take you out of yourself. A mental tonic."

Miss Marple sighed and shook her head.

"And what's more," continued Doctor Haydock, "I've brought my medicine with me!"

He tossed a long envelope onto the bed.

"Just the thing for you. The kind of puzzle that is right up your street."

"A puzzle?" Miss Marple looked interested.

"Literary effort of mine," said the doctor, blushing a little. "Tried to make a regular story of it. 'He said,' 'she said,' 'the girl thought,' etc. Facts of the story are true."

"But why a puzzle?" asked Miss Marple.

Doctor Haydock grinned. "Because the interpretation is up to you. I want to see if you're as clever as you always make out."

With that Parthian shot he departed.

Miss Marple picked up the manuscript and began to read.

"And where is the bride?" asked Miss Harmon genially.

The village was all agog to see the rich and beautiful young wife that Harry Laxton had brought back from abroad. There was a general indulgent feeling that Harry—wicked young scapegrace—had had all the luck. Everyone had always felt indulgent toward Harry. Even the owners of windows that had suffered from his indiscriminate use of a catapult had found their indignation dissipated by young Harry's abject expression of regret. He had broken windows, robbed orchards, poached rabbits, and later had run into debt, got entangled with the local tobacconist's daughter—been disentangled and sent off to Africa—and the village as represented by various aging spinsters had murmured indulgently, "Ah, well! Wild oats! He'll settle down!"

And now, sure enough, the prodigal had returned—not in affliction, but in triumph. Harry Laxton had "made good" as the saying goes. He had pulled himself together, worked hard, and had finally met and successfully wooed a young Anglo-French girl who was the possessor of a considerable fortune.

Harry might have lived in London, or purchased an estate in some fashionable hunting county, but he preferred to come back to the part of the world that was home to him. And there, in the most romantic way, he purchased the derelict estate in the dower house of which he had passed his childhood.

Kingsdean House had been unoccupied for nearly seventy years. It had gradually fallen into decay and abandon. An elderly caretaker and his wife lived in the one habitable corner of it. It was a vast, unprepossessing, grandiose mansion, the gardens overgrown with rank vegetation and the trees hemming it in like some gloomy enchanter's den.

The dower house was a pleasant, unpretentious house and had been let for a long term of years to Major Laxton, Harry's father. As a boy, Harry had roamed over the Kingsdean estate and knew every inch of the tangled woods, and the old house itself had always fascinated him.

Major Laxton had died some years ago, so it might have been thought that Harry would have had no ties to bring him back— nevertheless it was to the home of his boyhood that Harry brought his bride. The ruined old Kingsdean House was pulled down. An army of builders and contractors swooped down upon the place, and in almost a miraculously short space of time—so marvelously does wealth tell—the new house rose white and gleaming among the trees.

Next came a posse of gardeners and after them a procession of furniture vans.

The house was ready. Servants arrived. Lastly, a costly limousine deposited Harry and Mrs. Harry at the front door.

The village rushed to call, and Mrs. Price, who owned the largest house, and who considered herself to lead society in the place, sent out cards of invitation for a party "to meet the bride."

It was a great event. Several ladies had new frocks for the occasion. Everyone was excited, curious, anxious to see this fabulous creature. They said it was all so like a fairy story!

Miss Harmon, weather-beaten, hearty spinster, threw out her question as she squeezed her way through the crowded drawing-room door. Little Miss Brent, a thin, acidulated spinster, fluttered out information.

"Oh, my dear, quite charming. Such pretty manners. And quite young. Really, you know, it makes one feel quite envious to see someone who has everything like that. Good looks and money and breeding—most distinguished, nothing in the least common about her—and dear Harry so devoted!"

"Ah," said Miss Harmon, "it's early days yet!"

Miss Brent's thin nose quivered appreciatively. "Oh, my dear, do you really think—"

"We all know what Harry is," said Miss Harmon.

"We know what he was! But I expect now—"

"Ah," said Miss Harmon, "men are always the same. Once a gay deceiver, always a gay deceiver. I know them."

"Dear, dear. Poor young thing." Miss Brent looked much happier. "Yes, I expect she'll have trouble with him. Someone ought really to warn her. I wonder if she's heard anything of the old story?"

"It seems so very unfair," said Miss Brent, "that she should know nothing. So awkward. Especially with only the one chemist's shop in the village."

For the erstwhile tobacconist's daughter was now married to Mr. Edge, the chemist.

"It would be so much nicer," said Miss Brent, "if Mrs. Laxton were to deal with Boots in Much Benham."

"I daresay," said Miss Harmon, "that Harry Laxton will suggest that himself."

And again a significant look passed between them.

"But I certainly think," said Miss Harmon, "that she ought to know."

"BEASTS!" SAID CLARICE Vane indignantly to her uncle, Doctor Haydock. "Absolute beasts some people are."

He looked at her curiously.

She was a tall, dark girl, handsome, warmhearted and impulsive. Her big brown eyes were alight now with indignation as she said, "All these cats—saying things—hinting things."

"About Harry Laxton?"

"Yes, about his affair with the tobacconist's daughter."

"Oh, that!" The doctor shrugged his shoulders. "A great many young men have affairs of that kind."

"Of course they do. And it's all over. So why harp on it? And bring it up years after? It's like ghouls feasting on dead bodies."

"I daresay, my dear, it does seem like that to you. But you see, they have very little to talk about down here, and so I'm afraid they do tend to dwell upon past scandals. But I'm curious to know why it upsets you so much?"

Clarice Vane bit her lip and flushed. She said, in a curiously muffled voice, "They—they look so happy. The Laxtons, I mean.

They're young and in love, and it's all so lovely for them. I hate to think of it being spoiled by whispers and hints and innuendoes and general beastliness."

"H'm. I see."

Clarice went on. "He was talking to me just now. He's so happy and eager and excited and—yes, thrilled—at having got his heart's desire and rebuilt Kingsdean. He's like a child about it all. And she—well, I don't suppose anything has ever gone wrong in her whole life. She's always had everything. You've seen her. What did you think of her?"

The doctor did not answer at once. For other people, Louise Laxton might be an object of envy. A spoiled darling of fortune. To him she had brought only the refrain of a popular song heard many years ago, *Poor little rich girl—*

A small, delicate figure, with flaxen hair curled rather stiffly round her face and big, wistful blue eyes.

Louise was drooping a little. The long stream of congratulations had tired her. She was hoping it might soon be time to go. Perhaps, even now, Harry might say so. She looked at him sideways. So tall and broad-shouldered with his eager pleasure in this horrible, dull party.

Poor little rich girl—

"OOPH!" IT WAS a sigh of relief.

Harry turned to look at his wife amusedly. They were driving away from the party.

She said, "Darling, what a frightful party!"

Harry laughed. "Yes, pretty terrible. Never mind, my sweet. It had to be done, you know. All these old pussies knew me when I lived here as a boy. They'd have been terribly disappointed not to have got a good look at you close up."

Louise made a grimace. She said, "Shall we have to see a lot of them?"

"What? Oh, no. They'll come and make ceremonious calls with card cases, and you'll return the calls and then you needn't bother any more. You can have your own friends down or whatever you like."

Louise said, after a minute or two, "Isn't there anyone amusing living down here?"

"Oh, yes. There's the County, you know. Though you may find them a bit dull, too. Mostly interested in bulbs and dogs and horses. You'll ride, of course. You'll enjoy that. There's a horse over at Eglinton I'd like you to see. A beautiful animal, perfectly trained, no vice in him but plenty of spirit."

The car slowed down to take the turn into the gates of Kingsdean. Harry wrenched the wheel and swore as a grotesque figure sprang up in the middle of the road and he only just managed to avoid it. It stood there, shaking a fist and shouting after them.

Louise clutched his arm. "Who's that—that horrible old woman?"

Harry's brow was black. "That's old Murgatroyd. She and her husband were caretakers in the old house. They were there for nearly thirty years."

"Why does she shake her fist at you?"

Harry's face got red. "She—well, she resented the house being pulled down. And she got the sack, of course. Her husband's been dead two years. They say she got a bit queer after he died."

"Is she—she isn't—starving?"

Louise's ideas were vague and somewhat melodramatic. Riches prevented you coming into contact with reality.

Harry was outraged. "Good Lord, Louise, what an idea! I pensioned her off, of course—and handsomely, too! Found her a new cottage and everything."

Louise asked, bewildered, "Then why does she mind?"

Harry was frowning, his brows drawn together. "Oh, how should I know? Craziness! She loved the house."

"But it was a ruin, wasn't it?"

"Of course it was—crumbling to pieces—roof leaking—more or less unsafe. All the same I suppose it meant something to her. She's been there a long time. Oh, I don't know! The old devil's cracked, I think."

Louise said uneasily, "She—I think she cursed us. Oh, Harry, I wish she hadn't."

IT SEEMED TO Louise that her new home was tainted and poisoned by the malevolent figure of one crazy old woman. When she went out in the car, when she rode, when she walked out with the dogs, there was always the same figure waiting. Crouched down on herself, a battered hat over wisps of iron-gray hair, and the slow muttering of imprecations.

Louise came to believe that Harry was right—the old woman was mad. Nevertheless that did not make things easier. Mrs. Murgatroyd never actually came to the house, nor did she use definite threats, nor offer violence. Her squatting figure remained always just outside the gates. To appeal to the police would have been useless and, in any case, Harry Laxton was averse to that course of action. It would, he said, arouse local sympathy for the old brute. He took the matter more easily than Louise did.

"Don't worry about it, darling. She'll get tired of this silly cursing business. Probably she's only trying it on."

"She isn't, Harry. She—she hates us! I can feel it. She—she's ill-wishing us."

"She's not a witch, darling, although she may look like one! Don't be morbid about it all."

Louise was silent. Now that the first excitement of settling in was over, she felt curiously lonely and at a loose end. She had been used to life in London and the Riviera. She had no knowledge of or taste for English country life. She was ignorant of gardening, except for the final act of "doing the flowers." She did not really care for dogs. She was bored by such neighbors as she met. She enjoyed riding best, sometimes with Harry, sometimes, when he was busy about the estate, by herself. She hacked through the woods and lanes, enjoying the easy paces of the beautiful horse that Harry had bought for her. Yet even Prince Hal, most sensitive of chestnut steeds, was wont to shy and snort as he carried his mistress past that huddled figure of a malevolent old woman.

One day Louise took her courage in both hands. She was out walking. She had passed Mrs. Murgatroyd, pretending not to notice her, but suddenly she swerved back and went right up to her. She said, a little breathlessly, "What is it? What's the matter? What do you want?"

The old woman blinked at her. She had a cunning, dark gypsy face, with wisps of iron-gray hair, and bleared, suspicious eyes. Louise wondered if she drank.

She spoke in a whining and yet threatening voice. "What do I want, you ask? What, indeed! That which has been took away from me. Who turned me out of Kingsdean House? I'd lived there, girl and woman, for near on forty years. It was a black deed to turn me out and it's black bad luck it'll bring to you and him!"

Louise said, "You've got a very nice cottage and—"

She broke off. The old woman's arms flew up. She screamed, "What's the good of that to me? It's my own place I want and my own fire as I sat beside all them years. And as for you and him, I'm telling you there will be no happiness for you in your new fine house. It's the black sorrow will be upon you! Sorrow and death and my curse. May your fair face rot."

Louise turned away and broke into a little stumbling run. She thought, *I must get away from here! We must sell the house! We must go away.*

At the moment, such a solution seemed easy to her. But Harry's utter incomprehension took her aback. He exclaimed, "Leave here? Sell the house? Because of a crazy old woman's threats? You must be mad."

"No, I'm not. But she—she frightens me. I know something will happen."

Harry Luxton said grimly, "Leave Mrs. Murgatroyd to me. I'll settle her!"

. . .

A FRIENDSHIP HAD sprung up between Clarice Vane and young Mrs. Laxton. The two girls were much of an age, though dissimilar both in character and in tastes. In Clarice's company, Louise found reassurance. Clarice was so self-reliant, so sure of herself. Louise mentioned the matter of Mrs. Murgatroyd and her threats, but Clarice seemed to regard the matter as more annoying than frightening.

"It's so stupid, that sort of thing," she said. "And really very annoying for you."

"You know, Clarice, I—I feel quite frightened sometimes. My heart gives the most awful jumps."

"Nonsense, you mustn't let a silly thing like that get you down. She'll soon tire of it."

She was silent for a minute or two. Clarice said, "What's the matter?"

Louise paused for a minute, then her answer came with a rush. "I hate this place! I hate being here. The woods and this house, and the awful silence at night, and the queer noise owls make. Oh, and the people and everything."

"The people. What people?"

"The people in the village. Those prying, gossiping old maids."

Clarice said sharply, "What have they been saying?"

"I don't know. Nothing particular. But they've got nasty minds. When you've talked to them you feel you wouldn't trust anybody— not anybody at all."

Clarice said harshly, "Forget them. They've nothing to do but gossip. And most of the muck they talk they just invent."

Louise said, "I wish we'd never come here. But Harry adores it so." Her voice softened.

Clarice thought, *How she adores him.* She said abruptly, "I must go now."

"I'll send you back in the car. Come again soon."

Clarice nodded. Louise felt comforted by her new friend's visit.

Harry was pleased to find her more cheerful and from then on urged her to have Clarice often to the house.

Then one day he said, "Good news for you, darling."

"Oh, what?"

"I've fixed the Murgatroyd. She's got a son in America, you know. Well, I've arranged for her to go out and join him. I'll pay her passage."

"Oh, Harry, how wonderful. I believe I might get to like Kingsdean after all."

"Get to like it? Why, it's the most wonderful place in the world!"

Louise gave a little shiver. She could not rid herself of her superstitious fear so easily.

IF THE LADIES of St. Mary Mead had hoped for the pleasure of imparting information about her husband's past to the bride, this pleasure was denied them by Harry Laxton's own prompt action.

Miss Harmon and Clarice Vane were both in Mr. Edge's shop, the one buying mothballs and the other a packet of boracic, when Harry Laxton and his wife came in.

After greeting the two ladies, Harry turned to the counter and was just demanding a toothbrush when he stopped in mid-speech and exclaimed heartily, "Well, well, just see who's here! Bella, I do declare."

Mrs. Edge, who had hurried out from the back parlor to attend to the congestion of business, beamed back cheerfully at him, showing her big white teeth. She had been a dark, handsome girl and was still a reasonably handsome woman, though she had put on weight, and the lines of her face had coarsened; but her large brown eyes were full of warmth as she answered, "Bella, it is, Mr. Harry, and pleased to see you after all these years."

Harry turned to his wife. "Bella's an old flame of mine, Louise," he said. "Head-over-ears in love with her, wasn't I, Bella?"

"That's what you say," said Mrs. Edge.

Louise laughed. She said, "My husband's very happy seeing all his old friends again."

"Ah," said Mrs. Edge, "we haven't forgotten you, Mr. Harry. Seems like a fairy tale to think of you married and building up a new house instead of that ruined old Kingsdean House."

"You look very well and blooming," said Harry, and Mrs. Edge laughed and said there was nothing wrong with her and what about that toothbrush?

Clarice, watching the baffled look on Miss Harmon's face, said to herself exultantly, *Oh, well done, Harry. You've spiked their guns.*

DOCTOR HAYDOCK SAID abruptly to his niece, "What's all this nonsense about old Mrs. Murgatroyd hanging about Kingsdean and shaking her fist and cursing the new regime?"

"It isn't nonsense. It's quite true. It's upset Louise a good deal."

"Tell her she needn't worry—when the Murgatroyds were care-takers they never stopped grumbling about the place—they only stayed because Murgatroyd drank and couldn't get another job."

"I'll tell her," said Clarice doubtfully, "but I don't think she'll be-lieve you. The old woman fairly screams with rage."

"Always used to be fond of Harry as a boy. I can't understand it."

Clarice said, "Oh, well—they'll be rid of her soon. Harry's pay-ing her passage to America."

Three days later, Louise was thrown from her horse and killed.

Two men in a baker's van were witnesses of the accident. They saw Louise ride out of the gates, saw the old woman spring up and stand in the road waving her arms and shouting, saw the horse start, swerve, and then bolt madly down the road, flinging Louise Laxton over his head.

One of them stood over the unconscious figure, not knowing what to do, while the other rushed to the house to get help.

Harry Laxton came running out, his face ghastly. They took off a door of the van and carried her on it to the house. She died without regaining consciousness and before the doctor arrived.

(End of Doctor Haydock's manuscript.)

. . .

WHEN DOCTOR HAYDOCK arrived the following day, he was pleased to note that there was a pink flush in Miss Marple's cheek and decidedly more animation in her manner.

"Well," he said, "what's the verdict?"

"What's the problem, Doctor Haydock?" countered Miss Marple.

"Oh, my dear lady, do I have to tell you that?"

"I suppose," said Miss Marple, "that it's the curious conduct of the caretaker. Why did she behave in that very odd way? People do mind being turned out of their old homes. But it wasn't her home. In fact, she used to complain and grumble while she was there. Yes, it certainly looks very fishy. What became of her, by the way?"

"Did a bunk to Liverpool. The accident scared her. Thought she'd wait there for her boat."

"All very convenient for somebody," said Miss Marple. "Yes, I think the 'Problem of the Caretaker's Conduct' can be solved easily enough. Bribery, was it not?"

"That's your solution?"

"Well, if it wasn't natural for her to behave in that way, she must have been 'putting on an act' as people say, and that means that somebody paid her to do what she did."

"And you know who that somebody was?"

"Oh, I think so. Money again, I'm afraid. And I've always noticed that gentlemen always tend to admire the same type."

"Now I'm out of my depth."

"No, no, it all hangs together. Harry Laxton admired Bella Edge, a dark, vivacious type. Your niece Clarice was the same. But the poor little wife was quite a different type—fair-haired and clinging—not his type at all. So he must have married her for her money. And murdered her for her money, too!"

"You use the word 'murder'?"

"Well, he sounds the right type. Attractive to women and quite unscrupulous. I suppose he wanted to keep his wife's money and marry your niece. He may have been seen talking to Mrs. Edge. But I don't fancy he was attached to her any more. Though I daresay he made the poor woman think he was, for ends of his own. He soon had her well under his thumb, I fancy."

"How exactly did he murder her, do you think?"

Miss Marple stared ahead of her for some minutes with dreamy blue eyes.

"It was very well timed—with the baker's van as witness. They could see the old woman and, of course, they'd put down the horse's fright to that. But I should imagine, myself, that an air gun, or perhaps a catapult—he used to be good with a catapult. Yes, just as the horse came through the gates. The horse bolted, of course, and Mrs. Laxton was thrown."

She paused, frowning.

"The fall might have killed her. But he couldn't be sure of that. And he seems the sort of man who would lay his plans carefully and leave nothing to chance. After all, Mrs. Edge could get him something suitable without her husband knowing. Otherwise, why would Harry bother with her? Yes, I think he had some powerful drug handy, that could be administered before you arrived. After all, if a woman is thrown from her horse and has serious injuries and dies without recovering consciousness, well—a doctor wouldn't normally be suspicious, would he? He'd put it down to shock or something."

Doctor Haydock nodded.

"Why did you suspect?" asked Miss Marple.

"It wasn't any particular cleverness on my part," said Doctor Haydock. "It was just the trite, well-known fact that a murderer is so pleased with his cleverness that he doesn't take proper precautions. I was just saying a few consolatory words to the bereaved husband—and feeling damned sorry for the fellow, too—when he flung himself down on the settee to do a bit of play-acting and a hypodermic syringe fell out of his pocket.

"He snatched it up and looked so scared that I began to think. Harry Laxton didn't drug; he was in perfect health; what was he doing with a hypodermic syringe? I did the autopsy with a view to certain possibilities. I found strophanthin. The rest was easy. There was strophanthin in Laxton's possession, and Bella Edge, questioned by the police, broke down and admitted to having got it for him. And finally old Mrs. Murgatroyd confessed that it was Harry Laxton who had put her up to the cursing stunt."

"And your niece got over it?"

"Yes, she was attracted by the fellow, but it hadn't gone far."

The doctor picked up his manuscript.

"Full marks to you, Miss Marple—and full marks to me for my prescription. You're looking almost yourself again."

5. GREENSHAW'S FOLLY

The two men rounded the corner of the shrubbery. "Well, there you are," said Raymond West. "That's it."

Horace Bindler took a deep, appreciative breath.

"But my dear," he cried, "how wonderful." His voice rose in a high screech of esthetic delight, then deepened in reverent awe. "It's unbelievable. Out of this world! A period piece of the best."

"I thought you'd like it," said Raymond West, complacently.

"Like it? My dear—" Words failed Horace. He unbuckled the strap of his camera and got busy. "This will be one of the gems of my collection," he said happily. "I do think, don't you, that it's rather amusing to have a collection of monstrosities? The idea came to me one night seven years ago in my bath. My last real gem was in the Campo Santo at Genoa, but I really think this beats it. What's it called?"

"I haven't the least idea," said Raymond.

"I suppose it's got a name?"

"It must have. But the fact is that it's never referred to round here as anything but Greenshaw's Folly."

"Greenshaw being the man who built it?"

"Yes. In 1860 or '70 or thereabouts. The local success story of the time. Barefoot boy who had risen to immense prosperity. Local opinion is divided as to why he built this house, whether it was sheer exuberance of wealth or whether it was done to impress his creditors. If the latter, it didn't impress them. He either went bankrupt or the next thing to it. Hence the name, Greenshaw's Folly."

Horace's camera clicked. "There," he said in a satisfied voice. "Remind me to show you Number 310 in my collection. A really incredible marble mantelpiece in the Italian manner." He added, looking at the house, "I can't conceive of how Mr. Greenshaw thought of it all."

"Rather obvious in some ways," said Raymond. "He had visited the *châteaux* of the Loire, don't you think? Those turrets. And then, rather unfortunately, he seems to have traveled in the Orient. The influence of the Taj Mahal is unmistakable. I rather like the Moorish wing," he added, "and the traces of a Venetian palace."

"One wonders how he ever got hold of an architect to carry out these ideas."

Raymond shrugged his shoulders.

"No difficulty about that, I expect," he said. "Probably the architect retired with a good income for life while poor old Greenshaw went bankrupt."

"Could we look at it from the other side?" asked Horace, "or are we trespassing?"

"We're trespassing all right," said Raymond, "but I don't think it will matter."

He turned toward the corner of the house and Horace skipped after him.

"But who lives here, my dear? Orphans or holiday visitors? It can't be a school. No playing fields or brisk efficiency."

"Oh, a Greenshaw lives here still," said Raymond over his shoulder. "The house itself didn't go in the crash. Old Greenshaw's son inherited it. He was a bit of a miser and lived here in a corner of it. Never spent a penny. Probably never had a penny to spend. His daughter lives here now. Old lady—very eccentric."

As he spoke Raymond was congratulating himself on having thought of Greenshaw's Folly as a means of entertaining his guest.

These literary critics always professed themselves as longing for a weekend in the country, and were wont to find the country extremely boring when they got there. Tomorrow there would be the Sunday papers, and for today Raymond West congratulated himself on suggesting a visit to Greenshaw's Folly to enrich Horace Bindler's well-known collection of monstrosities.

They turned the corner of the house and came out on a neglected lawn. In one corner of it was a large artificial rockery, and bending over it was a figure at the sight of which Horace clutched Raymond delightedly by the arm.

"My dear," he exclaimed, "do you see what she's got on? A sprigged print dress. Just like a housemaid—when there were housemaids. One of my most cherished memories is staying at a house in the country when I was quite a boy where a real housemaid called you in the morning, all crackling in a print dress and a cap. Yes, my boy, *really*—a cap. Muslin with streamers. No, perhaps it was the parlormaid who had the streamers. But anyway she was a real housemaid and she brought in an enormous brass can of hot water. What an exciting day we're having."

The figure in the print dress had straightened up and turned toward them, trowel in hand. She was a sufficiently startling figure. Unkempt locks of irongrey fell wispily on her shoulders and a straw hat, rather like the hats that horses wear in Italy, was crammed down on her head. The colored print dress she wore fell nearly to her ankles. Out of a weatherbeaten, not too clean face, shrewd eyes surveyed them appraisingly.

"I must apologize for trespassing, Miss Greenshaw," said Raymond West, as he advanced toward her, "but Mr. Horace Bindler who is staying with me—"

Horace bowed and removed his hat.

"—is most interested in—er—ancient history and—er—fine buildings."

Raymond West spoke with the ease of a famous author who knows that he is a celebrity, that he can venture where other people may not.

Miss Greenshaw looked up at the sprawling exuberance behind her.

"It *is* a fine house," she said appreciatively. "My grandfather built it—before my time, of course. He is reported as having said that he wished to astonish the natives."

"I'll say he did that, ma'am," said Horace Bindler.

"Mr. Bindler is the well-known literary critic," said Raymond West.

Miss Greenshaw had clearly no reverence for literary critics. She remained unimpressed.

"I consider it," said Miss Greenshaw, referring to the house, "as a monument to my grandfather's genius. Silly fools come here and ask me why I don't sell it and go and live in a flat. What would I do in a flat? It's my home and I live in it," said Miss Greenshaw. "Always have lived here." She considered, brooding over the past. "There were three of us. Laura married the curate. Papa wouldn't give her any money, said clergymen ought to be unworldly. She died, having a baby. Baby died, too. Nettie ran away with the riding master. Papa cut her out of his will, of course. Handsome fellow, Harry Fletcher, but no good. Don't think Nettie was happy with him. Anyway, she didn't live long. They had a son. He writes to me sometimes, but of course he isn't a Greenshaw. I'm the last of the Greenshaws." She drew up her bent shoulders with a certain pride, and readjusted the rakish angle of the straw hat. Then, turning, she said sharply:

"Yes, Mrs. Cresswell, what is it?"

Approaching them from the house was a figure that, seen side by side with Miss Greenshaw, seemed ludicrously dissimilar. Mrs. Cresswell had a marvelously dressed head of well-blued hair towering upward in meticulously arranged curls and rolls. It was as though she had dressed her head to go as a French marquise to a fancy dress party. The rest of her middle-aged person was dressed in what ought to have been rustling black silk but was actually one of the shinier varieties of black rayon. Although she was not a large woman, she had a well-developed and sumptuous bosom. Her voice, when she spoke, was unexpectedly deep. She spoke with exquisite diction—only a slight hesitation over words beginning with "h" and the final pronunciation of them with an exaggerated aspirate gave rise to a suspicion that at some remote period in her youth she might have had trouble over dropping her h's.

"The fish, madam," said Mrs. Cresswell, "the slice of cod. It has not arrived. I have asked Alfred to go down for it and he refuses."

Rather unexpectedly, Miss Greenshaw gave a cackle of laughter.

"Refuses, does he?"

"Alfred, madam, has been most disobliging."

Miss Greenshaw raised two earth-stained fingers to her lips, suddenly produced an ear-splitting whistle and at the same time yelled, "Alfred. Alfred, come here."

Round the corner of the house a young man appeared in answer to the summons, carrying a spade in his hand. He had a bold, handsome face and as he drew near he cast an unmistakably malevolent glance toward Mrs. Cresswell.

"You wanted me, miss?" he said.

"Yes, Alfred. I hear you've refused to go down for the fish. What about it, eh?"

Alfred spoke in a surly voice.

"I'll go down for it if you wants it, miss. You've only got to say."

"I do want it. I want it for my supper."

"Right you are, miss. I'll go right away."

He threw an insolent glance at Mrs. Cresswell, who flushed and murmured below her breath.

"Now that I think of it," said Miss Greenshaw, "a couple of strange visitors are just what we need, aren't they, Mrs. Cresswell?"

Mrs. Cresswell looked puzzled.

"I'm sorry, madam—"

"For you-know-what," said Miss Greenshaw, nodding her head. "Beneficiary to a will mustn't witness it. That's right, isn't it?" She appealed to Raymond West.

"Quite correct," said Raymond.

"I know enough law to know that," said Miss Greenshaw, "and you two are men of standing."

She flung down the trowel on her weeding basket.

"Would you mind coming up to the library with me?"

"Delighted," said Horace eagerly.

She led the way through French windows and through a vast yellow and gold drawing-room with faded brocade on the walls and dust covers arranged over the furniture, then through a large dim hall, up a staircase, and into a room on the second floor.

"My grandfather's library," she announced.

Horace looked round with acute pleasure. It was a room from his point of view quite full of monstrosities. The heads of sphinxes appeared on the most unlikely pieces of furniture, there was a colossal bronze representing, he thought, Paul and Virginia, and a vast bronze clock with classical motifs of which he longed to take a photograph.

"A fine lot of books," said Miss Greenshaw.

Raymond was already looking at the books. From what he could see from a cursory glance there was no book here of any real interest or, indeed, any book which appeared to have been read. They were all superbly bound sets of the classics as supplied ninety years ago for furnishing a gentleman's library. Some novels of a bygone period were included. But they too showed little signs of having been read.

Miss Greenshaw was fumbling in the drawers of a vast desk. Finally she pulled out a parchment document.

"My will," she explained. "Got to leave your money to someone—or so they say. If I died without a will, I suppose that son of a horse coper would get it. Handsome fellow, Harry Fletcher, but a rogue if ever there was one. Don't see why *his* son should inherit this place. No," she went on, as though answering some unspoken objection, "I've made up my mind. I'm leaving it to Cresswell."

"Your housekeeper?"

"Yes. I've explained it to her. I make a will leaving her all I've got and then I don't need to pay her any wages. Saves me a lot in current expenses, and it keeps her up to the mark. No giving me notice and walking off at any minute. Very la-di-dah and all that, isn't she? But her father was a working plumber in a very small way. *She's* nothing to give herself airs about."

By now Miss Greenshaw had unfolded the parchment. Picking

up a pen, she dipped it in the inkstand and wrote her signature, *Katherine Dorothy Greenshaw*.

"That's right," she said. "You've seen me sign it, and then you two sign it, and that makes it legal."

She handed the pen to Raymond West. He hesitated a moment, feeling an unexpected repulsion to what he was asked to do. Then he quickly scrawled his well-known autograph, for which his morning's mail usually brought at least six requests.

Horace took the pen from him and added his own minute signature.

"That's done," said Miss Greenshaw.

She moved across to the bookcases and stood looking at them uncertainly, then she opened a glass door, took out a book, and slipped the folded parchment inside.

"I've my own places for keeping things," she said.

"*Lady Audley's Secret*," Raymond West remarked, catching sight of the title as she replaced the book.

Miss Greenshaw gave another cackle of laughter.

"Bestseller in its day," she remarked. "But not like your books, eh?"

She gave Raymond a sudden friendly nudge in the ribs. Raymond was rather surprised that she even knew he wrote books. Although Raymond West was a "big name" in literature, he could hardly be described as a bestseller. Though softening a little with the advent of middle-age, his books dealt bleakly with the sordid side of life.

"I wonder," Horace demanded breathlessly, "if I might just take a photograph of the clock."

"By all means," said Miss Greenshaw. "It came, I believe, from the Paris Exhibition."

"Very probably," said Horace. He took his picture.

"This room's not been used much since my grandfather's time," said Miss Greenshaw. "This desk's full of old diaries of his. Interesting, I should think. I haven't the eyesight to read them myself. I'd like to get them published, but I suppose one would have to work on them a good deal."

"You could engage someone to do that," said Raymond West.

"Could I really? It's an idea, you know. I'll think about it."

Raymond West glanced at his watch.

"We mustn't trespass on your kindness any longer," he said.

"Pleased to have seen you," said Miss Greenshaw graciously. "Thought you were the policeman when I heard you coming round the corner of the house."

"Why a policeman?" demanded Horace, who never minded asking questions.

Miss Greenshaw responded unexpectedly.

"If you want to know the time, ask a policeman," she carolled, and with this example of Victorian wit she nudged Horace in the ribs and roared with laughter.

"It's been a wonderful afternoon," sighed Horace as they walked home. "Really, that place has *everything*. The only thing the library needs is a body. Those old-fashioned detective stories about murder in the library—that's just the kind of library I'm sure the authors had in mind."

"If you want to discuss murder," said Raymond, "you must talk to my Aunt Jane."

"Your Aunt Jane? Do you mean Miss Marple?" Horace felt a little at a loss.

The charming old-world lady to whom he had been introduced the night before seemed the last person to be mentioned in connection with murder.

"Oh, yes," said Raymond. "Murder is a specialty of hers."

"But my dear, how intriguing! What do you really mean?"

"I mean just that," said Raymond. He paraphrased: "Some commit murder, some get mixed up in murders, others have murder thrust upon them. My Aunt Jane comes into the third category."

"You are joking."

"Not in the least. I can refer you to the former Commissioner of Scotland Yard, several Chief Constables, and one or two hardworking inspectors of the C.I.D."

Horace said happily that wonders would never cease. Over the tea table they gave Joan West, Raymond's wife, Louise Oxley, her niece, and old Miss Marple, a résumé of the afternoon's happen-

656 MISS JANE MARPLE

ings, recounting in detail everything that Miss Greenshaw had said to them.

"But I do think," said Horace, "that there is something a little *sinister* about the whole setup. That duchess-like creature, the housekeeper—arsenic, perhaps, in the teapot, now that she knows her mistress has made the will in her favor?"

"Tell us, Aunt Jane," said Raymond. "Will there be murder or won't there? What do *you* think?"

"I think," said Miss Marple, winding up her wool with a rather severe air, "that you shouldn't joke about these things as much as you do, Raymond. Arsenic is, of course, *quite* a possibility. So easy to obtain. Probably present in the tool shed already in the form of weed killer."

"Oh, really, darling," said Joan West, affectionately. "Wouldn't that be rather too obvious?"

"It's all very well to make a will," said Raymond. "I don't suppose the poor old thing has anything to leave except that awful white elephant of a house, and who would want that?"

"A film company possibly," said Horace, "or a hotel or an institution?"

"They'd expect to buy it for a song," said Raymond, but Miss Marple was shaking her head.

"You know, dear Raymond, I cannot agree with you there. About the money, I mean. The grandfather was evidently one of those lavish spenders who make money easily but can't keep it. He may have gone broke, as you say, but hardly bankrupt or else his son would not have had the house. Now the son, as is so often the case, was of an entirely different character from his father. A miser. A man who saved every penny. I should say that in the course of his lifetime he probably put by a very good sum. This Miss Greenshaw appears to have taken after him—to dislike spending money, that is. Yes, I should think it quite likely that she has quite a substantial sum tucked away."

"In that case," said Joan West, "I wonder now—what about Louise?"

They looked at Louise as she sat, silent, by the fire.

Louise was Joan West's niece. Her marriage had recently, as she herself put it, come unstuck, leaving her with two young children and a bare sufficiency of money to keep them on.

"I mean," said Joan, "if this Miss Greenshaw really wants someone to go through diaries and get a book ready for publication . . ."

"It's an idea," said Raymond.

Louise said in a low voice, "It's work I could do—and I think I'd enjoy it."

"I'll write to her," said Raymond.

"I wonder," said Miss Marple thoughtfully, "what the old lady meant by that remark about a policeman?"

"Oh, it was just a joke."

"It reminded me," said Miss Marple, nodding her head vigorously, "yes, it reminded me very much of Mr. Naysmith."

"Who was Mr. Naysmith?" asked Raymond, curiously.

"He kept bees," said Miss Marple, "and was very good at doing the acrostics in the Sunday papers. And he liked giving people false impressions just for fun. But sometimes it led to trouble."

Everybody was silent for a moment, considering Mr. Naysmith, but as there did not seem to be any points of resemblance between him and Miss Greenshaw, they decided that dear Aunt Jane was perhaps getting a *little* bit disconnected in her old age.

HORACE BINDLER WENT back to London without having collected any more monstrosities and Raymond West wrote a letter to Miss Greenshaw telling her that he kew of a Mrs. Louise Oxley who would be competent to undertake work on the diaries. After a lapse of some days a letter arrived, written in spidery old-fashioned handwriting, in which Miss Greenshaw declared herself anxious to avail herself of the services of Mrs. Oxley, and making an appointment for Mrs. Oxley to come and see her.

Louise duly kept the appointment, generous terms were arranged, and she started work the following day.

"I'm awfully grateful to you," she said to Raymond. "It will fit in beautifully. I can take the children to school, go on to Greenshaw's Folly, and pick them up on my way back. How fantastic the whole setup is! That old woman has to be seen to be believed."

On the evening of her first day at work she returned and described her day.

"I've hardly seen the housekeeper," she said. "She came in with coffee and biscuits at half-past eleven with her mouth pursed up very prunes and prisms, and would hardly speak to me. I think she disapproves deeply of my having been engaged." She went on, "It seems there's quite a feud between her and the gardener, Alfred. He's a local boy and fairly lazy, I should imagine, and he and the housekeeper won't speak to each other. Miss Greenshaw said in her rather grand way, 'There have always been feuds as far as I can remember between the garden and the house staff. It was so in my grandfather's time. There were three men and a boy in the garden then, and eight maids in the house, but there was always friction.'"

On the next day Louise returned with another piece of news.

"Just fancy," she said, "I was asked to ring up the nephew today."

"Miss Greenshaw's nephew?"

"Yes. It seems he's an actor playing in the stock company that's doing a summer season at Boreham-on-Sea. I rang up the theater and left a message asking him to lunch tomorrow. Rather fun, really. The old girl didn't want the housekeeper to know. I think Mrs. Cresswell has done something that's annoyed her."

"Tomorrow another installment of this thrilling serial," murmured Raymond.

"It's exactly like a serial, isn't it? Reconciliation with the nephew, blood is thicker than water—another will to be made and the old will destroyed.

"Aunt Jane, you're looking very serious."

"Was I, my dear? Have you heard any more about the policeman?"

Louise looked bewildered. "I don't know anything about a policeman."

"That remark of hers, my dear," said Miss Marple, "must have meant something."

Louise arrived at her work the following day in a cheerful mood. She passed through the open front door—the doors and windows of the house were always open. Miss Greenshaw appeared to have no fear of burglars, and was probably justified, as most things in the house weighed several tons and were of no marketable value.

Louise had passed Alfred in the drive. When she first noticed him he had been leaning against a tree smoking a cigarette, but as soon as he had caught sight of her he had seized a broom and begun diligently to sweep leaves. An idle young man, she thought, but good-looking. His features reminded her of someone. As she passed through the hall on her way upstairs to the library, she glanced at the large picture of Nathaniel Greenshaw which presided over the mantelpiece, showing him in the acme of Victorian prosperity, leaning back in a large armchair, his hands resting on the gold Albert across his capacious stomach. As her glance swept up from the stomach to the face with its heavy jowls, its bushy eyebrows and its flourishing black mustache, the thought occurred to her that Nathaniel Greenshaw must have been handsome as a young man. He had looked, perhaps, a little like Alfred . . .

She went into the library on the second floor, shut the door behind her, opened her typewriter, and got out the diaries from the drawer at the side of her desk. Through the open window she caught a glimpse of Miss Greenshaw below, in a puce-colored sprigged print, bending over the rockery, weeding assiduously. They had had two wet days, of which the weeds had taken full advantage.

Louise, a town-bred girl, decided that if she ever had a garden it would never contain a rockery which needed weeding by hand. Then she settled down to her work.

When Mrs. Cresswell entered the library with the coffee tray at half-past eleven, she was clearly in a very bad temper. She banged the tray down on the table and observed to the universe:

"Company for lunch—and nothing in the house! What am I supposed to do, I should like to know? And no sign of Alfred."

"He was sweeping in the drive when I got here," Louise offered.

"I daresay. A nice soft job."

Mrs. Cresswell swept out of the room, slamming the door behind her. Louise grinned to herself. She wondered what "the nephew" would be like.

She finished her coffee and settled down to her work again. It was so absorbing that time passed quickly. Nathaniel Greenshaw, when he started to keep a diary, had succumbed to the pleasures of frankness. Typing out a passage relating to the personal charms of a barmaid in the neighboring town, Louise reflected that a good deal of editing would be necessary.

As she was thinking this, she was startled by a scream from the garden. Jumping up, she ran to the open window. Below her Miss Greenshaw was staggering away from the rockery toward the house. Her hands were clasped to her breast and between her hands there protruded a feathered shaft that Louise recognized with stupefaction to be the shaft of an arrow.

Miss Greenshaw's head, in its battered straw hat, fell forward on her breast. She called up to Louise in a failing voice: ". . . shot . . . he shot me . . . with an arrow . . . get help . . ."

Louise rushed to the door. She turned the handle, but the door would not open. It took her a moment or two of futile endeavor to realize that she was locked in. She ran back to the window and called down.

"I'm locked in!"

Miss Greenshaw, her back toward Louise and swaying a little on her feet, was calling up to the housekeeper at a window farther along.

"Ring police . . . telephone . . ."

Then, lurching from side to side like a drunkard, Miss Greenshaw disappeared from Louise's view through the window and staggered into the drawing-room on the ground floor. A moment later Louise heard a crash of broken china, a heavy fall, and then silence. Her imagination reconstructed the scene. Miss Greenshaw must have stumbled blindly into a small table with a Sèvres tea set on it.

Desperately Louise pounded on the library door, calling and shouting. There was no creeper or drainpipe outside the window that could help her to get out that way.

Tired at last of beating on the door, Louise returned to the window. From the window of her sitting-room farther along, the housekeeper's head appeared.

"Come and let me out, Mrs. Oxley. I'm locked in."

"So am I."

"Oh, dear, isn't it awful? I've telephoned the police. There's an extension in this room, but what I can't understand, Mrs. Oxley, is our being locked in. I never heard a key turn, did you?"

"No. I didn't hear anything at all. Oh, dear, what shall we do? Perhaps Alfred might hear us." Louise shouted at the top of her voice, "Alfred, Alfred."

"Gone to his dinner as likely as not. What time is it?"

Louise glanced at her watch.

"Twenty-five past twelve."

"He's not supposed to go until half-past, but he sneaks off earlier whenever he can."

"Do you think—do you think—"

Louise meant to ask "Do you think she's dead?"—but the words stuck in her throat.

There was nothing to do but wait. She sat down on the window sill. It seemed an eternity before the stolid helmeted figure of a police constable came round the corner of the house. She leaned out of the window and he looked up at her, shading his eyes with his hand.

"What's going on here?" he demanded.

From their respective windows, Louise and Mrs. Cresswell poured a flood of excited information down on him.

The constable produced a notebook and a pencil. "You ladies ran upstairs and locked yourselves in? Can I have your names, please?"

"Somebody locked us in. Come and let us out."

The constable said reprovingly, "All in good time," and disappeared through the French window below.

Once again time seemed infinite. Louise heard the sound of a car arriving, and, after what seemed an hour, but was actually only three minutes, first Mrs. Cresswell and then Louise were released by a police sergeant more alert than the original constable.

"Miss Greenshaw?" Louise's voice faltered. "What—what's happened?"

The sergeant cleared his throat.

"I'm sorry to have to tell you, madam," he said, "what I've already told Mrs. Cresswell here. Miss Greenshaw is dead."

"Murdered," said Mrs. Cresswell. "That's what it is—murder."

The sergeant said dubiously, "Could have been an accident—some country lads shooting arrows."

Again there was the sound of a car arriving.

The sergeant said, "That'll be the M.O." and he started downstairs.

But it was not the M.O. As Louise and Mrs. Cresswell came down the stairs, a young man stepped hesitatingly through the front door and paused, looking round him with a somewhat bewildered air.

Then, speaking in a pleasant voice that in some way seemed familiar to Louise—perhaps it reminded her of Miss Greenshaw's—he asked, "Excuse me, does—er—does Miss Greenshaw live here?"

"May I have your name if you please," said the sergeant, advancing upon him.

"Fletcher," said the young man. "Nat Fletcher. I'm Miss Greenshaw's nephew, as a matter of fact."

"Indeed, sir, well—I'm sorry—"

"Has anything happened?" asked Nat Fletcher.

"There's been an—accident. Your aunt was shot with an arrow—penetrated the jugular vein—"

Mrs. Cresswell spoke hysterically and without her usual refinement: "Your h'aunt's been murdered, that's what's 'appened. Your h'aunt's been murdered."

INSPECTOR WELCH DREW his chair a little nearer to the table and let his gaze wander from one to the other of the four people in the room. It was evening of the same day. He had called at the Wests' house to take Louise Oxley once more over her statement.

"You are sure of the exact words? *Shot—he shot me—with an arrow—get help?*"

Louise nodded.

"And the time?"

"I looked at my watch a minute or two later—it was then 12:25—"

"Your watch keeps good time?"

"I looked at the clock as well." Louise left no doubt of her accuracy.

The Inspector turned to Raymond West.

"It appears, sir, that about a week ago you and a Mr. Horace Bindler were witnesses to Miss Greenshaw's will?"

Briefly, Raymond recounted the events of the afternoon visit he and Horace Bindler had paid to Greenshaw's Folly.

"This testimony of yours may be important," said Welch. "Miss Greenshaw distinctly told you, did she, that her will was being made in favor of Mrs. Cresswell, the housekeeper, and that she was not paying Mrs. Cresswell any wages in view of the expectations Mrs. Cresswell had of profiting by her death?"

"That is what she told me—yes."

"Would you say that Mrs. Cresswell was definitely aware of these facts?"

"I should say undoubtedly. Miss Greenshaw made a reference in my presence to beneficiaries not being able to witness a will and Mrs. Cresswell clearly understood what she meant by it. Moreover, Miss Greenshaw herself told me that she had come to this arrangement with Mrs. Cresswell."

"So Mrs. Cresswell had reason to believe she was an interested party. Motive clear enough in her case, and I daresay she'd be our chief suspect now if it wasn't for the fact that she was securely locked in her room like Mrs. Oxley here, and also that Miss Greenshaw definitely said a *man* shot her—"

"She definitely *was* locked in her room?"

"Oh, yes. Sergeant Cayley let her out. It's a big old-fashioned lock with a big old-fashioned key. The key was in the lock and there's not a chance that it could have been turned from inside or any hanky-panky of that kind. No, you can *take* it definitely that Mrs. Cresswell was locked inside that room and couldn't get out. And there were no bows and arrows in the room and Miss Greenshaw couldn't in any case have been shot from her window—the angle forbids it. No, Mrs. Cresswell's out."

He paused, then went on: "Would you say that Miss Greenshaw, in your opinion, was a practical joker?"

Miss Marple looked up sharply from her corner.

"So the will wasn't in Mrs. Cresswell's favor after all?" she said.

Inspector Welch looked over at her in a rather surprised fashion.

"That's a very clever guess of yours, madam," he said. "No. Mrs. Cresswell isn't named as beneficiary."

"Just like Mr. Naysmith," said Miss Marple, nodding her head. "Miss Greenshaw told Mrs. Cresswell she was going to leave her everything and so got out of paying her wages; and then she left her money to somebody else. No doubt she was vastly pleased with herself. No wonder she chortled when she put the will away in *Lady Audley's Secret.*"

"It was lucky Mrs. Oxley was able to tell us about the will and where it was put," said the Inspector. "We might have had a long hunt for it otherwise."

"A Victorian sense of humor," murmured Raymond West.

"So she left her money to her nephew after all," said Louise.

The Inspector shook his head.

"No," he said, "she didn't leave it to Nat Fletcher. The story goes around here—of course I'm new to the place and I only get the gossip that's secondhand—but it seems that in the old days both Miss Greenshaw and her sister were set on the handsome young riding master, and the sister got him. No, she didn't leave the money to her nephew—" Inspector Welch paused, rubbing his chin. "She left it to Alfred," he said.

"Alfred—the gardener?" Joan spoke in a surprised voice.

"Yes, Mrs. West. Alfred Pollock."

"But why?" cried Louise.

Miss Marple coughed and murmured, "I would imagine, though

perhaps I am wrong, that there may have been—what we might call *family* reasons."

"You could call them that in a way," agreed the Inspector. "It's quite well-known in the village, it seems, that Thomas Pollock, Alfred's grandfather, was one of old Mr. Greenshaw's bye-blows."

"Of course," cried Louise, "the resemblance!"

She remembered how after passing Alfred she had come into the house and looked up at old Greenshaw's portrait.

"I daresay," said Miss Marple, "that she thought Alfred Pollock might have a pride in the house, might even want to live in it, whereas her nephew would almost certainly have no use for it whatever and would sell it as soon as he could possibly do so. He's an actor, isn't he? What play exactly is he acting in at present?"

Trust an old lady to wander from the point, thought Inspector Welch; but he replied civilly, "I believe, madam, they are doing a season of Sir James M. Barrie's plays."

"Barrie," said Miss Marple thoughtfully.

"*What Every Woman Knows,*" said Inspector Welch, and then blushed. "Name of a play," he said quickly. "I'm not much of a theater-goer myself," he added, "but the wife went along and saw it last week. Quite well done, she said it was."

"Barrie wrote some very charming plays," said Miss Marple, "though I must say that when I went with an old friend of mine, General Easterly, to see Barrie's *Little Mary*—" she shook her head sadly "—neither of us knew where to look."

The Inspector, unacquainted with the play *Little Mary,* seemed completely fogged.

Miss Marple explained: "When I was a girl, Inspector, nobody ever mentioned the word *stomach.*"

The Inspector looked even more at sea. Miss Marple was murmuring titles under her breath.

"*The Admirable Crichton.* Very clever. *Mary Rose*—a charming play. I cried, I remember. *Quality Street* I didn't care for so much. Then there was *A Kiss for Cinderella.* Oh, of course!"

Inspector Welch had no time to waste on theatrical discussion. He returned to the matter at hand.

"The question is," he said, "did Alfred Pollock know the old lady had made a will in his favor? Did she tell him?" He added, "You see—there's an Archery Club over at Boreham—and *Alfred Pollock's a member.* He's a very good shot indeed with a bow and arrow."

"Then isn't your case quite clear?" asked Raymond West. "It would fit in with the doors being locked on the two women—he'd know just where they were in the house."

The Inspector looked at him. He spoke with deep melancholy.

"He's got an alibi," said the Inspector.

"I always think alibis are definitely suspicious," Raymond remarked.

"Maybe, sir," said Inspector Welch. "You're talking as a writer."

"I don't write detective stories," said Raymond West, horrified at the mere idea.

"Easy enough to say that alibis are suspicious," went on Inspector Welch, "but unfortunately we've got to deal with facts." He sighed. "We've got three good suspects," he went on. "Three people who, as it happened, were very close upon the scene at the time. Yet the odd thing is that it looks as though none of the three could have done it. The housekeeper I've already dealt with; the nephew, Nat Fletcher, at the moment Miss Greenshaw was shot, was a couple of miles away filling up his car at a garage and asking his way; as for Alfred Pollock, six people will swear that he entered the Dog and Duck at twenty past twelve and was there for an hour having his usual bread and cheese and beer."

"Deliberately establishing an alibi," said Raymond West hopefully.

"Maybe," said Inspector Welch, "but if so, he *did* establish it."

There was a long silence. Then Raymond turned his head to where Miss Marple sat upright and thoughtful.

"It's up to you, Aunt Jane," he said. "The Inspector's baffled, the Sergeant's baffled, I'm baffled, Joan's baffled, Louise is baffled. But to you, Aunt Jane, it is crystal clear. Am I right?"

"I wouldn't say that," said Miss Marple, "not *crystal* clear. And murder, dear Raymond, isn't a game. I don't suppose poor Miss Greenshaw wanted to die, and it was a particularly brutal murder.

Very well-planned and quite cold-blooded. It's not a thing to make *jokes* about."

"I'm sorry," said Raymond. "I'm not really as callous as I sound. One treats a thing lightly to take away from the—well, the horror of it."

"That is, I believe, the modern tendency," said Miss Marple. "All these wars, and having to joke about funerals. Yes, perhaps I was thoughtless when I implied that you were callous."

"It isn't," said Joan, "as though we'd known her at all well."

"That is *very* true," said Miss Marple. "You, dear Joan, did not know her at all. I did not know her at all. Raymond gathered an impression of her from one afternoon's conversation. Louise knew her for only two days."

"Come now, Aunt Jane," said Raymond, "tell us your views. You don't mind, Inspector?"

"Not at all," said the Inspector politely.

"Well, my dear, it would seem that we have three people who had—or might have thought they had—a motive to kill the old lady. And three quite simple reasons why none of the three could have done so. The housekeeper could not have killed Miss Greenshaw because she was locked in her room and because her mistress definitely stated that a *man* shot her. The gardener was inside the Dog and Duck at the time, the nephew at the garage."

"Very clearly put, madam," said the Inspector.

"And since it seems most unlikely that any outsider should have done it, where, then, are we?"

"That's what the Inspector wants to know," said Raymond West.

"One so often looks at a thing the wrong way round," said Miss Marple apologetically. "If we can't alter the movements or the positions of those three people, then couldn't we perhaps alter the time of the murder?"

"You mean that both my watch and the clock were wrong?" asked Louise.

"No, dear," said Miss Marple, "I didn't mean that at all. I mean that the murder didn't occur when you thought it occurred."

"But I *saw* it," cried Louise.

"Well, what I have been wondering, my dear, was whether you weren't *meant* to see it. I've been asking myself, you know, whether that wasn't the real reason why you were engaged for this job."

"What *do* you mean, Aunt Jane?"

"Well, dear, it seems odd. Miss Greenshaw did not like spending money—yet she engaged you and agreed quite willingly to the terms you asked. It seems to me that perhaps you were meant to be there in that library on the second floor, looking out of the window so that you could be the key witness—someone from outside of irreproachably good character—to fix a definite time and place for the murder."

"But you can't mean," said Louise, incredulously, "that Miss Greenshaw *intended* to be murdered."

"What I mean, dear," said Miss Marple, "is that you didn't really know Miss Greenshaw. There's no real reason, is there, why the Miss Greenshaw you saw when you went up to the house should be the same Miss Greenshaw that Raymond saw a few days earlier? Oh, yes, I know," she went on, to prevent Louise's reply, "she was wearing the peculiar old-fashioned print dress and the strange straw hat, and had unkempt hair. She corresponded exactly to the description Raymond gave us last weekend. But those two women, you know, were much the same age, height, and size. The housekeeper, I mean, and Miss Greenshaw."

"But the housekeeper is fat!" Louise exclaimed. "She's got an enormous bosom."

Miss Marple coughed.

"But my dear, surely, nowadays I have seen—er—them myself in shops most indelicately displayed. It is very easy for anyone to have a—a bosom—of *any* size and dimension."

"What are you trying to say?" demanded Raymond.

"I was just thinking that during the two days Louise was working there, one woman could have played both parts. You said yourself, Louise, that you hardly saw the housekeeper, except for the one minute in the morning when she brought you the tray with coffee. One sees those clever artists on the stage coming in as different characters with only a moment or two to spare, and I am sure the change could have been effected quite easily. That marquise head-dress could be just a wig slipped on and off."

"Aunt Jane! Do you mean that Miss Greenshaw was dead before I started work there?"

"Not dead. Kept under drugs, I should say. A very easy job for an unscrupulous woman like the housekeeper to do. Then she made the arrangements with you and got you to telephone to the nephew to ask him to lunch at a definite time. The only person who would have known that this Miss Greenshaw was *not* Miss Greenshaw would have been Alfred. And if you remember, the first two days you were working there it was wet, and Miss Greenshaw stayed in the house. Alfred never came into the house because of his feud with the housekeeper. And on the last morning Alfred was in the drive, while Miss Greenshaw was working on the rockery—I'd like to have a look at that rockery."

"Do you mean it was Mrs. Cresswell who killed Miss Green-shaw?"

"I think that after bringing you your coffee, the housekeeper locked the door on you as she went out, then carried the unconscious Miss Greenshaw down to the drawing-room, then assumed her 'Miss Greenshaw' disguise and went out to work on the rockery where you could see her from the upstairs window. In due course she screamed and came staggering to the house clutching an arrow as though it had penetrated her throat. She called for help and was careful to say '*he* shot me' so as to remove suspicion from the housekeeper—from herself. She also called up to the housekeeper's window as though she saw her there. Then, once inside the drawing-room, she threw over a table with porcelain on it, ran quickly upstairs, put on her marquise wig, and was able a few moments later to lean her head out of the window and tell you that she, too, was locked in."

"But she *was* locked in," said Louise.

"I know. That is where the policeman comes in."

"What policeman?"

"Exactly—what policeman? I wonder, Inspector, if you would mind telling me how and when *you* arrived on the scene?"

The Inspector looked a little puzzled.

"At 12:29 we received a telephone call from Mrs. Cresswell, housekeeper to Miss Greenshaw, stating that her mistress had been shot. Sergeant Cayley and myself went out there at once in a car and arrived at the house at 12:35. We found Miss Greenshaw dead and the two ladies locked in their rooms."

"So, you see, my dear," said Miss Marple to Louise. "The police constable *you* saw wasn't a real police constable at all. You never thought of him again—one doesn't—one just accepts one more uniform as part of the Law."

"But who—why?"

"As to who—well, if they are playing *A Kiss for Cinderella*, a policeman is the principal character. Nat Fletcher would only have to help himself to the costume he wears on the stage. He'd ask his way at a garage, being careful to call attention to the time—12:25; then he would drive on quickly, leave his car round a corner, slip on his police uniform, and do his 'act.'"

"But why—why?"

"*Someone* had to lock the housekeeper's door on the outside, and someone had to drive the arrow through Miss Greenshaw's throat. You can stab anyone with an arrow just as well as by shooting it—but it needs force."

"You mean they were both in it?"

"Oh, yes, I think so. Mother and son as likely as not."

"But Miss Greenshaw's sister died long ago."

"Yes, but I've no doubt Mr. Fletcher married again—he sounds like the sort of man who would. I think it possible that the child died too, and that this so-called nephew was the second wife's child, and not really a relation at all. The woman got the post as housekeeper and spied out the land. Then he wrote to Miss Greenshaw as her nephew and proposed to call on her—he may have even made some joking reference to coming in his policeman's uniform—remember, she said she was expecting a policeman. But I think Miss Greenshaw suspected the truth and refused to see him. He would have been her heir if she had died without making a will—but of course once she had made a will in the housekeeper's favor, as they thought, then it was clear sailing."

"But why use an arrow?" objected Joan. "So very far-fetched."

"Not far-fetched at all, dear. Alfred belonged to an Archery Club—Alfred was meant to take the blame. The fact that he was in the pub as early as 12:20 was most unfortunate from their point of view. He always left a little before his proper time and that would have been just right." She shook her head. "It really seems all wrong—morally, I mean, that Alfred's laziness should have saved his life."

The Inspector cleared his throat.

"Well, madam, these suggestions of yours are very interesting. I shall, of course, have to investigate—"

MISS MARPLE AND Raymond West stood by the rockery and looked down at a gardening basket full of dying vegetation.

Miss Marple murmured:

"Alyssum, saxifrage, cystis, thimble campanula . . . Yes, that's all the proof *I* need. Whoever was weeding here yesterday morning was no gardener—she pulled up plants as well as weeds. So now I *know* I'm right. Thank you, dear Raymond, for bringing me here. I wanted to see the place for myself."

She and Raymond both looked up at the outrageous pile of Greenshaw's Folly.

A cough made them turn. A handsome young man was also looking at the monstrous house.

"Plaguey big place," he said. "Too big for nowadays—or so they say. I dunno about that. If I won a football pool and made a lot of money, that's the kind of house I'd like to build."

He smiled bashfully at them, then rumpled his hair.

"Reckon I can say so now—that there house was built by my great-grandfather," said Alfred Pollock. "And a fine house it is, for all they call it Greenshaw's Folly!"

6. SANCTUARY

The Vicar's wife came round the corner of the Vicarage with her arms full of chrysanthemums. A good deal of rich garden soil was attached to her strong brogue shoes and a few fragments of earth were adhering to her nose, but of that fact she was perfectly unconscious.

She had a slight struggle in opening the Vicarage gate which hung, rustily, half off its hinges. A puff of wind caught at her battered felt hat, causing it to sit even more rakishly than it had done before. "Bother!" said Bunch.

Christened by her optimistic parents Diana, Mrs. Harmon had become Bunch at an early age for somewhat obvious reasons and the name had stuck to her ever since. Clutching the chrysanthemums, she made her way through the gate to the churchyard, and so to the church door.

The November air was mild and damp. Clouds scudded across the sky with patches of blue here and there. Inside, the church was dark and cold; it was unheated except at service times.

"Brrrrrh!" said Bunch expressively. "I'd better get on with this quickly. I don't want to die of cold."

With the quickness born of practice she collected the necessary paraphernalia: vases, water, flower-holders. "I wish we had lilies," thought Bunch to herself. "I get so tired of these scraggy chrysanthemums." Her nimble fingers arranged the blooms in their holders.

There was nothing particularly original or artistic about the decorations, for Bunch Harmon herself was neither original nor artistic, but it was a homely and pleasant arrangement. Carrying the vases carefully, Bunch stepped up the aisle and made her way toward the altar. As she did so the sun came out.

It shone through the East window of somewhat crude colored glass, mostly blue and red—the gift of a wealthy Victorian churchgoer. The effect was almost startling in its sudden opulence. "Like jewels," thought Bunch. Suddenly she stopped, staring ahead of her. On the chancel steps was a huddled dark form.

Putting down the flowers carefully, Bunch went up to it and bent over it. It was a man lying there, huddled over on himself. Bunch knelt down by him and slowly, carefully, she turned him over. Her fingers went to his pulse—a pulse so feeble and fluttering that it told its own story, as did the almost greenish pallor of his face. There was no doubt, Bunch thought, that the man was dying.

He was a man of about forty-five, dressed in a dark, shabby suit. She laid down the limp hand she had picked up and looked at his other hand. This seemed clenched like a fist on his breast. Looking more closely she saw that the fingers were closed over what seemed to be a large wad or handkerchief which he was holding tightly to his chest. All round the clenched hand there were splashes of a dry brown fluid which, Bunch guessed, was dry blood. Bunch sat back on her heels, frowning.

Up till now the man's eyes had been closed but at this point they suddenly opened and fixed themselves on Bunch's face. They were neither dazed nor wandering. They seemed fully alive and intelligent. His lips moved, and Bunch bent forward to catch the words, or rather the word. It was only one word that he said:

"*Sanctuary.*"

There was, she thought, just a very faint smile as he breathed out this word. There was no mistaking it, for after a moment, he said it again, "Sanctuary . . ."

Then, with a faint, long-drawn-out sigh, his eyes closed again. Once more Bunch's fingers went to his pulse. It was still there, but fainter now and more intermittent. She got up with decision.

"Don't move," she said, "or try to move. I'm going for help."

The man's eyes opened again but he seemed now to be fixing his attention on the colored light that came through the East window. He murmured something that Bunch could not quite catch. She thought, startled, that it might have been her husband's name.

"Julian?" she said. "Did you come here to find Julian?" But there was no answer. The man lay with eyes closed, his breathing coming in slow, shallow fashion.

Bunch turned and left the church rapidly. She glanced at her watch and nodded with some satisfaction. Dr. Griffiths would still be in his surgery. It was only a couple of minutes' walk from the church. She went in, without waiting to knock or ring, passing through the waiting room and into the doctor's surgery.

"You must come at once," said Bunch. "There's a man dying in the church."

Some minutes later Dr. Griffiths rose from his knees after a brief examination.

"Can we move him from here into the Vicarage? I can attend to him better there—not that it's any use."

"Of course," said Bunch. "I'll go along and get things ready. I'll get Harper and Jones, shall I? To help you carry him."

"Thanks. I can telephone from the Vicarage for an ambulance, but I'm afraid—by the time it comes . . ." He left the remark unfinished.

Bunch said, "Internal bleeding?"

Dr. Griffiths nodded. He said, "How on earth did he come here?"

"I think he must have been here all night," said Bunch, considering. "Harper unlocks the church in the morning as he goes to work, but he doesn't usually come in."

It was about five minutes later when Dr. Griffiths put down the telephone receiver and came back into the morning room where the injured man was lying on quickly arranged blankets on the sofa.

Bunch was moving a basin of water and clearing up after the doctor's examination.

"Well, that's that," said Griffiths. "I've sent for an ambulance and I've notified the police." He stood, frowning, looking down on the patient who lay with closed eyes. His left hand was plucking in a nervous, spasmodic way at his side.

"He was shot," said Griffiths. "Shot at fairly close quarters. He rolled his handkerchief up into a ball and plugged the wound with it so as to stop the bleeding."

"Could he have gone far after that happened?" Bunch asked.

"Oh, yes, it's quite possible. A mortally wounded man has been known to pick himself up and walk along a street as though nothing had happened, and then suddenly collapse five or ten minutes later. So he needn't have been shot in the church. Oh, no. He may have been shot some distance away. Of course, he may have shot himself and then dropped the revolver and staggered blindly toward the church. I don't quite know why he made for the church and not for the Vicarage."

"Oh, I know *that*," said Bunch. "He said it: 'Sanctuary.'"

The doctor stared at her. "Sanctuary?"

"Here's Julian," said Bunch, turning her head as she heard her husband's steps in the hall. "Julian! Come here."

The Reverend Julian Harmon entered the room. His vague, scholarly manner always made him appear much older than he really was. "Dear me!" said Julian Harmon, staring in a mild, puzzled manner at the surgical appliances and the prone figure on the sofa.

Bunch explained with her usual economy of words. "He was in the church, dying. He'd been shot. Do you know him, Julian? I thought he said your name."

The Vicar came up to the sofa and looked down at the dying man. "Poor fellow," he said, and shook his head. "No, I don't know him. I'm almost sure I've never seen him before."

At that moment the dying man's eyes opened once more. They went from the doctor to Julian Harmon and from him to his wife. The eyes stayed there, staring into Bunch's face. Griffiths stepped forward.

"If you could tell us," he said urgently.

But with his eyes fixed on Bunch, the man said in a weak voice, "Please—*please*—" And then, with a slight tremor, he died . . .

Sergeant Hayes licked his pencil and turned the page of his notebook.

"So that's all you can tell me, Mrs. Harmon?"

"That's all," said Bunch. "These are the things out of his coat pockets."

On a table at Sergeant Hayes' elbow was a wallet, a rather battered old watch with the initials W.S. and the return half of a ticket to London. Nothing more.

"You've found out who he is?" asked Bunch.

"A Mr. and Mrs. Eccles phoned up the station. He's her brother, it seems. Name of Sandbourne. Been in a low state of health and nerves for some time. He's been getting worse lately. The day before yesterday he walked out and didn't come back. He took a revolver with him."

"And he came out here and shot himself with it?" said Bunch. "Why?"

"Well, you see, he'd been depressed . . ."

Bunch interrupted him. "I don't mean *that*. I mean, why here?"

Since Sergeant Hayes obviously did not know the answer to that one he replied in an oblique fashion, "Come out here, he did, on the 5:10 bus."

"Yes," said Bunch again. "But *why*?"

"I don't know, Mrs. Harmon," said Sergeant Hayes. "There's no accounting. If the balance of the mind is disturbed—"

Bunch finished for him. "They may do it anywhere. But it still seems to me unnecessary to take a bus out to a small country place like this. He didn't know anyone here, did he?"

"Not so far as can be ascertained," said Sergeant Hayes. He coughed in an apologetic manner and said, as he rose to his feet, "It may be as Mr. and Mrs. Eccles will come out and see you, Ma'am—if you don't mind, that is."

"Of course I don't mind," said Bunch. "It's very natural. I only wish I had something to tell them."

"I'll be getting along," said Sergeant Hayes.

"I'm only so thankful," said Bunch, going with him to the front door, "that it wasn't murder."

A car had drawn up at the Vicarage gate. Sergeant Hayes, glancing at it, remarked: "Looks as though that's Mr. and Mrs. Eccles come here now, Ma'am, to talk with you."

Bunch braced herself to endure what, she felt, might be rather a difficult ordeal. "However," she thought, "I can always call Julian in to help me. A clergyman's a great help when people are bereaved."

Exactly what she had expected Mr. and Mrs. Eccles to be like, Bunch could not have said, but she was conscious, as she greeted them, of a feeling of surprise. Mr. Eccles was a stout and florid man whose natural manner would have been cheerful and facetious. Mrs. Eccles had a vaguely flashy look about her. She had a small, mean, pursed-up mouth. Her voice was thin and reedy.

"It's been a terrible shock, Mrs. Harmon, as you can imagine," she said.

"Oh, I know," said Bunch. "It must have been. Do sit down. Can I offer you—well, perhaps it's a little early for tea—"

Mr. Eccles waved a pudgy hand. "No, no, nothing for us," he said. "It's very kind of you, I'm sure. Just wanted to . . . well . . . what poor William said and all that, you know?"

"He's been abroad a long time," said Mrs. Eccles, "and I think he must have had some very nasty experiences. Very quiet and depressed he's been, ever since he came home. Said the world wasn't fit to live in and there was nothing to look forward to. Poor Bill, he was always moody."

Bunch stared at them both for a moment or two without speaking.

"Pinched my husband's revolver, he did," went on Mrs. Eccles. "Without our knowing. Then it seems he come out here by bus. I suppose that was nice feeling on his part. He wouldn't have liked to do it in our house."

"Poor fellow, poor fellow," said Mr. Eccles, with a sigh. "It doesn't do to judge."

There was another short pause, and Mr. Eccles said, "Did he leave a message? Any last words, nothing like that?"

His bright, rather piglike eyes watched Bunch closely. Mrs. Eccles, too, leaned forward as though anxious for the reply.

"No," said Bunch quietly. "He came into the church when he was dying, for sanctuary."

Mrs. Eccles said in a puzzled voice, "Sanctuary? I don't think I quite . . ."

Mr. Eccles interrupted. "Holy place, my dear," he said impatiently. "That's what the Vicar's wife means. It's a sin—suicide, you know. I expect he wanted to make amends."

"He tried to say something just before he died," said Bunch. "He began, 'Please,' but that's as far as he got." Mrs. Eccles put her handkerchief to her eyes and sniffed.

"Oh, dear," she said. "It's terribly upsetting, isn't it?"

"There, there, Pam," said her husband. "Don't take on. These things can't be helped. Poor Willie. Still, he's at peace now. Well, thank you very much, Mrs. Harmon. I hope we haven't interrupted you. A vicar's wife is a busy lady, we know that."

They shook hands with her. Then Eccles turned back suddenly to say, "Oh, yes, there's just one thing. I think you've got his coat here, haven't you?"

"His coat?" Bunch frowned.

Mrs. Eccles said, "We'd like all his things, you know. Sentimental-like."

"He had a watch and a wallet and a railway ticket in the pockets," said Bunch. "I gave them to Sergeant Hayes."

"That's all right, then," said Mr. Eccles. "He'll hand them over to us, I expect. His private papers would be in the wallet."

"There was a pound note in the wallet," said Bunch. "Nothing else."

"No letters? Nothing like that?"

Bunch shook her head.

"Well, thank you again, Mrs. Harmon. The coat he was wearing—perhaps the Sergeant's got that too, has he?"

Bunch frowned in an effort of remembrance.

"No," she said. "I don't think . . . let me see. The doctor and I took his coat off to examine his wound." She looked round the room, vaguely. "I must have taken it upstairs with the towels and basin."

"I wonder now, Mrs. Harmon, if you don't mind . . . We'd like his coat, you know, the last thing he wore. Well, the wife feels rather sentimental about it."

"Of course," said Bunch. "Would you like me to have it cleaned first? I'm afraid it's rather—well—stained."

"Oh, no, no, no, that doesn't matter."

Bunch frowned. "Now I wonder where . . . excuse me a moment." She went upstairs and it was some few minutes before she returned.

"I'm so sorry," she said breathlessly, "my daily woman must have put it aside with other clothes that were going to the cleaners. It's taken me quite a long time to find it. Here it is. I'll do it up for you in brown paper."

Disclaiming their protests she did so; then once more effusively bidding her farewell the Eccles departed.

Bunch went slowly back across the hall and entered the study. The Reverend Julian Harmon looked up and his brow cleared. He was composing a sermon and was fearing that he'd been led astray by the interest of the political relations between Judaea and Persia, in the reign of Cyrus.

"Yes, dear?" he said, hopefully.

"Julian," said Bunch. "What's *Sanctuary* exactly?"

Julian Harmon gratefully put aside his sermon paper.

"Well," he said. "Sanctuary in Roman and Greek temples applied to the *cella* in which stood the statue of a god. The Latin word for altar 'ara' also means protection." He continued learnedly: "In 399 A.D. the right of sanctuary in Christian churches was finally and definitely recognized. The earliest mention of the right of sanctuary in England is in the Code of Laws issued by Ethelbert in A.D. 600 . . ."

He continued for some time with his exposition but was, as often, disconcerted by his wife's reception of his erudite pronouncement.

"Darling," she said. "You *are* sweet."

Bending over, she kissed him on the tip of his nose. Julian felt rather like a dog who has been congratulated on performing a clever trick.

"The Eccles have been here," said Bunch.

The Vicar frowned. "The Eccles? I don't seem to remember . . ."

"You don't know them. They're the sister and her husband of the man in the church."

"My dear, you ought to have called me."

"There wasn't any need," said Bunch. "They were not in need of consolation. I wonder now." She frowned. "If I put a casserole in the oven tomorrow, can you manage, Julian? I think I shall have to go up to London for the sales."

"The sails?" Her husband looked at her blankly. "Do you mean a yacht or a boat or something?"

Bunch laughed.

"No, darling. There's a special white sale at Burrows and Portman's. You know, sheets, table-cloths and towels and glass-cloths. I don't know what we do with our glass-cloths, the way they wear through. Besides," she added thoughtfully, "I think I ought to go and see Aunt Jane."

That sweet old lady, Miss Jane Marple, was enjoying the delights of the metropolis for a fortnight, comfortably installed in her nephew's studio flat.

"So kind of dear Raymond," she murmured. "He and Joan have gone to America for a fortnight and they insisted I should come up here and enjoy myself. And now, dear Bunch, do tell me what it is that's worrying you."

Bunch was Miss Marple's favorite godchild, and the old lady looked at her with great affection as Bunch, thrusting her best felt hat further on the back of her head, started on her story.

Bunch's recital was concise and clear. Miss Marple nodded her head as Bunch finished. "I see," she said. "Yes, I see."

"That's why I felt I had to see you," said Bunch. "You see, not being clever—"

"But you *are* clever, my dear."

"No, I'm not. Not clever like Julian."

"Julian, of course, has a very solid intellect," said Miss Marple.

"That's it," said Bunch. "Julian's got the intellect, but on the other hand, I've got the *sense.*"

"You have a lot of common sense, Bunch, and you're very intelligent."

"You see, I don't really know what I ought to do. I can't ask Julian because—well, I mean, Julian's so full of rectitude . . ."

This statement appeared to be perfectly understood by Miss Marple, who said, "I know what you mean, dear. We women—well, it's different." She went on, "You told me what happened, Bunch, but I'd like to know first exactly what you think."

"It's all wrong," said Bunch. "The man who was there in the church, dying, knew all about Sanctuary. He said it just the way Julian would have said it. I mean he was a well-read, educated man. And if he'd shot himself, he wouldn't drag himself into a church afterward and say 'sanctuary.' Sanctuary means that you're pursued, and when you get into a church you're safe. Your pursuers can't touch you. At one time even the law couldn't get at you."

She looked questioningly at Miss Marple. The latter nodded. Bunch went on, "Those people, the Eccles, were quite different. Ignorant and coarse. And there's another thing. That watch—the dead man's watch. It had the initials W.S. on the back of it. But inside—I opened it—in very small lettering there was "To Walter from his father" and a date. *Walter.* But the Eccles kept talking of him as William or Bill."

Miss Marple seemed about to speak but Bunch rushed on, "Oh, I know you're not always called the name you're baptized by. I mean, I can understand that you might be christened William and called 'Porky' or 'Carrots' or something. But your sister wouldn't call you William or Bill if your name was Walter."

"You mean that she wasn't his sister?"

"I'm quite sure she wasn't his sister. They were horrid—both of them. They came to the Vicarage to get his things and to find out if he'd said anything before he died. When I said he hadn't I saw it in their faces—relief. I think, myself," finished Bunch, "it was Eccles who shot him."

"Murder?" said Miss Marple.

"Yes," said Bunch. "Murder. That's why I came to you, darling."

Bunch's remark might have seemed incongruous to an ignorant listener, but in certain spheres Miss Marple had a reputation for dealing with murder.

"He said 'please' to me before he died," said Bunch. "He wanted me to do something for him. The awful thing is I've no idea what."

Miss Marple considered for a moment or two, and then pounced on the point that had already occurred to Bunch. "But why was he there at all?" she asked.

"You mean," said Bunch, "if you wanted sanctuary you might pop into a church anywhere. There's no need to take a bus that only goes four times a day and come out to a lonely spot like ours for it."

"He must have come there for a purpose," Miss Marple thought. "He must have come to see someone. Chipping Cleghorn's not a big place, Bunch. Surely you must have some idea of who it was he came to see?"

Bunch reviewed the inhabitants of her village in her mind before rather doubtfully shaking her head. "In a way," she said, "it could be anybody."

"He never mentioned a name?"

"He said Julian, or I thought he said Julian. It might have been Julia, I suppose. As far as I know, there isn't any Julia living in Chipping Cleghorn."

She screwed up her eyes as she thought back to the scene. The man lying there on the chancel steps, the light coming through the window with its jewels of red and blue light.

"Jewels," said Bunch suddenly. "Perhaps that's what he said. The light coming through the East window looked like jewels."

"Jewels," said Miss Marple, thoughtfully.

"I'm coming now," said Bunch, "to the most important thing of all. The reason why I've really come here today. You see, the Eccles made a great fuss about having his coat. We took it off when the doctor was seeing to him. It was an old, shabby sort of coat—there was no reason they should have wanted it. They pretended it was sentimental, but that was nonsense.

"Anyway, I went up to find it, and as I was going up the stairs I remembered how he'd made a kind of picking gesture with his hand, as though he was fumbling with the coat. So when I got hold of the coat I looked at it very carefully and I saw that in one place the lining had been sewn up again with a different thread. So I unpicked it and I found a little piece of paper inside. I took it out and I sewed it up again properly with thread that matched. I was careful and I don't really think that the Eccles would know I've done it. I don't *think* so, but I can't be sure. And I took the coat down to them and made some excuse for the delay."

"The piece of paper?" asked Miss Marple.

Bunch opened her handbag. "I didn't show it to Julian," she said, "because he would have said that I ought to have given it to the Eccles. But I thought I'd rather bring it to you instead."

"A cloakroom ticket," said Miss Marple, looking at it. "Paddington Station."

"He had a return ticket to Paddington in his pocket," said Bunch.

The eyes of the two women met.

"This calls for action," said Miss Marple briskly. "But it would be advisable, I think, to be careful. Would you have noticed at all, Bunch dear, whether you were followed when you came to London today?"

"Followed!" exclaimed Bunch. "You don't think—"

"Well, I think it's *possible*," said Miss Marple. "When anything is possible, I think we ought to take precautions." She rose with a brisk movement. "You came up here ostensibly, my dear, to go to the sales. I think the right thing to do, therefore, would be for us to *go* to the sales. But before we set out, we might put one or two little arrangements in hand. I don't suppose," Miss Marple added obscurely, "that I shall need the old speckled tweed with the beaver collar just at present. . . ."

It was about an hour and a half later that the two ladies, rather the worse for wear and battered in appearance, and both clasping parcels of hardly-won household linen, sat down at a small and sequestered hostelry called the Apple Bough to restore their forces with steak and kidney pudding followed by apple tart and custard.

"Really a prewar quality face towel," gasped Miss Marple, slightly out of breath. "With a J on it, too. So fortunate that Raymond's wife's name is Joan. I shall put them aside until I really need them and then they will do for her if I pass on sooner than I expect."

"I really did need the glass-cloths," said Bunch. "And they were very cheap, though not as cheap as the ones that woman with the ginger hair managed to snatch from me."

A smart young woman with a lavish application of rouge and lipstick entered the Apple Bough at that moment. After looking round vaguely for a moment or two, she hurried to their table. She laid down an envelope by Miss Marple's elbow.

"There you are, Miss," she said briskly.

"Oh, thank you, Gladys," said Miss Marple. "Thank you very much. So kind of you."

"Always pleased to oblige, I'm sure," said Gladys. "Ernie always says to me 'Everything what's good you learned from that Miss Marple of yours that you were in service with,' and I'm sure I'm always glad to oblige you, Miss."

"Such a dear girl," said Miss Marple as Gladys departed again. "Always so willing and so kind."

She looked inside the envelope and then passed it on to Bunch. "Now be very careful, dear," she said. "By the way, is there still that nice young Inspector at Melchester that I remember?"

"I don't know," said Bunch. "I expect so."

"Well, if not," said Miss Marple, thoughtfully, "I can always ring up the Chief Constable. I *think* he would remember me."

"Of course he'd remember you," said Bunch. "Everybody would remember *you*. You're quite unique." She rose.

Arrived at Paddington, Bunch went to the Luggage Office and produced the cloakroom ticket. A moment or two later a rather shabby old suitcase was passed across to her, and carrying this she made her way to the platform.

The journey home was uneventful. Bunch rose as the train approached Chipping Cleghorn and picked up the old suitcase. She had just left her carriage when a man, sprinting along the platform, suddenly seized the suitcase from her hand and rushed off with it.

"Stop!" Bunch yelled. "Stop him, stop him. He's taken my suitcase."

The ticket collector who, at this rural station, was a man of somewhat slow processes, had just begun to say, "Now, look here, you can't do that—" when a smart blow in the chest pushed him aside, and the man with the suitcase rushed out from the station. He made his way toward a waiting car. Tossing the suitcase in, he was about to climb after it but before he could move a hand fell on his shoulder, and the voice of Police Constable Abel said, "Now then, what's all this?"

Bunch arrived, panting, from the station. "He snatched my suitcase," she said.

"Nonsense," said the man. "I don't know what this lady means. It's my suitcase. I just got out of the train with it."

"Now, let's get this clear," said Police Constable Abel.

He looked at Bunch with a bovine and impartial stare. Nobody would have guessed that Police Constable Abel and Mrs. Harmon spent long half hours in Police Constable Abel's off time discussing the respective merits of manure and bone meal for rose bushes.

"You say, Madam, that this is your suitcase?" said Police Constable Abel.

"Yes," said Bunch. "Definitely."

"And you, sir?"

"I say this suitcase is mine."

The man was tall, dark and well dressed, with a drawling voice and a superior manner. A feminine voice from inside the car, said, "Of course it's your suitcase, Edwin. I don't know what this woman means."

"We'll have to get this clear," said Police Constable Abel. "If it's your suitcase, Madam, what do you say is inside it?"

"Clothes," said Bunch. "A long speckled coat with a beaver collar, two wool jumpers and a pair of shoes."

"Well, that's clear enough," said Police Constable Abel. He turned to the other.

"I am a theatrical costumer," said the dark man importantly. "This suitcase contains theatrical properties which I brought down here for an amateur performance."

"Right, sir," said Police Constable Abel. "Well, we'll just look inside, shall we, and see? We can go along to the police station, or if you're in a hurry we'll take the suitcase back to the station and open it there."

"It'll suit me," said the dark man. "My name is Moss, by the way. Edwin Moss."

The Police Constable, holding the suitcase, went back into the station. "Just taking this into the Parcels Office, George," he said to the ticket collector.

Police Constable Abel laid the suitcase on the counter of the Parcels Office and pushed back the clasp. The case was not locked. Bunch and Mr. Edwin Moss stood on either side of him, their eyes regarding each other vengefully.

"Ah!" said Police Constable Abel, as he pushed up the lid.

Inside, neatly folded, was a long rather shabby tweed coat with a beaver fur collar.

There were also two wool jumpers and a pair of country shoes.

"Exactly as you say, Madam," said Police Constable Abel, turning to Bunch.

Nobody could have said that Mr. Edwin Moss underdid things. His dismay and compunction were magnificent.

"I do apologize," he said. "I really *do* apologize. Please believe me, dear lady, when I tell you how very, very sorry I am. Unpardonable—quite unpardonable—my behavior has been." He looked at his watch. "I must rush now. Probably my suitcase has gone on the train." Raising his hat once more, he said meltingly to Bunch, "Do, *do* forgive me," and rushed hurriedly out of the Parcels Office.

"Are you going to let him get away?" asked Bunch in a conspiratorial whisper of Police Constable Abel.

The latter slowly closed a bovine eye in a wink.

"He won't get too far, Ma'am," he said. "That's to say, he won't get far unobserved, if you take my meaning."

"Oh," said Bunch, relieved.

"That old lady's been on the phone," said Police Constable Abel, "the one as was down here a few years ago. Bright she is, isn't she? But there's been a lot cooking up all today. Shouldn't wonder if the Inspector or Sergeant was out to see you about it tomorrow morning."

IT WAS THE Inspector who came, the Inspector Craddock whom Miss Marple remembered. He greeted Bunch with a smile as an old friend.

"Crime in Chipping Cleghorn again," he said cheerfully. "You don't lack for sensation here, do you, Mrs. Harmon?"

"I could do with rather less," said Bunch. "Have you come to ask me questions or are you going to tell me things for a change?"

"I'll tell you some things first," said the Inspector. "To begin with, Mr. and Mrs. Eccles have been having an eye kept on them for some time. There's reason to believe they've been connected with several robberies in this part of the world. For another thing, although Mrs. Eccles *has* a brother called Sandbourne who has recently come back from abroad, the man you found dying in the church yesterday was definitely not Sandbourne."

"I knew that he wasn't," said Bunch. "His name was Walter, to begin with, not William."

The Inspector nodded. "His name was Walter St. John, and he escaped forty-eight hours ago from Charrington Prison."

"Of course," said Bunch softly to herself, "he was being hunted down by the law, and he took sanctuary." Then she asked, "What had he done?"

"I'll have to go back rather a long way. It's a complicated story. Several years ago there was a certain dancer doing turns at the music halls. I don't expect you'll have ever heard of her, but she specialized in an Arabian Night turn, 'Aladdin in the Cave of Jewels' it was called. She wore bits of rhinestone and not much else.

"She wasn't much of a dancer, I believe, but she was—well— attractive. Anyway, a certain Asiatic royalty fell for her in a big way. Among other things he gave her a very magnificent emerald necklace."

"The historic jewels of a Rajah?" murmured Bunch ecstatically.

Inspector Craddock coughed. "Well, a rather more modern version, Mrs. Harmon. The affair didn't last very long, broke up when our potentate's attention was captured by a certain film star whose demands were not quite so modest.

"Zobeida, to give the dancer her stage name, hung on to the necklace, and in due course it was stolen. It disappeared from her dressing room at the theater, and there was a lingering suspicion in the minds of the authorities that she herself might have engineered its disappearance. Such things have been known as a publicity stunt, or indeed from more dishonest motives.

"The necklace was never recovered, but during the course of the investigation the attention of the police was drawn to this man, Walter St. John. He was a man of education and breeding who had come down in the world, and who was employed as a working jeweler with a rather obscure firm which was suspected as acting as a fence for jewel robberies.

"There was evidence that this necklace had passed through his hands. It was, however, in connection with the theft of some other jewelry that he was finally brought to trial and convicted and sent to prison. He had not very much longer to serve, so his escape was rather a surprise."

"But why did he come here?" asked Bunch.

"We'd like to know that very much, Mrs. Harmon. Following up his trail, it seems that he went first to London. He didn't visit any of his old associates but he visited an elderly woman, a Mrs. Jacobs who had formerly been a theatrical dresser. She won't say a word of what he came for, but according to other lodgers in the house he left carrying a suitcase."

"I see," said Bunch. "He left it in the cloakroom at Paddington and then he came down here."

"By that time," said Inspector Craddock, "Eccles and the man who calls himself Edwin Moss were on his trail. They wanted that suitcase. They saw him get on the bus. They must have driven out in a car ahead of him and been waiting for him when he left the bus."

"And he was murdered?" said Bunch.

"Yes," said Craddock. "He was shot. It was Eccles' revolver, but I rather fancy it was Moss who did the shooting. Now, Mrs. Harmon, what we want to know is, where is the suitcase that Walter St. John actually deposited at Paddington Station?"

Bunch grinned. "I expect Aunt Jane's got it by now," she said. "Miss Marple, I mean. That was her plan. She sent a former maid of hers with a suitcase packed with her things to the cloakroom at Paddington and we exchanged tickets. I collected her suitcase and brought it down by train. She seemed to expect that an attempt would be made to get it from me."

It was Inspector Craddock's turn to grin. "So she said when she rang up. I'm driving up to London to see her. Do you want to come, too, Mrs. Harmon?"

"Wel-l," said Bunch, considering. "Wel-l, as a matter of fact, it's very fortunate. I had a toothache last night so I really ought to go to London to see the dentist, oughtn't I?"

"Definitely," said Inspector Craddock . . .

Miss Marple looked from Inspector Craddock's face to the eager face of Bunch Harmon. The suitcase lay on the table. "Of course, I haven't opened it," the old lady said. "I wouldn't dream of doing such a thing till somebody official arrived. Besides," she added, with a demurely mischievous Victorian smile, "it's locked."

"Like to make a guess at what's inside, Miss Marple?" asked the Inspector.

"I should imagine, you know," said Miss Marple, "that it would be Zobeida's theatrical costumes. Would you like a chisel, Inspector?"

This chisel soon did its work. Both women gave a slight gasp as the lid flew up. The sunlight coming through the window lit up what seemed like an inexhaustible treasure of sparkling jewels, red, blue, green, orange.

"Aladdin's Cave," said Miss Marple. "The flashing jewels the girl wore to dance."

"Ah," said Inspector Craddock. "Now, what's so precious about it, do you think, that a man was murdered to get hold of it?"

"She was a shrewd girl, I expect," said Miss Marple thoughtfully. "She's dead, isn't she, Inspector?"

"Yes, died three years ago."

"She had this valuable emerald necklace," said Miss Marple, musingly. "Had the stones taken out of their setting and fastened here and there on her theatrical costume, where everyone would take them for merely colored rhinestones. Then she had a replica made of the real necklace, and that, of course, was what was stolen. No wonder it never came on the market. The thief soon discovered the stones were false."

"Here is an envelope," said Bunch, pulling aside some of the glittering stones.

Inspector Craddock took it from her and extracted two official-looking papers from it. He read aloud. "'Marriage certificate between Walter Edmund St. John and Mary Moss.' That was Zobeida's real name."

"So they were married," said Miss Marple. "I see."

"What's the other?" asked Bunch.

"A birth certificate of a daughter, Jewel."

"Jewel?" cried Bunch. "Why, of course. Jewel! *Jill!* That's it. I see now why he came to Chipping Cleghorn. *That's* what he was trying to say to me. Jewel. The Mundys, you know. Laburnam Cottage. They look after a little girl for someone. They're devoted to her. She's been like their own granddaughter. Yes, I remember now, her name *was* Jewel, only, of course, they call her Jill.

"Mrs. Mundy had a stroke about a week ago, and the old man's been very ill with pneumonia. They were both going to go to the Infirmary. I've been trying hard to find a good home for Jill somewhere. I didn't want her taken away to an institution.

"I suppose her father heard about it in prison and he managed to break away and get hold of this suitcase from the old dresser he or his wife left it with. I suppose if the jewels really belonged to her mother, they can be used for the child now."

"I should imagine so, Mrs. Harmon. *If* they're here."

"Oh, they'll be here all right," said Miss Marple cheerfully . .

"THANK GOODNESS YOU'RE back, dear," said the Reverend Julian Harmon, greeting his wife with affection and a sigh of content. "Mrs. Burt always tries to do her best when you're away, but she really gave me some *very* peculiar fishcakes for lunch. I didn't want to hurt her feelings so I gave them to Tiglash Pileser, but even *he* wouldn't eat them so I had to throw them out of the window."

"Tiglash Pileser," said Bunch, stroking the Vicarage cat, who was purring against her knee, "is *very* particular about what fish he eats. I often tell him he's got a proud stomach!"

"And your tooth, dear? Did you have it seen to?"

"Yes," said Bunch. "It didn't hurt much, and I went to see Aunt Jane again, too . . ."

"Dear old thing," said Julian. "I hope she's not failing at all."

"Not in the least," said Bunch, with a grin.

The following morning Bunch took a fresh supply of chrysanthemums to the church. The sun was once more pouring through the East window, and Bunch stood in the jeweled light on the chancel steps. She said very softly under her breath, "Your little girl will be all right. *I'll* see that she is. I promise."

Then she tidied up the church, slipped into a pew and knelt for a few moments to say her prayers before returning to the Vicarage to attack the piled up chores of two neglected days.